THE RUSSIAN ORPHAN

THE RUSSIAN ORPHAN

They Call Him the White Stallion

Book One in "The World Changer" Series

As you read, imagine...

DEEDE BLAKE

Copyright © 2023 by Deede Blake

All rights reserved.

No part of this book may be reproduced in any form or by any electronic or mechanical means, including information storage and retrieval systems, without written permission from the author, except for the use of brief quotations in a book review.

This is a work of fiction. Names, characters, places, and incidents either are the products of the author's imagination or are used fictitiously. Any resemblance to actual persons, living or dead, events, or locales is entirely coincidental.

Developmental and line edits by Motif Edits
Cover design by YellowStudios

Paperback ISBN: 979-8-9881433-1-4
Hardback ISBN: 979-8-9881433-0-7
Kindle ISBN: 979-8-9881433-2-1

Published by World Changers Publishers, LLC

deedeblakeauthor@gmail.com

deedeblake.com

DEDICATION

I am dedicating this book to two deserving humans.

First, to Officer Brian D. Sicknick who died the day after domestic terrorists rampaged inside our American Capitol. Looking at the released footage of that event, it's more than obvious that your efforts, and at times, your cunning, saved numerous lives on that most horrible of days. Yea, you did nothing less than help save our democracy. When I fashioned the character of Sergei Radkov, men like you served as my example. Men who remain cool under fire and step up to do the impossible.

Our grateful nation owes you a debt we cannot repay. There are not adequate words in our language to honor you. May you reside in peace, knowing you are among the best of the best who made a difference that day.

To the friends and family of Brian Sicknick, know that he was a man who was loved and beloved. He was the very best of our American story. His life, more than any other, gives me hope for an American future.

Second, I dedicate this to my partner, Bob Van De Motter. You were the first to read my manuscript and, upon my urging, criticize it (although it was hard for you to do so). Thank you for navigating my frustration while developing this manuscript. Thank you for taking me by the hand, biding me to come with you, walking me to the end of the drive, and saying, "Look up." I did. And I fell into an impossible show of stars, a constellation of thought and imagination. You are the best of men. I love you without end.

FOR BOB
Came to me at twilight.
You held me until dusk.
Hope lives for dawning
Where bird feeders live
Woodpeckers peck seed
Doves rejoice their coo.
And coffee mugs steam.
You give me sanctuary.
This is best love.
With all my love, Dee

"One has to understand what the enemy is all about: the enemy's history, the enemy's culture, the enemy's aspirations. If you understand these well, you can perhaps move towards peace."
— Zbigniew Brzezinski

PREFACE

The contents of this book came from the confluence of several things stirring all at once in my geopolitical brain. First, like many Americans, I became disillusioned by the American political system. Let me rephrase that: As a patriot, I became damned angry at the goings-on in our American political system. And frightened. When I traveled to Russia and spoke with so many ordinary citizens there, I realized my fears were well-founded.

It's true that ordinary Russian citizens told me they prayed for America. They stated their prayers for America were based on a perception that America is heading down the same road Russia has traveled during the past century.[1]

Russians have walked a torturous road whereupon raw blood flowed in the streets of their land.[2] Russian citizens expressed the desire for the bloody Russian experience to be the last on the planet. They wanted no other people to experience what they have. And that's before we even consider communism, Russia in WWII, or the gulag system. More blood.

I considered: just what has our government done for its people with our system of taxation? It didn't help my frustration when I evaluated the top three responsibilities of government: security, work on behalf of its citizens, and providing an infrastructure—the means to access goods and services—that individuals cannot achieve on their own.

Security. Yes, we have a military. But what about citizen protections at home, and justice? The constitution devised our government to work for all citizens. Does it? If so, then one must consider why so many Americans feel excluded by its processes. Anybody check out our infrastructure lately?

And yet, every year there is a debt ceiling and we borrow more money to pay our debts. No one wants to discuss the hardship of repaying our national credit card debt with a hurting citizenry. We must. Else, our generation will make hungry paupers of the next. Yes, hungry. The need for American imagination and solutions is past due.

And here I was watching presidential debates to decide who might best lead our country. What candidate can evaluate our national needs and propose the best solutions? Instead, what do I see? Not a discussion of our real problems. Zero solutions. Worst of all, grown men relating their hands to their penis sizes. Good grief.

I hadn't expected to evaluate the hands of any politicians, the lady on the stage included. Certainly wasn't concerned with penis size. My policy is not to concern myself with a penis unless I intend on using it. Whether a candidate flaunted an Oscar Meyer or a Beanie Weenie in their britches wasn't of my concern as an American voter.

I couldn't get my mind off the lack of leadership. Do Americans need entertainment so badly that we must turn our nation's grave drama into a comedy? If so, we're in trouble. (If not, we're still in trouble.) Yet many adored the humor of those debates. I thought deeper. People need humor to offset pain. Show me a comedian and I will show you a person who has known pain, experienced it, and can call it out by name.

Pain. We were a nation in pain. We still are. Despite our political stances, associations, or concerns, we are a hurting people in desperate need of leadership. Leadership that will serve America, albeit with tough love upon a hurting nation.

Then there was the capitol invasion of January 6, 2021. I watched in horror as a group of approximately one thousand domestic terrorists invaded our capitol. A capitol building whose property belongs to every American and which every American keeps the lights on through their taxation. Worse yet, the intent was to assassinate Vice President Mike Pence to halt our democratic election process. These domestic terrorists wanted blood. Raw and flowing blood.

We may not like election results, but it's our process. I dare say the Democrats didn't like the outcome of the 2000 election. I thank God for Al Gore, who said it was time to go and provided leadership rather than incite murderous intent. I've always respected Al Gore for his leadership during those months. Today, I love the man for it.

And yet, murdering a vice president was not enough for that crowd of insurgents. They devised a hangman's noose for Nancy Pelosi. Not because she had committed any crimes, but because they didn't like her. Didn't like her. What county can sanction such a thing except with disgust? And fear. Those domestic terrorists actually intended to hang an eighty-year-old lady because they didn't like her. I shudder to consider what may have happened if they had succeeded.

Now, let us compare that to the Bolshevik Revolution, remembered by blood in the Russian streets. It's impossible to give a complete history lesson on the subject in a few brief sentences, but I'll do what I can. The word "Bolshevik" means "One of the Majority." The name itself was meant as a ruse. Bolsheviks were as much a minority as the US domestic terrorists of 2021. Lenin didn't win the first Russian election in 1917. In fact, the Bolsheviks were minority winners. How did they come to power? By blood, in the October Revolution.

Many people think the massacre of Tsar Nicholas II and his staff gave rise to Lenin's power. It did not. Lenin had already seized power. Tsar Nicolas had abdicated over a year prior. Lenin was afraid of Tsar Nicholas being rescued by the Czechs. So, he gave the order to massacre everyone in seclusion with the former czar, including his entourage. Not just the family, wherein there wouldn't be succession to the throne of power, but everyone in the home. One maid wasn't just bayonetted, but mutilated with multiple wounds. All this while WWI was still raging. Blood. Yes, power in Russia was taken with blood spilled by the hands of domestic terrorists. Blood. Raw and flowing blood. Then communism.

I'm happy at least the Russian are praying for us. God, we need all the prayers we can get.

After the presidential debates, I watched a documentary on Vladimir Putin. He is a charismatic man, but with certainty, a cold and calculating one as well. I imagined. Imagined the future. A better future. We don't know from where the next great leader in the world will emerge. I allowed myself to imagine Russia.

Enter Sergei Radkov. Enter Dr. Selena Frederick. Two World Changers. One Russian. One American. I feel safer just knowing they are in the world, albeit in my imagination.

Come with me, my reader. Come with me and imagine. Together, let's go on a journey. Journey to live in a world finding solutions through the works of us all. Allow ourselves to be inspired into action. Mere handfuls of humans are willing to step forward and do the hard work to serve a nation in pain. Let's join them. And by doing so, our servitude will change the world. We will be World Changers.

Forgive me my mistakes. I'm sure there are many despite the efforts of many. However, responsibility for them is mine and mine alone. Feel free to contact me through my website or the email address listed on the copyright page.

I don't speak Russian, and for those who do, I apologize if I've done a little butchering. Considering the Cyrillic alphabet, it's impossible to accurately translate all words into English. The Russian language consists of letters and symbols that simply don't exist in our language. I've taken some license with words like *spasiba*, which is less formal than *spasibo*.[3]

Spasiba has more of a slang feel to me. I like to think of spasiba as meaning "thanks" and spasibo, "thank you."

Spasiba,
Deede Blake
deedeblake.com

---

1. This time frame occurs when western news channels such as the BBC and CNN were available in Russian media outlets.
2. Of note, my Russian journey was prior to the Ukrainian invasion. Much has changed since, including media access available to Russians.
3. Both mean "thank you".

PROLOGUE

I GRAB my jaw with both hands. Chomping down hard, I try to keep my teeth from chattering. My wet body lays freezing under my bed with my stomach flat against the cold tile flooring. Cold. So cold. The Russian springtime rains drenched me as I foraged for food this morning. The icy wetness taunts my unnourished body with shivers.

My raincoat and goulashes have grown larger on me due to my shrinking size. I'm hungry. So hungry. I had hoped to catch a minnow or two in the recently thawed stream running below our apartment. But then I recalled Momma said Mother Nature instructs the baby fish to swim deeper, closer to the warmer earth, dashing my hopes. *Momma.* I want to scream out for her.

I must set my mind to work. I need to recall if I left any wet spots on the tile floor. Droplets that will show the traces of my wetness. My presence. *Think!* I order myself. I'm so cold. And hungry. I don't want to be scared, but I am. As I shiver from the cold, I shake with fear. I can't think. But I must. I will myself to focus. I ponder if the pair sitting on my bed detect any of my unevaporated drops.

One man. One woman. Neither one on a kind mission. They sit on my bed with its cosmonaut-patterned covers as though they own it.

A rustle of a wrapper. I hear a thin cellophane crunch when it hits the floor. The sound booms in my ears like a roar of thunder. Candy?

Yes. Chocolate. I want to grab it up with both hands and swallow it whole, without the luxury of taste. I cannot. I must not. The sitting couple know I haven't eaten. They know my hunger. I'm their prey, just like the minnow. I can feel it in my frozen bones and shaking skin.

"Want one?" asks the woman with thick legs and fat feet bulging from the tops of her blue flat shoes.

"Sure," says the man.

I pray for a silent stomach as I listen to the unwrapping of the morsel. Oh God. Candy! Chocolate! I can smell it. I clinch my teeth tighter as saliva flows from my mouth. My hands grip my jaws tighter. Tighter.

Momma told me about what it means to be insane. Is this it? I mustn't let my mind wander. "Focus!" Yes, that's the word Momma would use when my thoughts strayed from my homework. "Put your blue eyes on the page and focus."

"Yes, Momma," I'd reply. I must stay focused today. Momma would want me to focus.

I spy a slight movement of the woman's white-and-blue polka dot skirt. I hear wrappers rustling. I put my hands over my ears because the sound blasts so loud as the woman dives into the bag of sweetness.

"Oops. Can I have another? That one dropped on the floor," says the man's voice. The voice sounds with a deep bass thump, like the beating of the singing drum in music class.

Thud.

Another dark chocolate delight lands in sight, in reach of my arms. I want it. I want both pieces. *Focus, Sergei, focus.* I close my eyes so that I can't see the food. I'm focused now, I convince myself. My eyes reopen. The morsel is within reach, a simple hand snatch. Left or right. It doesn't matter. Unmoving, I stare at it. Study it like a cat studies a bird.

When was the last time I ate? Days, for sure. I couldn't steal from Kolinsky's Community Grocery again. I know that. They caught me stealing food from there two weeks ago. Thank God I escaped. Barely.

Blinking fast, I lose my focus and I'm there again. My thin legs running so fast as I blast through the grocery's front door. I cradle the loaf of bread next to my thumping chest like a ragdoll. Then, pandemonium ensues as I run between two elderly ladies burdened with shopping bags. Speeding, I almost knock the ladies to the ground. I didn't mean to. I shout back, "Sorry," as my legs run the longest way home.

Momma would like that I said sorry, but she'd punish me for stealing. I dash into the back alleys, race up ladders and across roofs, rappel myself down, and enter unlocked basement doors known to exploring children. Sorry, Momma. Sorry for all of it.

Perhaps Kominsky called the authorities to send in this bed-sitting pair today. No, too much time has passed. They would have come for me that very day.

Occasionally, an entity leaves food at our apartment door. Some person. Some angel. I don't know who to thank. After scooping up the food morsels, I shovel them into my mouth with both hands while the apartment door closes. There's been nothing left beside our door in over a week.

Hungry. So hungry. Tears fall from my eyes as I feel the pain of hunger in my gut. I wipe the tears with my sleeve. I won't cry. I won't.

Two days ago, I ate sprigs of tender spring grass that peeked their crayon color from underneath the melting snow. I munch down on as many tender reeds as I could find. After diving my hands into the icy stream water to catch a surface minnow, I swallow the slippery meal whole. The opening of my narrowed gullet forces me to feel the pain of my prey as it swims in the shallow acid stream of my gut. I feel like a monster.

Can an eight-year-old be a monster? Am I old enough now that I'm eight? Can an eight-year-old be insane? I recently turned eight years old. For the first time in eight years, my mother missed my birthday. There was no cake. There were no kisses. There was no Momma.

I was thrown a meat and vegetable ort from the patio of Mr. Pandit several nights ago. While searing his family's meal on the barbeque, the self-important government worker likes to tease me with a bite of his abundance. Mr. Pandit can never button his shirt all the way around his stomach. A view of gross dark hair around his gluttonous belly button pops through a slit in his shirt. I silently call Mr. Pandit a curse word. Momma says such words aren't nice and I shouldn't say them. No, I shouldn't, especially since my bastard neighbor cuts off a small morsel from his dinner. Sorry momma, but he's an awful man. An awful man with food.

The odor of the cooking food drifts down into my nostrils. I want to cry with hunger, but I only let my stomach cry.

"Bark like a dog," Pandit commands, hairy knuckles holding the grilling fork, my reward at the end of its sharp tine.

"Roof! Roof!" I respond while down on all fours, putting on a dog show for the greedy bastard. Sorry, Momma. Pandit tosses a chunk of meat down the hill, which lands close by on the ground. I scoop up the meager piece and swallow it whole.

"Roll like a dog on your back, bu-u-ut you have to eat on all fours like a dog."

I oblige the hairy man by rolling on my back with my feet flailing in the air. Pandit's belly laugh tortures my cold ears.

"Go get it, boy," says the man as hairy fingers toss the last piece of my meal four meters from my body. I arise on all fours and travel on my shins to a grilled onion slab. My teeth devour the vegetable piece. I know that will be all. I know when Pandit has had enough fun. As much as I hate these exercises, I hate the days without them even more.

On the day before this pair invaded our home, I ate as many pieces of a wet newspaper as tolerable. The bitter inky taste is not a craving, but a solution to expanding my empty stomach. It helps the pain. I've no choice. The rains mean no minnows, and the sparse grass blades are trampled into the mud. No passersby for a hungry boy to beg an apple. No grilling by Pandit. I'm too short to reach inside the tall garbage cans outside my village's restaurants. I sneak through alleys in the night to look for cat food, or food containers in trash bins. The containers are heavy but I manage to tip them over. Nothing. I'm determined to control my hunger until Momma returns home. Tomorrow I'll eat the grass in the mud if I must. I will.

But today. Today, I must refuse the temptation of dark Russian chocolate on my hungriest of days. Um, dark Russian chocolate. *Stop. Focus.*

Yesterday was double torture after eating newspaper for breakfast.

My stomach is inky on the inside as I belch the sour newspaper taste. Pandit's son, Afanasiy, thought he could bully me. Along with a few of his hefty pals who claim to be spawns of government worker dads. Cowards. I might be hungry but I'm not weak. They blast their jibes behind my back as I walk home alone after school. I ignore them. But I have a plan: when I reach the wooden bridge over the stream near home, I'll turn around to face the taunting boys. One by one, I will throw them into the stream. This is my plan. They're bigger, but I'm faster. Without blinking an eyelash, I lock eyes with chubby-cheeked Afanasiy, my blue eyes glued to his.

"What you going to do about it, you fucking beggar?" asks the hefty bully. My eyes don't move. My body isn't stiff. I'm relaxed. Calm. I appear to be in an unnerved state of hypnosis. I am. My eyes follow his fat cheeks as they wobble.

I feel a pang in my gut as a chilled wind blows my wispy blond curls. Momma wouldn't like my curls touching my shirt collar rather than trimmed above it, the way she likes to couture it.

I stare as hard as I know how into Afanasiy's eyes. I'm not emotional. I'm not scared. I'm hungry. All I can think about are his fat jowls that I would love to have barbequed on a plate. I don't know why I speak these words. Perhaps I'm a monster. I don't know what I should say instead.

My eight-year-old lips separate from my teeth. I think I'm feral. Maybe like a hungry wolf in the Siberian forests. Calmly, the words that fall from my mouth are, "I want to eat your face."

My eyes still don't blink. I don't move. I don't will it. I don't control it. It just happens. My lips don't cover my teeth but remain in a growl position, as though I'm a werewolf ready to shred my prey.

These bullies aren't accustomed to push back from a momma's boy like me. The boy whose pretty momma walks him to school every morning. The momma who's always ready with a snack when I get home. Now she's gone. Just gone.

There must be something in my glacial blue eyes. Sergei Radkov won't be low-hanging fruit on this day. I will not. Is it possible I will kill them or will I be killed? I don't know. I wonder, if I kill them, would I eat them? Would I really want the fat globules of Afanasiy's cheeks coursing through my blood, or would I rather die? My gaze doesn't abandon his.

I don't know which mouth speaks it, but one boy says, "Shit, I think he's been possessed. You know, like in that movie. Maybe he was bitten by a werewolf or possessed by a demon? I think he's getting ready to morph into a vampire."

The boy runs off in the opposite direction. The rest of Afanasiy's troop deserts him, running after the boy. After regarding the serious gaze of my eyes a second more, Afanasiy runs, too.

Now hiding under my bed, another chocolate drops to the floor and skids near the lady's fat foot bulging from her blue shoe. The silky skirt of white with navy-blue polka dots kiss her female legs just inches above the shoe. My eyes stare at the pieces of delight as hard as I had stared into Afanasiy's eyes. I want that chocolate. I do. *Focus.*

The government-working father must be the culprit who called for the aid of the pair now sitting on my bed. Had to be. How can I get out of this? Where can I go? Can I scramble from under my bed and run away? Where would I go?

The bed-sitting couple talks of coworkers, the soccer season, and things abstract to me. Momma taught me that word—*abstract*—when she was teaching me about art in a museum. The couple continues to chat. I continue to hunger.

What if I go for the closer piece? Not fast. Slow. I won't make a sound. I'll eat it later. Slowly, I go for the closer piece. My hand extends. I spread out my fingers and affix two of them around the fattest part of the morsel.

Slow. Slowly, now, slow, comes a whisper inside of me.

Before I can retract my arm under the bed, a large hand swoops down and grabs my wrist.

I dig in my heels, trying to create traction on the wet tile floor. I swing my other arm around the wooden bed slat above my head. My grip tightens around it, hoping for leverage against a stronger power.

"Let go of me, you." Gasping in an ocean of air, I squeal. "You meanie! My father will not like this, you, you bastard!" *Sorry, Momma.*

"You're the bastard, kid. No one knows who your mother whored with to create you," says the bass voice.

"My mother is no whore. Do NOT call my mother a whore!" I scream in agony as the man jerks hard enough to hurt my shoulder. My shoulder feels like it isn't even in socket. It hurts real bad.

"Don't hurt him. We got orders," says the woman with bulging feet, reminding the gruff man of their limitations.

"We always got orders," comes his retort. "And this kid is never seeing his momma ever again. Got that kid?" says the man as he scoops up my fighting body.

My arm is hanging funny. I can't move it. It's the worst pain I've ever known in my recently-turned-eight-years-old life. It forces me to give up. I know I can't fight. The man picks me up like a lumberjack and throws my kicking, screaming body over his thick shoulders. My face is scratched by the hairs on his neck.

Although I'm in pain, I stop crying. I won't cry anymore. My wounded shoulder upsets me, but I'm more upset about being defeated. This means I won't be at our apartment when Momma gets home. How will she know where to find me? I just want to be here when Momma returns. Is that too much to ask?

My sweet momma, who wasn't here a few months ago when I got home from school. My sweet momma, who's always here when I get home. Not on that day. Not on this day. Maybe never again.

My body recoils and I scream as I'm toted like a human lump from our apartment. The presence of Momma leaves me when the door slams. I shudder. She's gone, vanished. Just vanished. "Bye Momma," whispers lips covered with tears and snot as I'm thrown into the back of a car.

What did the man say? *Never going to see my momma again?*

PART ONE
THE COMMANDER

CHAPTER 1
VICTORY DAY

MAY 9, 2024
Victory Day Celebration of 1945 Nazi Surrender
Presidential Dacha, Ural Mountains, Russia

I was never afraid to die. I'm not afraid to die today. I'd prefer not to die on such a fine spring morning with the smell of Russian blooms faint in the air. But what the hell? Mostly, I wish not to die at the hands of my own people.

Yes, I'm a Spetsnaz commander. GRU. But at the end of the day, I'm an average man kicking life in his early forties. Just a regular guy like all the rest. Yet, at the end of *this* day, I hope I'll still be just a regular guy—a *live* one.

No, it wasn't my lot in life to wed a Russian beauty and gift my country with a litter of children. To do what exactly? Line up the kids, pat each progeny on the head, and say, "I'll see you in a year or two?" Kiss my wife, and leave?

No, this was not the path of Commander Sergei Radkov. Instead, here I stand in front of this godforsaken presidential dacha. I'm a soldier. A professional soldier. Commando. Spy. Spetsnaz. GRU. I've spied. I've fought. Hell, at times, I've *fucked* for country. I can tell you in honest words that Sergei Radkov has one ladylove. Her name is Russia.

I drip in sweat. The water from my brow is filling my shoes. I'm standing in front of the side entrance to the presidential dacha like a guard dog. Those that surround me and my dedicated commandos, know we are Spetsnaz. They know we would not think twice about dying. Nor killing…

Damn. If possible, I'm sweating more. Sweating more bullets than my AKS-74U weapon can fire. My heart pains as if a million rounds from my own weapon have shot through my pumping organ. My breath heaves as I take in my surrounding space. I can't imagine this scene before me. Yet, I'm starring right into it. Can't take it in, though. Can't believe it. Cannot.

Instead of being focused, I imagine my chest exploding. Bits of my heart muscle plopping with a thud on top of those fragrant Russian blooms. Leaving nothing of me except a few of my blond curls floating from the sky like bird feathers. I've experienced enough men blown to hell during my years of soldiering to understand my imagined scenario. Compared to this scene, I prefer it.

I'm afraid. I've not felt fear this deep since two social workers sitting on my bed captured me. They dragged me off to my new orphanage home. Made me an orphan boy. Fear. Goddamned fear. Cold-hearted, inconceivable fear. The great unknowns. It's food for the greatest fear mongers in all of mankind. I had long since squashed down that fear after that day when I was hauled away. I, Commander Sergei Radkov, have spent my life methodically avoiding the unknown. And now it's crawling up my spine like fire from a missile launch.

I do not, *do not*, have time for this bullshit. I snap my mind into focus as I scour the landscape for good options. I look to the left, to the right, ahead over the mountains ridge and behind me. Thousands on all sides. Fuck, fuck, fuck! Thousands against me and my mere eight commandos. All good men. None worthy of dying today. I shift my focus from scoping the expanse and look into the faces of the rebels in front of me. Micro vision each facial expression that I scan. All are here expecting a fight. Expecting blood. Expecting death. Men and women. Determined. I want to shout at them that blood is not pretty. Neither is death. It's in fact a very, very ugly business. It doesn't matter who bleeds or who dies.

It hasn't been a full hour since the standoff began. There has to be an option somewhere. Must be. I need to find one scant option and pray. Quick. I want to hold my silver Solovetsky cross that I wear around my neck. Rub it between my fingers and take a few meditative breaths. Okay, it's my security blanket, my cross. My adult pacifier. It relaxes me when I'm stressed. My connection to my country, its history, and the world my mother lived in. I conclude I have no time for such luxuries. Time to stop thinking like a pussy and start being the commander I am.

My countrymen surround the besieged presidential dacha. My compatriots, my goddamned compatriots, numbering into the thousands, likely the tens of thousands. Because of the terrain of the dacha's Ural Mountain perch, I assess any approximation to be useless. The number doesn't matter. Many. Too many. Too many came here to die today. Or to kill. Killing isn't pretty either. I've killed enough to know.

How so many rebels breached my security and arrived on my secured mountaintop is something I don't have to consider for long. It must be an inside job involving most of my initial hundred commandos defecting to the other side. I got that in the first three seconds of this little tea party. The sweat on my brow reminds me of just how fucked I am. I shove those thoughts to the back of my brain. Solution. I must find a solution.

I observe Vogo. Little fucker. His head and half of his short torso protrude out of the hatch of a BTR-90 personnel carrier. He's only five meters from me near the dacha side-entrance, with those under my protection inside. Vogo's thousands of rebel groupies are gathered below him as far as the eye can see. The little pissant always did like attention. He's in pissant heaven with a bullhorn pulled up to his little pissant lips. Fucker. His words egg on the crowd surrounding the dacha. They eat up his every word. Words such as "REVOLUTION!" The pissant should've been a rock star and left soldiering alone. I watch as he disgraces his uniform. I can't believe it. Vogo, in on this? I may not believe it, but damn if it's not right in front of me. Fucker.

Vogo Orlinsky is someone I consider to be a close and long-standing friend. We've been together since the English-Speaking Academy at eight years old. Along with Ivan the Silent, at fourteen years old the three of us attended Suvorov Military Academy together. Upon graduation, we three entered the Military University. Currently, our trio are all Spetsnaz comrades. GRU. At least until today. Today, I, Commander Sergei Radkov, can't say who the hell anybody is anymore.

I put Vogo in charge of security late last evening while I caught a few hours of sleep. Pissant knew I would. If my mentor and commander, Alexei, were with the team, then I would've defaulted to taking charge during his rest. But Alexi is not here. I suppose he is on another assignment. I wonder if Alexei...

No, not Alexei. He is more of a hardened patriot than I. I wonder what he would think and do about all this. If Alexei were here, he would've already shot Vogo. Probably smile while pulling the trigger. Alexei is a man who is often underestimated because of his short stature, just like Vogo. Alexei may carry a congenial manner but, inside, he is the strongest man I know. He's my mentor. *Our* mentor. I love him. Owe him my life. I'd never call him a pissant.

Vogo is the little pissant. We've been at each other's side since we were eight years old. Vogo, whom I've trusted for decades. Trusted with my life. I'm trying to process how in the hell he was on the side of the revolutionaries and allowed this armed crowd of thousands to engulf the mountainside. Vogo? Vogo... I shake my head.

Vogo might be a little pissant. But, without a doubt, no one except Vogo could have gotten the amphibious beast in which he stands to travel up the sharp ridges and craggy outcroppings of this mountainside. No one can drive like Vogo. Best pilot I know. Plane, helicopter, boat, tank. It doesn't matter. If it moves, Vogo can handle it. An amazing sight, even under the circumstances. Vogo. Only Vogo. Damn you, traitor Vogo.

Questions remain. Is Vogo in charge of this revolution? If not, who is? More importantly, what's the little fucker and his flock going to do?

My mind struggles to process every plausible answer. I don't like any of them.

Across the valley, black ore darkens much of the Ural mountainsides. Proof of springtime shows as the sun warms the mountainsides and melts the snow from the rooftops of the ore mountains. New flora has flung its color upon the brooding mountainous landscape. This rugged dacha mountain, combined with Russian engineering, provides support for layer after layer of the massive dacha complex. Now is not the time to awe at Russian engineering. Yet I can't help myself.

The dacha stands in stark contrast to its usual bearings on this day. The complex country home caters to the human experience via sensation and sight at every turn. Gazebo views inside guest housing float out onto private ledges. Elevators and staircases provide transport to structures which yield a privileged experience.

In a quieter time, a mountaintop viewer might see the burst of spring colors below as wildflowers dancing the barynya, a Russian folk dance, as their stems bend to the will of the wind in the warming sunshine. A particular dacha structure erected upon an extended outcropping gives one the experience of an eagle's soar. Straight down the cliff appears as you walk outside onto the balcony.

There are few sights of dancing flowers or anything soaring on this day. Only bedlam. I return my focus to what is in front of me. On this day, more than any other day, my mind wanders. My attention span isn't for shit today. Maybe it's because I sense death is close. Smell it.

When my thoughts return to what I'm witnessing, I take in the rebels more than the rebellion. Witnessing a maddening crowd as far as my eyes can see, but each body is an individual in the crowd. A BTR-90. Vogo. Betrayal of country by men under my charge. Fuck.

My mind forgets the other dacha structures which allow their inhabitants to be hidden from view altogether by their abutment to the thickening forest. Privacy. A rugged delight. One can streak naked as animals in the forest without the intrusion of human eyeballs. Yes, that is a privileged experience. I force delight from my mind.

I forget the dacha structures, woven around the mountainside until ending at the topside plateau. Despite the impressive invasion into nature's space, the native homes made of birchwood sit with rustic grace and a gentle demeanor within their singular world. I always compared them to a lover holding hands with the Russian Continental Divide. Yes, I forget them, along with all things unimportant. Lives are at stake today. Not just lives, but Russian lives. I usually never let my mind wander, but today, geez, I'm all over the place. Maybe it's because I think I may not make it. This is my day. End of the line. It's my turn. My turn to die. Die today. Accept it? Fuck that shit.

It'd been my task to ensure security for this dacha and its periphery on behalf of the president of my government. A government I've served since my childhood. A government, which lacks the abundance of many things, including food. Yet, it has served me since childhood. Although at times, sparsely so.

It'd been easy for me to plan this mission. Over the past years, the Commander in Chief has often commissioned Spetsnaz teams to secure this dacha location. This president demanded Spetsnaz, the best of the best, to provide his presidential security when the sovereign left the Kremlin walls of Moscow.

The president has dozens of other dachas. Some are, shall we say, somewhat unknown? However, this dacha seems to be the president's favorite. The chief commander visits this location more often than his other voluminous real estate choices. Planning security here was easy. Routine.

I, Commander Sergei Radkov, have never taken "easy" for granted. Never. Eliminated the unknowns. I enjoy the reputation of a dependable commander. Depended on because I don't let accidents happen. It's never easy. Not really. But I endeavor to make it seem that way. Time and again I've protected my homeland, my team, my president. No mistakes. No glitches. Easy as a smoothie on a Sunday afternoon. I'm not bragging about these things. This is who I am. This is what I do. This is what I was born to do. Not easy on this day. No. No smoothies today. God damn it.

Before I awakened to this day, everything had been routine. Smooth. Silky smooth. Damned easy. Although my task was made more challenging by my president, everything had gone according to all plans and protocols. This assignment took an especially intense turn when the president decided to host all the Russian Federation's elite military personnel along with additional high-ranking subordinates here for Victory Day. This arrangement wasn't something I expected this cautious president to undertake. But I made it look easy. I did.

How did it all take such a sharp left turn? How the fuck did it happen without me hearing a breath? A word? Revolutionaries. For fuck's sake. And most of my team in on it. Even Vogo, damn him. For the first time in my career, I can't put all the moving parts together to create a cohesive picture and develop a plan. I need answers. I want answers. I don't want to die before I get them.

No, the president didn't help. Arrogant bastard. I still don't understand my president. The leader knew well that by having all his top military advisors present together, he was asking for significant security issues. How did he reply when me and my commander presented the issue to him?

"It's Victory Day, God damn it. Instead of the usual la-de-da Moscow parade, this Victory Day will show the people that Russian leaders are serving their country. Let the fucking locals parade. The leaders are honoring their duty to secure the Russian nation. Just as you will, Commander."

Bastard didn't have to tell me my duty.

I emphatically disagreed with my supreme officer. The president thought himself to be fail-safe. I wasn't wrong in thinking my president to be downright fool hardy. As a commander, I understood I must accept my duty. Accepted it with a sigh but accepted it all the same. I didn't sigh at my duty so much as my belief that the president's mind was weakening. His arrogance had begun to weaken the man.

Now, here I stand. In front of the entrance to what should be a secure presidential dacha. Sweating. And I, Commander Sergei Radkov, am completely butt-fucked. I feel like I have a pile of fish bones stuck in my throat. Mission failure. I don't like it. Hell, with all my training, I don't have the skill set to deal with failure. Failure has never been a considered option. I struggle to swallow as I accept my mission's failure. My failure wad is stuck somewhere between my Adam's apple and the pile of fish bones. I hock and spit.

I missed a signal somewhere along the way. I usually feel something in my gut. Something. Nothing this time. I missed lots of signals.

Now Russians will die. My comrades will die. I will die. Maybe it's not my president who has weakened. He will likely die, too. All because I allowed myself to think it was going to be easy. Too easy. Just too damned easy.

We are still in the midst of a standoff at the dacha entrance side door. Minutes are ticking by. I still have no plan. *Think, God damn it*, I urge myself. Me and my small band of handpicked commandos are the only remaining protection between the main convention room holding the President of Russia and his invited staff and this maddening crowd.

Help should have arrived by now. There's been no reply to our SOS. And the rebels aren't making a move. Why? I'm sure whoever is in charge of this dance we find ourselves in knows just how long it should take for backup to arrive. A scorching, killing backup. The rebels should've stormed the dacha when they first arrived, and the group didn't need thousands. Doesn't make sense.

Hell, Vogo and the other commando traitors could've taken me and my eight out already. Something is off. Something is way off. I know it, but I'll be damned if I can figure it out. This is not a military maneuver. It isn't. It's more of a party. A fucking Victory Day Parade.

Blood vessels in my temples pulse. Vibrate. Tick like a time bomb. Whatever I'm going to do, it better be soon. This empowered crowd won't remain calm much longer.

My eyes evaluate the swarm of vehicles on the mountain plateau. A menagerie of metal clusters litter the mountain road. Upfitted vehicles contain various rifle mounts. Other vehicles provide transport as prior, current, and wannabe soldiers hang various weaponry out of vehicle windows. Most soldiers and a handful of wannabes are familiar to me.

I got it. Now I have it. I quickly assemble a plan and pray.

I remember certain persons inside those vehicles, others with rifles in their hands. Once, I had called them comrades and friends. I hope they still are. Every life here is banking on it. The thing I'm sure of is that I can't direct a bullet into a rogue comrade. I sure as hell can't shoot any Russian citizen without considering dying first. And I sure as hell am going to do everything in my power to protect my charges who are inside this dacha. That is my sworn duty. Period. And God damn it.

I order the remaining few commandos to remain vigilant, and if this plan fails, not to die over this day's events. There's nothing else the commandos might do to save the officers inside. Good commandos dying beside the doomed would help no one. "And that's an order, too, damn it!" I yelp, reinforcing my brief message to my small band of dedicated men.

While moving in front of them, I whisper in confidence to Ivan the Silent. "See they carry out my order, damn it."

Fair-haired Ivan the Silent gives an expressionless nod.

I fly one hand in the air. With my other hand I point my weapon toward the ground. I take a step forward toward the BTR-90. "I want to lay down my weapon," I shout to my countrymen and former comrades. No reason to bother checking my weapon safety. I know this weapon as well as I do any of my attached body parts.

Carefully, so very carefully, I lay my weapon on the ground.

CHAPTER 2
SERGEI BECOMES THE WHITE STALLION

WITH MY HANDS in the air, I walk a few meters to the side of the carrier. I pull myself up top, using the tires and side of the vehicle. It's a challenge even for me. I'm proud to say I'm a man who has worked to strengthen his body every day of his life. Every day since I was an eight-year-old orphan. I try to make it look easy. Engage my muscles. Stretch sinew tied to bone. All trained and honed and trained again since my orphanage days. It was survival then. It still is.

I spent my childhood free time running the orphanage yard perimeter, doing sit-ups in bed at night while others were sleeping, or chin-ups on the metal shower rod. Fitness was survival. Survival was everything. I wanted to stay alive long enough to run farther and stronger in life. I wanted my momma to be proud of me when she found me. In my eight-year-old head, I always thought she would. Now my body coordinates its climb with muscle memory and lifts me up like seasoned lovers in the night. In spite of everything else, I'm thinking of Momma.

Once I'm up top on the carrier, I say to Vogo, "Let me have the bullhorn, Vogo." I command more than request of my friend who has brought himself up from his hole to stand on the carrier beside me.

Vogo, who likes to be in control of any and every situation, looks at me reluctantly. He stands silent for a moment as his brown hair glistens with a red tinge in the Eurasian sun.

"It's okay, my comrade," I assure him in a softer voice.

My blue eyes look at my friend, and again request, "May I have the bullhorn?" I use the nicest, calmest voice that I can muster. "Please."

Vogo nods consent and appears he will indeed hand the bullhorn over to me. He looks down demurely. Pissant. Vogo has always hated himself for giving in to me. I know it.

We've been the best of friends, yet competitive to the point of near death. Since we began our military careers, I've always been his superior. Hell, even got better marks at English school. At Suvorov, I really surpassed him and blistered past him at the Military University. In Spetsnaz, there was no doubt whether I was Alexei's favorite.

Yet, Vogo is one of my two long-held and dearest friends. I've always loved him and had his back. I'm angry at him, but I love him as I stand beside him today, despite his betrayal.

So once again here's Vogo, giving into me. Even while he is holding all the cards. He hates it. I know he does. He's always given in to me, as though he were on autopilot. The quiet crowd watches as I look into his brown eyes as if to say, "Yes, pissant, I always bested everyone. I was always the class leader. I was always your friend. And you liked it. Hate me if you can."

Before he hands me the bullhorn, Vogo pulls the horn to his lips and speaks to the crowd. "This is my friend Sergei Radkov. He is a Russian patriot. He wants to speak to you all. Give him your attention." Pissant.

I nod to Vogo as I take the horn from him. I have no words. All I have is my heart. I let my heart use my vocal cords as I begin to speak. "Good Russian people, I've lain down my weapon. I know most of you think I'm your enemy, but I tell you, this is not so." I pause a few ticks to let that sink in.

Standing on top of the metal monster beside Vogo in the Eurasian sun, I continue my narrative off the cuff. "Russians, people of my heart, I've served you with great joy all my adult life. I've trained since I was fourteen years of age at the Suvorov Academy and then later at the Military University.

"Good people, I owe every morsel of bread that ever entered my hungry mouth to you. Every shoelace that ever tied my shoes, I owe to you. All of my education, I owe to you." I point my finger into the crowd so they understand I'm speaking to each of them.

"You see, I was an orphan. You know how limited such a child's choices are, yet the Russian people took care of me when I could not. So, very early in my life, I decided to take the path, no matter how hard, to serve my people. The Russian people who are my only family, and the only love that fills my heart."

The crowd whistles, cheers, and shouts, "SERGEI! SERGEI! SERGEI!"

Vogo's brown eyes blaze down on the carrier's metal surface as though he's a fire-breathing dragon planning a barbeque. I'm thinking he regrets handing me this bullhorn. Well, just wait, pissant. I'm just getting started.

Someone in the crowd near the tank exclaims, "He looks like my white stallion who swishes his tail in confidence as though he might run through the fields of Father Russia and rule the world from its plains!"

"Yes, and strong," says one person.

"Confident," says another, nodding in affirmation.

"Commanding," replies the first man who compared me to a white stallion. "Look at his blue eyes. He is so very Russian. Yes, he is a stallion."

I hear some of their words since they are front and center standing near me, but I don't respond. Then I hear a small group cheering, "WHITE STALLION! WHITE STALLION!" Soon, the cheer spreads like wildfire in summer throughout the entire crowd. I have no idea why the crowd is cheering this. A horse? For fuck's sake. I just need to stay calm and in control. Whoever they think this white stallion actually is, I'm going to need to be more convincing. And stronger. Yes, stronger. And more convincing…

I pull the bullhorn back to my lips. "I understand your anger. Brothers and sisters of Russia, I understand your fear. Not a fear of dying. Not a fear of getting hurt, but a fear of the future and what might happen to the Father Russia we all love."

Once again, the crowd roars. "WHITE STALLION! WHITE STALLION!" I give them their moment of revelry. Maybe this white stallion has to do with something other than me. Maybe I misunderstand. A mantra? I flatten my palm with a wave toward the ground to request attention from my compatriots.

"I cannot stop any actions that are the will of others today. But listen to me, my good Russians, as I have a plan so that many lives may be saved. NO ONE WILL DIE TODAY!" I shout with certainty.

"WHITE STALLION!" The crowd roars with enthusiasm.

"You are my brothers and sisters of great Father Russia. I need all of you here to live better and more peaceful lives for yourselves and those you love," I pronounce. Then I allow a short pause. It'll give the souls around me a moment to pause too. Hopefully, the members of the maddened crowd will consider safety over emotion for an iota of time.

"This man here," I nod and point at Vogo, "is your friend. He's my friend, too. We both know him. I propose that you allow me and three of my men to go inside the dacha. I'll try to persuade the men inside to give themselves up to Russian law and justice. The men will come out with their hands up and surrender themselves. Vogo can pick a team from among you, or your leadership can decide who will go with Vogo while I'm inside. I won't play any tricks against my people. The men will come outside, including the current Russian president."

I stop my speech just long enough to point to my lifelong friend. "Then Vogo and his team and my team will take all of them in this carrier," I say while emphasizing the vehicle by pointing to its metal frame. "To the closest prison, which is, per Russian law, wherein they will await trial in Russian courts."

Breathe, two, three. "They'll be guarded by both of our teams. It'll be in this way that the Russian people will have spoken, and our government will begin reform."

I don't know which laws the president has actually broken, but the economy has tanked. Once again, my nation's people are hungry for change. Hungry period. I hate it. I hate hunger. A revolution isn't so surprising, but I'm surprised it's happening on this day. I must give the revolutionaries something. A president in prison is better than a dead president. That'll have to do. For now.

Vogo's eyes and ears perk up when he hears me speak his name. He likes hearing his name. Vogo loves a stage. I know what he's thinking. *Sergei, who always won the cadet treat at the Suvorov Academy to go to the movies. While the rest of the cadets stayed in their barracks to study, Sergei's adolescent feet padded to the movies on Saturdays. Sergei, whose pockets were full of toasted sunflower seeds from the academy kitchen, and with the meager change for movie admission.* Childhood competition is bouncing between Vogo's ears just as it did when we were fourteen years old.

Jealous pissant loves hearing me call out his name to the crowd. He acts as though he cares about nothing or no one, but Vogo needs attention more than anybody I know. I hand back the bullhorn to him at the end of my proposition.

To the cheers of "WHITE STALLION!" I jump down from the tank, pick up my weapon, and walk through the dacha side door. Three commandos follow me. I hear the crowd roar. I'm not sure if the crowd's sentiment is one of approval or not. It doesn't matter. I'm going to do what I need to do.

CHAPTER 3
THE TEARS OF A WHITE STALLION

WITH MY THREE COMMANDOS, we blitz through the dacha corridor. We scurry down a hallway lined with opaque wallpaper containing black stick scenery. Intricately carved birch moldings the size of a lumberjack's leg hang from the ceiling. My team has no time for scenery today.

We're in a corridor that I, when I had the luxury of time to be a smart-ass, nicknamed "The Hall of Handshakes". Pictures line the walls of the hallway. There are numerous matted photos with lamp lighting above each, snapshots of the Russian president shaking hands with a variety of world leaders. An eye trained to look for minute details might notice that the light bulb illuminating the president's face appears a shade brighter than the person standing next to him.

The president makes for perfect photos. Perfectly straight shoulders. Perfectly straight teeth making a perfectly straight smile. The leader's pinpoint eyes focus perfectly straight into the lens. Perfect photos. With my uproarious sense of humor, I often joked to my comrades that I hope never to be placed between this president and a camera flash. No time for such musings today.

The commando team trots to the end of the corridor and clears it. The corridor curves to the left. There is a dead end. The commandos enter the door on the left. From there, we enter The Maze of Turns.

I slip a key into the last door of the trek. We enter the corridor with caution. The commandos face the convention entrance, which is fronted with bulletproof glass. Inside, the officials are gathered at a long table. Their world is noticeably in chaos.

I order the commandos to secure the position. One on each end and one in the middle. The middle commando lies belly flat at ninety-degree angles to the conference room and parallel to each door. Hand grenades and smoke bombs lay at his side. The weapons of each commando points to the center. Ready commandos. It's a beautiful thing. Soldiers without exact orders knowing exactly what to do. Love it.

I pick up the red phone on the wall to request entrance inside.

"Relinquish your weapon," hollers the reddest-faced general.

"As you wish," I reply and comply. I abandon my weapon for the second time this day. Lifting my palms above my head, a buzz ring is the cue for me to enter.

Inside, pleading eyes are on me.

"Mr. President." I say in respect along with a salute as I address my Commander in Chief.

The Commander in Chief returns my formality with a slight nod. Next, I address my other superiors in the same military fashion.

"This is our security, Mr. President," says one general.

"I know who he is, General," replies the irritated, gray-eyed leader with pinpoint pupils that see much. "What do you have for us, Sergei?"

"The situation is hot, Sir. Our military personnel are involved. The insurgents knew where the communication centers were located. The rebels disabled the area's cell towers. I did recon in the back tunnel. They captured it, Sir. Although you can't see the rogue commandos, the tunnel is wired. The commandos are hovering out of bomb range. The entrances are the only way out."

"What are you saying? That we just surrender? Is that your solution, boy? You expect I should just give myself up to this mob because you did a shitty job of providing my security?"

My jaws clench as shame slams into my heart with a jolt. Fish bones return to my throat. I don't reply. I can't reply.

"I'll shoot you myself," the president declares with itchy ire after reaching into a drawer for his Sr-1 Vektor. He yanks the handgun out and points it in my face.

My muscles strain in my stillness. I squarely face the gray-eyed man who is threatening my life. My president has every right to kill me. I failed him. But I'm one of the few faithful he has left at his disposal. I hope wisdom wins out for my president's benefit. My leader behaves as if he is relaying a routine order while steeling his gun between my eyes.

"Stop, Mr. President!" a general exclaims. "Do you want a wild crowd in here before we're ready?"

My president shoves his weapon back into the drawer. Neither of us blinks from our eye lock. It's not a pissing contest. But if I blink, then I'm automatically the last man from which the president should take advice. My president breaks the silence and speaks in a businesslike fashion, as though he's requesting a routine report on troop deployments.

"Can you disable the tunnel bombs?" he asks.

I shake my head to my words. "I can't advise it, Sir. I'm sure Vogo, whom I've served with in many lands for Father Russia, executed the wiring. No one can surpass him, Sir. Vogo will have lain many alternate bypasses and false triggers without even thinking about it. He has devised dozens of charges we used in the past. However, I've never once seen Vogo wire his magic without using his imagination to add a few unique charges. The man is second to none. It's a game for him, and he's crafty. Chances are that the next best expert in the world would likely blow the tunnel."

After listening to my explanatory monologue, the president wheezes through his teeth, "Is this Vogo not your friend?"

I dislike what he's implying. I don't allow myself the luxury of being incensed. My glacial blue eyes look through my long, dark lashes and lock onto the president's pinpoint gray ones. "Sir, I have known Vogo for many years. I know him as a friend. Vogo is a man of intelligence. I've watched him use treachery without mercy. He's received and excelled in the best training Father Russia can offer."

"Oh, here's Moscow," cries a general with excited relief. "Finally, someone is picking up the back line!"

"Moscow is silent," says a monotone voice over the speakerphone. Then the call is unceremoniously disconnected. The general opens his mouth to scream, but no sound exits his throat.

The president's face turns white as a billowy stray cloud on a crisp blue-sky day. He falls back into his chair. "I'll be damned if these bastards can march right in and kill me in my own home."

In reality, it's the people's property, but I'm not foolish enough to split that hair. "I have a plan, Sir. I can't promise you what will happen afterward, but it'll give us time to think and plan."

"I've heard your *plan*—outside, as you spoke to the people," the president replies, while tilting his head forward with a nod to enunciate his words.

"Gentlemen" is the only word spoken by the president as the leader rises. It's not just a word. It's an order. Shoulders straight. He leads the convoy through the Maze of Corridors, up the Hall of Handshakes until the parade of leaders reaches the door to the outside. I take lead in the front. My commandos fall into position. No man speaks. All officials prideful. Backs straight. Leaders of a nation carry on as though there is no threat to their security.

I walk to Vogo's position to certify that the leaders from the conference room are present. I assure my comrade (former comrade? I don't know) that the conference room, as a point of reference, is clear. Everyone present has given themselves up and is prepared to board the tank. Before anyone can move, there is a thundering explosion from the dacha.

A stack of black smoke coming from the location of the furnace room provides an immediate diagnosis. Holy shit. I'm sure the leaders sent secretaries and other underlings to burn documents by the box load. The furnace overloaded. It has blown. Simply blown. An explosion ensues, and the west end of the dacha is on fire. I still as I try to decide my best course of action.

In less than a second, shots ring out from the rebels. The word "NO!" blares from my mouth as I sprint to protect my president. It's my duty to die for him. I will. My body lunges to protect my Commander in Chief. I'm too late. The President of Russia, his subordinates, along with twelve leading unarmed military advisors, are all killed by speeding bullets in this faraway dacha. This faraway dacha built for peace and serenity.

It is a land forgotten by time. The mountain exists in a land which has forgotten time. It's a land which thanks God Almighty for the blessings the land provides to the natives. Simple. Rugged. Bare. It's not a scene like a wintery Christmas card of fluffy snow and icicled windowpanes as seen through the late fall, winter, and early spring months.

I stare into the face of the gray-eyed president whose lifeless body now lies beneath me. I look around at the leaders fallen beside my president. My head shakes with grief. My body shakes in disbelief. I *am* grief.

I watch as blood trickles out of the men's frames with a sticky red consistency, crawling along the ground like an amoeba in water. As grim as most might consider it, I thank the blizzard of the past season for having melted. I can't explain why, but I hate to witness blood reddening the purity of a snowy landscape.

More machine than man; I'm a machine that can no longer download. Zombie-like, I stumble to the east side door entrance of the dacha several meters away, where my commandos remain. I collapse on my haunches, my back against the dacha wall.

Ivan the Silent sits beside me. I watch the commotion with a hollow stare. My chest contains anger, shame, compassion, even love, but most of all, grief. I see Russians to the dacha's west who have sustained burns, injuries, death. Hell, someone must have thought this a tea gala. At least the revolutionaries thought to set up ambulances and medical support for this little ado.

To the dacha's east lie dead bodies on the ground whose protection was my responsibility. Around them, Russians, my Russian people, cheer with joy at the lifeless bodies of the fallen. All this gaiety while other Russians are injured or worse. The imbalance rips open my heart.

Then there is the press. Foreign. Domestic. No one's invitation was overlooked to this little tea party except for mine. As per the norm, the media is being the media. The press adds to the disarray by racing around like children on a playground. They poke microphones in anyone's face who will say something. Anybody. Anything. Fuckers.

I don't know when the first teardrop fell. I don't know how many fell, nor how long they fell. They just fell.

CHAPTER 4
BITS AND PIECES

I OPEN the door to my New York City hotel room and throw my purse on the bed. Next, my shoes go sailing through the air. The oriental rug receives their plonk. My body gets the last toss as I fling it onto the bed beside my purse. A wet spot grows where my body plops. I simply don't care.

My day moved from being good and successful to long and hard. Fast. One hell of a day.

Ten a.m. sharp started my day with a book signing. The event ran past the apportioned time. I sprinted in high heels from the bookstore to the conference. Students Against War (SAW) invited me to be a forum speaker. As a physician formerly associated with Doctors Without Borders, I can say plenty about the terrors of war on a population. Especially on the most vulnerable. Women. Children. The elderly. And not just the obvious terrors, but lack of clean water and food. Malnourished children and pregnant women. Malnourished elders and those with disabilities.

At the moment, though, my personal starvation is at the forefront of my mind. No time to eat since breakfast, and now I'm fending off hunger shakes while battling negative emotions from a day turned sideways.

Afraid my stomach might growl at the rostrum, I had grabbed a chocolate chip cookie and a bottle of water in the welcoming room before entering the conference. An elder Columbia University professor gave me a little, "tsk, tsk." I bounced him a wink and a smile. *Hey, if a chocolate chip isn't for eating, why have them there?* Tsk tsk.

My stomach groans at the remembrance, so I sit up and order room service. That chore accomplished; I lie back down in the same wet spot on the bed. It would horrify my mother to see my pouting behavior, but on this evening, I'm not Elizabeth Frederick's daughter. I'm a woman who does not give a rat's ankle about the soaking wet clothes on the bed, shoes on the floor, nor my disheveled appearance.

I prepared for this day rather playfully but professional. I even donned a suit. Not my favorite attire: khaki shorts or long khaki trousers with a plain tee shirt. Yes, that's the ticket. Guess I can't always dress as I did when on assignment in the field. This is New York City. Not Africa, South America, or Asia. I miss those khaki days, but life has turned me in a direction that I know I must see to the end, come what may. Do what good I can while I can. And the field will always be there. Always.

It seems the world believes I have a "platform," so I figure I need to dress for the role. Dress as a woman with a platform. Is it because I'm a woman who stands up for what she believes in, that folks think I have a "platform"? I don't know. I can't answer that question.

I chose a bright-pink suit to wear. Not a magenta nor a cotton candy pink, but a rich tropical pink. It's the color of the warm climate I grew up in. Oh, the memories of growing up by the ocean shores will never leave my soul. They were the last place I called home. Even to this day, I love tropical colors and clothes and amplifiers blaring a Buffet tune.

Me in all my glory: that is the persona I exhibit on this day. I pull my long dark hair, which has now grown to lapping my ankles, straight backward. I was concerned my lengthy curls might create a distraction, and I didn't want that. I secured it with a clasp, one of the tightest that I own.

Curls can dilute a woman's important words from what I've experienced. Yet I had every intention of feeling like myself and didn't twist my mane into a huge bun-wad like a Japanese geisha. Thought about cutting it all off, all that hair. Tempted at times to shave it all off like a Buddhist monk. Both my agent and my manager scream at the idea. "It's your brand," they say. Okay, so I keep it. Not so much as a brand, but sometimes I like the feel of it blowing in the wind and being wild and free. Wild and free. Novel idea. Never found a wild and free adult. Not really. In the words of my favorite philosopher, Bob Dylan, "We all got to serve somebody."

Well, the book signing worked out better than expected. But the conference? No. I, Dr. Selena Frederick—OB/GYN, author, and former DWB physician—left that conference, never wishing to return. One man. One irritating man. One voice. The cause of all my angst.

A total jerk in the fourth row. Joe Cook is his name. A reporter. An international correspondent. What in the hell was he doing there other than trying his best to provoke me? Instead of a potential asset to the conference cause, this reporter was an absolute ass.

To boot, I called him sir. Sir! "Yes sir," said a smiley-faced me. Damn. Man, those two words smack of *I'm so Southern*. I don't hide this fact, but Southern people are, to this day, misunderstood by many as mud eaters and religious snake handlers. I don't have time to overcome those perceptions. If anything causes wars, it's a people misdirected by erroneous perceptions.

So, I do what any professional would do: I attempt to capitalize on my misspeak. I no longer shy away from my Southerness in front of this New York City crowd. Screw that. I am who I am. I continued as the whole person I am and leave no parts of my personality behind.

The question-and-answer session went well until the jerk made his appearance. This jackass asked me so many irrelevant questions. Personal questions. My topic at this conference was to encompass the plight of women in war zones. And there he is, this jerk, this stupid man, asking me all these stupid questions.

I get it. Everybody isn't all about the things that concern me. In fact, some people may see me as a "Goody Two-shoes," too much of a do-gooder. But the folks who organized this conference care about the same world issues I do. They felt I was qualified to speak and were kind enough to invite me. I *am* qualified. I'm a physician whose association with Doctors Without Borders means I'm well qualified to speak on the subject.

Oh, then there's the book I wrote after my resignation from DWB. The book. Who would have guessed I would become an international best-selling author? Did I say something about life turning me in a different direction?

Let me tell you what this jerk did. I had my fingers in the air, pointing skyward, my digits representing every place I have seen sorrow. I was answering a question from the middle row, and I was in the middle of my explanation. "For example, how do you tell a starving pregnant woman in a war-torn country, where there is only a smuggled food supply, that this woman must decide between feeding herself and the baby she is developing and giving her meager scraps of food to her already-born children?"

While everyone else was considering the question, this jerk, this reporter, this Mr. Cook, rose and asked me about my education, my age, did I think I was qualified because of my youth, and damn him, my parent's death. Even about the life insurance policy! Can you believe it? I was fuming. You can ask me anything as a doctor or as a person. But my family? That is not a good choice of questions, especially when you're making some sort of insinuation about my parents' death and a stupid life insurance policy.

I rolled that bastard's question around in my throat before responding. Maintaining my composure, I had already resolved to allow my rich Southern accent to take over my speech, and not to fling my damn hair back from my face. NO! I wouldn't let him rattle me, but somehow, I needed to get my talk back on topic and control what was happening in that room. I was, after all, the doctor in charge.

But every time I answered someone else's question, the ass let out this audible little whistle. What in the hell was that about? I willed myself to focus and keep my train of thought on the questions being asked. To make it worse, the asshole actually had a tape recorder and a microphone that he pointed at me. Who does that?

I looked away from the man in the fourth row and pointed to the back of the room. "A question there, in the back." I couldn't even begin my reply. This rude man actually stood up from his fourth-row seat and jumped into the conversation to impolitely take over with his own agenda. An agenda that included asking about my parent's life insurance policy. Like I'm going to kill off my parents for money.

I simply replied with what I'm sure is a flustered face, "Yes, my parents had a life insurance policy. Many people do. And it's no one else's business."

Mr. Jerk continued to belt out his agenda. "You were recently named *Time* magazine's "Person of the Year," *World Changer's* "Most Interesting Person," and *Chic's* "Most Beautiful Woman in The World." Any comment?" blurted out the obnoxious ass. Blurted it right then and there before I could even begin to answer that question from the back row.

And there it was. The proverbial shoe had fallen.

"Confused," I retort with a glacial glare.

"Can you expound on your answer?" came the voice of jerkdom.

"It means *I'm confused*. I was unaware of being known in the United States, much less abroad. I've been fortunate to promote my book on morning and late-night TV shows and forums such as this one. A French magazine, *World Changers*, and *People* magazine, bestowed a great honor upon me, and so I ask why I am deserving. I'm a simple physician who answered the call to serve in troubled lands, just as every physician in America, yea, even the world, serves the human condition every day. I wrote a book. Lots of authors write books." I wanted to hit him with my book upside his head. The hard cover edition.

I swallowed down some of my irritation and continued. "As for *Chic*, I would love to say that I've spent time in France. Unfortunately, my experience was limited to an airport between connecting flights. I've never had the pleasure of Paris's sights and smells. Hence, I'm confused why a French magazine paid me such a compliment."

I knew I was losing the battle with my heightened irritation. My material was just too damn important. So little time to get my message out. There are persons out there who are hungry, sick, injured, war-torn, and dying.

I'm not sure of all I said, but I know this fell from my mouth: "Frankly, sir, I'm confused why you persist in asking impertinent questions about me. This is a discussion pertaining to the plight of women in war-torn countries. I'm joined by a room full of people trying to understand the worst plights affecting our world citizens. We're all here to contemplate solutions."

I continued in a fury. Damn me, I did. "All the questions you are asking me are a matter of public record. I think you've mistaken this room for a tabloid research room, which is where you should look for the answers to your questions."

The crowd made a slight rumble of laughter, then went silent. Silently silent.

The next question came from a petite Columbia University professor sitting in the back. Mr. Cook asked no more questions but let out one more audible whistle. Damn him for provoking me to lose my cool. Ass wipe.

I rejoiced when the conference ended. Rejoiced.

Oh, my eventful day didn't stop there. After saying my conference goodbyes, I walked back to my hotel room in the drizzling rain instead of taking a taxi. Thinking a little mild exercise might smooth my post-conference jagged edges. Yes, that's the ticket. I nostriled in the springtime mist.

I stopped off midway to peruse a newly opened shop. The boutique only sold scarves. Scarves made of any print or material one could imagine. Art scenes. Geometric designs. Hearts all aflutter. The ones that caught my eyes were those featuring flags of various nations. I had forgotten the Russian flag converted back to the red, white, and blue design in 1993 after the downfall of the Soviet Union in 1991. *How perfect.* My European book tour was set to end in Russia.

To wear separate US and Russian red, white, and blue scarves with a white pantsuit would be subtle but perfect diplomacy. Selena style, you know? I often steal from another one of my favorite philosophers, who goes by the name of Jimmy Buffett, and "quietly make some noise." I love my Buffett wisdom. It always draws me back to my roots on North Carolina shores, with their extended summers, suntan oil, and white sands.

These are the reflections in my North Carolina head as I filtered through the scarf racks. No matter what I'm doing, somehow my thoughts return to the last place I considered home... and to them. To that day. That time. That sadness. That history of joy arrested. I understand what it means to lose someone beloved in your heart. Can't stand being without them. Cannot. I guess that's okay, isn't it? To never let yourself be without them in your heart?

Anyway, I picked out a scarf with an American flag design. It had a bit more of a creamy-white shade than the other options. I chose the same coloring as the Russian flag. I tied them together in a sea knot my father taught me. *Nice,* I assure myself. *Thanks, Dad.*

Continued my journey on the New York street toward my hotel. I stop in at a children's bookstore. One of my author colleagues has a new release out.

I try to recall my Russian itinerary. My manager arranged a visit to an orphanage with a library. The Russian kids will surely love this book, even if it's in English. I review its bright illustrations of Native American life in the southwest as I turn each page. No wonder it's a Caldecott winner.

How very lovely it is. I turn the pages colored in Georgia O'Keefe southwestern hues. A gender-nonspecific book about a Native American brother and sister's unique journey growing up in the southwestern USA is enough to pique anyone's interest.

I count in my head the number of books I should pick up to donate to the orphanage library. Learning that I chose her book should please my friend, Jean Maria. The author, Jean Maria Whitecloud, and I made a fast friendship at a writing seminar before I completed my book. We keep in touch. I have a long list of persons I wish to visit but can never make the time. Unfortunately, Jean Maria is on that long wish list. I'll send her a note about choosing her book for my orphanage donation.

My mother, my dear but insistent mother, had a pet peeve about reading in her household. It was one reason, I suppose, why I found myself headed to the University of North Carolina in Chapel Hill at the early age of sixteen. I graduated from college at nineteen. Nineteen. The age I was when my parents were reported missing at sea in *Summertime.*

My dad, Dr. Joseph Frederick, was an experienced and responsible seaman. He loved sailing the intracoastal waterway, which was literally in our backyard, in *Summertime*. It was his life's joy. *Summertime*, his boat, was named after a tune from Porgy and Bess, not the season. *Summertime*, whose music system never left home without blaring Buffett.

Only bits and pieces remained of *Summertime* when she washed ashore. Bits and pieces of boat matter, scattered in disjointed pieces and discovered at disjointed times, along the same shorelines beloved by her former occupants. The bodies of my parents were never discovered. Piracy, along with dozens of other theories regarding what may have happened—whether by professionals involved in the investigation or the murmuring of locals—was a perpetual source of discussion. There was only one known fact: a sudden squall at *Summertime's* coordinates. Bits and pieces. Bits and pieces. Today, in a bookstore in New York City, they were on my mind.

I was delighted at my selection of books for kids of different ages that I plan on donating to the orphanage library. The clerk will have the books delivered tonight. Good. I have an overnight flight to London tomorrow night to kick off my European book tour. How heavy traveling with all those books will be, along with copies of my own book. A little exhausted sigh escapes from my chest. Minor details such as luggage are what can weary a traveler. I try to spread out the weight with lighter items and include a few books in my carry-on. But two checked bags are still a whole lot of weary.

Returning to the street after the bookshop, I continued to the hotel. I was loving my walk in the faintly falling rain. The mist felt good against my skin. Life was beginning to feel good again. Until I perceived the raindrops to be a slight bit heavier, and I'm without an umbrella.

My walking pace increased. Then, out of nowhere, a yellow taxicab speeds through a puddle formed at the curb by earlier rains next to where I'm walking. A spray washes over me as though I'm a novice surfer getting beaten by a wave. I could've sworn I heard the cabbie laughing. Is this National Bastard Day? If so, I didn't get the memo.

I'm freaking soaked. Soaked from the rain. Soaked from the splash. Head to toe. Soaked. My clasped hair is now heavy, as though it's a vessel carrying the water of 10,000 lakes.

My shoes squished as I walked. They sound like a duck wearing galoshes. My tropical-pink tailored suit, made of summer wool, itches my skin.

My neon-white ruffled shirt I'm wearing no longer lines both sides of my face like a parenthesis. The shirt ruffles are flat and have turned grayish from the wet smog and acid rain. The ruffling continues down in a V, forming a secret alliance with my cleavage. My gel cup bra wicked up water and increased my chest size by inches on each side. My boobs feel lop-sided. The suit is like a wet diaper. Feels heavy as a keystone.

I snap back from the trials of the day and return to my current moment in time. Arising from the bed, I peel the wet clothes from my body and let them drop to the floor. Um, yes, my comfy granny gown. After bagging my suit for hotel dry cleaning, just on cue, room service arrives. Smells wonderful. Soon, the book delivery arrives as well.

Grabbing a medical journal, I read as I devour my dinner. After eating the last bite of food on my plate, I draw myself a warm bath and let myself sail away.

CHAPTER 5
SERGEI'S SHAME

USUALLY, a soldier is in sensory overdrive. Today, this soldier can't process a thing. Not from my gut. Not facts or figures. Not from experience. Cannot. Not a thing.

Fuck me.

I sit with my back against the east dacha wall. The dead sleep in front of me. The west dacha burns as citizen firefighters strive to control the blaze. I don't move to help them. Let the rebels who caused this shit deal with it. I focus on the dead.

My eyelashes feel paralyzed when I try to blink tear-stained eyes to protect against the ashen soot. Seen men die. Seen men I considered my own blood cut down like animals by the ravishing of enemy gunfire. This soldier has seen life escape the eyes of enemies as my knife powered beneath their rib cages or my hands broke their necks. Yet, on this day. In this place. At this moment. At this ill-fated dacha, I'm drained to the point of thoughtlessness.

I'm a confident military man, but at this moment I'm a lost orphan, uncertain whom to trust. Where to go? Father Russia, tell me what to do. Indeed, I'm not sure who my commander is following this defeat. Every part of my being aches.

My heart feels like it has been waterboarded and can't possibly pump the fluid load. My soul weeps with sadness, but not one tear that drops from my eyes falls for me. It doesn't. The only tears are for my home. My Father Russia. My people. These things matter to me. Too much blood and death has littered the streets of Russia over the previous hundred years. So much blood in the streets of one nation. I shake my head as the consideration pains me. One nation, with all its religious structures, didn't remember how to pray The Lord's Prayer after seventy years of communism.

"What now?" I ramble to myself aloud. Not realizing the cameras of the press have found my face. Unaware, I allow myself to process my shame in the public media.

Thanks to an anonymous sponsor, me and Vogo have been buddies since both of us attended a private English-speaking school at eight years old. We were roommates and friends at the Suvorov Military Academy, along with Ivan. We three comrades attended the Military University together. Served in many lands and on many missions together for Father Russia. Vogo and Ivan were as close to me as twin brothers. Vogo and Ivan, my best friends since childhood, having met Ivan as a fellow orphan at eight years of age. Our trio climbed our way to Spetsnaz together. Elite of the elite. Best of the best. It was the heart's desire of three boys to become commandos. When had my friend Vogo become part of this coup? No idea. Not a clue. Not a damn clue.

Been together daily for months now. Not one slight hint of anything awry. I know every commando in my unit and every person involved in security detail for the dacha. Not a single thing out of place.

It amazes me that commandos under my charge participated in the coup. This realization hits me like a blowtorch in a snowstorm. But Vogo?

While my unmoving body remains propped against the wall of the east dacha, the west side explodes and burns. I'm despondent. Empty. Dismayed. Thought to be soldier's soldier, a man's man, and here I am, weeping like an infant watching the scene unfold. Compatriots applaud and jeer as the rebels lift the dead remains of the former leader and his generals and fling them in the air. More applause follows when the remains fall face-first to the ground. Rebels place two of the deceased officers in a lover's pose. I chew the bitter herb of sorrow as I recall my words, "No one is going to die today." It was possible to be sane then.

An orphan experiences much shame. A military cadet learns discipline through shame over his failures. Ah, films on Saturdays of yore. Only the best cadette earned the pocketful of toasted sesame seeds from the academy kitchen. This day contains the moments of my greatest failure and shame. No sesame seeds today. I would trade every last damn sesame seed I ever earned not to know today's tragedy.

It was my duty to secure the perimeter and personnel inside the burning dacha. Mine. I, Commander Sergei Radkov, understood this mission was of the highest importance regarding the president and his officers. This happened on my watch. The bodies of fallen officers are fouled and paraded in front of my eyes like a comedic circus. It's a horror movie.

I begged my commander to persuade the president to hold this meeting in Red Square rather than this dacha. Begged him.

I held my tongue while my commanding officer advised the president against the dacha plan on Victory Day.

"No!" resounded the Commander in Chief. The leader wanted his top advisors out of Moscow on Victory Day. Victory Day belonged to the people, not the military.

"I've heard rumblings of discontent," said the red-faced president who didn't like to be advised against whatever he damn well wished. "It's those OPEC nations and the US and NATO and their sanctions while Russians go hungry.

"I've improved our food supply to feed our nation with the aid of Russian scientists," the screaming president continued. "I've invested in the latest technology and Russian ingenuity. I've stopped oil shipments out of Russia until prices raise profit margins. With, of course," he stated conspiratorially, "exceptions made for trade negotiations that are critical to Father Russia. Russia must allow enough to satisfy its neighbors and friends. Fucking NATO nations can freeze for all I care."

"Yes, Commander, but—" The president cut the general off in mid-sentence and waved him off.

"As well," said the president with one gray eye winking, "I'm pushing Russian tourism. Perhaps you have seen it in the news? Who, in this region, can offer beaches more desirable than Crimea or Sochi? Our Golden Ring? Lake Baikal? Our mountains? I've even improved access to the Arctic tundra." The president flails his hands from left to right as though he were in a tourism commercial.

"But, sir," protested the general. "We must give weight to these grumblings—"

The superior commander again cut him off with the another wave of his hand. "I've heard these rumblings of dissatisfaction. Russians must learn patience. Measures need time to come to fruition."

"Sir, I beg due respect. People are hungry now. Social institutions such as orphanages are reporting hunger and malnutrition among their populations," says the pleading general. Still seeking to inform his president, the advisor cautions safety concerns to a deaf president.

"Just as well. It'll save us either prison costs or burial costs later for those orphans. Only ten percent of them don't end up in prison or dead before their time," the Russian president says without feeling. His gray eyes are blank.

I hated his words.

The confounded general almost laughs at the incredulity but catches himself. Thought better of it. Worse, my commander feared he needed or take the president at his unfeeling word. It's also my greatest fear. The leader of my country laughing off his failures to improve the conditions of the orphan class. My class. He may have been the president, but he was also a crass asshole.

Now, that general's blood leaches into the dacha soil along with his president's.

And here they are, by the thousands, in front of me. All the discontented. My people. I'm a soldier through and through. Despite all my training in being a professional soldier, there's no way I would cut down citizens of Father Russia. As much as I hate what the rebels did, they are my people.

Shoot Russian citizens? No, I can't pull that trigger. Especially pull it on angry citizens who are hungry. It's been a while, but I've never forgotten the feelings of my own childhood hunger. I was fortunate to have a sponsor who paid for my tuition to go to a private English-speaking boarding school soon after arriving at the orphanage. Military training provided boarding as well. These institutions elevated nutritional standards above that of the orphanage. Orphanage hunger was only a marginal improvement over an eight-year-old boy left alone. The orphanage never provided enough food. Hell, never enough of anything. The orphanage fed the children the bare minimum to keep them alive. Never enough. Never.

Hunger before being taken to the orphanage scarred my soul. No human, especially a child, should have to endure such hunger. No, it was not within me to fire on Vogo and the other rebels. They are my family. My only family. I'm an intelligence officer. How could Vogo take part in this? He's my brother in my heart. Did he know me too well? Well enough to know there are lines I wouldn't cross?

Exclude me? How? How did the pissant pull that off? More importantly, how did I, Commander Sergei Radkov, not realize a damn thing? My God, the coup of the century just took place. Not a word. Not a whisper. The silence should have alarmed me. I failed, and now so many will suffer because of it. Hell, they're already suffering. My shoulders slump with the truth. If Russians wish to hang me, damned if I won't be the first to place the noose around my neck.

Shame. It's unshakable. It's one of those things that you can't whitewash from your soul. The surrounding smell is nauseating. Distinct odor of burning flesh from the furnace blast. A sickening odor permeating and hiding its putridness in the thick black stack of smoke rising from the dacha boiler room. Escaping into the heavens as though it were a mighty invading army on a mission to overthrow God.

According to his nature, Quiet Ivan sits beside me without speaking. I look over at my friend. "I want you and the others to change out of your commando clothes. The rebels aren't giving us much attention now. That won't last. Sneak into the convention," I instruct. "Try to leave through the rear. Don't go to the presidential quarters. I suspect plundering will be at its peak there. The president kept changes of clothes in several places. Check the laundry. Probably your best chance of finding larger sizes. You know where they are. Use what you can. Then go underground."

Ivan gives his head a nod. "You?" asks the quiet man. The man has, if nothing else, word economy.

"I, comrade, am going to create a minor distraction for you. Then I'm helping our injured countrymen."

Ivan gives a nod and rises, then prepares the commandos for the next stage. I smile at the leadership of this man that I love as a brother.

I haven't yet begun processing this Victory Day oxymoron. Suffering from my countrymen motivates me to put it aside and rise to walk over to the BTR-90 tank. Loudly and firmly, while simultaneously knocking on the metal of the tank, I impolitely request Vogo dismount the BTR-90 and climb his scrawny little ass down for a man-to-man discussion. "Come down, pissant."

Vogo is having good fun with the bullhorn, but he complies without emotion. He motions for us to meet inside the carrier for increased privacy.

"Other comrades decided, Sergei," the anxious Vogo explains before I ask a single question. "The consensus was that you would never join us. The comrades thought this way would be easier. You know, when it was done." Vogo's voice contains a slight plead.

"You mean after I suffered the shame of my lifetime by failing my mission, or after I'm dead?" My crystal blue eyes glare into Vogo's brown ones like a light beam into darkness.

Want to belt my friend, who drops his eyes to the ground. Put a fist at warp speed to the back of the man's throat. Leave his teeth dangling like a broken accordion.

Vogo is right about one thing. I'd never have agreed to it. Would have thrown my friends and anyone else under the BTR-90 for suggesting such a thing. May have shot them myself.

I study him for a moment, as he glues his cowardly brown eyes to the ground. Resisting the urge to put my fist through the face of my longtime friend, I turn around and without a word walk off, disappearing into the crowd.

CHAPTER 6
SERGEI IS MORE THAN A SOLDIER

I MOVE from the east dacha toward the west. No one can help the eastern dacha dead now. As I make my way, I pluck up human carnage. Help ambulatory victims hobble to the medic station. Help carry those unable to walk on a stretcher. Others I throw over my shoulders or carry them in my arms to medical aid.

I lose a battle when I try to stop the blood gushing out of a woman's gut. Try to resuscitate her when I see her empty eyes give up her soul to the Holy Ghost. It's no use. The heart compressions only cause the blood to gush faster from her gut. Perhaps she's some child's mother. A wife or sweetheart. A daughter, an aunt. She matters to someone. Do these idiots not think of these things before they declare a glorious revolution at gunpoint? Do they not see bearing arms is a failure? A failure to find a better way.

I move on. Help to haul ice and water. Direct volunteers where they might locate certain items and supplies. Autopilot. My element. Direct and aid in any type of task. Do all that I can. Help.

"Looks like the president won't be needing these," quips the president's personal physician. The doctor grabs available supplies, and I help deliver them to the medic station. The competent doctor falls into the flow of saving lives.

I receive word that interim charge over the government has been given to Andre Smoltsky, Chairman of the Federal Council, which contains two houses of the elected government. Chairman Smoltsky is next in line for the throne of power in Russia. The demise of both the president and prime minister assures that. He is immediately sworn in and holds a news conference.

"I want to keep my current elected position. I will execute the office of president until our body nominates and confirms a temporary president. This is pending elections," explains the now-balding Smoltsky over a television.

"I'm calling for calm. Let's busy ourselves with the business of being Russians," blares the politician on the airways. I'm acquainted with Smoltsky. I have faith in his abilities. God alone can tell us what the future holds. Desperate times and desperate men. This gala affair wasn't arranged for the sake of continuing business as usual. Yet Smoltsky is politically wise, as he is part of what can be considered *old school*.

The medical staff attending the injured cheer at the Smoltsky news. This brings hope for improved support to the dacha victims. Two mere ambulances are located at the scene and the local hospital contains less than ten available beds and only one emergency room doctor. The ambulances transport victims to further distances to offer aid to the needy. This slows the return of the vehicles to the dacha to take more injured. Appreciated local services appears. However, the need continues to exceed the demand.

Hope for the needy increases since Moscow now has authority to open flight paths for medical evacuations. I expect medical services to be a priority. Soon, I hear the whirring blades of a copter looking for a landing. I rush to move patients back and forth until my services are no longer needed. Most nurses and one of the doctors collapses for a few moments' rest. I do not.

The afternoon shares its rays' delight as the days of the midnight sun lengthen. Soon the Russian landscape won't know darkness.

CHAPTER 7
THE ESCAPE

UNCERTAIN HOW I end up in the dacha's garage, I'm aware of being as much zombie as I am man. I grab my stored mountain bike and challenge the mountain trails through the forest.

My clothing is blackened and torn. Soot covers my skin. Flakes of ash hang in my blond curls. I must appear as old as Father Time.

To say the least, my political status is unclear ever since the coup. I assume there are still those who might wish my demise. I can't be sure if the Vogos of my country might consider hauling me to a prison resembling the Russian gulags of old. Maybe assassinate me or place my body in front of a firing squad.

It's conceivable the coup will fail. The president and his closest advisers have perished, but it remains possible for the surviving military to seize power.

Commander Sergei Radkov is the guy who failed to provide the presidential party with adequate security. Under this scenario, I might experience more than the shame embedded in my Adam's apple. A noose could easily be placed around my neck. For the time being, my training dictates an operative like myself should hide underground.

Over thirty-six hours have passed since the dacha event. No one seems to be coming to look for me, and most of the rebels have left now that the fun is over. Turned tail and ran, with their brothers in arms who suffered around the west dacha in trouble. Glad I was not a part of the rebellion. I would hate to have those bastards as my comrades. But then there *is* Vogo and the others.

Almost everyone is dressed in some type of military attire. I suppose my military dress doesn't stand out all that much. Still, I need to dump my military persona sooner rather than later.

I'm worried about Ivan and my other comrades. I don't know about their outcome. Prayer for their safety escapes my lips as I propel my bike through the silent mountain trail. In my heart, I know the commandos are well-trained operatives. On this day, my hope is for their training to be enough.

I stop at a tarn to bathe. Removing my clothing, I walk into the newly thawed mountain lake as though it were a warm bathtub. In reality, it's cold as ice water. Grabbing sand from the bottom of the tarn, I scrub my face, my hair, and my skin that is tarred from the explosion's flame and ash.

And tears. I scrub my tears from the harm caused to my countrymen and my failure to protect them. Since I was an eight-year-old orphan, I've never cried. Over the past few hours, I've cried more tears than I did as a child.

And fear. I need to get that shit off of me. I want to scrub it from under my skin and every deep spot in my soul where I've hidden it. I haven't been afraid since I became an eight-year-old orphan, either. I scrub the smell of fear from my clothes with rigor using lake sand. Rinsing my body and my belongings, I redress in wet clothes, mindful that I will have to drip dry. My mind is in overdrive. I work swiftly. No time to waste. Once again, I propel myself on autopilot. No time for fears or sorrows.

I remove the knife attached by a leather strap to my calf and cut off my pants legs to produce shorts. This will keep my pants from appearing to be of obvious military issue. My bike panniers! Yes! Time to get my head out of my ass. I had forgotten my panniers. I keep an extra shirt there. "Good, Sergei, good," I hear my mentor, Alexei, saying, as though I hear him speaking in soft tones through a distant loudspeaker.

I've been awake and working under stress for nearly two days now.

In my confusion, I overlooked my freaking bike panniers. Often, I load the mouths of the bike panniers with rocks to increase my toil across the mountain hills during my bike rides for a better workout. Other times, if going to the gym to lift weights, I fill the panniers with a change of clothes and any toilet items missing from my gym locker.

I maintain a membership in a town thirty miles away from the dacha. Often, I provided security for that particular presidential dacha. That dacha became the president's favorite place among his real estate choices, away from the demands of Moscow. Occasionally, I managed stolen hours to work out at the gym.

Routinely, I start by biking to the gym. Next, I lift weights upon my arrival. Then, I reward myself with several miles of swimming in the pool before enjoying the fragrant banya, the Russian community bath. I relish this last ritual. No such rituals will take place on this day.

I always went alone to the gym. I informed no one of my membership or of the gym's location. I had no issue with taking my comrades to the gym, per se, but none of my buddies enjoyed biking through the hills. They preferred to drink and play cards while off duty. Like a good soldier, I never discussed my destination or activities. It's the way of my training. Need-to-know only. Not going, no need to know.

I filter through the contents of the panniers. Anything nonessential, I dump into the lake. I want to keep my guns—*plural*—as well as my knife a little while longer. Next, I break down my rifle rather than leaving it to fly in the wind behind my back while biking.

Additional falsified papers, cash, identification, and disguise measures for a "just-in-case" moment are stored in my gym locker. Time-sensitive missions out of country are the norm. The items are geared toward foreign travel versus the use in my own land. As an operative, I have known many instances during my soldiering career where having such products on hand was useful. An operative has a plan B. I consider myself now on plan F. There had been a plan B yesterday. Plan B, C, D, and E have gone to hell in a handbasket. Americans say that, don't they?

In preparation, I remove the stitching of the thin pannier lining. As well, I had stored money, a passport, and papers behind the loose lining, then resewn it with a matching thread on a sewing machine kept at my Moscow flat. I was given the flat by the Russian state at eighteen, a gift for being an orphan. The flat is small, but I enjoy calling it "my orphan home" in jest. Between assignments, I often stay there. Suppose I feel at home in my orphan flat as much as anywhere.

The shame over failing my protection assignment is like a deep cut in my soul by a knife called "Sergei Be Ashamed." Several literal scars mar my body from stab wounds obtained during hand-to-hand combat in the field. One injury pierced my kidney and nearly took my young life. Memories of those injuries don't hurt as much as the current sadness in my heart. It's worse than any knife blade.

It's a sadness I wish I could slap out of my being. Carve it out with a scalpel.

Even so, as one of the best of the best, a soldier's soldier, I intend to keep my head screwed on straight. I know myself; I know my greatest strength is calmness under stress. Doesn't mean it's easy because damned if the past days haven't challenged all my strengths and exploited all my weaknesses.

Think about fleeing the county. I've money, papers, and a passport. But I can't desert Father Russia. Not now. Not when my country needs me the most. I'm staying even if it means I die.

Mounted on my bike, I race as fast as my legs can spin the bike chain through the remote trails. I know these trails as well as I know my weapon. Few humans use them. These trails are muddy this time of year. Melting snow runs downstream to the receiving lakes. The usual healthy rainy season this time of year hasn't occurred. It turned unseasonably warm in early spring this year, and the blue skies speak of drought more than they do torrential rains. These conditions make efforts easier for the cyclist on the run.

Make no mistake, it remains cold this time of year in the Ural Mountains, as well as in most parts of Russia. Russians bundle in coats and scarves on one day during this season. On the next, these same countrymen don swimsuits in public places. Open to observation are sunbathers on grassy knolls soaking up the sunny rays of spring.

The chill doesn't affect me as I pump my way through the forest. The skies are clear above the stagnant dacha smoke that is graying their clarity. A huge complex, the evidence of the dacha burning and surrounding forest remain in the air. Guess the dacha builders never counted on a fire and didn't provide a sufficient water source for fire. Almost the entire mountainside burned. Thank God locals contained it long enough to get the victims out.

I catch smells from the explosion in the wind. Sickening odor, the smell of charred human flesh refuses to disappear. At various parts of the forest, the trail is hazy from the heavy growth of linden and birch trees. The nauseating odor and the darkening haze envelop me like a straitjacket. There is no air. My chest tightens as nausea splashes bile against the back of my throat. I want to vomit, but I fight the nausea. I will overcome it like a soldier.

The more I move away from the dacha, the less I detect the smells of horror. Wish the distance could remove the horror wrapped around my heart. I continue to muscle my way up hills and control my speed downhill lest I bust my ass. Injury isn't something I need at the moment.

I've cycled from partial darkness to where there's lovely breaks in the forest between the overhanging limbs of birch and linden trees. The limbs are thin and short, allowing the warming sun to shine, offering the solar star's gift of warmth and light. No time to notice luxuries of nature. My mind focuses on my body and self-determined mission.

I fight sorrow. I fight shame. I fight fear. All my life, from the playgrounds of the orphanage to foreign battlefields, I've always fought. Always.

CHAPTER 8
SELENA IS A BABY ALONE IN THE WORLD

AROMATIC BEADS CREATE a bubbly froth in the whirlpool bath. I disrobe and step into the warm swirls, letting the water engulf my body. Splashing water on my breast and torso, I slide deeper into the warm cocoon. It's 8 p.m. on a Thursday night in New York City and I've absolutely nowhere to go. I don't have close acquaintances in the city. At least, not close enough. No friend to call or visit. No one I can join for dinner. Yes, I fill my days, but nights are hell.

Tomorrow brings a full day of packing before boarding a jet to fly off this continent to Europe and begin my book tour and speaking engagements. Yes, I'll travel to countries and see much that few Americans ever see. I wish nights alone in a hotel room on another continent differed from those in the states. They don't. I wish I had more wisdom on the subject but can only listen to myself sigh.

Yes, I'm a best-selling author, but will likely write only this one book. I'm an experienced physician. Some folks believe I might have much to offer the world. So, do I. Yet, I look at the out-of-date wallpaper and cry out loud, "WHAH, cry on, you little baby." My little pity party from earlier should be over.

Instead, I gaze at the wallpaper and say, "Know what? Loneliness is loneliness. Even I don't possess the right to tell myself I can't have my own brand of loneliness. Nor my own brand of self-pity. So, there. Go to hell, wallpaper. Dr. Selena Frederick, OB/GYN says go to hell, you ground-up, piece-of-a-tree victim." Can't say why I got so pissed off at the wallpaper. Just was.

Guess the wallpaper was pissed off too because it didn't dare to reply to my silly rant.

Struggling to get "real", I focus my mind on tasks—so many tasks I need to perform before leaving on my flight out of JFK tomorrow evening. I close my eyes but know that's a mistake. Know my mind will wander. Know I'll be transported back to *them*. Back to that place. That time. Back when I had a home and when people I loved lived.

Back to the days of Jimmy Buffett blaring on *Summertime*. In college, it had been worth the couple hours' journey from the University of North Carolina in Chapel Hill to home for the weekends. Back to my roots on the North Carolina shores, with their extended summers, suntan oil, and white sands. Oh, yeah. So worth it.

Autumn is my favorite time of year on the shore. The Atlantic waters feel as warm as a bathtub. Crowds gone, and the temperatures in the high seventies or low eighties. The setting provided a conducive environment for plowing through the tons of endless college reading at hand. Oh yes, Carolina to home on the weekends. Screw football. I would choose the shores over grunting male sweat any day. That was more my sister's deal, the Southern football craze. The Tarheels are historically more of a basketball school, anyway. Even a nerd like me didn't miss Carolina basketball.

Often, if my schedule permitted, I left Chapel Hill on a Thursday afternoon and began my reading and writing at sunrise the next morning on the cooler sands. Soon, Buffett played somewhere along the beach, either close by or across the sound. Locals never considered the nuances of the Carolina shore landscape. The sights, sounds, and smells are innate. Always there and ready for the taking—and for the tasting. Oyster harvesting took place right in my backyard. Only need a beer and a grill to enjoy fine dining.

I must admit I had an idyllic life until I received that fateful news from my sister on that fateful day. The day Debbie, my sister, called to tell me our parents were reported missing at sea. My brother-in-law, Bubba, was on his way to pick me up at college, just weeks away from my senior finals.

A smile breaks across my face as I close my eyes recalling the number of times that I've clarified, "Yes, that is his given name: Bubba." Straight from his home in the North Carolina mountains, and as Southern as his drawl and cowboy boots. As well, Bubba earned the moniker "Big'un" because the North Carolina State tight end was a big baby, large child, and gigantic man. And a bear-sized pussycat. Southern folks. The best!

In her past life, Debbie was a cheerleader in college for the University of North Carolina. Debbie and Bubba met at a football game between UNC and NC State. Tarheels against the Wolfpack. It was love at first sight between the representatives of the rival teams. Now the pair have added two little girls to the family. I'm thinking no football rivalry came to mind during the creation of each of my nieces. But then, with those two, maybe it did…

My father loved the sea. Loved his seaside community. One of the poorest counties in North Carolina back then, everyone in Brunswick County had a close relationship with the country doctor. The doctor made house calls. Certain patients couldn't afford to pay their medical bill, so they bartered their medical visits. Dad took the kindnesses folks offered instead of payment. Never once did we pay for a car wash at the local gas station nor an ice cream cone at the local creamery. Seldom paid for a meal out or a haircut.

Dr. Joseph Frederick was not a physician without opportunities, having received a top education at Duke University Medical Center. Joe Frederick had many choices, but this life was what he wanted. No one on the planet ever doubted that.

Elizabeth Frederick, my mother, was a teacher and librarian. When Debbie was born, Mom became a full-time doctor's wife, although she often donated her time to educational projects. She returned to teaching when Debbie became a teen and got her driver's license. *Mother freedom.* Or so Elizabeth Frederick thought.

Much to the surprise of poor Elizabeth Frederick, soon after resuming teaching, she discovered she would produce what she came to call "the joy of everyone's life." That joy became known as Dr. Selena Frederick, OB/GYN. Did I say I had an idyllic life growing up? I sure as hell did. Loved and doted on by everyone in the family—and Brunswick County for that matter—an unexpected bundle of joy. Maybe that's why I pursued obstetrics. Maybe it was the stories Dad whispered to Mom about rape victims and his disgust. Or the many stories he told about the healthcare struggles of women in poverty. Perhaps I simply wanted to share a fraction of the idyllic joy they gifted me in my early life.

So, without disappointment at being stripped of her "mother freedom," Mom began a literacy program in the community to make use of her spare time after my birth. I was raised as much by an unwashed itinerant farmer sitting at my family table as anyone, as my mother tutored her students while bouncing me on her knee. I always admired Mom for maintaining her passion.

Suppose guilt plays a wee bit of a role in my recent descent into pity parties. Without a doubt, I continue to possess a grand passion for the ideals of my platform. I suppose it's not just that I miss the hands-on treatment of what we were taught in Bible School at the First United Methodist Church of Brunswick County, of what Jesus called "the least of these." Maybe it's because, unlike my mother, I have no child to bounce on my knee. I don't have a nearly grown daughter or an adoring husband. Wherein my life may seem more exciting, I would elect to own my mother's "complete package," if you will. Dear old Elizabeth. Damn, I miss her.

Both of my parents won local, state, and national awards for their work. I describe them as the "real deal." Between my mom and dad, cross words were rare. And if a cross word did slip out, at once an apology followed. "I'm so cranky, honey. I'm sorry to take it out on you, babe." A kiss. A hug. Early on, we Frederick girls learned not to walk past our parent's bedroom after such an exchange. Carnal things took place there.

They never reappeared on that shoreline. Pieces of *Summertime* washed up later, but never the bodies. Those two fine people were deemed to be dead and buried at sea.

A year after officials pronounced our parents missing, Debbie decided the house on the waterway needed to be sold. I was livid.

Debbie explained that though she and Bubba could use the money from the sale of the house, that wasn't their primary concern. They had been through tough times before as mountain ranchers. Of concern was a college-aged Selena Frederick, who had just started her first year of medical school at nineteen years old. Debbie and family lived on the western side of the state. The upkeep on a coastal house is overwhelming for even full-time residents. This made keeping the house impossible. Debbie cried, too. My ire dissipated as the depths of our mutual loss shredded our torn and bleeding hearts.

Even though my parents provided well for my college education in a trust fund, their unspoken wish would be for me to apply the money to my future, come what may. No doubt about that by anyone on the planet.

As if memories could fall from my eyes, I open my lids and shake my head. I miss them.

I close my eyes again to abandon my day. Abandon the city. Abandon my side of the world.

The whirling jets of the whirlpool relax my muscles and allow both my body and mind to drift. My mind always drifts to two places: one, the last place I called home; the second, a miserable locale, where the persona of Dr. Selena Frederick, OB/GYN tried to save lives, birth healthy babies, and make a world of difference in an indifferent world. Tonight, like so many lonely, damn lonely nights, my thoughts move back to a desolate spot in a war-torn country. I don't remember the exact name of the place anymore. Does the place even have a name now?

All I remember is *him*. Young. Tall. Handsome. Clean-cut blond hair. Straight shoulders. Blue eyes that twinkled like Santa Claus.

In that desolate spot was a soldier named Sam. My best friend, until the night we had a onetime affair. Well, if you can call a onetime sexual escapade an affair. Sam died the next day.

Captain Sam Von Blake wiggled out army medical supplies for the field camp where I worked. I had gone with him on what turned out to be his last supply wiggle. What you must understand is that Sam Von

Blake was a married man, and he loved his wife. Sheila, Sam's bride, was the woman he missed with desperation and wanted in his arms that night he slept with me. He told me so. He told me he wanted to close his eyes and believe himself to be holding his beloved Sheila.

Under a half moon, Sam pulled the Jeep off the dirt path to hide behind a scrawny tree in a wide-open space of nothingness. Tears in his eyes, he talked to his best friend about how he felt afraid of losing Sheila. Not their tie. Not their relationship, but her face. The fading memory of her body. The feeling of being with her. The unbearable loss of memory that he was desperately trying to hold on to.

Sounds like a crock but guess you had to be there, under the moon that shadowed rocky hills covered with dust and dirt.

So, I held my friend. He closed his eyes, and, in the darkness, I loved his body like his wife. Yes, Sam and I cared for each other, but I understood his heart and his home were with Sheila. Period.

When Sam and I returned to the encampment, surely smelling of sex and glowing with drink from bootleg hootch, morning was creeping over the dry hills. A few mountain goats bleated on the hillsides, looking for scrapes of anything chewable to eat. Sam snuck into my tent for a hug goodbye before making his way to base.

"Thanks for last night," Sam whispered into my hair. "Especially exploring the sky from the back of the Jeep and counting stars despite the half moon."

"I'm not sure if they were stars as much as hootch-induced hallucinations, but it was fun, Sam. All the laughs we had while exploring the night sky. Other than that, nothing else happened. Nothing at all," I retorted with a knowing smile.

"Can I walk you down the aisle and give you away when you finally find a man worthy of making an honest woman out of you?"

I guffawed. "Only if you bring the hootch."

Sam gave me the most serious of looks. "Leave this place, Selena. Leave this hellhole and go find a man who will love you like the morning sun. Give you a white picket fence and a good life. You've done your tour of duty. You deserve the white picket fence."

"White picket fence?" I questioned. "Don't you have to whitewash those?"

Sam gave me a little smack on the behind. Both of us smiling, he did something he hadn't done the night before: his blue eyes studied my green ones so deeply that I felt electricity pass the synapses of my retinal nerves all the way down my spinal column. Sam grabbed me and pulled me into a kiss that both stunned and excited me.

He returned his blue-eyed gaze as he walked backward out of my tent into the dawn, leaving me standing there with shock and swollen lips. I can't tell you what passed between us at that moment. I really don't know, other than to say it was a moment. A moment where we both understood he needed to leave. No, it wouldn't be right for him to stay in my tent. Not at that moment.

Left standing inside my canvas residence, I heard Sam turn over the motor to the Jeep. Listened as he dislodged the emergency brake. Heard the wheels put in reverse and the vehicle leave at a meandering pace down the dusty dirt trail back to the military base.

I'm certain that Sam's mind was on the night before, up to the moment he backed out of my tent. My mind sure was there too. Doubt he checked the rearview or side mirrors. Doubt he drove in an unpredictable pattern on the empty road to improve his chances with a zigzag route. Doubt he saw the glint of metal from the sniper's rifle that buried a bullet in his brain.

"Damn! Damn it!" I cry in screams, my eyes flying open and flinging water against the wallpaper as I sit up in what should have been a calming whirlpool. I've grown since Sam's death and no longer believe it was all my fault. Now, I believe it *was partially* my fault. Now I believe I have another person to live for and try to make proud. Another person that I can't touch or even reach out with a phone call. Sweet Sammie.

I heave as I take in the last few years, the events as raw as though they happened yesterday. If I hadn't slept with him, maybe beautiful Sam would still be alive. Then again, maybe because of that night, Sam died in a kind of peace, instead of the man who cried into his hands at the thought of losing the memory of his love. If.

As you might hear in Bible School at the First Methodist Church of Brunswick County, "The Lord works in mysterious ways."

Perhaps so. All I know is that Sheila's husband—Jimmy's father—

my best friend—is forever gone. You can call it the Lord's will, fate, karma, kismet, destiny, his time, or any other damn platitude. Fact is, Sam's gone, and I miss him. My number one best friend who ever walked on this planet with me. In that way, he *is* my Sam.

I fill the whirlpool with more water. I don't care that my fingers now have the wrinkles of a ninety-year-old woman.

After his death, I realized I couldn't continue to perform at my usual level with DWB. Sam had said as much before he died. He told me to find a man to love me. That I deserved it. I don't know if I can follow my friend's advice and find a man to love me, but it was time for me to leave the work that, until his death, I had loved.

Desolate people live in desolate places. I had become more desolate inside than the desolate souls that I served. The time had come for me to leave the life of Doctors Without Borders. That was what I needed to do, and I never tried to deny it. I inhaled Sam's advice and finished my commitment to the cause.

Among my sparse possessions existed one-half dozen notebooks of what I called my "free notes." The notes journaled my years in service to the earth's most needy human souls. At times, I mailed notebooks to Debbie for storage.

I lost notebooks on the job while in the field. Forced to scramble to safety, I had to leave them. Other times, I left my notes behind, choosing to fill my trusty knapsack with items more conducive to saving lives. I hadn't considered what I might do when I completed my service. Wasn't sure I would be whitewashing Sam's idyllic picket fence.

Well, at least the tear that just fell into the whirlpool is warm.

Needed downtime. That's all I knew. I couldn't even talk to Debbie about Sam when I returned, and very little about my overseas experiences. I needed to be alone to process my past years. So, first I traveled to Debbie and Bubba's ranch to pick up my journals and spend time with my sister, Bubba, and their girls. Then I said goodbye to my family, the dog, horses, cows, and chickens, and set off in early September for the North Carolina coast. I found the coolest old and ratty first-row beach house and rented it through the fall and winter. I was in Selena heaven.

I drove by the old homestead. It was empty for the season. I parked my car, which Bubba loaned to me, on the side of the road next to the driveway. My presence would've gone unnoticed if I'd pulled into the drive, but my heart wouldn't let me get that physically close. At the same time, I wanted to jump out of the car. Scream at the Frederick homestead changes. Explore around back. Go inside. Sit on the wide veranda at the front of the house.

The veranda. We had welcomed so many visitors there. If too hot to sit on the back porch, the family sat on the wide front veranda shaded by mature trees. Lunches of tasty pimento cheese sandwiches that would leak their insides from the bread if you didn't lick around the edges to sop up the yummy goo.

Laughs. We had so many laughs just sitting out on the spacious front porch. For some reason, a long-ago memory popped into my head. There was a family that lived across from us and catty-corner a bit. When I say *family*, I mean to say there were several brothers, each with a home, and the widowed mother also with hers.

One of the brothers had been quite successful in his business. As a successful entrepreneur, he went out and bought himself a fifty-foot boat. You could call it a yacht, with white leather seats, a cappuccino machine, and two salons.

There was another brother, who some would consider a "slow adult"—Ernie. I don't know how slow Ernie truly was, but he could do two things well: count his damn money, and immaculately and reliably manicure lawns. Every day except in bad weather, Ernie could be spied driving his tractor mower with a cart hitched to the back. Before he started mowing the yards of neighbors as his source of income, he would scour the landscape for fallen pinecones, sticks, and debris.

On this particular day, as we sit sipping mom's homemade lemonade, we spy Ernie's mower turning the curve, but missing his cart. Not sure what happened to the cart, but in its absence, Ernie had hitched his brother's pride and joy of a boat to the back. And there went Ernie, with his tractor mower. Filled with pinecones and a wealth of dirty debris flung over the white leather seats of his brother's yacht.

We all rolled laughing. I remember my mother saying, "Did you see that?"

My dad shook his head in red-faced laughter, replying, "Yes, I saw it."

I don't know why that story came to me, but it did. I guess it's the recognition of the indigenous coastal folks who shaped my young life. I laughed hysterically at the memory. It became urgent that I leave the homestead at that point because I had literally wet my pants. That Ernie.

Back at my cottage rental, I spent hours lying in the shallow waters that were as warm as my current bathtub. Sitting in a chair by the beach, I reviewed journals. I wrote. I'm not sure why I wrote. I just did. And with a fury, too. I wrote and wrote and wrote until, alas: I completed a full manuscript.

On a lark, I sent the completed book to a writing contest. Glory be, if I didn't win. Part of the prize included a literary agent. Then the manuscript developed into a book contract, audibles, and a movie in the making. Whirlwind. Overnight, I, Selena Frederick, of Brunswick County, North Carolina, achieved celebrity status. The public actually listened to what Selena Frederick said, too. I know my medical credentials added credence to my words, but I didn't comprehend the power of those words. I only perceived my need to say them.

The thirst people possessed for compassionate understanding overwhelmed me. It did. I dedicated the book to "Captain Samuel Fletcher Von Blake." I paid homage to Sam in a way I hoped would inspire Sheila and Jimmy to be forever proud of him. I scripted a few words about the things he had done to help save others and lost his life doing so. Everyone loved the man who always wore a smile. His loss was a barren spot in anyone's heart who knew him. Captain Samuel Fletcher Von Blake, a US Army and humanitarian hero.

Months later, I received a thank-you note from Sheila that said, "Thank you for loving my Sam." I had no way of knowing Sheila had written the note while lying in bed with the lover she had slept with for months prior to Sam's deployment. Found out about it later through a mutual friend. It sickened me, knowing how much Sam was suffering at the time of his death. Still, Sheila was Sam's Sheila, and Jimmy was his boy. As far as I'm concerned, it will always be that way.

I open my eyes, feeling so lonely that I can't bear it. Cannot. Tears drop into the water as I recall my night with Sam and his last kiss. I reach for my pink toy.

"Oh Sam," I say out loud. "I should leave you at peace. I should let you go, but tonight I need you, Sam. God, I need you, Sweet Sammie."

The wallpaper didn't speak, but I bet those little stick figures watched.

CHAPTER 9
THE GYM

DUSK DIDN'T FALL, thwarted by the midnight sun. I arrive at the gym and lock my bike at the back, close to the trail. After retrieving my folded gym bag from my panniers, I make way inside. On the gym log, I sign in as Omar Stetzdal, one of my aliases, and stroll to the locker room as if to change into workout clothing.

As the lock to my private locker spins, I listen to reports from the television on the wall. Even though I think I'm alone, I act my role as a disinterested patron in case of an undetected eye. With my back to the news, I listen to every word as I remove my pouch from the locker and place it in my gym bag.

Someone enters the locker room. I duck my head deeper into my locker as I go about my business. Whether staff or patron, the gentleman stops at the row of toilets and takes a piss. Then leaves. No hand washing. Dickwad.

As I close my locker door, I see footage I wish I had retrieved at the dacha prior to leaving. The full press, both foreign and domestic, present at the lovely mountain retreat gone crazy. Someone thought of everything. Everything except letting me, Commander Sergei Radkov, know what the hell was going on. These thoughts processed through my mind, too, during the bike ride here, and I'm no closer to filling in the missing puzzle pieces. Hell, I don't even know what all the puzzle pieces are.

There I am, as though I were buck naked waving at the tele. Tears falling from my eyes in grief and dismay. Eyes not wanting to see unarmed men under my protection shot down in cold blood in front of me. Now the dead are lined up and shown with blood drained from their faces on a world stage. "What the fuck?" I hiss. Thank you so much, Mr. News Anchor, for warning of graphic content.

Film rolled while I spoke to the crowds atop the tank. Film rolled as tears made white lines on my black face after the explosion. Film rolled with my back against the dacha wall while I processed my shame. Processed my failure and its consequences. Film rolled as I processed my fear of what might once again happen in Father Russia, as it had at the start of the past century. So many lives lost and altered then. So many lives already lost and altered now. And the film rolled. On and on it rolled, with Commander Sergei Radkov the star of the show.

Pissed off now after the news report, I'm in full commando mode as I step into a shower stall for an actual shower. I dye my hair a dark brown. Crop it at the back and along the sides. Put the cut hair in a pouch in the gym bag. Other than changing my hair and wearing colored contacts, I decide against any fake disguises that the morning light might discern.

I do, however, add what looks like a boil to my chin. My favorite disguise accessory. The pus-filled wen looks as though it might burst open at any moment. Just the thing to cause people to look away and remember little except the ugly thing on my chin.

Donning a baseball cap, I peek out to investigate before departing the shower stall. Looking around, I notice someone has left their pants on a hook in the shower next to me. In fact, they have left everything, including shoes. No time to try on clothing for a fit. In commando mode, I stuff the pants and shoes into my gym bag. As my mother's son, I leave the unneeded shirt and put twenty thousand rubbles in the shirt pocket.

I take the back way down the stairs to an exit, although a sign says *No Entry*. Tough shit. I'm in a hurry. I turn the sign around backward and keep going. The side door is closer to my bike, but I will have to pass a few offices. Climbing down the stairs, I crouch on my tiptoes to reduce noise and time my movements.

There's a security camera in the stairwell, and it will spot me. I can't avoid it. I could disable it, but its placement is high, and it will take time and materials I don't have. The bill of my cap pulled down tighter, I change to a normal gait and look away from the camera. At the bottom, I flatten my back against the beige wall.

I hear voices. Feet moving slow. Two women are in the hallway and headed for the stairs. I bend down to tie my shoe. As the two women open the stairway door and enter, I catch the door before it closes. Less noise. Less attention. I peek out the open door and enter the hallway. I stroll past the offices along the passageway as if it were the normal thing to do.

Shit! The side door is locked. It was at times. It's not the first time I've checked this gym exit out. I check out everything in every place I go. It's the way of my training. It's what an operative does.

I'm irritated not to catch a break today, but I reach into the side pocket of my bag and pull out my keys and key aides. My "little helpers," I call them. In ten seconds, I have the side door open, but seconds count. My irritation is rising. I feel it. I remind myself I haven't slept or eaten in almost forty-eight hours. "Training. Stick to your training at all times, Sergei. It will save you," says the voice in the back of my head. How many times has my mentor said that to me? Alexei's voice sings in my head and soothes me like a lullaby.

"Natural. Act very natural." That's what Alexei would instruct. So, I slow the short walk to my bike although I want to run as though I'm on fire. With ease, I take off on the closest trail behind the gym.

I stop after a short distance to check out the pants and shoes that I snatched. Both items are too large. The pants are a little short. Moving the pants down as far as I can, I belt them there below my waist and let my shirt hang out.

The tennis shoes look like clown shoes on me, and I protrude a size twelve. Whoever owned these pants and shoes is short, heavyset, and has enormous feet. I consider these facts as I weigh the value of the items. I stuff socks into the toe box of the oversized shoes. That will do for now, though it's almost made the clown shoes too tight. I must deal with them as is and keep moving.

At a fork in the trail, by instinct, I stop to hide my army boots and shorts. Finding soft soil, I bury the three items in separate spots in the surrounding forest. I hide one piece on each side of the trail. Next, I take out the most critical items from my panniers. I add them to the gym bag, which has been made lighter by the removal of the boots and shorts. I add all the clothing and toiletry I can squeeze in. My gym bag, which is plain, black, and nondescript, needs to be ditched as soon as possible for another plain and nondescript bag. It'll have to do for now, but I'll change it later, along with these clown shoes. I'm getting a foot ulcer.

I push myself to bike a little farther while looking for a place to ditch the panniers and bike. All of my fatigued muscles burn, but I pedal through pain. I'm nearing a town which has a train station. I almost shout "Eureka!" when I notice caves on a downhill descent that are a few meters off the trail. After removing the panniers from my bike, I consider hiding them in one of the caves. The first cave isn't deep and comes out on the other end after about ten meters. At the entrances and around the sides of the cave openings are viny branches that have grown over but are still thin from the winter season. The vines won't totally obscure the cave openings and my goods. Still, it will have to do.

Rather than hiding the panniers on the ground inside, I place them atop a stony protrusion jutting out near the top of the cave wall. Out of sight. Good. I'm hoping the snaking vines will hide these items from view. As most folks, if they were to leave the trail to explore the caves, tend to concentrate on the mouth of the structure. Not that I want to retrieve any of these items. I just prefer for them not to be found.

From here, I move my bike deeper inside a second cave farthest from the trail. I hear voices. I freeze. Automatically, I fall to my belly and remove my knife from my ankle. I crawl to a position where I can peek through the vines.

"Look mommy, there's a man. He's acting like a snake," I hear a small singsong voice say.

"There's no man, honey. Come along." Adult voice. Female.

"But I want to go ask the man why he's acting like a snake," says the small whiny voice.

Damn kids. And, just as I think that thought, the little girl runs toward me.

"Come back, here. Come back here right now!" calls a powerful bass voice, moving toward the little girl. Adult. Male. About one point eight meters in height. Average weight and conditioning. Approximate age: thirty.

Female adult remains on the trail. The male calls to the little girl, but she's upon me.

"What are you doing?" asks the small voice. "Why are you crawling like a snake?"

"I'm looking for plants," I tell her. Do I even like kids? I'm not sure. Yeah, actually, I think I do, but damned if I know anything about them.

"Why do you have a knife?" she asks in a little curious voice.

I'm too tired for this shit. "How do you know I have a knife?" I ask.

"You do have a knife. I saw it," says the little girl as the father reaches her side.

"You're right, I do." I pretend to examine some of the viny branches. "I use it to cut plant samples," I explain to little Miss Curious. I thought Papa Bear would have dragged his offspring away by now, but no. No, he hasn't. He's looking on with curiosity, too. For fuck's sake. Can't a commando get a little peace and quiet around here and get a little work done?

"Why do you cut plants, mister? What did they do to make you so mad?" asks the babe.

"Oh, I'm not mad at plants. I love them. I'm a botanist. That's a person who studies plants. So, I'm taking a few plant samples today."

Baby Bear got out a "Why" to begin her next question, but Papa Bear leads her away back to Momma Bear. Thank God.

When they are out of sight, I slit the bike's tires. Removing the handlebars and seat, I hide them in separate locations in the forest. I bury my weapons in the cave floor at different spots on the highest ground possible to make the burial sites more flood resistant. From the cave, it's approximately a two kilometer walk into town. Child's play, except for the clown shoes.

As I enter the small village, there are caravan-style market tents lining the streets which sell many types of goods. Such markets are common throughout the villages of Russia, even until late in the evening, especially during the warmer weather. Perfect. I locate a tent displaying American blue jeans. Russians love American blue jeans. Hell, they love everything American except Americans. The jeans are probably counterfeit, but that's not my current concern. They sell my size, and I buy several pairs along with several long-sleeve polo shirts that are nondescript and have no logo. In the summer, it'll be cold in Karelia, my destination.

Another tent sells "American" tennis shoes. Even if they are British or made in a sweatshop, the Americans wear them, and that makes them attractive. I don't try them on. I feel like I have foot blisters the size of the Gobi Desert. I don't wish to draw attention to that or the ill-fitting clown shoes. I hope for reasonably good luck and purchase two pairs of my size and pray for the best. I want to put on a pair, but the clown shoes stuffed with socks along with the monster blisters on my feet might be rather memorable. Soon. Soon I will say goodbye to this obnoxious footwear.

Find a larger traveling bag, this time in a dark green whose color isn't discernable from navy or black at a distance. I also purchase a heavy coat and gloves unsold during the colder season. I sit on a bench seat outside of a tent and stuff my purchases into the new bag. Strolling past the tents, I espy a display of baseball-style caps. Grab a navy blue which has no logos or writing.

The smell from the explosion has burned out my nostrils, but not so much that I can't smell sausages cooking at a nearby vendor. I'm ravenous. Suddenly, I hope I don't growl and show my teeth. I purchase enough to consume and still have leftovers for the train ride. Maybe. What's three levels above ravenous? Because that's where I am, so the idea of saving some might be overzealous. I want to scream at the vendor to hurry, package them, and hand those sausages over. Finally, the vendor puts the warm meat into my hands, and I compliment my meal with bread and a few quarts of kvass. Oh yes, kvass!

Being a commando has made me quite hungry but more so thirsty. The liquid, which is concocted with blueberries and fermented bread, hits my tongue and I gulp it down. My thirst is intense. I barely taste the rich berry flavor in the first quart. The berry richness native to cold weather climates is a delight. I allow the flavor to linger on my tongue before I eat part of the sausages. The remaining tasty sausages call out for me to eat them, but I spare a few for the train ride. I mustn't overindulge or get sluggish. I finish the kvass though and purchase a few bottles of water.

After devouring this much-needed vendor fare, I make my way to the railroad station. "One ticket to Yaroslavl, please," I request of the ticket agent. I use my gym identity of Omar Stetzdal. I'll switch that identity again when I leave from Yaroslavl. For now, I purchase a first-class ticket and pray I don't have a cabin mate overnight, as I might get a peaceful night of sleep. I grab a newspaper and wait for the midnight train. I normally wait until a quarter before the hour to get up and go pee. Train toilets are not sanitary places and will likely overflow before the night is over.

Two words: clown shoes. I duck into a bathroom stall and remove my shoes. I have red soggy socks. Crap. No wonder both my feet hurt so bad. Having new shoes won't help much. I put my clown shoes back on and go to the kiosk to get Band-Aids. Well, no one there. I have to ask the ticket agent if they are open this time of night. She says she will help me in a minute. So, I wait. And I wait. I'm standing in two shoes that are holding a bloody river. I've sutures to sew myself up if I get cut, but not a single XYZ Band-Aid. The ticket agent has the phone to her ear. She's chatting away as though there isn't a man standing here with feet producing a bloody river the size of the Gobi Desert.

Thank God. She hangs up, five minutes prior to my train arrival. I buy antiseptic cream and four boxes of Band-Aids. Where I'm going, it's possible no one will know what Band-Aids are. I will have to dispose of the clown shoes when I get off the train.

I'll arrive in Yaroslavl in the morning and can take another overnight train to Kargopol. I'll need to hire a driver there. After an overnight stay, I can hire a driver to take me the several hours' drive to Karelia in northwestern Russia near Finland. It's a land that both time and man have forgotten. Forgotten long ago.

CHAPTER 10
THE EYEBALL

THE NEXT MORNING, I awaken and scream, "Go away," to my buzzing alarm clock. As the clouds of sleep recede from my brain, I realize sleeping late is not an option. My robust to-do list prior to my overnight flight from JFK into Heathrow contains far too many items. With reluctance, I withdraw from my cozy covers and six pillows and order room service. When I first checked into my room, I wondered why anyone would need six pillows on a bed. But I must admit, I enjoyed all six of them, and slept well.

I flick on the TV to catch the news while waiting for the hotel room Keurig to finish dripping a cup of coffee before I begin packing for my flight. The news is reporting the most amazing story. I stop in the middle of folding a pair of blue jeans, so drawn I am to this story. The report is stating the president of Russia, his top military staff, and his top advisors were killed in a coup. The prime minister as well.

The Vice Prime Minister has refused the presidential position, so Andre Smoltsky, next in line for the position as chairman of the Russian elected houses, will take over as president in the interim. My head is spinning over the intensity of the story. What most occurs to me as strange is that the news coverage doesn't focus on the fallen. Strange.

Instead, the report repeats reels of a most handsome Russian soldier. A commander who tried to talk sense to his people at the presidential dacha. His attempt to save lives, not just the president and his ilk but of all present, are apparent. An exploding furnace is stated to be the reason the soldier's plan failed. It's a fantastic story. Enthralled, I stop in place and sit on the edge of the bed as I sip my coffee.

The news report hardly mentions the victims and those injured in the tragedy. Such an oversight would normally upset me. Yet I can't help but focus on this soldier. This handsome soldier I must add, despite his small facial scar, is sexy as hell. His crystal blue eyes are the color of glacial waters I saw at Hubbard's Glacier on an Alaskan Cruise. Thousands of miles away, they capture me—and, I imagine, every woman in the universe, for that matter. The newscast is broadcasting a loop of the soldier's speech to his fellow Russians at what is reported to be a "presidential dacha," or country home. Another loop shows this soldier sitting at the side of the dacha in tears. Then one of him helping the injured for long hours.

Feeling enthralled, and without considering what I'm doing, I raise my hand to touch the soldier's face on the TV screen. I can't remove my hand from his beautiful face. My fingers, which have a mind of their own, explore every line of his face. I want to kiss him. I know it's stupid, but I could swear I felt my ovaries flip.

For some unknown reason, I'm drawn to touch this man's face. Don't want to stop. Don't want to leave him. He's a mere face on a TV screen, but it all feels so, well, so intimate. I want to touch the flesh of the handsome face that's thousands of miles away.

Before I realize what I'm doing, I land my right hand pointer finger squarely into the eyeball of the Russian while caressing the blooming television screen. Thank God the man can't feel my fingertips. When I understand what I just did, I couldn't tell you why I did it. I haven't a clue. It's just such a privately ludicrous thing. I blush. Thank God it's private, because even I think I'm acting as though I'm thirteen years old. Hell, I'm not sure I would have been this silly at thirteen. Poked them man in the eyeball. Thank God it wasn't real life.

A close-up shot taken of this soldier as he pauses for a moment of reflection before speaking all but makes my ovaries take another leap for joy. He's a poster boy for a sexy man. I'm mesmerized not just by the physicality of this man, but also his message. A little "Damn!" escapes my lips as I listen. I notice the *damn* was spoken in my most authentic Southern drawl.

I didn't foresee this reaction. I would have told anyone, anywhere, at any time, that for a woman my age to have a teenage obsession with a face eight thousand miles away is, well… nuts. Yet, this man's face later comes to me in my dreams. He is my dream man. I felt connected to him the first moment I saw him. Having him come to me in my sleep was unavoidable. It just was. And in my thoughts. Constantly. His face will appear to me on this very night—and I think will continue to forevermore—when I reach for my pink toy. What can I say? The man freaking moves me.

Reality returns as breakfast arrives and shocks me out of my trance. "Thank God," I murmur, knowing I must return to reality. I do have a flight to catch.

Intrigued, I continue to watch the Russian news reel while I eat eggs and toast. I miss my mouth a few times. Reality can only tug so hard.

After eating, I sigh and turn off the TV. Reality wins out. One does not need a college degree to figure out that packing wouldn't happen if I didn't turn off the tube.

Here I go again. Packing away my solitary life into a few bags.

I have come to live out of a suitcase while promoting my book and platform. In truth, I understand I've lived a transient lifestyle since the day I left for college. I visit my sister, Debbie, and her family occasionally. But last time was when? How many months ago? Too long, and with visits way too short. Wish I had visited them before leaving for Europe. I miss them terribly. But my life has existed in a constant state of flux over the past year. *Swoosh*.

I do miss them, but at the same time I understand my family has adjusted to not seeing me ever since I left for Doctors Without Borders. They all hope I will settle in the mountains with them, but they are wise enough to understand that I march to a different drumbeat. I understand it too.

For whatever reason, I've been graced with an opportunity to express what I feel is important in the world. It's my destiny. I feel it in my bones. Along with this opportunity comes the lack of opportunity for me personally. You know, like what is important for me personally to obtain for myself in life. To settle down. Have a home. Have a freaking hobby. On that front I'm totally defunct. I'm trying, though. I'm just not there. Not yet. Maybe having my ovaries twist and turn over a faraway Russian is a sign that I need to get busy on that particular project. I smile.

Sighing at my thoughts, I box items for storage that I will send to my sister. Debbie can access my storage locker. Sis will label and arrange my belongings with care. Neither of gets why I need the locker. Both of us understand one hundred percent what's behind my need to keep old high school annuals, the ropes from dad's tying instructions, mother's book outline that never got written... The list goes on. *Them.* I need to hold on to them.

The closest thing to having my own home is a storage locker. My address? Unit number 23A.

CHAPTER 11
THE PLANE

THE NONSTOP COVERAGE in Russia continues to capture my imagination as I pack and prepare myself for my European journey. The news coverage continues to highlight the Russian commander. *Charismatic* doesn't do justice in describing the handsome man. I wonder if he's unmarried. If so, he would have his choice of Russian beauties. Hell, he would have his choice even if he were a married man. Reality is cruel to the imagination.

I wish I spoke a word or two of Russian. Attempts to learn a few critical words for the European tour drove me all but mad with frustration. So many tongues on one continent proved insurmountable. I decide I will try to pack my brain with critical words of a language just before traveling to the given country. The pace of the European tour is daunting, much less trying to cope with language. Scandinavian countries alone are a challenge beyond what my brain can manage. Perhaps "good morning" and "thank you" for warming the crowd as I travel between nations will be all that I can manage.

I'm unsure about the languages of other countries, but I realize Russian, with its Cyrillic alphabet, could require a lifetime of study. For sure, not a task accomplished on a plane ride. The language blows my mind.

History made English the international language of business. With wisdom, world citizens understand the value of learning English. I have the opposite of their plight. I feel grateful not to be on the other side of the coin: a Russian needing to tackle English. I admire those Russians who conquered my native language. It's challenging enough to speak "Southern" in the United States of America.

Along with me, I drag along "Old Trusty." I began giving inanimate objects names as a child. Guess I never grew up. Old Trusty is the moniker given to my knapsack that I carried through jungles, deserts, and war zones. Trusty is now geriatric, but I'm determined to use the old boy until his dying day. A bit of a sentimental good luck charm.

After paying bills and running errands, I shower. I take a few minutes to consider the Russian soldier. Enough said. Uber arranged, but late. Damn New York City traffic, but at least I'm en route to JFK.

As I arrive a few minutes late to the airport, a few individuals recognize me and introduce themselves. Surprised, I show the smile that Elizabeth Frederick taught me while I talk with folks and sign autographs. In my mind, autographs are a curious thing to covet. Yet I understand some folks are into it.

I invested in a first-class ticket, knowing I have trouble sleeping on an airplane. My agent scheduled an itinerary that has me running as soon as the plane lands at Heathrow. The schedule doesn't include time to recuperate. First class seems worth the investment for a transatlantic flight, and for a soul that needs rest.

After boarding the airplane I buckle into my seat. I feel comfortable until when who should appear but Mr. Fourth Row. I'm unamused.

"Well, hello Dr. Selena Frederick."

"Please call me Selena. I enjoy being informal."

"Great, call me Joe," the fourth-row man says with a shit-eating grin.

"Jooooooe," I say with my slow Southern drawl and a nod of my head to acknowledge Mr. Cook. Kindly. Damn Southern upbringin'.

"I'm astonished you're even speaking to me, but I'm glad you are," says Joe.

"Oh, I'm not one to hold grudges," I say nonchalantly, "but if one of your goons puts a camera in my face, they're gonna require surgery." I'm teasing and give Joe a wink.

Joe gives his infamous whistled reply. "My, but the *lady doth protest too much.*" With a split face he asks, "Since we're on the subject, how about an interview?"

I repress the impulse to laugh. Then I give my sweet Southern smile taught to me by mother and ask, "Oooh, were we on the subject?"

"I could have sworn we were on the subject," says Joe, failing his innocent man act.

I don't know what I'm thinking. Suppose I'm amused by this incorrigible man, after all. Part of me wants to tell him to take a flying leap. At 30,000 feet would be nice. Instead, my lips end up saying, "Okaaay, but with a caveat."

"Shoot."

"Thirty minutes total. Right now, on the plane," I demand.

"I'm sure my team can handle that."

"I'm not finished," I say with my own shit-eatin' grin. "At the conclusion of thirty minutes, you and your crew give up your seats in first class to someone in economy."

"Lady," Joe whistles. "You drive a tough bargain. Ya sure I couldn't offer to lay a little dough on ya? Take ya to dinner?"

I roll my eyes and give him a half look and murmur. "*Puleeze.* I'm capable of feeding myself, and J*ooooo*e... you can't afford me."

"You're a different sort, for sure. My experience is that celebrities die to be in front of a camera. I'm usually appreciated."

I look disinterested.

"Ah, come on, Doc."

"It's *Selena*," I say while looking away from him.

"Okay, Se-*len*-a. You have a deal. Just understand I'm connecting to Russia from London, so my flight is long. And I'm a geriatric geezer with an unhealthy prostate."

I chuckle in spite of myself. I press the call button for the flight attendant. I explain the interview agreement and request her help to find four economy-class passengers who may find first-class seating helpful. Perhaps a passenger with children or an elderly couple. The flight attendant gives a wink and says she would enjoy the task. I like her.

Once the plane takes off and the pilot clears for passengers to move around the cabin, the crew gathers equipment from the overhead bins.

Joe begins the interview by talking about my time with Doctors Without Borders. The reporter refers to a lot of text I wrote in my book, which he obviously has actually read. His knowledge of my book's content surprises me as well as impresses me as he skillfully dissects its pages.

I can't help but soften a little toward the reporter hailing from the fourth row. Obnoxious, yes. But I like him despite his rough edges.

"What's your opinion of the current situation in Russia?" quizzes Joe. "Do you anticipate civil war?"

"Well, I only know what I've briefly seen on the news. I don't believe it's important what I think, and the same goes for anyone else outside of Russia. I believe it's important what the Russian people think. Things appear calm there for now, and like other world citizens, I hope it continues. I can only speak in terms of hope. I hope for peace, and no more senseless death. Everyone wants a resolution that will satisfy the mass of humans that make up what the world refers to as Russians."

"I wouldn't be a journalist if I didn't ask this next question."

I nod a *go ahead*, suspecting what's coming. I would prefer to stick to my platform of peace, healthcare, improvement in poverty—issues that affect women.

"I'm wondering why, in God's name, does a lady like you, who a considerable number of folks call 'the most beautiful woman on the planet,' would devote her life to helping those in the greatest hell holes on earth? You could be spending your days instead sailing on a yacht with a hot adoring lover."

"Joe it's not for me to give dating advice. That's far from my expertise."

"No, but women's issues are. And as an OB/GYN specialist, sex is definitely in your wheelhouse."

I want to laugh, and I'm sure I have a goofy grin on my face. "Are sex and dating the same thing?"

"Sometimes."

Okay, he's got me. I give a slight pause. "Perhaps it's because I'm disinterested in gentlemen who try to convince me they are great lovers with a large penis because they can afford to buy the sailing vessels with the biggest oars. Now, if the guy scrubbing the deck is single, then perhaps we can talk. Between the two, he's likely the better gentleman." I notice Joe is not whistling but looks quite serious.

"What do you want in a man?"

I pause and he qualifies.

"Women around the world see your advice as solid. They have a right to know what kinds of decisions Dr. Selena Frederick makes for herself. I want to better understand the choices you personally make on behalf of those women."

The question is sincere. Damn, he got me again. I'm going to enjoy watching him pack up and move to economy class. I slowly begin my reply. "I can go out on the limb and say it's unanimous that women want a person of good character as a partner. I see that as a baseline. The unique quality that appeals to me in a gentleman of suitable character is strength. I'm a strong woman. I would need a strong man. Another woman would value other qualities based on her own particular needs."

"Wimps need not apply?" asks Joe with a grin.

I screw up my face.

"Do you plan to get married in the future, maybe have a coupla kids?"

"I don't know, Joe. I take life one event at a time. Right now, I'm concentrated on my European tour. And trying to do as much to benefit others as I can along the way. Who knows what's next for me after that?"

I can tell Joe is hankering for more, so I continue. "If I meet a gentleman who I perceive to be 'Mr. Right,' if you will, I'll embrace marriage and the blessing of children. But it's difficult for me to affirm what I will do in the future. I have no reference for that."

Joe didn't delude himself into thinking I was unaware of me giving him a ten-minute freebie.

"Thank you for talking to me, Dr. Frederick. You are an insightful woman. Delightful, as well."

I nod more than speak my thanks. I sit grinning as Joe and

company move to the back of the plane. Soon, I'm joined by a young woman with a baby. They're both delightful, mom and babe. The mom lets me enjoy holding the baby for a little while. I love cuddling the little one and whisper sweet songs from my childhood to the child. Mom allows me to feed the babe a few snacks, and I even help out with a diaper change. Bliss.

After the mother settles her infant to sleep, I lean my chair back and sleep the sleep of saints.

CHAPTER 12
SERGEI'S JOURNEY

MY OVERNIGHT JOURNEY via train is hell. First, I have a cabinmate, and the man won't shut up. Worse, he keeps looking at my face with recognition. Then he turns his head to inspect my wen as though he has never seen a boil before.

I don't even bother to catch the man's name. A man whose whole family tree I know within five minutes. "Say, I have a pin if you want to pop that thing."

Here I am, feeling soaked blood moving from the bottom of my feet to the top of my socks as I formulate a reply. "I think I prefer the way it is instead of gushing blood and pus. Excuse me. I'm eager to get ready for bed and sleep. Tough couple of days, you know."

I try not to be curt, but probably was a little. I'm waiting for the train to move once all passengers have boarded and entered their rooms. Less foot traffic that way. So, I gather my bathroom needs, sliding my Band-Aids into my gym towel, along with toothbrush and paste. The hell with shaving; I'm a traveler. I grab a pair of clean socks and new shoes.

God, I hope blood doesn't bleed through the socks on my feet when I remove my shoes before going to bed. This guy will surely notice. My lie is ready. The socks stuffed in the clown shoe toes are dripping red. Shit, I only have one pair of clean socks.

I make my way to the toilet at the back of the train. It has overflowed with pee. Worse, the toilet doesn't have a lid. I too have to pee, but I don't want to make the overflow problem worse. Guess I will have to hold it.

I need to nurse my foot blisters without putting anything on the floor. Shoes first, I put everything in my hands into the sink. It is not exactly clean, but it will have to do. I prop a long leg on top of the sink. Thank God I'm physically fit, as standing on one leg in a space a fraction the size of a linen closet with poor lighting and a pee-drenched floor is not a task suited for a couch potato.

I remove my shoe and blood-soaked sock. I let them fall to the floor, since I plan to dispose of both. My wound needs to be cleaned. I remove the toothbrush and paste rolled in my towel and store them inside a new shoe. I gently turn the sink's water on and direct it onto the towel, barely wetting the end. I clean the ulcer wounds and dry them well before adding a pinch of antibiotic cream. I use the larger Band-Aids, but damned if they will stick. They must be a hundred years old.

Pissed off, I don't give up. In the meantime, someone bangs on the door. I don't even bother to reply. I end up using smaller Band-Aids to tape on the bigger one. Half-assed ingenuity, but I can slip on my socks without disturbing the bandages. I put on a new shoe, which, God love me, is tight. I will try the other pair in the morning.

Another bang at the door. I answer with the most ague-saturated voice I can muster and reply, "I'm sick."

Quickly, I repair the second foot and put on the second tight shoe. I add my toothbrush and paste to my towel. Damned if I'm brushing my teeth in here.

The garbage can is full and miscellaneous pieces have overflowed to litter the floor. I dump more garbage onto the floor and stuff my clown shoes and bloody socks near the bottom of the can. After I replace the garbage, I attempt to wash my hands. No, there's no soap in the dispenser. Of course not. I use a full minute of vigorous friction underneath the running water.

I return to the cabin, say goodnight to my cabinmate, and retrieve a pillow from the overhead bin. No damn blanket. Great, just great. I'm tempted to leave my shoes on but am to the point I don't care. Let Mister Nosy see my feet. I have a story.

At least my cabinmate is silent. I take my coat and spread it over my feet and bottom half of my body. That should help. I turn my back and fall off into a deep sleep until I'm awakened by a disturbing noise. I sit up in fight-or-flight mode, my ears keen to assess the source of the noise. It sounds like a trainwreck when falling from its metal rail. Let me adjust that: it's like *twenty* trainwrecks going over their metal rails.

I look over at my cabinmate. Damn. How does so much snoring noise come from such a skinny man? It was a long, long night. Did I tell you I had to pee?

It overjoyed me when we arrived in Nyandoma—the closest station to Kargopol—as the few hours of gray night were opening their doors to the dawn of a new day. I taxied to the only Kargopol hotel. The taxi driver gave me a car driver referral for the next day's journey to Karelia. Rays of the warming dawn seeped through the windows of the Kargopol hotel room. The simplest of Russian towns, lounging beside the Onega River, I've always liked Kargopol with its rugged quaintness. True Russia.

My stomach growls as I'm reminded of a Russian breakfast cooking downstairs. I don't bother to unpack but instead descend the stairs as ham and eggs waft into my nostrils. Thank God, my new shoes are a better fit. Small joy, but I'll take it. A tabby lounging on the stairway greets me with a forlorn meow and an offer to rub its belly. Another small joy. I stop and sit beside the cat.

"What do you think of this insanity, buddy?" I ask as I stroke the soft mane of the multicolored feline.

The cat burbles a lazy meow.

"Me too, buddy, me too," I reply.

The hotel serves many hunters, anglers, and other sports persons who stay at the hotel when they visit the town to fish or hunt in the forest. To advertise its trademark, the hotel graces its entrance with a large mounted brown bear. Its huge ursine teeth drip from its lips and sharp, pointed claws appear as if the animal just stepped out of a bear's nail salon. The brown bear plays his role well.

On my way to the basement restaurant, I tip my blue cap to the mounted animal as I walk by. I give myself a smirky smile as I think how cool it would be to paint that bear's nails a sexy red. I think I might be getting punch-drunk from lack of sleep.

I suck up my breakfast as if rabid. Because of my upcoming journey to Karelia, I recognize it may be a while before I enjoy a meal on the scale of Kargopol's offerings. I plan to fatten up while the opportunity lies available on the table. One thing about Russians: we are a people who, when we eat, eat darn well. Especially at breakfast. The server fills the table with dishes for my choosing. Even with my robust appetite, I eat a mere half of the offerings. A Scottish breakfast somewhat compares to the Russian, but only somewhat.

With a coffee cup in hand, I lean back in the chair to take in the rustic lodge decor. Heavy timbered logs reach across the low ceiling in this cellar cafe. Abutted by a dense forest, the hotel café displays animal heads of many types, including foxes, wolves, bears, and stags with such heavy antlers that I wonder how the animals kept their head upright.

The hearth contains a blazing fire on this sunny yet chilly May morning. For the first time since the dacha, I enjoy my surroundings while sipping the remainder of my coffee and finish the rice porridge. I recall this spot as the place of the Russian sasquatch sightings. Seventy people witnessed the same event. The sasquatch had a young one who had drifted into a clearing. The sasquatch burst from the forest, snatched her young, and ran back into the forest. A soldier pursued the beast and its young. The soldier who ran after them claimed he caught up with the pair. At that point, the soldier stated he fainted from the putrid sasquatch odor. Hmm. All I know for sure is that seventy people saw something.

I should sleep after breakfast but have an excess of energy and want a little time outside on this sunny morning, especially since spring rains are expected later in the day. After a few hours of walking the quiet roads of Kargopol, I fall asleep on a grassy knoll beside the river's edge. As much as I love this place, I know I can't stay. Too many souls traffic through this small haven abutting the Kenzero National Park. Now a UNESCO biosphere, the rich forest provides interest to handfuls who wish to enjoy untouched Russian nature.

I awaken after a brief nap, knowing I saved the best of Kargopol for last. My mouth is on the verge of salivating as I make my way to The Cathedral of the Nativity of Christ perched atop the hill overlooking Kargopol. I can't explain how good it feels to be released from my intense operative mode. I have a lot of thinking yet to do, but stimulating my mind may help.

The church is no longer a functioning place of worship due to age and a destructive fire centuries ago. The cathedral's front is now used as a religious art museum. The entire city burned in the 1700s, as well as part of the church. Somehow monks, with the help of residents, saved the painted wooden "heavens" fitted in the church's dome.

During the years of communism, local monks hid the heavens, or dome paintings, along with a wealth of religious art. I swallow hard in awe each time I stand before a piece of this primitive art. In my heart, with no doubts whatsoever, I believe these unique pieces of art were under the protection of God Almighty Himself. I can't say why most of the world doesn't know about this art and will never see it, but nevertheless, God himself sought to save it and inspire a few with the amazement of its existence. In this place, I, Commander Sergei Radkov, who had never been inside a church until I was in my twenties, experiences humility before God, as the art offerings massage my heart with unique Russian history and culture. I do love my land. It's something that this poor orphan boy can claim as his own.

When I return to the hotel, I find sound sleep until the morning. After another Kargopol breakfast, my driver arrives, and we begin the several hours' journey to Karelia. We pass by the mounted hotel bear who is now wearing bright red fingernail polish. Wonder how that happened?

I feel free. I know it's short lived, but for now I converse as an old friend with the driver as we trek across the remote land. Wearing a baseball cap like mine, the driver chats about soccer and his son most of the way. His son plays soccer. I sense these shared experiences between father and son are this man's whole life. The driver and his wife have only the one child. It warms my heart just to watch the man's face light up when he mentions his son.

Honestly, I envy the boy. I never had the joy of lighting up my father's face. Dear ole Dad. Whoever the hell he is.

We arrive at the movable wooden bridge to cross the Kenzero Lake. A frozen lake during the winter, Kenzero Lake, meaning *highest point*, is uncrossable until the lake thaws in the spring. It's a "red" place, as red means *beautiful* in Russian. It will take another seventy kilometers to reach the village. The crisp and chilly air is as fresh as anything that's ever entered my nose as the car motors its way down the dirt road. Grass-covered hills hail dandelions sprouting up on the side of the road. The clear blue lake with its natural beauty peeks through on the driver's side of the dirt road. As though to spite winter, the grass in this glacial region comes out in early spring in a deep green color found in a rainbow, as if to thumb its nose at the bitter season. Cows and sheep feed in the spring meadows, oblivious to their slaughterhouse destination.

My senses alert me to the village being nearby when I smell the cow dung. Cows roam the unpaved town streets of Vershinino Village, my Karelia destination. Few people on God's good earth are hardy enough to live in Verishinino Village bearing the frozen living conditions. Of Finnish ethnicity, most inhabitants are interrelated kin folk. Thank God for the hardiest. After all, someone must look after the cows. *Mooooo*.

The cows consider themselves to be the most prominent of citizenry in the village. These regal citizens leave their piles wherever nature calls. The piles stay as placed, mostly on the main dirt road, until the rains wash them away. A few dogs parade the village streets. The canines follow strangers with curiosity, as if they're Spetsnaz spies. They leave their piles, too.

Upon arrival, I head for the community center concerning a cottage rental. Vershinino Village in the Karelia region offers only a few housing options on the lake. The village has a hotel which boasts six rooms. I prefer to be alone and opt to rent a house containing three bedrooms and its own banya. More than I need, but the spot will suffice nicely.

The bathroom toilet is a hole in the floor. There is no running water in the cottage, but a full barrel of lake water is in the kitchen. I suppose the cleaning staff makes trips to the lake with lighter buckets to top off the barrel between rentals. One sink exists in the Karelian cottage, which is in the kitchen with the water barrel. However, there is no plumbing or piping. Only lake water. I'm grateful to have a refrigerator and amazed it actually works. Lake Verishinino is not for the fragile. Nope. Is not.

After signing the rental agreement with a woman named Ludmilla, I inquire as to the possibility of renting a boat. Ludmilla smiles, showing her black teeth and says her husband has a flat-bottom boat and he can take me out on the lake. I convey to Ludmilla that I prefer to explore on my own and can leave a substantial deposit for the boat. Ludmilla appears fifty. In biological years, I suspect Ludmilla to be a few years younger than me. She smiles her black-toothed grin and says her husband will drop by before lunch. I inform Ludmilla that her husband can find me at the cottage or the community center. Otherwise, walking on the village road.

In the intermarried village, everyone knows the location of anyone in the village at any given moment. The village is home to approximately one hundred residents. Children on bikes with their dogs trot alongside to spy on visitors. Curious young eyes observe the stranger's movements.

So do the eyes of the long-lashed cows. The cows carry on like gossipy humans. They notice everything and everybody who dares to sojourn their dirt streets. They gather at street corners, not allowing anybody to pass or walk among them. It's bovine real estate.

There is a tiny local market two hundred meters up the hill from the cottage. I pick up milk, cookies, sour cream for the cookies, a bottle of Crimean white wine, a couple gallons of distilled water, and coffee. The woman totals my purchase by spinning the small balls on an abacus. As I step outside, sitting in front of the market is a man with a boat hitched to a truck. My ride has arrived.

I repress a laugh. In my head, I measure the flat-bottom boat to be about four meters long, and handmade. I nearly question the man if the boat will float but choke down the jibe. The boat has a fifty-horsepower motor on it, so if it does float, it can fly. My smart-ass musing causes me to wonder if the boat *needs* to fly to keep the craft on top of the water. Kenzero is the coldest of lakes. One icy plunge below the frigid surface is likely the last plunge a person will ever take on earth in such waters.

"You go out in it much?" I slyly ask the man with leathery skin, who I assume to be Ludmilla's husband. The husband appears a decade older than Ludmilla.

"Every day," the man replies. "Where about ya going?"

"Oh, just to the close-by islands. Maybe over where the communal farm was," I respond.

"So not far, then."

"Nope."

"She's yours if you want her," the husband says with approval. "Not doing any fishing?"

"No, just taking in the scenery alone. Away from the city," I confirm.

"Came an awful long way just to do that."

"Well, lots on my mind. Far seemed good, so here I am."

"When you want to take her?" asks the expressionless man.

"Hoping for this afternoon," I say. "Hoping for just after lunch."

"How about I pick you up at the community center after lunch?"

"Sure," I agree. "I told Ludmilla I'd give you a deposit."

"No need," says the leather faced husband. "I know where you live."

I nod. "That you do."

I walk back to the lake home on sore feet and store my purchases. I change into dirty clothes. Caring about one's body odor is a wasted effort in Verishinino. I stretch and begin my exercise with an endurance run. My feet are sore, but exercise is more important. I've been through much worse in the field. Much worse.

I speak and nod to the kerchief-wearing babushkas who are walking on the roads outlining the village. For my efforts, I receive stony stares, if given a glance at all. Wonder if they think I'm hitting on them? Geez.

Race up the hill to the only Verishinino church and back down the other side to a marina where several boats are docked. I continue exercising by repeating the village track. Two dogs follow me with wagging tongues, keeping pace. They are friendly, so I don't mind the company.

At 11:45 a.m., I return to the house to chug a bottle of spring water, pick up my wallet, and make my way to the community center for lunch. It's the only establishment that serves food in the village. Cooking in the cottage kitchen is not a consideration I entertain. I muse to myself that an applicable moniker for the cottage is "The Amoeba Hotel". I hope for improved sanitation at the community center. The Verishinino Hotel guests, consisting of hunters and anglers, eat their meals at the community center since the hotel doesn't offer food. Lucky people. It's awful.

The meal begins with the Russian staple of borscht, a beet-based soup. The kitchen serves the soup without sour cream. This is an atrocity. Russians eat everything with sour cream. I'm incensed, especially since I left my supply of sour cream at the cottage. Hell, I would've brought it if I had known. Like salt and pepper, I would expect sour cream to be served. I hope they will offer cream and sugar with the coffee. Damn.

Along with a salad, fish is served. An ugly fish. The fish resembles an Omul but is hardly a delicacy. Whatever the type, it's a tiny, bony, spiny thing with empty gray eyes that stare at me. The fish contains more bones than meat. I muse to myself that I will exert more energy picking through the fish's bones than there are available calories in the entire meal.

It's a Russian tradition to start a meal with a soup and bread. Next is a salad, then the main course with vegetables. Not so in this village. The humorless babushka who cooks and serves the meals at the community center dumps everything on the table at once.

Every village house has a garden with potatoes. So, every meal contains the starch. I observe my plate and attempt to decipher: just how were these potatoes cooked? The offending potato-cook serves a salad made of grated beets and cabbage with one-half of a cherry-tomato chunk on top. So generous. Don't forget the stale brown bread with coffee or tea made with the damn lake water. I've eaten better food from a can during missions for the military with bullets flying at me. I don't quite know what those canned meals contained, but they tasted better than the community center rations, and are less mysterious.

The meal cost 1,150 rubles. Hell, I can get a burger and fries at the Hard Rock Cafe Moscow for less. I don't expect steak and fries, but is clear water too much to ask? Not for the frail. No, Vershinino Village is not. The village market stocks ham and cheese. A cold sandwich eaten outside the cottage might be a better option in the future.

The "boat husband," as I joke to myself, appears in front of the center the second I walk outside. Excellent timing. Who needs cell phones in this village? They seem to have better communications than Moscow.

The man still has not shared his name with me. Oh well. I decide not to ask such a personal question. Although the man spies me with a hint of recognition. It's to my advantage that folks in the village have no desire to become acquainted with outsiders, nor to serve them well. Leave your rubles, get the minimum, and go home. Do svidanija! Goodbye.

Kenzero Lake contains many small islands. Some uninhabited. Others have sparse or seasonal human habitation. An example of sparse, there is one island inhabited by one man. Another, with only six year-round humans. Another rises in the summer to a grand population of fifteen. Since the lake freezes, the year-round inhabitants must have the items needed to exist during an icy sub-Arctic winter.

The lake locals won't waste their wisdom on one's curiosity. They will turn their heads instead of answering. The island of the dead. It's the burial site of the nonliving natives. What perplexes me is what happens in the wintertime when the lake freezes? It's a guarded local secret. Best to not know.

I spent a few weeks on Kenzero Lake islands in the past while on a mission to find a rogue agent. Bastard sold Russian intelligence secrets. Reports of sightings of the agent floated around the Kenzero locale. So, I was sent by Moscow to assess if the traitor was hiding out around the islands. This occurred while I had blond hair and blue eyes, perhaps a decade prior. No need to disguise for such a mission. None of the locals show hints of recognition, except the boatman. I feel a twang of concern for the man's recognition of me since the rogue agent was located living on the island where the dead are buried. Unfortunate for him, the lifeless provide no shelter or food. Dumbass should have known better. After a few nights is the cold wind and freezing rain, and nearly starved, he was ready for an alternate fate. Begged me to shoot him. I wasn't going to let a traitor get off that easy.

The event was the news of a lifetime to the locals. The curious folk found the happening to be fodder for gossip to the nth degree. Every tongue was a-chatter with their kinfolk concerning every detail of the investigation. That could be the hint of recognition I see in the boatman's eyes. Or perhaps, he's just summing me up.

The boat husband requests I display my boat skills. I oblige by cranking the motor and explaining how one handles a boat. Ludmilla's husband signals a leathery thumbs-up.

I take off to the island where I recall a small wooden church standing guard, its onion dome and spire containing "remembrances." Remembrance items are presented to God by women mostly, if not solely. The women bring in a piece of their best handiwork of quilting, shawls, embroidery, etc. and hang them across a rope in front of the church altar. The woman gives her offerings to the glory of God. In appreciation, she expects God to fulfill a special prayer in her troubled heart. At times, the requests are brutal, like expecting God to strike someone dead that the babushka hates.

Such practices, although taking place in the Russian Orthodox Church, are a tradition dating back to pagan times. Such traditions linger in remote places in Russia like Kenzero Lake. The pagan and the Christian, holding hands together to soothe the unchangeable ways of a harsh Russian life.

With a tug of curiosity, I'm eager to discover if progress occurred on this island inhabited by a population of ten people. After mooring the boat, I trudge up the steep hill to the church. The same community sign which existed a decade prior remains unchanged. The sign honors the fallen in the war against the Nazis. However, new tokens adorn the simple memorial refreshed with new plastic flowers. The tokens are another pagan tradition. An inch-high wooden carving of a dog, a metal ring. I don't understand most of the tokens but find them interesting.

I climb the steps and push open the wooden front door of the domed church. The same remembrances are hanging across the altar rope as per a decade prior. Locals believe it to be a curse to manipulate a remembrance once the worshipper places the item at the altar. I'm not one to mess with a kerchiefed babushka's remembrance. However, I wonder how long they expect the remembrances to stay in place. Hundred years? Fifty? How long will it take for God to need them? Humans never used the items.

I sit outside on the steps of the church. A tail-wagging yellow dog hustles up to me and takes a little sniff. Gently, I pat the dog's head and pull an apple from my coat pocket that I picked up at the community center. I eat the apple while breathing in the fresh air. The air wafting through my nostrils is a welcome change from the air in the rented cottage, especially near the bathroom hole which was dug decades ago.

In the cottage is a sitting room outside the bathroom. A library, if you will, containing several bookshelves filled with books sitting in front of an old couch. The couch appears more worn and dirtier from disuse than actual use. God Almighty can smell the bathroom stink in heaven. Immediately I shut the bathroom door. Next, I shut the door between the library and the kitchen to control the filthy bouquet. Better, but the odor was like a strong chemical. I imagined the fragrance was still strong enough to leach through your skin like a parasite. Yuck. At least someone appreciates books.

So yes, I find the fresh air on this lake hill a pleasure. I climb onto a knoll and take off my parka coat. The locals shared that Karelia had been experiencing several days of drizzling rain. The driver and I caught what I hope is the end of the rains during our ride to the village. Now the sun is showing Karelia its rays. The warm rays dance around the grass blades and twirl with the dandelions. My fair face welcomes the warmth. I fling the apple core into the field. The yellow dog runs to retrieve it. As I get up to walk back downhill, the dog returns alongside me.

The yellow canine nudges me, trying to get me to take back the apple core. I inspect the soiled thing. "How about something like this?" I ask the canine while picking up a stick and throwing it down the hill instead of the ruined piece of apple.

The dog runs and catches the stick midair before it can touch the ground. I give the dog's ear a good rub with a few "Good Dog!" rewards. I slow my cantor downhill and shorten my stride to play catch with the dog for a while. When I reach the boat, I don my parka before shoving off. The wind is glacial while gliding across the lake in the open boat.

While I'm arranging to shove off, the happy-to-have-a-friend yellow dog jumps into the boat. I coax the canine out by picking up the stick and tossing it uphill. While the dog is retrieval happy, I shove off the boat. Cranking its motor, I speed the homemade boat up the lake. The dog jumps into the icy lake and swims after me. It doesn't take long for the pooch to think better of it before turning to swim back to land, the stick hanging in his canine mouth.

Dogs aren't a common sight in Russia. In Russia one only sees dogs in the countryside. Rarely in the cities or urban areas. Dogs were used to control the masses during the communist era. Seeing someone torn to pieces by dogs in the streets, much less the gulags, was not an unusual scene. Dogs are property protectors in the countryside and remote areas. City folk have different security needs.

On the next island I make my way up the hill. I don't know what I'm looking for by making this trek, but damn, I badly need answers. Only I would go to one of the most remote places on the planet to find answers. Go figure. An operative, especially one on the run, can end up in strange places. Done that before, more times than I care to count. Just never figured I would be doing it in my own country.

A WWII monument exists on this island as well, but the plastic flowers are near decay. I make a mental note to offer money to Ludmilla for new flowers and request her husband replace them while out on the lake. Once, this larger island with the same area as Verishinino had a vibrant community. Until the communists came and instituted a collective cow farm here. The project failed miserably.

I remove my parka, and my head borrows its fluffiness as I lay atop the hillside. The hilltop where I now lie, covered with green grasses and dandelions, once existed as a cow pasture. I feel tired, but clear-headed. A nap here under God's glorious sun would be nice. Alas, I need to plan what I should do about my bizarre situation.

I face a cloudless sky. Not a cloud, nary a mist, a direct view into heaven. This island hasn't always been deserted. I allow my thoughts to drift into the clouds away from me to the former residents of this village.

The number was thirty. Thirty names on a monument from one war. Souls embraced on this earth with dirty plastic flowers and a few tokens. And embraced by those who remembered. Was there a single soul left who remembered? I imagine the presence of the thirty lost souls to be right here, in this place, for as long as people remembered.

The number was ten. Ten houses where the thirty souls abided and lived their lives until their country called them to patriotism. A broken Pact of 1939. A German invasion into the Fatherland. The invaders had brought tanks and troops rolling into lands that didn't belong to them.

These thirty were a microcosm of the estimated twenty-five million Russian souls who lost their lives as the Germans dropped their bombs, marched their soldiers, and rolled their tanks into the nation of Russia. Twenty-five million. Military and civilian. Brave men and women stepped into brave shoes to do what brave people do. Twenty-five million.

Another number existed, nine hundred. For nine hundred days the invader surrounded the sainted city with a new communist name to the south. A city who had lost its name and identity that was given to the great Russian Czar a few centuries prior. The communists yanked the czar's namesake city from him. Communists who were more Swiss than Russian. The Party gave the city a more communist namesake in their own image.

In most countries, towns have some form of a main street. In most Russian towns, Lenin Street is the major thoroughfare to this day.

The enemy, represented by the man with the trademark dark mustache, never controlled the czar's staunch city. His *Heil Hitler* bandits rolled into nearby Peterhoff on the Bay of Finland and made a mockery of it. What their bombs did not destroy, their thieving hands did. Hitler never possessed Saint Petersburg, then named Leningrad, because the heart and soul of the Russian people wouldn't allow it.

Some folks exalt victory to a Russian-mustached bastard, Stalin. I've long since decided the victory belongs to my people, not to one man. Such was life in those dark times of Russia.

The thirty of ten houses left their island home to protect their homeland. Thirty souls that once breathed but too soon would not. Brothers, fathers, husbands, uncles, sons who left in clumps or one by one and stepped into brave shoes and never again walked the grounds of their lake home. Their bodies never returned, but their souls stayed in the forest and lingered in the trees of their glacial lake habitat.

No males remained except the young. Women carried on life in the village without aid from their men. The women became babushkas. Soon the young boys grew to be young men with only memories of their fathers' teachings. The boys learned the ways taught by frigid lake life, learned to cope with its harshness as their fathers did before them. Once grown, they took young wives from surrounding villages. They would propagate life on the lake into another generation.

The communist-Russian life change arrived with its obnoxious surety that it knew more than these hardy people. A government started by a Russian who was in exile in Switzerland before he came back to Russia to revenge his brother's death. A damned calamity. This revenge and hatred caused millions of Russians to lose their souls long before losing their lives in the cruelest ways imaginable. Russian against Russian. The oppressed had cause to revenge so much more. The communists changed this lake island village into a Soviet collective farm. Hadn't enough been taken from these people already? These people who asked for so little? Truly, what gave you the right, Lenin? And you, Stalin? Motherfuckers.

You mustached bastard. What gave you the right? Wave your violent hand, frighten people to bend to your will and way of thinking? What made you think you killed God and became Him? What gave you the fucking right? I shake my head with rage as I mourn the brutal and unnecessary death of so many of my countrymen. So many. So very many. One of them may have been Momma, but I could never find a record of her. Records mean nothing. Not in Russia.

Then the number became four hundred. Four hundred cows munching their way to fatness and milk. In a few decades, the collective farms failed. The number now is *zero*. The life here is now zero. Zero.

Somehow, the babushkas persevered through those dark times, even during the seasons without sun. Babushkas who looked fifty when they were thirty and ninety when they were fifty. Alas, the babushkas placed their last scarf on their head to enter the chapel and lay down their last remembrances on the altar of worship and prayer, then died or moved to a nearby village. Most likely, they did not leave the lake. The Kenzero whose icy waters made up their life's blood.

This is Russia. This is a microcosm of all of Russia.

I sit up, a decision made. It's as clear as the heavens above to me. I know what I need to do. Go back. I won't cower here. God damn it, if I am going to die, I'm going to die as a fucking *Russian* fighting for his people. I live in a world too damn full of mustached bastards.

Without delay, I return to Verishinino Village. I enter the community center office at closing and beg to use the phone. There would be a charge, of course. Of course! I call my driver friend, who replies, "Yes, I can be there in a couple of hours."

"Can you pick me up a cell phone on the way in? I need to make some urgent calls. A burner phone is alright. I will, of course, repay you and with a handsome tip." The driver doesn't hesitate to agree. He has already experienced me as a man of handsome tips.

In the meantime, I grudgingly eat dinner at the community center. As earlier, same borscht without sour cream. Same stale brown bread. Same cabbage and beet salad. Though a different concoction with beef and potatoes that is not half bad. Same tea made with lake water. Forgive me, Momma, for my misbehavior, but I've had enough of this nonsense.

I hate selfish and lazy behavior, circumstances be damned. I take my cup into the bathroom, which has clear running water in the sink, rinse the cup with fresh water, and fill it. I take the cup to the old babushka clinking about the kitchen. "Warm this up for some tea," I instruct without ceremony.

She eyes me as if to say, "What, the lake water tea not good enough for you?"

"I won't be running with the shits for four days because you're too cheap or lazy to use fresh water. Warm it up," I say without apology.

The old woman gives me an *up yours* look but does as I request. I observe her, watching her every move. My trust level isn't high. Neither is my tip to the old woman. Tipping is not a necessary custom in Russia, but zero is not a tip I normally leave, especially in a poverty-stricken area. I like to tip above average. I have been blessed and possess more than most. Over tipping is a duty. Perhaps it's the communist in me.

I have enough time for a quick banya visit before the driver arrives. Grabbing bottled water to drink because of the importance of hydration as well as toiletries, a towel, disposable slippers, and a change of clean clothes, I make way to the backyard banya. The structure contains three chambers. The assembly area is the first chamber, where I remove my coat and shoes. I slide on paper banya slippers. Each chamber has short doors, one leading to the next. With my greater-than-six-feet height, I must duck to enter each doorway. With low ceilings, each chamber of the banya can preserve heat.

In the next chamber, I disrobe and wrap myself with a towel. I set my water on a table. The banya is a "black banya." The black soot ceilings from the burning wood which heats the stones in the furnace is how I can tell. This room is warm, with the purpose of bathers growing accustomed to the heat. I swig water from the gallon jug while sitting for a few minutes to allow my body to adjust to the sweltering temperature. When ready, I proceed into the third chamber.

To make the stones on the banya furnace steam, I pour lake water taken from a barrel with a scoop pot. The banya feels its usual two hundred degrees. Ludmilla left a bunch of eucalyptus branches to enhance the banya experience. Perhaps left by prior bathers, on second thought. Hell, they even charged me one hundred rubles for the disposable slippers. What was the banya fee for them?

I'm not in the banya for the spa experience. Here to wash. I dip a white and red-rimmed metal bowl into the lake water barrel and fill it. I use the bowl as a scoop pot and dump water several times over my head, shoulders, and body. Next, I sit on the bench where I lay my towel to keep from burning my legs and beat my back with the eucalyptus branch. The idea is to sweat and cleanse the pores.

Once I feel my back has had a good cleansing, I shampoo my hair and rinse. My body is cleansed and rinsed in the same manner, and I return to the middle chamber. Gulp swigs of water, then cover myself with the towel. I leave the banya house to walk down a wooden path to the lake. I lay my towel on a wooden step. It's time for me to jump into the icy waters of the lake, completely naked, to close my pores prior to dressing. During the winter, banya guests often roll naked in the snow after a banya bath. Today, the icy lake will have to suffice.

This step completed, I towel off and walk up the steps to the banya and dress. I collect my things and return to the cottage to pack my meager belongings. With a smile, I leave my water and the unused sour cream, hoping the next tenant can use it.

Soon the driver arrives. We journey the dirt road away from the village like two old comrades.

"There's a spot before the bridge where you can get a signal from the town below. Sometimes, anyway. You have to climb a hill, but it's not too bad," explains the driver.

I nod in approval. When the driver spies the hill, he stops the car. I jog up the hill with the phone. The driver takes a leak on the other side of the car.

I'm nibbling my lip as the phone rings.

"Hello."

"It's me. I need to meet you," I confide into the phone.

"Where, when?"

"Same place. Same time. Three days."

I hear a familiar low whistle. You bet. "How will I find you?"

"Find a scenic bench. I will find you."

With that, the call ends. I trot back to the car. Within a few hours, I'm at the train station in Nyandoma. I request to buy a one-way ticket to Saint Petersburg.

PART TWO
WHO IS SERGEI RADKOV?

CHAPTER 13
WE KNOW WHO YOU ARE, SERGEI

IT SEEMS you have to go through Egypt to get to the moon these days when traveling in Russia. Instead of direct, I have to journey all the way to Yaroslavl in the Golden Ring of Russia before I can make my way to St. Petersburg. If I had known that, I would've requested my contact meet me in Moscow since St. Petersburg means an extra day of travel. The tourist season is not yet in full swing, but the trains of Russia are teeming with international reporters. More travelers, fewer trains.

A cabinmate enters my first-class cabin on the train. He is cordial but quiet and seems as travel weary as me. I allow him a little private time and walk outside of the room. My ears absorb the sound of the train tracks below, and I view the swiftly moving landscape from the hallway window. When nothing but the sound of breathing is audible in the cabin interior from the hallway where I'm standing, I reenter the cabin with hopes of rest.

Rest may have been possible, except for one thing: no window shades. I try to sleep as the midnight sun streams through the night as the train chugs its way across the Russian expanse. A few hours of the slight grayness called night provides some respite.

Waiting for the grayness to fall, I sit up most of the night and observe the landscape from my window. Most of the passing terrain is rural, sparsely populated, and barren. Near the population centers, the scenery is lovely with quaint villages and the amenities that such a place can offer; away from them, though, it appears the railroad cuts through the most uninviting scenery Russia can offer. Here is no-man's-land. I drink it in, observing my country inch by inch as I never have before.

The train arrives in Yaroslavl in the morning, but my connection to St. Petersburg is not until midnight. Yaroslavl is an ancient Russian city in the Golden Ring. Despite its age dating back to the eleventh century, Yaroslavl is a contemporary modern city on top of its ancient history where two rivers co-join. There is plenty to do here, but I don't have the mindset to indulge. If smells are a measuring stick, it should be easy to find a good meal.

I'm not hungry, per se. I finished cheese and bread on the train the night before and enjoyed washing it down with Crimean wine. Coffee. Yes, that's what I would enjoy. A cup of coffee, strong and black, made into molasses syrup with sugar. I stride around downtown for a little while, then order a cup of Java at a cat cafe. Never owned a pet. My orphan situation didn't permit such luxuries. As an adult, this soldier rarely saw home, so 'twas impossible for me to care for another soul. On occasion, I ran across stray cats while home in Moscow. Of course, I couldn't bear to let an animal remain hungry, so I would search for a home for the feline orphans. Hunger is not something that any of God's creatures should know.

I order myself a nice brew of French press. I sit in a chair and watch the felines have their way with the café and its patrons in the beverage only area. One tabby comes up to me and makes her way into my lap. I humor her as the animal climbs up onto my shoulders and makes a bed around my neck. "Look. I like you, but I can't tilt my head back to drink my coffee. Come here little one," I say to the tabby, who seems determined to use my neck as her new sleeping pad.

I reach up and remove the cat from my neck and place the sweetie in my lap and stroke her. She rewards me with the music of her purrs. It satisfies something inside my soul to think there is another soul in Russia who loves me, albeit a furry soul. Hell, it will satisfy me if someone *anywhere* loves me. At this point, I think I'm the most hated man in Russia. The purring kitty gives me a friend even though the friendship lasts the time span of a cup of coffee. I feel lost and wonder what music I will soon face. It won't be as pleasant as the kitty's purrs.

I finish the last gulp of coffee and give the cat a parting ear pinch, but I'm distracted from my exit when the news comes on across the television. The news program is about the dacha coup but focuses more on *me* than the actual events, or the lives that were lost on that fateful day. Instinct dictates I should run, but I make myself stay.

"Who is this man?" the talking head asks. "Who is this man who was so brave and tried to save lives in a situation that was hopeless and scary, and whose agony is so visible on his face?"

"What the hell?" I ask out loud, without thinking.

I avoided media reports while in Kargopol and Karelia. Well, Karelia didn't have television. Didn't want to see the dead. Didn't want to see the injured. Didn't want to remember. Too painful. Much too painful. I, Commander Sergei Radkov, failed in my duty to them all.

The server overheard my comment and replies, "Yes, that must have been a mess. Russians needed to do something, though. Russia can't continue like this. I'm barely keeping my doors open. The donations to feed the cats have dried up too. All this while the oligarchs eat like fat cats while the rest of us starve. Hooray to the people who stood up. It's time the world stands up to all the fat cats who are feeding off the rest of us like vampires."

I make a noncommittal nod. The news anchor returns to discussing the reel. "Yes, Tanya, he looks quite distraught. We have confirmed the name and background of the soldier who has enthralled Russia. Perhaps, even the world. His name as Commander Sergei Radkov. His comrades say he is respected and a true patriot of Father Russia. Comrade Radkov hasn't been seen since leaving the presidential dacha and isn't available for comment."

Tanya chimes in. "I've spoken to many people who are calling him the White Stallion. Some are saying they would like to see him appointed to replace Smoltsky as president. Many Russians think he has love for his country and our people, and that's what Russians need. Those Russians are hoping he will come forward and put in his nomination before the committee."

"Of course, the position is temporary pending elections, so Russians say they will get a sample of what he can do as interim," Tanya continues. "Here's what some had to say."

The broadcast turns to reels of ordinary citizens commenting on why they think I should be president. *Me?* What? The reporters interview a few of my military academy instructors, and a few active and retired prior commanding officers. Most I've not seen in years. The media even interviews an American soldier who says I was the most professional soldier he had ever known and would be proud to serve under me. That's good to know since I don't recall the man.

Really? I can't believe this report. This dumbfounds me. I feel like I'm on another planet. Why in the world should people want to nominate me as president based on my greatest fuck up? Damn, Russians are acting like Americans.

I've heard and seen enough. Bamboozled, I pick up my confused ass and leave the cafe. Leaving the server a generous but not enormous tip so as not to draw attention. I put 10,000 rubles into the jar to feed the cats. That should provide kibbles for a while. Can't let my new furry friend go hungry. Meandering out the door, I do my best to appear as a tourist without a concern, but my head is spinning.

After leaving the cafe, I walk through the city with my sore and tender feet. Yaroslavl is full of shops, restaurants, and street vendors, including carnival-style shopping tents. I try to process the newscast while going about my business, but my head is in a whirl. Until ten minutes ago, I thought I might be dead in a few days. Still might end up that way.

Shopping through the carnival tents, I quickly bore from the idleness. Hit pay dirt though, finding some much-needed new socks. Other than that, there's nothing to purchase. My only needs are a few explanations and some answers. Of greater concern, what in the hell am I going to do when I find these answers? More importantly, what in the hell is going on among all these moving pieces? I feel the strings of a puppeteer. Someone put on that dacha event. I know it. It was made to look organic, but I know better. Who is holding the strings?

I wander among ancient Russian Orthodox cathedrals and structures. Saunter past the city's infamous green and gold domes, breathing in the sunshine and winds of the crisp, sunlit spring day. My stroll brings me to a tour of the Khram Il'i Proroka with its emerald-green onion domes atop the building's stark-white exterior. I never tire of looking at Russian icons surrounded by heavily gilded gold ornamentation. The creation of such grandeur reaches back centuries in our historical religious homes. Double is my curiosity, since so many, so terribly many of their kind were destroyed during Soviet times. Estimates of remaining religious structures post-communism are one-third. Two-thirds of the history, beauty, beliefs, and culture of my people are gone. Just gone. Destroyed by mustached bastards.

I experience the shared feelings of shame and torment along with my people as I continue my Yaroslavl march. So much of my nation's story eliminated, by what? Ignorance? Intent? Hate? "Fuck," I murmur while shaking my head. No one possesses the right. No one. The result is shame. Unadulterated shame. A damned bitter shame. No matter what you think about it, it's impossible to discuss Russian history without discussing the Russian Orthodox Church.

Cathedrals, monasteries, and churches stripped of their icons, religious art, and tapestries. Bells and other metal objects used in religious services melted down by communists and repurposed. Some buildings were upfitted for government service use, such as the monastery on Solovetsky Island. It became a gulag. A religious building converted to a house of murder. I look into heaven and whisper to the Mother of Mothers, "Dear Mother Mary of Christ, save us from ourselves. Intercede for us."

The bastards. I hold my Solovetsky cross between my fingers and pray in silence. I beg for God's hand on my nation, my people, and our future. The last thing I want to happen in my nation is for us to revert to Soviet times or anything of that ilk. After seventy years of the repressive government, not a single soul remained in Russia who could remember how one prays. No one knew the Lord's Prayer. Not a soul remembered the prayer of Jesus in the vastest nation on the planet. My people, so rich in culture, were deprived of elements that are vital to every member of humanity.

Of course, that which the Russians didn't destroy themselves the Nazis dropped their bombs upon, like a cat toying with a mouse. I reflect as I stop at the World War II memorial, filled with flowers and tokens of respect and loss. My eyes study every person's name chiseled into the obelisk. Once again, my fingers find my necklace cross, and I pray for those lost and their descendants. Those who continued life after their passing. "These were the bravest," I speak aloud. No one is within earshot, and I'm graced with silence for my communion.

Next, I meander to the golden domed Uspenskiy Kafedral'nyy Sobor. The current structure is a resurrection of the old one, the replica being completed in 2010. The German mustached bastard destroyed the ancient one with his bombs. May the flames of hell forever lick his asshole for what he did to my country.

I soak in the opulent art, and it takes my mind off of my troubles at hand. Before I know it, hours have passed as I study the sixteenth-century frescoes and compare one with the other and then begin again. I love anything that makes my country special. Like most of my countrymen and women, I'm vested in the pride of being Russian.

I love art and music. I think it's my connection to Momma. From our small apartment, she gave piano lessons to make a little money when she could. Other times, I would watch her face as she played the instrument alone, lost in her own sound. Even as a young boy, my mother taught me art, and together we took the train to see many exhibits. Momma had a way of making art come alive, just like her music. Even to a young boy. Yes, Momma, I remember.

After climbing the bell tower of the cathedral, I have a bird's-eye view of the city below. Imagine myself to be a bird. Free with the way of the wind and soaring over the city while watching humans and knowing their secrets. Not a single care in the wind. *What in the hell? What in the hell? I'm so confused.*

After the tower, I stop to explore the multicolored glazed tiles on the exterior of the Church of the Epiphany. Such amazing artists, these ancients of my people. A sadness hangs over me, not knowing any of my family. It creates more than a small void in my heart. In my soul. The discovery of such places on this day helps me connect with my personal history and my Russian people. It's special in my heart. What hurts me most is knowing I have no one with which to share all this. *All this.*

Much sadness belies my people, but also ingenuity, craftsmanship, and careful artwork laid down in one generation and catapulted into the future centuries. Behold my people. My Russian people.

Perhaps one day I will find a child to mentor and share our nation's history with. Perhaps an orphan. My heart yearns to share with someone of my ilk, to reveal things so powerfully wonderful about who we are as Russians.

I see a city marker close to the river walk beside the mighty Volga and the smaller Kotorosl River that embraces the city. The marker states: *Yaroslavl — Founded 1010*. Continuing down the river walk, I sit down on a bench just to watch the birds fly. *Why? Why? Why?* Why am I in the midst of this? Is this the will of God, or is there a human puppeteer?

The news coverage enters my silence. What has brought this focus on me? A ruse? One to get me to appear in public? My appearance accomplished; God knows who might administer my fate. Things are not passing the smell test for Commander Sergei Radkov, Russian Spetsnaz. No, they are not.

I push those thoughts out of my mind for now and let them be what they may. I enjoy the sensations of the icy river wind on my face, the blue sky, the birds living their lives around the riverbanks without a notion of trouble. I don my coat to prevent the last bite of the cold season from making a meal out of me. Brrr. Again, I feel the need, an absolute need, to nod my head in silent prayer.

I can't say that I'm a particularly religious man, as I grew up without religion. An experience changed my heart. It began years ago when, as a young soldier, I made a miscalculation in hand-to-hand combat with an enemy and it nearly cost me my life. A knife blade entered my kidney. Lying on the ground in a pool of blood, Alexei, my mentor, administered first aid to stop the blood, then scooped me up and carried me on his shoulders to a medical unit where surgery was performed. Still, the wound nearly ended me and my career. I dug deep and fought hard for all that was mine. Beginning with my young life.

Once stable, I was transported back home to Moscow to recover from the wound. Weak and anemic, I was ordered to bed rest. Like most young men, I became restless during this healing process. Being a fighter, I blew off the doctor's orders and took a few hours' train ride on a pilgrimage to my namesake, Patron Saint Sergius of Sergiev Posad, who built a lavra, or monastary, in the fourteenth century. I recall this former pilgrimage as I sit upon my Yaroslavl bench under icy blue skies.

The venerated lavra, anchors the township in a Golden Ring hamlet. It's at this Russian holy site where I experienced a change of heart. Where else but the holiest site in all of Russia?

Saint Sergius built the lavra structure mostly by himself, but sometimes received the aid of other monks. Sergius became the most venerated saint of Russia. After completion of the monastery, the Virgin Mary appeared to him and another monk. The Holy Mother declared the monastery would be under her protection throughout its existence.

The kind mother of Jesus kept her word. During the seventeenth century, an army made up of thirty thousand Polish–Lithuanian soldiers invaded the monastery. Two thousand locals fought against the overwhelming forces. When a mere two hundred Russians remained, for a reason unknown to history, the Poles just left. Took off. No explanation.

Napoleon took his crack at the sainted town, but due to muddy rainstorms, he could neither find it nor access it. Hitler bombed all around Sergiev Posad but for whatever reason couldn't direct a bomb into the monastery itself. Mustached bastard found Yaroslavl though and—to use commando slang—bombed the shit out of it.

For many Russians, Sergiev Posad is the real beginning of Russia. Others claim the start of Russia to be in Rus, with the first capital of Russia being Kiev. Losing that piece of real estate via Ukraine's succession was to Russians the equivalent of New York State declaring its independence from America and saying, "By the way, we're going to take the Statue of Liberty, and Niagara Falls, too." Even without taking into account considerations such as politics, it's little wonder why the two neighbors and former countrymen don't have any loss of love for one another.

Recovering from the knife wound in my injured kidney, I was left weak as a hungry kitten. Yet, in my determined youth, I was eager to get out of Moscow for a day to regain my strength. Anemic, weak, tired, with pale skin and sunken eyes, I reasoned the quest would be difficult on me, but so was hanging around the Moscow orphan flat all day. There were moments I thought the quest that day would accomplish what the knife did not.

On that day, youthful Sergei, being full of piss and vinegar as youth tends to provide in great quantity, begins my journey inside the Trinity Sergius Lavra, Russia's holiest of holy sites. All I know is that I share the patron saint's name. Someone—some person, somewhere, at my birth—had cared enough to give me that name. That is the scope of my knowledge about my own history, other than the fading memory of my mother's face. God, I still miss her. All the way to my bones, I miss her.

The babushkas cover their heads, setting the standard for all women who enter the lavra. A choir sings to the right side of the entrance, with priests sitting in gilded chairs next to them. I make my way in the long procession line of pilgrims to show veneration to the saint. I learned the choir sings during the whole procession, which is every day, all day. So many volunteered voices conjuring music so often. Amazing!

Many believers kiss the icon enclosed in a glass casing and cross themselves with three fingers. Others kneel. Others lean their heads all the way over to touch the glass with the top of their heads. A unique experience for each pilgrim, but an experience it is. I stare at the icon of my namesake and take in the saint's face as though I'm looking for a family resemblance. Ridiculous, I know.

I stare perhaps too long considering the lengthy line of pilgrims waiting for their iconic moment. Can't help it. It's more than a religious experience for me. It's a Russian experience. Looking into the eye of the iconic saint, I simply utter spasibo—"thank you" or "God save you."

I'm reluctant to leave the sight of the saint's face, but find myself continuing along the procession, viewing a few other relics, then make my way out of the monastery. I purchase a liter container from the gift shop to fill with Holy Water at a well that furnishes water from a stream that passes through a cross in a small chapel next to the kremlin wall around the monastery. Like most ancient Russian communities, Trinity Sergius Lavra has a kremlin, or citadel wall. Parts of the monastery kremlin remain on the side where the fountain is found on the holy grounds of the lavra. The stream of water from the fountain passes through a cross contained inside of a tiny chapel just inside the kremlin walls. For that reason, many consider the water to be blessed and holy.

Weakened from the vigor of that day, I thought my body might collapse. In my twenties then, yet I felt like an old man. Holding onto the side of the well for support, I lean with the plastic bottle underneath the stream of water. For reasons I don't understand until this day, I speak these words as my weak back spasms in pain: "Dear Jesus, make me well. Heal me. Heal me as only you can."

I take a long swig of the Holy Water and am aware of strength returning to my core. A painless bolt of lightning crosses through me. A healing bolt. I take another swig. Then I see it: a ball of light, shining yellow like the sun, silhouetting the face of a woman I recognize as the Virgin Mary. She speaks to me. "You are made well. You have been chosen." Then she disappears as fast as she appeared.

I shake myself beside the well, as if trying to find reality. You don't have to believe this story. Hell, I wouldn't if I were in your shoes. Guess that is why I have never told a single soul about it. What I can say without hesitation is that from that day onward, I've had no problem calling on a higher power. To this day, I don't know what the Holy Mother meant. One thing is sure, I was healed at that moment, on that day at the well of Saint Sergius Lavra in Sergeiv Posad. My experience was real.

After recalling this miracle of my youth, I allow my eyes to look up and see the clear skies of heaven from my Yaroslavl bench. My heavy heart feels the need to pray to a power stronger than this soldier's heart. I nod my head in reverence and pray in this moment with my Solovetsky cross between my fingers, pleading for the intervention of the Trinity on behalf of my country, as well as a good word from the kind Mother. After I finish my riverside Yaroslavl prayer, I stroll back into the city.

Now hungry as a Russian bear, I use my nose to find which restaurant has the most enticing smells that would best please my appetite. I find a restaurant serving steak. Mmm. My creeping hunger gives a thumbs-up. After Karelia, I'm ready to indulge in different fare.

I finish my late afternoon meal and drink a few more glasses of the house vodka while listening to a band playing the blues. Love the blues. I consider the blues imported from the southern USA to be like Russian ballet. Once you discover it, it's time to stop looking because it won't get any better than that.

I leave the restaurant sated but shop in a grocery I espied earlier in the day. Food is needed for the train ride, and a book to help distract me from all the things bouncing around in my head like a beach ball in the wind. Even though I have many questions beginning with the fateful dacha day, the thoughts and images that reoccur most often are of those injured and dead. A person can stand only so much of that. I'm a soldier. I know that nugget too well.

There's a supply of fruits and vegetables at the grocery. Cabbage salad gets old really quick for a worldly man such as myself, despite my humble beginnings.

This sated soldier with brown hair and an ugly wen grabs ham, cheese, and bread. Next choice is figs and a pint of strawberries and blueberries each. Pick up instant coffee, then stroll over to the book section to see if I can find something entertaining. I pick up a newspaper and find a treasure on the book aisle, a collection of Tolstoy's short stories. My sore feet are killing me.

I have, of course, read all of the great Russian author's novels, but little of his short stories. Seeing the book entices me to change my plans and head to the town of Tulia and Tolstoy's Polyana home. But the Spetsnaz commando in me dictates it would be too risky, and I need to stay on task. Polyana is one of my favorite spots in Russia, with its long dirt roads and rolling grassy knolls and as much fresh air as one's lungs can hold. Horses are available at the stables for an excursion on the roads that recount the past life of Count Tolstoy. Unfortunately, many other tourists love the same thing. Too risky. If I can hope for one day, I hope to go to Polyana with a book and read all day on a grassy knoll.

My grocery loot is gathered in a couple of plastic bags, and my treasure doesn't exclude a nice Crimean wine. Love the stuff. I meander to the train station. It'll be a few hours before my train's departure, so I take a seat in the back of the waiting area and cover my face by reading the newspaper.

Viewing the headlines, I almost blurt out an audible "What the hell!" It seems the proud written press has confirmed the commando hero of the coup. The name Commander Sergei Radkov is spread all over the printed page, along with my face. The paper lists everything I've ever done since the first time I filled my diaper.

Thank God Ivan and the others aren't mentioned. Though I would like to know if my dedicated commandos are safe.

Love this part. The report states confirmation of my identity was delayed since none of my loyal compatriots wanted to name me. Well, somebody did.

I have become nervous about my identity. It isn't something an operative wants splattered all over the media as though I'm a heinous criminal on the run. I become nervous about the adequacy of my disguise. Hell, nervous, period. I lift my newspaper higher.

Can't understand why the media is calling me a hero. A hero who failed. Has fallen on his face. And the failure cost? Premium.

And calling me the White Stallion? Are Russians so hungry for a hero? The paper states a member of the dacha mob thought me to be like his favorite stallion. Intelligent. Confident. Strong. In control. Knew his place in the world. Could conquer any world that came to him. Something about a wispy tail. A horse? A tail? They left out sexy. All bullshit.

What do they want from me? Really want from me? The newspaper states citizens want me to come forward so the people can congratulate me for my bravery. Other parts of the article state Russians want me to consider being the leader of the new United Russia. Me? I don't get it. The newsreel in the cat café was confusing. The newspapers are on board, too. I thought the café news reel might be a one-off in sensational reporting. Geez, my face takes up the first half of the front page. So much for a mere fifteen minutes of fame. I pray for less.

Damn. Do they not understand this "brave Russian soldier" has fucked up miserably? Honestly, I couldn't make this shit up in a comedy. A comedy of errors.

I read the rest of the newspaper and start on the Tolstoy book, trying to act as if I'm any guy with brown hair and a wen. And sore feet. Can't wait to kick these shoes off.

Midnight arrives midway through the book. I close it and take a bathroom break before boarding the train, hoping to avoid the toilet on the journey to St. Pete's. The spy in me senses no problems on the perimeter or within. Another cabinmate this time. I'm glad I took time to wash my vitals and change clothes in a public restroom prior to eating in Yaroslavl. Trains contain enough smells without me adding my body odor. I'm sure my cabinmate appreciates my lack of stench.

My cabinmate, Maxim, tells me he is returning home to see his family living near St. Petersburg. Maxim was a career sailor in the Russian Navy. Now retired, the veteran hasn't been home in years. His family shamed him into taking the pilgrimage home. I don't discuss my military background, as every able Russian male has one because of conscription. Instead, I state I'm a Moscow merchant traveling in an effort to recover from the grief of losing my wife. That halts the conversation about me.

I listen amicably to Maxim's stories, although I've heard the same stories in one form or another before. Have those tee shirts or know someone who does. Maxim brought a wonderful bottle of French Rose and shares the fruity liquid in a plastic cup with me. In return, I share my grocery goods and wine with him. Maxim talks a little about the coup but doesn't show signs of recognizing me. I listen but don't respond to that issue.

Unlike the night before, I shade out the sun and drift off to sleep. The train will arrive in St. Petersburg in the early morning hours. I'm ready for what comes next. Even if it's a firing squad.

CHAPTER 14
SERGEI PRAYS

I FEEL LOST. Lost in this familiar city. Lost as a soldier. Lost as a Russian. Lost as a man. Lost in my mind. Lost in my soul. Lost to the bone. Lost. During my lifetime, I never felt absolutely lost. Even as a boy orphan. It's a matter of survival to be in control and smart at all times. I try to be smart. It took one second for an eight-year-old to figure out that showing an iota of weakness wouldn't be an option. The savages would eat me alive.

Guess I thought Momma would come for me one day. Or a miracle father would show up. Until then, I was going to be the best little Sergei ever. Learn my English, best at the academy. There was no one to give me direction, so I had to navigate on my own. Even an eight-year-old boy knows not to get lost in a jungle.

I check into a St. Petersburg hotel. After entering my room, I plunk down my scant luggage. Immediately, something overtakes me. No warning. An overwhelming awareness that the alternative to inaction is to be severely ill. I think the craziness of the past days has caught up with me. Must be. I'm nauseated. My heart is racing like a speeding train. Alone in my room I'm in relative safety but having a panic attack. Urgency flushes through my body. An urgency as strong as a bolt of lightning would be to a golfer holding an iron in the air on tee off. A golfer pissing his pants while watching a lightning bolt pass him by in favor of the flagpole. A flagpole set ablaze, thunder arriving late on the scene.

Yes, urgent. My heart is racing faster. My face in the mirror is red. The tips of my ears are crimson. I've never had this experience. Damned if I know what to do but I know I must calm my racing heart. I fall on my lost knees and do the one thing I can: pray. Lately, I can't seem to pray enough. "Dear God, I haven't talked to you nearly enough. I haven't given you one good reason to hear this prayer. I'm so confused and asking for your help." I shake my head. "Dear Lord, Mother Mary of Jesus once told me two things.

"Mother Mary said I was healed, and it was true. I shall not ask for another healing, although my soul is as empty as that of Judas. The Mother of Mothers also told me I was chosen. I don't understand what she meant. I believe the Holy Mother. Dear Lord God in Heaven, I do so believe her. I don't comprehend what she *meant*. Please help me in my ignorance to find my way. I can do naught but your will, as I truly have none of my own. I have never known my father. Deserted by my mother, or she was taken from me. My country and its people are all I have. I've never been so afraid for them as I've been since recent events. Help me to help my people. I pray of you, my sovereign God. Forgive me of my many sins."

I was about to end my prayer but instead continue to speak to my God. I'm not finished emptying my lost soul. "Dear Lord in heaven, wherever my mother is, please watch after her and hold her in your hands. I don't know my father, but I shall honor him as is right, and ask for your hand upon him. I pray in the name of the most Holy Jesus. Amen."

Calmer now. So much calmer. I cross myself with three fingers and make my way to the shower. After a cold shower I make haste downstairs for a tasty lunch of beef stroganoff, salad, borscht, pickled vegetables with an extra serving of pickled mushrooms, brown bread, and blinis with homemade blueberry jam.

Sauntering my sated body back upstairs, I turn on the television. In my head, I'm thinking I need to face this political situation and figure things out. Why do I feel like the thing I most need to face is me? I've never lacked confidence in exactly who Commander Sergei Radkov is.

In the words of an American philosopher—I think his name is Bob Dylan—"the times they are a-changin'."

I have emptied as much of "me" as I can, so I search for a news station with an update on the political situation. The military supports the new government. That is good.

The forming government is focusing on dissolving the power and fortunes of the oligarchs and distributing their wealth back to the populous. Most oligarchs were captured at their dachas while the coup was taking place. As well, corrupt government officials of the past had their assets seized and the money returned to the treasury. The government plans to place the oligarch properties and those of errant government officials on the market. The news report describes a plan to auction properties that do not sell within two years.

That is a problem. At least I think it to be a wrong move. Who could buy these massive properties? Would that not invite corruption monies from the outside to enter Russia? It's a plan that sounds good on paper but not in practice. Would it not be better to turn the estates into resorts or museums, making them accessible to all Russians for a reasonable price? Alas, even to anyone in the world who wishes to explore Russian history through this particular avenue? The proposed plan isn't a good plan in my mind. I try to look through the lens of a commander as my eyes remain glued to the screen.

As far as who is in power, the Chairman of the Federation Council of Russia, Andre Smoltsky, is sworn in as the new president on a temporary basis, per his request to resume his elected office as chairman as soon as possible. At least until a presidential appointment can be confirmed by council, and then pending post-reform elections. The First Deputy Prime Minister will slide in as Prime Minister. Government power and responsibilities are being redistributed among the executive and legislative branches, and constitutional amendments have been signed into law.

Hmm. Smoltsky. Why does he not want to keep the presidency? I find it odd... Then again, maybe not. I wonder: The country is still in chaos. The economy remains tanked. Pre-coup problems still exist. So, whomsoever takes the presidency now will inherit the pre-coup problems. Rather than be the one to take the heat and danger, why not let some other schmuck take the position? Smoltsky probably expects the next leader to fail. Then he can step back into the presidency and look like the sainted savior of Russia. I wonder…

"And then there is Sergei Radkov, who has not come forward," says the anchorman. The news broadcasts a clip of the people shouting "WHITE STALLION! WHITE STALLION!" at the fated dacha. "Will they choose Comrade Radkov as the new President of Russia, do you think?" asks another of the talking heads.

"Well, he's certainly charismatic, a proven commander and leader, and popular with the people. Russians have really gotten behind this White Stallion. I haven't spoken to a single person who doesn't think he would be an excellent ruler for Russia," replies an unfamiliar mouth.

"First thing Commander Radkov needs to do is resurface." On and on talk the heads about what I *should* do.

Ready to turn the newscast off, I halt my finger on the *off* button because who, but who, should pop up? None other than Vogo, filling my screen. I let out whistle like my old friend, Joe Cook. Vogo talking up a storm. *Now he finds his ability to speak*, I muse. Wish he had talked this much to me before the freaking coup.

"He's my friend. I've known Commander Sergei Radkov since childhood. Russia would be lucky to have him as a leader. Commander Radkov didn't take sides at the dacha but tried his best to do his duty against overwhelming odds. That is the Sergei Radkov that I know. As to why he's not parading himself in front of the cameras, well, that is the Commander I know as well: a modest man. Sergei loves Russia and our people more than any man I've ever known. Sergei is an expert operative. As such, I expect he went underground while he decides what he can best do to serve his country. The people are right to love him."

Well, you got some of that right, Vogo.

I'm speechless. I'm struggling to come to terms with what to think, say, or do. Only a few days ago, I was looking at dead bodies littering the ground. My eyes are on the electronic square, but my mind is all over the place.

Then the blue-eyed iconic Sir of Russia, Andre Smoltsky, is the next guest. The newscaster asks him: would he, as interim president, nominate Sergei Radkov to be president? My back stiffens as I perk up.

The chairman answers yes, he would, his crystal blue eyes peering from his fair face. "Sergei would be one of my top three choices if the house council agrees. Commander Radkov is the one person the house members will respect, and the people will trust. I wish he would come in. I would like to talk to him."

"What next?" I ask the ceiling.

If Smoltsky thinks I'm going to be his little fall guy, he can bend over and get butt-fucked. I, Commander Sergei Radkov, am not going to be his puppet. I will always serve my people and if I have to teach that old fat cat just how to lead a country, I will do it. I won't fail. Not this time. Sell oligarch properties and swell the treasury, indeed.

Smoltsky will quickly learn this Russian is not a crusty politician talking out the side of his mouth. There is a puppeteer out there and one way or another I'm going to flush them out and—

My thoughts stop. It's as though my mind is as clear as a brook with babbling water.

I inhale. Exhale. Then, "Oh my God! OH MY GOD! Oh, oh my dear God in heaven," I cry out in revealed amazement. Crazy revealed amazement as I recall my earlier prayer.

Chosen? No way. I cannot continue this thinking. There is just no way.

Silent. I close my mind and remain silent for a long while. Then I decide. I will serve my country any way Father Russia needs me, no matter what. I will pray every day for the higher power to lead me, no matter what. This isn't a one man show. If this is how I'm chosen, then okay. To honor Mother Mary, who healed me, I will say okay. I acknowledge right up front that if that's so, I'm not in charge. I must do the hardest thing I've ever done in my life: relinquish control.

Without a doubt, I have no idea how to do that. My survival has always depended on me maintaining control. I guess this just means I will have an invisible commanding officer. Yes, that is it. An invisible CO. I will take my orders in private from Him. He outranks me. I get that.

At some point, I flip the channel to the BBC, if not to entertain myself then perhaps to get another slant on the situation embroiling me. Instead of the Russian situation, the BBC is interviewing this beautiful American doctor I have seen in magazines but not live in person. She is fascinating, not to mention sexy as hell. So, I think, and I'm sure every man in the world agrees.

Dr. Selena Frederick is wearing an ankle-length shimmering green dress. With dark hair, her huge green eyes look like emeralds. The slits on the sides of her dress show her perfect figure and long, toned legs as she walks on stage. Her appearance defines conservative and classy. She oozes something. Not sure I can find the right word. Something.

I ogle this beauty and try not to let the saliva drip out of my mouth. She is so *it*. She oozes *it*, whatever "it" is. I listen to every syllable of her words as she answers the interviewer's questions. It's more than her exquisite beauty and intelligence. I'm trying to process this "Selena," this "Dr. Frederick," as a whole person. But damn, she is a lot to process. While I'm trying to figure out this explosive attraction I have to her, there is an explosion bulging behind my zipper.

Something more about her, though. Something. Truly, not a toy for the playboy type.

Dr. Selena Frederick is not a woman trying to make her way in the world with beauty and intelligence alone. Heart? It's not just that Dr. Frederick is so accomplished. She is not all about herself. It's as though the young doctor's beauty and intelligence don't occur to her. She must know. She must. She just doesn't care about it. My groin is growing. If this keeps up, I will need bigger jeans.

And that smile with those ruby red lips. I'm telling you; she has these cherry lips that are as curvy as her body. As I sit in awe of those lips, she opens her mouth and the sweetest, most humble words fall out, covered in her native accent. God, the way she speaks with her words slowly dripping off her tongue like honey. Umm, I long to twist that tongue inside my mouth.

I'm telling you, watching this woman is more exciting than any action-adventure movie. My heart is racing. I swear, if this is love, I will take it.

I never in my entire life considered I would have an overwhelming desire to meet any woman. One thing is for sure: I want to meet this one. Okay, so Dr. Selena Frederick is well out of my league. But damn, what a fantasy.

After the Selena interview, I turn off the square box. What man could think of a damn thing after Selena Frederick? Yet my mind needs to return to Russia.

Wowzer, how much can one brain take in? I feel like my mind is filled with more than my brain cells can process. Okay, maybe there are other cells processing too. Processing Selena Frederick doesn't help me resolve my homeland issues. Reluctantly, I steer my thoughts to review my acquaintance with Andre Smoltsky, which dates back to my days at Suvorov Academy.

As a politician, Smoltsky had taken an interest in the academy and visited on special occasions. In fact, he had been the keynote speaker at my graduation from the academy. I don't know him well, but I have no reason to mistrust him.

This whole crazy cascade may be a ploy, but it would be difficult to pull it off in such a public manner without fallout. Then again, someone pulled off a coup. Perhaps that was the point—but why?

The television says I am popular with Russians. Whatever that means. I have appeared in the news and the press in recent days. Could be merely fifteen minutes of fame. A diversion. Maybe I will disappear altogether with the next news cycle. Perhaps the Russian people are experiencing desperation, the same as I am, and worried about their futures. Desperate people do desperate things. Choosing a leader shouldn't be one of them. I understand I'm a commander. A leader, but not a politician.

The commander in me decides not to be desperate. I plan to meet my contact in the morning. That is my plan. Gather information. Step back. Assess, then act.

CHAPTER 15
ME, SIR?

I STRIDE from the platform onto the ferry headed for Peterhoff and find a seat near the rear. Me and Commander Sergei Radkov have known each other since the Second Chechen Campaign when I was assigned to the region as an international correspondent. He was just a kid in an officer's uniform then, wearing his young face. Hell, I was a kid then too. I'm not sure I even knew what a prostate was then. Could just whip it out and pee.

Damn bloody nine-year mess that war was. The rest of the world didn't seem to care much about a Russian civil war fought against Jihadists. Russians measured their dead not by numbers of the fallen so much as the loss of whole ethnic groups in that war. Vanished. Gone. No one left to procreate the next generation. I can't help but whistle as I recall the blood and brutality. God damned shame.

Russia tried to warn America about what was coming. Hell, *I* tried to warn America about what was coming. My words didn't sink into Washington or the American psyche. Not even the bombing of the World Trade Center in 1993 did it. It took more than 3,000 deaths on September 11, 2001 to convince America that something was coming. God damned shame.

I look up from my ferry seat to find a tall man with brown hair and green eyes, and what appears to be an abscess on his chin, standing before me.

"Is that seat taken?" the man asks.

I give an ear-to-ear grin and say, "No, please help yourself. Misty day it seems, out here on the Bay of Finland."

"Yes, it doesn't look like the weather will be kind to us. Even so, the crowds will come. They always come," replies the wen-faced man matter-of-factly.

"Oh, nothing stops the Chinese," I say. "They'll be here even if we have a tsunami," I add musingly. "Damned old Chinese women have the sharpest elbows known to mankind. No fat on 'em. Better guard your rib cage."

"I've heard," answers the brown-haired man, trying not to laugh his ass off. "Last time I was here, a few of the Chinese tourists actually slid under the rope cords surrounding the throne of Peter the Great and took turns taking pictures of each other sitting on the throne."

"I care for my rib cage the most," comes my grumpy retort.

"I understand. I suppose when you live in a country containing one point four billion people, you require outstretched elbows just to move around. I suppose it's an automatic defense measure," he says.

"Well, they are from the peasant class. Never got to leave home or go anywhere before in their life. Very uneducated lot. But I do understand why they flame up the Russian's ire. To boot, they are quite impolite. Not at all like the Chinese living in my American homeland. Americans of Chinese descent are for the most part model citizens. Here, I just wish they would leave my rib cage out of it," I say as I continue to converse to the stranger.

"I'm not sure if this drizzle is going to disappear today. I think I may go to the Upper Gardens first. Maybe miss some of the morning crowd. Let the old Chinese women have their way with Peter the Great while I'm in the garden," offers the stranger as a solution. "I enjoy the trickster gadgets Peter thought up to insert into his garden plans. Especially the mushroom-shaped structure that rains around the edge when you sit on the seat. It's said that ole Peter liked to take women there to steal a kiss in his bachelor days."

"Not a bad idea," I reply, then look away with another low whistle, keeping my mouth from stretching into an ear-to-ear grin.

We both disembark to enter the Russian Versailles. The stranger strolls to a different side of the central Grand Cascade Fountain from me with all sixty-four of its fountains. I watch from the grotto above the Samson Fountain while the stranger observes at ground level as Samson tears open the jaws of the lion and squirts a twenty-foot vertical jet. I can't get enough of it.

True to Russian tradition, the fountain is not without its symbolism. The lion stands on the Swedish coat of arms—the fountain represents a victory by Peter the Great in the Great Northern War. I never cease to be amazed at these fountains. Especially since they work in concert without a pump and were engineered in the eighteenth century.

The stranger makes his way from the Grand Cascade to the Upper Gardens, which are smaller than the formal Lower Garden but not without their charm. The czar showed a lot of genius for entertainment and fun. I watch from the grotto as the man makes his way to the mushroom structure and finds a nearby bench. I join up with the wen-faced man and sit beside him.

"Nice get-up ya got there, comrade," I tease.

"The best I could come up with on short notice," returns my grinning friend. "I seem to have a conundrum," Sergei continues, getting to the point.

"How so?" I ask. "It seems to me you've got this tiger by the tail."

"But is it real, my friend? I don't know if, when I surface, whether I'm going to be shot or made president. I think getting a medal for the dacha fiasco is worse than getting shot."

I let out a whistle.

"Have you heard anything more on the ground than what is available on the news?" Sergei questions.

"Nope."

We both sit in silence while watching the play of two squirrels in a tree.

"It seems to me," I start slowly, "what you need to do is what you do best, Sergei. That is, rising to the challenge. I think Russians are taken with your sense of duty, your realness, the fact you didn't take sides and remained solution oriented." Then to jibe my friend I say, "That was just damned un-Russian of you! Bold I would say."

Sergei laughs briefly but transitions to a more somber tone. "I was thinking I should contact Smoltsky and at least hear what he has to say. Perhaps I can get a feel for things," Sergei says in a low, conspiratorial voice.

"I think that's a wise choice," I reply. "Whatcha got to lose?"

"Can you set it up?" Sergei asks of me.

"I think so. When? Smoltsky sounds eager to hear from you."

"As soon as possible. How about tomorrow, noon? I will call him to make contact," Sergei confirms. "By the way, I didn't see you at the dacha," Sergei asks more than comments.

"Oh, I was in New York taking care of family business. Wouldn't you know I miss the correspondent event of this century?" I quip.

"It was quite a gala affair," Sergei says in what I know to be a regretful tone.

"Yep, but I got to meet and interview the most beautiful woman in the world."

"The American doctor?" Sergei asks with enormous eyes.

"Yep, that's the one."

"Is she the way she appears on television?" asks Sergei, looking like the young officer in Chechnya.

I consider. "I would say yes. I should know. The first time we crossed paths, I kept interrupting her while she was answering questions from the crowd at a conference. I wanted to see if she was as nice as she seems. I have a hard time accepting that anyone could be that nice."

Sergei looks quizzical.

I pause then continue. "She kept her cool until about the fifth time, then she let me have it. She's smart and kind, and her heart is in the right place. Make no mistake, though, she's tough as nails if you push her," I declare.

"I think if she were here right now, I would get on my hands and knees and beg her to marry me. I just think she is so *it*," says Sergei, still wearing his youthful mask.

"You and every man on the planet, my friend. It turns out we booked the same plane to London before I connected to Moscow. She let me interview her right there on the airplane. It should air tonight."

"My plans are made. I can't believe she let you interview her after the way you harassed her."

"Well, it wasn't quite that easy. The deal was that me and the crew had to hand over our first-class seats to someone in economy class after the interview."

Sergei throws his head back and has a good belly laugh. "She made you move out of her sight on the plane? That is hysterical."

"Yeah. She sat next to a mother with a crying baby the whole trip. Dr. Frederick bounced the babe like it was her own."

"I would take bouncing a baby instead of looking at you, too, Joe."

"I told her I was an old man with a bad prostate, but she was nonplused."

Sergei's face went red with laughter.

"Hell, if I thought the Doc could help my prostate, I would have dropped my jockeys and taken a finger wave right there at thirty thousand feet."

With that, Sergei roars and grabs his aching stomach. Tears begin to dribble down his face as he gasps for air.

Poor me could only nod. "I told you she could be tough." I say with a sigh and a whistle. "Well, if I can get my geriatric carcass off this bench, I'll see if I can arrange your contact with Smoltsky," I express without concern.

"There is a private boat waiting for you at the docks," Sergei informs me as he slides me a phone. "Text me yes, no, or later."

"Got it," I confirm and reply as though teasing, "But do I have time to see that fountain make that vertical leap just once more?"

"Nope," replies Sergei.

"Well then, I must insist on the first interview with Russia's new president," comes my knowing reply.

"I don't know about being president. Let me get through Smoltsky first," Sergei begs.

"I want to interview you soon, my friend, whether you become president or not. You're a hot item and I want to be the first to put you out there," I reply to my good friend.

"Oh, when I get ready to surface, I'll ask you for your services, good friend Joe," Sergei assures me.

"Soon then?"

Sergei looks at me with amusement. "Get your geriatric ass on that boat."

"Aye, aye, skipper," I jibe while saluting. I pick up my crusty behind and head to the docks.

Within an hour, I'm speaking to Andre Smoltsky's private secretary. "No, I don't want an appointment. I just need to speak with him. I have some information for him. Tell him Joe Cook called. Andre knows my number. Tell him as soon as possible."

"I will tell him when he gets back, Joe," assures the male clerk.

———

Within a few hours, I receive a text from Joe that simply says "Yes". I smile. Good. The ball is in motion. Let's see which way it's going to play.

I now have time on my hands, and I'm restless as hell sitting in this hotel room. The thing I'm most excited about is the thought of seeing the beautiful American this very night. Anticipation grows as I imagine not taking my eyes away from her smile. In my twisted mind, I'm on an imaginary date with her. Just looking at her smiling at me while we eat dinner. Yes, that would be good. Just watching her mouth open and close while she eats. Beautiful teeth splitting apart to make beautiful words. I may never get around to lifting my eyes to see her extraordinary emerald eyes.

An American doctor who used her skills in treacherous places. In places, at times, made dangerous by the likes of me. For the second time in a long while, I feel an erection coming on. Can't say why a thought such as that would have that kind of effect on me. Maybe it's recognizing that she is so much more than me. Maybe it's because I'm actually letting myself have a fantasy for once. A fantasy that goes beyond the physical about a woman who is so much more than I could ever be. Not even on my best day.

Selena Frederick won't come on the electronic square for several hours. I don't know if my libido will survive its hyperactivity. Damn, she is so *it*.

I should indulge in another shower but instead opt to adjust my pants before leaving the hotel room. I have to get the hell out of here for a while. Strolling down the Pushkin streets of St. Petersburg, I find a copy of Selena Frederick's book at a corner bookstore. The book will engross me in later hours.

I continue my walk through the streets of the magnificent city of St. Petersburg. The soreness in my feet isn't gone but improving. I throw a bit of a limp into my disguise. I shouldn't be wandering out in the streets like this, but I must get in some exercise, and I must get outside to freaking breathe. Tonight, I will work out a new disguise.

Hmm. Which art offerings should I indulge in? Tsarskoye Selo Museum of Fine Arts. Yes, that is good. I haven't been to this gallery in many years, so much of the art is fresh. I want to shout out to Momma that, yes, I still hold the love of art in my heart, just like her.

I spend a few hours perusing various art pieces and letting the artists' emotions flow into my soul. The thing I appreciate most about Russian art is that it's so emotional. A nation that has known so much blood in its streets, especially since the days of Napoleon, would be remiss not to have a wealth of emotional art. *What am I going to do about this presidential thing? This can't be real.*

I depart the gallery with aching legs and screaming feet. I'm becoming physically weak from my slackness in exercise. Yet I arrange an Uber to Nevsky Prospect instead of walking like a real Russian. I declare myself on holiday from everything today. Maybe I will take a run later or work out in the hotel gym.

I walk around the prospect until I run across a club where I know there'll be blues playing, even at this early hour. First things first, though. I find a restaurant serving Georgian food. Ah, the best in all of Russia is Georgian fare.

Peeking inside the eatery window, I espy an eclectic collection of heavy tapestries depicting Georgian life, from saints to generals in battles to a crazy cat professor with glasses. Handsome Georgian carpets adorn the wooden floors. The tables are pine, showing off their natural multicolored grains. A runner of Georgian tapestry lies longways across the ornate pine table grains. Lovely. This looks like a good place.

I'm seated by a steward wearing the traditional Georgian Khevsur chokhas with its trapezoid shape and heavily ornamented chest and back piece, along with gold ornamental sleeve ends and around the outline of the tail.

A hot bowl of lobio. Yes, that is the way I will start. Instead of salad, I feast on an appetizer of dolma stuffed with meat and cheeses and wrapped in grape leaves. The main course is hard to choose, but I decide on shaslik over the heavy pasta of khinkali since the lobio and dolma will be so filling. No meal is complete without a bottle of Georgian wine. YUM! Forget France. Forget Germany. Forget California. If you want excellent wine, go to Russia or its neighboring regions. I rarely skip dessert at a Georgian restaurant but am too stuffed to even consider the dessert menu. I might need larger jeans, for real.

Instead, I enjoy a cup of coffee upstairs on a veranda that overlooks the prospect. Despite the chilly air, I relax alone at this early hour just to be away from my confining hotel room. I decide not to watch any news until tomorrow. Only Selena, the pretty American doctor, will be tonight's viewing. Then I'll devour her book.

As for the Russian issue, what will be will be. As I sip a second cup of the steaming brew whose vapors tickle my chilly nose, I consider what I may have to say to Smoltsky on the presidential issue. The solution I find in the steaming cup is the only thing my heart knows: Commander Sergei Radkov will serve his country and his people. And that's that. Not political. Maybe this *is* what my country needs. But I need a plan B.

If the Smoltsky call is suspicious, I will go back underground. Maybe leave Russia. Go to a nearby country? Stay in the region but remote. If I leave, I want to wear my own skin. Show my own face but fake my name and profile. I have the money. I can kick back for a while. I will sit, watch, and wait. I miss my friends. Hope Ivan, Alexei, and even the pissant are okay.

After I suck in my last coffee drop, I leave the restaurant and walk down to the club playing my favorite music genre. I start with a glass of kvass, as I'm feeling quite heady from the wine. The band is not bad.

They play good ole Muddy Waters, a little Stevie Ray Vaughan, a little Allman Brothers, and a female vocalist throws in her Bonnie Raitt rendition. Oh America! We just love to hate you for your music!

I leave the club after about an hour and return to the hotel. Not able to put it off any longer, I read through Selena's book. If I was not in love before, I am now. This lady could've done anything with her life. She could have married another doctor, had kids, and lived in a perfect house with a perfect white picket fence. Instead, she served the neediest of the needy. She served. Damn. She is my hero.

At 8:30 p.m. I have the TV turned on to the right channel. The Selena channel. I can give up many things in life, but I won't miss this interview. My longtime friend, Joe Cook, and the most extraordinary Dr. Selena Frederick. To my frustration, Selena's spot doesn't air at the beginning of the program. Seconds seem like hours. "Ah come on! They are airing the most half-cracked stories," I complain to the air.

Then, there she is. Casual in a simple white blouse and jeans. I'm sure this moment is the loveliest I have ever seen her. I smile, remembering the story Joe told me about the terms of their interview. When it is over, I go back to reading her book. My mind relentlessly pops visions of her face, her smile, her body across the pages of her words. In love with an image? Crazy, right? I just don't know what to do about it. This fantasy brings me joy. I think I should continue it. Selena Frederick is as perplexing as my nation at the moment. My heart fills with puppy love, and I haven't a damn clue what to do about it. Maybe this is an exercise in giving up control.

As the evening wanes, I do something I've never done. A midnight sail on the waters of St. Petersburg, which is essentially a city put together by a group of connected islands. At midnight during the late spring and summer season, all the bridges open. I've seen it from the shore, but never from the water. Despite the springtime chill outside, I make my way to the canals in the dusky midnight sun. After obtaining a ticket from a charter, I sail the night away with a champagne glass in hand. Very un-undercover of me.

I have stopped giving a care. Hell, despite my best efforts, I might be dead soon anyway. A lifeless corpse found somewhere, or not found at all. If that is to be my fate, then I'm going to live. Right here, right now, in the borders of the country I love. My heart aches. What my heart wants is to have a woman I love beside me as I sail around the sainted city. I've never had such yearnings. Never. I wish I could turn to the face of the beautiful lady, and ask, "Dr. Selena Frederick, would you like to have a glass of champagne with me? See the lights, beautiful lady, do you see the lights?"

When I return to my hotel room in Pushkin, I take off my shoes while sitting on the side of the bed and fall backward. It has been a full day. Let tomorrow be tomorrow. Until then, come what may.

Kneeling beside the bed in reverence to God, I pray hard to my Lord. I know He is busy with better than me, but I beg: "Allow me to serve my country in the best way possible, please Lord God, lead the way." I pray for the lost souls at the fateful dacha and their families. I pray for my Russian people. I ask—no, *beg*—for God's hand in my life. When I arise from my knees, I sit back on the bed's edge and cross myself with three fingers and massage my Solovetsky cross. For not being a religious man, I'm finding God a comfort. For the first time since the incident, a small sprig of peace is welling up in me.

"Oh, Solovetsky, I missed you this time," I say out loud as my fingers tickle the cross. My original plan had been to go to Solovetsky after Karelia. The monastery on Solovetsky was converted back to being a monastery after its horrific history as a gulag during the communist regime. No gulag was a spa vacation by any means, but Solovetsky, at the Arctic Circle, was notoriously horrid. Hitler had visited there in the 1930s when he and Stalin were still butthole buddies. Solovetsky is where Hitler got his ideas for the concentration camps that murdered so many.

I always go to Gora Sekirnaya, a hill meant for special punishment of gulag prisoners, when I'm at the archipelago on the White Sea. More than a million prisoners lost their lives in the gulag at the murderous hands of the communist regime. With so many who needed killing, who had time to keep good records? Maybe it was two million. There were a few foreign inmates, but mostly it was Russians killing Russians within the gulag confines. If ever you want to yell "REVOLUTION!" then by all means, don't do so before visiting that place. I know that if by some miracle I become president, the avoidance of bloodshed will be my top priority.

Whereas confinement in a typical gulag involved a slow and a brutal death, the isolation camp at Sekirnaya was particularly inhuman. For some minor infraction, the guards would march weak and malnourished gulag prisoners up the steep hill to Sekirnaya. They would leave the prisoners there to starve or freeze to death. After which point in the winter, the guards would unceremoniously push the stiff bodies down the steps to await a mass grave burial in the spring. If the guards were really in a nasty mood or just wanted to have a little extra fun, they would strip the prisoner naked and tie them to a tree to die from the elements.

In the summer, the overseers enjoyed even better cruelty delights. They would tie the naked prisoner to a tree and let the bugs from the neighboring swamps literally eat the prisoner alive. It was best if the souls of the victims died overnight, but sometimes they would linger for days. It was not just men but women too. As well, they were not beyond killing pregnant women. What were these people's crimes? Being teachers, engineers, artists, poets, or God forbid prior military officers.

Oh, and for God's sake, don't be a prisoner of war returned from Germany to Russia. Stalin considered it the responsibility of each Russian to die for their country. To be captured by the enemy was a cowardly disgrace. I could never reconcile why the bastard didn't simply let the Germans shoot the prisoners. They would have been better off.

I would go to the island monument at Sekirnaya to pray for the victims and light four candles when at Solovetsky. One candle for Solovetsky gulag victims, one for the Sekirnaya victims, another for all the victims of all the gulags throughout Russia, and another for the spin-off of Hitler's Solovetsky in the form of concentration camps. While there are many who pray for the German brand of victims, I think it's only right that they, too, receive Russian prayers. Thanks to America claiming victory in WWII, most of the world is familiar with Hitler's concentration camps. Only a handful have ever heard of Solovetsky, or the horrors of the Russian gulags of which Solovetsky was just one of 30,000. To worsen the issue, the Americans record history incorrectly. It was Russia who defeated Hitler and ended the war in Europe. Not the Americans. Even though it is certainly a valid argument that the Russians got lucky.

I'll be damned if I'm going to let this happen to my Russian kinsmen again. I'll be damned!

Solovetsky is a place of reverence to me for another reason: one can charter a boat from Solovetsky to Zayatsky Island. Zayatsky, where the White Sea crashes along the shores of the remote Arctic tundra isle. Newly thawed, the White Sea is so blue and pure. The sea is not azure, like in tropical climates. There is a cleanness about it, with fresh air lifting the White Sea gulls, black wings decorating their white bodies.

About six people stay on that island year-round, most being scientists who rotate on and off the island, or perhaps a monk. Scientists who wish to study the stone-monument labyrinths built as far back as 2 BC that cover the three-hundred-meter island. Then others who wish to study this environmental microcosm and relate it to the broader world environment in hopes of gleaning new insights. These are hardy disciples of science and soulful worship since the White Sea freezes from fall to spring. Frozen and wet, there is no way off the island.

Labyrinths with their crude stone monuments were constructed there three to five thousand years ago. The only thing that is known is that the isle is not a burial place for ancient man. There are no bodies buried there. The latest scientific theory is nomadic people placed the labyrinths while stopping at this location during their cyclical travels. They built these monuments and labyrinths to honor those who had died along the way in what was probably an annual journey.

I like this idea. From the earliest of times, people loved and honored one another. They were connected. They were family. They were clan. As an orphan, the idea of clan is romantic to me. I think I feel love converted to a religious experience by the history of Zayatsky. The isle touches my spirit like no other place.

Sitting on a bed in this warm hotel room in what many people consider the most beautiful city in the world, I muse. Frozen White Sea? No, I won't complain of the sharp glacial wind that cut my nose today, nor the chilly mist that wet my bones. Blanketing myself with thoughts of the White Sea protects me from my current life concerns, replete with the charm of the freshest air one can breathe. Somewhere between the sound of a birdcall and my remembrance of the island journey, I pull my covers to my chin and fall asleep.

The next day I arise and, while dressing, turn on the TV to examine what is happening in the world. First, I click on a British channel which is showing the beautiful lady again. I watch her walk across the stage with her sexy legs and sit her rounded rump into a chair. That rounded rump and me standing in my jockey shorts with shaving foam on my lower face, a razor suspended about six inches from my lathered chin. I decide lowering the razor is a good idea. I wish I could rub my hands over that round rump and kiss those ruby red lips. Once I remember to breathe and get oxygen to my brain, I'm reminded every man in the world watching this program is wishing the same thing. Fuckers.

Selena attaches a microphone to her shirt as though she has been doing this since childhood. Speaking with a friendly mouth, saying hello to the interviewer in her native Southern American tongue. Damn.

Emerald eyes glow with light. A "within" light. A light that radiates from her spirit and mesmerizes both man and woman. Lips as red as the rubies of India speak with concerns of others. Concerns about pregnant women in war-torn countries or those whose lands have been hit with natural disasters. She speaks of commonsense things that wealthier nations take for granted, such as the value of clean water in less fortunate places.

I hold my position in front of the TV, taking in every morsel of Selena Frederick as her time slot allows. After the program ends, I return to the bathroom with a "wanting more" sigh and shave. I need to breathe in and out a few times first though. After all, there is still that razor in my hand. The brain cells that process Dr. Selena Frederick have overheated and used up all my oxygen. Were those brain cells? At any rate, I find myself shaky thinking about the beautiful lady whom I accept is way out of my league.

She has moved me all the same. Moved through me. Moved me in a way I've not been moved in a very long time. Well, forever, actually.

It has been a while since I sexed a woman. I became tired of the game. Tired of never lying but never telling the whole truth. Never able to be Sergei Radkov, instead forced to allow another man to fill my skin. Allowing my persona and looks to connect long enough to sex a willing woman then move on.

It's time for me to mosey downstairs for a Russian breakfast. I eat as though I don't have a concern on God's green earth. The news cycle is unchanged in my room after my meal's completion. I hope to see a rerun of the lovely Selena, but the media doesn't cooperate. Exercise would be nice, but I don't want to tire myself. Taking along my book, I rent a car and drive out of St. Petersburg toward Peterhoff. There is an out-of-the-way grassy spot only reachable by human ambulation in a small local park. I text Joe to confirm the number, then wait until my cell phone shows 12 p.m. I dial the number from the text.

Smoltsky answers. "Sergei, how are you?"

"I am well, Mr. Chairman. Or should I say Mr. President?"

"Oh, call me Andre," the president says with cordiality. "You have stirred quite a sensation among our people."

"So, I've heard."

"Have you heard I want to put you up for nomination as president of this glorious land?" Andre's voice trails off to become serious. "Sergei, I can't think of a better person to lead Russia. That is the God's truth. I want you to lead this country, Sergei. You won't let it become what it was a century ago. You're not a political man, but I've watched you play politics when you needed. Your eyes are sharp. Not having a worn and hardened politician like me will be the best thing for the Russian people. The people will get behind you, Sergei. They will."

"Sir," I begin, forgetting the new handle of "Andre." "All I can say is that I will serve my country and its people. I'm not a politician and I don't wish to be one. But I will serve Father Russia in any capacity I can."

"Won't you come in, Sergei? We have a lot to discuss."

"I will see you soon, Andre. I can't say when, but soon."

"I know you, Sergei. I know I can put you up for nomination. Then the committee members of each house will interview you. Are you up to that? I can help you prepare for it."

"It's your choice whether you put me up as a nominee. I'm agreeable to the hearings. As far as prepping, with all respect, Sir, I want to do it on my own. Not that I don't think the most valuable advice I can get is from you. It's just that if I can't hold my own against six hundred or so Russian representatives, then how am I going to handle the Americans, Chinese, British, and Finns?"

Andre roars with laughter. "Sergei, that is why I chose you. You've always been able to couple your intelligence with your charm. I've always known that about you, and I've admired you more than I can say for many years past."

"Thank you, Sir." I can't get into "Andre" mode.

"How can I reach you?"

"I will let you know. I'm coming in."

"Excellent!" exclaims the chairman.

I text Joe. "It's time. I'm ready. Call me on my usual cell to arrange the interview." I get up from my grassy spot and laugh at my damp bottom. I throw the burner phone into the garbage.

I sense I'm being used as a pawn. I'm not sure to what end, nor by whom, but I sure as hell am going to find out.

CHAPTER 16
SERGEI'S WAY

I RETURN my auto rental and walk to the hotel. I reassemble my personal cell phone. Already there is a message from Joe, and I return his call.

"So how did it go, my friend?" Joe asks right off the bat.

"Says he will nominate me for president."

I hear a whistle in my ears. "Come a long way, my friend. One hell of a journey."

"Well, I'm nowhere yet, but I *have* been on one hell of a journey," I tease with my friend. "Time for you to interview me," I say in a more serious tone.

"When?"

"Now."

"Before the nomination?" Joe whistles.

"The Russian people should see me before anyone else. Before the nomination process, I think the people need to get a look at what they're asking for."

"You were never one to move slow, Sergei. There's a conference room at my hotel," continues Joe without a whistle and moving fast as the train I know him to be. "Can you do it this afternoon or tonight?"

"I think so," I reply. "It's just, Joe, I need time to buy a suit."

"Don't *buy a suit*, Sergei. The people love you as you are. The last thing you want to do is look like the status quo. Be yourself and go buy a nice pair of slacks and a shirt."

I think for a moment. "Joe, that is able advice, but at some point, if I am to be president, the people need to have confidence that I can carry out the role. I'm going for the suit."

Joe whistles. "Sergei, why in the hell am I trying to advise you on anything? You're ten times smarter than me. Do the suit."

I laugh. "What time?"

"About seven-ish."

"That is fine. I just need a suit and a shower. And I need to change my hair color."

"I'll work on the arrangements." There is no whistle.

"Okay. I'm checking out of my hotel room. I'm going to Moscow tonight on the late train."

"Got a problem with driving?" questions Joe.

"I turned in my rental. I wasn't sure how long this would take."

"I got wheels. When we wrap, I'll check out of the hotel and Hugo can drive us. I'll work the piece and Hugo or you can drive. I'm gonna film the drive. You know that, right, Sergei?"

"I do now. Sounds a bit overboard but is okay with me."

"Well, it's history, man, and I'm recording and documenting it."

"Good old Joe," I muse before hanging up.

I pack and check out of my hotel. Carrying my one bag, I make my way to a fashionable men's shop I know in St. Petersburg. The Iranian tailor recommends a fashionable gray suit made with a new sleek fiber. The texture is comfortable and wears well.

"Do you like?" asks the tailor.

I prissy a bit in front of the mirror, running my hand down the slick textured fiber. Left turn. Right turn. A peek at my butt and the fit across my shoulders. "Hell yes," I reply.

The tailor makes a few adjustments on the spot lest he lose the sale, as his client is in a hurry. Meanwhile, I search for just the right shirt. I fall in love with a plum-colored one by an American designer. Nixing a creamy white for the colorful plum, I pick up a tie with the colors and design of the Russia flag in abstract that also incorporates hints of gray and purple into the fantastic color scheme.

By the time I choose black dress shoes, the tailor is finished. I express my appreciation to him, and though tipping a tailor is not customary, I leave him enough rubbles for a nice meal. "Get yourself a nice dinner as my appreciation for your prompt service."

I leave the shop and pick up hair dye on my way to Joe's hotel. Joe answers the hotel room door and gives me a hug as I enter. "You hungry?" he asks.

"I'm getting there."

"Good. I'm past there. How about room service while you shower? We'll eat, then I'll change. I'm wearing a suit too," Joe says with a smile.

"Good taste," I grin.

"Whatcha wanna eat?"

"Anything. A burger is fine." I shrug as I head to the shower. I emerge afterward with blond hair and blue eyes, wearing underwear and a tee shirt, and missing the wen on my face.

"Didn't want to mess up my clothes," I say apologetically.

"My God, Sergei. I've been in the military and interviewed in locker rooms of professional athletes. I've seen men in their underwear before."

I chuckle at the same time room service knocks on the door. I dart into the bathroom to let the man empty his cart. He doesn't need to see my underwear.

"I got us a bottle of wine. It's not a good idea before we tape, but what the hell? It's just one bottle. We can each sip a glass after the wrap."

I agree. The cheeseburger and fries seem the best I've ever eaten.

My friend and I complete our meal with our usual friendly banter and complete our preparation plans for the taping. It's six thirty. We leave the hotel room and make our way downstairs to the conference room.

I study the questions and continue to pour over them as we await the cameraman.

"You sit here, Sergei." Joe instructs. Take the head of the conference table."

I sit where instructed and look around the conference room. The room is, well, sterile. White walls with a few pictures. The room could pass for a hospital room. The buoyant, flamboyant side of my whacky personality can't feel what it needs to feel here. Yes, the moment is serious, but not somber. In my opinion, this room should contain corpses.

The camera man comes in with his paraphernalia, helped by a hotel employee.

"Hugo Cooper," the man says as he shakes my hand.

"Pleased to meet you," I respond.

"Are you guys ready?" asks Hugo as he fiddles with his equipment.

"Yes," replies Joe.

"No," I say.

Joe looks at me with alarm.

"It just doesn't feel right," I express. "I would prefer to do the interview in the chairs in your suite."

Joe whistles.

Hugo glances up from his equipment irritably and remarks, "You guys need to make your minds up."

"Hey dude, this is going to be the next president of Russia. If he says stand on your head and count to a million, then you stand on your head and count to a *billion*. You got that?" Joe is red-faced. "If the man says it's not right, then it's not right. And you know what? It isn't fucking right!"

Everyone spends a moment inhaling a breath. "I'll be right back," Joe informs us, waving an index finger.

Gratefully, Joe returns within the half hour. I'm tiring of asking Hugo how he likes St. Petersburg and making small talk. The same hotel employee joins Joe, pushing an empty cart.

"Come on, guys. I've got it worked out," explains Joe. The men load the equipment and head for the elevator. The elevator takes us to the top and the hotel employee inserts a card into the penthouse.

Joe pulls the blinds to block out the midnight sun, then thinks better of it, so that the city of St. Petersburg can be seen in the background through the camera lens. Joe and I seat ourselves in two burgundy leather chairs, which are set in front of the expansive penthouse window. Hugo adjusts for the lighting.

"This is more like it," Joe says as we straighten our ties in front of the mirror. Both of us burst out laughing. "We're like two schoolgirls getting ready for a high school prom," Joe says through laughing teeth that spit out a shower of saliva.

I laugh and reply, "Joe, you can take me to the prom, but I'm not dancing with you."

With that retort, even Hugo bends over, rolling in laughter.

"Okay, we'll get serious," Joe says, calming down after our little ado.

Hugo checks his cameras as we take our seat. "Sergei, you're a bit taller than Joe. Can you maybe slump a little to even up the height? Maybe scoot your arse a little closer to the end of the chair? Maybe we could prop up your feet?"

"No," remarks Joe. "He is a tall and strong leader. I would rather set him up even higher on books than do that."

"Okay," Hugo replies. "But Joe, you're going to look like a weenie."

"Then a weenie I am."

I sit up straight with my shoulders back as the camera rolls. Joe gives his introduction spiel. Of course, he asks me the softball questions first.

"Are you surprised by President Andre Smoltsky's statement that he is going to put you up for nomination as the new president of Russia?" begins Joe.

"I'm very surprised."

"Have you talked with him about it?"

"Briefly," I reply presidentially and honestly. "Only to discuss the nomination process if he does indeed put my name before the houses."

"Do you think he will?"

"This is a decision only he can make. I'm certain he will discuss it with many of his colleagues. At the end of the day, it's his decision, and it's an important one. In many ways, the onus of Russia's future is on him. I believe he will consider many candidates, both men and women, and act according to his counsel and his conscience. Russians need to give our current leader as much time and space as they can for him to make the best decision on their behalf. "

"Will you be disappointed if he doesn't nominate you?"

I answer thoughtfully and with intense sincerity. "I haven't had time for the idea of being president to sink in long enough to concern myself with any disappointments. I only wish to serve my Father Russia and the Russian people in any capacity I can. If I can't serve Russia and its people in any capacity, then that would be my greatest disappointment."

The interview moves to the fated dacha. I respond to each question with truth and emotional reserve. Soon I tire of it but continue with a professional demeanor. It's something I must face head-on.

"I can't tell you much more than what the people have seen with their own eyes on television," is my response. It's probably not advisable, but I want to be honest with my people. "Make no mistake: what's not being said is that I failed the men who were shot, and possibly the furnace victims as well. The president and company were under my protection. Russians are always under my protection. It was my failure to detect the coup that led to a domino effect at the dacha. If the situation had gone differently, it's possible the furnace whose motor needed repair, wouldn't have been overstuffed with box loads of documents and blown at that moment."

"You couldn't have known," Joe says, trying to give me a break.

"But I *should* have. I see it as the greatest failure of my career, and I see the faces of the dead every night that I sleep."

"Sergei," Joe cajoles. "Didn't most of your own team join the rebellion?"

"They did. That is what makes it so hard for me personally, and I think makes the event so difficult to understand. It doesn't absolve me. I am a man of duty, and I failed at my duty. I'll not lie about that. It's up to the Russian people whether they can forgive me for it."

"Why do you think members of your team joined the rebels?"

"Make no mistake: they didn't organically join the rebels. It was pre-planned. There's a mistaken belief that the event was organic. Perhaps somewhat, but not totally. Even a medical station had been set up in advance to handle the injured. This tells me a fight was expected and it wasn't a sudden uprising. It was pre-planned, and the Russian people have the right to know that. I might be many things, but a liar to my people I am not."

Joe presses on but moves away from the topic of the rebellion itself. "What did the late president say to you when you entered the dacha for the last time?"

"That is a conversation that I hold in confidence with my prior commander. I don't divulge the contents of private conversations with my superiors, even when they are no longer alive."

"Might you do it for the history books at some point?" asks Joe, continuing his full-court press.

"I can't say yes or no. Perhaps in the future and for that reason, but this moment is not the right time. Each person who died that day has family, friends, and a community to consider. Their pain is fresh, and I'm not willing to risk putting salt in their wounds. Russians don't hurt Russians, and that much is final."

I continue. "Make no mistake, Joe. To discuss conversations with my superiors is not something I'm likely to ever divulge. I would have to see a higher—more noble if you will—reason that would make the situation better if I do. Otherwise, that information will die with me."

"But, Commander Radkov, twelve Russian leaders lost their lives that day at the hands of other Russians. Do you not think Russians and the world have the right to know what was discussed in that control room?"

"Those things are true, but honestly, does it matter? Would knowing change the outcome? I am of the belief it would not," I reply. "I think the crowd was emotional, and it was a tense moment. When they heard the furnace blow, they thought it was gunshot and those with guns started shooting. The day was deranged, and deranged things happened."

Changing my tone, "In Ecclesiastes, the writer says there is a time for all things under the sun. Now is the time to heal. The time for Russia to enter a healing stage has come. It's my hope being truthful will help that process. As well, Russians need to move forward to a future of prosperity. It's what all Russians want at the end of the day."

Joe moves on to the kinds of decisions I would make as president. "Do you think the embargoes against Russia can be lifted?"

"I do. First thing that must happen is to allow the Crimeans and Ukrainians to speak. I think there should be one more election in

Crimea when the government in central Russia is reformed. It's their lives. They have the right. I've always been told by the Crimean people that they want to be Russian, not Ukrainian. Maybe that is propaganda, but I've heard it said to me by the Crimeans. So, for them to be able to vote without being pressured by any form of fraud or threat will make the Crimean voice clear. I think that is the important thing. To allow Crimeans to speak with a clear voice. This will remove one arm of the embargo.

"Ukrainians have oft said their withdrawal from Soviet Russia in 1991 wasn't so much about sovereignty as being fed. That was before the invasion. Crimeans say they feel safer with Russia in charge, but Ukrainians don't hold that position. We have much to mend with the Ukrainian population. No matter what, Ukrainians are our literal brothers and sisters, our Russian brethren. They fought like hell for Russia during the Nazi invasion. Much is owed to this population. We must begin with respect and peace. No matter what else happens, they are our neighbors."

I shrug. "You must remember, the initial Ukrainian government was set up by the likes of Michael Flynn and Paul Manafort with a puppet president who later lost his position because of corruption. This made the people of Crimea prefer the safety of their Russian heritage rather than be ruled by others at that point. I think because of the recent events, both groups have the right to see how Russia evolves with its changes. If Crimea stays, then they are Russian. Come what may, from that day forward they are Russian. If they decide to go, whether as Ukrainians or as an independent Crimea, then they will be our neighbors and deserving of peace and respect."

I come up for air after this lengthy description of my position on this complex issue then continue. "I think the Ukrainians have spoken. I respect the will of the Ukrainian people. Personally, I hope both groups stay Russian. I would request two things from them both: peace and patience. Patience is something that few in the region have left, beginning with me. But we must have the patience to build toward a lasting peace in the region. I would humbly request both groups to examine the new Russian trend, then decide. Until then, peace, forgiveness, understanding from all nations will move prosperity forward as we dissolve our differences. May the people's will be done. It's the only way to deal with our Ukrainian neighbors, as well as all nations that touch our borders. We have much in common with our neighbors and share an ancient history that binds us more than another government thousands of miles across the ocean. Yea, even in Moscow and Kyiv. I will draw on that bond to promote peace and prosperity for the region. We must re-cement this broken bond, especially with our Ukrainian neighbors. I think we can begin with respect and follow with trust." I end, then start again because this issue is extraordinarily complex.

"As well, I would make it clear to other nations that they must show respect to all in this region and stay out of our affairs. Allow us to resolve our own conflicts in our relationships. If there is peace in the region, then their influence is not needed and, by necessity, must be offered peacefully or not at all. And, with the sole focus of prosperity in this region."

The Russian commander in me hopes the asshole of POTUS puckers. I'm talking to him. "I have nothing against the West per se, but I'll vehemently request the West step back and let us resolve our own regional issues to develop a lasting peace. It's time."

Joe continues with hard-hitting questions over the next hour, for which I give "Commander-Sergei-Radkov-type" commonsense replies.

Joe begins to wrap up. "Do you understand that you are a man, a leader who could change the world?"

I think and answer with sincerity. "Joe, I haven't thought in those terms. But I can say without conceit that, if given a chance, I hope I can change the world we live in for the better. But making things better doesn't just happen. You must study situations, then make decisions and plans. Sometimes even make concessions for us to live in a better world. The first thing we must accept is that the status quo is unacceptable."

"What are you going to do now, Commander Radkov, while waiting to see if you will be nominated for the presidency?"

"I'm going home."

CHAPTER 17
GOING HOME

AFTER THE INTERVIEW, we load up and put everything into Joe's Mercedes rental. Hugo calls a filming buddy in St. Petersburg, Mikhail, to aid with the filming and the nine hours of driving. Off flew we four fellows holding wine glasses amid the midnight sun to Moscow. I consider it silly the way the newsmen are recording my every breath.

"It's history, man. Ya gotta give us that." Joe says to confirm his position.

"Maybe yes, maybe no," I remind him.

"Either yes or no, it's history, my friend, and I want it on film."

I let myself smile at the notion. Coming to terms with my destiny, I take advantage of the time on the ride to allow Joe to throw out questions for which I respond and note the subject categories on a pad. I make suggestions to Joe for a category to formulate a question, and Joe obliges and develops a question, spurting it out in his most dignified voice. Joe multitasks while bantering with me and reviews the earlier interview. Mikhail or Hugo, depending on who was driving, has the camcorder rolling from the front seat. I consider it a warmup to the possible house hearings. Who knows? Perhaps this will be my life. Rolling down the road with cameras in my face.

Our group arrives in Moscow in the early morning hours. I request the driver drop me off at the metro station in Moscow. I make my adieus to my co-journeymen with handshakes of kinship. Actually, I'm fewer than five hundred meters from my flat. After the car pulls away from the parking area, I sneak out of the station on the opposite side and circle back. I don't go to my "orphan flat." Instead, I enter a studio which I rent across the narrow street from my official home so that I can keep an eye out on my orphan flat when I feel queasy about my security. I get this feeling often. It's a precaution I enforce at home and abroad while on assignment. Indeed, I'm a very cautious man. It has kept me alive.

After reviewing the surveillance equipment in my studio, I nap for a few hours, but am roused by a call from Smoltsky.

"Are you in Moscow, Sergei?"

"I am."

"I saw your interview with that international correspondent. Smart move."

"Yes, as you know, he is freelance. Joe agreed to have it shown in the Russian media first."

"I'm grateful for that. Good politics, you know. Then, the rest of the world will see what to Russians is old news. Let Russia lead."

"Agree. Joe spent most of the night working on it. He pushed to get it aired today. Guess it has already run."

"Joe Cook, as they say in America, doesn't let grass grow under his feet. The man has a huge professional network. With a phone call, the networks carry his interviews," chimes in Smoltsky.

I'm smiling at the other end of the phone. "I've known him for a long time."

"Sergei, because of the crisis, both houses want to interview you right away. Can you be ready by tomorrow?"

"I'm ready today."

Smoltsky chuckles. "You'll need to interview with committees in each house. I'll try to arrange one of them for tomorrow."

"That is fine. Though, if I may speak freely, President Smoltsky, I was wondering if there is a place large enough for both houses?" I know there is. For fuck's sake, it's Moscow with over thirteen million people.

"Why do you ask, Sergei? What are you thinking?"

"Well, not just for me, but for any candidate for nomination. Thinking it might be helpful for all the representatives to be present at the interview. Out in the open. Invite the media. Let the committee members from both houses ask the questions taking turns, but have all members present since they will be the ones casting their vote."

Smoltsky should think along these lines, but I tap dance. "By presenting the process in this forum, it allows the members to appear as important guest, which they are. With good fortune, I may chance a meet with a few of them. As well, it'll give the Russian people a chance to judge for themselves."

"Sergei, you are going to make one hell of a politician in spite of yourself," wheezes the chairman with delight. "The committee members are ready and anxious. Both committee houses are encouraged because you understand the need for rebalancing our government and the need for elections as soon as possible. Are you sure you're ready?"

"Yes, Sir, I'm ready."

"Very Well," I will text you the information.

"Thank you, Sir."

"Mr. President to be, you must learn to call me Andre at all times."

"Yes, Andre. Old habits are hard to break. From now on, you will always be Andre. No more Sirs."

"Very good. And wear that suit again. That was sharp."

"Thank you, Andre. I will be sharp!"

We hang up and I review the security footage, not seeing anything amok. Let me wait now after this call. If there is danger, it will happen soon. I don't necessarily distrust Smoltsky, but there is something in my gut that says to be wary.

No fresh food in the studio, since I haven't been here in a while. And damn it, I'm not wearing that same suit. Still in operative mode, I let the three-hundred-and-sixty-degree computer screens do their work while I prepare a simple pot of rice. Wash the snack down with plain water and the plain rice fills my stomach.

Before showering, I check the TV for any interviews with the sexy American. No such luck. I think she's in France by now, but my days have been so screwy. I can't recall my own itinerary over the past few days.

After showering, I look through my closet for a disguise. "Oh yes, I have missed you," I say out loud with a grin. Pulling out a navy-blue pant suit with a long coat, I survey the look. A long, dark-haired wig to honor Selena is my choice this time. I sit on the edge of the bed and speak her name a few times. Just want to hear her name. A girdle with extra butt is needed, but the bulge in front is not. Time to put Selena Frederick out of my mind.

After a close face wax, I put on heavy make-up and brown contact lenses. A silk scarf around my neck covers my Adam's Apple. Lipstick designs perfectly pouty lips. I don a pair of blue leather flats and the amazon female leaves the studio.

Soon afterwards, I receive a text from Smoltsky with the details of the hearing: *Interview tomorrow at 0900. Tsvelkova Arena. Call me direct for questions.* Only Smoltsky could have made such elaborate arrangements this fast. I send a text to Joe Cook.

The lady arrives at the lower Arabat District by foot. Then she makes a short voyage via the metro. A train arrives in less than two minutes. Metro train promptness is a source of pride to the Russian populous. The blue flats are killing me. Hell, the blisters on my feet haven't healed. But my ass gets a few looks.

Despite all the fine artwork on the walls and ceilings hanging above the marble floors, I hate the metro. The eyes of Russians never meet. Russian eyes always look downward with dour expressions when on the metro. Not that the eyes look away. They don't look at all. So Soviet. So damned Soviet.

The hearts and minds of my people are stuck in a past, and the fear will take many generations to overcome. Somehow, the metro is a holy place of worship with all heads bowed, paying reverence to a living past of death. Death of the Russian soul arriving at another Russian destination in the chariots of their destruction, the people's metro. Much blood was shed for the construction of such chariots. I'm damned tired of the notion that Russians must die in order for the masses to progress. Damned tired.

The lady gets off the metro exit at the top of Arabat Street. Arabat, my favorite street in all the world. Once the home of the KGB, it's now a walking street for arts and shops, restaurants, and music. Street music plays those sweet blues on guitars, mandolins, violins, you name it. An international street where my favorite sign outside of an establishment is "only rubles accepted here." Oh Arabat, you have remained so very Russian after all.

I sit for a while and listen to a band that has huddled in the middle of the street. Bass guitars, drummers, fiddlers, a front man singing the blues. I'm in heaven. My butt itches to dance, wishing I had Selena Frederick in my arms to twirl around in the street. Hell, my butt itches, period.

Of course, I would have to lose the extra ass currently hanging onto my butt to dance with the pretty lady of my dreams. Ten thousand rubles is a good-sized tip, but the lady leaves the big note as she walks past the money hat on a journey to food forage. The rice has filled me but not satisfied me. Not by a long shot. Despite my current looks, I'm a Russian man, and I damned well eat like a Russian man.

Alas, I arrive at The Hard Rock Cafe. Well, my last actual meal was a burger. I guess two in a row won't kill me. I'll eat here to honor Selena's American heritage. A beautiful name for a beautiful lady.

The server makes his second ahem as the lady looks up from Selena thoughts to order a burger and beer. It's a perfect spring day in Moscow. Taking an outdoor cafe table on the street, I listen to the sounds of the musicians who fill the air with their ear food. Oh yes, this is Arabat. The smell of other eateries fills bi-gender nostrils, but nothing so strong as The Hard Rock at the moment.

A beer arrives. I indulge in people watching and speak in a feminine French voice to the surrounding guests with their children from England. Then to an elderly Swede couple, and a few women from Crimea. The people watching fare in the street contains people from all walks of life. Of all ages, including groups of teens. Crowds of elders. A group of twenty of so Buddhists in colorful toga garb with shaved heads on both genders parading in the street and chanting while beating a small goat skin drum with what looks like a bone. The cult members talk to the international community about joining their sect and pass out one-page pamphlets. From what I can gather, the hard-core Buddhists of the country, whom personally I consider the true Buddhists of peace in my nation, are not at all pleased with this cult, their behavior, nor calling their perverted form of religion Buddhism. Too cultic. If I were in a western nation, my viewpoint would be considered conservative. When did that happen?

After the meal, the lady saunters down the lively street, taking in its smorgasbord of delights. The only place I can recall as similar to Arabat Street is the area around the Roman Baths in Bath, England. Wherein there are signatures of the Romans, Celts, and Normans in that English city, it's still decidedly British.

No, Arabat, you are one of a kind. The lady finds a few shops selling men's clothing of her liking as the blue flats meander closer to the capital. Several summer suits with monochrome shirts are to her male liking, always tying his colors to the tractor design of the Russian flag. This flag still represents the Russian people. Not able to decide on a favorite, I purchase several silk ties with the Russian flag design, as such items are plentiful in this area.

After finding matching shoes, I think I'm done with this heavy ass, bra, scarf around my neck, and uncomfortable shoes. Done. Finito. Homeward bound. No such luck. No such luck because as the lady is arranging her awkward packages, what do her eyes see? Has to see because the damn window is full of them? Nothing less than White Stallion tee shirts in ninety percent of an Arabat shop.

"Oh, for fuck's sake," I say out loud, forgetting the smooth female voice mastered decades ago. Thank God no one notices. I should walk away. Know this wasn't the kind of place I should be perusing. Know I should take my heavy ass and blue leather shoes and hurry back to the studio. There is safety in those walls. Safety. I should check the security. I'm going before both Russian houses in the morning and will ask them to appoint me as the next President of United Russia. Be safe. Leave. Don't give into curiosity. I can't be caught on Arabat Street in Moscow, Russia in this get up. That is what I'm going to do. Time to say, "Bye Horsy" and head off for safer ground.

But she walks closer to the window and studies the horse. They did the shirt in abstract art. Silky, sassy white coated stallion with a swishy tail. She likes the swishy tail painted on cloth with each white hair discernable to her eye. The tail flips a bit on the end. Confidence. Yes, that's it.

The stallion is confident. The body of the animal is all muscle and toned and honed to perfection. Strong.

The eyes. How did the artist capture a look so deep into the eyes? It was just a bit of black paint. Just a dot. There should be nothing there. Yet, those eyes don't contain emptiness. "Intelligence," says a female voice.

Five minutes later, a hand with a perfectly polished red fingernail hands the merchant a 5,000 ruble note. The tall woman with long dark hair waits for change. Her velvety voice thanks the merchant as she curls her red fingernail to show its feminine style and perfection while accepting the change. The amazon beauty sticks the bag into the package with the shoes. What can she say? The lady likes the shirt's colors.

Shuffling to the other side of the block, the lady catches an Uber, since she has an armful of goods. The Uber driver leaves her off at the metro closest to the studio. Upon arrival, she gingerly lays the loot on the bed. The blue flats fall from her feet.

The male would like to drop this heavy ass on the floor and see how far he can fling the bra with the make-believe tits. But the mission is not done. Not yet. Damn it. More blisters on the feet.

Computer scans are clear. Like a proper lady, she touches up her make-up and pouts her lips with a little more Fire Engine Red. Thank you Lancôme. She slides back on the flats and takes off in search of food.

In the book section at the grocery, she finds Selena's book, *Lives on the Line*, displayed as the latest best seller. She grins.

She picks her food items and the ingredients for her stroganoff recipe, a favorite. Lots of sour cream. The wine section stocks Crimean favorites. Crimeans grow exceptional grapes.

After returning to the studio, I delightfully dispose of shoes, pantsuit, ass, tits, wig, and makeup. I shake my naked butt in a little dance. Thank God I'm a man. I like it.

CHAPTER 18
SELENA PINES

FROM MY HOTEL ON ST. Germain Street in Paris, I review my notes and itinerary and a little long-lost college French.

I flick on the television, hoping to catch an earlier interview of myself. Never hurts to critique oneself. Instead, I catch an interview by none other than my heartthrob, Sergei Radkov. "What a way to be preempted," I mutter. In this month's issue of *World Changers*, I've been replaced by Sergei as the magazine's title lead, "World's Most Intriguing Person."

I love it. Can't think of anybody else I'd want to be followed by. What woman wouldn't pay any price to see the blue-eyed man? Crystal-blue-eyed man. Clear. Clear like the sky on a cloudless day. Blue eyes that don't so much look through me, as I imagine look for me. I wish. I'm as starstruck as a thirteen-year-old. Still, I wish his pouty lips would kiss me. Damn. *Am* I thirteen? When did I not grow up? When am I going to settle down with a real man?

You know, I'm spinning in place. I fall into each day going to a new place but doing the same thing. What in the hell am I going to do when this is all over? I've traveled to so many places in the world, yet I have no idea where on this planet I would like to live. Sometimes I think I might return to the Carolina coast, but my old home has changed too much. *They* are not there. Should I honor my dad by continuing his work? I feel loneliness hovering just thinking about it. There's no one there to anchor me. Is that the right word, "anchor?" I'm unanchored.

I'm in such pitiful shape that the only thing I can think of is falling in love with a hot Russian and having his babies. My God, I'm pitiful. I've heard it said when you stop looking for love is when you find it. I can say that's untrue. Otherwise, I would have been head over heels by now. And how in the hell can I fall in love when I'm in a different city every couple of days? Maybe first I need to decide on a home. Shucks, maybe then just look at my opportunities and pick one. That will be home. I'm becoming a spinster.

Never thought this would be my life. Thought I would finish med school and move home with the love of my life and work with dad. Go back to my beginning. I've been moving through life and not living it for a long time now. When am I going to live instead of drifting day to day, following a predestined fate? Would the world really fall apart if I didn't do this? No. But not doing it would make future me quite unhappy. I would hate myself for not following this path to the end. This endless path.

The only place I really want to visit and see is Russia. Maybe that's why I've been given this Sergei crush: to motivate me to spend time there. Soon I'll be there. I get giddy just thinking about it.

My agent wants me to do an in-depth Scandinavian and Baltic tour when I finish in Russia. I may, but damned if I'll not extend my tour in Russia so that I can see more of that vast country. Sorry destiny, but can't I take off several months for a break?

My pen drops and I scoot closer to the television. Sergei Radkov is speaking. Speaking of peace. Sergei Radkov, speaking of prosperity for all. Sergei Radkov speaks with wisdom. I swoon. He is so out of my league.

I use my fingers to outline his face, wanting so very much to touch him. I'm careful not to poke his eye with so much as a pinkie this time. He is just so... so... *it*.

When I make my way to bathe, the pink toy is in tow. God, it's been so long since I've had actual sex.

The Russian man's eyes are upon me. Lusting. His mouth kissing. Whispering. His body glorious. Masculine. Male. Prone. So much man.

So much man making love to me. An imaginary lover taking me to the place that only a lover can. Oh God. My stress is relieved for a little while. I have it bad. Me and every woman on the planet.

After dressing, I dine alone at a recommended French restaurant. I'm asked for my signature twice. I enjoy the attention and brief conversation. Damn, I'm lonely. Pure and simple. No wonder I act like a thirteen-year-old with the latest teen magazine. I give myself permission to act thirteen. Loneliness is a harsh condition. I can be as young and immature as I choose within the privacy of myself.

That decided, I close my hotel room door and imagine Sergei Radkov on my arm. Taking me in his arms. I imagine looking into his blue eyes. Dancing. Touching. First kiss. Exploring. Caressing. Coveting his body. Wanting him to be mine and not sharing this slice of him with the world.

I don't admonish myself for acting like a schoolgirl. No, I do not. But damn, I'm going to need that pink toy again.

CHAPTER 19
REUNIONS

I PUT away my groceries after changing clothes. Opening a beer cooled in the fridge, I opt to let the white wine chill.

Security screens clear.

I chagrin myself a little for not preparing for the interviews, which are now hours away. I concentrate on keeping my nerves steely. Depending on my intelligence, my knowledge, my experience, even my inexperience to provide sharp, fresh replies to probable questions. Instead, I spend most of the night devouring Dr. Selena Frederick's every word as though she is my lover. I eat her—chapter by chapter, line by line, word by word. When I finish reading her book, I read it again. Then again. My eyes, already tired, will not close with exhaustion. I tarry on until I have chewed and digested every last word of her manuscript.

I will let her be my guiding star, I decide. I will let her spirit fill me as I address the people of my country. This is so much better than preparing canned replies for tomorrow. I think that type of preparation is not, in this instance, the best for me. I think better on the fly and pulling from what is in my heart.

If ever I believed Selena Frederick to be a strong woman by her mildness—a beauty who took her care to the ugly, a star in the darkness, a dichotomy, an enigma—then I'm more than convinced now. I realize she spent her career patching up victims whose injuries may have been inflicted by the hand of none other than myself, Commander Sergei Radkov. When I pulled my commandos away from disease, Dr. Selena Frederick rushed in to care for the sick and save the forgotten. A pregnant woman under her care could bear a life that might one day be a future kill for my party. Selena has given her all to provide food, clean water, medicine, vaccines, health to those God named mother and child.

The two of us walked in the same pastures, but on opposite sides of the fence. She may have even been the drop-dead gorgeous American doctor who once patched up Vogo in a commando raid gone bad. The events relayed to me were that the female physician was firm in her position that her organization wasn't there to take sides in the conflict but was present to preserve the life and health of the indigenous people. While she favored no military and wasn't a military doctor, her medical oath allowed her to treat a soldier—a devil, an enemy of the people—to the best of her ability. She was a healer. That is who and what she was, period. She had no other lenses.

After the doctor patched him up, Vogo grabbed the American doctor by the ass and forced a deep tongue kiss upon her. As soon as she was let loose by him, the doctor slapped him upside the head and said, "Just because I treated your wounds doesn't mean I won't create another one." The commandos rioted in laughter at this as they left with their newly bandaged comrade.

I remember Joe's story about how she negotiated throwing him to the back of the plane. It's damn funny, but it tells me how smart she is at getting what she wants. Could even be a bitch, in commando language. What do you want, pretty lady? It would be the happiest day of my life if your passion threw *me* to the back of an airplane, though it would take more than a thirty-minute interview to do it... Okay, maybe not.

I wonder out loud, "Was it her? Might she have been the one that day with Vogo?" With that on my mind, I lie on the couch and doze for many hours until I receive a call. Damn, I was having one of those dreams.

Smoltsky asks me if I'm ready.

"Yes," comes my drowsy response.

"I'll send a security team to pick you up," he informs.

"Don't bother. I can provide my own security as I have no other cares. If I carry the vote, then I'll put my security in the hands of the professionals."

"Sergei, take the damn security team. Russia can't take a chance on losing you."

"As you wish, Andre."

I allow myself to fall into a deep sleep. After arising and reading the online news while sipping coffee and eating microwaved muffins, I review the uneventful security loop on my computer. With my second cup of coffee in hand, I realize with relief there is no activity around my flat. Quiet. Too quiet. I recall the days before the dacha coup. It was quiet then too. I'm leery of quiet, but all seems well.

Turn on the TV for a little background noise and pull out a knife to chop onions for stroganoff. I hope this to be my dinner, but then I'm unsure if I will be home anytime soon. Guess I should freeze it.

While cleaving the meat into Julienne slices, my ears are gifted with the sound of the beautiful lady on an early morning French television show. Kitchen tools in hand, I stop my activity and freeze in front of the television while I drink in the voice of this lady like I'm a groupie.

"Thank you for getting up so early to be with us today, Dr. Frederick," the female television host opens.

"Reminds me of my early days as a student and medical resident in America," muses the woman, her emerald eyes lightened by her green silk shirt and dangling Native American earrings that contain hints of green peridot. A burgundy skirt with a green and gold trim in a Native American design falls to her calves. The cameraman takes a shot of gold sandals showing burgundy toe polish that is so sexy. Would love to polish those toes.

The interviewer opens, "Tell me, Dr. Frederick, I was looking at your tribute to Captain Samuel Von Blake in your book's dedication. Who was he? Was he the only American that you personally knew who died during your time 'in the field,' as you call it?"

Selena listens to every word of the question before answering. In my opinion, the television audience would forgive her if she whacked the woman upside the head for asking such a stupid question.

Selena wets her ruby lips and answers, "I wish that were true. I dedicated the book to Sam because he, of all the nonmedical people I ever encountered, worked the hardest to preserve life or improve quality of life when humanly possible." With a smile of remembrance, "And at times, when it was humanly *impossible*."

Selena disguises it well, but from my Moscow studio I understand Dr. Selena Frederick and Captain Samuel Von Blake had been lovers. I have no criticism of that. I understand how it is in the field. More so, I understand that look of love. I've never known love. There's never been anyone to love me, nor has there been anyone for me to love. However, I keenly recognize the look of love. Maybe because I crave it. *Really* crave it from her. For this, I'll not feel jealousy toward the deceased captain who gave his life in service to his country.

The interviewer continues to question Selena about the deceased captain. I want to jump through the television and strangle the lady. I yell out loud, "Leave her alone, damn it! Leave her alone. She has suffered enough." Not sure where that came from. Shit, I would call that rage.

Selena remains calm, although her emerald eyes show a sad hue. "I was in the same 'theatre,' if you will, with Sam twice. Sam risked his life several times to help us at the camp in both theatres. He was killed the second time."

"So, you felt obligated to recognize him?" asked the ridiculous lady.

While in Moscow, my ears steam red.

"I think," said Selena, "'obligated' is not the correct word." She pauses a moment, then continues her thought. "You see, everyone loved Sam. I'm sure his family knows that better than anyone. Because this camp experienced loss in so many ways when we all learned of Sam's death, I wanted to remind his family why he was beloved by so many. For all the sacrifices he made for us and others. I believed a simple dedication to him was the least I could do. Not to mention, such a person of sacrifice embodies the spirit of my book."

The French interviewer with the Botox forehead and sagging throat asks Selena what comes next after her current book tour. What a terrible interview, just wasted when you consider the talents of this pretty lady.

"I truthfully don't know," says Selena with honesty. "The tour is extensive, so I take it day by day. After that, I'm a piece of driftwood."

Drift my way, pretty lady. Drift my way.

"Do you think you would return to the field, or to some scary place? I hear you're already going to Russia on your tour. With the current situation there, does that frighten you?" asks the saggy throated hag.

"Russia?" asks Selena. "I've been in more dangerous places. I was pleased to have my book recently released in English and Russian there. No one can predict the future. For now, it seems calm, and the government is progressing. It doesn't frighten me in the least."

"Yes! Let her have it, Selena!" I yell at the television. "I will protect you, beautiful lady. Nothing will happen to you here. I will see to it with my life. Oh, come to Russia, Selena. Come here! I want you to see my country."

Selena continues to muse with the early morning interviewer in need of a new facelift. "It's possible that if I were to go to Russia—such a mystical land with so many areas of beauty, a unique history, and a vast number of things to do and see—that I may never leave. I guess that would answer the question of what I'm going to do next with myself," says the smiling beauty.

"So, you plan to go?" responds the older woman.

Duh.

"Certainly," replies Selena. "Russia is on my calendar. It's scheduled at the end of my European and Baltic tour. My agent speaks of an extensive tour in Hawaii, parts of Asia, Australia, and New Zealand. I'll see what happens. I'll see my sister and her family first, though. I miss them. Definitely looking forward to my time in Russia, however."

"I'm sure Russia would love to have you," assures the older host, as fake as a mannequin, and segues into the next show before going to break.

"Oh, beautiful lady," I murmur out loud to the black box. "My country wants you to come."

I turn off the television, feeling overloaded at the thought of Selena Frederick touching Russian soil. I attend to my cooking.

After washing dishes, I look through my new clothes. I press them to perfection and line them in the order I plan to wear them in the upcoming days, while my bones are being picked apart by the committee on international television. I prefer to pour myself a glass of the Crimean wine and settle back on the couch to reread Selena's book as a little jazz and blues track plays in the background. But one hell of a duty is calling. I sigh.

Review the security tape. Nothing. What kind of security is this that I am being provided with? Nothing yet? Rookies.

Showered, shaved, and dressed, I top off my breakfast with stroganoff nibbles while cooking. Kneeling, I pray, carrying out my mission plan. I pray with fervor for all things sacred to me. I even pray for the strength of Selena with her eternal sharpness and calm under fire.

I drink a bottle of water as I watch the live footage of my apartment security once again. Nothing. Nothing? Hmm. At 7:59 a.m., a car pulls up. That will be the one. Damn!

I shoot out of the studio door, take two steps at a time down the back stairs, and sprint across the street before the two men have even gotten out of the car.

Can't resist startling them as I tap on the tinted driver's window, and boom, "Hey, you guys. Here to sell pot? I heard you have some good reefer. Why not roll one out of your bag?"

"Damn you, Sergei!" shouts the explosive Vogo who jumps out of the car. The driver, Alexei Plokhy, the man who mentored me in my early military years, remains seated in the driver's seat an extra minute while laughing his fool ass off.

"Sergei! Sergei!" the older man exclaims through his laughter. "Or should I call you the White Stallion? You make an old man pee his pants. Nobody but you, Sergei. Nobody but you," says the man with his signature brown leather tam on his head.

Both men hug me like brothers. Alexei had been on another assignment during the dacha incident. Vogo doesn't doubt that I've forgiven him. He doesn't even have to ask me for it. We hug as two reconciled brothers. Pissant.

"Well, I guess we need to scope the old place out," says Vogo. The pissant looks around as though he's looking for something.

"Why?" I dare to ask.

"Because I may sure enough need to roll a reefer after you scared the shit out of my ass," replies the emotional Vogo.

I allow a chuckle at the expense of my old friend.

"Besides, we need something to do over the next hour."

"You know Moscow traffic. Let us go now. Maybe I'll have a few minutes to ready myself before the start."

"Okay by me," throws in Alexei.

We three amigos meander down the streets of Moscow with me and Vogo in the back seat of the black Mercedes Benz with tinted windows.

"You know, if someone shoots at us, I have to throw myself on you and take the bullet for you," chides Vogo.

"Vogo, you're too damn little to throw yourself on me," I throw back, tit for tat.

"Ah, but take a bullet for you, I shall," retorts the pissant. Remembering the recent past, my response is to raise a questioning eyebrow at the shorter man's banter.

From thence, there is no discussion until we arrive at the arena. We three men revere the passing landmarks of the Russian capital in quiet. Three men who have known each other for so many years. Men who together watched as their brothers died. Men who carried one another on their backs. Men who had grown together, learned together, lived together are now reduced to silence in awe of the upcoming event. I'm glad to have them close. Despite everything, they are my support. They understand, at such times, the value of silence.

PART THREE
THE NOMINEE

CHAPTER 20
PICKING MY BONES

THE MERCEDES ARRIVES BEFORE 8:30 a.m. at the arena, which was overhauled overnight into a parliamentary convention center. They set the stage at the front, and it will hold the questioning committee members. Members of the lower house on the left, the upper house on the right. Tables with chairs line the stage in front with me, the guest of honor, in the middle. I'm given a staff of three to help me should the need arise. A male and female appear to be recent college graduates, and a more mature male political operative. I might need them.

"Your team is here to serve at your pleasure, today and beyond, should you wish," informs Smoltsky, who has made his presence known.

The four of us, feeling awkward, aren't sure how to address one another. I nod in greeting. I guess they can refer to me as a nominee?

"The press is national and international," says Smoltsky.

This is hardly a surprise to me as I broadcast a wink at my friend, Joe Cook.

"All press present have agreed not to question you today. They're here to report on the events as they unfold. You'll answer enough questions without the press adding on. Vogo is in charge of press relations today. Any problems, refer them to Vogo to pull their press passes," continues the current president.

Wonder why an underling isn't doing this spiel, I think as I shudder to consider what Vogo pulling a press pass would look like. I flash him a nodding grin. I also shudder to consider what my bones will look like after the committee picks over my carcass.

Smoltsky finishes with the outlay of the room and all protocols, down to how the members will file in. The members with the most seniority and their staff will sit below in the chairs and desks with me. The other members will fill the gallery in the stands. In symmetry, lower house members are on the left and upper house to the right. The nomination committee will be on the platform atop the stands.

I'm ushered to a waiting room. As the time draws near, I relieve myself but drink more water to hydrate. There's to be a thirty-minute break every hour and a half. My demeanor remains one of complete comfort and confidence. Complete bullshit. My knees are knocking. I adjust my tie and suit coat.

In the waiting room, I listen to the lower house file in on the left as the upper house files in on the right. Next, the men and women of the upper platform file in. Then Smoltsky leads the way, with me the nominee trailing him like a puppy. I take my seat. Andre takes his seat on the upper platform in the middle. The sergeant at arms requests all to rise as the Suvorov Band plays the national anthem. Love that band.

Andre Smoltsky is in his element. He explains why we are there and the grave task at hand, as if no one knew why. Then Smoltsky, left to right, introduces the questioning committee members on the platform as though no one knew who they were. Hell, they have name placards in front of them. I surmise those introductions are for the benefit of the serious-faced representatives, giving them a chance to show their dour faces but wish to waggle their closed smiles as if to say, "Hey everybody. See me on the tele?"

Smoltsky then asks me—I'm sure more for political reasons, though he labors to make his questions appear like protocol—"Commander Radkov, are you willing to swear to this committee that you have not received advance copies or notification of the questions being asked today or tomorrow by this panel prior to our seating today?"

"I do so swear."

"Commander Radkov, have you received any advanced help through contact with any members of this committee or delegation, or prepped in any shape or form for this interview via an arrangement by any house members prior to this seating?"

"I do so swear that I have not."

"Commander Radkov, do you promise to answer all questions from this panel as truthfully and honestly as you can within the scope of your knowledge?"

"I do so swear."

Smoltsky outlines the protocol, ad nauseam for the gathering, and turns the first question over to his colleague on his left.

A thick-lipped man who God graced with blond hair remaining on top of his head despite his sixtyish age, says, "Good morning, Commander Radkov."

"Good morning," I reply, focusing on keeping my voice strong. I try to blot out the rest of the world and focus on this one committee member as though we're talking one on one.

"My question deals with international relationships, Commander."

I'm not sure if the representative is condescending or trying to puff up his own importance.

"I've noted in an interview with an American reporter that you believe the abominable embargoes against our nation can be rescinded. Just how is it you think this can be done?"

"To begin with"—my eyes know I must give a *don't fuck with me* show of strength with this first ass wipe or I'll be unceremoniously sunk—"only part of your assertion is correct. The interview was with a reporter who happens to be from Brooklyn, New York, in America.

"However, I've known him since the Chechen War. Joe Cook was the only American correspondent who tried to help the world understand the enormous situation that is still in the consciousness of many Russians. He agreed to use a Russian outlet before any other media outlet."

Realizing that wasn't his point, the thick-lipped man decides to pursue me down this rabbit hole. He thinks he will ensnare me. Good.

"Why did you not pick a Russian reporter?" quizzes the thick-lipped man with real hair.

"I picked the reporter I trusted," is my short retort.

"As well, I don't see these honorable proceedings as just a Russian event," I continue. "The nomination of a president for the country with the largest land mass in the world is an international event." Without pause, I address the embargo while the committee member's face reddens.

I speak for about ten minutes on Crimea, then the Ukraine. This is the Russian way. The big shots give long speeches on a single topic while everyone else falls asleep. Maybe I'll mix it up a bit if I can.

On this issue, I end with, "If you heard my recent interview, then you know where I stand. If I were an American, it's the same as if the state of New York in America was to secede from the United States and say, 'Oh, and by the way, we're taking the Statue of Liberty and Niagara Falls with us.' There's no difference. Despite the insult, decisions were made. Lines were drawn. Whether Russians like the decisions of the Ukrainians or not, the invasion shouldn't have unfolded. Cooperative diplomacy over the reasons given would've been far better than the actions taken. Despite our dislike of it, the Ukrainian region made a decision over a score of years ago. Whether they choose to reverse that decision is something for the Ukrainian people to decide. Russia should have accepted the decision and sought to develop cooperative diplomacy for the sake of stability in the region. I would have used economics."

I continue eye to eye with the thick lipped man. "I don't have access to the top-secret documents concerning our involvement in Ukraine. If I did, then I might have another viewpoint. Are there persons with Nazi ideals in the Ukraine? Probably. There are probably some in Russia. The United States has many. You will find these peoples of evil ideology on almost every continent. However, I'm not aware of such ideology being broadly held by the Ukrainian government, nor widespread throughout the populous. Are there Nazi training grounds in Ukraine? Possibly. However, rolling tanks into a sovereign nation isn't the way to handle such threats. I only need to remind Russians of German tanks rolling through our country, resulting in devastation for both countries."

I pause.

"At this point, it's much more rational for Russia to build a lasting peace with Ukraine that will benefit and prosper us both. If borders are to be drawn, the Russian people must respect their sovereignty. We don't have to like it, but we must respect it. Otherwise, rebellion will continue. Death will continue. Disease will continue. Starvation will continue. Russians will continue to suffer economically. We must work toward prosperity for all concerned. We live in a world ready for peace. Let us join the world."

The room, except for the dour panel, explodes in applause and cheers. This is unexpected. I expected this viewpoint to be unpopular. However, I had decided ahead of time to be man enough to take the hit.

Covertly smiling, Smoltsky brings down his gavel and reminds the room of the need for appropriate behavior so that the proceeding's time limits can be respected. Smoltsky invokes the time limit, but he allows me five more minutes to expound on this complex issue, with the promise that I might follow-up at a later time.

"I've decided that the keystone concept for my nomination is the word 'imagine.' So, let us take a stroll back in history as we *imagine* a world at peace. The Ukrainian people are our people. Many Russians consider themselves to be descendants of Rus from the Ukraine. The first Russian capital was Kiev, known in recent times as Kyiv. I understand why this irks every Russian to the marrow. This is the ancestral home of our beginnings. However, the history of hunger and politics has drawn a line between us, and Kiev is no longer within borders of Russian influence. Yet we must imagine the Russian and Ukrainian people moving together in peace so that we both may have prosperity. Geographical lines are just that: lines on a map and nothing more. In peace, Russians can still visit and honor their ancestral roots. Imagine…

"I can forgive the people of the Ukraine for their decision in 1991, as, among other things, it was based on hunger. Russia failed during Soviet times to provide proper resources to that western part of our nation. The part of our nation that produced a significant portion of our food. The very Ukrainian farmers who fed us starved. All Russians who were alive then, during the fall of the Soviet Union, are familiar with supply issues. We can't pretend they didn't exist. This issue was particularly bad by the time goods reached that far western part of our nation. Or, more precisely, those goods rarely reached that region at all because they no longer existed. In the breadbasket of Russia, food was taken from the farmers and sent to the cities. Ukrainian farmers starved. I have hungered; I have starved. I understand it."

After a sip of water, I speak but want to draw in my interviewer. How can I stop being so very Russian?

"Now, let us consider where we are and what peace would mean. If we're to create peace in our region, then we must build the bridges of peace. I envision not just the removal of embargoes, but also growth. Growth of tourism, for example. What better way to put money into the pockets of ordinary Russians and Ukrainians than foreign money? Tourism and growth for both of us. Imagine safe air flights and trains between our countries. Tourists able to see the beauty of Russia and cross safe bridges to see the beauty of the Ukraine. Imagine money in the pockets of vendors and craftsman. A rise in income for our museums and beloved historical sites, here as well as in Ukraine. Let the world in to see Russia and bring their dollars, euros, yen, and the like. A region at peace means prosperity for both sides. As a person who has known unrelenting hunger over an extended period with no food in sight, I can forgive any decisions made during times of incessant hunger. Such a life is not living. It's not even surviving. My word of hope to the Russian people is… *imagine*."

There is squirming and a bit of mumbling, and Smoltsky gives one brisk gavel strike to quiet the noise. I like the noise. That means the crowd may actually be awake.

Smoltsky told me earlier that in the United States, the president cancelled everything on his schedule to watch me, a man who may become the new leader of Russia. I hope POTUS's asshole is puckering. Get out of our region, Mr. President. Russia is a new nation with new goals. And, if I have any say in it, we'll create a better world at large. Join us or get left behind.

THE RUSSIAN ORPHAN

The next committee member asks about the environment and alternative energy. Thanks to reading Selena's book, I sail through that part of the interrogation like an expert.

Next, the colleague to the right of Smoltsky is given the floor. "Good morning, Commander Radkov. My name is Yaro Nikolsky. My question deals with international affairs but has more to do with the military and its operations. Is it your position that Russia needs to commit to moving the military back to our own borders and remove our presence from other conflicts? Is it my impression that you want to downsize the Russian military and reduce our superior presence?"

"Never," I say simply but firmly. I find the ire of Selena when pushed too far. The spirit of the American lady is with me.

"Mr. Nikolsky, look into my eyes as I tell you this: I'm a Russian soldier, a commander. I've given my life to soldiering for Father Russia. As an orphan, I was lucky to have a silent benefactor at eight years old, whom I don't know and can't thank even to this day. I attended an English-speaking private school so that I might learn the international language of business. This reduced my sorrowful time at the orphanage, yes, but it also prepared me for what I would do in service to my one and only father, Russia. Then I trained at Suvorov, then the Military Academy. I gave my life and career to the needs of my one parent, in foreign lands and at home. Go against my Fatherland's protection? Never. If I do, then do not waste your bullet to shoot me. I'll use my own."

"Yes, but you must admit such measures would weaken the Russian military," banters back Nikolosky. Good.

My eyes lock onto the man and don't waver, even when his self-assured attitude tries to wave me off. "Mr. Nikolsky," I say with force, "there are international areas where we need to reduce our presence and other areas in Russia where we need to strengthen it. Even after the dissolution of the Soviet Union, Russia is still the vastest nation in the world. We have eleven adjusted international time zones, three oceans, and twelve seas. Russia has huge amounts of coastline under her protection. We have an Arctic tundra and a subtropical climate. Seventeen nations border Russia. Russian security needs are greater than any other nation on the planet. It's those needs and especially the integrity of our borders that concerns Russia the most. Those borders and their maintenance require the most energy to protect the innocent Russian citizens here at home. Especially in threatened areas. Our country need not delve into the warmongering of other lands. His own children and his own home give him plenty with which to keep busy."

With that, there were a few knowing murmurs, but they kept the sound to a minimum. Nikolosky holds his banter. Too bad. I was ready for him. The exchange was "out of the box" for Russian governmental procedures. I want that. I hope I can create more of such exchanges.

But my answer is received as hoped. Smoltsky adjourns for the first break, wherein the gallery goes wild with a standing ovation. I'm the first of the delegation to be led out. Me and my security team return to the waiting room, and Smoltsky soon follows.

Entering the waiting room, Smoltsky exclaims, "You are nailing it, Sergei! I'm so very proud of you, Sergei, so very proud." He puts one hand on my back to pat it like a father.

"You're getting your commonsense approach out while letting them know you're a strong and reasonable man who loves his nation more than life itself. God Bless Russia!" exclaims the older man.

I think Smoltsky might pee his pants.

Vogo looks on and shakes his head with a laugh. "Sergei. Always Sergei."

Ivan is here and has the duty of protecting the waiting room from invaders. I'm overjoyed to see him. I hug my comrade and kiss his cheeks. "So glad to see you, brother. So glad to see you," I tell him.

As usual, Ivan says nothing, but smiles. I know he is glad to see me, too. I's rare to hear Ivan speak. Long ago, I learned to read his eyes.

I take off my tie, drink water, relieve myself, and drink more water. Just stay calm. Hmm.

Five minutes before it's time to reconvene, a horn blasts and I put my tie back on, ruffle my hair, and prepare to stand tall with straight shoulders as I reenter the arena. All have already taken their seats as before. Smoltsky and his gavel call to order the gathering and remind me I'm still under oath. Smoltsky turns the floor over to the next person on his left.

The committee throws me questions on commerce, rebalancing political power, elections, and finally the big one: America.

"Mr. Radkov," begins Representative Ishayev, who looks like anyone's grandmother with her loose tweed skirt and navy turtleneck, which looks like she may have worn it thirty years ago when she was first elected to office. I didn't miss her pointed omission of my title.

"I'm going to turn the conversation inward to our national issues. I've heard you discuss needing to rebalance power within Russia and your wish to see elections take place as soon as possible. First, I would like to know what your vision is for rebalancing our government's power. Do you see Russia as a democracy, a republic... an American colony?"

Her words drew a few chuckles of laughter. "Furthermore, what can Russia expect from your vision of Russian-American relations?"

I imagine "Damn Ruskies" being murmured by the American president in the White House at that very moment.

Knowing this woman to be hard as nails, I remain quiet during her rant and take notes on a pad to assure that whatever she says comes back to bite her scrawny ass.

"Ms. Ishayev, you are wise to structure these questions together in this format." The gray-haired woman in old clothes makes a conciliatory nod.

"First, this vision of Russia need not be mine, but that of the people of Russia. I think that is to be answered by the elections, which I will expound on in a few minutes. There's no nation on earth with a perfect democracy, but many have democratic practices. An election in and of itself is a democratic practice."

I take in a deep breath. "Republic? I hope not because they don't seem to stay around for long. As we have seen with our own eyes recently, changes of power and government rarely happen without bloodshed. A republic puts the power in the hands of the individual. But the individual's cooperation with their neighbors and countrymen is often sorely lacking. Such an ideology does not propagate a fair society. Worse, individuals with power often exclude others not of their ilk from power. No, this is not what I imagine in Russia."

I make unbreakable eye contact with the elderly woman. "I can think of no nation who has suffered more than Russia over the past one hundred years, yea, going back to the days of Napoleon. I also can't think of any country who has seen rawer human blood flow in its streets than Russia. Russians are not a violent people, but they do respond bravely to violence against them. It's time for these good people of my country to decide what type of nation and people they want to be, and how they want to be governed. I hope they choose to be a country encompassing the same rights for all citizens, and not just certain individuals."

I allow a moment, pray for the calmness of Selena, and begin my next windy retort. Ishayev is frowning but doesn't comment, so I take the lead and begin.

"As for the United States of America, it's not a bad nation. Its people are not a bad people. Americans want the same things as the Russian people: to be free. To go to work every day and raise their children. Food, shelter, and a few luxuries."

I wonder if the ears of the American president have perked up.

"However, the Russian people are not American people. Our heritage and our history are vastly different. We didn't start at the same place, nor did our governments evolve to the same end. For example, think solely about Americans calling themselves the 'Great Melting Pot' because of the past immigration of many nations, languages, and religions that have made their way to America. Yes, they are a vast and powerful nation."

I switch gears. "I would argue that Russia is as vast and powerful nation, but with a much *greater* melting pot than America. The difference is that the American melting pot came to their shores. The Russian melting pot has always been here, as part of the fabric of our society."

Ishayev actually rolls her beady little eyes. I pause, but I'm not done yet. No, I'm not. "Russia has Mongolian and Asian people near our Chinese border. We have nomadic peoples in our tundra regions. Russia contains many ethnic groups throughout every region, on every mountainside, surrounding each lake and body of water. Our people speak over thirty different dialects. There is a population of Buddhists, and an even larger population of Muslims. God only knows how our

Jewish citizens survived so many years of persecution, but I'm glad to have them here. We see Russian Christian Orthodox throughout our land, but there is a mixture of Catholic and Protestant Churches in our nation as well."

I take a deep breath. "Our people are derived from people of every imaginable ethnic group in every region. The Uggs, and the Finns, and many Scandinavian peoples. The Tartars, the Cossacks, the Chechens, and many, many more. We have an estimated one hundred and twenty ethnic groups in Russia speaking over one hundred languages. This is the fabric of Russia and always has been."

I do my best not to put my tongue in my cheek for my last words on the subject, which is sure to be repeated often in the media. "As far as Russia being an American colony, my dear lady, you must read the most recent science. It's more correct to say the Americans are a Russian colony, since science has verified it was Russians who crossed the Bering Strait so many thousands of years ago into the Americas."

There is a roar of laughter, at which point Smoltsky brings down his gavel.

I continue to answer the rest of the elderly woman's questions but circle back to America.

"Do we want to be like the Americans, who remain in gridlock, in hopeless debt, and can't agree on anything, much less find solutions to their problems? I hope not. We should be a nation of more than rhetoric. Someone asked me if I thought we should be more like the Americans. My reply was, 'God, I should hope not.' No, I don't think we should go the way of the Americans. I hope to form a better government than the United States, regardless of any similarities we coincidentally share with American ideals. Russian focus should be on rebalancing power so as to increase the meaningful input our people may have in their own governance. A people driven by solutions, not ideology. Imagine. Just dare to imagine that."

Looking straight into the eyes of the committee member, I add: "Ms. Ishayev. You asked me about government reform. I think we need to start at the beginning, with campaign reform. Not just available, secure voting. More than that. Putting forth individuals who are willing to serve and solve the problems of our great nation. That requires rebalancing our government and power structure, especially at the regional level. I call upon all of Russia to imagine. Imagine we have a country that looks at our problems and solves them as a whole people. We can't resolve problems if we can't first imagine solutions. That is my message to my people. Begin to imagine. Don't settle for the status quo."

I have one more thing to say. "And Ms. Ishayev, I'm not Mr. Radkov. I'm Commander Sergei Radkov. I've worked hard for that title, put my life on the line for it, been injured in battle and nearly died for it. I expect to keep it."

Smoltsky calls for a break amid a silent room.

Afterward, the next committee member is friendlier. "Commander Radkov, I would like to thank you for your service to Father Russia."

I nod with appreciation as the question from the committee member continues. "I might like to see if I can steal the couple of minutes and ask about how is it you view Russian guardianship regarding preservation of Russian history, culture, and artifacts."

I didn't expect this question, but I know much. Like any other Russian, I've seen much.

Unbeknownst to me at the moment, at every bar and watering hole in Russia, every metro, in every taxicab, voices are abuzz and cheering slogans such as, "Damn right! Radkov for president! WHITE STALLION! WHITE STALLION!"

Soon I will learn that during the hearing sessions, the streets of Russia began to flow with vodka, with the citizenry cheering and shouting in support of my nomination as though I'm the home soccer team outscoring our rivals. I think some citizens are shouting just to shout. Vodka can bring out a person's primal need to roar.

As the Russian citizens roar, I field questions on the economy, the media, and corruption. I focus to stay bright-eyed and engaged.

Unknown to me, Russian citizens in the St. Petersburg region are jumping up and down with joy in the streets. The city if filled with marching bands playing and beating the drums while navigating the city streets. Soon, in every large Russian city, marching bands and celebrating citizens have filled their Lenin Street. Russians love their marching bands.

The meeting is called to a close with a Smoltsky *BAM*! A long overdue two-hour lunch ensues. Smoltsky arranged for lunch to be catered for everyone, and I meander about and talk with many of the representatives and staff. After a while, Smoltsky pulls me aside.

"I think you need to see this."

Along with our teams, we enter the waiting room. "Look at this," says the older man. Smoltsky switches on the newscast coming from all over Russia. People are marching in the streets everywhere with signs and shouting, "WHITE STALLION! VOTE FOR THE WHITE STALLION!"

"It's not just in Moscow and St. Pete. It's in Novgorod, Yaroslavl, Arkhangelsk," says the gavel bammer, who flips from station to station.

"Even small villages. Isn't it great?" he asks.

"No," I reply. "I want to put a stop to this now before it gets out of hand. Russia can't submit to mob rule. Get me linked up live," I demand.

They pull the press into their unique positions as I arrive at a podium placed in the center of the stage. I hear someone saying, "Going live in three, two..."

"Good citizens of Russia," I begin. I can see my white teeth gleaming in the teleprompter. White teeth inherited from whom I have no idea.

"I have heard that many of you have arrived in the streets of Russia to support me. Thank you. I want your support. At the same time, I must request that you go home. You see, there is a time to speak. I would never tell a Russian citizen not to speak. There is a time for all things under the sun. A time to speak, and a time to listen. A time to hear. Now is the time for all Russians to hear and to listen well. Once you've listened to everything that I am being asked, and have digested it well, then it will be time for you to speak in a voice of celebration... *if* my nomination is carried, and *if* you agree with me."

After a brief pause, I continue, "No matter what you think of them, these representatives come from your collective voices. It is their solemn duty to decide whether what I propose is the right direction for Russia. We're a great country with great people. However, make no mistake: we also grapple with a complex history and complex problems. These representatives are being asked to make decisions for our nation that will last a long time. These are unprecedented constitutional decisions. The committee members don't have an up-to-date handbook, only their wisdom. I ask you to please give them a chance to listen to me with their own ears. Give them a chance to listen to their own inner voice. It'll only be a few more days now. I beg of you all. Please go home and listen. Let the committee members make their decisions without pressure. Believe in the process. And may God bless our great Father Russia!"

I leave the podium. The representatives all give me a standing ovation. For which I nod at them and return to the waiting room and say no more.

Smoltsky soon follows. "Thank you, Sergei. You're right. We don't need mob rule. Everyone is trying in their own way."

"I know," I nod.

Smoltsky suspends the committee meeting for the rest of the day to let things settle down and allow the committee members to process the ground that was covered this day. It's been a lot.

Smoltsky looks at Alexei and Vogo. "I guess you guys need more help keeping the next president of Russia safe?"

"I'm on it, Sir," replies Alexei. "He'll need a full detail and then some," states the man, not wearing his brown leather tam.

From there, the security detail takes me out to one side of a cleared parking lot where a helicopter lands as gracefully as if it'd been born in that spot. Two men push me inside and climb in behind me.

"Like your new transpo, bro?" Vogo teases from the pilot's seat. When we were kids at the English-Speaking Academy, we two fellows would tease one another and come up with our brand of English slang. Oh, the days of yesteryear.

"Nope," I reply. "I know the pilot."

In my hotel room on Saint Germain Boulevard in Paris, I'm following Sergei Radkov on television as he responds while the Russian house presidential committee bombards him with question after question. I poke the side of my face with a forkful of food because I'm so engrossed in what Sergei is saying. I seem to be developing a habit of that lately.

When did I start calling him Sergei like an old chum?

A few times, I yell, "You tell 'em, Sergei!" I'm so in sync with this man.

I've never been a hero worshipper. Never been one to seek out famous people. Folks ask me for my own autograph, and I comply, but I want to ask them why. Does taking this small piece of another person make you better in some way? Honestly, I appreciate being able to simply talk with them more. Not for them, for me. I'm a lonely soul, and who can't resist wanting to be surrounded by people who are interested in you? It's a cheap thrill, but I take what I can get.

Sergei Radkov, however, is someone I'm honestly guilty of hero-worshipping. Hell, I gave up a day in Montmartre just to watch a committee interrogation. If that isn't hero worship, I don't know what is.

My eyes drip with tears in response to Sergei's responses. Especially his impromptu media address to his people. People who are celebrating him. He sends them home so they can listen and let the committee members make their decision without pressure. Who does that?

This man gives the world hope. He gives me hope. *Much hope.*

CHAPTER 21
OLD TIMES WILL NOT BE FORGOTTEN

SOMEWHERE NORTH OF MOSCOW, I'm flying in a helicopter with old comrades. "Where we headed guys?" I ask.

Vogo jumps in to answer that one. "Tomorrow, if the committee interrogation is complete, we're taking you to your favorite dacha to wait out the committee's decision. Today, much closer," he grins.

"That's good, because I didn't even pack my bag. I don't have a change of clothes for tomorrow."

"Don't worry, we'll get you back in time to change," chimes in Alexei.

Ivan is silent.

"That is, if you can get the pilot out of bed in time," I poke fun at my friend Vogo, and we all chuckle.

The helicopter, along with the rest of the security detail in front, behind, and alongside us, descend.

"Oh my God!" I exclaim. "It's been years since I was last here."

"Yes, everyone is excited you are coming," responds Vogo.

Vogo's family home. Sometimes I'd visited during the holidays during my childhood, at other times for the entire summer, depending on his family's plans. Orphanage escape. Freedom. Good times. My joy at being back here again overtakes me. Moisture fills my eyes.

Me and Vogo were rowdy boys back in the days of old. Hell,

always rowdy, taming only with age. Well, a little, anyway. Later, Ivan joined the rowdy pack.

Vogo's wealthy family provided him with private instruction on horseback riding, polo, fencing, martial arts, and target shooting. I got to join in. The family even let Vogo drive an old 1957 Edsel with an electromechanical push button transmission around the property lands. Little nine-year-old Vogo would stand straight up to drive with the seat pushed all the way back. His head barely cleared the steering. Oh, the benefits of being a late-in-life child. At times, some parents grow to not give a shit about raising children anymore. In Vogo's case, his were so tired of child rearing that they just let him run wild. I think that's why he craves attention. Never take Vogo to a strip joint. The man will drop his whole paycheck, not so much for sex but attention from the girls.

We don't call him "a pissant" for nothing. Vogo is short and slim. Barely made Spetsnaz because of his height. Small but fierce. We were once in hand-to-hand combat on a mission. Vogo was jumped by a guy who had at least six inches of height on him. Vogo ducked his opponent's fist then sprung straight up on top of the guy with his legs around the guy's waist like a monkey. The enemy's arm span was too long to land a punch with Vogo up close on his torso. Before the opponent could figure that out, Vogo had hit him two times in the face and stunned him. In a flash, Vogo pulled his knife from his ankle sheath and stuck the blade directly into the man's eye socket for a kill.

If that wasn't enough, Vogo pulled out his knife, did a backward somersault as the dead man was falling, and rolled to one of the two opponents I was fighting. As one enemy lifted his leg for a round kick, Vogo rolled in and split the man's femoral artery up to his groin. As the guy lay bleeding out, Vogo hopped up and got behind the guy I was fighting, stopping a few meters away. Stood there with his arms crossed and bloody knife in hand. When the guy decides to run for it, he turned to find Vogo waiting with a grin. The foe then turned back around and decided to take his chances with me. That's when Vogo leaped on the man's back and broke his neck.

My pissant friend. Never underestimate his theatrical drama. Actually, grinned at me after the man fell and said, "Thought you needed a little help, bro. Should've let me take all three alone."

That was typical Vogo. A pissant.

I found it a mystery as to how Vogo's family held on to the homestead during communism. His father being a Party leader didn't hurt. Back in those days, Party was everything. Throw in a little corruption and you could hold on to a lot.

As happy arrivers, we enter the front door. The cook meets our crowd at the door.

"Olga! Olga! You are here. What a pleasant surprise!" I cry.

"Yes, Vogo brought me up here. Who else would feed your crowd?" says the old woman that I love.

Olga usually works at my favorite presidential dacha, near Lake Baikal. Some years before, Vogo and I rescued her from her drunken husband, who was beating her in front of a grocery. The public incident enraged me.

We took the beaten woman to the presidential dacha and arranged for a doctor to look after her. The kitchen happened to need a cook. Olga spoke up and said, "I can cook." And boy could she. Olga makes the best stroganoff. Lots of sour cream.

Today, Olga holds the position of kitchen chief at the dacha on Lake Baikal. Truth is, she's chief of the dacha and grounds at large. The lady is boss of her domain. The former president rarely visited that dacha, but Olga continued to cook, freeze and can food, try out new recipes, and feed the staff as though the president was in residence. She runs a tight ship.

The former president liked the larger dacha in the Ural Mountains, so security staff rarely got to venture to the lakeside presidential residence. However, Olga was often sent to other places on the government dole for large events. She would occasionally run into us young men she referred to as "the boys." Besides a cook, Olga was the closest thing I have had to a mother.

The rest of the crowd stands stunned at the opulence of Vogo's family home. Olga directs them all to their quarters.

"Thank You, Vogo, thank you," I say to my friend and comrade.

I look at Ivan, feeling so overjoyed to be at Vogo's, and begin to ask, "How does it feel to be back..." before trailing off.

At that moment, I realize Ivan has never been invited to the palatial country home. I want to fall through the floor. Both of us ignore the comment as though I hadn't said it. Damn me and my mouth.

Vogo breaks the awkwardness by saying, "Come on Sergei, let me show you to your quarters."

After we climb the sweeping staircase and turn left, I know our destination. When Vogo opens the door, I exclaim, "My old room! I've missed you! My God, there are clothes all over the bed."

Vogo chuckles, "Like old times."

I remember.

The first time I visited Vogo, I had nothing to wear except my school uniforms. Vogo's family were the type of folks who dressed to the nines for dinner. Just a kid, I still understood enough to be embarrassed. Intuitively, Vogo wore his uniform to dinner, too. The next day, when I returned from adventuring with Vogo, a complete set of clothing was laid out on my bed. Play clothes, dress clothes, fencing clothes, riding clothes, a martial arts uniform and all in several sets. Shoes to wear for every occasion.

I asked Vogo at the time who provided the clothes for me. Wanted to thank them. Wanted to thank them the way my mother would have insisted.

"I don't have a clue," Vogo guffawed. "This is how rich people work: they do something for you, don't thank them. You just accept it and go on. They usually don't want your thanks. Embarrasses them, ya know?"

I didn't know. It wasn't the way Momma had taught me, but I accepted Vogo's explanation.

"Are you responsible for this?" I ask my friend, returning to current times.

"Nah. Mostly Olga."

Looking over at the suit, I grin. "I guess the pilot can sleep in tomorrow morning." Damn, I probably have more suits now than, well... any president.

That gave Vogo his signature guffaw. "Not presidential quarters, but I thought you would feel more at home in your old room."

"I do." With hesitation I sigh and say, "My friend, I hate to ask anything more from you, but I want you to do something for me."

"Name it."

"I would like to go on a horseback ride."

"Done."

"We'll need three horses."

"Who is the third rider?"

"Ivan."

"Can he ride?"

"Can't say, but I'll walk his horse if I have to," I reply with a twinge of sadness.

Vogo understands. "How about in thirty minutes?"

"Yes, meet me in the kitchen. I want a nibble of whatever Olga is cooking." I give a knowing grin.

"Do you mind clueing in Ivan and Alexei?"

Vogo gives a nod and leaves the room, closing the door behind him.

I hang my clothes up and sit on the edge of the bed. The earlier exchange with Ivan rattled me and brought back memories I had long buried.

I'd spent the school term at English school, and then the summer romping with Vogo. Ivan was left at the orphanage to fend for himself. Left with the savages. Ivan became one of them.

The young voice of Ivan rings in my ears. "You left me Sergei. You left me. I killed someone. Sergei, I killed someone."

I climbed down from my bunk and held my ten-year-old friend.

"Shh. Hush now. You never should've been put in that position. Hush now."

Once I returned to my upper bunk, I decided Ivan was right. I did leave him. I had no choice. I was just a kid. When adults said go, you went. What could I do about it?

I decided that when next asked to go to Vogo's again, I would try to talk my way out of it. When that time came, talking was of no use. "You're going, kid. Those are the instructions," said the schoolmaster.

Ivan and I talked the next day during the orphanage holiday and decided we would both go to Suvorov Military Academy at fourteen. This would get us both out of the orphanage for most of the year.

"Keep yourself as fit as possible. Stay strong. It's hard on orphanage rations but bulk up your muscles as much as possible. Run as much as you can. Keep your grades high. It'll take a few years, but we'll both get there."

This seemed to give Ivan hope. Hope was the best I could offer as a child. Damn me to hell.

The summer before we both entered the academy; Ivan came to me and informed me he didn't think he could go with me to Suvorov. He'd had gotten his girlfriend, Katarina, pregnant. The two of them planned on running away together.

I spent two days trying to reason with my friend, but we both knew Ivan's baby would be placed in an orphanage, just like him. Ivan couldn't bear the thought of that. I was heartbroken for my friend, but once again, what could I do? I was still just a kid.

On the third day, tragedy struck. The girls Katarina's age were housed in the basement with stairs leading straight up to the cafeteria. The stairs were so crumbly and old that pieces of rock would occasionally shed off when walked upon. The substandard concrete stairs should've been closed off and shut down a generation before. They collapsed. Katarina died, along with ten other young girls. Ivan's unborn child made eleven.

I was at the orphanage on that occasion. I had to peel Ivan off the wall. Ivan, who once was gregarious, had already quieted down after "the incident" back when he was ten years old. Now, after Katarina's death, he hardly spoke at all. To this day, he is called "Quiet Ivan," or "Ivan the Silent."

Several more times I was sent to Vogo's and Ivan was sent back alone to the orphanage during school breaks from Suvorov. Ivan was constantly on my mind, but that didn't help Ivan. I never meant to desert him. Even after we were in college at the Military University, Ivan was always just there. He never talked, but I kept him by my side as often as possible.

Tears stream down my face as I sit on my former summer holiday bed. Those damn memories. So long ago, and still so painful. I understand I owe Ivan something, but I'm not sure what.

I shake my head to remove the young voices of me and Ivan from my head. It's over. Past tense. Over.

Changing into jeans and a shirt, I settle for the tennis shoes that Olga provided for me since I didn't have any riding boots. I make my way downstairs.

Olga wouldn't let we three leave without taking in a little snack. She serves homemade bread, ham, cheese, fruit, and cookies along with some milk, like we are still little boys. All three of us withhold our chuckles, then burst out laughing.

"What?" asks Olga.

"We love you Momma Olga. You make snacks fit for a king."

"Wait until dinner," the old woman quips back.

"We'll be sure to work up an appetite," responds Vogo.

When we finish our snacks like good boys, we head out to the horse stables. The stable boy has the horses readied, and we mount. As usual, Ivan says nothing. Then he trots his horse like a pro. Vogo and I sit on our horses with mouths agape. It's obvious that of we three men, Ivan is the best rider.

"Look at you," I say while gazing over at him. "And here I was worried you might not be a rider and we would have to give you pointers."

"I own a horse," replies Ivan in a rare comment.

"You *own* a horse?" questions Vogo. "When did that happen?"

"I guess I bought my first one about ten years ago."

Vogo and I give each other a quizzical look. Quiet Ivan.

"How many horses have you had?" I ask in a curious tone.

"This is my third one. I had a half of one once. I shared ownership with someone else."

"Wow," says Vogo.

"I guess you like riding, huh?" I say. It's as much a comment as a question. Guess I'm stunned at how little I actually know about this friend that I've been close to for most of my life.

"I always wanted to learn to ride, so I did. It became my passion. I don't get to ride as much as I like, but I drive out to the stables as often as possible when I'm in Moscow. It's a good hike to get out to the stables, but it's worth it."

I wonder if Ivan should be the one called "The White Stallion." All I can say for sure is that I'm overjoyed he survived the coup and is by my side now on my security team.

"I guess that just means we'll have to race home after our ride," throws in Vogo.

We three comrades ride around the estate like the longtime friends we are. As we ride through streams, we joke about everything, including splashing each other. Climb hills, trot through fields and grassy knolls like twelve-year-old boys. The skies smile upon us with all clouds blown away. The sun kisses our skin and our smiles while we three adult boys explore as much of the massive estate as possible.

As dinnertime rolls around, we line up at the old spot where Vogo and I would begin our race so many decades ago. Ivan defeats the both of us, arriving at the stables as though he were riding Secretariat.

"Come on, you slow pokes," chides the quiet man while giving the stable boy his reins.

My heart leaps with joy at seeing my friend so happy. Ivan has been through so much, but it didn't stop him from becoming a vicious operative. I know my friend as many things. One is a merciless killer. An interrogator who torments like no other. Ivan knew how to find a person's tender spot and apply relentless pressure. He wasn't a man who spoke but listened and watched. He's an unofficial expert on human behavior. I wish he would find love in his life more than I wish it for me. But I wonder if Ivan lost the ability to love those many years ago. The thought scares me. I, too, lost the ability to love in many ways during those years.

Ivan was teased by our other comrades in Spetsnaz for using his cock as a weapon. He did. I've been in locker rooms, in gyms, military barracks, athletic rooms of all sorts. I've showered in community showers since I was a kid, but I've never seen anything like Ivan's. His manhood isn't just long, it's wide. He likes to wear a ring around the uncircumcised head. Just the head looks like a portobello mushroom.

"Whatcha thinking about, Sergei?" asks Vogo as we walk toward the mansion house.

"I was thinking about the time Ivan told that man he was going to put his cock up the man's ass if he didn't tell us the location of the cache of weapons. Ivan pulled over a chair, jumped up on it, threw down his pants, and put his balls right under the man's nose, screaming next his cock was going up the man's ass if he didn't give up the location."

Vogo and I bend over, laughing. Through his tears Vogo says, "I've never seen any man's eyes get so big."

I retort, "I've never seen any man's cock get so big." Vogo and I laugh with tearful red faces.

Ivan is quiet. Not even a blush, but he smiles at his silly friends. Already, I've heard him talk this afternoon more than I ever have.

We three pals walk together and throw jibes at one another and laugh about old times.

"Don't wear your suit to dinner tonight, Sergei. It's casual night. Olga wants everyone to be comfortable and have a good time. Good wine. Good beer. Good vodka. Good food. Good company. What is better? *Da*?" Vogo informs more than questions.

"I'll tell Olga that I will only be comfortable if she is comfortable. Either she sits down and eats with us or I'm wearing a tux," I retort.

"Ah, bro, you don't have a tux. We're good, but not that good," shrugs Vogo.

I snicker.

In fact, when dinner is served, it is comfortable. Olga joins the company of her food eaters, and it is like a family holiday. Not that I can recall any of those. Our group talks and jokes and even sings. They toast me. I smile big and struggle not to cry with the love I have for the people in the room. Maybe I've learned to love and found family after all.

"Well, I wish it were for his wedding, but I guess getting nominated for President of United Russia will have to do," winks Olga.

"No, I think Alexei will be first for that," I return. On it goes until the midnight sun became dusky and all my old pals and the rest of my security team who were not on duty that night are scatted off to bed by Momma Olga.

I kneel to pray before bed. My thoughts of Ivan have shaken me into the reality of our life. Where we came from, where we have been, our struggles, who we are now.

It is not my country nor the trials of the next day, nor my friends, nor anything else I think about when I wrestle the covers around my neck. It's the American doctor that steals my most peaceful moments. I dream of her. God, do I dream of her.

CHAPTER 22
HERE WE GO AGAIN

THE NEXT MORNING, after giving Olga a bear hug goodbye, I take to the skies with my security team. The helicopter lands in the same spot at the convention center as yesterday, and along with my surrounding twelve-man security team, we proceed inside. Extended security has swept the convention center and cleared all attendees. Snipers are in place.

Surrender. Surrender to all of it. I guess it's time for me to put my faith in these guys. Damn, I hope they do a better job than I did for the last guy.

At the sound of the horn, I enter the arena for the morning session. An air current from a supersized fan couldn't move this air, it is so somber. Every human is still. So quiet. Waiting. Quiet as though we're waiting for a church service to begin.

Even Smoltsky doesn't pound his gavel so hard as he calls the meeting to order. He reminds me of my prior committee oaths. I nod.

The questions concern labor, immigration, terrorism. I take a hard stance.

Representative Obarin quizzes me on the management of natural resources, particularly mining and mineral rights.

I put my hand over the microphone and give Alexei, who is

standing to my left, a look that he understands. The bald man leans his ear next to my mouth.

"Watch the gallery for the puff-ups," comes my whisper.

He turns and leaves my side as though he is on an important errand. He stops at the door entrance and leans on the adjacent wall to face the gallery.

I'm ready. "Russia is a nation of extraordinary natural resources. Not just oil, but gold, diamonds, gems, and uranium. It's the uranium that I will focus on during the allotted time."

Half of the representatives lean forward. The press double-checks their equipment. Something is about to happen. They sense it.

"Russia owns nine percent of the world's uranium supply. The United States, who owns five percent, buys up to half its supply from us. The West may embargo our food, but the United States will buy our uranium."

Reporters jot. Cameramen hold their breath as they zoom in and out on my face.

"Let me explain this. Mineral rights in Russia are owned by the people. Whether the Russian treasury actually sees the cash benefits from the sale of Russian uranium is something that I don't have the answer to. If I am president, I promise the Russian people I will find out. If anyone in this room, or outside of this room, has their teeth nibbling around the edges of profit from uranium sales, I promise you a fair prosecution—but prosecution you will see."

I pause for a moment. Others think me to be gathering my thoughts. Alexei knows it's his cue to scrutinize the room.

Continuing, I say, "In America, mineral rights are owned by corporations. They put the uranium profits into the hands of wealthy mining companies. Even uranium contained on Native American lands. Of course, they let their First Peoples do the backbreaking, life-shortening work of digging the uranium out of the mines. They tell these miners how fortunate they are to have a job, and their leaders, well…" I shrug. "I'll let the Americans and their First People nations work that out for themselves."

"This is an issue that is important to Russians. Russian oligarchy owns part or all of those mining companies in America. This is quite a good deal, eh? Make money on mining American uranium, sell it back to them at"—I squinch my face—"a marginal profit, let's say, along with selling them some of ours."

The room goes dead. Alexei notes a few red faces, and so do I. A few pairs of eyes bore holes in the floor.

I keep my eyes on Smoltsky. My gut doesn't completely trust the man, though I have no reason not to. Quite the opposite. Guess that's what I don't trust. You find the power; you find the money. Everything else unfolds.

A low whistle breaks the silence. The sound reverberates in the room. A few representatives look askance toward the sound, while others maintain their Russian stoicism.

I recognize that whistle. It doesn't ruffle me at all. I continue.

"This is the problem for Russia," I begin. "One day Americans will wake up. One day, they will become aware that as the citizenry works, obeys laws, and struggles to live their quiet day-to-day lives, their land and resources are being raped. The American people are the only ones who can stop their current situation, and they will. Eventually. I believe it is destined."

Representatives and reporters with writers' cramp lean forward. They want to absorb every consonant and vowel of what I'm saying. I strive not to disappoint them.

"Russia has many other natural resources. Uranium yields are apparent. After all, why does Japan want to claim the Kuril Islands between Russia and Japan? My journalist friend, Joe Cook, once asked me, why do both Russia and Japan want a bunch of rocks sticking out of the ocean? Islands only inhabited by less than 20,000 people?"

A smile can't contain my smirk. "I replied to my friend using American salt: 'There's gold in 'em hills.' And that gold is uranium."

In the gallery, Joe Cook nods with the memory and shoots me a thumbs-up.

"Russia is a blessed land. Not only do we have vast amounts of oil, gold, diamonds, and gems, but land itself. I would rather discuss a product Russia and the rest of the world have in short supply. That product is food. Food scarcity is real."

I'm talking with passion. "The world will soon crawl toward nine billion people. Scientists say the ideal population is one point five billion. Some think three to four billion may be sustained. Scientist can debate that, but yes, we're fishing out our seas. Yes, world hunger is real. Distribution is one problem, but it isn't the only problem. We can talk about all the evidence of that for days. One fact that I find stark is migration of great white sharks from their usual habitat. The great whites have even made their way all the way to the eastern shores of the United States. That's almost half the way around the world from their Australian Great Barrier Reef home. The shark's journey is to find food. They aren't there for Disney World, my friends. Population control is a must. It must take place worldwide, and soon."

Silence. God, I would love a challenge. I go on. This is probably the greatest issue in our world.

"While the United Nations has committee meetings, the poor starve. As we sit here, every second there are two deaths. However, there are also four point two births taking place. The math difference is easy to comprehend."

My eyes look directly into the cameras. "Russia is one of the few nations that has a relatively acceptable record of population control. We need to do more. More importantly, we must consider our trade with nations who don't have systems of population control. One of the worst offenders in the world is the United States of America."

The Commander in me takes flight. "This, my friends, is why we must, *we must* focus on our borders. Land is a premium. Russia enjoys vast lands with low population density. The hungry will come to us, my friends. I'm not a cold man, but I understand Russia must preserve its resources for Russian peoples foremost. This is also a major reason why Russia must achieve peace in our region. We must. It isn't only about humanity per se, but about the *preservation* of all humanity. Russian sacrifice is not enough. Solving such problems will involve world sacrifice. Let us begin in our own region."

I stop. I'm way past the allotted time. Even the stoic Russians are looking around. If someone needs to speak, it's unclear if they can. In my gut, I feel success. I need success. My country needs success. And damn it, the world needs success. And I plan to change it. I plan to be a World Changer. I'm starting to capitalize that phrase. World Changer!

Like Dr. Selena Frederick, I want to change the world and make it better. She is my shining star.

Finally, the silence breaks, and the next representative asks me, as a military man, who has influenced me the most. It's a softball question. The ninth inning is in play.

"Dwight Eisenhower."

"Another American, I see," comments the representative. "How about the Caretaker's mistakes? In Vietnam, for instance?"

"You asked me my greatest military influence, not presidential nor leadership." Pause. "Not just for his substantial role in World War II, but his postwar stance."

I quote the American General and President Dwight Eisenhower, reciting his "Prosperity Through Peace" speech. I can quote the great American general's words from memory and do so with passion. It's like poetry to me. I don't need a single word for reference.

"Every gun that is made, every warship launched, every rocket fired signifies, in the final sense, a theft from those who hunger and are not fed, those who are cold and are not clothed. This world in arms is not spending money alone." I continue to speak Eisenhower poetry, per verbatim and without reference. Total recall propagates my words.

"It is spending the sweat of its laborers, the genius of its scientists, the hopes of its children. The cost of one modern heavy bomber is this: a modern brick school in more than thirty cities. It is two electric power plants, each serving a town of 60,000 population.

"It is two fine, fully equipped hospitals. It is some fifty miles of concrete highway.

"We pay for a single fighter plane with a half million bushels of wheat.

"We pay for a single destroyer with new homes that could have housed more than 8,000 people.

"This, I repeat, is the best way of life to be found on the road the world has been taking.

"This is not a way of life at all, in any true sense. Under the cloud of threatening war, it is humanity hanging from a cross of iron."

After a pause, I speak my last remark. "My Russian people, I challenge you to *imagine*. Close your eyes and imagine the world you want to live in. No person has ever done anything unless they first imagine it. Not a man in space. Not a medical discovery. No achievement of any degree. Nothing. We can't solve problems unless we first imagine that we can find a solution. Imagine a world with different priorities. A world at peace. A world with an abundance of food and necessities. A world concentrated on clean water and food instead of weapons that destroy. Imagine our neighbors as friends. Imagine. Just imagine."

"Imagine we dismantle that cross of iron. Imagine Russia leading the world in problem solutions. Imagine Russia leading the world community in ideas. Imagine we become the bringers of peace. Imagine Russia changing the world we live in for the better. Imagine."

The room is quiet. The atmosphere ticks up a somber notch. Not a single sound. Not one. No throat clears. No pen clicks. No papers shuffle. No whistles from Joe. Nothing. Then, the room suddenly explodes in an ovation of applause. The entire room is on their feet, Smoltsky's gavel be damned. Smoltsky lets them have their cheer. It's over. *It's over!*

Once again, I board the helicopter and off we fly toward the dacha at Lake Baikal. "Wait, I need to go pack a bag."

"Phew, Olga has taken care of that. Did you think she would not for her Sergei?" asks the pilot.

I give a nod and a smile. Now I know I have more suits than Smoltsky and probably even the American president. It's over!

Within the hour, the media reports that when I discussed population control, the world paused. I love it. The world needs to pause.

Media reports a tale from a White House leak. That when I discussed uranium, a small drip of saliva escaped from the mouth of the President of the United States and dripped onto his chin. In the Oval Office, the president's senses were glued to me like a fly on flypaper. Good. I listen intensely to POTUS's words when he speaks, too. Quid pro quo.

In my hotel room in Munich, I'm jumping with joy after seeing Commander Sergei Radkov in front of the presidential nominee committee in Russia.

"Wow! Wow!"

I continue to watch Sergei work the conference room making a thousand handshakes as the media covers the event. Ten thousand hugs. He must feel good about his committee performance. He should. He was spectacular.

A talking head speaks over the footage of Sergei's post-committee celebration, saying many of the representatives are of hardline Soviet thinking. It's hard to say how the vote will play out. But Sergei's space is bursting with jubilee, and I'm smiling harder than I ever have as I watch the convention attendees grab for a piece of him.

The media channel switches from the conference to the streets of Russia where people are celebrating. Once again, marching bands are marching. Strangers are hugging. Kids are waving miniature Russian flags. I'm smiling even harder than before if that were possible.

Even so, I would rather the screen go back to Sergei. Sexy Sergei. The man of my dreams. I want to soak in every ounce of him. See those crystal-clear blue eyes. Wisps of blond curls. His demeanor. His voice. His intelligence. His ability to influence others and lead. This man will change the world. Imagine. He challenged Russians to imagine, and I do so right along with them.

I'm developing a pink toy urge, but I ixnay that impetus. I want to see and hear as much Sergei as I can. It's just that he's so damn sexy on top of everything else. He looks so good in that suit. I would love to win the female lottery with its grand prize of removing that suit from him with my teeth.

Imagine.

CHAPTER 23
WHIRLY BIRDS AND WHIRLWINDS

THE TEAM BOARDS seven different KA-52 Alligator helicopters.

"We blowing up something, Alexei?" I ask.

"National security," quips my friend.

As the presidential nominee, I'm in transport from the convention center to the presidential private airport. My eyes grow wide when I see the airplanes. On the tarmac sit two Tu-162 M2 supersonic fighters and four MiG-31 BSM interceptors.

"The grapevine said Russia didn't get these, but we did after all," I exclaim in disbelief. "Wowser!"

"More where those came from, my friend," replies Alexei.

"How did you get those?" I ask, still in awe.

"You see, I have a cousin," begins Alexei.

"Never mind," I reply, cutting him off.

"Hope you don't mind copiloting, bro. Only four seats and one is for the copilot," chimes in Vogo.

"You can fly this thing?"

"Of course," Vogo shrugs. "Who else would Father Russia have test his new fighter?"

"I'll be damned."

"Come on, co-bro, I will show you how to fly this bird. Won't take it up to a full 2,220 kilometers per hour. Will ease off a bit so those slow interceptors can keep up."

"Slow, yeah. Real slow interceptors."

I climb into the cockpit and take in Vogo's flight instructions like a kid at Disney World. Less than three hours later, the planes fly east past Lake Baikal and land at Dzhida Airforce Base near the Mongolian border. A trip that would have taken over seventy hours by car.

Copters waiting. I slip into the cockpit beside Vogo. The team of copters fly south toward Irkutsk through the Sayan Mountains. The team executes the security plan smooth as silk. Or so it seems. Commander Sergei Radkov should've learned his lesson about smooth security plans by now. Damn it to hell.

Upon reaching the borders of Lake Baikal, I hear Ivan screech, "Missile!" Piloting the front helicopter, he veers to his left to throw off guidance and casually blows the ground-to-air missile out of the air in a glory of red flames.

"Up 5,000 kilometers," shouts Alexei, "and increase—"

"No!" I shout into my headset. "Vogo, you take point. You have the best maneuverability. Up one thousand kilometers. Slow by one hundred kilometers per hour. The rest of you stagger up every 3,000 kilometers. Head toward the mountains, then up 3,000 kilometers until over the range. Then drop below the range. See if we can throw 'em off."

Alexei shouts back, "Sir, you are my resp—"

"God damn it! No time for this! I've fucked up responsibility enough to know what it is. *You* are my responsibility. Vogo has the best chance here."

After a moment, Quiet Ivan speaks up. "Sir, I'm thinking it may have been a one-off. Want us to go back and light him up?"

"No. There may be civilians down there. Besides, the culprit has probably hunkered down on a hill or in a cave."

"Fucker," murmurs a pilot. I'm not sure who since my mind is racing. Then it happens.

Not one, two, but three missiles light the air.

"Get behind the range, fellas. Max speed behind the range!" I scream.

Vogo is at max speed when he veers over the top of the mountain and descends. A missile explodes on the other side as we take cover. Close, so close.

Not able to get over the range in time, Ivan ascends up at max speed but won't make it over the mountain in time. My God! Please God, don't make me watch my friend die. Please, not this one. Not Ivan. Ivan shoots downward as the missile approaches him. He blows it to pieces across the sky.

The third missile is in play. I'm concerned Sasha, one of Alexei's young recruits, isn't going to make it. I want to close my eyes but know I can't. I must see. It's my training. My eyes are wide open.

The young commando surprises me. Sasha's helicopter nearly scrapes the top of the mountain before ducking down. The sky is red with fire. I don't know if his helicopter is safe, damaged, or terminated. Those men in that helicopter might be burning alive.

Through the fire, I see the helicopter hobble out. "Are you hit?" I scream.

The copter straightens. Sasha replies, "Just shrapnel, Sir. We aren't looking pretty but not dead either, only battered and bruised."

"I'm slowing, fellas, down two hundred kilometers per hour. Sasha, check your systems, especially fuel."

The copilot answers. "All systems check, Sir. Body damage, but nothing critical."

I close my eyes in relief. "Looks like we're taking the long way in. Somehow those fuckers knew our flight path. No doubt about that. Leak, fellas. Not a word of this. It'll stay with the crew. Not a peep."

"Aye, Sir," came a barrage of replies.

The helicopters land on the Lake Baikal dacha helipad. It's a damn miracle to have made it. I run down the hill and through the back door. Why do I feel like a little boy running toward Momma?

Olga is cooking in the kitchen. I only partially slow my trot after running downhill right through the door. I pick up Olga and whirl her around like a helicopter blade.

"Put me down, Sergei," she screams.

I follow her request after one more twirl. "The hearings are over. Be here at the dacha for a few days… if I'm lucky." I give a sigh and a shrug. "A little rest will sit well with me while the powers that be determine my fate, and that of Russia. What is for dinner?"

"Chicken Kiev."

"Yum. That stroganoff you made last night was extra good. I could eat it every day. You know, I'm a Russian who loves his sour cream."

"Well, then. I'll put your very own bowl of it beside your plate," winks Olga.

"You spoil me, Olga."

"Go up and change. Dinner will be ready soon. I prepared the presidential suite for you."

"No, Olga. I don't feel right doing that. I'm not president yet."

"But Sergei, I put all your things in there."

"Tell you what, fair maiden," I tease. "I'll stay in the room beside the presidential suite and move the things in there."

"Okay. I just want to understand one thing," she says in a near scolding voice like a momma.

My eyebrows give an inquisitive raise.

"Am I going to be seeing my Sergei more if you become president?"

"You can bet on that." I must smile. I just must.

The others enter through the back door, having walked instead of running down the hill. At the same moment, a petite young girl in her early twenties enters the kitchen. She has her long blonde hair pulled back in a braided bun. Large blue eyes and perfect skin grace her face without an iota of makeup. A natural beauty.

Ivan blushes. The only time I've seen Ivan blush is when he sees this girl, Irina. The girl is a spitting image of Katarina, Ivan's deceased girlfriend. Irina has been at the dacha for a few years. I've noticed the two of them stealing glances, but there's no gossip of anything more. Besides, Ivan has a few years on the girl. Still, her resemblance to Katarina stirs him. That much is for sure.

"Oh, excuse me, Sir. I didn't hear the helicopters land," says the girl.

"Come on in Irina. It's good to see you. You look well."

"Thank you, Sir. I hope you win your nomination," she replies.

Always a sweet girl, but like Ivan, she is quiet. Unlike Ivan, she is shy. Ivan is not shy when it comes to women. How he lures so many women into bed without saying a word is beyond me. It was Ivan who taught me how to seduce women with my eyes. We were fifteen. I was glad for the helpful tip. I was still a virgin, but Ivan, well... Ivan already had more experience than most married men.

I give her a nod of appreciation. "I appreciate your support, Irina."

She blushes, then addresses Olga. "Ma'am, I finished the rooms as you requested. Would you like for me to set the table?"

"Of course, Irina."

Without delay, the girl gives a slight curtsy and leaves to go about her task.

"That's the hardest working girl I've ever seen," comments Olga. "The others wait for orders. She asks how she can be of help. Perhaps I can ask the new boss to give her a raise?"

"That can be arranged," I smile, while noting Ivan's eyes follow Irina's departure from the room. Her body is not frail, but petite. Like Katarina's. Although Irina seems more fit somehow. Perhaps it's because she didn't grow up on orphanage food.

"Okay, you guys know where the rooms are. Pick you one. I'm not a hotel clerk. No one eats at my table unless they have cleaned up first," bosses Olga.

"Aye, Aye, Captain," responds Vogo. The team scatters.

My room adjoins the presidential suite. In the suite itself across a huge bed are my jeans and shirts and shoes and suits and socks and underwear and riding boots and toiletries. Olga has arranged for everything. Dimples implode my face as I consider my affection for her. Especially noting a Russian-blue suit with a white shirt and tractor-designed tie. That Olga. The suit would be perfect for an inauguration, and I'm sure that was her mindset. I hope I don't disappoint.

I look around the presidential suite. The entire wall on the right is a blazing fireplace. Above the fire is the expanse of a gold gilded mirror containing leaded glass outlines. There's a settee and a chair in front of the roaring fire which someone has started. The massive bed completes the wall on the opposite side. Sheets are specially made for the famous bed. I have often wondered just how many people could sleep in that bed at once. The president could participate in an elaborate orgy in that bed. Hugh Hefner would have felt intimidated, even in his younger years.

A masculine writing desk of heavy mahogany sits in the back corner. I salivate, loving the look of the now-empty desk. Behind it are half floor-to-ceiling windows across the wall capable of providing abundant lighting, though the mechanical blinds are now closed. That is, if there is any light outside. A door on the other side of the desk leads to a toilet, which contains an enormous closet and dressing area. A duplicate toilet area is present on the opposite end of the wall beside the fireplace. It has a more feminine feel.

I've seen this room several times before, but the feel of it is so different now. Gathering my Olga loot, I carry handfuls of clothing through the feminine toilet into the adjoining room next door. The guest room is nothing to sneeze at.

The room is smaller than the presidential suite, but contains its own fireplace, settee, and writing desk. The writing desk is made of a veneer with swirls of a yellowish hue. Gold pulls on the drawers have ornate carvings and a brassy shine. I find the desk gorgeous but think more of the masculine mahogany desk in the presidential room. This room doesn't contain what I call "the twenty-acre bed," but it's a king size. Bookshelves with old book smells line the room. I like the room. It's bigger than my orphan flat in Moscow.

Okay, so I like architecture, and really salivate at ornate furniture. I spent my life in a humble apartment, then an orphanage, then in a school of military barracks, then camped out in foreign lands. I've furnished my small flat with pieces that I like, but it's an odd occasion that allows me to enjoy it. Seeing ornate furniture is like otherworldly. I have lived two ways: extraordinarily sterile or extraordinarily unsterile.

I start a fire in the fireplace. After showering, I stroll outside to walk around a bit, since the others haven't come to the dining area yet. Alexei meets me on the back brick patio. From here, we have a view of Lake Baikal.

"I love the lake," comments Alexei.

"Me too," I reply. A lazy yawn blows through my lips. "I like it so much better here than the Ural Mountain dacha. Here at Lake Baikal, there are hills and mountains and the lake. The other dacha is larger and heavily ornate. A lot of unique engineering and architecture, though," I concede. "I adore the simplicity here."

"Word is, the former president had over twenty-something palaces, chalets, chateaus, and dachas. I think we've only seen a handful," says Alexei, shaking his tam-covered head. "Incredible Russian properties that are just *there*. Empty and unused. Kept up for a 'just-in-case' occasion, just like this one."

"The first thing I'll do if I'm nominated president is decide which ones to liquidate and put the proceeds into the treasury. Russia only needs this one as a presidential retreat. Some of the other properties should be evaluated for other uses, such as museums or places of historical value. If so, they need to be converted for such use. Allow the public to enjoy them. Hell, they paid for them."

"I think you're going to make it, Sergei," responds my former mentor. "You're right about those properties. Hell, some could even be converted into hotels or retreats for public use."

"True. I think liquidation is a hasty decision. The properties may generate money faster if converted to other uses. Who in Russia will buy them, anyway? The oligarchs whose assets were seized by the US and NATO? Outsiders?" I give my shoulders a shrug. "I'm in the mindset of conversion. Otherwise, we start where we left off."

I can speak with an open mind and heart around my longtime mentor, comrade, and friend. "I'm glad you weren't at the other dacha, Alexei. It would've broken your heart."

"It did break my heart. I had taken some time off to look after Momma. The old woman's health is waning."

"Ah, I thought you might be off on assignment. You know, I'm okay here without you, if you need to return to Moscow. I understand how much your mother means to you. She always tickled me. So sweet, but at the same time, so feisty. I haven't seen her in a while, but I can bet she makes for a bossy babushka."

Alexei laughs. "That is true, my friend. She is bossier than hell, but I've never known a better woman or mother. My cousin is looking out for her now. I pay her to stay with Momma while I'm away. The two like each other and sit around knitting together."

My smile is knowing. Alexei has more cousins than the world can count. The woman might be a cousin, or she could be a prostitute. No one ever knows with him. Everyone is Alexi's cousin.

My cell phone rings. Smoltsky. The breathless man tells me the committee has put me up for nomination. The vote will go to both houses in the morning. I request him to ask for a secret vote. This will ensure that any representative who votes against me won't need fear repercussions if indeed I carry the vote.

Smoltsky thinks it a good idea and will put it before the two houses. "Hang in there, Sergei," he says.

"You bet."

"Shoot, that was fast," comments Alexei.

"Not as fast as I'm going to eat my dinner when Olga is ready for us," I grin, then my face grows somber. "I have a problem, Alexei, and I don't know what to do. Well, it's more of a feeling than a problem."

"You, Sergei? You have a problem—er, a feeling—and you don't know what to do?" Alexi replies slowly. "I suppose there's always a first," shrugs my former mentor.

"I'm thinking I'm very much in love with a woman and there is nothing I can do about it. Can't get her off my mind."

"Is she married?" quizzes Alexei.

"No, no, nothing like that. I haven't even met her."

"So, you are in love? In love with a woman, you've never met? The committee should have asked that question." Alexi nods, as though he is ultra-sure of his words.

What can I do but give a short laugh? It sounds ridiculous even to my ears when I say it out loud. "I can't stop obsessing about her. Fantasizing about her. I live to see the broadcasts of her interviews, or of her speaking at conventions. Already read her book like six-dozen times or more."

"Sergei, Sergei. I know who you're talking about. Dr. Selena Frederick. I'm in love with her, too. Sorry to fantasize about your fantasy, but I fantasize about her, too. What can I say, my friend? I'm a man."

"I know. Every man in the world is in love with her. But I'm really, really, *really* taken with her. It's not a onetime fantasy. It's a continuous fantasy. And it's not just her body or her looks. It's what she thinks, and how she walks and smiles, and does everything. I got it bad. If I met her, I'm not sure I could speak." I realize I sound like a schoolboy. Damn me.

"Well, Sergei, I've never known you to have trouble speaking to the ladies. Remember, Mr. Presidential Nominee, she isn't Russian."

"I don't care about that. I would give it all up for her. There's no doubt in my mind about that. I would." I nod to convince myself as much as Alexei.

Alexei gives a Joe Cook whistle. "Man, you *do* have it bad."

Olga rings her dinner bell. The old lady loves that thing. A real dinner bell that could awaken the cosmonauts in the space station. Soon we're all at dinner with another night of toasts and revelry.

Before bed, I kneel to pray. I give thanks to God, pray for my nation, then pray for Selena. Not for me to have her, but for her safety and health on tour. I tell myself I won't fantasize about her tonight, but damn, my dreams have a mind of their own.

The next morning I arise at my usual early time. After breakfast, Olga and I stroll out to look at her new greenhouse. She and her kitchen team leave behind a buffet for the others.

Her greenhouse is impressive. Growing fresh vegetables in the winter, and a substantial garden in the summer. The wise old woman invests in cows and sheep to graze the hillside and for milk, cheese, and slaughter. She is raising chickens next to the barnyard that lay fresh eggs.

My mind wanders. Might Olga be on to something? Might community greenhouses be an answer to food distribution to the needy? Whether in urban areas or Siberia? On the rooftops of residential buildings? I've always wondered if the planting of more evergreen trees, even on rooftops in cities, might help the environment, slow global warming with the increased oxygen production. Could mankind begin to erase its footprints, especially with a reduced population?

During the COVID-19 crisis, I wondered if evergreen planting would help. It's published that oxygen increases human interferon, hence aiding the immune system. I've read medical studies that state hyperbaric treatment has helped with COVID-19 symptoms. It's now well-known there are viruses circulating in the atmosphere at all times, and many play helpful roles. The increase in desert dust from global warming is causing more viruses to fall from the upper atmosphere into our earthbound environment. Would more oxygen in our environment be helpful or cause an ecological disaster? If I'm approved as president, I'll get scientists on it right away.

Yes, my mind is wandering, but after all, I'm challenging my people to imagine. Is it possible that such a simple step of planting more evergreens in forests and on rooftops could possibly improve multiple environmental issues? I have no idea. But as a problem solver who hopes to be a World Changer, I want to know. Love capitalizing that phrase. World Changer. That will be me if I'm given the vote. I hope it's me if I don't get the vote.

Coming back to earth, I address Olga. "You amaze me, Olga. Where did you get the money for this?"

"I asked for it," she quips.

"Oh, I got that message," I smile with a tease. "You know, dacha budgets won't be in my job description, per se."

"Oh, I will have no problem asking the president directly," she quips.

I'm sure she will have no problem at all going straight to the President of Russia to get her budget approved.

We explore more of her substantial greenhouse. There is a gray kitten, a Russian Blue, who stares at me with his big green kitty eyes. The kitten seems to make himself at home and purrs to my ear rubs.

"Oh, that blue boy is a stray," says Olga. "I hope he'll earn his kibbles by keeping the rodents out of my greenhouse and the barn, too."

"Just hope he doesn't prefer to eat your chickens," I contemplate. "I think you might need a feline strike force like the one at the Hermitage to handle this place when it turns cold."

"Don't think for a second that I won't get a strike force if I need one. I'll see what this little one will do first." Olga picks up the kitten to stroke him. Carrying the furry bundle, she points to the corner that gets the most sun. "I'm going to invest in a few citrus trees to see if I can grow them here in this spot." Olga speaks as though she has a preapproved budget.

"You're doing a great job, Olga," I compliment.

"I do a little more each year. I planted some cherry trees this year. See if they will make it. A gardener helps me with all this, but I told him to stay away while you are in residence. Less is better, I think. He took care of the animals this morning and is probably at home at his fire by now."

My reply is a single smile.

"Moscow is still sleeping. They won't be up for another couple of hours. I think I'm going to take a walk around the lake." My eyes twinkle at the thought. "Maybe later, some of my security will take a horse ride with me. Who knows, maybe shoot a few clay pigeons, or better yet, go hunting and shoot something for Olga to cook."

"Don't you dare!" she chides. "I'll let Alexei know what you're up to."

I take a long walk around the estate property, breathing in the fresh air of the blue lake. My mind is not on my country. Nor viruses, oxygen, or evergreens, but the beautiful American who without one word to me is stealing my heart. Stealing my heart with her presence in the world. *You're such a schmuck, Sergei,* I tell myself. Selena Frederick is a fantasy. A fantasy I should dispose of. Yet this fantasy warms my heart. I feel happy when I think of her. Is that really so bad?

Yes, if the committee asked me anything close to a Selena question, they would've deemed me insane. Yet I would give my left nut to have her standing beside me at this moment. Anything. I would give anything. Get to know her. Read her expressions. Kiss those damn ruby lips. Yes, I would give anything.

Later on, Ivan, Alexei, Vogo, and I take a troika ride instead of horseback riding. We hook up the sleigh with three nags ourselves since Olga has run off all nonessential staff. We four men in ten-year-old mode have a blast as we ride the troika down the dacha road, around hillsides and dales until our stomachs groan. Commandos in childhood. That's what we are.

Our foursome cleans up for lunch, and Olga serves us a smorgasbord of meats, cheeses, fruits, and her homemade bread. There are jams of all types. My favorite is the blueberry from Olga's own vines. And homemade blueberry kvass. Yum.

After lunch, we unhook the troika and let the nags out to pasture. The security team could use a rest from the last few hectic days as much as I can. I foresee more hectic days soon. The off-duty commandos return to their dacha quarters. I read Selena's book again in a quiet atrium, not that I haven't read it enough times to have it memorized by heart. It's like religious time for me. Religious *fantasy* time, I remind myself. This is the only way I can commune with her. Damned if I won't take advantage of every chance I get to commune with the lady of my imagination. Pathetic? Yes. But I feel happy, contented. I'm not drinking, gambling, or whoring. I determine my private fantasy isn't hurting a soul. I ask no one to understand it. Hell, I don't understand it myself.

Is the orphan in me fearful that he might come to love a real person? No, the orphan isn't allowed to feel fear, is he?

Before it seems possible, it's closing in on dinner time. I don't want to abandon my Selena time, but even a deranged lovesick puppy must eat. Time to shower and change and go downstairs.

Sitting back on the patio with a glass of wine, I'm joined by my friends, Vogo and Ivan. I'm sure Alexei is painstakingly taking care of my security. The man is anal. Thank God.

Ivan is quiet, as is his norm, but I draw him in with talk of horses. Shameful as it is, horses are the only thing I'm aware of that Ivan loves, or at least likes. Well, besides females. But then, who remembers passing lovers' names enough to indulge in a conversation about a female? Even I have no female name I can provide. I'm finding it hard to converse with Ivan since we aren't in the field as much. How did this happen? Am I abandoning him again by not addressing how the dacha event may have affected him? Damn. But before long, we three friends are bantering back and forth, laughing with heads thrown back.

Olga rings us to dinner, and we sit down to a steaming bowl of Olga's borscht soup, bread, sour cream, and jams. As an extra, she has made pelmeni—dumplings stuffed with mincemeat and pork. The cook made a fresh salad from her garden as the next course. Then she brings in her shashlik, a Russia kabob which is made of steak or lamb and fresh vegetables.

Just as everyone thinks she has outdone herself; she brings in trays of perozhina cookies rolled in powdered sugar and rich dark cocoa that melts in your mouth followed by just a little nut crunch. Of course, there are samovars of tea and French press coffee. All eat past their fill. No one can eat just one cookie. She has made different ones using different recipes, all decorated to perfection. Got to try one of each, right?

My cell phone rings. Smoltsky. "Excuse me while I take this."

"Good news, Sergei. You are the next president of the Russian Federation. I need you back tomorrow to be sworn in," says Smoltsky with no pretense. "Two p.m.?"

"I'll leave early, but just to give security plenty of time, can we make it three p.m.?" Recalling our earlier helicopter attack gives me pause to wish for days instead of an hour.

"Yes. Of course, Sergei. And congratulations!"

After we hang up, it hits. I'm the president of my country. My knees are so weak that I think I might fall. I give myself a few minutes. I'm unsure if I can speak. Finally, I do, and speak out loud. "Dear Mother. Dear Holy Mother. You said I was chosen. Thank you for choosing me and loving our country." Confirming I can hear my own voice, I return to the table.

"Bad news, guys," I say sorrowfully, grinning inside. "You all must have whirly birds in the air before Olga's rooster crows, because I'm being sworn in as the next President of Russia at three tomorrow afternoon, Moscow time."

PART FOUR
SISTERS AND ROOSTERS

CHAPTER 24
SELENA MUST

IN MY HOTEL room in Bern, I caught the news of Sergei being confirmed as President of Russia. On the air, Smoltsky outlines his return to the chairmanship post and Sergei taking over as acting president pending election reform and elections. "This is good news for Russia," says the aging man with his tuft of blond hair over his balding head and clear blue eyes. "Good news for the world."

I'm so excited! This has nothing to do with me, but Sergei Radkov puts me in teenybopper mode. I calculate time differences and plan to arise early the next morning. Once dressed for my conference, I'll get to watch Sergei's swearing-in ceremony. Or so I thought.

My cell phone rings just after I see the good news. I think about the advantages of working out in the field. No cell towers, much less phones.

"Selena," Bubba says timidly.

Shit. "Oh, my God, Bubba, what's wrong?" Alarm bells blow like the building is on fire. It's Bubba calling instead of Debbie or one of the girls. Instantly, I sense a big problem.

Debbie, over three months pregnant, surprises both Bubba and me. She not only passed out, but her blood pressure skyrocketed. She's anemic. The doctor has gotten her blood pressure under control, begun intravenous doses of iron, and put her on bedrest. A bedrest that might last the entire pregnancy.

"Selena, I thought I was going to lose her," cries Bubba. "She's so pale. You know how she runs around all the time, taking care of everybody but herself. These country doctors here seem to be doing her some good, but I'm just not sure about them."

"Bubba, from what you've told me, the doctors are doing the right thing. Might I remind you that our father was a country doctor? Rural countryside doctors have likely delivered more babies than I have," I assure him. "I'm getting on the next plane out of here."

I drop my phone while trying to retrieve my agent's number. I pick it up and breathe a few breaths. I'll need to call my logistics manager to explain my situation as well. Help! I need help. I'll ask them for help.

The agent's concern is more on "striking while it's hot." I cut him short, telling him in no uncertain terms I have zero concern for that. Fuck him. I mean it. I've made him plenty of money and worked hard. Screw him. Dr. Selena Frederick is not his property, and I'm going to my sister, and that's that. I'll reschedule all engagements when and if possible. But for now, I must tend to a family emergency. I tell the agent to handle the press release. I'll fly out as soon as possible, and no, I don't know for how long. I let money talk. "I grant you carte blanche. I'll give you your portion of anything I can't reschedule."

When I call my manager, she's far more amenable. "What can I do to help? Selena, breathe," she says.

"Sorry, I'm hauling clothes from my closet while phoning. This is what I need you to do: First, get online and see if you can get me a ticket out of here tonight. Try Charlotte, Raleigh, Atlanta. You might have to fly me from Basal or Zurich. I don't care about the price tag. Time beats dollars." Why didn't I call her first so she could work on this before I called my asshole agent? He's on my shit list.

"Okay," she says, giving me a simple response.

"Second, get in touch with anyone on my schedule for the next two weeks. Hell, make it a month. I just can't say how long I'll be gone until I get to the States. Let them know I have a family emergency and will reschedule if possible. As always, give my deepest apologies."

"I'm on it. I'll get back about the flights ASAP."

"Thank you. You're a dream."

I took her guffaw as a "Goodbye."

Continue to throw clothes, books, and possessions into my travel bags. Thirty minutes later, my manager rings and says, "The best I can do is a flight from Zurich into Atlanta at 7:20 p.m. There's one seat left. Can you make it?"

Check my smartwatch. About 3:30 p.m. now, and my bags are almost packed. The ride to Zurich will be an hour. I'll take an Uber to the airport. "Yes, I can make it. Get me that seat."

Click my Uber app and schedule a pickup ASAP. Add a note to the driver to wait for me if I'm not downstairs. I promise compensation.

No time to shower. I wash my essentials, put on deodorant, and brush my teeth. Don't floss. Grab my toiletries, weigh my bags, and close my hotel room all within twelve minutes. Of course, the damn elevator takes longer than that. If I wasn't on the eighth floor with full bags, I would take the stairs. Out of breath, I turn in my key at the front desk and assure the clerk I have no problem paying for the night.

The driver is waiting out front. A short-haired lady of about fifty and a markedly German appearance helps me with my bags. The Mercedes zooms toward Zurich.

CHAPTER 25
SISTERS

A TWENTY-FOUR-HOUR FLIGHT, and no sleep. I took a rare Diphenhydramine to help me sleep in an economy class seat on the way to my clan, but drugs didn't even help. After arrival in Atlanta, I pick up my luggage and take off to the car rental area.

No cars! Not anywhere with anybody. Not a single rental. Why didn't I try to book a car while I was on the way to Zurich? Damn, I didn't plan that far ahead.

I pull out my Uber app for the minimum five to six hours' drive to the mountains of North Carolina. When I see the price tag, I shake my head and hit the confirm button.

Well, I better go pee, I consider. Last thing I need is a bladder infection.

An unwelcome text from Bubba fills my iPhone screen: Debbie lost the baby, but she's stable. At least that's what the doctors say. I want to cry. Saying "I'm sorry" isn't adequate. Instead, I send a quick text back updating my travel status.

The Uber driver keeps me waiting for an hour. I can't complain. It's a long drive for me and doubly long for them. It's just that I'm so anxious to get to Debbie. The Honda sedan pulls up, and my luggage is thrown in the boot.

Off to the North Carolina mountains I trek, with a happy Uber driver who will rake in good pay for this trip. I'm cool with that. Anybody who will dive this long deserves good pay. Unless we end up in a ditch, I'll tip them well. They might need enough for a hotel room.

I'm off to help my sister. Even though she's sixteen years my senior, we are close. I feel love for her as my heart burns at our loss. She's a mother who lost a baby. For the loss of a life that I only knew about a few hours ago, a hole burns in my heart to lose them. I'm off to be with the sister who's always treated me as though I was her own baby. The love I have for Debbie swells my eyes, but losing her little one fills me with grief.

Different, the two of us, Debbie, and I. Me with my world galloping, as though I might conquer all evil all by myself. As if I were Superwoman and can fly without wings. I left my family behind to confront this thing I label as "destiny." More than any moment before in my life, I realize how much I need them. I need *them*. I have turned my nose up at letting their life become mine, as I trot from one corner of God's green earth to the other. They should hate me. Truth be told, in recent times I've seen more of the inside of hotel rooms than anything else. My life is full. Very full. It's also empty. So very empty. Superwoman? Bullshit. I cry. Compared to Debbie, I don't make a difference at all. She is the one who is superwoman.

Debbie with her two children, a husband named Bubba, the ranch. Her home. Her place. Her love and heart for it all. The woman works tirelessly without complaint. That is love. Not just for her husband, but for all of it. She has more love inside her than I do in my pinky nail. My tears fall, loving her, hurting for her. Eager to be beside her.

The Uber driver leaves me to my grief. After the tears dry, I wonder if I'll ever possess a place of my own. Someone of my own. I wonder what it would be like to be married to Sergei Radkov. Would he be someone I could make a life with? I have no way of knowing. Why am I thinking about this shit right now?

Sergei Radkov is a fantasy. Everything I learn about him I adore. What's the chance that I'll ever meet the President of United Russia, anyway? What would he see in an American doctor? *Maybe a mistress*, I muse with wryness. I may not be able to have Sergei Radkov, but I want someone like him. Maybe these wild thoughts I have of him are a template, a matrix for the man I might actually one day meet and take things to the next level with. Maybe.

I pull out my iPhone. There are no videos of Sergei's inauguration, which I think is strange, but then again, I'm on a cell phone. There's a wealth of pictures of him at many points during his life. Oh, there he is. Commander Sergei Radkov looks so handsome in his blue uniform with gold ornaments for his inauguration. It reminds me of the Prussian uniforms in the days of old. Sergei has always been a handsome man. Since his teenage years, he's carried his shoulders straight with the wispy blond hair and eyes like a crystal blue lake ice in an Arctic region. Despite my thoughts a few minutes ago, I'm moved when I see his face. I feel vulnerable to him. Damn, I should have specialized in psychiatry.

One snapshot shows him at eight years old when he first entered the orphanage. Child Sergei looks emaciated. My heart breaks looking at the picture of this gaunt boy. An article tells the story of how his mother disappeared one day without explanation during the last years of Soviet times. Sergei stayed at their apartment alone and went to school while waiting for his mother to return. The boy nearly starved doing so. I start to cry again. Shit. Do I need an antidepressant?

The article speculates about Sergei's unknown father and continues to talk about an unknown benefactor, his schooling, his military career. I can't help but wonder what Sergei is like in person. This man. This notable man. This World Changer. That is what he says he aspires to be. A World Changer who challenges his people to imagine.

I spend the rest of the trip barely seeing the landscape zip by as the dark hours fall on the car rolling along the interstate from hill to dale. The valleys challenge the driver to climb higher and higher mountains. I smile at the cows and horses and an occasional sheep. I make out slight animal outlines in the dark each time a house's burning light shares its rays in the rural fields. And the smell of dung. As we climb toward Debbie's home, I can smell it as it draws nearer.

I think about my nieces who are both absolute tomboys on the ranch. The girls climb trees, shoot low-powered shotguns, ride horses, herd cows. *Girl power.*

Alas, we arrive at the ranch. I let myself in through the unlocked front door. Four arms around my waist meet me with cries of, "Aunt Selena! Aunt Selena! We've missed you so much!"

Now that's a welcome. "My God, how you've grown! Where is your dad?" At another time, I would've asked them why they were up so late. Not tonight.

"Dad's at the hospital with Momma," says the elder, who looks so much like Debbie these days. I know these words don't bode well for Debbie's health. "Are you going to stay with us, Aunt Selena?"

"I sure am, but for now I'm going to see your momma and daddy after I find your momma's keys."

"Momma leaves them on the hook over the kitchen counter," helps Elizabeth, the oldest and named after our mother.

The youngest is Lena, short for Selena. Both are beautiful. The girls are still so young, with lots of time to develop into many things. I wonder what both of these two lovely stinkers will become.

"Found 'em. Okay girls, I want you to both be good while I'm at the hospital. It's the middle of the night—or morning, I should say. I'm going to lock the front door, and I want it to stay locked. Have you eaten?"

"Yes, Aunt Selena," says the youngest mouth. "Elizabeth cooked us a pizza. She cooks good pizza." I spy a box for frozen pizza in the garbage.

"You girls, okay?"

"Yes, we been watching some of our favorite movies."

"Okay, but keep this door locked."

"Bye Aunt Selena," they singsong together.

I jump in Debbie's car and race off to the local hospital. I find a sleeping Debbie in the hospital bed and Bubba on a cot. Despite my tiptoeing, they both awaken when I enter the room. I give them a hug. Debbie looks pale. I've never seen my gorgeous sister look so bad. Her paleness tells me that my beloved Debbie lost her baby and a lot of her own blood.

"The girls?" asks Debbie.

"They're fine. They fixed themselves a pizza."

Debbie manages a weak grin. "I guess leftover meatloaf and green beans didn't occur to them."

"Of course not," I reply.

Bubba speaks up with his deep Southern mountain range drawl. "They brought me this here cot. I thought I needed to stay with her tonight, just..." He didn't finish.

"I'll stay with her," I chime in. "You go on and look after the girls."

"Now, ya'll don't be a-hoverin' over me like I'm an invalid. You two go on home and get some rest. Selena, you must be tired after flying from halfway around the world. I'll be up and about in a few days," scolds my sister.

"Oh no you won't," I say. "I cancelled everything for the next month, so you're going to have to put up with me for a while. And dear sister, I spent a lot more time sleeping in cots over the past years than I have a bed."

Debbie has no strength to argue.

"Good night, hon," says Bubba to his wife as he plants a kiss on his wife's forehead. "I guess it's almost time to feed the animals and make the girls' breakfast." Debbie's husband leaves us women to our own devices.

I settle into my cot but sit up, knowing Debbie might want to talk a bit.

"Bubba and I were hoping for a boy this time," says Debbie dreamily. "Of course, another tomboy would've been just fine."

I choose my words with care. "Debbie, there's nothing that can replace this loss. I don't want you to think about this at all right now, but you're young enough to have another child if you and Bubba want."

"Oh no, nothing like that," confirms Debbie. "This was a little slipup, you know? Bubba and I planned to make the best of it though, and with joy. We would've named a boy after Dad. We were getting used to the idea of having another little one around. It just wasn't meant to be."

Debbie sighs. "All those lovely plans of joy in such a short time. I was just beginning to suspect. Been so busy and all. Then it was over. The little one had such a short time to be in our hearts."

I don't believe in *meant-to-be's*. Not really. But I would never argue with my sister, who's trying to cope with a loss, and whose eyes are drawing heavy with fatigue. What my experience tells me is that the soul of this lost child will always stay with Debbie. She'll feel sad during times like what would have been the child's birthday, or when the lost one would have started school or graduated. During holidays. It's what women accept as mothers. From the time conception is known to us; we are mothers, and nothing changes it.

"You sleep now. And remember, a whole month. You have your sister for an entire month," are my last words.

I fluff my thin hospital pillow a few times and lie down on my cot. Sleep soon takes me. In this realm, he comes to me. Looks at me. Talks to me. Loves me. Sergei Radkov is with me in this realm.

CHAPTER 26
DOCTOR

I AWAKEN her with my presence in the room.

"What time is it?" she mumbles with one eye open.

Hair tangled, signs of fatigue around her eyes. Crumpled clothes. She is the most incredible vision I've ever seen. I'm a country doctor. I don't get many visions like this one, although her married sister is a beauty as well. "It's late. My watch says about 0600," I whisper because of the sleeping Debbie.

The vision sits up on her cot. "Y'all got any coffee around this place?" asks the sleepy goddess.

"There are machines in the canteen, but it's pretty awful. There's some in the nurse's lounge that's better. I'll get you a cup."

"I'm okay. Will ask the nurse if I can bother them for some," replies the woman of natural beauty.

"I don't mind," I whisper, suspecting she knows I'm Debbie's doctor by my lab coat. "I could use some, too. How do you take it?" Looking at the sleepy beauty, I wonder if I'm whispering or if my voice isn't coming out at all.

"Just a drop of cream," she says.

"So, bougie," I attempt to tease, but sound like an idiot. I tiptoe out to complete my coffee boy task.

She's rinsing her mouth out in the sink when I return. She must not have anything with her. I was told she arrived in the middle of the night. I'll let her know the gift shop downstairs sells toothbrushes.

She creeps out the door to join me, the overqualified coffee boy who hauled two coffee cups down the hallway. I hand her a cup.

"Sorry," she apologizes. "I got here late last night. I must look like Cousin It from *The Addams Family* right now. I only have the capacity to care about two things at the moment: Debbie and *coffee*. Thank you so much for the coffee. I don't want to treat the hospital like a hotel and bug the nurses more than necessary, but I don't even have a toothbrush." She gives a matter-of-fact grin.

I'm enchanted. I can tell she's already brushed most of the tangles from her ankle-length hair. Coffee in hand, she fidgets unconsciously with her mane's remaining superficial tangles with her other hand. I tell her about the gift shop, and ask, "Where did you come from? Do you live around here?"

"Oh no, no, no. Actually, I flew in from Zurich. Otherwise, I would've been here sooner. Arrived last night," she whispers, aware how sounds vibrate in hospitals.

"Wow, you traveled a long way."

"She's my sister," my vision shrugs, taking a sip of the black coffee with a spoon of melted creamer.

I extend my hand. "I'm Dr. Hayden Pugh. I'll bet you are *the* Dr. Selena Frederick."

"She told you, huh? Was it over twenty times?" she smiles.

I chuckle. "No, just nineteen. Actually, I'm familiar with your work. Loved your book."

She gives me, Hayden Pugh, a smile. I hope I don't have a heart attack.

"Thank you. How are Debbie's labs?" Dr. Selena Frederick, rock star, asks.

"Her numbers bumped up a bit. Once stabilized from the transfusion, I gave her iron and erythropoietin to bump up her red blood cells. Also gave her an IV with folate and multivitamin. Hoping she can go home in a few days, but I might need her to come back to complete her iron therapy and possibly the erythropoietin. I might need you to give her subcutaneous erythropoietin at home. We'll see. Depends on her labs."

"Sounds like a good game plan," replies Dr. Frederick.

I must look goofy. Instead of being a professional, I'm giving a pep talk. I'm a halfway handsome doctor about her age, I say to myself. I'm glad I got a haircut yesterday because instead of looking scraggly, my neatly cut dark hair is above my ears. Wonder if the cut brings out my ocean blue eyes. I like that, "ocean blue." Goofy Dr. Hayden Pugh has ocean blue eyes. Maybe she has a thing for big blue eyes. I try to open mine wider.

"You staying here long?" I ask, instantly forgetting my ocean blue eyes.

"I cancelled everything for the next month. I'll take off longer if I need to," she explains.

"That'll be sufficient if your sister improves as expected. I know she's glad you're here," I say, trying to keep the conversation going. She has these ruby red lips and a sophisticated Southern accent. Bewitched. I'm bewitched.

I realize I should get off the topic of Selena, so I transition. "Tell you what: I have other rounds here at the hospital. I'll circle back and check on your sister soon."

"Sounds good," says those deep red lips.

"Anything else I can do for you?" I ask. *Please, I'll do anything. Anything.*

"Does this hospital have a cafeteria? It just occurs to me I haven't eaten since breakfast on the airplane. What was that, a day ago?" Selena reflects as if trying to create her own timeline. Dryly, she says, "I'm not even going to tell you the last time I showered." She rolls her eyes as if to insinuate, *It's getting-ripe-time.*

I smile at her don't-give-a-care attitude. Hope my dimples show. "Yes, downstairs next to the canteen. Don't eat the scrambled eggs. The eggs are half raw and swimming in lard. I can ask a nurse to bring you some soap and a towel to shower in the room," I offer.

"That's okay. I don't have a change of clothes. I'll call Bubba in a little while after he's finished feeding the animals and make a quick run back to the house."

I end our encounter by saying, "Okay, see you in an hour or so."

Ocean blue eyes. *Remember, I have ocean blue eyes,* I cajole myself as I take off down the hall, eager to return.

CHAPTER 27
TROUBLE

I NIX THE SCRAMBLED EGGS, as Dr. Pugh recommended. Congealed yellow globs swimming in lard were beyond yuck! Found boiled eggs, though. My tired, jetlagged ass wants bacon, but all I see is fat with rare stripes of lean meat. The small cafeteria doesn't serve any wheat bread, much less multigrain. Guess I'll settle for white toast. I add a cup of low-fat peach yogurt to my tray and call it breakfast.

Returning to Debbie's room, Dr. Pugh is already there. "Finished a little early this morning. Thankfully, your sister is already awake and asking for you. Would hate to have awakened her earlier."

I nod.

"I filled her in on what the two of us discussed earlier. She's aware that I'm prescribing her bedrest, which is to be well-policed."

"I just lost a baby for Christ's sake. Women lose babies all the time," growls Debbie.

"No, you didn't just 'lose a baby.' You lost a baby and *almost died*," Dr. Pugh retorts. His face is stern, and his brows furrow together. "Late for your pap smear, too. As your doctor, ma'am, I'm going to insist that you schedule one after I see you in my office," he throws in.

I give a slight gasp.

Poor, poor Debbie. Somehow, I haven't processed how bad off my sister was. I, Dr. Selena Frederick, OB/GYN should've known. The thought of the near loss of my sister shocks me. I can say I'm sleep-deprived and fuzzy-headed, but it's no excuse.

"Unless there aren't any unforeseen problems, I'll check on you this evening during my rounds," says Dr. Pugh to his patient.

"I used to like you," says Debbie to her doctor petulantly before giving him a wink.

"I still like you," he says and winks back.

I like Dr. Pugh. He can handle my sister. That takes a lot of talent.

"Can we speak outside?" he asks me.

I'm sure I'm pale. I give a simple reply. "Sure."

"How was breakfast?"

"Not steak and fries."

Dr. Hayden Pugh shows all his straight teeth. Teeth that look like a dentist's dream. Childhood braces, I suspect. "Sorry about in there. I didn't realize you didn't have the whole story."

"I didn't have *any* story. I concentrated on being a sister, not a doctor. Should've known, though. The idea that I could've lost Debbie hit me hard. It just didn't occur to me that I could have actually lost her." I say, giving my poor excuse.

"I see," says Dr. Pugh. "When she came in, her hemoglobin was five. I wasn't sure if I could save her. Your sister scared the hell out of me."

My legs wobble. Dr. Pugh grabs my arm. "You okay?"

"I'm... sorry," I say, flushing. "I didn't ask questions when I got here a few hours ago. Debbie was weak but awake. Just didn't comprehend it was so bad. I'm alright now."

Dr. Pugh releases my arm, though I feel a twinge of reluctance in his grasp.

"Anything else I can do for you for now?" asks the kind doctor.

I'm in a trance. *I almost lost Debbie. Debbie the indomitable.*

"Sure you're okay?" he asks with concern.

"Yes," I whisper.

When I reenter the room and close the door, a singing voice says, "Cute, isn't he?"

"Very cute. Might I remind you you're a married lady?" I hear the strongest laugh since I arrived. "Don't even think about it," I warn my matchmaking sister.

"Who, me? I'm a meek woman. I don't possess the brain cells to think," she quips.

"Never seen you meek in my life. Runs in the family. But you're right about the brain cells. Those needn't do any thinking," I tease back.

Debbie smiles. "Lord, is this what it takes to get my sister here to take a swing at happiness?"

Bubba arrives with Calla lilies tied off with a purple bow in a clear vase. Thank-you brother-in-law for your arrival and getting me off the hook with my sister.

"My favorite," says Debbie. Her smile reaches each ear. "Come here, Big'un. Let me give you a kiss."

"Hold on here, lady. Sorry, babe, but we can't practice baby-making for a while. That doctor has already given me the lowdown on that," chirps Bubba while leaning to kiss his wife.

I blush. "TMI, guys. With that, I'm going to the ranch to shower. I smell worse than your goats."

I pick up my handbag. "I'm going to leave you two lovebirds alone for... whatever. That's the cause of all this trouble, though, isn't it?"

Bubba gives a big boy laugh as I leave the room.

Back at the ranch, my shower feels like it was delivered by God himself. Hot and sticky weather outdoors, even in the mountains, as July is counting down before making its corner turn. "Dog days," I murmur out loud to myself while putting on a shirt.

There is a noise outside. "What's that? A crow?" I pull back the wispy curtain to find a rooster on my windowsill. "Don't crow at me, you feathered beast. I know how to castrate. And, my feathered friend, I know how to fry chicken," I shout at the annoying beast with yellow eyes.

With that, the rooster lets out a loud squawk and flies off the windowsill.

CHAPTER 28
DAY BY DAY

SHE PULLS into the parking lot of the hospital. Who does she happen to find in the parking space next to her? Me! I'm sitting in my practical four-wheel drive RAV4. For the first time in my life, I wish I had a flashy sports car. Ordinary Dr. Hayden Pugh, country doctor, is rifling through papers and notes in a file folder. I sigh. Ordinary.

I jump out of my car when I spy her. I just want to talk to her about everything. And nothing. "Fancy meeting you here," I say, then realize she might think I'm a stalker. An ordinary stalker.

"Yes, seems to be my current stomping grounds," Selena replies.

"I was looking at a patient's file. I think I'm missing something, but I can't discern what it is. I'm thinking about sending the patient to a specialist at Duke. Maybe you can take a peek later if you get the chance? If you don't mind, that is."

"I don't mind at all. Just remember, my patients rarely had the benefits of such things as labs, medicine, and supplements. Mainly they just got bandages, and those were often handmade."

"I admire what you've done, Selena. It must've taken a toll," I say, wondering if I'm being too forward by using her first name.

"Yes," is her simple reply.

"Say, would you still like to get that steak and fries you mentioned?

I know a place close to here. You need to keep up your strength, too. Debbie is going to need you a lot over the coming weeks."

"Thanks, but I ate Debbie's leftover meatloaf and green beans that her girls passed on last night. Besides, although this was an unplanned pregnancy, I believe Debbie is taking it hard. Both she and Bubba had become excited about the baby before the worst happened."

"Understand," I say with ease.

Switching gears, I attempt small talk. "The ranch. That sounds so nice. That's what I love about this area. Everything's so simple. So uncomplicated."

"I can't say about 'uncomplicated,' but life is simpler for sure. Where do you hail from?"

"New York City, if you can believe it." I can't believe that she's asking something about me. Me! *She is being nice*, I scold myself.

"Lost your accent out here in these backwoods," she comments.

God, I love watching her lips move. I feel like a thirteen-year-old Hugh Hefner. "That's what all my Northern friends say," I reply, smiling while loving every second talking to this beautiful and exciting woman. "Where is your home now?"

Selena takes a moment to consider. "Unit number 23A."

"Excuse me?" I question, not comprehending.

"A storage unit. Mountain Storage Unit 23A. That's where I'm storing my things for now. Just don't need a permanent home since I travel so much. Sometimes I'll rent a flat at my current location to get a breather in between destinations. I appreciate those times, but I try to come back here regularly to see my clan before it's time to take off again.

"I'm glad you're here, though," Selena adds.

"Yes, I'm the only OB/GYN doc in the county now," I reply as I try to wrap my mind around Selena's life. "Do you still practice?"

"Not right now. Not since I left Doctors Without Borders. Just speaking engagements and book signings keep me on the move."

"Wow. Think you'll go back into practice when you finish your tour? Maybe planning to come here?" *Say yes. Say you'll be coming back here for good.*

"I can't say. Taking things day by day. My agent is discussing another tour at the end of this one. There's also talk of a movie deal. I'm not sure how involved I'll be with that. Just want to be sure the correct story is told with the right focus, you know? I can't help my patients now, but I do want their story told."

"You're the right one to do that, Selena," I say in a complimentary fashion. Hope I'm not sounding too flirty. Well, maybe I do want to sound a little flirty. Maybe just interested? Yes, that's it. Sound interested in her.

"Thank you," she replies in a gentle voice. "Well, I better get upstairs. Duty calls," says the beautiful woman with an easy smile.

"Yes, it does," I say as a knowing man. I want to fall on my knees and beg her to stay here and just talk to me. I want to beg her not to leave. Yeah. That would go over well.

As Selena makes her way back inside, I call out behind her, "Selena! I'm glad you're here, too." *Why, oh why did I say that?*

Selena looks like she doesn't know what to say. She flashes me a smile.

Oh God, she *does* think I'm a stalker.

The day is wearing on in Debbie's hospital room. I read medical journals, pulling out one after another from a bag I toted to the hospital. The jetlag is killer, but I need to stay awake. I answer emails on my iPhone. I make a few calls outside the door because Debbie is resting. Sleep is a great healer. Sleep, sister, sleep.

With my iPhone out, I peek at a few pictures of Sergei. The press is talking about all the plans President Radkov is making for Russia. Sergei says something, and the media hangs on to every word. The media can't get enough of the man. I understand that. I understand it well. I can't get enough of him either. I plug in my earphones to listen to President Radkov spill out words in his language.

Less than a week has passed since his presidency began. Days, really. The media is already reporting what a hard worker he is showing himself to be. Up early and working until bedtime every night. The new President of United Russia has started the process of evaluating the value of properties owned by the former administration. Some will be put toward public commercial use, while others are being evaluated for their historical worth. The president will keep only one presidential compound, on Lake Baikal. That compound, while for presidential use, doesn't belong to him but to the people of Russia. President Radkov has been clear about that.

"I hear he's quite fond of that presidential retreat. The idea of leaving the compound behind when he leaves office will be one of those things that he'll feel sad about doing, but I'm certain he'll do as duty dictates," says a talking head on YouTube.

"The White Stallion. That's what he's called by the Russian people. The strength and fortitude of the man makes that an appropriate moniker," says another face.

He is. He sure is. God, I wish him well, I'm thinking. I know at some point I'm going to have to release this fantasy. I don't want to. Wish I could go to Russia as soon as Debbie is well. I just want to be in the same country as this man. Just want to be there and feel he is close by. I'll never even see him face to face while I'm there, but I'm drawn to be in his country. Take it day by day, I say. Day by day, I sigh.

Around six p.m., Dr. Pugh shows up for his rounds. In his hand he has a takeout plate with steak, potatoes, and salad. "Sorry, I didn't know how you like things. Got you medium-well. Forgot to request fries instead of the baked potato. Baked will taste better warmed over, anyway. There's a microwave in the lounge."

"Thank you so much." I'm flabbergasted by his concern and kindness. "Let me pay you for this," I quickly offer.

"No way," replies the doctor. "I told you, got to keep your strength up, too. I had lunch at the place I was talking about earlier, so I got you this takeout for dinner."

"I can't thank you enough," I say, hoping he sees my earnest look.

Dr. Hayden Pugh's eyes dance.

"God, I envy her," says an awaking Debbie in a sleepy tone. "Toast *and* broth for lunch. It doesn't get much more gnarly than that."

"Did you say 'envy?'" asks the smiling doctor as he pulls a meal from another takeout from his bag. "This one's for my patient. I'm advancing your diet."

"For me?" Debbie replies. "You are a love."

He is.

Dr. Pugh pulls open Debbie's chart. "Let us see," he says, speaking mainly to me. "Her iron is up to forty. RBC is three point two. Hgb, seven point one. TBIC is 172. Retic count much better. Met pak much improved. I had to replace some electrolytes, but now they're all within normal limits."

"I have no idea what any of that means," replies Debbie. "If my numbers are so great, why am I so God-awful tired? I haven't slept this much since I was a baby."

"That means you have come a long way, my little pretty. Make no mistake, though, you still have a way to go," says Dr. Pugh in a half playful tone. "Debbie, you're just going to have to take it day by day. I'm going to get physical therapy to take you on brief walks starting tomorrow morning. They'll do this four times a day. Take it slow," he warns. "One step at a time. One thing at a time. If you do well, I'll let you take short—and I mean *very* short—walks when you get home. Selena will be the boss. You must take it day by day, inch by inch."

"Yes, one day at a time," I add, knowing my sister will want to fly after her first step home. "I'm an expert at that."

"All I know is that I am going to feel a lot better once I eat that steak," replies Debbie grumpily.

"Well, the steak will help your iron," I say. "I'll warm it for you. I can tell you're dying to eat." Gathering the food loot, I take it to the lounge to warm her portion first in the microwave.

Dr. Pugh follows behind me and makes a fresh pot of coffee. "She's doing well at this stage," he comments.

"That's my assessment as well," I reply to the kind doctor. "Debbie is a tough lady."

We continue to make small talk until I remove Debbie's plate from the microwave. I thank Dr. Pugh again as I go to settle Debbie in for her meal.

Dr. Pugh is gracious with his "happy-to-do-it" words but forgets to pour himself a cup of coffee.

CHAPTER 29
CALL ME HAYDEN

ON HIS EVENING rounds the next day, Dr. Pugh announces he will discharge Debbie to her home the next morning. His explicit instructions are detailed. I'm impressed.

"Dr. Pugh is a handsome man and has a nice build. He's smart, sweet, and funny. Has an adorable personality. Even if he's interested in me, I don't have enough time to explore a relationship with him." I respond to Debbie's nagging as though she's saying I should ask him to the prom or something.

"Oh, he's interested. You would have to be blind, deaf, and dumb not to see that," says my sure-as-hell sister.

The doctor stops in while Debbie receives her outpatient therapy. Just to say "Hi," not to make a marriage proposal as Debbie hopes.

A few days after she is discharged, Dr. Pugh stops by the ranch, stating he was in the neighborhood and thought to check in on his patient. Everyone sees through that, including me. Especially me. Okay, he's interested. So what. Am I supposed to jump the bones of every interested man?

I welcome the doctor with Southern hospitality. Debbie and Bubba are ecstatic over Dr. Pugh's arrival, but mum's the word between them. I'm sure they would love nothing more than to classify me and Dr.

Pugh as an item. But they act coy, which makes me want to pinch them.

The girls love having the good doctor visit, as well. Dr. Pugh finds things to talk about with them. The books they read, their summer fun, the start of the new school year. Of course, they have to show Dr. Pugh their horses. Amiable, he strides along beside them to the barn. As we say in the South, the girls think him to be the "cat's me-ow." He is a fantastic person. I'll say that. After the barn tour, he asks to speak with me outside on the porch.

"Sure, Dr. Pugh. Let me fix us something to drink. It's hot out there." Each with a glass of tea in hand, Dr. Pugh sits in one of the wicker chairs and I sit in the veranda swing facing him.

"Selena, do you think you might call me Hayden?" he asks.

"Yes," I smile. "Damn Southern upbringin'. We're all about using proper titles and showing respect. Everyone over twelve gets called 'sir.' Even then, the ones under twelve get called sir and ma'am too, but only in a stern voice." Total bullshit. I'm not sure why, but I'm trying to be distant without being unkind. Should I be distant?

Hayden laughs. "I understand. My first 'sir' was from an elderly lady. I almost fell out of my chair. I went to check the mirror to see if my hair had turned gray."

I chuckle.

"Selena, do you think... or might I interest you... um, would you like to go out to dinner with me tomorrow?" he asks shyly.

Hayden says the last part so fast that I have to decipher his speech. "I would love to, Hayden, except tomorrow night is a big night for Bubba. He's making his famous barbeque. You should drop by and get a plate."

"Sure they won't mind?"

I guffaw. "Bubba losing a chance to brag? The man is convinced he's a chef extraordinaire these days since Debbie can't do the cooking. Truth is, Debbie's one of these women who, when she makes one of something, she actually makes two and freezes the leftovers. That way, when she's busy with the girls, there's always something to pull out of the freezer for a quick dinner. Bubba's thawing and rewarming but proud all the same," I explain.

"But tomorrow... tomorrow, Bubba is making his special barbeque," I say. "The pig is already on the spit. Bubba plans to wear his special apron that I ordered for him off Amazon."

"Sounds lovely," says Hayden with a fixed ear-to-ear grin.

Should I lead him on?

We continue to talk on the wide veranda porch, with Bubba taking an occasional peek out of the window at us and trying to act nonchalant. Seems he's immediately reporting the goings-on back to Debbie. I know he is. I roll my eyes at the pig-cooking man. It's so obvious that it's embarrassing.

We chat for another half hour before Hayden takes his leave. I walk him to his car.

"I've enjoyed talking with you, Selena. Glad I stopped by."

I respond with a "Me too." I mean it. It was nice to talk to a peer, and a hell of a lot better than staring at a hotel room wall, which seems to be my pastime lately. Maybe, just maybe, I should get to know him. He's a good man. There isn't one reason I shouldn't want him. Want him bad, even. But for whatever reason, he just doesn't flip my ovaries like Sergei Radkov. Do my ovaries need to flip to get to know him?

I don't go inside directly after Hayden leaves but instead sit in the swing. I like Hayden. I do. A sweet guy. Something about him just doesn't inspire romantic feelings toward him, though. Damn, will my obsession with a Russian man who is totally inaccessible to me now cause me to close the door on other prospects? What's going on in my head? Even I think it's insane. Insane.

I consider. Perhaps therein lies the reason I'm so drawn—so damned drawn—to Sergei Radkov. Something about him. Just *something*. Crazy but true. Perhaps I've chosen this inaccessible man to fall madly in love with so that I won't have to make any choices. I can't say. What I do confirm in my mind is that Hayden, wonderful Hayden, doesn't give me the same feelings. Not his fault. Nothing wrong with him. I've made no choices of any kind. Not yet. Hayden has made his. His choice is here. The country doctor has found his place. He has found home. He seems happy here.

What makes an adult choose a home? The place they want to settle into and make a life. A job? Family? A somebody? Whatever their reasons, they choose. Me? My dumb, insane ass wants to be where I was before I turned nineteen and received the worst news I could imagine. That news changed my home and my life. I had a home, and it no longer exists. When am I going to get that through my head? My life is adrift on the same sea where my parents lost theirs. I'm going to be a nomadic spinster if I spend much more time in this life I'm living. Not that I don't love every opportunity to do what I'm doing. It's just that it's so one-dimensional. It's only the one thing and nothing else. I do a lot of good. I know it. It's just that the life I live is so incomplete. Do I have to give it up to do something else? What? Where? When? Don't have those answers, but I'm asking.

I'll be back on tour in a short couple of weeks. I maybe could give up the second tour and come be with Hayden if that's what we both wanted. No. I fear ten years down the road, I'll realize that I copped out and settled with a man I didn't love. Like an awful lot, but don't love. I'm a passionate creature. What then?

Hayden Pugh deserves better than that. He deserves a woman who will love him like the morning sun. I'm sure of that. It's okay if we keep each other company for now. Be good friends. There isn't enough time for us to be more. Even Hayden is wise enough to see that.

Would I regret giving up every other chance in my life for the likes of Sergei Radkov? Perhaps not. Damn Russian. Oh, what a fool I am, even thinking this. Sergei is my ideal man. In time, I hope to find my ideal. That is all. My ideal partner. I want to find a man whose name lights up my world.

What I, Dr. Selena Frederick, need to reconcile in my heart is the need to find home first. It's said that home is where the heart is. Yes, find my heart, and not just in what I do for a living. That's what I need to do. I seem to have lost my heart somewhere along the line. I haven't found home. Not yet. Maybe I need to find my heart first. Hayden is many things. Many good things, but he isn't home. My heart feels it—or more accurately, *doesn't* feel it. Doesn't mean I can't invest in getting to know this special human.

I look at the dusky sky with streaks of pink across the horizon. I smell rain coming across the mountains. I enjoy my family, seeing the girls and how happy they are, love the animals and the ranch. Why couldn't I make these mountains my home?

Truth is, I can't, because that would be living a lie. I would live my life wearing someone else's skin. It would be a good life, and a good skin. Just not mine. I must wear my own skin wherever it takes me. Ideas of what I might do after my tours end bounce in my head. An NGO, maybe. Glad I had this talk with myself.

I love the ranch, but there is one thing I hate about it: that damn rooster. Every morning he crows from my windowsill at daybreak. One of these mornings I'm gonna wring that rooster's neck and cook him for supper.

CHAPTER 30
THE ROOSTER CROWS NO MORE

HAYDEN ACCEPTS my invitation and comes over the next night and everyone has a jolly time. Especially Bubba. Get a few beers in this man and some barbeque, and Bubba the mountain man gains the ability to conquer earth.

Hayden and I talk comfortably with each other. We talk about his patient. I review the patient's chart over predinner drinks. "Seems you get her labs straightened out then she plummets again. Your suspicions are right. There's something more going on, but I'm at a loss as to what. Best guess is probably metabolic. You ran more tests than I could ever think of. Helping her find a higher God is a good idea right about now."

Hayden chuckles at my suggestion. "Yes, I mentioned that to her. The patient is not in favor of making the journey to Durham. Now I can tell the patient that I had another physician review her case and they agree with me. An *eminent* physician," he says with half a joke.

"I'm not eminent in her particular area, though. If I were, I might have some answers. Confounded as you, I'm afraid." I roll the patient's situation over in my head. "I think some patients just dislike it when they perceive they're a can being kicked down the road. So, stress that you infrequently refer patients out but are at a loss and want to take every available opportunity to help her get well, or some such wording. Perhaps she won't feel so much like a tin can. It's just a matter of perception, mind you."

"'Tin can?'"

"Oh. Forgot you're not from the South. Let me see if I can explain this. In the old South, when the population was lower and things were much less developed, we were more a walking sorta people. Kids especially would walk up and down old dirt roads and find a tin can on the side of the road. They kicked the can as far as they could while walking down the road. When they caught up to it, they'd kick it again."

"Ah," says Hayden. "I hear all these little sayings here in the South. I'm going to have to ask for more explanations from you. Might make up some of my own."

We chat about family, friends, childhood days, and school experiences, with sporadic laugher thrown in. We say good night on the porch and Hayden kisses my cheek. I'm glad he doesn't expect more.

We continue to date most nights. Some nights Hayden comes to the ranch, interacts with the family, and spends time on the porch with me.

"Dr. Pugh is like a teenager gone a-courtin'," says Debbie.

Debbie is getting around better every day. The mother of two is tired, but mornings find her in the kitchen cooking breakfast. I always make her take an afternoon nap after our walks. We two sisters help the girls with their homework in the afternoons, since school is now in session. Debbie insists on cooking dinner, but Bubba and I clean the dishes. Debbie can't stand to sit and watch for long, and jumps in to clean the dishes, too.

I sit Debbie down and lay things out. "I'm leaving in ten days. Wondering if I should delay my departure at least a few more weeks?"

"No way!" Debbie exclaims. "Bubba has already hired a lady to come in and do the heavy housework. I like that idea. Never had a housekeeper. Now, sis, I've been good about letting you do most of the work around here. Today, I'm beginning a new program. I'll do one strenuous thing each day and that's all. I'll get more advanced later, but for this week, that's my plan. Today you and I are going for groceries. Promise not to pick anything that weighs over five pounds."

"I don't mind, Debbie. You're my one and only sister. Almost lost you. Can't you let me help a little longer until you're totally better? That'd make me feel better." I beg, "Please, let me help."

"Nope. Are you sure that you're not wanting to stay longer to get better acquainted with Hayden?"

"I'm sure," I answer.

"I thought so," says Debbie. "Selena, you have a destiny. Since you were born, I've known that you're special. More than to your family, you're a gift to the world. I know it's hard on you. I'd like for you to have a home and family like me. But you aren't me, Selena. You need to dance to your own drum, as much as we'll all miss you. I love you too much not to understand that."

Destiny? I hug my sister.

On Saturday, Hayden and I take a horseback ride. We sit on a grassy knoll and breathe in the mountain beauty. "Beautiful here," I admit. "The only thing I hate is the damn rooster who crows at my windowsill every morning. I'm going to google and research if there's a way I can get him to go away."

Hayden laughs. Says he did a chicken impression when he was a youngster. He gets up and demonstrates his strut. I laugh so hard I'm unable to speak. Hayden sits back down next to me as we both laugh at our silliness.

Before I can say what happened, Hayden kisses me. Kisses me on the mouth, sliding in his tongue. Kisses me the way a man does when he means to kiss a woman. I freeze.

"I-I'm sorry. Guess I should've asked permission to do that," stammers Hayden.

"No, Hayden. I just wasn't expecting it, is all."

"Then can I kiss you again?"

"Hayden, you're aware I'm leaving in a week, right?"

"Yes, but that doesn't mean I can't see you when you come back. How long will it be, a few months?"

"Don't know how long. May start another tour after this one. I'll be in Russia for a while. The Russians are big readers and—"

Hayden cuts me off. "Selena, are you going to use a storage unit as an address forever?"

I don't answer immediately, then choose my words carefully. "Hayden, you can't possibly understand this. *I* don't completely understand it, but I'll try to explain it to you."

"I'm listening."

"I haven't had a home since my parents died. Been wandering ever since. I haven't found a home yet. Not a physical home, but one inside me. Not like you. The only thing I know for sure is that it's not here. Not permanently."

Hayden holds my face. "Then come and stay with me until you find your place. Come be with me. Let me share my home with you until you find your own. I'll follow you anywhere. I will wait as long as it takes."

I use a gentle touch to remove his hands from my face. "It can't be like that, Hayden. You can't spend your life waiting for me to show up. More importantly, wondering if I'm happy. The wonderful Dr. Hayden Pugh I have come to admire deserves better than that."

Hayden searches my face for a long time. "I guess the rooster doesn't crow anymore, does it? See, me, Hayden Pugh, New Yorker, has made up his first Southern quip. Guess this *is* my home."

We two ride the horses back to the barn and tend to them in silence. Hayden extends his hand for a shake. "Goodbye, Dr. Selena Frederick."

I don't walk him to his car. We never see each other again.

PART FIVE
THE SHE

CHAPTER 31
SERGEI IS PRESIDENT

I HAVE FEW INDULGENCES. Growing up as an orphan, I understood what nice things were. Those were things owned by other people. During my adulthood, I didn't yearn for any more than necessary. An occasional good vodka, maybe paying a little too much for a nice dinner is as far as adult Sergei splurges. That's the extent of extravagance enjoyed by the orphan-turned-commando, and now president.

I learned to dress well and carry myself with pride and confidence. The ability to dress as a man of means was curriculum during my Spetsnaz and GRU training. The training hadn't all been about being Rambo with hand grenades and secret codes. Though the in-depth training on pretending to be gigolo, among other undercover personas, fit well with my personality. It was fun wearing someone else's skin for a while. Then, as indulgences go, there is this desk in the presidential chamber at the dacha on Lake Baikal.

So much of my exposure as the new leader of Russia to the "fineness" of life relates to things being heavy, gold-gilded, or ornate to the point of gaudiness. Here at this dacha on the shore of the world's oldest and deepest lake, I enjoy my life of simplicity away from the city.

The presidential desk, made of carved mahogany, is a finer thing to

Russia's new president. The desk stands with strength like a yeti on a mountainside. Strong. Indomitable. Its legs carved by man, but its beauty made by God in the wood's grain. In a chamber with many things heavy and gold-gilded to love, I love this desk. 'Tis a good thing that I do. I spend more hours than any human should staring at the desk's top.

I exhale an audible *"thththrp"* with my tongue in the silence of my chambers. Not even halfway through reviewing the military budget perched in a thick bound file on my beloved desk. *Thththrp*. I spend as much time at this sole remaining presidential dacha as time allows. The Lake Baikal presidential retreat remains the only dacha not put up for sale or repurposed after I took my presidential oath. It's more than a resort. It's a haven. If I don't have meetings in Moscow, then I stay here to perform my work. Why not? It's the age of emails and computers.

Lake Baikal is no less than a gift from the heavens to Russians. The Lake Baikal dacha breathes its life among the Buryat people. The lake's waters are not just the deepest and oldest of all lakes in the world; it also wins kudos as the clearest. As far as I'm concerned, the most inspiring natural setting in the world. Just this one spot is what I've preserved on Russian earth as a presidential retreat.

Three long months have passed since the presidential inauguration. National and international opinion polls show me to be a popular president. Whatever that means. Get this: I read in a news article, *His wispy blond hair clothes a brain of sharp intelligence and with his warrior's heart makes him an immediate international superstar. A gentleman's magazine voted President Radkov as Bachelor of the Month*. Who thinks up this shit? I'm not a playboy. Well, not anymore.

When asked about my notoriety, I smile with a straight grin, browed by a damn big Roman nose, and state the title probably means I'm the luckiest man this month.

The Prime Minister resigned promptly after I assumed office. I replaced him with a less partisan woman whom I think will run the office with efficiency and respect. She is the first female prime minister of my nation. When asked if I intend this move to pacify women in Russia, I'm sure my eyes dance as I retort, "One may say it's about time. However, Russia is more fortunate than that. Eliana Tsorkra has proven herself to be a reliable and capable person who the Russian people can depend upon. For that, I say it's about time." Russia's patriarchal nation cheered. Damn glad because I would've been pissed otherwise. My remark wasn't political but the damn truth.

They call me "The White Stallion," and I work like one. I trot from early morning until late at night, every morning, and every night since the inauguration. Never consider taking a day off and eat most meals in my chamber. I'm a self-tyrant who works in flight between Moscow and Lake Baikal. I spend more hours in my chambers than on the hiking trails outside of the dacha chalet.

I love the chalet style of this presidential resort. The main chalet rests on a bluff overlooking the lake. It's my favorite place to take a walk and think of her. She has been away for a while, but back on tour now. Her website hasn't updated her schedule. I hope the woman that I idolize is alright. She has revealed a bit of her thinking about her future. She states she is in the mindset to pursue work at an NGO or perhaps a missionary position somewhere in Africa. It's so like her. Always giving.

The chalet design comprises several bedrooms around the main bedroom chamber. My chamber has everything I need. I yearn for nothing more while in this space. Other than that, *She* never leaves my mind. I suppose soon I'll lose her public presence to Africa and never hear of her again. In the meantime, my mind creates in my chamber. Works there. Cozies there. Eats there. Sleeps there. Imagines the face of Selena Frederick there.

My desk is placed in one corner of the spacious chamber, positioning me close to the massive fireplace. I'm happy for it now that Russia is turning dark and cold. A mirror crafted in the ornate Russian style of gilded gold hangs above the fire. Reflected light from the mirror adds a touch of brightness. As the mirror reflects the light around the room, two skylights provide even more light via an architectural extension. The upper windows of the room, constructed of bulletproof glass, extend halfway up the wall to the ceiling. Very bright in here—when there is light in Russia, that is.

A settee of Victorian-era styling, along with two wide-winged side chairs, provides coziness in front of the crackling fire. What I would give to see a mane of dark hair sitting here. I cherish this coziness and work like an Alaskan miner's mule in front of the mirrored fire, wishing She was sitting beside me. The dacha remains unchanged by its new occupant. I find it perfect. Except for one thing: a mane of dark hair belonging to my She.

Then there is the bed. The bed graces the space against a partial wall across from the fireplace behind the settee. This bed is enormous. I've never seen a bed so huge. It seems to go on for miles. Made of heavy dark mahogany, the monstrosity prides itself with intricate carvings of Russian life. Being a smart-ass, I commented one day that I'm thinking about adding on a parking garage for my car next to the twenty-seventh pillow.

As I walk out of the presidential chambers, there lie waters of a gurgling spa. Warm waters formed by a natural geothermal spring rest smack in the middle of the outer chambers, available as well to visitors or family members close to the president. A dome-shaped glass of sky-blue tint lights the warm space. Tall windows extend from the ceiling to halfway down the twelve-meter walls. The walls meet the floor made of Persian-style tiles. Blues and greens weave designs on the tiles, providing a breathtaking interior. I'm up for a midnight swim in any season. I love to swim, especially in these geothermal waters. Not laps, but wading suffices to relax my stiffened muscles at day's end, then my body collapses at night on the supersized bed. My tired body presents an exhausted mind to bed, transporting me to the realm of slumber as though cradled in angel wings.

I'm mostly a stair-taker, as I seek exercise excuses. Behind the spa, an elevator is available to upper and lower floors from my chamber level. The dacha floor just above the private sleeping chambers is a room with a billiard table and a seating area. As well, the space expands to the exterior. A dining room welcomely seats one hundred people in front of floor-to-ceiling windows. Juxtaposed over a hanging bluff, the space meanders outside to extensive outdoor decking overlooking clear blue Lake Baikal. The impression is as though a person is soaring on the back of an eagle at night, underneath a star canopy, whether inside cuing balls or smoking outside on the deck. I adore it but have never eaten nor cued a ball there.

If one is not so inclined to nature, then an art gallery and a ballroom exist on the uppermost floor of the presidential chalet. I've never used the ballroom, nor have I had time to indulge my art passion in the gallery. Sometime. One day.

The bottom floor houses a state-of-the-art kitchen, as well as housing for Olga. There are other rooms available for visiting overnight staff, in addition to visitor cabins and smaller chalets dotting the dacha grounds. The dining area makes a horseshoe around the kitchen proper. For the benefit of staff meals, tables and booths sport red and white tablecloths that give the area a fifties-era soda shop vibe. A gym and shower lie at opposite ends of the kitchen, as well as the laundry. Sometimes, I eat and work in the kitchen and spend a little time with Olga. And oh, I forgot: Oliver. Let's not forget Oliver, the Russian Blue feline. He owns the place. On rare occasions, I sneak him up to my chamber to rub his ears while I work at the settee. We're orphan pals.

Smoltsky put my security in the hands of Alexei and Vogo, with Alexei assuming the senior role. I don't change it. The duo, along with Ivan, is happy I chose this lake location to secure myself, the man who has developed into the new leader of the world's vastest nation. The location poses security challenges, but nothing the well-trained team can't handle. Their friend and president feels at home in the chalet-style dacha. That is what matters to my security team.

I've left my security in the hands of the men I most trust. Alexei, Vogo, and Ivan, and others who have spent enough time as Spetsnaz agents. They have served their time. Each agent had the choice of whether to join the presidential security team or continue in their current position. Each responded, "I will serve my president at home or on foreign soil." My guys, my pals, my anchors, and my rocks. Although, during mundane times for security, I lend team members out to the military to instruct new recruits.

My predecessor acquired the dacha as a real estate holding. I saved this one resort for presidential use but made sure the dacha's existence is well known to the Russian people, as well as its purpose. Its ownership is squarely in their hands. Hope those that follow in my shoes appreciate it as much as I do.

I have one other luxury. I possess taped interviews and conference talks of Dr. Selena Frederick. My favorite interview is of Selena with Joe Cook. I have missed seeing the charismatic doctor on the international stage while she is away. She is a person with so much to offer the world. Wherever she is, she changes the hearts and minds of people. Dr. Selena Frederick is a World Changer. No doubt about it.

To see her for a few minutes as I drink my vodka at night before bedtime gives me energy overdrive to keep plodding along in my position. She inspires me. Yes, I would be the first to call myself a stalker. What can I say? I'm a fan.

I kneel at night, every night, before the giant bed and pray for her. Prayed when she had a family emergency for her happiness, her health. Those are my most private and my most coveted moments. To talk to God almighty about Selena is an honor. Then with a sigh, I climb into bed and fall face down among a gazillion pillows and dream of Selena's flow of long, dark hair beside me.

CHAPTER 32
RED IS BEAUTIFUL

IT HAD all started in the late spring when the windowsills of Russia were full of floral blooms. Trees leafed in green adorned the buildings and highways of the capital when I took office. A stiff chill is now in the air. If not during the day, the glacial blast makes its presence known during the evening. Summer has closed her doors and opened a new season of Russian coldness. The coldness will spawn its counterpart, darkness, into life as the days shorten to near nothingness. It doesn't seem evil. Not to Russians. Darkness is part of the beauty of our world.

I like to walk, yea, even take a run in the early morning hours while in Red Square long before the hour of the tourists' arrival. When at the Baikal dacha, I do the same even after the lite falling of snowflakes blow in my face from the lake winds.

I still work like a white stallion—or an Alaskan mule, or any damn beast of burden. I push myself and everyone around me. I'm doing the one thing I know how to do: I'm fighting. Still a boy orphan, more than I care to admit. A man soldier. Maybe I am the White Stallion. Damn me to hell, but my people need this. They need someone who fights for them, and I will fight for them until I die. I may've been born to do just that. For sure, at some point, I was chosen. Chosen by the Russian people. Chosen by Smoltsky. Chosen by the Russian houses. Chosen by the Holy Mother Mary herself. Chosen. And I will fight for my God-given place in this world to perform what I've been chosen to do.

I spend as many days at the dacha as possible. Otherwise, if not out of the country on presidential duties, I stay at the Kremlin apartment in Red Square. I haven't as yet stayed in the Presidential Palace. I don't need it. I save my people the money. Arriving at Red Square late this evening in September, I complete my reviews of an environmental study. Still thinking about those evergreens. I'm set to begin the new week, beginning with my early morning exercise routine the next day.

Security expects the president to rotate his physical workouts and jog most early mornings in Red Square. Every morning I first go into Saint Basil's Cathedral, erected by Ivan the Terrible in the sixteenth century, or one of the other nine churches attached to the cathedral to say my morning prayers alone and ask for God's guidance for yet one more day. This pleases the Orthodoxy to no end. Some mornings, I invite clergy of all ranks in the Red Square Cathedrals to join me in prayer for our churches, our nation, and our world. I figure God doesn't mind a few extra voices.

I think what catches the clergy off guard is that sometimes I lead in prayer, while other times the highest-ranking clergy who are present lead. Sometimes it's impromptu. Sometimes a scheduled breakfast. Sometimes I invite clergy from other religious communities in our nation. Jews, Catholics, Buddhist, Islamist, Protestants. I ask the Russian Orthodox to take a back seat and let one of the other clergies lead or participate in the service in a meaningful way. It's hard for them to allow this in the heart of their Red Square home. I know a few clergy want to balk, but I think all understand the advantages of inclusion. Besides, the last time a clergyman balked at me, I quoted *the first shall be last and the last shall be first* scripture. "You can argue with me, but first you need to go argue with Jesus," is what I say to them. No petty problems seen since.

Soon, tourists arrive to see the square, the Kremlin, the cathedrals, the artillery, the State Museum, and Alexander Garden. All unfolding to create the massive mosaic that is the crown jewels of Russian culture. A culture as ancient as time.

Red Square with its red-bricked Kremlin Wall to the west encourages foreigners to think the color entitles the name of the square. Few know that red means beautiful in Russian. By happenstance, the Kremlin Wall is the color "red" in English, but that word doesn't have the same meaning in Russian. Oh, Russia, my native land. How much I love him.

I embrace stolen moments of reflection in the Alexander Garden. On this Monday morning in Moscow, the dew has fallen on flowers of yellow, red, purple, and orange and upon green grass that has turned crunchy, when the night temperature fell below zero. The flowers were chosen by the horticulturist, who maintain the bravery of the floral colors despite their exposure to the frightfully chilly night. Not to worry, though. The flowers will always be in perfect rows, in perfect color, and perfect height, despite the weather. The Kremlin gardeners stay busy with constant botany rotations. Symmetry. Perfection. The beauty of a Russian garden.

After jogging around the perimeter and through various pathways, and around the perimeter again in my solid-gray jogging pants and hooded sweatshirt, I shoot a smile at my breathless security detail wrapped up in their winter coats, scarves, hats, and gloves. I continue downstairs to the gym for my hour workout with the personal trainer, but not before shooting a bit of ribbing at my mentor, friend, and now head protector.

"I can tell you've given up the cigarettes, aye Alexei?"

"You can tell that, Sir?"

"Sir" sounds so unnatural to my ears, coming from Alexei. Now an older man, my Chief of Security was once my mentor and teacher during my military career. Not to mention saved my young behind more times than I care to count. At the present time, I understand I must allow Alexei the pride of speaking to me with the honor of presidential nomenclature such as "Sir." It is a matter of pride for him, and a matter of leadership for the security team.

"Yes, I can tell you have more breath," I giggle at the slumped-over man who now holds his tam in his hands.

Alexei looks up. Not even half a year earlier Alexei would've told me, "Fuck off, Sergei!" Now he peers up meekly at his boss and says, "As you can tell, Sir. As you can tell."

"Remember your waistline, though. That will slow you down too. Come dressed in your warm-ups and running shoes tomorrow. You can change into your day clothes after a shower in the gym. It would be good for the whole detail to come so dressed and ready to run. They don't need to be dressed in their best clothes when I jog. The team can shower afterward while I'm in the gym. Plan a long path, da?"

"As you wish, Sir, da," wheezes out the man with the handheld tam.

I can hear his thoughts: *I love him like a brother, but the man is a fucking machine. He's gonna kill me tomorrow. That is, if I can get out of the bed in the morning after today's effort. Thank God for mothers with liniments that stink to high heavens but soothe your sore muscles.*

I know Alexei is cussing and spitting and calling me every name he can think of. I almost laugh out loud.

I bury a smile and nod as I stretch my legs, arms, shoulders, and torso. Making my hellos to Nikoli, my trainer, I begin my weightlifting routine. What I like best is the shower after the routine, with its three faucet heads and warm ceramic seat where I can sit in a warm mist and allow the pelting water to relieve the soreness in my hunched back. Some muscle soreness is from the workout. The rest is from my military history.

Afterward, I don a robe and slippers before making my way upstairs to my presidential chamber to dress for the day. I spend the early morning hours on a conference call with Smoltsky and several other committee members with the houses of government to discuss election reform. Seems that many long-serving members of the houses are planning on stepping down. Not surprising.

My political basket is loaded with younger house members who spout change and are more aligned with their president. I've assigned many of those members the oversight of a new task force committee to investigate corruption, with the idea that the corrupt be brought to justice. The youthful members embrace this with glee, honored by their new positions and their president's endorsement. These representatives will be the makers of the new Russia and its laws. The result has been many hardliners cutting and running before the wrong stone gets turned over. Smoltsky doesn't like this, but in my mind, I don't work for Smoltsky.

I'm still looking for the puppeteer. Somebody staged a coup. I'm not worried about the hardliners leaving. The puppeteer will never leave. Only death or prison will take them out.

I continue this Monday with the economy, military recommendations, environmental studies, and an afternoon visit by the Iranian president to discuss border issues. We two men like one another. It's a treat to host him. The Iranian president rose to power through his military history, the same as me. As leaders, we don't talk in circles. Our conversational journey is forthright, and though Muslim, the foreign president still indulges in a glass of vodka prior to dinner.

The Iranian president didn't bring his wife, knowing me to be single. I muse to myself that all the leadership wives must hate me for mucking with their socialite wings. Recommendations occur. Names drop. Yes, even a "chance" introduction to a beautiful and intelligent woman of single marital status is placed in the path of the President of United Russia.

I can't say why, but I have no interest in those women. Maybe because they are all alike. I've known, and yes, bedded many women in my time, but this seems to be a matter of boredom in my early forties. *I'm getting to be an old man*, I muse. Still very much a man, but at this point in time, I perceive these women to be more trouble than they are worth.

As remote as she is to me, the only woman I can imagine myself being paired with is the beautiful American woman, Dr. Selena Frederick. I ask Alexei to keep an eye out on her itinerary each day, to see if there is any local footage or website update of her wherever she might be on her current tour. "Between us guys, aye friend Alexei?" It's my one indulgence. I love just looking at her. Call me a stalker if you like. Call me a pitiful stalker if you like, but she is my fantasy woman. She is my She. I wouldn't ever want her to find out through a leak in the grapevine that I've been swept away by her. So, it's just Alexei and me. If Selena Frederick knew about my stalking, it might scare her despite her toughness.

"Da," the chuckling man with a balding head says. "You and every man on the planet, my friend. No shame there. No, no shame. Lucky is the man who gets to hold that beauty in his arms. It's between just us two guys."

After the Iranian president leaves, I'm in my chamber wearing my favorite flannel lounging pants made of Scottish merino wool and my Hard Rock Cafe Moscow tee shirt. Polling over additional environment and oil reserve studies when I hear a faint knock at my door.

"Do you have a moment for a private word, Sir?" Alexei asks.

"For you Alexei, always." I can tell Alexei has something behind his back as the security chief enters. I furrow a questioning brow but wait for what I suspect will be a slight surprise between friends. I'm wrong. It's one hell of a big surprise.

Two empty glasses plunk down on my desktop. A bottle of my favorite Beluga Gold Line vodka follows. Alexei's fingertips, his dark hair gracing hairy knuckle tops, pull two cigars from his breast pocket.

"Guess what I found out today, Sir?" asks the older man as he lights the two imported cigars after pouring two glasses of the smooth clean liquid.

"That you're smoking again?" I grin.

"Making an exception, Sergei," says Alexei in a moment of lesser formality. "It's infrequent that I can bring such good news to an old friend, much less to my Commander in Chief."

"Well damn, man. Let me hear this news," I reply while blowing out smoke, followed by a sip of vodka and a smile.

"She's coming here, Sir."

"She? *The* She? My one and only SHE?"

"Yes. Yes. And YES!" exclaims the backsliding smoker as he gives me a high five.

"When?"

"Can you believe in a mere few weeks? I gave orders to expedite her visa so as not to delay her arrival. She actually forwarded her arrival date and extended her visit to sightsee Russia."

I fall back in my chair. It shouldn't mean one thing to me that Dr. Selena Frederick is coming to my nation. Despite the coup, I'm pushing tourism in my homeland. I've strengthened local police power, especially in the larger cities, who bear the heaviest brunt of tourism. There have been a few kidnappings of foreigners though, especially of high-profile persons in United Russia. You better believe President Sergei Radkov sent Spetsnaz to resolve those. And Spetsnaz did. I've gotten political pushback on the matter. Not being military, the incidents should land in the laps of local and regional police. But my opinion is clear: such actions within the borders of Russia are not mere crime, but terrorism. Superior force is needed to manage terrorism. You better believe I'm asking to have as many Spetsnaz operatives churned out as is feasible, too.

On occasion, I lend staff from my security detail to protect high-profile targets while visiting Russia. I'll do no less for the lady of my dreams. She definitely meets the standard of "high profile." Kidnappings are blocking progress toward safety in my country. Bunch of thugs who aren't Russian, for the most part. They'll not get their hands on Selena Frederick. "I want you to handle her security personally, Alexei. Put Vogo as my lead while you take this assignment."

Alexei lets out a little laugh. "You and Vogo? The team will take bets on who will shoot who first, Sergei."

"I can handle Vogo," I reassure my friend and presidential security chief.

I think for a moment. "Alexei, you know we still have a leak problem, right? It's bad enough that a bunch of thugs think our country is Mad Max's Thunderdome. I understand your concern for me. I'm not fool enough to think I'm safe, but I can handle myself better than a defenseless woman in a foreign land."

"Sergei, I'm your Security Chief. We are in hard times, whether it's thugs, leaks, the economy, or plain old chaos. Although you're my main concern, your concerns are mine. Fact is, keeping Dr. Frederick safe is in our national interest. I work for a wise president." Alexei smiles, then tilts his head a little and asks with a teasing smirk, "Might you want to throw a little soiree to honor the American author as your guest?"

"Are you kidding? She would think me some kind of... *ass*," I reply like a timid man. "Keep her safe is all that I ask. I wouldn't want her to feel that she is being sexually harassed by the President of United Russia while she is here."

"Who said anything about harassment? A little gathering. Or a big gathering. Just enough of an honor so that you might meet her. Surely, with her notoriety, she has met heads of state before?" asks Alexei.

"Maybe," I reply. "For now, I want to be sure she is safe and sound. I can't use my office to pursue an infatuation, Alexei."

"Who said *pursue*?'" replies the stubborn old goat. "What I said was 'honor her.' She has done many honorable things."

"I'm afraid I can't envision myself honoring her. More likely to stammer and spill my drink all over her dress. Then try to help wipe the drink off her dress and tear it. Then faint because I realize I touched her boob in the process," I reply while bobbling my head.

"You describe a hilarious comedy, my friend. Sounds like you either got it really, *really* bad, or you have lost your touch. I can remember suave Sergei taking a few female targets in elevators, in their husband's beds, on beaches, swimming pools—wherever the need to fuck for country might ask you to busy yourself," replies an unamused Alexei.

"I passed that torch. I also think that may be why I'm taken by this American, Alexei... between you and me. She just has that 'something' different. I could never take her for only pleasure's sake, though for any man it *would* be a pleasure."

"Of course, Sergei. No one knows. It's our secret. If the worse our Russian president is guilty of is an infatuation with a remarkably beautiful and intelligent woman, then so be it," comments Alexei, giving in.

I explain myself further. "I think that is what causes me to look at Selena Frederick with so much interest. The women I've known, whether targets or nontargets, have been more about themselves. Yes, they wore perfumes whose memories linger in your nostrils for years. Some put the word 'kink' into sex. Most were as damn beautiful as any man could want. But, at the end of the day, my friend, they were all about themselves. Their needs. Their problems. What they want," I expound with a shrug.

I, President Radkov, as a man, continue to contemplate my feelings as I prop my feet on top of the environmental study. I draw a long toke on my cigar, followed by another swig of vodka. "What attracts me to this lady is the idea that she isn't all about herself. She has given herself to service of others in more combat zones than I have. You should read her book. She wrote more about the service of others than of herself. That is what she chose to share with the world."

I ramble on. "Now she thinks of being a missionary in Africa. Acts as though she has no idea of her head-to-toe beauty. Yet she must be aware. It simply isn't important to her. She's about herself in the sense that she is a healer and servant to others, and that is it. Her whole platform is about service to others, and she spends her life traveling around the world to improve the circumstance of the unfortunate. My God, if you heard about the stuff she did while in service with Doctors Without Borders, it would knock your socks off. And she took little credit for it, other than to say she was there. Damn. She is about as unselfish as they come. I feel proud to care about her as I do."

My dreaming eyes float to the ceiling as Alexi replies, "I've heard that she is as she shows herself to be in public. She is a kind and well-mannered lady but can be feisty if pushed the wrong way."

"Her feistiness is what I don't want to know. That would be my worst nightmare," I say. "She is way too smart not to smell a rat, especially if I set something up just so that I can meet her. I wouldn't want to find myself on the wrong end of her wrath, especially with her in the right."

"Oh Sergei," laughs Alexei. "You've lost your touch if you can't schmooze your way out of a little female feistiness. I had more faith in you than that, my friend."

"Alexei, this is going to sound really, truly, absolutely strange to you. However," I pause to choose my truthful words with care, "I never cared before."

With that, Alexei throws his head back in full belly laughter with a bit of red vodka nose marring his face. "*You*, Sergei? You who have bedded women in the castle five minutes after they shook hands with the Queen?" Alexei continues his hearty laugh.

I stay stone-faced but allow my lips to up turn just ever so slightly, knowing what my longtime friend is saying to be true. "I know it's silly, Alexei. For God's sake, I don't even know this woman. It's possible I finally meet her, and the switch will just turn off. Somehow, I doubt that. She seems so different, is all." Considering the idol of my infatuation, I shrug. "That's why I like her. That is why I find her interesting."

"I can't say that I blame you, friend Sergei," Alexei says, then rebuts in a more serious tone, "Actually, I think a nice woman as lovely as she would be perfect for you."

"Yes, my friend," I say with a wry smile. "But would I be perfect for her?"

Alexei answers, almost with offense, "God Damn it, Sergei! You're the President of Russia. You're the leader of the vastest nation in the world. What more could a woman ask for in a man?"

Only Alexei can speak to the President of United Russia in this way. He has earned the right more times than I can count.

"My friend, those things matter not a damn to her. I like her that way," I say.

Continuing to draw up remembrances with my friend, "So, you see, my friend, I'm quite intimidated by her. I've never been intimidated by a woman before. Most of the women you knew about threw themselves at me, not the other way around, even in the field. Remember? That was always the goal. My game. Knowing them and bedding them gave me access to many things. It revealed secret passageways or how to avoid security in and out during the chase. The bedding was secondary, though pillow talk helped speed things up. But the bedding was secondary."

"Oh, I remember. I had to watch a few times if you recall," inserts the old mentor.

"That you did," I confirm. "Here is the thing though, my friend," I say with firmness as I set down my vodka glass and refill both glasses. "I never used them. They initiated everything and used me or thought they did. Yes, when I bedded them, it helped the mission, but I would've made my target anyway." I shrug. "Those women made it faster and easier, is all."

"That you would've done," agrees Alexei. "And it wasn't only that you had a plan B, C, and D. It was that your plans were always so beautifully integrated. Sergei Radkov always kept all the moving parts within reach of each other, but never intersecting. I always admired that about you."

We're quiet as we remember days of old. Raids we made. Information obtained. Information planted. People we'd been. Clothes and disguises. Making long-range plans for targets while raiding in the meantime. Damn, we were good. Some of those long-range plans included the wives and mistresses of targets from which we took a variety of things.

"Thank you for telling me about her, Alexei," I say, breaking the silence of memories. "But, I think, meeting the beautiful lady won't be in my cards. Even if we happen to find ourselves sleeping in the same city," I say conclusively. And sadly.

"Well, envy me my assignment then," teases Alexei.

"That I do, my friend. That I do."

CHAPTER 33
LOST

I STEP up to the conference podium in Helsinki, Finland. I adjust the microphone and begin to speak.

"Today I've been asked as a physician to speak to this group of single women as though there is a medicine for singleness. I'm not going to speak to you as a physician. Instead, I will speak to you as a single woman. Last night, I scribbled down some words expressing how I feel as a singular human. I think these words apply to men as well. I actually gave this conglomeration of ideas a name: 'Lost.' It goes like this:

"I have been lost. I believe in being found. I believe in the power of silence. I can see the strength of speaking the unspoken.

"I believe in the power of forgiveness. It's a process, but I've forgiven every single trespasser in my life. May they go in peace and find goodness on their journey to a better way of living.

"I believe in being a respecter of every person. I deserve and demand to be respected. I am kind. I am loud. I am soft. I can deal with life as seriously as I can death. I can shout down from a mountaintop.

"I don't need a man who is musclebound, but one who is strong. A strong man who can handle being with a strong woman such as myself. Such a man will think it damned easy to hold such a butterfly in their hands. Never once would it occur to him to quash the butterfly he holds.

"Not so long ago, I approached this idea of mating as simply dating and making friends. I still do, but I think being truthful is better.

"Truth is, most of us are here, meeting in this place, at this time, because love has failed us, or we have failed love. Yet, we want to be loved. It has taken a lot for me to speak out loud and admit that I want to be loved by a partner that I can love back. I applaud each of you for having the bravery to admit the same.

"I have always thought that I passed by the love of my life and the blessing they could bring. I thought I was involved with the wrong man at the wrong time and simply walked past the right one. I thought I went into the wrong door on the wrong corner or crossed the wrong street instead of going straight. And missed them, this lover I was searching for.

"Problem is, although I'm still searching for my mate inside my soul, it wasn't until recently that this bright light turned on in my head. It made me consider something. Is it possible, just perhaps possible, that if I walked past the love of my life yet I'm still searching for them, that they are still searching for me?

"I think approaching each man based on his own merits and letting friendship, laughter, and pleasant conversation unfold is the way to go. 'Loves of your life' are rare. I may not be lucky on my first nor my one hundredth try. That doesn't mean other seekers aren't without merit on our journey. They help us to grow and define what it is that we value in a partner. They make us ready. Dare to imagine the ultimate.

"Recently, I came to realize the awesome capacity I have to love. It came through the idea of children not yet known to me. I have a friend with a daughter who is thirty-five years old. The daughter broke off a ten-year relationship with the man she thought would be the father of her children.

"My friend has two adult children in their thirties but has reason to believe they may not marry or produce grandchildren. Sometimes you simply don't get the things you want most in life.

"My friend's daughter announced her intention within the next year to foster children as a single mom. My friend was very ambivalent about it at first. Not that she had reservations about the biological part of accepting these children. No, she feared such a beautiful, well-educated, awesome woman as her daughter had given up on herself. Had given up way too soon on the possibility of love in her life.

"The daughter said to me, 'I'm not trying to lead by example here, although if that happens then it's okay. What occurs to me, though, is that I've been trusted—and I emphasize *trusted*—to provide love to these tender souls who may have never known love before. Some God, some greater power, some force has trusted me, *me*, to love these children. Hence, this force must believe I have the capacity to do so, or else I wouldn't be trusted to love them.'

"Damn. That's mind-blowing.

"I, too, have an enormous capacity to love others who are not related to me. The love we find may not be the way we've been formatted to think about it in our heads. If I could make one recommendation to you, it would simply be to grow your capacity *for* love. The more you love, the more your capacity to love will grow.

"So, I'm open to love in my life from whatever source, from whatever place it's sent to me. Love of my life, I believe in you. I believe you are out there searching for me, and you'll find me. I have the capacity to love you."

I'm happy my words receive a standing ovation. The press is all over it. Within twenty-four hours, my words are being quoted on dating websites around the world. I'm overjoyed that my heartfelt address served to assuage the loneliness of others.

In the mountains of North Carolina, Hayden Pugh says out loud, "She was just lost. So very lost. I hope one day she's found."

In the apartment of the Russian president, Sergei Radkov drops his glass of vodka.

CHAPTER 34
TO RUSSIA WITH LOVE

I BOARD A PLANE FROM HELSINKI, Finland, to Moscow, Russia. I'm going to the land of Sergei Radkov! And feeling like a groupie at a concert going backstage.

Damn, I thought I would never get here. Unbelievable what it took. I tried to get Jim, my agent, to bump Russia forward on my agenda. Asshole argued for business reasons. Just when I finally strong-arm Jim into agreeing, I find out no one has even applied for my visa. No visa! But didn't I sign the papers? Lost email. Unbelievable. Almost didn't get to come at all.

I let both my agent and my manager have it. I spoke words that Elizabeth Frederick, God love my lost mother, would have been horrified to hear fall from my mouth. I haven't been that upset in a while. I'm usually calm and flexible. Yet this is something I've waited for so long... the land of Sergei. It's hard for both my agent and my manager to understand my persistence since they don't have a clue about my little secret.

I pushed Jim for three months in Russia. He said I didn't even need three *weeks*. I've never yelled at that man before, but right then I did. I put my foot down. Jim wants me to start a tour right after Russia. We compromised on me having two months there, and I demanded he not begin developing my next tour until I've been in Russia for a month, as

I may extend my visa. On the other hand, I agree to interrupt my time in Russia for short-term bookings in Sweden and Norway if necessary. I don't want to.

Finally, I get across to Jim that this request is for me, Selena Frederick, and on my dime. I'm burned out. Fried. I need to come up for air. Air to feed the soul of a better me. Touring a country that includes Siberia may not be everyone's thing, but I'm not "everyone." I let my agent know in no uncertain terms that I won't do another tour without a break, even if it means passing on booking opportunities that may never return. At which point, I would stay in Russia, anyway. So, he didn't have any wiggle room. To boot, I refused to renew my contract with him until I had been in Russia for one month, either. I didn't leave him much choice. Jim suspects he is skating on thin ice with his client, as well he should be.

How does a woman in her thirties grow such a hard nose while going to Russia to find herself? I can't say, but I do know I intend to find out. It's time for me to put my life into perspective. I'll have to see how I feel in one month. I may close this chapter in my book of life and head somewhere like Africa to work. On the other hand, it's phenomenal to have so many opportunities.

I mentally go through my list of long-neglected friends. Sadly, there's no one I have faith can counsel me on my current feelings. Not about Sergei, not about Russia, not about my career. Most would feel disappointed in me. That hurts, but you know what they say about the truth. Oddly enough, I feel my only counsel is Sergei Radkov.

I know that sounds stupid since I don't actually know the guy. It's more about observing him. Learning from him as I watch him stabilize his country from afar. My feelings toward him are still hypersexual, but I'm attempting to convert that energy to using him as a mentor. A mentor who is invisible to me, but a mentor all the same. He's not just changing his country, but how the world at large thinks. A man who challenges others to imagine a solution to problems. A World Changer. I'm so excited that I'm giddy.

The plane arrives on time with no delays at Domodedovo Airport in Moscow. I bid farewell to my cabinmates, who had been kind to ask for my autograph, as I gather my belongings and deplane. I filter through immigration and collect the rest of my bags.

"Hello, my name is Alexei. I'll be your interpreter, your guide, and your driver while you're in Russia," says a short and stocky man holding a sign.

"Well Alexei, it seems to me you and I are going to get acquainted with each other pretty well over the next few months."

"As it seems, Madame," replies Alexei with a dignified smile and takes my heaviest bag, containing mostly books, but he manages the bag and opens the airport door for me, too. Somehow, Alexei arranged a coveted parking space in front of the airport. I'm impressed.

The middle-aged man opens the back door like a gentleman, and I'm seated in the back. He puts my luggage into the Mercedes' boot and settles himself with a buckled car seat. His chubby fingers remove the brown-colored leather tam from his balding head and places it on the leather passenger seat. Alexei puts the car in gear and drives us to the hotel.

I insist on helping to carry my bags from the car to inside the hotel instead of waiting for a bellhop.

"I understand it's the Russian way since Russian men are so gallant," I say to Alexei as we both check into our hotel rooms under the publishing house's name. "Guess it's my darn Southern upbringin', or at least my parents' preaching on self-reliance."

He smiles. "You're right, Ms. Frederick. Russian men are proud of being gallant. We're a patriarchal society, but part of being a man is how you treat women. At least, that is what our mothers teach us."

I smile. "Please call me Selena, Alexei. I enjoy being informal."

"Of course, Selena."

"I know what you mean about mothers. I can hear my mother's voice fussing over my luggage. 'You brought 'em, you carry 'em.' My dad would've said, 'Think those bags are going to carry themselves?' That would be my folks." We continue in a friendly exchange until we're checked in. I like Alexei right away. He reminds me of a short Bubba, the brotherly type. And built like Bubba, too. He may be short, but the man doesn't have an ounce of body fat, even though he's wide as a footfall tight end.

The elevator chime rings, and we enter the elevator with our bundles of luggage.

"So are your mom and dad still living in the southern USA?" asks Alexei.

"No," I reply, focusing to keep sadness from my voice. "Both died in a misfortune at sea when I was nineteen."

"I'm so sorry to hear this, Selena."

"Spasibo," I say, using one of my few Russian words.

Alexei helps me lug my bags into my corner room, leaving his baggage outside the door. I can tell even this muscular man thinks my bags to be heavy.

"Spasibo, Alexei. I know those are a handful."

"Just a few steel rods, eh?" He grins. "More than happy to help, ma'am," he says while removing his tam and giving a courteous bow. "I'll be right next door should you need me. Do you have any plans for this evening's dinner tonight, ma'am?"

I smile, thinking about the common use of "sir and ma'am" as part of what I musingly call my "damn Southern upbringin". I wonder if Alexei has done a little googling on my culture to help me feel more comfortable. Such a sweet man.

"No, Alexei. What I would like is room service, if anything, for dinner. I'm planning to catch up on emails and phone calls this afternoon through the night. I'm getting hungry now, though. Up for some lunch?"

"If you say 'food,' Alexei is ready," says the impish man, beating his chest like Tarzan.

I laugh heartily at the short man with the brown leather tam. It will be nice to have company for lunch. I reconsider his dinner invitation just for the sake of company, but decide I truly need to rest.

"About half an hour, okay?" I ask.

"Perfect," replies Alexei.

"Aw-shucks. Just remembered, I wanted to look in the gift shop for a minute. Want to meet me downstairs?"

Alexei pauses. "You know, your editor considers me your security as well. There have been a handful of foreigner kidnappings recently.

Fortunately, they have all been safely resolved. Still, please make sure I'm close by if you decide to leave."

"I see, and thanks for having my back," I say with a tone of gratitude. "I may go down in the morning to the gym and work out before getting dressed, but I won't leave the hotel."

"That's good," replies Alexei. "Come get me when you get ready to go down."

Aye yie yie. She is going to be a handful. What if I told her most of the kidnappings occurred in hotel elevators? One even happened in a hotel gym. Aye yie yie.

I go to my hotel room and turn on the television and call Sergei.

"What is she like, brother Alexei? WHAT IS SHE LIKE?"

"Well," reflects Alexei. "She said, 'Aw-shucks,' but other than that, not so impressive."

"Alexeeeeei," growls Sergei. "I'm going to strangle you with both hands."

I give a roaring laugh. "At first, I couldn't speak because she is so lovely. Then I couldn't stop talking because she is so lovely."

"Sounds like my idea of her. Don't cut to the front of the line at St. Basil's in the morning. Plan to stand there for a while. I can't believe she'll be so close to me, and I can't even talk to her."

"Sergeeeeei," I growl. "Now it's me who will strangle you with both hands."

"I'll see you tomorrow."

"Siiiirgaaay..."

"You must trust me on this, Alexei. Screen ticket holders closely. No press tomorrow. I'm looking into that lady's eyes tomorrow."

I wonder who is going to kill me first: Sergei or Selena?

CHAPTER 35
THE OLD MAN

SELENA and I enter Red Square at ten a.m. sharp. The entry to Saint Basil's Cathedral queues up immediately. We enter the cathedral queue at ten thirty.

An old man using a cane says, "Now you go ahead, young lady and sir. I'm an old man. I have all the time in the world."

"No, you go ahead," insists Selena.

"That would mean I'd have to pick this old cane up one extra time. No, I'll stay put here." He checks out Selena's ass. *Aye yie yie.*

Selena gives an extra broad smile to the old man with the crystal blue eyes. "Where are you from?" she asks.

"Kansas," replies the old man.

"Ah, the American breadbasket," says Selena.

I say nothing but try hard not to pee my pants from holding in my laughter.

"Yes, least when I'm there. I travel a lot. Especially after the missus passed. Keeps me busy, you know?" states Mr. Geriatric.

"Oh, I understand," replies Selena. "I travel a lot, too."

The old man stares at her smiling mouth. I can only imagine what the old dude is thinking.

"So, where you two from?" asks the old man.

"North Carolina," responds Selena. "This is my tour guide, Alexei. He can tell you about where he's from."

I politely tell the old man my name and where I was born. Now maybe it's the old man's turn to nearly pee his pants in laughter.

The three of us chat amicably in line while waiting for the tour of St. Basil's Cathedral. The old man almost loses it when Selena helps him up the steps. I'm thinking it might be torture for him. It's obvious he's playing his need for aid for all it's worth. "Name's William Johnson," he says, extending a hand. "Friends call me Bill."

"Hi Bill," smiles Selena.

Of course, the old goat stands as if struck dumb and stares at her lips.

As we enter St. Basil's, I begin my tour guide spiel, but I'm interrupted by "Bill." The old man asks, "Young man, is it okay if I listen to what you say about this church? I figured I'd just see it. Didn't realize there was so much to learn. Is that alright? I'll give ya a little tip."

I want to kill him. Speechless for a moment, I look to Selena.

"Of course, you may. Happy to have you joining in," replies the long-haired lady.

Bill takes in Selena as she chats with us, and she takes notes. Notes? Who the hell takes notes? No one except Sergei, when we toured the Statue of Liberty while on assignment in New York City. A smile cracks across my face.

At the end of the tour, Bill thanks us and extends his hand for a shake. I thought Selena would never get her hand back. Bill pulls out some rubles to hand to me. I give him the stink eye and graciously decline.

Bill ambles his way toward the presidential apartments. There is a presidential palace, but Sergei hasn't seen the need to use the grand home. The smaller apartments overlooking Red Square suits him better. Selena and I continue to take in the sights of Red Square. Sights I see often. It occurs to me that I'm a lucky man just for that. Indeed, I am. Just ask the beautiful lady that Sergei and I have shared time with this morning. Or should I say Bill?

Sergei is in his quarters viewing Selena and her tour guide below. In the presidential apartment there is a corridor with half windows overlooking the square. I'm unsurprised the commando in him has pulled out his binoculars to spy closely.

He says through his mouthpiece, "I feel, well, too much like a spy." So, he lays them down. Then he says, "Oh hell," and picks up the binoculars again.

I try not to crack up. Sergei listens in via a transmitter I'm wearing. I'm not sure he even remembers I can hear him. He mumbles things like, "Her voice. God, it's her actual voice. Who wouldn't give up blues music forever just to listen to her voice?"

Hope I'm not expected to respond. The next few hours are spent with Sergei watching and listening to Selena and me while we explore Red Square. Later, I'll tease him about screwing off on the job. The man deserves a few hours to care about what Sergei Radkov cares about every now and again. Outside of his official position, that is. Sergei is as enthralled as a kid going to the movies for the first time.

We stop to rest on a bench in Alexander Garden. The same garden where Sergei enjoys his private strolls and contemplations. Selena is wearing her long hair tied back with a ribbon and pulled across one shoulder as she sits with me on a bench. She looks cute. You know, beautiful, but in a fresh, girl-next-door sort of way. Not a stick of makeup.

I hear Sergei say, "God, I'd love to be that bench."

Selena becomes curious and gets up to stroll over and talk to the gardeners. I interpret as she converses with a female gardener about the flowers that are being planted in the lovely Russian garden.

Selena sits on her knees on the cold ground with the gardener, deep in conversation. The purples, pinks, yellows, and whites of the crocus, hellebores, snowdrops, and winter jasmine fascinate the woman, who is more beautiful than the flowers. Selena asks an extraordinary number of questions with great interest. The gardener smiles and replies to the beautiful lady while working her trowel.

Sergei yells down from his bulletproof window, "Give her a flower. Give her a flower." We both know how exacting the Russian gardeners are. That isn't something that will spontaneously happen. I'm not sure if I should ask the gardener for one, just to see.

Under his breath Sergei swears, "Beautiful lady, one day I'm going to give you so many Russian flowers."

I love it. One day.

Then he says, "That gives me an idea."

Love it better. An idea. I try not to smile, but I do.

Selena continues to enjoy her morning as she explores more of Red Square and its treats. It's difficult for even me to keep all the Russian cathedrals and their churches straight in my mind. This lady already had this information in her notes when she arrived and asks more damn questions than I can answer. Thankfully, an English-speaking monk is in one of the lesser cathedrals and answers her questions while I stand around looking stupid. Once I got past explaining there is a winter cathedral and a summer one contained in each cathedral complex, I was lost.

I explain that since all large Russian cathedrals are incapable of being heated in the winter, there is always a winter one with low ceilings and low doors next to its grand sister cathedral, which is used in the summer.

Thanks be to God that the monk hears Selena say, "So much history. So much beauty. So very... very... *red*. Yes, red," clarifies Selena, more to herself than anyone standing nearby. She speaks out loud, processing the overwhelming Red Square.

With that, the monk's red Russian pride is happy to step in and share his vast knowledge. Whew!

As morning rolls into afternoon, Selena and I agree to enjoy an Asian Fusion restaurant in an underground mall next to the square. Sergei's snooping time is up. Time for him to give up screwing off and change back to being president again. Can't help but feel a little sad for him, seeing as I'll be the one trotting off with the woman who has American-girl-next-door looks.

When Sergei realizes we are leaving, he says, "I'd like to trot a white stallion across Red Square, swoop up Selena, and race off with her on the stallion's back. Damn, the way her rump is attached to her spine. Make her smile once more, Alexei. Once more."

I turn to put a piece of paper in the trash so that the spy can get a look at her face. "Well, did you have a good day here at Red Square?" I ask Selena when I turn around.

Yeah, Sergei gets his smile.

After the tasty meal and a good amount of conversation, we drive back toward the hotel. "Do you need anything?" I ask of Selena.

"Actually, I do. I picked up these post cards at Red Square and I plan to fill them out tonight. It would be nice to get postage stamps so that I can get them in the mail. If there's a post office that is convenient."

"That's no problem. I'll take you on the way to the hotel. There's one nearby."

We arrive at a downtown location and park. "I'm afraid we'll have to walk a little, ma'am. It's difficult at times to park in the city," I inform her like an excellent guide.

"I don't mind," replies Selena. "I would love to go through a few of these shops, but I know how much men hate that."

"Enjoy yourself. I love to watch women shop," I shrug. "It's strange for men, but it seems to make women happy."

"Hmm," sounds Selena. "Are you married, Alexei?"

"No, I've never been married. Only to my job," I smile. My guard is down with her and I'm sure my eyes that have seen much are also speaking much.

I elaborate. "In truth, I was in the military for a while. I never believed I would live long enough to make a husband of myself. My father was in the military, too, and left a widow with a child to raise. I was actually about the same age when I lost my father as when our president became an orphan. Thank God for my mother. But I wanted to honor my father, who was a Russian hero, by going into the military. Didn't want to follow that part of my father's path by leaving behind a widow; I understood all too well the reality of my work. Now, I'm a happy tour guide who looks after his mom."

"I see," says the sweet American lady.

"My mother never remarried. She loved my dad so deeply that to this day she still mourns him. If she's ever seen another man, I'm not aware of it. So, I became the man of the house at an early age. But mainly, I would never want to leave behind a woman to mourn me like that." *Damn, when I start talking to this woman, I can't stop.*

There's something to the look in my eyes that doesn't get past Selena. "I don't know about Russia, but many women in America would consider marrying a man for that earlier comment about shopping alone," Selena smiles.

I blush and give a little relief chuckle, knowing she is trying to get me off my topic of sadness. As we stroll through alternating residential areas, with shops and restaurants in between, the smell of an olio of foods is in the air. We make our way through quaint narrow backstreet lanes.

After a brisk walk, we arrive at the post office. The building is old, with furniture and hardware from the nineteenth century. Selena whispers she's reminded of old western movies that she enjoyed during her childhood in America. The postal vendor even wears a white shirt with cuff stays on his biceps.

"Just like home a century ago," Selena whispers.

I want to tell her about my visits to America. Ah, maybe later. I always have a cousin somewhere.

Selena dares a "Spasibo" to the postal vendor.

He gives her a nod and replies, "Puzhalsta."

I like this lady.

On our way back to the car, Selena says even though she finds Moscow to be a modern city, it has pockets of quaintness, such as the post office. Even with the glacial winters, she finds the roads and highways are a dream compared to what's found along American byways. I love her assessment. Moscow is an ancient city with old parts hiding amid the new.

She hasn't been to the metro yet, but I promise to take her within the next few days. The metro stations are tourist sites in and of themselves. Lenin built "the people's station" with art and statues atop marble floors which hang below painted ceilings. Many people in Russia still revere Lenin for that.

With our chore accomplished, I inquire as to the type of shops Selena is interested in exploring.

"I'm not sure if I'll see anything interesting today, but tomorrow is another matter. After the book signing in the morning, I'm hoping to explore Arabat Street. I'll explore a little there, but I'm hoping to have lunch at the Hard Rock Cafe. Can we do that?"

"Sure."

"I have two young nieces. They would love a Hard Rock Cafe Moscow tee shirt. They're at that age," she explains.

Can't help but to allow a grin to cross my face remembering Sergei's well-worn Hard Rock shirt. Maybe I'll pick up a new one for my president and longtime friend.

"Also, I'd like to get some sort of Russian china for my sister. Something nice that she can use, like a platter. I read which towns in the Golden Ring may be the best place to search for china. Might be better to search for that later. What do you think, Alexei?" she asks.

"You've been doing your research, Dr. Frederick, that is for sure. They have beautiful things in the Golden Ring shops and offer much better prices than Moscow or St. Pete's. They have such things here and on Arabat. These backstreets will be cheaper if you find something you like. Arabat will cost more, but whatever you find will be of high quality."

"Oh, and I would like to buy a matryoshka doll or two... or ten," kids the smiling beauty beside me with huge green eyes. "It seems those are a popular request from home. Thinking I will need yet another suitcase before I'm done."

Oh God, my back.

"Did I pronounce all the syllables in the name of that doll right?"

I'm impressed. "Yes. You pronounced the 'little matron' doll name correctly. It seems the two of us will be doing a lot of shopping together."

"Then you'll see a lot of joy," teases Selena in return. "Please correct me when I misspeak in your language. I thought I could tame a few phrases on the airplane. Boy, was I mistaken."

Selena pops into a few shops but makes no purchases. We return to the car and make our way to our hotel rooms, but not before scheduling a dinner date at the hotel for later in the evening. Selena wants to conserve her energy for the next day. Besides, the Aquamarine Hotel has a wonderful bar and restaurant, not to mention a spa. She says she dreams of a manicure within in a few days, as book signing makes her nails shabby.

I'll be sure to make that happen.

She says she is thankful the women of Moscow are uber-adept at the needs of feminine beauty. How does this woman know so much?

CHAPTER 36
THE METRO

TRUE TO HIS PROMISE, Alexei takes me via metro to the bookstore the next day, here in the land of Sergei Radkov. I'm in as much awe of the metro station as I was at the Kremlin with its palaces and cathedrals. Alexei starts the day early. The powerfully built man is eager to share his knowledge about the art themes in different areas of the metro. Proud of the efficiency and ease of using the metro system, he explains how cars are scheduled to arrive every two minutes or less. However, Alexei brags that because of Russian efficiency, he rarely has to wait over thirty seconds. True to his prediction, when one car leaves the metro station, another arrives.

"Wait until you see how prompt our trains are. You'll see," muses my escort as he looks into my impressed face.

"Can't wait," I say with enthusiasm.

I've seen so much in a short time just in this small area of a city boasting thirteen million persons. Each sight, each smell, each sound of this city's heartbeat makes me want to know more. Feel more. Despite my world travels, I didn't grow up with large city amenities such as mass transportation in eastern North Carolina. Thoughts of Sergei enter my excited brain. I wonder if he prefers the big city of Moscow or rural life. Both? I do.

The most impressive thing about Moscow to me is that it not only exists but exists as the capital of the largest nation in the world. Originally settled for its poverty of place to avoid the Mongol Tartars over eight hundred years prior. The name of the city itself means "poverty of place."

The Moskva River ran through the settlement but wasn't a particularly good fishing spot. The land was poor for farming and slow to develop. The early Muscovites thought the area might provide protection from the treacherous Mongols, since the area appeared too poor to make a raid worthwhile. Now the sprawling city boasts thirteen million people. Wowzer. I contemplate what those early settlers might make of it all now.

I'm deep in thought as the metro car arrives. We squeeze ourselves into the crowded car. After the first stop, we grab seats across from each other. "It is quite busy this time of day," Alexei explains during the hustling stop but says no more. In fact, no one in the metro car speaks, not even if they are traveling together.

I compare the metro ride to being in a North Carolina church. All is silent. Eyes are on the floor as if in prayer. I bow too. Espying glittery gray female Ked tennis shoes, I realize they're the same as those purchased anywhere in America. While some Russians dress better than others, none appear sloppy. To use a New Testament term, none "stinketh." All citizens have a respectful level of cleanliness. I doubt that if their dour mouths ever spoke, they'd never even speak dirty words. Of course, I know better. I've learned a few of those words. Thank you, Alexei, for that information over a nice Crimean wine.

"This is our stop," says Alexei.

We exit the metro car and bustle downstairs to exit with the rest of the crowd. I note art, statues, and gold-gilded ceilings. As an American, I wonder how many Russians notice these things, surrounded by a wealth of art when using "the people's station." I wonder if Sergei Radkov loves art like I do, or at least likes it. I see art as a gift that God gives the artist, so that the artist can offer it to mankind. Love the stuff, but my college days were full of science and labs. Not much curriculum time devoted to the humanities. I'm a novice.

"That was an experience," I say as Alexei and I make our way down the stone steps into the sunlight and the outdoors, bringing forth another area of the capital city. The sunshine on my face is glorious, but the wind off the river blows brisk and frigid. My eyes fill with tears as blasts of wind curl my eyelashes.

"Wow."

"I know," smiles my companion. "Some days it's terrible. Should visit here in the deep winter."

As we traverse the block around a few buildings, the wind loses its terrible power but still threatens.

"What impressed you the most about the metro?" quizzes a curious Alexei.

"I think it was the silence in the car. It wasn't just being around strangers, their minds absorbed in their business—it's like an unspoken rule. A teaching. A culture. Like being taught as a young child to be quiet in church."

"Yes, yes, you are a perceptive person," speaks an excited Alexei as he talks about his culture, his people. "Left over from Soviet times," shrugs the tam wearer. "No one cared to be seen or heard. 'Unnoticed' was the ultimate state of being. You didn't want to become an object of notice, and you certainly didn't want even the most innocent of statements overheard by anybody."

After a few more sidewalk steps, Alexei continues. "I can still remember my mother talking about how she and her family had to be so careful as not to be overheard making the smallest of complaints while living during Kommunalka, the communist period of living in communal apartments. Your co-inhabitants would turn you in to the authorities just to enjoy having more space for a short while. Adults, and at times even children, were dragged off to gulags for reeducation. That is Russia's past." Alexei's voice becomes solemn.

I give my sweet new friend my silence but remain engaged.

"It has been said, 'What Americans take with lawyers, Russians take with blood.' The metro system is an example of that," explains Alexei professorially. "If you consider it, the metro has taken a lot of Russian blood to build, starting with the Bolshevik Revolution."

"That's intense, Alexei, but I'm sure your assessment is correct," I say as my eyes widen like those of a schoolgirl, taking it all in. Shit, I've seen a lot of stuff. Been *in* a lot of stuff. Russian history is as bad as it gets. Russians are a people who have suffered pretty much every sufferance I can imagine. Even after positive changes like President Sergei Radkov, they still suffer much.

"I can still remember my mother telling me to look around before walking out our door onto the sidewalk. Momma would spy up and down the street and avoid going out if there was a police presence," reminisces Alexei.

I can't speak, but my eyes widen as I realize this man lived during those times. Was raised in them. I have a sudden feeling that I'm being watched, followed. I should be ashamed. This history is nothing to be silly about. I shake off my feelings.

"Sometimes, it was just a gut feeling of danger. It began during the old days of communism and got handed down to my generation. If I had children, I'm sure I would teach them the same wariness, or at least awareness," reconciles the short but muscularly sturdy man.

"I see," I add. Letting Alexei's words whirl through my mind to parse their full meaning. Words which Alexei spoke openly.

Alexei goes silent. I have only simple words to offer in return. Another blast of wind scorches our faces as we make our way along the riverfront to the bookstore.

———

I go quiet as I mull over this woman who is so gorgeous that I can barely stand to look at her. I engage in short, painful glances of this incredibly lovely woman. Russia is a nation full of beautiful women. Women who are sexy beyond the word with their spiked heels and cosmetics. What Russia sparsely owns are women of beauty. Can't blame them. The place Russia is, has been, and remains has stolen that from many Russian women. Perhaps it always will. Or perhaps my president will pave a path toward change. He has already started to champion the rights of women and children in our society. Perhaps improvement in opportunities and respect of the female gender in our society will help to strengthen their souls. Such changes because of the leadership of my president. I'm honored to call him Sir. I'm honored to call him my friend.

Men need to change too. To change first if you think about it. We are a patriarchal society. We are still very much a man's nation.

A beautiful woman and a woman of beauty. The ultimate description of Selena. The rarest of her species. Dr. Frederick is more than beautiful and intelligent, I assess. The American is poised, self-assured, and caring of others. Kind. So very kind. Kind toward everyone she meets. Kindness can change the world humanity lives in.

I'm understanding Sergei's infatuation with this woman. Hell, I'm madly in love with her myself. In love with a woman that I reckon, even on my best day, I couldn't have. No, Alexei Plokhy isn't made for Dr. Selena Frederick. But Sergei. Ah, Sergei. Just right. Even after so many years, I've found a better understanding of my friend, boss, and leader of my nation because of his infatuation with this woman. It says a lot about him that he's chosen her. Beyond that understanding, I recognize that, as crazy as it seems, this woman is perfect for Sergei.

CHAPTER 37
WHO'S ZOOMING WHO?

ALEXEI and I enter the bookstore on the windy Moscow riverfront with its trendy shops and eateries. Alexei introduces me to the bookstore owner, Fyodor, who is a slight man with clammy hands and a vigorous handshake. I smile as the man with sweaty palms nervously pumps my hands up and down while exclaiming how honored he is to have his bookstore be the one to premier Dr. Selena Frederick in Russia. He will never forget it. Just never forget it.

Fyodor is a person who takes a moment to get used to. Receiving my hand back, I thank the slight man whose last name I'm sure I can't pronounce, though his first name is easy: Fyodor as in the famous Dostoyevsky. I suppose his name destined him to become a bookstore owner. Russians so love their authors and their books.

"It's very nice to meet you, Fyodor. Can you excuse me a moment while I go to the toilet to freshen up?" I imagine the wind has blown my curls straight, and I must look like I've been riding in a convertible at two hundred miles per hour.

"Sure, sure," Fyodor assures me with his nervous personality. The man not only tells me where the toilets are located upstairs, but he escorts me. The male and female signs over the doors are a dead giveaway, but I give him a smile of gratitude anyway.

When I descend the stairs from the toilet, Fyodor is in a nervous riot about going to lunch. Though nervous, he is also kind and expresses his desire to treat me to an upscale Moscow restaurant. I explain my desire for a plain ole burger at the Hard Rock Cafe. Not a strict matter of wanting American food, I confirm, but a chance to do Arabat Street shopping while scooping up a few Hard Rock Cafe tee shirts. A customer might only buy the tee shirts and not eat at the restaurant, but that seems like cheating.

I get the two men to agree to a Hard Rock luncheon after my book reading and signings. Fyodor and I discuss the passages I earmarked for reading, and he is most pleased.

"Oh, I loved that part. So real, so very real," exclaims the unreal energetic man of slightness. Fyodor takes off almost in a sprint to take care of a "just won't do" issue.

Alexei whispers in my ear, "Wonder where he got that horrible head piece. Looks like he's wearing a dead mouse on top of his head. Perhaps his cat caught it this morning. That thing might include the cat."

I shush him, but Alexei doesn't stop. He seems not to like Fyodor for one reason or another. One man is strong. The other is weak. Both headstrong. Hard to say why there is friction between the two. Maybe because Fyodor is quite effeminate?

"Never got the male baldness shame, though I do cover mine," says Alexei as though it's a matter of pride. "More because my head gets cold."

"Women definitely have their vanity," I say. "In my experience, women from many countries use swear words concerning their varicose veins and stretched skin from pregnancy. I always thought hemorrhoids should be their major complaint, but women are much more torn up about their blue-veined legs and their rolling bikini skin than they are about their inflamed assholes. If a man goes to extremes to hide nature's natural process, then so be it. Let the man have it."

My comments floor Alexei, but he ends up with an eye twinkle when he says, "I agree, but I don't understand why they go to such *ugly* extremes."

I give him my stink eye.

The bookstore opens to the chime of ten o'clock, and Fyodor

unlocks the door to a mass of huddled people. I fight exasperation. Were people there for me, or is there a going-out-of-business sale? Fyodor scrunches in as many people as possible in chairs, and some folks stand. Others sit around on the floor or stand against the wall.

Fyodor whispers to me he will not have enough copies if all these people buy my book, and that includes the ones he put in back for my personal use. To boot, it would take more than the time allotment for me to scribble my name in each one. I nod along as Fyodor describes these issues. I suggest he presale the books. Before I leave Moscow, I'll sign them. I will have my agent do priority shipping.

"Well, I'll stay until you push me out the door or we sell all copies," I assure him. "I had personal time planned for this afternoon, but I'll use it to make as many of your customers and my fans happy as I can."

Looking at Alexei, I ask, "Can you do me a favor?"

"I think you only need to ask."

"There are twenty books in my luggage. I need for you to run back to the hotel and retrieve those books. Here's my room key. The books are in a piece of luggage in the closet. The pink one. Can't miss it."

"What about lunch?" Fyodor breaks in, shifting from one foot to the other.

"We can worry about food when we're done," I say as though I'm in commando mode, but still smile kindly at the overwhelmed man who doesn't handle stress well.

"That will be twenty more books if you can do that, Alexei. If it's easier, you can just roll the suitcase here."

"Selena, will you be okay here alone?" asks my protector.

"I'm sure I will. While you're en route, let's see... it's a little after three a.m. in New York..." I calculate out loud more than converse. "Make a call to my agent." I pull a card from my wallet. "He'll take the call. Have him make a call to my publisher when they open and have more books forwarded to our next bookstore stop, and to here. If we catch them early enough, we have a better chance of the books making it in time.

"Here, take my phone. This is my access code. My agent will think it's me," I instruct.

Alexei nods understanding but asks if I'm not too trusting. "Lady, you have skills to take care of business, but I wonder if you're not the most trusting person in the world." He looks hesitant. "Selena, are you sure it's okay for me to go into your hotel room and rifle through your things?"

I give him an exasperated smile. "The way I see it, Alexei, there's nothing in there of importance to steal. There is nothing in there that I'm ashamed of. These books are too important to care about such things."

He acts as if he doesn't want to let me out of his sight for a second. "As you wish, Selena. Promise me you'll not leave here until I get back. I'll make it back as quickly as possible."

"I promise," I assure him with busy eyes nodding and smiling at the standing-room-only crowd.

Alexei makes a short stroll in front of Fyodor and stands nose to nose in the man's face. "I'll remove your balls with a hanging wire if you let anything happen to this woman."

Un-freaking believable.

Poor Fyodor stands as if he's too frightened to move. I have to nudge him when it's time to make the introduction.

I get the yellow panic signal from Alexei's cell phone while I'm across the street. I bring the car around. Before Alexei reaches the corner, I slam on the brakes with a screech to let him in.

"Waking up the neighborhood, Ivan?" he scolds.

I say nothing. Never do.

Alexei gives me instructions and jumps out across the street from the bookstore. He doesn't want either of us to go into the American's hotel room alone and sift through her personal things. I laugh out loud after Alexei gets out. It's not like we're not ex-Spetsnaz. In the past, we have done such things without a conscience, at least a thousand times before, but under other circumstances.

In the hotel room, I open the suitcase with the books. Work is done. Time to play. I smell her perfume, musty, not floral. Sexy as hell. Note her neatness and order and find her underwear drawer. Um, the lady likes a lacy tomboy style cut thigh high. So very comfortable and sexy. I sniff the crotch. I'm a man who loves the smell of woman.

I keep looking until I find what I really want. Her dirty drawer. I think I will take the red ones. After all, red is beautiful. Matching bra too, but the bra is likely too easily missed, so I'll keep the underwear for later fun. I smell the crotch of her used underwear and inhale the scent of her. Love the smell. I'm fucking aroused.

I spray a light mist of her perfume at the top of her underwear band. Standing at the bottom of her bed, I pull up the covers and top sheet. The bra is spread on top of the sheet to coax my imagination. Licking the crotch of her underwear, I suck it until it is dripping wet. Um, the taste of her. Love the taste of woman. I'm an animal.

Feeling the American in my mind as I tame my animal spirit. The American is beautiful, but to be honest, she's not my type. Yes, I could pleasure her, and she would pleasure me, but she is too smart. She would challenge my bullshit. I envision another vision. Another woman. Irina.

I like two extremes of women. Somewhat inexperienced. Hell, totally inexperienced is even better. Inexperienced women with vanilla ideas of sex. As vanilla as the bean on the vine. Innocent. That is Irina. Yum, vanilla is my favorite flavor. You can add many other flavors to vanilla. That's my specialty.

The other, a dominatrix. Both types have the same issue: control. A dominatrix is afraid of not having control. An innocent fears being controlled and is insecure. There is only a pubic hair of difference.

I enjoy converting women. To what? Well, that is my secret. Let's just say I can bend a staunch vanilla who won't even admit to touching herself, much less letting me watch. Within a couple of days, I'll have her sexing two men. To please me. Please me by seeing her pleasured so many ways and in so many areas of her body's real estate. Begin by gaining their trust, my friend. It all starts with trust, whether or not they actually should trust me.

Having the manhood that I do doesn't hurt. It can make a dominatrix beg for me on our first time out. Yes, I make her say please. Put her whip down and beg at my feet.

When I finish, I spread my seed across the bottom of her bed, then return the covers. Tonight, the American will sleep with a part of me in bed with her. I smile. Satisfied.

A man laughs at the pink bag as I pull into the elevator. My fist breaks open his Adam's apple. The elevator chimes, and I exit with the man unable to breathe on the floor. I smile. Satisfied.

I watch across the street as Selena begins her reading at ten thirty, starting with her thanks and acknowledgements to the crowds on both the first and second floors of the bookstore. The American especially thanks them for coming out in such frigid weather. At least to her it seems so as she hails from a warm climate. Selena tells the crowd who she is, as if they didn't know, what her experience and background has been, and what prompted her to write her book.

From there, she opens her book and reads passages about people in war-torn nations, people who are hungry and without food, people caught in natural disasters amid mother nature's sideways blitz, and people traumatized by human depravity, including rape. Many attendees have tears in their eyes. I listen through a transmitter I left behind near her dais. At the end, attendees ask many questions about her work, which obviously kindles a fire in Selena's heart. Many comment on the hardships of Russia in their past histories and Selena nods with understanding, using the warm glow of enlightened light that her audience has lit. Selena simply hugs a few. This lady is something special.

There are many concerns about human dignity and the crowd has questions about everything from healthcare to immigration. At last, Fyodor, with his antsy impatience, speaks to the crowd and says Selena's book will be for sale at the table on the other side of the cash register and Selena will be seated at a desk beyond that. As well, if a person already has a personal copy in hand that they want to have signed, to please step over to the other side of the room so that he can give them a note to show the book is not an unpaid copy.

Everyone complies, although folks continue to walk up to thank Selena for coming as she attempts to make her way through the crowd to her desk. She never stops smiling. Never stops listening. Never stops.

Russian attendees even tell her they are praying for Americans because they fear America is headed toward blood in its streets, just as Russia has known. The compassionate Russians feel the political signs are there. Selena hugs them as she thanks them for their concerns. Behold the heart of my Russian people.

Ivan shows up, and all but throws the pink suitcase from the Mercedes. Screeches off before I can get the door shut. What a damaged piece of human flesh, that one.

I get a few strange stares pulling Selena's pink suitcase, but what do I care? Just glad to get back inside the bookstore. Gonna have a talk with Cousin Ivan, though.

Selena writes requested notes, signs, smiles, answers questions, and listens to stories. Within minutes, she is no longer American or any other culture. She is Russian. The crowd adopts her as one of their own.

Of course, who should be there with a film crew but our old friend, Joe Cook? Never seems to miss a moment to get her on film. Selena blows him a kiss. Joe kisses the air back.

My return gives plenty of time for the twenty books to be scooped up by customers. All books sell. The clock strikes three o'clock before the last book is penned. Fyodor wonders if Selena can return for another reading before she leaves Moscow.

"I'm not sure, Fyodor, but it may be possible. If not before I leave Moscow, then maybe before I leave Russia. With this kind of response, I may see if I can extend my visa, if needed. We'll see. I've sandwiched in a lot of pleasure with work, so maybe I can have my arm twisted to stay on a little later. My publisher wants to extend my book tour into more yunvisited Baltic cities, and hence is motivated for me to do signings there. That has not happened yet, as publishing hasn't been able to keep up with demand in other places."

"I can see that, Selena," replies Fyodor. "When an author can't keep books for her personal use, I'd say the demand is strong. You must strike while the fire is hot."

"So true," replies a tired Selena whose hands must ache. "How about that food we discussed? I think I'm so there."

Fyodor shakes his head with regret that he can't go at this late hour but would like a raincheck for another time. "Just can't do it. Just can't possibly. Sorry, just can't. Just can't."

"Well then, I guess it's just me and my pal Alexei," concludes Selena.

I grin from tam edge to tam edge.

Selena says goodbye to Fyodor and the staff at the bookstore. We depart. Instead of walking back to the metro, I call an Uber, which arrives within a few minutes. Never in a million years would Selena guess the driver is Ivan reinvented. The wind has died down since the early morning, but the temperature has turned colder. Brrrr.

I ask the Uber driver to take us to Arabat Street. We stroll down Arabat Street while peeking into a few windows in hopes of spotting treasure. Selena seems to find more interest in the musicians who are playing along the closed street. With her arm in mine, we stroll into a few shops. I feel ten feet tall with this beautiful lady on my arm.

I crinkle my nose if I think the price is too high and that she might do better elsewhere. She invests in a few postcards, but other than that, Selena keeps her credit card and cash in her pocket, although the temptations are many. My crinkled nose keeps her thrifty. She thanks me for looking after her.

We eat inside the Hard Rock Cafe as Selena isn't accustomed to the Russian cold. The smell of cooking burgers and ribs with fresh sides makes Selena's stomach growl out loud. She grabs her abdomen as both of us let out a sophomoric chuckle.

Talk is amicable. About our homes, our childhoods, our family, and lives while slurping beer and dipping fries in catsup as though we're high school mates. Afterward, we stroll through more shops and stop to listen to street musicians from time to time. I can't remember the last time I had more fun with another human being. Ever the Russian gentleman, I grab the loot bags as Selena completes her shopping. As a Russian man, I won't even allow her to carry her newly bought postcards. I tuck them in with the bag containing White Stallion tee shirts.

She couldn't resist the tee shirts representing Sergei with the word "imagine" in Russian.

We arrive back at the hotel in good spirits but feeling the fullness of our earlier meal. We agree a light dinner with a drink or two would be a fitting end to the day. Selena takes off to the gym to work out, and I bring in another operative to monitor her while she practices martial arts katas in the gym. I don't want her to feel overly spied upon.

I call Sergei and send his Selena feed from my cell phone. "She had one hell of a day," I tell him. "I'm worn out, and where is she? At the gym, working out. A real hellfire, that one, but I must tell you, this is the best assignment I've ever had."

Sergei laughs. "I know about her success today. Joe Cook sent me his film. Joe thinks she is a World Changer and doesn't know it. At any rate, I'm happy for her success today."

"Well, he was right about you, Commander."

"You know, I once called you that, friend Alexei. Commander."

"The world is a changeable place, my friend."

"That it is. Tell me about the rest of her day."

I tell Sergei about the Hard Rock Cafe and the fact that they now have matching tee shirts, as well as the white stallion ones. I tell Sergei about the music Selena listened to in the streets of Arabat as well as the shopping. "She loves the blues. Shook her hips a little."

"Oh, heart of my heart. You didn't touch her shaking hips, did you Alexei?" asks my teasing president.

"We just had fun. Selena is like being with a best friend, but in a feminine way. You know, a fun that only a charming woman can bring."

"You're not falling in love with my woman, are you friend Alexei?"

I guffaw. "*Your* woman? Is she, now?"

"No comment," comes Sergei's rapid reply.

"I'm in love with her, Sergei. Everyone who meets her is in love with her. I can't help it."

"Neither can I. Neither can I," comes my commander's subdued response.

CHAPTER 38
HI-HO! OFF TO THE ORPHANGE WE GO

WE EAT HARDILY at the hotel's breakfast bar to prepare for the rigors of the day. Dinner had been a late salad with friendly conversation the night before. Learned Alexei is an only child, discussed his father being a career military man, same as Alexei in his earlier life. Sadly, his father was killed in action in Afghanistan in the early part of the Russian invasion when Alexei was young. These few pieces of information connect my Russian guide more fully by joining his corners to his middle.

"Always been just me and Mom since Dad died. Mom worked in the secretarial pool at the Federal Assembly until retirement," says Alexei.

"I lost my parents when I was nineteen. Knowing you lost your dad so young makes me appreciate having mine as long as I did. I'm fortunate to have a doting sister, though. She and her family are ranchers in the mountains of North Carolina."

"I never really left home. Although, I might not see my mother for more than a year at a time," explains Alexei. "I traveled so much in my early years that I didn't need another address. I know that is hard to understand, but that was my life then."

"Oh, I understand. That's my life now." I feel I can be confidential with Alexei, so I ask him, "Alexei, did you ever regret it? Traveling so much that you never had a home of your own?"

"I didn't. I have a home with my mother, and she came from a large family, so we have a lot of close relatives. Stay with her now 'cause I don't want to leave her alone," Alexei shrugs while ingesting his porridge.

"I see," I say. Inside, I tell myself, the difference is that he has a home. Still.

Then sweet Alexei says something to me that's so revealing. So affirming of my grief. So everything.

"You know, Selena," Alexei says while rolling his big brown eyes up at me while holding a piece of toast in his hands. "Our situations are not the same. I was very young, only eight years old, when I lost my dad. The same age our president was when he lost his mom. Truth is, I can barely remember my father's face. He was gone so long in between home stays that my young mind almost lost the memory of his face when he died. The piece of my father that I carry with me most is his shoes."

I can feel my eyes widen, knowing Alexei isn't done yet, and he is about to rock me in a direction I've never known. He takes a sip of orange juice and a bite of toast.

After swallowing, he says, "His 'hero shoes.' Truth is, he was just a man. But, in my mother's eyes, he was the greatest man that ever lived. I had her to console me. Another truth is, I think I consoled her more. She loved me and took care of me. Never doubt that. But I think I consoled her more. Gave her company many nights when I thought her yearning for my father would kill her. Me, just a kid. Carrying my father's shoes at my side, knowing one day I would have to step all the way into them."

Alexei pauses as though he's considering what to say next. I stare at his face, trying to absorb his words. I'm not sure how long I left my fingertips on the rim of my coffee cup.

Alexei removes his eyes from his point of reference and looks into my soul. "You see, Selena, the timing of your parent's demise was very unfortunate. Your parents were gone, your sister was out of the house.

Your friends leaving college upon graduation. You had no one to console you. You had no one to console. You were left carrying *two* pairs of shoes to step into. You were ahead of your time in intelligence, but still only nineteen years old emotionally. Everything you have become, everything you are, your brand upon this earth stemming from complete and utter goodness, extends from the two pairs of shoes that you carry inside. You're still trying to figure out how to make your feet fit in them."

He breathes in deep and gives me the most loving look I've ever known. "Selena, I don't think you are grieving over finding a home, as much as you're grieving over filling two pairs of shoes that will never completely fit."

I stare at him. Maybe glare, I'm not sure. I let one teardrop fall. Just one. The only one that I couldn't hold back, although I want to cry for a year. The teardrop plops into my coffee cup. I use the cloth napkin on my lap to dry my eyes.

"Thank you, Alexei," I mutter. It was the only thing left to say. I can find no more words to utter. I wish I had one, just one, to console him, but I don't.

———

After breakfast, I drive us out of Moscow to our overnight stay in Novgorod The Great, not to be mistaken for Novgorod Volynski in Ukraine. Tomorrow, the orphanage visit will take place. It takes six to seven hours to drive from Moscow to Novgorod. I talk as much as possible.

Selena is so brave. I know our breakfast talk rattled her. I talk to uncover any blanket of silence. Selena is too brave for that. So, I determine we'll talk as two good friends about everything and nothing.

Talk about my love for the area of Russia we are traveling. Novgorod was one of the ancient capitals of Russia and built around the ninth century. The city always had its own patriarch but remained a capital in past centuries.

A state-of-the-art library was built in early Novgorod and filled with old documents of Slavic mythology. It also acted as a navigation capital and economic center. Peter the Great had derived much of his navigational knowledge from the Novgorod library. There were works placed in the library from the likes of Galileo and da Vinci. Unfortunately, those works were burned by Ivan the Terrible. Ivan thought Novgorod to be too rich and too educated. I shake my head at the smallness of men.

"Tyrants," I say. "Russia has known one after the other. You can understand why Russians are so excited about President Sergei Radkov. Change, finally, a change for our homeland."

"Oh, that I do," she answers. "No country deserves good leadership more."

"I can't wait to show you this unique Russian city on our journey to the orphanage. We have an overnight stay planned there. I wish I had scheduled us more time."

Continue to talk about the great city as though I'm a college professor as we drive along the roads of Russia, as though we're high school pals going to the mall. Yes, wish I had scheduled more time in Novgorod.

"The drive has a lovely view of the Volkhov River and its outflow into Lake Ilmen, forming the most breathtaking river basin in the land around Novgorod Veliky. At least in my opinion. This is the place of dreams in my mind. This place, something about it... you know."

She smiles. "I do. I know exactly what you mean. I understand why you love it here."

"Along this road, I dream of retirement in this river basin with my fishing line in the water. The best in all of Russia, indeed all of Europe," I reflect. "One day, I'll make here my home. One day."

Selena squeals as she spies the cutest little boy in overalls on the riverbank. The boy is with an older man who looks to be perhaps his grandfather. The duo is fishing with simple fishing poles. Selena says the scene reminds her of the old days of her childhood home. My smile is enormous as my eyes adore my own dream of home.

"I love it," she says to no one in particular.

I understand.

I show her as much of the old city of Novgorod as I can with our limited time. Selena looks about in awe at the ancient city. Absolute awe. I love it! Love sharing this with her.

"Oh, to leave Moscow and make such a place my home," I say as we venture through the streets. "But for now, lovely lady, I'm in your service. And it's the greatest of service."

She guffaws. "I'm just glad you're here now showing me one of the most amazing spots on the planet."

She gives me her signature smile as she prepares to say something important. "Not sure how practical it would be for you, but if you knew what type of place you would like here, maybe you can invest in a holiday home for now? Bring your mom here. Show her what you're doing. Bet it would make her happy to see you enjoy it."

My gait slows. "You know, Selena, that is a tremendous idea. Always thought of it as something for the future. Down the road, you know? Why not start today?"

I shrug, but my face splits wide open. I feel as though I'm a kid at an amusement park for the first time.

"Thank you, Selena, thank you. I would love nothing more than to share such a place with Mom."

The next morning, we're en route to the orphanage which once was packed with four thousand orphans. Only about five hundred residents litter the playground now in the eight-to-eighteen-year-old range. As well, a small nursery for babes up to twelve-months-old. Mainly infants from the region stay here until they can be placed elsewhere.

The drop in orphanage residents isn't because of a drop in demand but because of an accident long ago that killed ten children, and an unborn child, after a staircase collapsed in one of the main buildings. Only then were several of the buildings deemed unsuitable for habitation or use. What remained would have to do in housing those infants. Housing, cafeteria, nursery, and school for the older children were crammed into the two remaining buildings.

The orphanage eagerly allowed Selena's visit because she brought gifts. Without charity from Russians or benevolent outsiders, the quality of life for many of these orphans had at times been beyond horrid. Some orphanages don't have any instruments of play for the children. No play gyms. No balls. No reading books. At best, a field where children can run and play according to the whims of their own imagination is the single luxury afforded by many of its kind. With approximately 750,000 citizens in the orphanage system, Russia can barely afford to feed these children, much less provide luxuries.

After the fall of the Soviet Union, many Russians turned to drugs and alcohol. Russia was not only a nation of poverty, but a nation in chaos circa the time of the fall. No loaves of bread graced the shelves of any market. Many government employees weren't paid for nearly a year. There was no food. But damned if Russia didn't have vodka. Vodka to a Russian is like running water to a civilized nation. You can always find a vodka fountain somewhere in Russia. Russian blood flows as vodka. Who needs sticky things like serum and plasma in your blood when you can have vodka? Aye? Da.

As the disease of alcoholism spread, so did the increase of children with fetal alcohol syndrome and Down's syndrome in such facilities. Mental retardation is considered a condition for which a person should be tabooed from society according to Russian customs. Imperfect. Few parents opt to keep such children, but those who do usually end up handing them over to the state. No public or private resources exist to assist those parents who might desire to keep their imperfect children. Lock them away. Keep imperfect Russians from view. That has been the Russian way, and still is to date. Just like the former gulags of the Soviet era.

Lock them away. Lock away anyone who doesn't agree with communism. Lock away anyone with a noticeable disorder, especially a brain disorder. Bring those educated and smart people off their high horses and throw them in a gulag to teach them better. Soviet Russia considered intelligence a disorder as much as it was considered a threat.

So, they locked them away. By the millions. And many millions died. Millions died while being taught to "think better." As I explain all of this to Selena, she shudders. She becomes quiet while chewing on this dark part of Russian history as we drive the highways outside of Novgorod. Orphanages and gulags. If that doesn't make a human shudder, nothing will.

"Wonder if the new president will want to make life better for orphans and other imperfect Russian humans," Selena questions out loud while gazing out the window at much better scenery than we are about to see.

I must find a way to tell her. Tell her more. Especially about Sergei.

Children are sentenced to orphanages for all sorts of reasons: parental abandonment, parental abuse, stark poverty, and an inability to feed and care for the children. Social workers strive to find relatives to care for them. But there is no foster care system, so social workers find orphan placement difficult. Most relatives are struggling with their own families. Hence another reason Russian adoption is so low. The innate instinct to care for one's own takes precedent over one's charity toward extended family. It's not cultural. Russian people are loving human beings despite their recent dark history. It's a matter of means. I dribble these facts to Selena as I drive, and I can tell she's absorbing every word of it.

I consider these things as well while we bump along back roads not quite so well paved in silence. My heart is with Sergei and Ivan, who have not only survived this system but thrived despite it. Although, without the help of that mysterious benefactor, whom I wonder about as much as Sergei, it's not so likely Sergei would've been as successful. Those are the odds. Only about ten percent of the orphan population doesn't die young or end up in jail.

If you think about it, Ivan wouldn't have thrived as well without Sergei. He wouldn't have had Sergei to guide and lead him. I guess it's a lesson on how humanity is connected and can help each other.

The benefactor arranged for Sergei to be sent to a St. Petersburg English-speaking school in the autumn after his arrival at the orphanage. As a boy, he had to return to the orphanage during school breaks but otherwise spent his time in school, thereby avoiding the human erosion that occurs from the basic incarceration the state-operated orphanage system utilizes. Sergei's inborn leadership helped him not only get through the experience but also instilled skills that brought him to the place he's in at present. The skill to love something greater than himself. His country. His fellow orphans. The skill to be more than one person. A diversified human who survived a savage orphan land and the human who learned the language of business and civility in another. The skill to fight like hell, and more importantly, to get others to fight with him.

He was damned lucky, but there was also something innately strong about that young man who was once under my charge. Recognized it immediately. Sergei tapped into that "something" and let it guide him. I'm glad because I dearly love the man. Always have. From the time he walked into my lineup, still a smart-ass youth. I worked my ass off to develop the youthful Sergei to his fullest potential, with his quick wit and damned sharp intelligence. He was a once-in-a-lifetime recruit. I never spent one second with him where it wasn't my honor to be in his presence. It was like a little brother had walked through my door who was superior to me, yet it was my job to develop him into a man, a soldier, a commando, and a commander. Yes, I damn well love the man.

One night around a campfire in Syria, Sergei and Ivan shared a little of their orphanage past with me over warm beer and a starry night. Well, Sergei did. Ivan just nodded. Guess this visiting the orphan trip has me remembering things I wish I didn't know.

Well, here it is. When he first arrived at the orphanage, Sergei took brutal and bloody royal ass-whippings from the older savages. Ivan too, but he wasn't fresh meat like Sergei. An eight-year-old kid who had just lost his mom. Fuck me, this is the truth.

What he noticed was that other kids his age were taking beatings, too. Beatings were a daily thing for the lesser and the weak. Sergei got tired of it, which makes me smile—that's the man I know. A man who doesn't just tire of problems but figures out how to take care of them. When the savages learned Sergei had a sponsor, the jealous ones really laid the beatings on him. Sergei realized he wouldn't survive alone. He would die before he made it to his "fancy-pants school." Ivan nodded, but never spoke his story. Almost forgot Quiet Ivan was there.

Listen to what this kid did. One night, Sergei banded together with other kids his age and younger. The boy leader convinced the younger orphans they should form a gang. They should stand together. Alone, they would each be beaten. Together, the assholes couldn't inflict as much damage if they had to fight the whole group. If one of the gang members got attacked while alone, the group would pick off the attackers one by one and get their revenge. This was Sergei's early coordination of covert operations. I smile. My God, the covert memories we share. Sorry, I digress.

Anyhow, while away at the English school, he picked another kid to take his place as leader, one whom he thought to be the strongest of the group. Name of Ivan Worliski, now known as "Quiet Ivan," or "Ivan the Silent." Sergei had no way of knowing that his choice to leave Ivan in charge of the kiddie brigade would haunt both of them for the rest of their lives. I knew how haunted he was, long before Sergei did. It's one reason I worked so hard to develop his strength as a man. Ivan, well, he was much harder to read. Still is.

After Ivan accidentally killed an older kid who had attacked him, no one crossed Ivan, or so the story goes. Prior to becoming a man and soldier, Ivan was a vicious kid who would just as soon split an enemy kid apart as look at him. Although this certain incident was deemed an accident in self-defense, Ivan committed his first killing in the orphanage. Ten years old. No one dared fuck with Ivan Worliski nor anyone under the silently fearless boy's protection. The beatings stopped. I was glad to hear that as the campfire flames crackled under the moonlit Syrian desert, but then I understood. Understood why Ivan was a man who would just as soon kill as not. Pitied the boy. Feared the man. But he was a true friend to Sergei, and still is. I think Sergei is his only family.

Ivan didn't have what Sergei had. Just didn't. Sergei has a warrior's heart and natural leadership. Ivan is a silent warrior. A silent warrior with no heart, but who loves Sergei more than his own life. Would die for him without a flinch. I know. I've seen it. Sergei and the other ragtag orphans were Ivan's family. Boy Sergei gave that to Ivan. Sergei gave Ivan a sense of family in that orphanage. Ivan is fiercely loyal to his family, as a wolf is to its pack. Back then, as a soldier, Ivan's family was his commando group.

Of course, I can share none of this with Selena. When I drive up to the front of the orphanage, I've almost forgotten the most beautiful woman in the world is in the car with me. I was lost in memories. So many memories of Sergei, Ivan, and Vogo, little pissant. Oh, stories of Vogo will have to wait because we are here. Here at this decrepit place.

The orphanage name is carved in stone but now hardly readable after years of wear from the Russian winters. Selena jumps as though her heart flew into her throat. A look of horror crosses her face as she takes in the view of the fenced institution. "It's a warehouse," she whispers under her breath. "May God bless these children. It's a warehouse. Forgive me, Elizabeth Frederick, but this is a fucking warehouse."

I know who Elizabeth Frederick is, as well as Selena's whole biography. Feel bad about asking her about her parents in the elevator when I first met her. I knew but was trying to act naive. I was an ass.

Who could find words after seeing the horror exposed to these children? I'm silent in the driver's seat while giving Selena a moment. The American lady caring so much for the children of Russia moves my heart. So, when my eyes begin to burn, I wipe them as though resolving an itch to hide a tear forming in the corner.

"I'm so glad I drug those books all the way from America to Europe, then back to America, then back to Europe, Scandinavia, then finally here," says Selena. "Alexei, in my life I've seen much… but I need a moment to process this emotionally."

"You know, I've forgotten to tell you about the library here, which was given the name *The Enlightenment*", I begin, trying to make things as upbeat as possible. "Before he was president, none other than Sergei Radkov started the library here. He was once a resident here. President Radkov has always involved himself as an adult, giving charity to the orphanage. He never forgets his roots. Remembers them every holiday."

"Sergei Radkov?" asks Selena with interest as her back straightens her slumping posture. "This is where he was an orphan? Sergei?"

"Yes, this is it," I assure her. "Are you ready to go inside?" Why did she call President Radkov Sergei?" Damn.

"Yes. I think I'm ready," Selena replies.

After removing the bag of books and candies from the car trunk, we walk at a slow pace to the administrator's office. Just seems like a place you don't want to rush into.

"Dr. Frederick, we're so happy to have you here," the English-speaking woman says as she introduces herself as Patina Svorvin.

"I'm excited that you're able to accommodate my visit. I hope these books will make a pleasant addition to your library." With a fret Selena adds, "I hope I've brought enough candies for all the children. I included a few extra just to be sure."

Dr. Selena Frederick brought seven hundred Tootsie Pops and seven hundred Tootsie Rolls for the Russian orphans. Sure, it'll be a gracious plenty.

The school's cafeteria is set up for the visit and the children are already there sitting cross-legged on the floor wearing eager eyes. Not enough chairs are available for over four hundred children, which doesn't include the nursery babies and the couple dozen staff members and teachers of the institution. The director agrees to interpret for Selena. My full-sized movie camera will film the visit. I love every second of it. Selena has grown in minutes from a woman barely able to hold back tears to a woman smiling in earnest for the benefit of children.

Selena greets the residents. "Hello, my name is Selena Frederick. I have come here today to bring a few books from different parts of my country that show a little about American life. I'm sorry the books aren't translated into Russian, but I hope the pictures will help you figure out what's going on in the stories. The fun part is that you get to make up the words to the stories yourselves."

Selena looks into the faces of hundreds of bewitched children. They tug at her heartstrings. Easy to tell that. Hell, they tug at mine.

She holds up the colorful Native American book by her friend, Jean Maria Whitecloud, and begins to read. Ms. Svorvin interprets as Selena reads the text and shows the pictures. "Don't worry if you can't see the pictures from where you are sitting now. Several copies of this book and others will be in your library for you to look at when you get a chance." The pretty American walks through the crowd of gawking children so that more can see the pages. Hell, I'm so enthralled by the story that I want to meet this Ms. Whitecloud.

When Selena finishes reading the book, the children put on a traditional Russian dance for the American doctor. Instead of sitting in the chair provided for her, Selena sits on the floor as she watches the traditional Russian folk dance and merry faces of children who are glad to show off their skills to a foreigner. When it is over, Selena claps loudly along with the orphanage staff.

Then Selena takes questions from the children.

"What kind of cars do people drive in America?" Even tougher questions follow like, "What kind of houses do Americans live in?" The question doesn't seem too difficult, but if one considers you are talking to children who may not have a memory of being outside this institution, then to talk about normal American life could seem cruel. Selena handles it like a pro, showing a picture in the book where some Native Americans carve a home from caves in a tall mountain cliff. One such home belongs to the author.

Even getting on a school bus to ride to school is a foreign notion to these kids. I'm sure Selena would prefer questions about such things as the weather. Ones that don't insinuate "Normal Americans have this and that and you don't." I get it. Been all over America. Selena did such an excellent job of it by just being herself. By being honest, and not focusing on the privileged but on many types of groups.

She did, however, have to brag about the warm beach and waterways in the spring, summer, and fall in North Carolina. The children *oohed* and *aahed* at such things as ocean water warm as a bathtub. Crabs on the beach. Making castles in the sand. She left out swimming, boating, and riding the waves. Kept it very simple.

One child asks, "What songs do children sing in America?" Selena decides to have a sing-along with the children. She has them stand up and teaches them the simple one-word song, "Amen," and explains that it's the ending to a prayer, or a statement of hope. Selena directs them to sing the song together, then divides them into groups of three to practice before having all of them join together again. Before long, the kids are all making a train and singing "Amen" together, their hands on one another's shoulder and belting out a choo-choo train of Amens. The administrators and teachers join in the cheerful Amen train, clearly holding back tears from their eyes while watching the joyful children.

When the song is over, the staff gives the children their candy. Selena sits down in the middle of the group and some kiss her on the cheek. Others give her a hug. Some simply say "Spasibo." One little girl has a comb in her pocket and wonders if she can comb Selena's ankle-length hair. Selena agrees to let the little girl slide the comb through the ends of her long hair. The little girls *ooh* and *aah* as though they have never seen hair being combed before. By then, the boys are on a sugar rush and start horseplaying, so the director brings the event to a close.

The administrator thanks Selena with an extended handshake, and Selena palms her with probably all the rubles she has on her person. I nod while I speak my goodbyes and send my video feed to Sergei and Joe Cook. The feed is in the news that afternoon.

Later, Sergei tells me he watched the video, then watched it again. He pauses in places where Selena is laughing with the children. Said he loves the way the blue-jeaned lady wearing a simple tee and tennis shoes broke out in song with the kids. If ever he had thought her beautiful before, he is even more convinced now. States he recognizes what's in his heart is love. Maybe, but President Sergei Radkov is in love with a stranger.

Well, ya know what? If he met Selena Frederick, she would not be a stranger for long. Can make you that promise. I just met the lady, and already I can talk to her about both painful and joyful things with equal openness.

"You'll think me a puff, Alexei, but I'm wiping tears of joy, tears of hope, tears of my own experience. This love for her is a crazy love."

It's rare to hear Sergei ramble, but he does. "I don't know what to do when a man is in love with a woman. It isn't something I've been taught. It's not something I've ever experienced. I didn't grow up in a place where love was observed, although I have seen many couples who love one another deeply and can't imagine anything except living their whole lives together."

The man doesn't stop to breathe. "Alexei, I understand right here and now that I want to live the rest of my life with Selena Frederick. That is, if she will have me. Oh God, please let her accept me. One way or another, I'm going to make it happen."

"Sergei, breathe, just breathe," I say to my president. "She will happen. It's just a premonition that I have."

"'Premonition?' Huh. I've been told people in love sometimes do rash and even stupid things. I've seen such interactions in the movies, whether they be comedy or drama. Of course, as a voracious reader, I've read of such notions."

Sergei is silent. I am a bit shocked by what he says next.

"I'm in love. I'm going to do something extraordinarily rash and stupid, just like any other man who is in love."

Ladies and gentlemen, this is not the Sergei Radkov that I've known for decades.

"I give in," he says simply. "Let us plan how I might meet 'the She.' I'm going to make her my She. I'm sending her a soiree invitation as soon as I check my calendar and can mesh it with hers. I'll let you know when I leave the invitation at her hotel room. Take a long lunch."

I grin and decide that if push comes to shove, I might just have to have a flat tire. I hang up the phone and leave the restroom in a gas station off the highway. I'm a proud papa.

CHAPTER 39
PRETTY FLOWERS FOR THE PRETTY LADY

ON THE RETURN trip from the orphanage, Alexei recalls a nearby neoclassical city where we might catch a good meal on the waterfront of Lake Seliger. We've not eaten, so a good meal would be welcome. Alexei decides on a restaurant that will be a nice place for a late lunch.

I enjoyed my visit with the children so much that I thought nothing of food. Sergei's former home. Damn. I'm a mess of emotions. A joyful high from happy children to sorrow for the past of the man who has captured my imagination. And I'm in his country. Finally! I would love nothing more than to thank him for allowing me to see it. Hear it. Smell it. Taste it. Touch the fiber of his country. Be in awe of it.

Now that we are back in the car traveling the Russian byways from the orphanage, my stomach grumbles. Loud. Alexei gives me a snicker as I throw my head back in the laughter of embarrassment. Alexei is such a pal.

"If you can hold on for a little under an hour, we'll be at the place I told you about. I'm hungry too. This will be a nice meal for us."

"Well, as we say in North Carolina, 'I can eat the butt out of a bull.' But yes, I can hang on for another hour," comes my consensus reply.

And so it is that sweet Alexei makes a detour to an outlying city, and we dine at this high-end restaurant in the middle of nowhere overlooking the lake. My God, I'm not sure what I'm eating, but it's an orgy of tastes. I lap it up like a hungry animal. Hell, I *am* a hungry animal.

I'm stuffed, but Alexei orders dessert and coffee. "Trust me, Selena. You'll want to try this. They have the best Ptichye Moloko in all of Russia, also known as the Russian Rafaello. It means 'bird's milk,' and it's legendary."

It was. The server brings a cake with an airy soufflé that is so rich and creamy that I feel my thighs growing with the first bite. There are these soft biscuits with a layer of dark chocolate that I suppose is the equivalent of American icing, but somehow different. The souffle's middle is somewhat like a creamy marshmallow. Damn, it's both light and heavy. I feel like I could fly away in delight with each mouthful. If my ass wasn't so heavy, that is. Didn't keep me from taking a piece of Russian Napoleon cake to go, though. Calorie-free. Must be.

After the meal, Alexei suggests we stroll the streets of the neoclassical city and its nearby monastery. Good idea. Alexei shares the city's claim to fame as the place where over six thousand Polish prisoners of war were massacred in World War II.

"Sorry for the gloom after such a joyful day with the children. Another part of Russia's dark past, I'm afraid. Plenty of that lurks among even the loveliest of places in my country," Alexei surmises with a sigh.

My tour guide pal advises I explore the shops for items of my liking. Yeah, there is nothing better than a male shopping pal who will tell you about six thousand deaths then advise you to pull out your credit card. I consider a Christmas ornament depicting the décor of the snow-laden local monastery dressed in its Christmas finery for Debbie.

I often buy Christmas ornaments for dear Debbie every time I can when visiting new places. Debbie collects ornaments and other Christmas décor like I collect dust. Being a rancher's wife hardly allows one to walk past your barnyard, much less see the world. When Christmas comes, Debbie will decorate the ranch fences with lights and wreaths of fresh flora from ranch lands. There are Christmas trees enough to advertise a Christmas tree farm right there on the ranch if so inclined. Debbie doesn't erect one or two trees for the season. She has one everywhere you turn beginning with two mainstays that grew next to the fence posts where a driver turns into the ranch. The family room, the dining room, a small one in the kitchen, on the veranda and the upstairs landing. She even erects one in the stable. The woman is a Christmas beast.

From the day after Thanksgiving until January the second, I know Bubba will be grinning shaking his head. Despite her eccentricities, the man loves every inch of his wife. He told me that he loves to see her joy every time she receives yet another ornament that will end up being stored somewhere in an outbuilding on the ranch. I'm sure he could use the space for other things. Bubba says he figures what the hell, it's worth it. If this is all it takes to make his woman happy, then he considers himself a lucky man. Debbie is a damned lucky woman.

Alexei snatches glances at his watch from time to time but doesn't hurry me. Instead, he's eager to recommend an ornament in lieu of the one in my hand. Hell, I buy them both.

It's not surprising we arrive in Moscow late in the evening. I yawn as we make our way up to our hotel rooms with my one little package in hand. Alexei and I are saying "Good night" to each other when I open my hotel suite door. I let out a shriek of surprise as my eyes espy the hugest flower display I've ever seen, perched on the coffee table in front of the couch in the sitting area.

"Oh, my God. How beautiful. How extraordinarily beautiful," I exclaim, still standing in the doorway, unable to move.

Alexei responds to my reaction and runs over to see the cause of the commotion. Drops his camera bag right in front of his door. We enter my suite, both saying, "Wow," at the same time.

"I wonder who they are from?" asks Alexei.

"They're so beautiful, and so fragrant," I mumble, trying to find words for my surprise as I stick my nose just above the flower petals to suck in the smell of each blossom. Then I begin to sneeze. I grab a tissue as my eyes water and let out several *achoos*. How could I forget that I have an allergy to most floral blooms? So, sue me. I got a bit excited. It's not every day a lady gets flowers. Flowers!

"I don't know," I reply. Then I let out a sneeze strong enough to whoosh a ship over the horizon in one puff.

"I love flowers, but... allergies, you know," I explain to Alexei. And let out a series of righteous sneezes. "That's why I seldom mess with floral perfume; mainly stick to musk based. Ah ah *ahchoo!*" I step into the toilet to wash my hands and recover from the blast of scent. When I come out, Alexei asks if I would like for him to remove the flowers.

"Don't you dare. I took an antihistamine. I'll be fine in a few minutes. Besides, I don't even know who sent them yet." With my eyes still teary, I pick up the embossed card and read:

Dr. Frederick,

I saw on the news today where you visited the orphanage of my childhood and left a gift of books for the small orphanage library. You may not know this, but that library is near and dear to my heart. I know firsthand how much a storybook's adventure can change a child's life. Especially a child in such circumstances. I don't have enough words in my Cyrillic vocabulary to tell you how grateful and very moved I am. Your actions did not go unnoticed.

I shall never forget your kindness.

With deepest respect,
Sergei Radkov, President of United Russia

I'm sure my eyes must deceive me. "Oh my God, Alexei, look at this. President Radkov sent me these flowers. Look, it seems the note may actually be in his handwriting. How kind of him. *Achoo!*"

Alexei studies the card as though he doesn't know what to say.

"I'll need to send him a thank-you note, but I have no idea how to do that," I say with teary eyes from the last sneeze.

"Not to worry. I have a cousin where he works," Alexei says. "Just give it to me. I'll make sure it gets sent to the right place."

My teary eyes now clearing, I say, "I'll write the note right now. Shucks. I don't have formal thank-you cards. I guess the hotel stationary will have to do. I feel embarrassed."

"President Radkov is a very informal man," replies Alexei. "I'm of the opinion that he will like the informal stationary better. He sees much embossed and formal stationery and cards. This informal stationary will be a pleasant change."

"You're right, Alexei," I reply, making my way to the writing desk.

"Same time for breakfast?"

I look up from my thoughts and reply from my desk chair, "Sounds fine, Alexei."

We smile at each other and wave our good nights. I sit at the desk wondering what to say to the president in my note. And I sit at my desk wondering what to write, and I sit…

Finally, I begin. Finish. Then scratch most of it out. All that I wrote was before I got myself together. I'm together now. I think.

I write on a fresh page:

Dear President Radkov,

I cannot possibly explain to you the joy and absolute surprise I felt when I opened my hotel suite door this evening to the most delightful floral bouquet I think I've ever seen.

Believe me when I tell you I received more joy today being with the children than they did with a few books and a little candy. Those children are truly deserving, the pride and future of Russia.

I have been following your successful presidency from afar. The people of Russia have a lot to be excited about when they look to their future. I will include you and your country in my prayers as I am,

Yours truly,
Selena Frederick

It has begun. Something has begun, though I don't know what it is. I feel it in my gut though, damn it. It has begun.

I wanted to tell Selena that Sergei would like *any* correspondence from her, even if she wrote it on her dirty underwear. No, wait, any man who got his hands on it would never throw that underwear away! Er... perhaps a dirty sock? No. No man would ever throw that away, either.

After I walk the meter or so to my hotel room and shut the door, I turn on the TV prior to calling Sergei with an update. Nice surprise: Selena's smiling face with the children is on the international news. Joe Cook has worked his magic. And my filming isn't bad either. Well, not too bad. Who cares? My heart is beaming as bright as the sun.

The media turns to Patina Svorvin, who says the phones are ringing off the hook with people both inside Russia and outside the country wanting to adopt children from President Radkov's former residence. Patina states wherein they are overwhelmed with joy to have so much interest, they will have to cipher out who is serious in their inquiry, since this is a lifetime obligation. It's not unusual for people's hearts to be moved by such a thing then lose interest when their experience or circumstance changes. Ms. Svorvin assures any listeners that she is more than happy to start the process and, as it should be, only the applicants with the truest of desires to adopt will survive that journey.

"Yes, yes!" I exclaim with a muffled shout. My fists pump the air in approval. Sergei tells me he spoke the same words and made the same pumping motion earlier in the evening when seeing the news reel.

"This lady is such a World Changer," he says. "She changes the world wherever she walks. The ground underneath her feet simply shifts. This is not a debt that I can repay. I'm so moved that I can barely speak. Leave it to a 'She' with ankle-length hair, green eyes, and a smile as bright as the morning sun to make me weak as a kitten lying among lions."

Should I tell him about her allergies? Damn, I have to.

CHAPTER 40
ANOTHER DAY AT THE OFFICE

I START another morning with Selena at a book signing on the other side of Moscow. Like the prior book signing, Selena is hoping for another standing-room-only experience in this bookshop located in an eclectic Moscow neighborhood. On one street along our journey there are walls of graffiti honoring everything from lovers' names in hearts, to tributes to deceased musicians, to words of revolution. One musical folk singer has been deceased for several years, yet fans are still leaving baskets of flowers with decorative ribbons and notes. The musician died young.

A man who is standing at the graffitied wall with his guitar touches the photo of the dead musician. The thirty-something-year-old man cries like a baby as he touches the musician's likeness drawn on the wall below the photo. Other people are there as well to see this musician's place on the wall, snapping selfies on their smart phones as though they had just made it to Mecca. Selena doesn't grasp the musician's Russian name, but for sure, she understands the musician was a beloved man in his short earthly time.

"Viktor Tsoi," I tell her again. He was the leader of the band Kino. The most influential of his time. A very beloved Russian artist.

"That is quite obvious," she replies. "Would love to hear his music, with the words translated."

A teary-eyed man opens his guitar case and plays a rendition of the musician's sound.

"Well, it's not translated, but there it is," I say. "So very sad. He died at twenty-eight-years-old in an accident." My own eyes nearly tear. This is Russia. Behold the heart of my people.

Selena listens and taps the beat on her hips with the guitar player. The man turns his guitar toward her and plays to her. She hugs him at the end. Aye yie yie. One day, some fruitcake is going to stab her while she's hugging him. Hugging him. A stranger. While she has a freaking book signing to get to. Aye yie yie. I love her as my friend, but there are moments I could strangle her too.

After a few streets on our journey toward the bookstore is the bridge across the Moscow River. There's a huge sweetheart ring of flowers in the middle of the walking bridge. Of course, Selena must stop to see it. I explain many couples like to come to this place to get married or propose. We walk across the bridge where there are many locks attached to the bridge railings. It's customary for couples, if they so choose, to place a lock on the bridge and throw away the key in the river, symbolizing the forever nature of their union. Very romantic.

After crossing the bridge, we're surrounded by older but well-kept buildings, eateries, onion-domed religious sites, a multitude of shops and galleries, and traffic. As well as a marching band playing, which thankfully keeps to the left of the sidewalk. Selena questions why marching bands walk the cities of Russia so routinely and play their tunes.

"Must be a Russian thing. I don't really know. Never thought about it," I reply. As they said on the Titanic, "And the band played on."

We arrive near the eclectic bookstore, which looks more like a library. There are old and new editions of any type of literature or text one might imagine, and in several languages. What Selena nor I aren't prepared for is the crowd of people already in line outside of the bookstore as we approach the popular establishment. It's still an hour before the book reading and a half hour prior to the store opening. She's gleeful.

I jerk Selena's arm. "Here, let's see if we can go around back." Too late. Selena is recognized, and the crowd makes their way toward the popular author.

Fuck! Shit! Damn! I hit the red panic button on my phone while stepping in front of Selena to protect her from the onslaught of the crowd.

This is on me. Why didn't I check for crowd conditions before approaching? I was too busy escorting the beautiful lady and soaking in her big smile framed by her billow of shiny hair.

"It's okay, Alexei," says Selena. She steps in front of me to stand. "I shouldn't hide from my fan base. These are people of like-mindedness."

I swear to you, I'm going to strangle her before the day's end.

"Can I get an autograph?" asks a fan.

I want to scream at him, "Fuck no! You can't have an autograph. Buy a book and get it signed, you dimwit."

A black sedan pulls up and parks in the middle of the busy street. Not a single car horn honks.

"Of course," replies the beautiful lady with white teeth shining on this extraordinarily sunny and warm fall day.

Of course, she says, "Of course."

Two men step out of the black sedan. Another dark sedan pulls up behind the first one, and three men step out of that vehicle. Together, the five make a perimeter around the crowd. And call in several other sedans. Somewhere close by, there is an aroma of blueberry muffins and fresh coffee in production. Aye yie yie.

Oblivious, Selena chats up her crowd, her face smiling at one person at a time and signing anything they shove in front of her. The crowd is friendly and respectful, but I'm still gonna need an antacid. Selena walks through the crowd as though she belongs there and tells every person she hopes to see them at the signing and thanks them for coming to meet her.

For the first time, I'm angry with her. I understand I'm simply scared, but damn it, crowds don't make for good security. You can't do anything with your life if you're dead.

I call Tanya Jaroslav, the bookstore owner, and request she admit me and Selena right that moment, or I'm taking Selena back to the hotel and tying her to a chair. Tanya is a cousin. She knows just how damned serious I am. We take a not-so-gentle stroll to the back entrance, and I give a not-so-gentle tug to Selena's arm, telling her the bookstore staff is ready for her arrival. I chance an innocuous nod at the sedan men as I lead Selena inside. The black sedans disappear. I request Tanya give us a minute as we enter the back storeroom.

"Are you crazy?" I scream. "Do you not realize how dangerous crowds are? Hugging strangers too. One of these days, a fruitcake is going to stab you in the gut in broad daylight. Why? Because they fucking can. You make it easy for them. I'm trying to protect you, but you need to help me out here."

Selena looks at me dumbfounded. She starts to say something, then walks off. Just walks off. Damn it to hell, she is such a... *a woman*. A God damned oblivious woman!

Selena does her meet and greet with the bookstore staff. Tanya opens the doors to what will clearly be more than standing room only. The crowd has grown with a fury in just the prior few minutes. This establishment is four to five times the size of the first Moscow signing. The crowd hurries in so fast that the place looks like a Goodyear blimp on its way to bursting. The door is open, with people hovering outside on the sidewalk and beyond. I have long since hit my panic button. Again. Ayie yie yie.

Tanya acts as though this is another day at the office as she introduces Selena to the crowd. Selena comes to the podium acknowledging everyone, including the people backed out into the street. The door is propped wide open so they can hear the speaker. Why did it have to be one of the nicest autumn days I can remember? Selena makes a joke about using a larger venue, but then she would have to rubber stamp her signings because she knows her hands have limits.

"So, we'll all just persevere together, and it'll all be okay," she says.

Why do people love that? They do. Selena must be Selena. Despite my fear, my concerns, I know Selena must do Selena. I'm thinking this lady's security is far above my pay grade. Turn in my timecard. Yeah. Bullshit.

At the end of the reading, those who bought books line up in the usual way for the author's signature. Of course, Joe Cook and his camera men were present since the beginning and follow the events until day's end. Once again, all the books are sold out, including the supply set aside for Selena. And the crowd is still lined out the front door.

"I ordered extra. I heard what happened at your last signing. Got a lot of preorders for the next shipment, though," states Tanya.

It is six o'clock before Selena leaves the shop. "Oh God, I think my hand is going to fall off," she groans as the last fan leaves.

Selena goes over and hugs Joe Cook, saying, "You're anything if not tenacious, Joe Cook."

Yeah, hug Joe. He's a safer bet than a stranger.

Joe gives a grin and a low whistle, "Man, you're killing 'em, Selena. Ya gotta be pleased with the turnout."

"Oh, this?" Selena says tongue in cheek. "It's just another day at the office."

Joe smiles in response as I tug Selena's arm. Gently this time.

"I have arranged special transportation for us with a cousin. He'll get us back to the hotel and take us later to the Bolshoi Theater. You'll not want to miss this Irish tenor. He is the talk of the town."

Selena says her goodbyes to Joe and his crew. "See ya next time, Mr. Tenacious."

"Not if I see you first," teases Joe. A low whistle is heard as the door closes to the establishment.

We crawl into the back seat of the waiting sedan and are off. Selena whispers, "I could've sworn the sedan took off before my door was closed. Everyone in Russia must know this guy drives like a maniac. They're all getting out of his way. And he parked right in the middle of the street."

We each run to our rooms once at the hotel. Selena emerges a half hour later in a red silk dress that's gathered at her bosom and flows down to her ankles, the fabric only slightly longer than her dark hair. The dress splits up the sides to her knees, showing off her athletic legs when she walks in her patent leather red spiked heels. Her wealthy bosom shows a reasonable amount of cleavage in the V-neck dress. The sleeves are three-quarters length with a flouncy funnel-shaped ending.

Selena adorns her hands and arms with elbow-length white gloves. Breathtaking.

I emerge from my hotel room in a dark tuxedo and jacket. I leave my tam in my hotel room.

Upon seeing one another, both of us say, "Wow!" We both giggle and at the same time say, "Look at you." More giggles. Each of us says "You look great" and bend over with belly laughs as though we're in high school. All anger is gone. Vamoose.

We meet our ride to the famous Bolshoi Theatre for the opera.

"Well, Alexei, I think this will be a perfect ending to another day at the office."

"Yes, it will be." I grin. "Except, as you say, 'I could eat the butt out of a bull,' is that it? Did I say that right?"

Selena chuckles. "You did. As for me, I'll eat both the front and hind quarters and refuse to share while I'm at it!"

I throw my head back in laughter, then look outside my window at the lights and the noises of my home.

———

Somewhere in Russia, a burner phone rings. "Are you on board?" I ask.

"I called you, didn't I?"

"When?" I want to know.

As if he is the important man on the line, he speaks with a shrug in his voice. "I'm going to wait a bit. Give a little more time. I'll be in touch. Stay ready."

"Done."

We both hang up.

CHAPTER 41
COUSINS

"GOOD NIGHT," says Alexei to his cousin who drove the black sedan to the opera and dinner. The quiet man doesn't reply.

As we enter the hotel, a receptionist flags me down. The young woman with a serious face and perfect English hails me as Alexei and I are making our way to the elevator.

"Doctor Frederick, I have something for you," says the woman, who is waving a note in her hand.

"Spasibo," I reply as the young woman hands me the note. Enjoy using my one word of Russian-speaking knowledge. Oh well, if that's all the Russian I'm to learn, then I figure I might as well learn to use it.

I open the note in the elevator. "Zowie. Look at this, Alexei."

Alexei takes the note as the elevator bell rings. "Zowie, for sure. You're invited to a ball at the presidential retreat on Lake Baikal. You'll be in Irkutsk on that date. It's close by."

"Lake Baikal is vast though, Alexei," I reply as I set my things down on the hotel coffee table and get my itinerary out.

"See this, Selena?" The note at the bottom says, *Transportation Will Be Provided as a Courtesy.*

"Man, they arranged everything. You're right, Alexei. I'll be in Irkutsk. What a stroke of luck. Wonder how far away it is to the retreat?"

"Well. The RSVP asks for your hotel, so they will contact you. All will work out, Selena. Don't worry."

"I'll answer the RSVP right away and let you forward it to your cousin at Red Square. President Radkov must have gotten his thank-you note!" I say like an excited thirteen-year-old who just won concert tickets.

Alexei grins.

"Oh, Alexei. I'm going to spend time tomorrow finding something to wear. Have not the slightest idea what I should wear." I shake my head as though lost.

Alexei chuckles. "What is wrong with what you're wearing now?"

"Between you and me, it shows too much boob for a presidential ball."

Alexei throws his head back in laughter.

"Can you tell me where I might buy such formal clothing in Moscow? Might your mother be able to recommend somewhere?"

"She can, but I can do better. Where is your laptop?"

I grab my laptop from the safe and boot it up and sign in. Alexei takes over and brings up a website and says, "Now Selena, go through this array of gowns and check the ones you want to try on."

"Oh my God, Alexei. These are gorgeous. I've never seen anything like this, ever." I'm not exaggerating.

"We should celebrate. I'm having Prosecco delivered to the room. I'm going to run next door and take off this monkey suit while you peruse the list," says my Russian pal.

"Be sure not to wrinkle your monkey suit or ya might need to get it dry cleaned before we take off to Vladamir," I call out behind him.

Alexei giggles for some reason that I don't fathom as he leaves my room. Maybe he doesn't need any Prosecco.

I'm engrossed and *ooh* and *ahh* over the lovely evening gowns. Feel like a princess going to a ball. I come to one that is lavender and has just the right amount of slink through the waist and a sexy slit up the side. Hmm, too provocative? The V-neck has a lacy material over the cleavage. The dress is sleeveless but has a velvet dark-purple weskit-style jacket that can be worn with the evening gown. It's short sleeved, but there are matching long lavender gloves that should fit below the elbow. As well, there's a pair of spiked high heels of dark purple velvet with a lavender floral ornament on the arch above the open toe. Now those are what you call kickin'.

I peruse the jewelry selections for this outfit of a smoky lavender color. I hadn't planned to purchase jewelry. Selections are rentable and that's good. I'm excited. Giddy. I might actually meet Sergei Radkov. Can you believe it? President Sergei Radkov. Decide on a stunning purple alexandrite necklace with matching drop earrings. To quietly make a little Buffett noise, I splurge and rent an alexandrite ring to wear on the outside of the glove. If Jimmy Buffett was standing here, I'd give him a butt bump.

Alexei returns as room service rings with the Prosecco. "Look at these Alexei, tell me what you think," I spurt out, not realizing the man is busy pouring the bubbly liquid.

Alexei strolls over and sits beside me after handing me a fluted glass. "Let me see what you came up with."

I slide the laptop to Alexei, and he places it in his lap. "I feel like the father of an anxious bride," he winks. "Ahh, the lavender one, yes. It'll be beautiful on you with your dark hair. I usually place lavender as a spring color, but this has... I don't know, I guess I would say a smoky or gray tinge to it. Maybe silver."

"It does. It's a unique color for the season, but is it conservative enough? At least, I hope it is." I frown while considering my choice. "Do you think I should pick something even more conservative, Alexei?"

"Absolutely not," says the Prosecco-sipping man. "Selena, what is important is that you wear what you find comfortable and believe looks good on you. That is 'conservative,' in my opinion."

"I just don't want to make a rookie faux pas."

"Trust me, you will be the hit of the ball. Err, the belle, I think, is what you say in southern United States?"

I smile and give him a little pinch. "Thank you, Alexei. Now I have a big question. This is top secret."

"Well, I don't know if I can answer top secret."

I giggle like a girl. "Well, you see my jewelry choices?"

"Yes, they are quite nice."

"I'm thinking about renting that white fox fur coat to wear with it. It's the one that's so white it has a smoky lavender sheen."

"That is killer, Selena."

"It is," I reply, much too excited. "They say it's returnable at their St. Petersburg location, which is where we're going next after Lake Baikal. Depends on how much the rental will be for those extra days."

"Can you not splurge and buy it?" inquires Alexei in a polite way.

"I could never wear something that exorbitant in the USA. Folks will say I stammer on about things like income inequality but wear this fur coat. I'm talking about one night's rental only, but one photo can distort the truth."

Alexei frowns in misunderstanding.

"I mean, I love animals, but in a place like Siberia it's either us humans or the animals." I attempt to explain. "People won't survive without the right clothing, including animal furs. I guess you can say I place humans over animals, though I'm not insensitive to animal needs, especially in ecological considerations. Even in medical testing, I think animal suffering and animal dignity needs to be factored in and never taken for granted." I shrug at Alexei, who has become my advisor on top of everything else. I hope I've cleared up my position.

"Ah, I see," says the advisor with an empty glass. He lets a broad smile show that he is enjoying me letting him in on my top secrets.

"It's not just the appearance of hypocrisy. People in the States, unless they're in the jet set, don't wear such things. I'm not a jetsetter. I would appear foolish wearing it there but would enjoy wearing it here for such a special occasion. Just this once because it's so perfect."

"Selena, you're in Russia. Do as the Russians do. These furs are a part of our life here. Our culture. It's your duty to wear that coat. Let me top off your drink," says my advisor.

"Not too much. I hope not to have a hangover in the morning. I'll go to the gym before breakfast and work off some of this dinner."

Alexei replies as he strolls over to retrieve the bottle, "I understand what you are saying, Selena. You wouldn't likely be able to enjoy the coat again. But I think you should wear it. People around the world understand the brutality of Siberian weather and the need for extraordinary clothing."

"Exactly. It's a matter of perception, not reality. Although I will be colder and shabbier in my parka, I will wear it for the sake of perception. By the way, how far away is it to this shop?"

Alexei grins. "Selena, I told you to leave it to Alexei. We won't be going to the shop tomorrow. The tailor will come with the dresses, the coat, the jewelry, shoes, and outfits in the morning."

"What? You're kidding? They're dragging all of that here? How do you know that?"

Alexei's eyes twinkle. "The local tailor does this all the time. I called him while I was changing clothes. A cousin," shrugs Alexei. "Your appointment is at 0900. Hit the send button, and you are done, dear."

"What would I do without you, Alexei?"

"Probably be a lost American in Russia," grins the man with a tad of enjoyable arrogance. We click our glasses and make plans for the next day.

"Besides, President Radkov doesn't allow his guest to be photographed without permission. Considers it rude."

"Still not sure about the coat, but can I ask you one question, Alexei?"

"Sure."

"Just how many cousins do you have?"

CHAPTER 42
BELLE OF THE BALL

IT IS nine o'clock on the dot. The parade begins the moment Hector, my cousin tailor, arrives. He brings gowns and goodies as though he is Santa arriving on a troika. My cousin is balding and looks a little like me, except I'm better looking. And sexier. Probably younger too. Wink.

Hector understands English well but speaks in broken sentences while using the foreign tongue. Two assistants accompany him, and both are quite fluent in English.

Hector tries to convey to Selena that he intends to take his own measurements of her body. Before Selena understands what is happening, one assistant has half-removed her shirt with her arms over her head in the air. The other assistant has Selena's pants down to her ankles and requests she step out of them.

I know this drill. They will strip Selena fully naked within seconds. I can already see the flush in the pretty lady's cheeks. I leave the room after expressing my thanks to my tailor cousin, with my back turned, of course. What does Selena say about such moments? Something about her "darn Southern upbringin'?" Yes, she is mortified already. This much is obvious. Imagine if I were to view her exposed body. A person can only do so much like a Russian when in Russia. Hell, we are a country of communal baths. Russians truly don't give a rat's ass about nudity. We know the difference between nakedness and sex. And... we can do a lot with both of them.

This will be an experience for Selena. Hector will measure everything from her toes to her shoulder blades. Selena will fear death by exhaustion before my balding cousin is done with all of his measuring devices. Not just a measuring tape but slide rule, pieces of plastic that fit various places on the body. Cousin will make an actual outline of her feet drawn on paper. He will place her in different positions with her nude body on a long sheet of art paper and draw her outline and its measurements. Then, he will put all that data into an app. Perfect fit. Every time.

As an OB/GYN physician, I'm sure Selena doesn't fancy herself a particularly bashful person. In her book, she describes how medical students strip sometimes to practice examinations on each other. I can imagine this experience might be different somehow. But Selena will adjust to it. I have confidence in her.

Meanwhile, being aware of the upscale tailoring process, I slide into my room to allow Selena "space." I use the time to update my Commander in Chief. "She is enjoying herself, Sir. Both of us stayed up late last night choosing an outfit for her online. Your lady is with Hector as we speak. She is in expert hands."

I know Sergei is wincing a bit at the formal "Sir" but we both understand it must be so. We have casual communications with each other in private, but the president grasps the need for protocol. It's still hard for him. My job includes assuring adherence to discipline and protocol. Especially now, after the coup. As much as the president understands it, he misses the informal times. I do too. Truth is, it is the greatest honor of my life each and every time I call this man "Sir." Each and every time.

"How was the opera?" my president asks.

I can tell he wishes to keep the conversation about Selena going for as long as he can. I'm imaging his eyes growing hooded with his thoughts of her.

"Oh sir, I wish you had been there with her. That Scottish tenor could mesmerize the fairies of our land. Voice smooth as silk."

"Perhaps one day I will be, Alexei. Just don't introduce her to the tenor, aye Alexei?" teases Sergei. "Every man in the world is my Selena competition, but while I'm in the fantasy zone, I might as well dream I'm the only man vying for her."

"Um, too late," I say, gritting my teeth.

"What happened?" asks my president. My Sir.

"We-e-e-lllll, the tenor knew she was in the crowd somehow and he recognized her from the stage, handed her a rose, and sang to her and I know he has called her a few times." I think I say all that in under one second.

Silence.

Finally, I hear a sigh. "Does she seem to like him? Want to go out with him?"

"All I can say is that he has called her, and she has spoken to him in a polite manner. She thanked him for the rose and the song. She has not asked to review or alter her itinerary."

"Did she *sneeze* at his flower?" Sergei asks with so much venom and jealousy that I laugh.

Needing to cheer him, I say, "Never fear, my friend Sergei. When she meets you, she will be so hypnotized that her eyes will only see you and no other man."

"Have you been spying on my fantasies, Alexei?"

"No, but I have spied before," I say in jest.

"That you have, my friend."

"The tailor knows what to do after the measurements?"

"He does."

"Coat too?"

"Instructions in place."

I hear the cheer return to my president's voice before he says, "Well, I guess Sergei Radkov, new President of United Russia, needs to get back to work on our nation's economic problems. Or practice my tenor voice."

"I don't envy you the economy, Sir. Though I've heard you sing. The tenor voice might actually be the more difficult problem. Even so, I don't envy the project of our nation's economy."

"Me neither, friend Alexei, me neither."

We hang up and I lie across my bed for a rest. This lady has all but worn me out, although I enjoy every second of her company. She starts at the gym at six in the morning. Sasha, another operative, covered Selena's security this morning unbeknownst to her.

God Almighty, help me. Selena is worse than Sergei. When I'm with them, I pretend to enjoy their workouts too, for my health. Guess I've grown to be this old fart who likes to box the bags a bit, but honestly, I no longer care about the shape of my ass. Can't say who is going to kill me with exercise first, Selena or Sergei. Ayie yie yie.

Nap until Hector texts me. My eyes pop open, and I run next door as though I'm on a battlefield. I tap on Selena's door.

"All done?"

"Yes, I am, Alexei. Thank you for being so patient. Look at this gown. Hector has made it fit me like a glove. Speaking of gloves, aren't these purple elbow-length ones to die for?"

I smile as a father who has brought joy to his favorite child. "You look... I cannot find the words."

"Are you sayin' I'm gonna be the belle of the ball, Alexei?"

"Ah," I chuckle with a snort. "I get what that means. I've seen *North and South*."

"With Patrick Swayze?" chimes in one of the tailor's assistants.

"Oh yes, that is the one." I agree.

"Did you see *Roadhouse*?" quizzes Selena.

"I did," responds the assistant emphatically. "Oh yes, I did. With the bedroom dancing scene? I could never imagine such a thing."

"It seems I must see that one. I believe I've missed something," I pretend to wonder.

"You must see it," says the assistant. "We won't spoil it for you."

"*Roadhouse*? One word?"

"Yes, I think so," replies the assistant as the amicable conversation drops.

Serious Hector shows his team out the door as though he's late for his next appointment. The man receives his thank-you's to his back as he and his team pull an Elvis and leave the building.

"Up for some art?" I ask Selena.

Selena pulls on her tennis shoes. "I need a change of pace after that tailor experience. I've never seen a medical exam as intensive as getting fitted for that gown. Decided I lacked experience on what I should expect and didn't quite have my mind prepared for it. But when in Russia…"

Selena looks reflective as she ties the last loop of her shoestrings. "Then again, maybe my Southern upbringin' is catching up with me in my old age," she groans.

"So, to answer your question, Alexei, you bet I'm ready for some art." Her million-dollar smile returns. "Are you ready to rumble?"

Her tongue is in her cheek, wondering if I will understand the context. "I AM READY TO R-R-R-RUMBLE," I bellow from my gut as I roll my r's.

Selena giggles like a schoolgirl. "Then, let's go Joe."

I pause and roll my eyes. "You know my name is Alexei, right?"

"I do," she replies.

As Selena hoped, she thinks she has pulled just a little piece of wool over my eyes.

"That's all I need to know," I reply, while appearing clueless.

Damn, this is fun. In truth, I understand Selena's saying well. Hell, I've been places in America that Selena has never heard of. Hellfire, I'm certain I've been to New York City more times than her. You, reader, know more than you should. This information is on a need-to-know basis only. You simply do not need to know.

CHAPTER 43
HANGOVERS AND KIDNAPPINGS

I SPEND my last day in Moscow touring three art galleries, after I go by the bookstores to autograph the preordered books. I'll be sad to leave this city. The city of Sergei Radkov, the man I admire above all men. I'm focusing my mind on upcoming events and hoping the gala ball pans out. Alexei is confident, but I must restrain myself so as not to be overly hopeful. Anything could go wrong. The weather, the transportation, lost luggage, the end of the world. Literally anything.

Russian art is the most moving I've ever seen. Certainly, the most emotional. Art pieces pull at me. Only force of will can drag me away from a portrait. Moving on to another piece results in an equally intense stare. I can stand in front of any piece until, as they say in my native land, the cows come home. 'Tis a shame most American artists will never see Russian art up close. Skilled masters painting toenails to perfection. Awe.

The last stop is at The Gallery of Erotica. As an OB/GYN physician, I find this one "the bomb," but most tourists are not so open-minded. Certainly, my mother, Elizabeth Frederick, wouldn't be. Don't misunderstand me. My mom is a great lady, but there are times I struggle to apply her values to my life. Notice I said my mom "is" rather than "was." I struggle with that too.

The night brings a trip to the ballet. I realize all that great American ballet which I've experienced in places like the Lincoln Center and the Met in New York City can't hold a candle to even secondary theatres of ballet in Russia. The difference is mind-blowing. The best of American performances can't compete with the extraordinary perfection of the Russian ballet artist. The choreography. Floating arms. Leaping feet. Once again, the American artist will be the losers, not being able to experience Russian artists on their home turf. I'm blessed.

Come to think of it, I can't say that I recall the name of a single American ballerina. In Russia, they are household names. I recall the ballet in America saving applause until the end. So very rigid. In Russia, if an artist does a few moments of solo, they take to the front of the stage at the end. Receive applause, blow kisses. Even beat their heart with their fist. Returns to the dance, and it continues.

Russian dancers revel in applause. A soloist may have tears in front of a wildly applauding crowd. Like all things Russian, so intensely emotional for their art. Makes me wonder if Russian art in its many forms is so emotional partly because of the support renowned artists receive from their countrymen. Does this increase an artist's desire to achieve perfection? One thing that's obvious is the artists perform for the people, not for themselves. A spectator feels it. It is truth.

Alexei and I eat dinner after the ballet. My mind is drifting in and out during our meal, thinking about the upcoming presidential ball while I chat with Alexei. Sergei Radkov is running through my brain like a freight train. I'm talking incessantly. Damn, I'm nervous.

I can't think of a Southern quip to describe my nervousness. Well, there is one, but I refuse to use it. It's awful. Okay, I'll tell you, just so you can see how terrible it is.

"Nervous as a whore in church." Six words that say so much about the wrong thinking of humans, especially toward women. Tell me, what little girl grows up thinking she wants to grow up as a woman who gets paid to allow men to release their bodily fluids into her body's orifices? And if there is shame, then where is the shame of men? And don't get me started on church being for the sinners and belonging to Jesus, not to man. A "whore" is someone who should never be nervous in church but feel at peace. Okay, soapbox over. Truly awful, as I said.

Sorry that Southern expression exists. At any rate, degradation toward all women should never be spoken. If the problem was simply words, then it would be one thing. But those words come from our thinking. Actually, if I were to consider my own sins at the moment, it would be these Black Russians I'm drinking. Damn, they're good.

I'm normally a woman with a calm interior. But I've nervously sat here and drunk six Black Russians. Six. That's more booze than a six pack of beer. Holy moly. Time to slow my row.

These tasty drinks seem innocuous. I never considered they might kick my ass. With vodka, Kahlua, a source of orange infusion, and a slice of orange garnish, the drinks taste like an after-date milkshake, but in truth, are human-ambulation-inhibiting fluids. I think I spoke all those syllables. Right?

"AIF's," I giggle to Alexei. "Great medical term. I think I got those wetters light."

Alexei has a big-brother frown.

"Anybody can misspeak, Alexei. I got those letters right. I think. See, I'm fine."

Is that Alexei sitting across from me? Did he switch places with someone? I decide to check out why Alexei looks so weird. I stand up. It's a mistake.

I manage to get Selena into her hotel room, remove her shoes, and cover her with care, as though she were my dear mother. I take my sweet caretaker's arse to my room and pray for Selena to be okay through the night. I'm not looking forward to calling my president, but I do. I report that the lady in question doesn't tolerate Russian vodka so well. In fact, she is presently quite shit-faced.

Sergei is silent on the other end. Fuck! I pace the hotel floor with my phone in hand, waiting for him to speak. I pull my phone from my ear to look at it. Don't ask me to explain. I don't know why. Yes, it's connected. Still, Sergei doesn't speak. Finally, I hear a sigh.

"Alexei, I'm concerned about this, but Selena is a grown woman with her own mind. I know she is in the best hands she can be in."

Then Sergei laughs his ass off. "Six? *Only* six? The lady is a lightweight. I love it."

Wish I did.

It's early the next morning, and it begins with over a three-hour car ride to Vladimir for a book signing. I carry all the hernia-inducing luggage downstairs and load the car. Selena's books. Selena's clothes for ballet, orphanage visits, and presidential balls. Selena's life. Selena's life passes through my hands in the form of suitcases.

With care, I nestle Selena in the backseat to allow her the most rest prior to starting the day. Selena says she feels as though she is an old lady returning home from the hospital. She manages to express appreciation, though. She states this is the worst hangover she has ever known. Then she falls off to sleep. Poor baby.

I awaken her as we make our way into the incredibly lovely city known for its golden-gated entrance. Mongrels looted the city a millennium prior and dragged away the city's original notorious golden gate.

The book signing goes long. Selena muddles through, but it is not her best day. Not her best day at all.

Selena read about the city cathedral's fifteenth century frescoes prior to our arrival. Outside the bookshop, a golden dome crowns the white stone walls of the Assumption Cathedral. Even with a throbbing headache, Selena is hoping for success at the book signing, but also that time will allow at least a peek at the interior of the famous historical site. As her day lengthens and customer after customer buys every book available, she reassesses the possibility of sightseeing is approaching nil. Silly girl.

Although darkness has fallen, I take her to the famous cathedral after dinner. We stroll. We have company following. Company that has followed us from Moscow. Two men. I'm concerned about their presence, but even more concerned as to what I might have to reveal to Selena.

I rap on the front door of the cathedral, but it's closed. It was supposed to be left open. Fuck! Sorry, God.

I don't have the operations support here that I had in Moscow. All the same, I push the red button on my phone. As well, I pretend to scratch my neck, but activate my personal GPS in a necklace I always wear in case I lose my phone in an interaction.

Nonchalantly, I show Selena around the extensive perimeter. The area is well lit by surrounding lights. So far, Selena is not aware of any issues. I have on my tour guide hat, but I'm looking for an alcove to tuck Selena. The two perpetrators are circling the cathedral in the other direction. We'll meet. Oh yes, we'll meet.

They pop out from around a corner and walk toward us with weapons drawn. Tokarev TTs.

"Get behind me, Selena."

"Not on your life," she bounces back.

Ayie *fucking* yie yie. God knows I'm sorry, but I have no time to tell him.

"We only want the woman," says one of the thugs.

"Then come and get me," replies Selena.

What? Does she not know those guns are used by hitmen? I want to hand her over to the thugs—*after* they've been strangled to death. By me.

"Dr. Selena Frederick, we *will* come and get you. Your lackey need not suffer. Not much, anyway," the man smiles.

At least she is getting them to maneuver closer to us. I'm thinking, *That's good*. Then I hear a voice behind them.

"Gentlemen, it's not of God's liking for you to commit violence anywhere, but especially not on His sanctified grounds," says a monk in a brown sackcloth tied with a rope.

"Fuck off, Father," says one of the thugs.

The two gunmen have positioned themselves sideways to look at the monk, then at us, and back again.

The holy man opens his hands gently while taking a short step forward. "Gentlemen, what reasonable thing can we do to keep you from committing a sin against God on His sovereign grounds? God's name is to be praised here. Even Satan knows that." Another half step.

"Over with the others, priest," says one of the thugs.

I speak, drawing the thugs' focus on me. "You must know how serious this is..."

In one swift move, the nonthreatening monk takes the legs out from under both thugs. They fall to the ground. I cover Selena. The split second when I realize no shots are fired, I kick the weapon from one thug's hand. Selena kicks the other.

The monk knocks out the thug I'm grappling with, while Selena, God love Selena, has the other thug on the ground with the arch of her foot across the man's neck. The man's face is eating dirt. Did I tell you she is wearing heels?

"Move and my foot will be obligated to break your neck. It's an ugly neck and I really don't care if I break it," she threatens.

The man stills. The monk removes the rope from his sackcloth.

"Can you hold him in place a moment more, miss?" asks the monk.

"Glad to, Father." Selena replies.

The monk ties the thug's hands behind his back. I drag the unconscious man over and the priest uses the remaining rope to tie the hands of the second thug to the first, orienting them back-to-back.

"You can let go now, lady. If you don't mind, can you gather the weapons?" asks the monk of Selena.

He looks at the conscious thug. "We can do this one of two ways," explains the monk in the most generous of tones, as though he is talking to school children. "I can knock you unconscious, or we can stand the two of you up and you can walk inside like a man. Or do you prefer to be treated like dead prey?"

"I prefer to stand."

"Wonderful. I'll awaken your friend. I do so hate to injure God's creatures on His Holy Grounds. May His name be praised."

The Father looks at me. "On three?"

I nod. We hoist up the thugs, and the priestly monk points for Selena to open the side door.

She does and holds the door open like we are family parading in for a holiday. Nothing like a beautiful woman holding two Tokarev TTs inviting you in for the holidays. Damn, I knew she practiced katas, but I had no idea of the extent of this lady's martial arts talents.

"Spasiba," says the cherubic-faced monk of my stature who is now missing a sackcloth tie. "In here. This closet shall suffice," he directs. "I'll get more rope to tie their feet."

Both thugs are cussing in God's house like they are in a mafia bar. I swipe their legs from under them and they fall to the floor.

"You broke my fucking arm! I think my fucking arm broke when I fell!" screams one.

"Good. That is God's punishment for your filthy mouth. If you speak another word, I'm afraid your arm won't be broken. It'll be crushed," I threaten.

The monk returns. He has extra rope to secure their bodies and feet together. There are also four women's scarves. "A little something for their blasphemous mouths," he explains.

"I can tie their bodies," says Selena. "I know nautical knots that won't come loose."

"Open your mouth," instructs the father when he has a floral scarf ready to cinch a thug's mouth silent.

"Fuck you, Father."

Before he can get the words out, the monk has hit the man's neck with a barely noticeable tap. The thug falls unconscious. The monk pulls the man's head by the hair below the crown and stuffs the scarf in the open mouth. He then looks at the thug's cohort and asks, "Easy or hard?"

The thug opens his mouth. Next, the monk puts scarves depicting Christ around their eyes. "Figure they need to see Jesus," he says without a single expression.

Me? It's all I can do not to laugh my fool ass off. We have these gunmen gagged and tied, unmovable, with a view of Jesus in a cathedral. It doesn't get better than that.

With the closet door closed, I say, "Selena, meet my cousin, Igor. He is former Spetsnaz."

"Glad to meet you," she laughs with her lips spreading to show all of her white teeth while she shakes Igor's hand.

Igor introduces Selena to a personal guide who shows the amazing American woman every awe-inspiring inch of the great cathedral.

I make a few calls concerning our captured thugs, and Igor and I sit on a bench to catch up on life.

The tour ends, and Selena, being Selena, hugs Igor and the cathedral guide with goodbyes. She slips large-denomination rubles into the church donation box and pulls a copy of her book out of her handbag, signs it with an appreciative note, and slides rubles inside the cover for the guide. I love this American woman.

Now we are back on the road, traveling by darkness to Sergiyev Posad, the township of the famous Lavra, and the genesis of the Russian Orthodox Church. At our overnight B&B, a woman in pink foam curlers and only three teeth in her mouth greets us. The next morning, the lady in pink foam serves the largest breakfast Selena says she has ever seen. The meal lasts us until dinner. I knew it would. If I know one thing, it's where to find the best food.

Before the book signing, I take Selena for a tour around the grounds of the holy site. Selena senses something magical while inside the Trinity Lavra.

The word, "Magical," slips from her lips. "I feel like an American child on Christmas morning," she whispers. "For now, I need to sense what I'm feeling, but I'll explain it to you later."

With a knowing smile, I nod.

The doctor, who processes things in scientific terms, can't explain her sensation. I love it. Selena whispers she feels bound up by saints, transported through time, bundled up in goodness. If she never left this tiny spot on God's green earth, she believes she would die a happy woman.

Who would not? *Not if they were constantly being touched with blessings by the hand of God Almighty Himself,* I consider. Damn. My Russia feels more amazing to me every day that I'm with this lady.

After leaving the Lavra, Selena explains her experience. "Despite attending Sundays at the First Methodist Church of Brunswick County, I've never experienced this degree of spirituality. I remember my mother saying, 'You never know where or when the hand of God is going to touch you.' Doggone if Mom didn't know a thing or two. I mean, here I am, thousands of miles from home, and I've spent lots of time in many places, holy places, thousands of miles from home. Never was I more aware of the distinct hand of God upon my shoulder than in this place. It was heavy. God's hand is heavy."

I can only smile, watching the green eyes of this beautiful woman speaking with amazement as her moving lips describe her experience here, in the most holy site in all of Russia. If I thought I could experience this much joy every day, I would hand Sergei my resignation and become a tour guide. Yet, I shouldn't be here. Sergei should. Sergei Radkov should be here in this place with Selena Frederick. What I would give for him to be able to take her hand and, like a proud Russian lover, and show her his home.

After leaving the township, Selena states she regrets having to drive during the dark hours. She is aggrieved to miss the sights of a bucolic countryside full of scenic beauty. "On the other hand, I've been given experiences few others ever have. I suppose missing the sight of yet another onion-shaped cathedral dome, wouldn't be my life's greatest loss," she reconciles.

"Yes and having so few hours of daylight doesn't help us. Come back," I smile at her. "Come back when we have the midnight sun to show us every delight Russia offers. For now, our midnight sun is hiding her face."

"She's away getting a *face*lift," Selena quips.

After nearly a three-hour drive, we arrive at the hotel in Yaroslavl. Yaroslavl is located on the outer western edge of the Golden Ring. A mounted bear outside the quaint local hotel welcomes the traveler, as well as the bear depicted on the establishment's sign. Yawning, Selena ekes out, "Suppose Russians love their bears."

The observant lady notices the farther away from Moscow we drive, the scarcity of English-speaking persons increases rapidly. Most of the folks at the book signing the next day don't understand a word she says. I act as an interpreter this time. Slows down her talk, but Selena is happy to accommodate.

Back at the hotel at day's end, Selena and I pack our belongings for Irkutsk and Lake Baikal the next day. The exhausted lady apologizes for not consulting her itinerary for many days. Says it's because I do such a jam up job of looking after her. "Somehow, you don't tire and keep me on schedule," she adds, with what? A loving smile?

"My new friend, Alexei. He spoils me," she winks.

Calculating in my head, I surmise about five thousand miles and at least a nine-hour flight the next day. So worth it. The night after, Dr. Selena Frederick will attend a presidential ball. I smile.

PART SIX
I AM A MAN WHO SAW A WOMAN

CHAPTER 44
THE RUB

ALEXEI and I have another long day, starting from early in the morning extending to a late-night check in at the hotel. The flight from Yaroslavl to Irkutsk takes over ten hours in the air, exceeding five thousand miles. That's further than New York City to London, but all in the same nation with no oceans crossed.

Yaroslavl is in the southern center of Russia and Irkutsk is a northern city though nowhere near the nation's most northern point. Another day's flight and thousands more miles would be required to reach northernmost Russia.

We're both acutely aware we're in Siberia now. Gloves and heavy boots are donned, along with several pairs of woolen socks to step on this snow-laden earth. Hats, scarves, and heavy coats are a must. And I'm still cold.

Irkutsk is called the "Siberian Paris." This small Siberian city competing with Paris's stature is not something I can imagine, but I arrive with my mind open. Irkutsk is lovely, as is every city, town, and postal code I've visited so far in Russia. I consider Paris to be chic, artsy, and trendy. At the same time, of ancient history.

Irkutsk is a large city surrounded by a rural area. It's a gathering place for nature adventurers before making their way to Lake Baikal for all kinds of natural experiences. Early developers of the area considered Irkutsk to be the Paris of Siberia during earlier times centuries ago because of its ancient architecture. The city grew over the past century as a restful haven inhabited by builders of the transcontinental railroad. Yet, considering the loss of sunlight, it is definitely a city of lights.

Alexei and I agree to skip lunch and suck in a big breakfast. At breakfast, Alexei says, "Before the book signing, I've rented a four-wheel-drive vehicle for us to take a ride. Can take a quick drive along Lake Baikal and take you to see the ice cruncher, the *Angara*. It is old, unlike the sleek nuclear-powered ones of today. We can stop if you like ships, or you can view it as we drive by. Russians are quite proud of it. *Angara* is superior to anything in America in this particular technology. So, we celebrate it."

"Let them celebrate with good cheer," I toast with my coffee. "Hope we don't run late, though. I have a ball to attend tonight!"

"Is that tonight?" teases Alexei.

After our early breakfast, we make our way in a Mercedes Benz SUV along the Angara River embankment on our way to the famed lake. I view lovely, gilded onion domes and neoclassical arches amid snowcapped mountain tops peeking through the dusk from both lack of light and thick snowfall. Alexei gets me to the book signing just in time.

"Oh, I forgot to tell you. The home office called this morning. You need to be ready for the ball at five P.M." Alexei informs me.

"That is rather early. How will we be transported to the dacha?" I ask.

"That, dear lady... that's a surprise."

I look at my grinning companion warily. "And just what does that mean?"

"Exactly what I said," replies Alexei with a firm grin.

"Surprise it is, then." I'm not one to give in easily, but I trust Alexei on all things Russian. The man has gotten me everywhere I need to be so far. I suppose a little trust is in order. Even if it is to meet President Sergei Radkov. I'll admit I'm nervous. Nervous as a cat, maybe? Way too mild, but much better than other quips I know. Much more politically correct, and true to what I believe. I'm freaking out and trying my best to hold myself together somehow. Definitely not my best self today. Damn, I'm meeting Sergei Radkov. I begin to sweat even though I'm dadgum cold.

A nice spa treatment in geothermal waters amongst the snow-laden outdoors would be a relaxing start prior to beginning my hoity-toity dress. But duty calls. Indulging in such a luxury would mean bombing at the book signing. For the first time, I leave the bookstore later than the time allotted, but before I sign the last sold book. One hour to dress.

"Damn, Alexei, in just one more hour, I'll be on my way to meet Sergei Radkov, President of United Russia. For the first time in my life, I find the thought of a meeting scary."

I can't wait to report to Sergei that Selena feels scared to meet him.

"I'm scared too. I'm scared she won't like my face. That she won't like me. I've never in my life, not once, ever cared about such a thing. I care too much now," replies the president.

I take a moment, choosing my words carefully. "Sergei, I can't promise how Selena will react to you or any of our plans. I've known her for a short time, but this is what I've learned: I've learned that everyone loves her because she loves everyone. Plain and simple," I say with a shrug in my voice.

"And am I an *everyone*?'" asks the president.

"An American quote I learned from Selena goes like this: *therein lies the rub*."

"How do you mean?" he asks.

"I've watched Selena. She is always kind to everyone. Even people who clean the toilets in the hotel or airport. A server. The chef. Always smiles and says 'please' and 'thank you,' you know? Asks the server to give compliments to the chef. And like you, she tips even taxi drivers way too much. Despite being familiar with the Russian custom that tipping isn't necessary. And the amount expected for other professions is much lower here. She even leaves the maid a tip every morning before she leaves her room. Bellhops and room service hotel staff love to service this beautiful lady for more than her looks. She palms them a grateful tip. She isn't showing off. It comes from a kind heart."

I take in a deep breath and continue trying to make my point to Sergei. "Always talks to her fans like she has known them all her life. They hug her. She hugs them. One fan complimented her on the barrette in her hair. Selena removed it and gave it to the woman."

"Um, doesn't surprise me. She's a woman with an amazing heart. I got that from reading her book, although she never discussed anything she did as extraordinary. Actually, gave credit to others whenever she could. She might say her heart was moved to do this or that, but that is about all. Dr. Selena Frederick, as you explain, is a very giving woman," expounds Sergei.

"However, one night, we dined with a wealthy British couple," I continue to explain to my longtime friend. "Selena was cordial. She listened. Her demeanor was professional. She processed their words and conservative opinions with grace but didn't respond to those opinions. The same as everyone else, she gave the couple smiles, but they weren't the same smiles I've seen her give to a server or a maid."

"The rub," says Sergei.

"Yes. I'm not sure how Selena will react to the rub."

Sergei is silent in thought. "Guess I'll have to pretend to be a server. It'd make me happy just to see her smile at me with those big white teeth and ruby red lips that I want to make sore with kisses. Her smile. If I can give her cause to give me that smile, I would clean every toilet in Russia."

"If she gives you that smile, Sergei, I can't promise you ruby-red-lipped kisses. But I can promise you won't get such kisses if you don't see such a smile."

"The rub," contemplates Sergei.

"Yes, Sir. The rub."

CHAPTER 45
YOUR RIDE, MADAM

I DRESS IN HASTE. So damned nervous, I poke my mascara wand into my eye. "You're going to make a fool out of yourself tonight if you don't get a handle on your... well... your *lust*," I speak out loud.

Give myself a pep talk while I dress. "Okay, he's handsome. He's gorgeous. He's athletic and smart, and I think he wants to do good things for others. What's not to lust about that man? Any woman in the world he wants would have him. Why would he settle for a fling with a doctor from the states? Russian women are beyond-belief beautiful. These notions I have about him aren't real. Sergei Radkov is just another man. You may meet him and think him a total jackass."

Continue to chat out loud to myself like a mad woman while I dress. "In fact, you may not even get to meet the man. If you do, it'll be brief. Even if he tore off my lavender dress and sexed me on the dance floor... oh damn, it's been too long. Not since Sam, and that was only one night. Geez, I don't remember before Sam. God, do I even remember how it's done? I'm an OB/GYN doc and I'm not sure I remember how to be with a man." My pep talk makes me even more nervous.

With that, I peek at the clock. Touching up my face, I apply mascara with care. I don my sleek dress. Ooh, I coo at the slinky feel of the dress. Alexei knocks at my door. Showtime.

My eyebrows raise as I smile. "You look amazing in your tux, Alexei."

Alexei is holding a large plastic bag with a hanger that he places on the settee. "Selena, you will be the most beautiful maiden at the ball in that dress. You, my lady, are a knockout tonight."

Leaning down as if to speak confidentially, I say, "You can call me Cinderella. I may not be the most beautiful maiden at the ball, but damned if I won't have the most beautiful dress!"

Alexei looks at me. "Who is 'Cinderella?'"

"Oh, she's from an American fairytale."

Alexei holds up a stop hand. "Spare me. Remember, Russia is the land of fairytales. I still can't remember who does what in those stories. Not even as a kid. Too many, just too many. But I would take any wager that you are the most beautiful maiden at the ball."

"Oh, you are so on. Like a pot of neck bones," I declare, standing up as straight as a Russian ballerina. "This dress just makes me feel like a princess, thanks to your cousin."

Alexei holds his stomach from laughing so hard. "Oh Selena. The things you say. 'Neck bones?'"

"Tell you about it sometime. Shall we go?"

"Well, first, let me get your coat." He opens the plastic bag.

It's the fur coat I was so gaga over. "Alexei, I nixed the coat. I really can't wear it. How did you get it here, anyway?"

"I've more than one cousin in the fur business," he smiles. "And Selena. This is a gift from a Russian friend. In Russia, it's against our custom to refuse a gift."

I'm flabbergasted. "Alexei. I don't know what to say."

"Say you'll be happy to wear it tonight. It's much more appropriate than your heavy coat."

"I'll be happy to wear it tonight," I smile. I can't believe it. That Alexei.

I admire Alexei in his tux in the elevator. No words spoken. Nothing but a smile. Can't help it. He invested in a cummerbund that matches my dress. Thank you, cousin tailor. Even a snippet of a lavender flower is tucked in the lapel. He's just too much. I love this little bald man who is holding a fedora that matches his dark overcoat and scarf instead of his tam.

I feel buxom in this fantastic lavender gown, but I'm thinking I remain conservative in appearance. My body feels curved in this slinky dress that rounds me through the lavender fabric, showing off a better figure than I possess through the unbuttoned fox fur coat. Dark purple gloves match my shoes and my alexandrite jewelry sparkles. My ankle-length hair has an extra lift and curl thanks to my curling iron. My styling has lifted my waves to the length of calf height. I do feel like Cinderella going to the ball. I do. Hope I dance with the prince.

A limousine picks us up and we travel down the river path to a clearing where a helicopter waits. Even more amazing, a snowmobile with an overhead cover sits ready at the road bottom to carry us uphill to the helicopter. A plastic tarmac to walk from the car to the snowmobile, and a second one from snowmobile to helicopter covers the snowy ground. Someone thought out these tiny details. I'm most happy they did. Cinderella would hate to ruin her kickin' slippers in the snow.

"Surprise," grins the impish Alexei.

"So, we're traveling by helicopter?" I ask. It's a statement more than a question.

"Your ride, madam," replies Alexei, making a full bow.

I giggle and sit in the cockpit next to the pilot. The ride takes an hour. The pilot flies low in the middle and along the sides of Lake Baikal, showing me the best views in the dusk.

Looking back at Alexei seated behind me, I relay my delight and pleasure. "I feel like royalty."

"Tonight, madam, you are."

Much too soon, the helicopter lands and once again, we're met by a snowmobile. The ride is up a steep hill to a bluff with a shadowy view of the lake. The snowmobile stops at the entrance of a large rustic dacha overlooking a bluff whose front steps are shoveled and de-iced. I want to have a better look at the whimsical architecture, but realize that won't be possible, as dusk is darkening the landscape despite the copious dacha lights. Even though the entrance is well lit, the surrounding area is otherwise in a blanket of full darkness.

I allow a clerk to take my fox fur at the entrance. I put the pickup ticket in my purple satin etui. Alexei escorts me to a glass elevator, and we make our way to the top. Upon arrival at the floor, Alexei leads me to be seated at the one and only table at the ball. This vast room and only one table. I'm wondering if I'm meant to sit here, but Alexei expresses confidence that it's fine.

We're the only ones here.

The table allows a front-side view of the band now filling the stage as the lights dim. Like a proper gentleman, Alexei pulls the chair out for me and makes a gentleman's request to be excused. I'm the only person in the room. In the whole room. Hell, I'm sitting at the only table in the whole room. Very strange.

I nod and listen to the quartet playing soft chamber music with a harpist joining in at the end. I'm not familiar with the piece but think it lovely. But then, with mostly science classes at Chapel Hill and no orchestra near Brunswick County, North Carolina, I'm not familiar with most classical music. My father was a pianist, but he was more likely to play Jerry Lee Lewis than Beethoven. *But why am I alone enjoying this? Is the quartet simply warming up?*

When the song ends, I clap my purple gloves together and give a nod to the musicians. A short intermission ensues as the bandstand curtains close. Lights return, and I hear the shuffling of instruments behind the curtain. I sit with my hands in my lap at the lone table with a lily-white cloth. A server arrives and asks if I have a drink request.

"Might you have a Crimean white?" I ask.

"Certainly, madam." The white gloved man disappears behind an alcove and soon reappears with a wine bottle on ice.

"That should last awhile," I remark to the server, who smiles while filling my glass.

"Is there anything else that I can do to make you more comfortable, madam?"

"No thank you, I'm quite alright."

What's taking Alexei so long? This is strange with this one table. We must be extremely early. My nervousness has relaxed some but is back again. I must be mindful not to gulp the wine. I want to snatch that bottle in the cradled ice and upturn it.

I hear heavy footsteps clonking behind me on the empty wooden floor. To my dismay, thinking a bull was making the clomping noise across the floor, a slim man of short stature is instead responsible for the heavy footfalls. Very odd that this man makes so much noise with his steps. He approaches my table. The man appears fit and strong in his well-tailored tuxedo. Well-groomed with medium-length brown hair, he wears what appears to be a permanent scowl tattooed across his face.

"I'm security. May I see your bag, ma'am?"

Somewhat startled by his briskness, I ask, "My bag?"

"Your purse, miss."

"Certainly," I respond while handing the man my purple etui. Stranger and stranger, but I have no reason not to comply.

The man hands it back to me and commands, "Open it."

I'm unsure how to take this. I've never met anyone so rude. I've been treated so well by everyone here in Russia. I'm rather taken aback. I've gone toe to toe with warlords who weren't as self-possessed as this tiny ogre. However, without a word, I comply and open my etui and hand it back to the man.

The security man dumps all the bag's contents on the table. He spreads a wand over all the items now lying on the crispy white tablecloth, including the bag itself. Then he turns the bag inside out. Picks up my tube of lipstick and eyes it with brown-eyed curiosity. He winds the tube of light-pink lipstick all the way out and sniffs it. For real?

I sit silent during the process. I remove my ring and gloves. He might want to wand them too. Maybe he thinks I have Borgia poison in a ring compartment. Whatever.

The pert security man leaves my empty etui and contents on the tabletop. I don't have the slightest hint or instruction whether I may put my items back into my etui or what.

Before I can reorganize my things, the man asks me to stand up. I comply. The man runs the wand over me from head to toe and all angles of my body. He asks me to remove my shoes. I comply. The brown-eyed bully turns my shoes inside out as much as he did my purse. I put the ring from my removed gloves on my finger as I wait for the man's assessment of my shoes. I don't want to lose that ring. A little loose, but I think it's safer on my hand. Maybe this much security is necessary, but damn, no wonder they've only had time to put out one table.

The man asks me to step away from my chair. Guess he's afraid I'll hit him with it. Wordlessly, I comply. Then he frisks me up and down. Especially down. I'm incensed long before his fingers reach my underwear. It's not the first time I've had such an examination processed against me, but I'll be damned if I expected to have it done here. Not in this place. Really? I'm surprised this oaf doesn't make me place my hands against a wall.

Now, I've been patient while this man completes his pat down. Until. UNTIL this bastard makes his way up the split of my dress to inspect my underwear. Oh, hell no! I whirl around and make a half turn and back away.

"You may not touch me in such a way. I refuse. I'll gather my things and leave," I say, flushed red with the ire of a Southern American woman.

I begin to pick up my items on the table and replace them in my bag. So pissed off, I don't even respond or give notice to a booming voice coming from another alcove.

"Enough!" says the voice. "That will be enough, Vogo. I think Dr. Frederick has shown plenty of proof that she is not a physical security risk."

I don't even look up but continue to fiddle with my items and place them back to their former posts inside my dainty etui. The gemstone arrangement on the outside of the bag sparkles. I'm leaving. That's final. Screw Cinderella and her ball. I'm so disappointed I want to cry, but I refuse. Absolutely refuse to let the degree of my disappointment show.

"I'm sorry, Dr. Frederick."

My irked eyes roll up to a face I recognize as that of Sergei Radkov. The man of my most intimate dreams. I fight the sensation of a different type of hot. My knees wobble. I will my ankles to pick up the slack.

"My name is Sergei Radkov," says the face to a speechless and frozen me. President Sergei Radkov presses his hand forward as though to shake my hand. I press my hand forward to meet his. I think. Somehow, it's extended. However, as I palm his hand, he bends down to kiss mine. Fuck me. My hand sizzles as his lips touch my skin. His lips linger on my skin as though he's going to keep and protect that hand forever. Damn, I might need to change my underwear, but I'm short a pair at the moment.

My mind stops working. I'm speechless. But I can't be. Words. I must find words.

As he rolls those damned crystal blue eyes up to me, I consider their aquamarine color. I bumble out, "Hello, President Radkov. I'm Selena Frederick." I think I got all those syllables correct. There seem to be so many letters. So many consonants and vowels stuck in my throat.

A breath helps me recover as we stand face to face and look at each other. Angry. Yes, I'm supposed to be angry, but I can't find my ire. Embarrassment. Yes, that's what I feel. I'm dripping with embarrassment. I'm sure my face is flush with it.

Our eyes are locked in a gaze I'll never forget. I see stars and flashes of light and I hear angels singing. I see Sergei's eyes twinkle, and I'm sure my flushed face is now wearing a smile. Sergei's damned kissable lips make a slight upturn. Just enough to show his freaking cute dimples.

"Please sit down, Dr. Frederick," President Radkov requests as he takes a seat across from me. "May I call you Selena?"

What? He's sitting here? Across from me?

Not knowing what else to do, I comply and sit down. Oh yes, I was supposed to be leaving. Well, now I don't know where I'm going, but wherever it is, I'm hoping I can take this man with me. *Don't flirt*, I instruct myself. *Do not flirt.*

"I'd prefer that," I say while completing my etui housekeeping and placing my folded gloves beside it. I've set my etui aside to the far corner of the white linen table.

I would like to ask the president what this is all about, but my mouth muscles collapse. I must remember my manners, but damn. As I look up, Sergei is sitting with back straight in his chair and staring at me as though in a trance. Crystal blue eyes the color of a Carolina blue sky are processing me in silence. His wispy blond hair frames his face, accentuated by an inch-long scar barely noticeable except up close, resting below his right cheek. Sergei is unmoved, as though he's sitting at attention. *What is going on here? I* don't feel unsafe. Just disturbed.

Before I can stop my sassy mouth, I ask, "President Radkov, might I kindly ask you why you've invited me here?" Flashes of inconsistency zoom through my brain, and I know I need to put my schoolgirl crush in another compartment. I find myself sitting straight in my own chair.

"First, you must call me Sergei, and I will call you Selena."

"Alright, *Sergei*," I pronounce with a strong emphasis on his name, "Why am I here? I was under the impression this was a ball. Yet I only see one table and one guest."

As I ask, I'm flummoxed at how strange it actually is. I feel my flight-or-fight instincts kicking in. I want to run. Damn, this is a hoax. My God, it's a hoax. I've been in this situation before by men who, down and dirty, just wanted to screw me. Well, I'm no schoolgirl. He won't be putting this American woman's notch in his belt if that's what he's after. I'm a woman, not a toy. Schoolgirl has left the building. I'm pissed, and more disappointed than I can put into words. I fire him a glare that should burn his eyes out.

"You are here to enjoy yourself, Selena. Please relax," says the President of United Russia, Sergei Radkov.

I want to pick up my etui and throw it in his face. And my glass of wine. And the whole damn bucket of ice with the bottle still in it. But right on cue, the curtain to the bandstand opens, and what looks to be a folk group appears on stage. And of course, they dim the lights. Ass wipe.

Several dozen musicians adorn the stage. Each musician is wearing a costume that reminds me of *The Sound of Music*. The musicians hold various native musical instruments in their hands. Several hold a balalaika, which is a variation of the American six-string guitar. At this moment, I feel the presence of my father. He was every bit as much of a teacher as my mom. He was more than musical. He enjoyed musical instruments as much as music itself. He had quite a collection of instruments from all around the world. And I mean he had them everywhere. In his music room. Bedroom. Living room. The house library used most by my mom. His office.

Someone was always sending a gift of a unique instrument. Dad loved describing how they made their sounds and what a musician could do to develop varied tones. Hell, he could give a lecture on mother's wind chimes. His Native American name was "Ears hear Music". Anyone who came to our house realized his love of music immediately.

Most of the musical instruments are richly carved and gilded with native designs. In spite of my current mood, I'm enjoying picking some of them out. As we say in the south, my dad would be in hog heaven. One woman plays a domra, which is similar to a three- or four-string mandolin and is played with a plectrum. A heavyset older man holds a banyan, an instrument similar to an accordion. A svirel player commences with a solo whistling his lovely sounding hand-carved flute. The flute, my favorite instrument. I'm forcing myself not to be enchanted by its bewitching melody.

A young woman with long blonde hair in braids joins in with a hand-painted zhaleika, which is known as a folk clarinet. A middle-aged man who appears to be blind, or at a minimum visually impaired, holds an instrument with a leather strap around his neck called a gusli. The instrument is a type of zither, as its strings are parallel to the resonance board. The man holds the instrument and plays it like he was born with it in his hands.

There are all sorts of lutes, flutes, and tambourines. A boy plays a volynka, which is a type of Russian bagpipe. Under other circumstances, I would be enchanted. Totally bewitched. Damn near was anyway.

Who wouldn't have been? But I'm way too upset for enchantment. And hurt. Embarrassed. Damn, I've been sideswiped. Music is magic, but I will not let myself get spellbound until I figure out what is up in this here room. My North Carolina slang is following me all the way to a Russian Presidential Ball. Is this a ball? Thinking I'm just President Radkov's call girl in a fancy dress.

Am I the only one to show up? I'm thinking I'm the only invite. *Transportation provided.* Few people would turn down such an offer from President Sergei Radkov. He's a bit of a hot ticket item right now. *Where is Alexei?*

On the one hand, I realize the man sitting in front of me is the President of Russia, and respect is in order. On the other, I'm so pissed. Getting madder by the moment. *Don't cry.* I try to suppress the bile in my throat as I piece together what's going on. I don't like being manipulated. Sergei Radkov is playing with me. It hurts. I've had this intense crush on this man, adored him even, and he's spent his people's money just to try and screw me. An American. I might be worth two notches. I suddenly hate him.

When the curtain closes, two servers arrive to deliver silver trays of food. The server puts the silver tray in front of me and lifts the lid. Salmon stew in cream with dill is exposed. The second server places Sergei's dish before him in the same manner.

"I don't wish to have stew tonight, but spasibo," I say in a sudden but kindly manner to the server. "Would you take it away, please?" I try very hard to remove the venom from my voice. It's not the server's fault. At least, I don't think so. At this point, who the hell knows?

Sergei frowns.

My server looks to Sergei. He tries not to show disappointment, and nods. The server takes away my dish while Sergei's server lights the table candles and fills our water glasses. Good. Damned if I'm going to drink this man's wine. The lights are dim in the rest of the ballroom, except for the lights anchoring the stage.

"That'll be all," Sergei says to the server in English.

The English is a nice touch, but I'm not going to sit here and eat in front of this man. I couldn't if I wanted to. I take a sip of water to wash down the bitter bile now flushing my mouth. I straighten my back firmer and instead of glaring at him, I stare away from the eyes of Sergei Radkov. Sergei Radkov, now better known as President Ass Wipe. My eyes are blazing a hole in the wall of this ballroom. Wish it were his skull.

What does he do? I'll have you know; President Sergei Radkov eats as though nothing is happening. Asshole. Nothing is happening, except for my heart breaking. I keep my composure perfectly straight as Sergei slurps every bite of his stew.

The curtain opens, and a man appears singing what sounds like a yodel and strumming a lute. Don't get me wrong. His voice is a smooth tenor and quite soothing. Thank you, Mr. Yodeling Musician. I need a little soothing.

I suppose the yodeler represents a Russian ethnic group and is culturally symbolic. Damned if I'm going to ask. After a few minutes into the song, the yodeler comes over to the table and walks around us a few times while playing his lute and yodeling his song before returning to the stage. I smile at the man. This isn't his fault. My smile does not extend to Mr. Radkov, however.

Again, I should be delighted. My wide-open eyes lock on to Sergei as though they're going to nuke him. There is nothing in my demeanor that spells delight. I'm sure he is more than aware of that.

The song ends. Both of us give the yodeler a courteous clap, and the curtain closes. I wish for different circumstances wherein I might give all these musicians a better reception. But my wishes? My wishes are down a well somewhere. And I'm a bit preoccupied at the moment giving their president the stink eye.

"Did you enjoy the music?" asks the president while his server clears his soup plates.

"Yes." Pert. Very pert.

Sergei looks at me. His eyes look, well, sorrowful. Damn him. Now he's killing me. Asshole's killing me. I look away.

Sergei waits. Waits until he's sure he has good eye contact prior to proceeding. "Selena, can you please just try to enjoy yourself and enjoy your food? My cook, Olga—"

I cut him off before he finishes his sentence. I try to recover. "My regrets to your cook. Mr. President, what I would like to know is, where is Alexei Plokhy, the man who escorted me here?"

Sergei guffaws a little. Guffaws!

"Selena, Alexei is fine. You will talk later, I promise," he says in the sweetest voice.

Now the guffawing man is killing me again, but in an irksome way. I say nothing.

"For now, please enjoy the music and we should have salads and a delightful meal served soon."

Oh, no. He's not getting away with this. I lean slightly forward. "Mr. President—"

He cuts me off. "Serg—"

I cut him off. I will not burble. I will not babble. I will not. "*Sergei, will you be so kind as to tell me where I might find Alexei Plokhy?*" I just want to find Alexei and leave.

He stares at me. "Selena, I assure you, Alexei is staying away on purpose," comes Sergei's near-laughing reply as the servers arrive and place a salad in front of us. I make the same suggestion as with the soup. Sergei gives his nod, and the server removes my plate. Sergei pretends nothing is unusual and dives into his salad as though he is a ravenous animal.

"Fine, then," I say while pushing back my chair. "If you will excuse me, Sergei, I'm going to look for my escort."

"Selena, please sit." Sergei blows out a breath. "I'll tell you about Alexei."

I draw my chair back to the table and let my posture relax into a listening position.

"Damn, Selena. You would've survived a Russian gulag."

I'm nonplused. My eyes are now like emerald lasers burning the shit out of his crystal blue ones. *Zap.*

The curtain opens and Sergei waves his hand. The curtain closes. Sergei's crystal blue eyes look hard into my emerald ones. I don't blink.

Sergei sets his jaw. He knows I won't allow him to save this cluster of a night.

"Alexei is my personal Chief of Presidential Security. He protects me. I assigned him to you for your protection while you are in Russia."

"What? *What?*" I ask, dumbfounded. "You *spied* on me? Alexei is a spy?" Tears fall from my eyes, and I don't try to stop them. I'm nearly falling forward from my pert perch. I'm more upset by Alexei's betrayal than I am about this scam by Sergei.

"Alexei?" I whisper as a tear runs down my nose.

Sergei begins to say he's sorry. I don't let his lips form the words.

"Excuse me," I say and rise to my feet. I clutch my etui and turn toward the ladies' room alcove.

I'm aware the back of my hair is bouncing against my lavender dress as this curvy lady is making hay to the ladies' haven. My lavender shoes click on the wooden floors. I want to take the shoes off, and my slinky lavender dress, and hurl them both at Sergei Radkov. The damned etui too. And the purple gloves and the alexandrite ring. Damn, I left my gloves. My proud back straightens, searching for dignity.

Once in the toilet, I sit on a settee in a waiting room off the main part of the utility area of the toilet. It's opulent, but I can barely see as tears roll from my swollen eyes. I'm so disillusioned. Such a fool. I really thought Alexei to be a friend and here he is a... a... a damned spy.

I'm not sure what I do and do not deserve. One thing I'm sure of is that I don't deserve this. It hurts. To the marrow it hurts. I'm disgusted as I remember my pink toy moments. Moments wasted on this jackass.

I don't sense I'm in any real danger. I can't say what my status is. Just certain I've been played for a fool. I've come across treacherous men in my time. Some were nothing less than mass murderers. But this? This is a different kind of treachery. Can they not just say "Ha-ha, we pulled one over on you!" and let me leave Russia and go home to America? What's the chance of that? What in the hell have I done wrong except trust someone? I can't fathom why they would do this to me.

Tears flow even harder. I hurt. Dear God in heaven, I hurt. I've lost a friend and now I'm all alone in the far reaches of this foreign land. What did Alexei say I would be without him? "A lost American in Russia?" Well, Alexei, I'm that. Congratulations.

I hear a male voice, and I turn my body around on the settee so that he can't see my tearful face. Well, good luck with that. The room is made of wall-to-wall mirrors. I look down to study the carpet and dry my eyes with a tissue. I want to wipe the mascara blotches from my eyes, but damned if I'll let him see me giving a rat's ankle about mascara. My Elizabeth Frederick ladylike demeanor is returning. Stick with me, Mom.

To tell you the truth, I'm a little shocked. The President of United Russia is actually standing in the ladies' toilet. He is president, after all. Guess he can go wherever he likes. Damn. Damn. Damn him!

"Selena, I'm so very sorry. I didn't mean for tonight to be like this at all," says the Russian president. "I'll send Alexei to see you as soon as he gets back. Olga, my cook, has sent him into town on an errand."

"I don't want to see him," I reply, trying to remove the tearful shakiness from my voice.

"He'll be most hurt to hear that. He's very fond of you," comes a soft voice.

How does he do that? Be such an ogre, then speak so gently?

I want to die when I hear Sergei Radkov move toward me. He sits next to me on the settee. I don't turn my body toward him. He won't see my teary mascara-blotched face. Not face to face, anyway. He can look in any damned mirror he wants, but I'll be damned if he sees me face to face. I close my eyes. He won't see my pain. He won't.

"Selena, I'm a man who saw a woman," begins the man sitting beside me. "A very beautiful woman in a foreign land thousands of miles away. I admired her greatly but thought I'd never have the slightest chance of knowing her. I kept admiring her. I read the book she wrote. Then, I read it again, and that has been the only book I've read since.

"Just so I could connect with her somehow," he says as an afterthought.

I turn to look up at this tall man. I'm wearing a weak smile, but only for a fraction of a second. *He read my book? Sergei Radkov is a fan?*

Maybe, but it doesn't change a thing.

Sergei continues, "Then one day I found out this lady, this woman, this incredible lady I thought to be beautiful inside and out, would come thousands of miles over the ocean to visit my country. I did nothing, because of my position. It wasn't like I could call her up and ask her to dinner and a movie. There was no way for me to ever meet this woman of my imagination. Not even while she was in my country. Not even when we were in the same city."

Softly he says in a near whisper, "To meet *you*."

More strongly he says, "I reconciled myself to thinking I never would, but you were on my mind every day. Have been for months now."

I breathe in deeply but don't reply. I can't. I can't speak. My eyes are boring a hole in the lush angelic-styled carpet.

"I sent my very best operative, a man I've trusted with my life over and over again, to protect you, Alexei. There have been a few kidnappings of high-profile foreigners here since the coup. I'm trying to put a stop to it. I would die if something happened you, Selena."

He takes in a lungful of air. "You're not the only person I've protected. There are many. But you are the only one I gave my best personal operative. The best of the best. I'm glad I did, because there were no less than three attempted kidnappings that Alexei, Sasha, and Ivan foiled. You know of only one."

"Ivan the driver?" I ask, finding my voice. "Either a friend or a cousin of Alexei's? I can't keep them straight."

Sergei gives a slight titter. "Don't worry about that. I have known Alexei for many years, and I can't keep his cousins straight either. Nor do I know who truly is a cousin and who is not."

With that, I'm unable to hold in my laughter thinking over my times with Alexei. Now looking up at Sergei, I ask, "Were those kidnapping attempts for real?"

"They were."

"I never suspected a thing. Except for the one."

"That's why I gave you my best operative. My personal protector. I didn't want you spending time in my country worrying about such things. I wanted you to have the very best experience Russia can provide for you."

"So, Sergei, let me see if I'm getting this straight: you had the people of Russia pay for a helicopter ride, a dinner, two bands, and God knows what else, just so you could meet a woman?"

"Not exactly. I assure you the Russian people didn't pay for a thing."

I look at him quizzically.

"I make a salary, you know. And there is still yet another band. The best is yet to come," he says, giving me what some people might call a shit-eating grin.

I let out a long, "Okaaaaay," wondering what exactly is next.

"Well to complete the story, I was doing great. So proud of myself for not kidnapping this woman I idolize myself, for myself. Then she did something that moved my heart so much it convinced me I must take a chance and do whatever it takes to meet her. That is when this half-baked plan got cooked up."

I shake my head, questioning, "What was it that I did?"

"The orphanage."

I let out a long "Aaaaaah," as though to say, "Now I get it."

"Selena, it's impossible to tell you how much you touched my heart. My heart which had already been touched by you. I know I'm much too old for this, but I was like a smitten teenager. I'm sorry I acted so stupidly," Sergei pronounces. He beats his forehead with the palm of his hand. "Please forgive me, Selena. Please forgive me," he says again, a little softer.

"So, you and Alexei did this all... for me?" I ask feeling myself softening.

"Oh, it was more than us. All my staff jumped in. They were all so excited to make this night special for you."

I bite my lip, but Sergei continues to rattle on like a self-absorbed child telling a story.

"I was going to have my chef from Moscow come up, but Olga, my cook, was so excited about what foods she could put on the menu and table decorations and what not, that I simply couldn't take it away from her. I'm like her adopted son since I met her and vice versa. Olga looks out for me like a mother."

I let out a slight laugh, but it's an accepting laugh. Yes, he's a grown man being mothered, but I'm thinking of the mother Sergei doesn't have. It's a happy laugh because I do feel happy for him. I consider myself an insensitive idiot. I hope he doesn't misunderstand my laugh. I leave a hint of a smile on my face. It's natural, not forced.

"Yes, all the ladies on staff picked out clothes for you, because they knew you would need to stay overnight a night or two. It's not safe to fly back tonight without undue safety risks. In fact, we'll have a bad ice storm coming through here tonight. Even Siberia comes to a halt in such conditions until the ice makes its way through. We'll be stranded here several days, for sure."

"Oh no, I have a book signing..."

Sergei throws a hand up. "Don't worry, it's been rescheduled. St. Pete will get the ice after us. They realize it. Alexei has handled it."

I nod.

"Selena, if you never want to look at my face again, I understand. I've arranged a guest room for you here in the main dacha, but there are visitor dachas in the compound. I only ask that you wait until after tomorrow to leave. The weather is getting nasty, and my staff is exhausted from trying to present you with a memorable night."

"I see," comes my weak reply. Hell, I really don't know what to say. I'm in overload. Doesn't happen often but I sure as hell am overloaded now. All this was for me. For me! Now I damn sure am a fool.

"What I would like," comes Sergei's gentle voice, "is for you to enjoy your dinner and the next band. I'd appreciate it so much if you would consider it. Olga and the staff have worked so hard to make every detail comfortable for you. You don't have to. You can go straight to your quarters, but it would mean a lot to me, personally"—he points the fingers of a hand to his heart—"if you would stay and eat."

"Give me a few moments to freshen up," I agree.

"Of course."

Sergei takes a few steps out of the ladies' room but stops at the door and turns around. "Selena, thank you," he says in a heartfelt rasp. "You're a beautiful lady who wrote one hell of a book."

I return a sweet smile with a simple "Spasibo" and fix my mascara for the second time in a night.

CHAPTER 46
STORYTELLING

I SIT in anticipation at the table, waiting for Selena to return from the lady's room. It's been tense. My fingers cross underneath the table. God, I hope we've cleared the air and can be "real" with each other. Whew.

Despite our rocky start, I'll never forget her simple first words to me: "Hello, President Radkov. I'm Selena Frederick." Not Dr. Frederick. Not Dr. Selena Frederick. Simply Selena Frederick. She's humble. I'll never forget how those words rolled off of her ruby red lips. God, her lips kill me. My lips sizzled as they pressed against her skin when I kissed her hand. Sizzled.

A smile crosses my sizzled lips when I see her returning to the table. Selena has cleaned her face. Her makeup is in place. I can tell she has brushed her hair. You'd never know she was a crying mess minutes ago. That hurts me. A lot. She has spread a little pale pink lipstick on those ruby red lips. So sexy. I want to kiss every trace of it off those killer lips. I stand up and pull out her seat in a gentlemanly fashion. Damn her rounded ass.

"Spasibo," she says.

"You're welcome. Hope you're feeling better," I say as I adjust myself back in my seat.

"I am," replies Selena concisely, adding her smile.

I'm smiling so hard, my lips are hurting my teeth. "Good. Now Olga can stop crying in the kitchen."

"Oh-oh," mutters Selena, dragging out words with extra syllables in her Southern style. "Is she upset I didn't eat her soup and salad?"

"Yes, that. But she has this idea that she has let me down, which is silly, but is Olga."

"Can I thank her personally after dinner?" she asks.

"Probably not. Olga will fuss that her kitchen is a mess, and she isn't dressed in her Sunday best."

Selena laughs. "I understand. I'm familiar with a lot of mothers, adopted or not, who are like that back home in North Carolina."

"They make the world go around," I say, smiling big. It wanes a bit as I remember my mother lost so long ago. When Momma pops into my head, it's hard to smile. I struggle to recall what my mother looked like. Other than her long curly blonde hair, big eyes, and sweet smile. The finer details of Momma are fading in my memories. A beautiful woman, my mother. I remember being a proud boy who was walked to school with the most beautiful of all the school mothers. Yes, I was so proud then.

"I'm glad you have Olga," says Selena.

Jolting me from my memories, I reply, "Me too."

"In America there's a saying: *the way to a man's heart is through his stomach.*"

I throw my head back in laughter. "I can't speak for other men, but that was true for me when I found Olga."

The servers make a slight interruption as they deliver chicken Kiev and roasted vegetables.

"Tell me a story about you," I request of the sexy American while taking a Kiev bite.

"I'm afraid there isn't much to tell besides what's told in my book. A woman without a home. That's what I've been since my parents died."

"I understand that," I remark.

"Yes, I think you do." She shoots me a bittersweet smile as she cuts her chicken with a knife before continuing her narrative.

"So difficult to explain. I grew up with loving parents in a community of loving people. I've a loving sister and two fantastic nieces that I love to pieces, and a brother-in-law who is like the brother I never had. They live on a ranch in the mountains of North Carolina." Selena takes in a breath while forking a piece of chicken. "After my parents died, it was like there was a hole blown through me that was so huge I could never hope to fill the void."

Selena sits here with chicken on the end of her fork tine, and I stop chewing to listen to her.

"I finished all the plans I made before they died. I finished college. I finished med school. I finished my residency. Then I didn't know where to go. I was lost. I didn't have a real home. Not anymore. Even though I could've gone back to where I grew up, nothing was the same. That must sound ridiculous to you compared to your experience, but all I can say is that was mine."

I swallow then give her a firm look but speak gently. "Selena, you are right. It was your experience, and your journey." I pause for a moment to form my words. "And I had mine. It was what it was for both of us. What matters is who we are today. It's okay to make things better for tomorrow, as well we should, but it's who we are today that matters."

She gives me another quiet, bittersweet smile and takes in the piece of chicken that has been hanging on the end of her fork. I perceive she is pondering my words as she chews.

"You're right, Sergei. I've existed in the future for many years. I was always asking myself, 'What am I going to do when I finish med school or my residency, or when I leave DWB?' That was all okay, but it would be very easy to lose who you are today because you are so focused on the long and winding road. If you make yourself strong today, then you will probably be strong at the end of tomorrow's road. I'm not sure I was ever truly strong. I'm just a woman who did strong things."

I look at her and consider her for a few moments. Finally, I develop my reply. "Yes," was my only word. We sit and eat in silence for a few minutes.

I break the silence. "What made you leave DWB?"

"A friend of mine was killed. I'd lost friends along the way, and death was not new to me by any means. But losing this friend was very personal." Selena pauses and takes in a deep breath before plunging into full disclosure. "The friend was a man that I had admired for a long time, and he was married," she says with a tilted head but no regret in her voice.

She is letting me in. Thank God she is letting me in and not holding back. Not a game player, this lady. I put my fork down to absorb her storytelling.

"We had a onetime affair on a lonely night. And then a sniper's bullet killed him the next day. Intuition stated I had to heal myself before I could heal others. Surprise! Here I am!"

I study her for a moment before I give her a smile. I sense a discomfort. She may feel she's under a microscope. The air is as thick as the juicy chicken she is cutting. This feeling is of her own making, but it's her feeling all the same. I don't like it.

Fearing tears might wet her eyes, as she looks at her plate and cuts another piece of chicken, I say, "I am so very sorry, Selena."

"Me too," is her brief and whispered reply.

As if trying to find a distraction, I make conversation about the jazz and blues band that will play during dessert when we finish dinner.

Out of the clear blue sky, I look the green-eyed lady in the eyes and say, "Selena, I'm so sorry that I made you cry. I was so stupid. The very last thing I ever want to do is make you cry. I'm sad now that I know you have cried a lot already."

There it is out there. I want her to know how I feel.

Her expression makes me believe she finds my words comforting. Like my nouns and verbs wash over her like a warm bath. I hope so. Her face lightens.

"I realize you sacrificed a lot for tonight, and I gave nothing. I want you to know I understand that now, and I'm sorry, too."

Thank God she understands. She understands I'm a man saying that, at a minimum, I want to know her. Damn, I think it's possible she wants to know me, too. As she looks into my face, I get this inkling, this *tiny* inkling, she wants to know me as much as I want to know her. Maybe crossed fingers under a table do actually work.

"Spasibo, for everything," she says, charming me with her Russian word. "You and your staff and Momma Olga have worked so hard. Please make Olga aware how much I appreciate her and the team's effort, and that my inappreciative behavior was a misunderstanding on my part and not directed at their superior efforts. To them, I would most like to say, I'm sorry."

"Olga is the best. I see the touch of her hand trying to make everything special," nods Selena, affirming her statement.

If I wasn't in love with this woman before now, I just flew past the definition of love and landed somewhere beyond the icy clouds in the sky over Siberia. My next quest will be to make her understand my feelings. Slowly, yet quickly. Not much time, ya know? Hoping in my heart that my desire to kiss her, bed her, be a man to her won't overtake my desire to make her understand my love for her. Damned hard, this love business, especially with so much lust involved.

Selena changes the subject. "For the first time, I'm taking in this room. Purple. Funny how my outfit matches the room. Just worked out that way. I love this wallpaper that represents moments in Russian history with drawings of persons and scenery. Simple but elegant."

"Yes," I reply. "Russian tastes gravitate to the heavy. Gold gilding amasses in places and carved wood in others. Heavy purple velvet curtains folding beside the windows and around the stage. The wallpaper breaks up some of that heaviness," I respond, not believing I'm into talking about wallpaper. And curtains.

"I love the rich purple color of the curtains. The way they fall to create those bishop sleeve bottoms is lovely. Against all the gold, they create magic. They're awesome," Selena comments.

"Russians love heavy gold. Hell, heavy anything. Just make it big. And heavy." I push my tongue into my cheek, because I want to tell her what else is big. And heavy. Take it easy, Tiger. I could sit here all night and talk with her about wallpaper and curtains. Just need to keep 'big and heavy' out of the conversation. What can I say? I'm a man with a head full of this woman, a heart full of love, and a groin full of lust. I need to concentrate on the first two of these three things.

We're finishing our last bites of dinner when Selena turns her head to look toward the footfalls she hears behind her. They belong to Alexei.

The impish man walks up to the table and hangs his head. "I'm sorry, Selena."

Selena throws down her napkin, stands up from the table, and puts her arms around Alexei. Hugs him like a Russian bear.

"Are you kidding me? You saved my life more than once." Selena beats her fist into her heart and says, "You're my people, Alexei. You can be my cousin anytime."

All three of us howl with laughter. From his tiptoes, Alexei kisses the top of her head. No one would ever suspect we're in a presidential setting. Oops. I'm just not your usual kind of president.

Alexei says his good nights. The curtain opens as the band begins playing their bluesy jazz instrumentals. We continue our small talk as the music plays. We lock onto each other's eyes but then dart away as if to say, "You can't read my private thoughts. Too personal. Too tender."

Between songs, the servers bring a dark chocolate marshmallow dessert that has a bite of dark chocolate cake and vanilla ice cream to boot. Dark chocolate shards make the dessert look more like an ornament than something edible. Russians love dark chocolate. Selena says she likes the dark chocolate a lot, but truth be told she is also fond of rich milk chocolate.

"However, chocolate is chocolate," she says while scooping the dessert into her mouth. She makes yummy sounds with her first bite.

She asks me if I know the name of the dessert.

"Something Olga cooked up. She is always creating things."

Selena picks up her glass and hoists it in a toast. "To the creator."

I clink my glass with hers. "To the creator."

We take our sips, and each of us exhales at the end of this scrumptious meal.

I begin the next conversation. "I noticed in your book, both of us were born in March. Many people love all kinds of gemstones, but I've always loved aquamarine. My mother wore it often."

"Me too," replies Selena. "I've started wearing more of it lately. I got pieces of costume jewelry when I was a kid that had aquamarine gems. When I got older, I was never a big jewelry wearer, but would gravitate to pearls and other things. Now, I guess I'm circling back around."

Selena's eyes are bright, and she's smiling. Her personality is so comfortable. We just met tonight, but I already feel like I can talk with her about anything, from childhood hurts to purple curtains.

"Yes, my mother had a few nice pieces that she liked to wear when she dressed up. God only knows what happened to them. Many times, I've wondered if she was born in March also, or if she wore them just because she liked the color," I reply without solemnity. Solemnity is a weird thing. It just hits you at its own chosen moment, or it doesn't.

"The important thing is that you remember that detail, Sergei. Wherever your mother may be, I can guess it would comfort her to know you remember such things. As well, it's just one of those things that no one or nothing can take away. You may not know where her aquamarine gems are, but you know where your memory of her is."

"Perhaps. Perhaps she abandoned me and doesn't care what I remember," I shrug, speaking in a matter-of-fact manner.

"What do you think?" asks Selena like a concerned friend.

"I think not. I want to think not," I say with a slight lean to my head, as if to negotiate the strength of my words.

"I remember some things," I tell her. "Things she told me to do, and especially how to be safe. Always protective of me. Took excellent care of me. Always kind to me. My mother read me stories and tucked me into bed. Helped with homework. One day, without explanation, she vanished. So, I think not, but then, I was just a kid."

Selena mulls her words in her mouth and rinses them with a swig of wine. "Sergei, if you would like my opinion, I don't believe your mother abandoned you. It's more than a hunch: it's a professional opinion."

My eyes laser on her with intensity. "Tell me why you conclude this, Selena."

Selena considers her reply carefully, and I appreciate that. She is the type who makes sure nothing has been left unfactored.

She leans forward. "I've seen many women give their children away, and some abandon them, even newborn babies. They do these things for many reasons. I've seen mothers do this across many cultures and underneath all sorts of dire circumstances. Your mother doesn't fit that description."

I nod as my eyes drop. Seemingly, I'm considering the white tabletop linen while I breathe in her words rather than indulge in the magnetism of Selena's bejeweled emerald eyes.

She continues, "The things you say to me don't fit that pattern. Perhaps you can't, but you're not recalling alcohol or drug abuse. I suspect you would if it had happened. Especially if you recall, say, your mother's aquamarine jewels." Selena gives me a moment to let that sink in.

I'm considering things in a new way, and her words are helpful.

"Sergei, you're a very intelligent man. I assess you must have considered all these things. I don't want to risk insulting your intelligence. Do you want me to continue?"

"Yes. Sometimes things sound different when said in another's voice," I say to her, but don't make strong eye contact.

The healer continues. "You speak of a loving mother who took care of you. Unloving mothers don't tuck their children in at night nor read them stories. At best, they will tell their children to go to bed. I've seen some who don't even care where their young children are, much less whether they're sleeping. You speak of her being protective of you and caring about your safety. That is a loving mother of the highest order."

Selena allows me a moment to process this until my eyes unfold themselves from the tabletop linen and return eye contact with her. It's strong eye contact. I nod for her to continue.

"The evidence shows your mother vanquished into thin air. The evidence of your words suggests she didn't abandon you. It's important to both you and her for you understand that difference."

"Thank you, Selena," I say in a soft voice. I'm in so much awe that I struggle to pull air through my nose and down into my lungs. I'm hoping she doesn't misunderstand my gaze. I have no intent; nothing is scripted. What is there in my eyes is just there. What is coming from my heart shows through my eyes. I'm looking at her heart, not her beauty. Not her boobs. Not her legs. Not her hair. Not her curves. Not her ruby lips. Not her ass. Her heart.

I break the electric silence. "You're wrong, Selena. You are a very strong woman."

Selena doesn't speak. She doesn't deny it. It's she who is now studying the table linen. I sense I touched something inside her essence. Something hidden. Something wounded that fights to heal. I get it, I think. The stronger you are, the more you struggle with the volume of your strength. It's almost like a liquid you can measure. Pour out what you need in a measuring cup. Is this enough strength for what I need? Do I need to find more and refill this vessel? Was the vessel accidentally broken? Inner human strength is unmeasurable and subjective. Yet humans are constantly trying to quantify it.

I break the pause in conversation. "Tell me something about your parents," I shrug. "A memory."

Selena thinks for a moment and allows a smile to return to her face after the tense prior conversation. "Oh! I remember an aquamarine one."

"Oh, goody!" I reply, with my eyebrows moving up and down.

Selena giggles at my comedy, and I suspect the use of the American term. I cross my legs and grin while she begins. I'm all in on storytelling hour.

"Well, it was the last argument I can remember between my parents. They rarely fussed. The two of them were always loving and supportive of each other. I even called my sister, who lives on the complete opposite side of the state, to ask if Mom and Dad were having problems. Sometimes they would discuss things with my older sister that they wouldn't discuss with a younger me."

"What did she say?" I ask with intense interest.

"Well, she told me to walk by their bedroom door right then and I'd have my answer. I did, and carnal things were definitely going on in there. My sister knew all the way on the other side of North Carolina. Guess you could say my folks had a pattern."

Selena's eyes widened at the word "things," causing me to shoot back a knowing grin.

"My sister said that in her opinion, at my parent's age, such arguments were their idea of foreplay."

I had to put my hand over my mouth to keep from spraying a mouthful of wine into Selena's face.

"Anyway," Selena continues after both our laughter clears. "My mother was having what we in America call a wedding shower for my mom's good friend's daughter, who was to be married that summer. Often when a couple gets married in America, close friends and relatives put on a gathering called a shower wherein guests present the bride with gifts to help furnish the new couple's household."

I nod in understanding.

"My mother's shower was somewhat formal in that she sent out invitations and only females attended. The event was to happen outside on the screened porch and the deck. Tables extended all the way down the walkway to the dock on the intercoastal waterway. Nowadays, people at a shower are more interested in jumping in the water, getting together, and having a barbeque and beer in the backyard. But my mother was old school. Mom did it the old way, and I assure you that when my mother did a thing, it was to perfection."

I make another nod but add a grin this time. *Like mother, like daughter.*

"So, she bought a large number of aquamarine placemats and tablecloths, with paper lanterns and aquamarine ribbons tied up everywhere. Mom picked aquamarine because the color was perfect for a spring event on the waterway." Selena set the scenario but slows a little as she shares a small piece of the woman who was her mother.

I continue to gaze at her with interested bemusement as Selena's animated voice talks about the place she once called home.

"Well, as Mom was considering everything, she thought she might be short a few matching napkins. So, she requested my father, who was exhausted after being up most of the night with patients, to go to the place where Mom bought decorations to pick up more napkins. You must realize, this place is at least ten to twelve miles out. No development existed between our house and civilization within that distance besides a gas station at that time."

I give another nod and add a look of bedevilment. I'm following the story with relish, and thinking I suspect where the story is going.

"Joseph Frederick asked my mother; *Can't those old biddies just wipe their mouths with paper towels?*"

I howl in laughter. I like her dad already. A man I'll never meet.

"My mother was patient," Selena assures me. "Mom asked 'Please,' understanding my dad to be tired, and gave him a kiss out the door." Selena takes in a breath to give emphasis on the next part. "Well, he made the worst faux pas and returned with *turquois* napkins."

"Oh, the poor man, especially after the paper towel remark. Your father had sunk himself in deep," I chime in.

"Exactly," agrees Selena. "My mother had a fit. My dad said he was not going back. Then they had a big argument over whether blue plus green makes aquamarine or turquois. Dad said aquamarine. Mom said turquois. It was on like a big boiling pot of neck bones, all over the damn color of the napkins."

"Oh, so please tell me. Did your poor dad make a twenty-mile round trip for more napkins?"

"Oh yes, after they came out of their carnal room. I'd have expected my father should be more tired, but his disposition was as though he'd just gotten up from eight hours of sleep."

I giggle, "I bet."

"So that was my folks and their aquamarine story. I always thought aquamarine to be a light sky-blue color. Almost like the color of your eyes. I'm leaning with my mom's opinion. Blue and green must make turquois."

"Not necessarily," I reply. "We mine a lot of aquamarine here in Russia. I've seen aquamarine the color of your eyes. I say the blue of my eyes and the green of your eyes make aquamarine."

Selena giggles, "Well, I won't disagree, or else you may send me out to buy napkins in a blizzard."

"Oh, I assure you, Selena, your mother well-compensated your father for his troubles."

Selena gives me a knowing smile as our eyes make accidental contact, both of which share a concealed glint. Whatever that glint held, it caught me off guard. Selena too, I think.

"I've not told a story about my parents since they died," Selena confides.

My eyes pick up on how much she still misses them, even after all this time. The two of us sit in silence. Each with slightly upturned lips and eyes darting, then holding. Then darting again.

Yes, those neck bones are boiling and will soon be ready to add to a Thanksgiving stuffing.

CHAPTER 47
ON LIKE A POT OF NECK BONES

THE LEAD SINGER in the band steps forward to a microphone as though to adjust its height before the next number. I take the prompt and lay my linen napkin on top of the tablecloth. I leave my seat to stand in front of Selena and give her a humble bow.

"May I ask for this dance?" I ask with an outstretched hand.

Selena accepts in silence, but I sense she is as nervous as me. I'm trying not to shake. Not to mention, I'm fighting the need to adjust my pants. Damn, I'm already sizzling with the touch of the skin on her back.

"I haven't danced in a long time," she whispers in my ear as the lights go dark except for a circular haze that encompasses the singer.

Her breath caresses my face. The smell of her wine is in my nostrils. Fuck me. "You can relax, Selena. I'm not a great dancer, but I'm going to enjoy this dance as though it's my first *and* my last," I whisper against her pretty face.

She smiles.

I smile back and put my hand around Selena's waist as the vocalist belts out in a strong, sultry voice, *"When a maaan loves a woo-maaaan..."*

Selena gives a slight snort and leans to whisper in my ear, "Wonder where that came from."

Alexei. Alexei informed me it's her favorite song.

"No idea," I lie as I move Selena's body with a confidence I don't really have. I lower her down from her waist for a playful dip. Slowly. Showing off my upper-body strength, I lift her back up closer to me. Hey, a man better use what he's got to impress his lady. I study her face as we move. Study the face of the woman of my affections. In no way am I disappointed in the woman I've always perceived her to be.

I smell her musky perfume. I want to kiss her so intensely that I barely hold my restraint. Hate to appear a barbaric Russian, but that is what I feel like. Primal. I want to ask her before the first kiss though, like a gentleman. Want to hear her say "Yes" to me. Want to hear that one word. Then all bets are off. I might still be a gentleman, or I might be a caveman.

I move my hand underneath Selena's hair, touching the back of her dress. Lowering her for another dip, her long mane drags the floor. Shit! I try to pick up her hair instead of the lady. I leave her bent at the waist. The two of us laugh at the comedy.

"There are some real disadvantages to having long hair," a charming Selena says while giving me a shy yet confident smile in the dim light.

Damn, where does she get that confidence?

"I was afraid I would step on it," I confess.

"Next time, I'll wear my hair up. Gotta be prepared for anything."

Next time?

We laugh, and smile, and look. Occasionally, our gazes shy in another direction. Damn, if this keeps up, I'm gonna be a worse bad boy than I intended. What did Selena say? It's definitely on like a boiling pot of neck bones. And I'm ready to gnaw on those bones.

I want to run my fingers through all that hair, touch her face, kiss those lips, leave her lavender dress on the dance floor. I want to take her right here and now. My bad boy pants tighten. I push "bad boy" from my thoughts and put him in a corner for time out. At least, I try. He's a wild child.

When Selena catches the next glimpse in my eyes, she detects my strong desire for her. I know she does. It's obvious. The overgrown bad boy in my pants is not helping. The one thing I don't want to happen is for her to think the attraction I have is merely physical. But what can I say? I'm a man. A man who hasn't bedded a woman in a while, but I only want to bed *her*. No other woman.

It occurs to me that she, too, has a need. Her eyes twinkle, and I'm enough of a man to sense yearning. A man lusts. A woman yearns. This woman is yearning. I'm not sure for what. I want to think those are bedroom eyes. Ah, therein lies the rub friend Alexei told me about. God, I want to rub. I can tell you that. I bend down to lean my face against hers. That is all the rub I need to be thinking about at this moment. I do. And it's heaven.

The music stops. All is quiet. It seems no one in the room is breathing. I stop my lead dance movements but don't want to break from her. I force myself to take a step backward. As if I were a man of the nineteenth century, I bend down to kiss her hand. Reluctantly, I release her soft hand back to her care.

"Would you like to see the art gallery?" I ask as light returns. "It's right off the hallway here. I love art, but I haven't seen the collection myself. The past few months have been so busy." I'm speaking softly after swallowing the invisible lump in my throat. I don't want to discuss my other lump.

"I can believe that," Selena replies. "Let me get my purse. I have a habit of losing things if I let them out of my sight."

"Of course," I say.

We make our way down the hallway with me taking her hand. The same hand that nearly sizzled the skin off my lips. We turn the corner to the left into the gallery.

"I'm not sure about the collection. Possibly the art was purchased with the property, or they may have brought in some pieces. An art historian in Moscow keeps track of such things," I inform her.

I unlock the door to the gallery with my master key and turn on the lights. "Light" is the operative word.

"Wow," Selena exclaims. She's observing the open space with plentiful skylights that would direct sunlight downward so as not to affect the paintings. That is, if sunlight was present.

The gallery room is large and airy. Curved white benches with arched backs and plush seat cushions are placed in exact positions where an observer might sit to take in the artists' every brush stroke. When one approaches a painting, the setting is so very intimate.

The most intriguing garden grows in the center under the skylights, suiting the room's flair for airy space. In the garden there are statues and urns and busts and sculptures. This space too, is intimate.

Selena comments, "Observing a painting here in this setting, I feel as if I'm having a private conversation with the artist. Thank you for bringing me here."

As if she can't find the right words to describe her experience, Selena looks up at the taller me, and adds, "It's so lovely. Someone had a true heart for this space."

She appears to be in a trance, trying to take it all in. I love it. Damn, she's so beautiful.

"I think you're right, Selena, but I'm unable to say who. I know nothing about the history of the dacha. I only just recently learned there was a gallery here. Even then, I did not really know what beauty lay behind this locked door. This is the first time I've been inside."

"What a woooonderful adventure we're having then," says the beautiful woman that I can't take my eyes away from. She's drawling out syllables with her Southern American accent and it's killing me.

We move to observe several pieces, chatting between ourselves about the artists' brush strokes, artistic themes, and the very Russian trademark of captured human expression in their visual artistry. I remark that I know the locations in a few of the landscape pieces, or at least the general location. There're a few paintings of Lake Baikal, the mountains, and cultural groups of Russia. We mosey across the main gallery into a secluded alcove gallery. One could say the alcove gallery was of erotic art.

Selena isn't at all put off by the artistic content. I'm sure she has seen plenty of intimate body parts in her time. We make our way along the line of paintings until we come to a full wall-sized painting covering the rear of the room. Neither of us can remove our eyes from it. The portrait depicts a full-frontal nude woman standing next to an enormous bed. She is only wearing aquamarine jewelry. The woman appears to be removing her blue satin robe and letting it drop behind her. The look of the woman in the painting controls the overall tone of the setting. Her look isn't as much "Come hither" as it is "I'm coming to you."

The portrait lady has hair a lovely shade of blonde that falls almost to the floor. She possesses hair that is almost ankle-length, like Selena's. Unspeakably lovely, the lady wears green eyes similar to Selena's, but the painted lady's eyes are more elongated than Selena's round ones. We both stand in entranced silence, as though we're in prayer. The portrait is breathtaking.

"The anatomy is so perfect. Even the toenails," Selena says, whispering as though she's back home in a North Carolina church. "There's something more here. I can't quite put my finger on it. It's as though the artist had a true love for her, but I'm not quite seeing requited love in her expression."

"Hmm," I say unconsciously while intensely studying the painting. "I'm not sure about the eyes, Selena. I'll have to study them more. However, although the bedding is different, I'm sure that is the bed in my bedroom chamber."

"Really?" Selena says automatically. "Suppose this was a prior owner's wife, or mistress, maybe? Not just a muse, though. It would be interesting to know who painted this. Sort of for laugh and giggles. It seems a matter of intrusion by us on a private moment. I may be crazy, but that is how the portrait moves me to feel."

I pull out my cell phone from my tuxedo pocket and turn on its light for more illumination. Curious, I run the light along the bottom of the painting and pick out a signature that looks like an *S* with a line to the right of it.

"Someone whose first or last name starts with an 'S,' I think. I suppose they don't want you to know more than that. Not a signature I'm familiar with among Russian artists. I know many, but by no means all," I consider. Yet, I feel I know that signature from somewhere —but where?

"'Tis curious," replies Selena with her round green eyes taking in the facial details of the lady subject. "I'm not sure about it, but there's something in this lady's eyes. The artist caught it, if not in spite of him or herself. It's like a revelation to them, you can tell. You can feel it in your chest."

"You're like me with art," I reply with a knowing smile. "Like music. Sometimes you get carried away with it. The artist takes you to another existence."

"I'm sorry to hold up the line," Selena teases, looking behind her at no one. "Can I come back to see her before I leave? There's something about this lady's eyes that has captured me. I guess my curiosity is in overdrive."

"Stay as long as you like and come as many times as you like," replies this very pleased man at her love of art. "I'm intrigued by this painting as well. There's something familiar about her. I can't put my finger on it, but she captures my curiosity as well."

"Weeeeell," replies Selena with that drawl again, "she *has* slept in your bed before."

I give an embarrassed laugh. "Yes. That she most likely has."

"This might sound crazy to you, but do you want to know what I see in this lady's eyes?" asks Selena.

"Love to."

"What occurs to me is a distance from the artist. Like she cares for them and is trying to portray the look the artist wants, not what she truly feels. That is curious, because the artist would have to be her lover, whether male or female. You can tell the artist loves every inch of her with every inch of their heart. It's obvious by their portrayal of her. I see fervor in the brush strokes. Not just perfection, but a perfecting. The artist would die for her. I feel it. But what's in her eyes is almost a submission. I perceive the artist saw that when they painted her. It may have hurt them. I think it did. But the artist loves her still. I can feel it. It's like the artist understands it."

"Very possible, Selena. In Soviet times, people had many relationships just to survive. Always about survival. There was no space for love. Even a young couple who got married and had youthful love would eventually realize it wouldn't take much to separate them forever." I shrug. "Someone says something to the authorities, and whether or not it's true, their partner, man or woman, would get sent off to a gulag. In a marriage, the other partner would have to denounce their partner in prison to stay outside of it themselves.

"Homosexual love is still not accepted in Russia." I'm sure Selena is aware of that. "I'm thinking about how I might change my people's attitudes to be more accepting. In an out-of-the-way place like this, though, during Soviet times, private same sex intimacy might occur."

Selena nods. Having experienced many horrid stories during her time spent in war-torn nations, I realize she has known the sickening depravity some humans bring.

I continue my musings. "During Soviet times, especially during the days of gulags, it was Russian-on-Russian. I'm sure as a clinician you've not been too far removed from the same things happening in nations undergoing civil war. The thought of what my countrymen did to one another hurts me to the bone. I'm not a man to brush the past under the carpet. A lot of my own suffering was because of it."

I continue like a history professor as she gives me her silent attention. "Women in gulags had babies to get away from the hardship of their gulag work on little food rations. I'm talking about women cutting down trees with a saw and hauling them away by hand. These women, of course, would put the babies up for adoption. The child was a means to an end, since pregnant women were assigned to light duty. Survival at its worst."

"The fathers were the prison guards?" she asks.

"Yes, almost always," I reply with certainty.

"I've read about the gulags in writings by Solzhenitsyn but have forgotten some of the dark details. That experience by so many Russians is unbearable for me to think about. I can only imagine how it affects you."

"Thank you," I murmur.

With that solemn insight, the two of us pull ourselves from the painting and complete our tour of the alcove and the opposite wall of the gallery. I stand behind Selena to give her space—hell, to give *me* space, because I want to touch the back of her hair. Such perfect curls in a mass falling far down below her back, encompassing her physically, while nothing encompasses her spirit but art. God, I love that.

There are a few times I look away from the paintings to the round muscular bump between her back and her thighs. Now that, my friends, is art. My primitive man wants to rip her dress off and lay her down right here. Lie with her and take my own artistic journey from floor to wall to alcove to garden. Then, across benches and look to the sky.

"Well, I think we've seen most of it, but I would like to come back to see it again soon," says Selena.

My thoughts of Selena's bump, that mental portrait of her luscious rump, are interrupted. I reply, "I would love to bring you back here, or you can always come on your own. See those two chairs there?" I point into the center garden. "I can't be sure, but they appear to be comfortable sunning chairs under the skylights. Make a great place to read a book. Perhaps we can try them out with coffee in the morning?"

"How awesome would that be?" replies Selena agreeably.

Damned awesome, but I'm sure reading won't be foremost on my mind. I smile like a good boy and recommend we go below to take in the natural pool of geothermal water.

CHAPTER 48
GEOTHERMALS

IN THE ELEVATOR, I comment to Sergei, "I heard there are a few geothermal sites in the area. I'd love to have swum in an outcropping near Irkutsk surrounded by a spa. I hear it's two-thumbs-up experience. Alas, duty called, so no time for luxury."

"I'm familiar with where you're talking about," replies Sergei as the bell rings in the glass elevator after taking us down two floors. "Been there once. I love to swim in it. Float, really. Can't do actual laps like I can in the Moscow pool. God, I was a fish in a former life, I think. Love to be in water. Suppose it's because I didn't get to do much of it as a kid. Too cold," he shrugs. "Later, I attended schools that had heated indoor pools. That's when my fish grew scales."

"I get that, having grown up around warm water. I'm a fish too, scales and all," I reply. "Although, not so much in pools as in the ocean."

Cinderella and her prince step off the elevator to what might be bedrooms along the outer walls. It's hard to say for sure since all the doors to the rooms are closed. In the middle of the space, a pool of water bubbles to the surface. Bright, colorful tiles surround the outline of the irregularly shaped fresh water source. An open area around the water has a venting mechanism incorporated into the domed glass ceiling. I surmise the dome's design allows the humid air to escape, even in blizzard weather. Impressive engineering.

My eyes soak in the windows, the blue dome ceiling, and the outrageously gorgeous multicolored tile flooring which looks Mediterranean. More precisely, the tiles might be more Turkish, or from one of the more recently formed "Stans." A comfortable space is created with unimposing tables and sculptural chairs. Large plants grow in big round clay pots whose limbs try to kiss the sky. Once again, the architect has worked magic using natural ceiling light as I noted in the gallery. This dome protrudes several floors below the upper architecture. I assess all the alcoves of the upper floors, such as the ones in the ballroom, help to achieve the mid-height dome architecture of the dacha design.

Sergei's eyes are on me as I'm taking in the inner sanctum of his personal space. This prince of a man allows me to enjoy the moment. Just enjoy without words. I like that, even though I can feel his eyes checking out my backside. Women just know when that stuff happens. That's okay. I've checked out his backside, too. Although for some reason I peg him as more of a boobs guy.

"Go for a swim?" Sergei inquires casually.

I'm sure I'm blushing despite my efforts otherwise. "I'm not reeeeeally dressed for a swim," I say, waving my hand to bring attention to my formal wardrobe.

Sergei's mouth forms an ear-to-ear grin. "You modest Americans. Underwear swim," retorts the president-turned-teenager.

"Um, that's a brilliant suggestion," I reply with one raised eyebrow. "Except I'm not wearing any."

Eager, Sergei already has his tie and cummerbund off and laid upon a bench. "Well then, I will take mine off as well. That way, you'll not be alone." Not waiting for me to reply, he unbuttons his shirt. "Come on, I won't look. So warm. Feels so good, Selena."

Modest American, huh? Well, I've seen more female body parts than he ever will on his best day, and a darn many male ones, too. Without a word, I put down my etui on an opposite bench and walk over to request Sergei unzip my dress. I feel his eyes on my ass. I'm sure of it. Serves him right for playing Mr. Casual. I take his challenge and taunt him like a cat flipping its tail. Oh, President Radkov, it's so on. You can bet it's on like a pot of roiling neck bones, and I can't wait to eat 'em.

Elizabeth Frederick wouldn't like this. I hear her "tsk tsk" from heaven. *Sorry mom, but when in Russia, do as the Russians do,* I think as I turn my eyes to heaven. Like other Europeans, these people are immodest about nudity. Not just nude sunbathing. Russia is the nation of the banya, community bathing. Sergei Radkov can get an eyeful of my ass if he wants.

I remove my shoes. Remove my jewelry and take the combs from my hair. Gather my long hair and twist it to make a large bun on my head. The combs hold up my mane perfectly. Standing, I remove my dress, which slides off like melting butter on a slanted hot potato. Maybe I'm being a bad Southern lady, but I'm not in America nor the South. When in Russia…

I was a medical student once. Hell, my classmates, both male and female, stripped naked for each other to be examined. If a classmate had sex on their mind, they kept it to themselves. Unspoken taboos were put in place by the student group. Such as discussing the body of classmates outside of our learning lab. I see no reason to turn myself upside down over nudity in a nation that finds American modesty laughable.

Sergei has already made his way into the pool. As I make my way to its entrance steps, Sergei comes over to offer his hand to the naked Cinderella. True to his word, he keeps his eyes downcast.

The warm, soothing waters embrace me with enough swirling bubbles to hide my physique. Sergei has turned all the lights to dim mode. Multicolored track lights surround the pool. And there's always the light of the moon. A sliver of light waning between clouds, which will soon disappear with the oncoming ice storm. I feel transported. To where, I can't say. Another planet? The most wonderful place on this planet? Now I understand why Sergei loves this dacha despite his lack of knowledge of the gallery. Guess that was a bonus for him.

I would feel his presence in this pool even if I wasn't swimming right beside him. What I find more amazing is that I've heard him say publicly that the dacha belongs to the people and is meant for the president's use only during their term. And that there would be no other such properties held by the Russian government under his term. That means one day he will give this up.

"You like?" comes Sergei's softball question, knowing it to be impossible not to like this.

"No. I love."

"Me too," is Sergei's pleased-as-punch reply. "Come with me over here," requests the prince while taking my hand. "There are two built-in chairs, and I put water on the ledge for us. Easy to get dehydrated, if not careful."

I comply. True to Russian engineering, the seats are arranged in such a way that the water comes just over the level of one's chest. The chairs slope so that a couple of average height might talk intimately to one another while the soothing waters flow around them.

I open a bottle of water and drink. "I hope I'm not putting on a peep show for your security team."

"No," assures Sergei. "I stationed security around the perimeter and outside the entrance door of this floor. Alexei vouches for my security in your presence."

The thought of the tam-laden man gives me a smile. Grateful he and the other guys can't see me, though. I still have a pinch of my damn Southern upbringin' in me. Just a pinch. Sometimes I think I lost that upbringin' in a bag somewhere in a foreign airport. Other times I think a suitcase flies open, and those years of upbringin' jump out.

"Good. Not Alexei that I worry about nearly so much as the man you call Vogo. Guess Vogo is doing his job, albeit a bit excessively," I state.

"Oh Vogo. How do I describe Vogo? A man of extremes. His presence is felt long after he's gone. The man sees to it," nods Sergei for emphasis. "However, he has saved my life many times, and I've saved his a few, too. There's no one I would trust more to give up their life for me and die cussing and spitting while doing it."

I laugh. "I see. Have you known him a long time, or is he somewhat like another Mother Olga?"

It's Sergei's turn to laugh. "I've known Vogo much longer than

Alexei. I've known him almost as long as I have known Ivan, which is when I first arrived in the orphanage as a child."

"So Vogo and Ivan were orphans also?" I ask, curious.

"Ivan was. Vogo, no."

"I see."

Sergei is thinking as though he is weighing something. I'm about to tell him I'm sitting here buck naked talking to a man I barely know, so surely, he can share a little history. Instead, I take a sip of water.

"It's a very, *very* long story, Selena. Very."

"I have two ears. Neither is full at the moment."

Sergei smiles. God, I love his smile. I adore this man. Guess that's why I'm sitting here with him in my birthday suit, with Elizabeth Frederick rolling over in her wet grave. Wherever that grave may be. Such thoughts always weigh me as though I'm standing on Jupiter. I shovel the sadness into another corner of my soul as I wait for Sergei's response.

I've never loved a man before, not even Sam. That was different. Sam wasn't mine. Sergei isn't mine either because I'll only have this speck of time with him. But, for the moments I have, I'm going to make him as much mine as I can. My heart is open. Foolish and unregulated, but open.

I wish I could ask Elizabeth Frederick, "What do I have to lose?" I'm scared. I'm freaking shaking, but this man told me he saw a woman whom he admired and wanted to know but thought it impossible. He went through a lot to make this possible. This moment. It's possible these are the only moments we may ever have. And I will be damned if I won't give this man a chance to know me. And do everything I can to make sure he never forgets me. I'm never forgetting him.

This man, with those big blue eyes—now more sapphires in the light than crystal blue—would give any woman cause to move an entire mountain with the blink of his eye. Sergei may not be mine, but tonight, I'm his Cinderella and he's my prince. Everything else be damned.

"Okay. Let me see how I can make this as brief but meaningful as possible," says Sergei. "Let me start with Ivan."

"Ivan, the blond man with spiked hair and who was the driver and

Alexei's friend... or cousin... or one of those 'attachments' that Alexei has a lot of?" I ask.

"Yes, that one," affirms Sergei. "Though he's not a cousin, only a comrade. Ivan was at the orphanage his entire childhood. When I arrived, we were the same age, but both of us were still just young kids and scared as hell. Ivan hardened, though. Kid only knew orphan life. Never seen him laugh. Not really. Seldom seen him smile. Smiles more with his eyes than his lips. I learned to read his eyes over the years. If you don't know him, he is a scary man."

"Yes, he is hard to read. Not sure if he is scary or if that is only his outer exterior," I agree.

"Ivan is a man to be afraid of. You're safe with him as long as you do nothing against me. To his credit, he is very loyal to me. I'm loyal to him. Been together a long time, the two of us."

"I see," I nod. Sifting through the catalogue in my mind of dangerous men I've been in the uncomfortable position of encountering. Those men were animals and easy to read. Whatever Ivan's rage might be, it's well controlled. Even so, it would take little to convince me Ivan possesses the ability to kill without emotion.

Sergei continues to tell his history. "Anyway, after I had been at the orphanage for a few months, they informed me that I had a sponsor. Someone who wouldn't adopt me but would help with my development, as it were."

Shaking his head in the negative as if knowing my thinking, "No, I never received information about who this sponsor was, nor anything about them. Whether they are man, woman, or a charity, I simply don't know. Believe me, I've tried. That knowledge is as tight as any Russian or American cover-up I've ever seen. And I can tell you, Selena, both nations are quite good at covering things up, but Russia is better. Russia doesn't leave any loose ends. Ever. Americans just lie better."

Nodding while making eye contact and listening to Sergei tell this story that he shares with me. Although I have many questions, I don't interrupt. I take a swallow of water.

Sergei swallows a gulp of water as well. "This sponsor sent me to an English-speaking private school with boarding near St. Petersburg. The boarding didn't extend to school breaks or during the summer, so I would have to return to the orphanage. When I returned, Ivan and I would be just as tight as ever. This is where Vogo comes in."

Sergei chugs water and wipes a little renegade bit around his mouth with the back of his hand. "The English school is where I met Vogo. Again, we were the same age, and we both started at the same time. Along with a few other boys our age, we were roommates. Vogo was an absolute wild man. What can I say? At that time in my life, he was just my type of human. The two of us hung out together. Vogo was wild and bold. Untamed. Still is. Guess that's why I seemed to have more in common with him than the other boys. Even though his father was a massively wealthy man, a Russian industrialist who made weapons for Father Russia."

My teeth show as I smile while I consider Vogo as a youngster. "You and the wild man? Pul-eaze continue."

"I told you. Long story."

"I like long stories." Another swig.

"Well, I would hang out with Vogo at the English school. Together we made up eight-year-old dreams about going to Suvorov and being in the military and Spetsnaz. That was right up Vogo's alley. Later, I shared the dream with Ivan. Encouraged Ivan to make and keep himself physically fit. Work hard in school to get the grades. At fourteen, we could apply to Suvorov together and stay out of the orphanage for the most part. He listened. We achieved the dream," Sergei shrugs. "Me and Vogo and Ivan all hung together while at Suvorov. After graduation, we three attended the Military University together. After that, we joined the military, and moved into Russian special forces."

"So, you've been friends with Vogo since English school as a boy?"

"Yes. More than that, Selena. If it hadn't been for Vogo and his family, I'd probably not be who or what I am today. Very likely I wouldn't have had the skills."

"How so?"

"On holiday break, when I was about nine years old, I received an invitation to stay with Vogo and his family instead of going back to the orphanage during the holidays. Missed Ivan, but I had one hell of a time for a near month at Vogo's family home. For any boy, much less an orphan, spending time on a working farm with an endless amount of land equaled heaven. Land, pigs, cows, sheep, chickens, fresh food—and lots of it—a fishing pond, martial arts lessons, fencing lessons, a shooting range, horseback riding."

"Must've thought you died and gone to heaven. Hog heaven, as we say in America, or at least in the southern states. My sister and her family live on a ranch, but I'm sure it's much simpler than Vogo's home. I can see how you could pick up skills not otherwise available to you."

"Vogo's home was a boy's dream alright. As far as dying, there were a few times I was sure I might with Vogo the wild. At first, I was unsure about the 'heaven' part."

"How so?" I ask with continued curiosity.

"Well, the first night there, I was told to wash and dress and put on my best clothes for dinner. My best clothes were my school uniform. My only clothes were my school uniform."

"I see."

"When I went to the dinner table, I was so damned embarrassed. Never in my young life had I seen such a thing, nor had any concept of it. Such a dinner. Vogo's mother dressed in an evening gown and his father wore a tuxedo. Full evening dress just for a Wednesday night family dinner. Vogo was the youngest of six siblings. All the rest of the family, whether married or single, lived in the enormous mansion above the farmlands and were all dressed the same as their parents."

I hope my expression shows I understand his childhood embarrassment. "I see," I murmur in a low voice.

"The thing that saved me," Sergei nearly laughs with the memory, "was Vogo."

"Hmm," I respond, opening another bottle of water.

"A defiant nine-year-old Vogo sat there with his school uniform on too so that I wouldn't be alone in my school dress."

"Surely his parents didn't mind so much, since you were young boys?"

"Oh, they minded. Vogo was a very spirited child who was a late-in-life mistake, and all his brothers and sisters were much older and adults."

"I can believe the 'spirited' part," I blush, remembering I was a late-in-life baby too.

"Oh, spirited to the Nth degree, but the two of us had the best time together. Both of us got up early, gobbled down breakfast, and ran up and down and all over the farmlands. Rode horses a lot. By the end of the school break, I rode well enough for me and Vogo to race. No one bothered us if we didn't arrive late to any of the lessons set up for Vogo. They let me take part. A few times we raced the horses so we wouldn't be late!"

I have a knowing laugh. "I don't know a lot about little boys, but I know about little girls growing up on a ranch. Imagine my nieces race their horses as well."

"Oh man! Such fun! That next night when I went to clean up for dinner, there were two sets of tuxedo-style clothes for me, as well as riding pants and play clothes. Never in my whole life did I have so many clothes. And shoes. Don't know who brought them there or who paid for them. Just there for me. All laid out."

"I can imagine how overwhelmed you must have been."

"Definitely, but excited at the same time. Clothes were better than getting toys. I was, in fact, very grateful, but I didn't know who to thank. Vogo told me not to thank anyone. Said it was just the way rich people do things."

"What a perceptive kid."

"Oh! That he was. The two of us did all kinds of things. Vogo was a man of the world for a nine-year-old and pretty much on his own. Guess his parents were tired of raising kids."

Sergei snickers at his boyhood memories. "Oh God, he actually had a little car that we drove around the farm. Had to stay at the farm with the car, though. That was the rule. Short Vogo could barely see over the steering while standing with the front seat pushed back, but he sure as hell could and would drive that car, and not slow. Loved to pop the clutch and make wheelies. Later, he taught me to drive. After that, they let us drive the farm combine and reaper."

"You're right. The experience exposed you to many skills in a short time." I'm sure my eyes are wide.

"Oh, I haven't gotten to the big stuff yet. When we returned to school as normal, there was no reason to think that wasn't a onetime invitation. But then, I received an invitation to spend that summer with Vogo. Truly, I missed Ivan and the other kids. Kept in touch and wrote each other as often as possible."

"Please do tell me about the big stuff," I ask, and hear my down-home Southern style. It follows me like a shadow.

"Guns."

"You're kidding me? What, nine-year-old children?" Then I remember my nieces.

"Yes. Not much older than that. Had an instructor and all who taught us how to shoot shotguns, rifles, and later, handguns. The man overlapped as our fencing and martial arts instructor. Not only did he take us hunting, but we also camped out for about a week. Lived off the land. The instructor taught us to track and do many things not every boy learns."

"Amazing," was the only word I could say. I know about such natives. My father was from a First Peoples tribe, after all.

"So you see, Selena, I learned much from Vogo and his family."

"Yes, I suppose you did. Were you invited back again?"

"Yes. I returned several times and stayed another summer. Other times, I would go back to the orphanage and see Ivan. Took my English books when I went back to the orphanage and taught Ivan English. Although he learned as much from the books as possible, Ivan didn't speak often, and that was a disadvantage. But he worked very hard on pronouncing English words. Tried to share as much of the benefits that I received with Ivan. Hated to leave him at the orphanage, but the truth was, I really didn't have a choice. I was told to go. Ivan understood that, and he knew I was still his friend. Took care of each other as best we could."

I'm amazed. In absolute awe. "Then the two of you met up with Vogo at Suvorov?"

"Exactly, and we've all been together since. But Selena, the stories of our time together as soldiers aren't something we can nor do talk about. Not even between ourselves. Just the other times."

I nod my head in understanding. "When did you meet up with Alexei.?"

"Ah, we met that old geezer at Spetsnaz training," Sergei said in a loving tone. Alexei was our instructor. "Tough as nails. One thing you didn't do with Alexei was act cocky, or else he put your behind on the ground. Put all three of us on our young asses many times. The man looks disarming, but I'd never underestimate him."

"Alexei? Sweet Alexei? I can't imagine him in that role," I muse. "But now that I think about it, I guess I can." Remembering the kidnapping attempt. I was in better hands than I knew.

Sergei nods. "Ah, yes, sweet Alexei. All his former students and comrades grew to love him like an older brother. The man has saved my life several times. Once, in the direst of circumstances."

I'm all ears now.

"The two of us were in hand-to-hand combat against six enemy combatants. I received a knife wound in my kidney. Without Alexei, I'm sure I wouldn't have made it. Sweet Alexei may be short in stature, but he is a giant among men. That is why I chose him to protect you while you were here."

I can't help but smile at the thought of Alexei as a Special Forces instructor. A man who still lives with his mother. Go figure. Not to mention, he protected *me*. "Did you continue to go back to Vogo's family home?"

"A few times, but soon after we started at Suvorov, Vogo's father was killed. Murdered, actually. Shot execution-style in the head. They never found out who was responsible."

"How horrible for Vogo."

"I thought so too, and when Vogo got back from the burial, I of course told him how sorry I was about his dad. You know what he told me? Vogo said he didn't care because his father was a stupid bastard anyway and was about as much use below the ground as above it. Then he said, *Now I can be an orphan like you and Ivan!*"

"That's strange, but fourteen-year-old boys, no matter how wild, are deeply insecure humans. Anger over abandonment issues, including death, can manifest in different ways."

"It was strange, but we never talked about it again."

"I see," I say, with the gears spinning in my eyes.

"It's your time to tell me a story, Selena."

"Geez. Out of stories. I really can't bring one to mind at the moment. Maybe later?"

Sergei understands my brain is in overdrive with all he's packed into my head in a short amount of time.

"Okay," is his simple response. Sergei picks up his fourth water and chugs the entire bottle.

I swing my arms around in the water gracefully, as if moving the water to displace it like a swimmer.

The bottle topples over when Sergei put it down. Our eyes meet. He stares at me. He locks his gaze on mine. I'm not sure what he's thinking.

In a gentle tone that's so damn hot, he asks, "Can I kiss you?"

I'm not surprised that he wants to but am still somehow caught off guard just the same. I'm scared, again. Damn, it's been a long time. Do I know how?

I take a moment before replying. His eyes are upon me. Heating me like a blow torch. "I could tell you it's against my teachings for a woman to, first of all, be in a pool of water naked with a man she hardly knows, much less kiss him. That is true, but not the truth. Truth is, I've not kissed a man in a long time. I wonder if I remember how. Thinking maybe *I* should kiss *you* first." I say the last sentence slowly and with intensity, and so damn insecurely.

Sergei's eyes lock on mine and don't move. He doesn't speak. He's just, well, open. This man who wants to know me is open. There is something in this intense man's eyes that shows approval. Damn, I find his natural intensity so damn sexy. Then his eyes twinkle. Twinkle. And, if possible, that is even sexier. I shake with chills in this humid water.

Slowly, very slowly, I take minute steps to move my body closer to his. My hands raise above the water to expose my wrinkled fingers. Both of us make a nervous chuckle and Sergei sweetly kisses one of my wrinkled fingers as a mother would kiss a child's boo-boo. We're both nervous with anticipation.

Using the hand with the kissed finger, I touch the side of his face, drawing a line around its features the way I did on the television in the hotel room back in New York City. My other hand stretches to run its mass down the side of his face, down to his neck, all the while keeping my gaze locked on his eyes. My lips slightly part. Sergei leans forward at a relaxed attention and awaits my moves. At first my lips don't touch his but kisses the scar on the side of my prince's cheek.

Sergei holds steady, but his eyes flutter as though he's a caged bird waiting to be set free. My lips work their way across his jawbone and pause just in front of his lips. Allowing my lips to give the slightest touch, I pull back a little, then allow myself to kiss him a little more strongly, adding pressure, then again pulling back.

Finally, I give Sergei the moment he's been waiting for and put my mouth on his to share the joy of pleasure that two mouths can make. Damn, his lips sizzle, and this alpha male takes over. Sergei Radkov takes me into his arms, and my legs wobble on the pool bottom. I feel like I'm filling the pool with my wetness instead of the other way around. I've never been kissed like this. Sergei kisses the way a man kisses a woman when he wants her. *Wants her*. Not just sex but wants her. All of her.

His soft tongue plunges. Indulges. Teases. Plays. Relishes. His throat moans, verbalizing his want. His pleasure. His lips suck. His mouth works. His hands rub my back, but he remains a gentleman. I feel his engorgement against my belly.

I'm not sure who ended the kiss. His hands cup my face. We both breathe and stare. Stare for seconds, minutes, days, a millennium. This is a kiss that I will remember the nanosecond before I die. No matter the future—our future—our *right now* will be on my mind for eternity.

"Oh, dear lady, beautiful Selena," Sergei says, caressing my face with his fingertips. "I think you remember well. Now, it's my turn to start."

In a split second, my prince scoops me up as though he were taking me to bed in a romantic novel. His arms around me draw my naked breast against his. His lips don't hover, nor waiver. Sergei Radkov kisses me like his lips mean everything he is saying. And feeling. Damn. I remind myself to breathe.

His engorged manhood ends just below my navel. Sergei Radkov is a man, after all, and a lot of it. I'm in deep water in more ways than one. I'm in a humid geothermal pool, but I'm sure the drop of sweat on my forehead is new. And I'm wet. Not just on the outside, but from the inside out. I think I might be overflowing this pool.

When the kiss is over, I move my upper torso back from him about a foot. Mouth agape, I can't breathe, much less speak. I feel like I'm smothering. Floating. Yet my feet touch the bottom.

Sergei speaks for me. "Are you ready to get out? Towels, a robe, and pool shoes are on the bench for us."

"Sure," I mutter, and I might have slurred that.

Sergei takes me by the hand and the two of us stride our nudity toward the steps. Each of us showing respect to the other and focusing ourselves on something besides the beautiful nakedness of the other.

Instead of a towel, Sergei picks up my robe and stands behind me. He holds the robe open as I put in my arms and tug it around me. Cinderella pulls the soft and heavy white terry cloth about her nakedness, crossing it in front with the loose drawstring.

Sergei leaves his hands gripped loosely on each arm behind me and speaks into my hair, "Come and I will get you warmed in front of the fire."

He enrobes as I fiddle with the towel and use it to dab my face and wet spots on my head. While wondering what Sergei means by "warming me," he covers himself behind me. My hair falls loose down my back as I remove the hair combs. I turn to see Sergei frozen as he observes each strand falling one at a time down my backside, covering my legs down to my ankles.

With the slight touch of his fingertips on my back, Sergei leads me into the inner sanctum of his bedroom chamber.

CHAPTER 49
THE SANCTUM

SERGEI LEADS me into his bedroom chamber. I stand in the doorway of his sanctum to take in the rustic yet modern ornate room. Like all things Sergei, it's amazing. I'm mesmerized as I enter the space, my eyes flitting about like a butterfly. They freeze on the blazing fire. An entire wall of fire. My entranced gaze on the fire melts, and my eyes soak up the detailed gold gilding leaving this Cinderella's mouth agape. Carved wood. Windows. Skylights. Decor.

Sergei allows my eyes time to explore, understanding the need to let me take it in. I like that about him. His patience. At least with me. His mouth is upturned just enough to show his dimples. It's like he enjoys watching me enjoy. Exactly like in the art gallery. He's watching me watch. Absorb. Process. Reads my thoughts. It's like we exchange surreal communication about our surroundings in these quiet moments. Moments that I'll always cherish.

"Come sit by the fire so you can warm yourself," suggests Sergei while waving toward the settee.

"How lovely. I understand why this place is special to you," I remark, still in awe.

Sergei gives a brief snort. "Actually, most of my time here is spent working. Selena, are you warm enough in that robe?"

"My toes are a little chilly, but I'll make myself at home and tuck them under me."

"I have something you will like." In a moment Sergei returns with a heavy fur throw-type quilt made of soft white sheepskin to warm my legs and torso. "Would you like some wine? The staff brought another bottle of the Crimean and put it on ice."

"Oh my, your staff aims to please," I reply as Sergei places the quilt around me. "If you don't mind, I'm going to drink more water first. Little dry after the swim." I lick my tongue across lips that feel dehydrated.

"Okay," says Sergei, pulling two water bottles from his bar fridge. Handing one to me, he sets the other on the coffee table.

The president makes an executive decision and stokes the already roaring fire. I think he perceives I may need more mental space to acclimate, more than wanting to keep the fire roaring.

Instead of admiring this man's backside or his shoulders that muscle through his robe, for a few blessed moments I remember my father. A flashback reminds me of my dad stoking the fire at home on cold winter nights on the waterway. Especially on Sunday afternoons when my mother would set aside family reading time in front of the blaze. Page by page, the short winter afternoon would transition from dusk to darkness, then bedtime. I jump out of my flashback as Sergei hits a button on a side panel and the glass doors of the fireplace open.

"Neat trick," I remark, amused.

"Well, wait until you see this." Sergei first stokes the fire a little to move all the coals below the grate. Then the commander, currently in charge of electronics, pushes up one lever on the side panel. A tray of wood on a grate slides through a back panel and sets a tray of new wood down on top of the old one. Sergei repeats the process three more times across the fireplace.

"Never in my life have I seen anything like that," I remark. Can't seem to keep my gaping mouth closed as my eyes follow Sergei's action.

"Russian engineers," winks Sergei with a shrug and a grin. Damn, he's adorable.

He strolls over to the settee to sit beside me once he has the fire roaring. I lift the fur to make space for him. After Sergei nuzzles into the settee, I lay the quilt over him. Each of us revel in a quiet moment as we let the soft comfort warm us. We nuzzle like long time lovers.

Sergei cedes a portion of his revelry as he bends over to pick up his water while asking me, "How have you enjoyed my country so far?"

"My time's felt so short. Flown by like a jet. I could spend a year here and barely touch on the interesting places your country offers. So much art and history oozing everywhere. Not to mention Russian engineering," I tease with my tongue in my cheek. "I highly recommend it, President Radkov," I say, now speaking with certainty. "I'm enjoying your country very much. You'll get a good report card."

"That's good," says a grinning President Radkov. "Have you considered what you're going to do when you leave Russia?"

"A little, and not really. Maybe touring the Baltic countries. Problem is that the publishing house might not make deadlines. Book signing dates might need to be moved forward a few weeks. There are conferences on human rights I plan to attend in Scandinavia that are tied to the end of the book tour."

I shrug. "I may have to do a little backtracking. Perhaps it's fortunate that I'll be delayed leaving Russia by a few days, thanks to the blizzard. You know, President Radkov, I may have a visa issue," I taunt while taking a swig of water, wearing a hint-hint smile.

President Radkov retorts, "I'm proud to say my country is welcoming to foreigners and handles visa issues promptly." He provides a wink and a nod with an added nose crinkle.

"What I mean to ask is, what are your hopes and dreams, Selena?" he asks pointedly. "What do you want out of life when you finish your book tour—or tours, plural?"

"What does Selena Frederick dream about?" I question as if talking to myself. *Besides your damn hot body?* "For the first time in my life, I have no hopes. No dreams. No answers for the 'what's next' question. Of course, I'm a trained physician and can go nearly anywhere to practice. Maybe involve myself with more activism."

I pull the fluffy fur skin tighter to my chest and continue. "I could go to where my sister lives and be a country doctor the way my dad did. That was Dad's life, though. He stepped into it with both feet and never looked back. And it was a good life. No such epiphany for me." A wry smile crosses my blank face.

Sergei listens to me with his wealth of patience. I consider if he's asking me if I ever want to marry and have a family. Seems that question follows that line of inquiry often. My friend Jean Marie Whitecloud once assured me the world would be losing a great mother, if not. She's sweet like that. She has that macro connection to the world that's not as innate for me. Besides, I'm sure Sergei gets the same questions.

"I understand," Sergei says to me. So simple are his replies at times.

"I'm actually at the same sort of crossroads. I've no idea what I'm going to do with myself after the elections," he continues, as if gathering his thoughts. "My work has been as a soldier and a spy. My only love has been for Father Russia. Served my country, always. That's my skill set," he finishes, as though he's looking for answers in the blazing fire.

"You have time," I say. "In your shoes, I hope I would take that time. Hell, I would need that time. Believe me, Selena Frederick is a prime example of not being able to rush epiphanies. Sometimes, it's simply a matter of being at the right place at the right time, I think."

"You're right. Much heavier things on my plate than my future for now, I'm afraid." Quizzically, he asks, "Did your father ever share with you how he found his particular epiphany?"

"Oh yes. Many times. Another one of those long family stories that got repeated over and over."

"Neither ear is full at the moment," replies Sergei with his boyish grin.

I shoot him a laughing smile and begin. "Let's see. Dad was a Native American from New Mexico who received a scholarship to college, then to Duke University Medical School."

"So, you're part Native American, or should I say of the American First Peoples?"

"I am. Either or. I've been told I have one hell of a warpath."

"I have reason to think that may be true," replies a jesting Sergei.

I make a fist and bore a playful noogie with my pointer finger into Sergei's arm. A teenage boy returns a smile. A large smile. He makes me feel so... accepted. Yes. Like he loves having me beside him alone in his chamber. His inner sanctum in physicality and in spirit. Just the two of us. I love it, too.

"Anyway, while at Duke, he took a three-to-four-hour drive to see the ocean for the first time. A friend took him out on a boat during that first trip. That was it. My father decided that was home for him. Not a large and busy beachside town," I stress. "But a poor one. At the time, Brunswick County, where I grew up, was one of the poorest counties in North Carolina."

"The rest is history, as they say?" asks Sergei.

"Yep. Dad opened a small medical practice and lived upstairs in a small apartment. Then he met my mom, married, and then came my sister and, sixteen years later, me."

"That's a beautiful story," Sergei says with approval. "I wish I could tell you how my parents met and made decisions, but I can't. One of those holes in an orphan childhood, you know? I'm glad you have this beautiful story in your heart and memory, though," Sergei says while his fingers make a small circle on my left chest to indicate my heart. "How did your parents meet?"

I let out a small laugh. "That's another beautiful but long story," I say while looking up at Sergei.

Sergei points to his ears. "Empty ears, and I love beautiful long stories."

My dimples deepen. We're like two old friends catching up. He's not trying to sex me. Sergei Radkov is trying to know me. My stomach flips. I'm filled with a kind of glow as I consider how to tell this man my story.

"Let me see if I can remember how this goes." After a moment's consideration, I begin. "My father had just started his practice in my hometown. Mom was a teacher and librarian in Myrtle Beach, South Carolina, which is just over the border in South Carolina from where my father lived in North Carolina."

"Ah," remarks Sergei.

"Well, my mother had always been interested in adult literacy. Due to low literacy rates in Brunswick County, she wanted to start an adult literacy program, but could never raise the funds. Unstoppable, Mom jumped through hoops to get a teaching certificate in North Carolina. If the county would provide a meeting place, she agreed to volunteer her time two nights a week."

"Your mom was a cool lady. No wonder your dad fell in love with her," injects Sergei.

"Oh yes, he did. At first sight." I pause and lean over conspiratorially. "I think it was her *big boobs*."

Sergei laughs seriously out loud. "Oh Selena, I'm going to have a drink. Your story deserves a toast. Will you have some wine with me?"

"Sure."

"Keep telling your story. I'm listening." Sergei says while opening the wine and dispenses the fruity liquid into two glasses.

"Actually, my mom was sort of my dad's patient. To get her North Carolina licensure, she had to go for a bit of a mini physical. My dad was the only doc in town where the literacy program was to be, so my mom made an appointment for the physical. Well, you can guess the rest."

Wine glass in hand, I expand the story. "My dad said he opened the patient door expecting he was going to see another toothless old hag and instead, it was the most beautiful woman he had ever seen. In his words, *he gave her a thorough exam*."

"I bet he did," remarks Sergei, seated comfortably beside me and making lots of eye contact as I tell my story. "Your dad was a comical man."

"He was a total character. My mother was the serious one."

"So, he asked her out for a dinner and a movie?" asks Sergei.

"Oh no. Way too poor for that. Dad found out about the literacy program, so one night he walked in and sat at the back."

Sergei gives a deep belly laugh. "You know, your dad knew how to pick up chicks."

I laughingly agree. "My mother asked him if she could help him with anything. Dad said, 'No, oh no, just wondered what an adult literacy program was like.' Mom guffawed and completely ignored him."

Sergei lifts his wine glass for a toast. "Here's to love at first sight."

I grin and click my glass against his.

"Please finish your story. Love it."

I turn more to the side to face Sergei a little better on the settee while sipping my wine. I reposition and tuck my feet. Sergei tucks his feet, too. Sergei is enthralled with my storytelling while in the comfort of his inner sanctum. I could sit right here and exchange stories with this man until the cows come home.

"Well, my dad claimed he only did it for the view, but he kept going back to every meeting of the literacy program. Mom said that was bullshit. Her take on it was that Dad discovered there was an ass to match her boobs."

Sergei tries not to spit out his wine. "Your parents were truly a hilarious pair."

"Yes, they were. Mom with her proper British, and Dad wearing his New Mexico bad boy. Elizabeth and Joseph Frederick were quite a pair."

Sergei watches the animation in my eyes. Talking about my parents and recalling happy memories is a good thing for me. He knows it. If that doesn't warm a woman's heart, I'm not sure what will.

"Well, to get on with the long-drawn-out story my parents always found time to tell," I continue. "Finally, Mom allowed my dad to walk her to her car after class. Although she would get into her car and drive home, both secretly wanted to stay together for a while but didn't let on. My mom's conservative upbringing dictated otherwise."

Taking a sip of wine, I'm looking into my patient listener's face while entertaining him with my continued storytelling. "This went on for a few weeks. Then, one night, my dad said, 'Come on, I want to take you somewhere.' Well, my mom pitched what Southerners call a hissy fit, saying that if he thought he was going to get into her pants because he had a doctor's license, he could think again."

"Very proper, your mother."

"Extraordinarily. She was from an uppity British family, and they were all no-nonsense folks. But Dad, being Dad, stopped her ranting and raving by kissing her on the mouth, right then and there in front of his Buick. Dad claims it hushed her up. Mom claims otherwise."

"Oh, I like your dad's style," Sergei says as he makes a fist beat on his chest, giving me deeper dimples.

"Well, my dad took my mom to a plot of land he had recently purchased on the intercoastal waterway, thanks to owner financing. It would later become the place of our family's house and homesite. The land had a dock for a boat, but no other development. Dad shared all of his plans with mom."

Beginning in what comes out as a sing-song voice, I explain, "He was going to build a small house, then expand it, but he thought it would take time. Many people in the county were on government medical assistance programs; others were uninsured and couldn't afford to pay my dad at all. Often, he bartered services, even decades later when I was growing up, for meals at the cafe, gas at the station, or even a car wash. At some point, he even said he might start living on a boat to cut costs."

Sergei seems enthralled with his killer crystal blue eyes on me.

"It wasn't his best moment when he told my mom that to marry now would be selfish of him. He had nothing to offer a woman and wouldn't for some time. All he had were hopes and dreams."

"What did your mother say to that? Ah, let me guess: she let him have it?"

"Sort of. Story goes she simply asked him to take her back to her car. Mom was silent in the car, then let him have it when they got back."

"Oh no... not the silent treatment?" groans Sergei.

"Oh yes, and my mother could do silent," I assure him. "She told Dad he was a coward and didn't deserve a woman whom he had no faith in to begin with. Second, it was quite belittling for him to suppose that all women desire a man only for the sake of a house and a steady income. Furthermore, if he needed to have those things to share his love and not give a woman a chance to endure his hardships with him, then he deserved to be alone instead of with a good woman. Mom got out of my dad's car without ceremony and drove home. Dear old Dad didn't attend the next literacy meeting."

"Geez, so they almost didn't get together?" quizzes Sergei.

"Hard to say. Dad asked the man who ran the service station across from his office to watch over it while Dad was gone. Mom found out that much. Dad said he needed to go on an emergency trip to New

Mexico for a few weeks. Then, of course, Mom was worried sick about him. It crossed her mind he might never come back, unlikely as it seemed."

"Weeks of agony for your mom, I guess. What is the saying? Something about absence making the heart grow fonder?"

"Yes, that's the saying, and it *did* grow fonder. That's why she wanted to kill him when he got back."

Sergei chuckles loudly. "I don't know your parents, but with little that I know, that sounds like them."

"Easy to figure out those two passionate creatures," I say with assurance. "Seems my dad drove straight to New Mexico without stopping. Hell, even these days it would probably take three days to make such a trip. Well, as soon as he got there, he spent a few days in this hogan of the tribe's medicine man. Dad was to do a ritual wherein the great spirit would reveal his destiny. That was my grandmother Black Hair's recommendation."

"Your mother didn't like this?" asks Sergei while taking another sip of wine.

"My mother was livid. Dad told her that after the hogan, he spent weeks playing the piano at a local bar in the nearest city where he had sometimes played during high school and college. The owner built it up on the radio and such and Dad claimed he raked in a lot of money."

"So, your dad, the doctor, went to New Mexico to play the *piano* to make money? Oh, and let's not forget, sweat it out in a hogan? I assume a hogan is a simple housing structure?"

"Yes, a hogan is a housing structure used by the Navajo people. But that's only part of the crazy story. What he used the money for, though, was to buy my mother a diamond ring."

"Ah, that must have made her happy."

"Well, he said he had to kiss her to shut her up first. Soon they married," I say, ending the story.

"That is truly beautiful, Selena. What did you say your parents' names were?"

I grin at his interest. "My mother's name is Elizabeth. My father's Christian name is Joseph. His First Peoples name is Ears Hear Music.

Even as a boy, Dad always sang and played musical instruments," I say, smiling at my father's memory.

I realize this was the first time I've been without pain long enough to even speak my parent's given names since they died.

"Well, let us do another toast to Joseph and Elizabeth… to lovers at first sight," Sergei suggests.

Our glasses click and then there is silence. Silent silence. We look at one another and have that terrible and awkward "what next" question in our heads. Our silence seems to sing as loudly as the Winchester Cathedral Choir. Neither of us can hear our own silent voice ringing in our own heads because of the choir noise ringing in our ears from the other's silence. Finally, Sergei cuts to the chase and speaks the things on his mind he wants to know and asks the questions I want him to ask. Still, his sincerity takes me aback.

"Selena, what do you want in a man? What's important to you?"

Though a bit taken aback by his directness, I contemplate his question. I wrap my arms around my knees as if storytelling at a campfire. "Besides the basic things, the basic 'sober, honest, loyal, good communicator' baseline stuff? I believe there are three things that I want in a man that are specific to me as a woman."

"Tell me."

"First, I want a man who understands that I'm a strong woman in many ways, and he needs to be a strong man. By 'strong,' what I mean is that he needs to be a man who can take me by the hand and gently, very gently, tell me when I'm wrong. That's a strong man."

Sergei gives a slight smile. "I've actually done just that this very evening, in the presidential toilet."

I guffaw. "Second, I want a man with so much joy in his heart that waking up next to me and saying, 'Good morning, sunshine,' comes naturally."

"'Sunshine?' I'm sure I can *naturally* call you anything you like. And a few other things, that just come naturally."

Damn, he makes me smile. "Third, I would like a man whose heart is so big from loving so much that on our best day—*and* on our worst day—he can say his life is better because I live in his chest."

"That would be the easiest of all," says Sergei. "After all, I've loved every person in my homeland enough to die for them. My chest is large, and there is no doubt in my mind that Selena Frederick already fits in." He pauses.

"I'm stunned. Stunned by the deepness of your thinking. You, Selena Frederick, are one hell of a woman."

His voice is sincere. His eyes speak truth.

I don't know want to say or think. I mumble, "You see, Sergei, I think I've put myself in a quandary because it might be quite difficult for one man to possess all three of those qualities and possess them well. I suppose I've never been one to settle."

Sergei smiles. It's a loving smile. His smile fades, and he becomes solemn while he is considering his words. "Selena, I need to tell you some things. It's important that you know. I must tell you. I don't want you to find out elsewhere."

"You don't have to explain yourself to me. Neither of us is a child. We both have lived prior lives."

"I know," Sergei says simply, with a whisper. "Selena, you must know I was a soldier. You understand a soldier kills."

"Yes," I whisper back, giving his discussion the solemn tone that it deserves.

"I was a Spetsnaz operative and a spy. I did many things out of love for my country. Whether it was to kill a man or to bed a woman to obtain secrets, I did what was needed. I never questioned it. I'm not ashamed of it. It was what I did. I never bedded the women to use them. It was always their idea, in fact. And I never killed a man just to kill. I didn't enjoy it. It was strategic."

I nod and think for a long moment before I speak. Sergei plants his eyes on the fur of white that surrounds the two of us as he listens while I speak.

"Sergei, I was once told by a man that it is who we are today that matters. Today," I emphasize. "We must work for the betterment of tomorrow, but not lose who we are today." I allow my eyes to gaze so direct and so hard into his crystal blues as he raises them. I'm thinking my look is so strong that my green eyes cover his blue ones like a blanket with my stare. "I like who you are today," I say.

I watch Sergei's chest deflate as though he's been holding his breath and his lungs suddenly burst like a balloon. I'm thinking I stunned him with the gravity of the words I've just spoken. Sergei coughs to clear his throat, which sounds paralyzed. Sergei finds his voice again.

"Selena, I heard you once say—or perhaps it was in your book, where you said that you believed you probably walked past the love of your life and just missed him. That you had walked by him, or gone into the wrong door at the wrong time and weren't paying close enough attention, and forfeited a great gift from life?"

"Something like that, yes."

"When I read your book, I remembered the great market fire in Burundi."

"Yes, I remember it."

"I realized we had both been there at the same time. In fact, I went to that market daily. We could've walked right past each other, but you see..." Sergei takes in a deep breath as though he needs more oxygen. "You were there to save life. I was there to take it."

Silence. Both of us look at each other with so much respect, and maybe even love. Despite our words, it's love that boils to the surface of my heart. I'm just not sure what to do with it.

"Selena," says Sergei in a soft voice. "I want to give you honesty. Honesty isn't something to be thought about later. I'm a master game player, but with you, no. There are no games."

I nod because words aren't welcomed into my mouth.

"It made me wonder how many times I may have played the game against you without realizing it. Might I have been the one that hurt some of those you tried to save? Or trained someone who did? I never hurt women. Nor children. I will say that," says Sergei, stressing his moral limit.

I believe him.

Silence once again. I'm having a hard time finding the right words. Instead, I take his big hand and put it next to my face to love it.

I find my voice. "Sergei, I treated men, women, and children who came into our encampments. It wasn't the type of post where you only hand out prenatal vitamins and deliver babies. My hands were full performing many types of surgeries, and as a healer I couldn't refuse treatment under any circumstances, not even in foreign lands."

Silence. I look into Sergei's two crystal blue pools and speak with every intention of strategically bypassing his heart and going straight for his soul. It's my belief that your heart processes love, but your soul owns it. I feel love whirling in my chest and building in my soul. I just don't know what to do with this kind of love. I've never known it. My fingers trace his lips.

"We all do things in our line of work that go against a deep moral code within us. For me, it was doing abortions." I let my fingers fall to my lap as though I'm admitting guilt.

"Abortion went against everything deep within me because I wanted to save every drop of precious life that I could. Yet, I found myself in a position, for many and varied reasons, helping a woman abort her child." I sit in self-judgement. "You see, I'm a killer, too. My sin is no less than yours."

Sergei's eyes are following my every syllable as though he is in a trance and waits for me to continue.

"We must believe deep in our hearts that these violations of life's moral code are for the greater good. At that time, we think we're doing the right thing. We must believe that, to do what we do, to help the ones we can in the way they need it. Otherwise, we would have no chance of doing any good at all."

"Thank you," Sergei says softly after a moment. Looking into both my eyes, he sees me. Sees all of me.

"Will you hold me?" I request.

"I would love to." Sergei pulls me close to him and kisses the top of my hair.

I listen to his heartbeat as I snuggle down with my head against his chest and stare into the glorious fire with the white throw wrapped around the two of us to ward off any unforgivable chill in the Siberian night.

After a few minutes pass, Sergei speaks gently. "Selena, you have three choices: You can sleep in the room next to mine. You can sleep in my bed, with me, and I won't touch you if you wish. The third is that you can sleep in my bed with me, and I will touch you, and I will make love to you." He picks up my face to look him in those incredible eyes of his. "I think you know which one I prefer."

"I think you know what I prefer," is my soft reply.

Sergei's lips come to me slowly as his hands touch the outlines of my face. He drowns his blue eyes in my emerald ones, possibly—depending on whether you're Elizabeth or Joseph Frederick—making aquamarine. Slowly and softly, he works his mouth around mine.

I feel the softness of his tongue massaging mine and I'm sure there is nothing on this side of heaven that can make me float in thin air like his touch. His arms cradle me. His tongue caresses mine. Sergei Radkov is without a doubt the man for which I've waited my whole life. I gasp as lips and mouth journey the side of my face down my throat and reach my collar bone. I evidence my excitement with a rush of warm fluid escaping into the back of my robe. My woman is dripping wet with arousal. My heart is dripping with want of him.

"Oh Sergei," I mutter and place my lips on his face and neck and run my fingers through his wispy hair.

"God, you feel so good to me, Selena," Sergei whispers into my ear with his manhood already attuned to his physical wanting. "Woman, I'm going to take you to bed and give you my body, my lust, myself." His voice is strangled with yearning.

Our faces rub in a caress, as we find the other's eyes. Outside, the birch and linden trees are trusting their souls to God, as the fireplace roars and we absorb the warmth of its wooded sacrifice. "Come," says Sergei, and stands up to take my hand.

Suddenly, he says while his eyes grow wide, "No! Sit back down." The fingers of his left hand are running through his blond curls as though he's distressed.

I'm puzzled when Sergei sits down beside me with a look nearing bewilderment. He rubs his hands nervously between his legs.

"Selena, with all the planning and trying to have it all perfect, I totally forgot to arrange for condoms. I'm sorry."

"Oh." That's all I can leak out of my mouth.

"I can excuse myself by saying I didn't think this far ahead. I never imagined that we..." He looks away. "That we would get this far tonight. I thought I'd be leaving you at the door of your bedroom tonight. I didn't let myself imagine that we'd connect the way we did."

I nod, not knowing what to say. Yes, our connection is unexpected, despite my desiring it. Evidently, so did he.

"Confession time, Selena: it's been a while for me, not to mention I've been crazy busy. I haven't met a woman that I desired. Not since I saw your face." He clears his throat.

"I've never had sex with a woman without a condom," he quickly confesses. "I would never risk having a child with the possibility of my child ending up in an orphanage, perhaps even without my knowledge. Would never risk it," he says, shaking his head for emphasis.

I believe him. A knowing laugh loosens in my throat. "Sergei, I've never had sex without a condom, either. My parents ingrained that nugget into me from the time I learned what the word 'sex' meant. Professionally, as a doctor, I've always felt it necessary to take my own advice."

"I see," replies Sergei. "For me, it was not wanting to risk the potential of creating a child. I should've cared more about the health issue, but I didn't. Believe me, with all the physicals I've endured in the military—and it's even worse now as president—one thing I know is that a man can't be much healthier than I am. In everything."

I smile. "That's good." But then shoot him a "What are we going to do about it?" look.

Sergei has the same look. "One of the guys probably has one, or God, I hope more than one," he says, looking at me seriously. "Let me get dressed and I'll go see." He mumbles, "My greatest disasters in life happened when I didn't have a plan B. Hell, tonight I didn't even have a plan A."

"I don't see much of any other way either, but I admit I'm a tad embarrassed at the invasion of privacy." I blow out a breath. "There's one other option. I'm on the pill. Pregnancy won't be an issue. I'm willing to take a leap of faith with you if you're willing to take a leap of faith with me."

"I saw your pills when Vogo had the contents of your purse removed. I worried you might have another guy," says my prince.

I give him a loving smile. "Nothing like that. I just like to control my cycle, especially while on tour. Female matters can get messy."

"Oh," replies a glad Sergei and bites his lower lip just a little.

"Selena, if there is one woman, I don't have to worry about what kind of mother she would be to my child, it's you."

The sweetness of his words heats my heart like a warm, heavily iced cinnamon bun with a steaming mug of cocoa. My hand reaches up to touch his face and give him a little peck of a kiss, but Sergei isn't having it.

He takes me into his arms and kisses me with passion. "I'm going to make love to you, woman. Right now. I will take your leap of faith."

Sergei takes me by the hand and lifts me up from the settee. He picks me up and carries me beside his bed. Removing my robe, I return the favor and remove his. We stand before each other as if we want to capture this moment for eternity.

Our only light is the blazing fire as the howling wind outside sings its tortured chorus. The sky drops ice in pecks on the rooftop, in what sounds like frozen sheets. Mother Nature's rage doesn't discourage us as our eyes blaze, studying each other's heated soul as our two bodies stand in front of one another.

My hand touches his maleness. "You are so much, man. So beautiful," I say running my hands dreamingly to the sides of his hips and behind. My lips kiss his hard chest.

Sergei groans. Bending down to kiss my lips while touching my breast, Sergei's mouth climbs down from my chin, then steps down the ladder of my throat, as though he's on a trip to Mecca. His tongue escapes and licks one nipple and then the other.

"Oh yes," I moan. Gasping, enjoying the feel of his moistness against the backdrop of the raging fire and the sound of falling ice.

Sergei climbs further down the ladder on his knees and grasps the bump on my backside. His large hands hold their position for moments while his eyes explore my woman. He rubs his face softly in my public hair, then without ceremony, he jerks my womanness into his mouth.

I scream as my pleasure gushes and overflows. "Oh God, Sergei, I want to taste you." Pulling myself back from his magic, I give him my hand to lift him up and lower myself. I begin. Oh, I begin. Rolling. Twisting. Pulling. Sliding.

Sergei speaks words of male pleasure in Russian as his head falls backward from lack of muscular support. "Oh Selena, I must stop you now. I want to be inside you tonight for a long, long time."

I rise to my feet and Sergei picks me up to lie on his enormous bed. He hovers over my outstretched body and lays himself between my legs. Softly, he kisses my mouth. My breasts. My body rises and falls to meet his soft touches.

"Are you ready for me, Selena?"

I feel his breath on my teeth. His eyes in my eyes. His heart beating in my chest. "Da, da," I say, remembering his language. Sergei makes a sizzling sound with a "Sssaah" of pleasure.

Sergei enters me gently, sliding his hands beneath my bottom and lifting me to meet him while making circular motions, which morph into deeper churns as his manhood pulses inside me while his tongue travels its path around my breasts. Gyrations. Squeezes. Moans.

I pull my legs around his backside and let my body rise and fall to his motion while kissing his face, his neck, his collar bone. I tighten my woman around him and squeeze, then release as he strokes me. My squeezes drive him primal as sweat forms on his back. His moans are a cry.

He slows to caresses the front of my abdomen then lower while supporting me with the other hand. He stops and pulses while he runs his fingers across my clit. I squeeze him.

He falls on his back and pulls me on top of him. I like that. In my experience, I find males seldom understand their role to help balance a woman in that position. Sergei Radkov does. Oh, better the pleasure this expert lover provides, and I squeeze the hell out of him often as I slide my wetness around him. He howls.

Sergei leans upward to kiss my lips. My face. My neck. Oh God, my neck. Moving his hands higher up my back behind my hair, I lean back and rock for another brand of pleasure. Oh, to watch his pleasure. Sergei releases one hand and extends it down to my womanhood. His mouth wets his fingers and massages my sex with one, then two fingers, working from one area to another in a circular motion. Above my hip bone, inside my thigh, and right above his action.

I pant, moaning with excitement.

Sergei takes me to my end as he circles me while I rock and

squeeze. He leaves himself throbbing. Lifting his back to support me, he holds me. Coos in my ear, making sure I have time to recover and to realize he has held himself back to give me more.

I found his reassuring "Ummm's" in my ear to be the best part of the entire experience. A woman would give her whole life just to hear those fleeting seconds of a formally nonexistent word that is spoken in all languages. A secret word spoken in a hidden garden. An inner sanctum.

Sergei holds my face to gaze into his lover's eyes as he slowly churns. There is no other touching during our motion. All body language is read through our eyes. It's heaven. It's truth. It's us. Slowly, Sergei bends his head and softly kisses my lips, my shoulder. Oh, my shoulder. Moves his hands to the small of my back to better enjoy my breasts. He loves them.

Allows me to pull up straighter as he steadies me by holding both sides of my bump, which he seems to like the feel of since he continues to massage my maximus with one big hand on each cheek. Slowly. Slow churns. Moves his hand above my hip bone and pulls me down by my lower waist to dig himself inside of me as deep as I think possible. Holds and pulses. Just holds it. I moan and squeeze.

Holds himself inside me deep, like all that exists of himself is given to me. Every plane of his existence is offered up to me.

"Selena, can you give yourself to me again?" comes a whisper in my ear.

"Yesss," extends my one-word answer.

Sergei murmurs, "I'm almost ready to give myself to you. Oh Selena, beautiful Selena, are you ready to take me?"

"Yessss." I slide faster and harder.

"When you take me, leave your eyes open." Sergei requests while moving his lips around the side of my face and ear. "I want to see your eyes when you take me. When I give myself to you." Face to face with me now, he rubs his lips in short spurts as he travels my face. "I'm giving myself to you."

"Yessss, Sergei, YES! Give yourself to me, I want to take you Sergei."

Sergei churns. Hard. With his eyes upon me, he lets himself go and releases a primal scream.

I scream too.

We become immobile and fall over sideways onto pillows. Weak but joined. Somewhere in the night ice mixes with snow as the two of us sleep from our rigors, unmoved in each other's arms. I drift into the early stages of sleep. A wolf cries out to its pack, but the cry is faint in President Sergei Radkov's bedroom chamber.

Five minutes of blissful rest pass. Nothing stirs. Then someone's belly bellows louder than that damn wolf in the forest of the Siberian tundra.

I laugh. "That's mine."

"Are you sure it's not mine? It's hard to tell."

I laugh again. "No, no. It's indeed mine."

"Are you hungry, Selena?"

"Yes, but I'm alright till morning. I should've eaten Momma Olga's soup and salad."

Sergei whispers conspiratorially, "I'm hungry too. Let's sneak out of here and go raid the fridge."

"Won't we wake up your Olga?"

"Not if we're quiet."

"What will I put on? The robe won't be enough."

"I'll give you something. You have clothes in the other room, though I'm not sure what's there. The ladies took care of everything."

"Um," I try to say neutrally. I wonder too.

"Here are my favorite pants. Just roll up the bottom a little." Sergei hands me a pair of tartan blue-and-green warm-ups made of a soft fleece. I like the way they smell. Smell like Sergei. Now the pants will smell like our sex.

"Let's see, here are a pair of wool socks and a sweatshirt. Throw over your robe and voilà, perfect," says Sergei.

I do as he requests, giggling all the way as Sergei dresses the same. I love it. For absolutely no reason at all, we're having fun pretending to be like children sneaking downstairs to devour Santa's cookies.

Sergei takes my hand and leads me to the door. Just for good measure, he tells me to shush and tiptoe. Of course, it's utterly ridiculous. An army tank can drive through this dacha, and no one would hear it with the thick walls and heavy wood, gurgling pools, and stone fireplaces with crackling fires, and dampening precipitation heavy with snow and ice.

A giggling duo holding hands walks down the back hallway and takes the stairs down. We meet the presidential security detail at the bottom of the stairs, and I suppose the Russian words Sergei whispers inform the man what's going on. Our mission continues as we journey out of the sanctum.

———

The older man says to the younger man: "Is all in place?"

Younger Man: "It is. Small complication. With an American whore now."

Older Man: "The American doctor he is reported to have this major crush?"

Younger Man: "Yes"

Older Man: "All the better! Keep all in place."

Younger Man: "Sure thing, Dad!" Speaking with sarcasm.

CHAPTER 50
HUNGRY LOVERS

LIKE TWO CONSPIRATORS, we tiptoe to the expansive kitchen with its several large walk-in refrigerators and workstations for everything from vegetable cleaning to desserts. Yes, Olga has a well-organized kitchen. Red booths on the perimeter of the cooking area look like a throwback from an American 1950s diner-style soda shop. Charming. Nothing awry. Not one thing is out of place, and everything shines like a new dime. My Olga never disappoints.

"I'm afraid to touch anything," Selena whispers. "Everything's so immaculate and well ordered."

"Come on," I whisper back, holding tight to her hand. "Think I know where Olga keeps the leftovers." Our feet tiptoe over to one of the stainless-steel refrigerators and I pull the top off a container. "Oh yes, salmon stew. Into the microwave it goes."

"Yum."

"And here's the salad. And here are the langoustines and shrimp cocktail that Olga gave up on serving earlier."

Selena gives an exaggerated *sorry* grin with a crinkled nose.

With her ruby red lips and wearing my clothes, I perceive her to be even sexier than she was less than an hour prior, when the passion flowed through our bodies like the Volga River through Russia.

"Need bowls to warm up the stew," whispers Selena.

"Why don't we put the whole thing on the stove?" I whisper back.

"I'd hate to ruin this stew by reheating. Olga may plan to serve some to the staff. Besides, we'll need bowls anyway to eat it," says Selena's soft voice.

"Will it ruin it to heat it in a pot?" I question.

"Fish falls apart easily, so the leftover portion might be. Can heat our portion on the stove though if you prefer." About that time, a gruff-looking older woman walks out of a side room wearing her housecoat and pink sponge curlers.

"Olga," is the only word I speak. Then add, "Come here, Selena, let me introduce you to Momma Olga."

"Momma Olga," says Selena, extending her hand for a handshake while pointing to herself then simply saying, "Selena."

Olga gives Selena a polite nod and a sleepy smile. Olga and I converse in Russian, then I realize I'm leaving Selena out.

Selena picks up on my unspoken thoughts. "Sorry, I can't pick up a single word. Tough language, that Russian."

"Momma Olga says that we need to sit down in a booth, and she will take care of everything."

"Sergei, Momma Olga has already worked too hard. She should go back to bed. I can clean up afterward."

"Momma Olga won't consider it, and I would rather argue with a tree than her. I would have to order her to do it, and I dislike being heavy-handed if I can avoid it."

As if off the top of her head, Selena smiles and walks a few feet over to the front of Momma Olga and bows, adding a "Spasibo" with a hug.

The old woman blushes and kisses Selena on the cheek. We sit in a far booth that is the most private, but Olga still gets in an occasional wink and nod to show me her approval.

Momma Olga reheats the soup, but in the meantime brings us fresh homemade bread rolls that would melt in your mouth along with fresh butter. The old woman includes a small fruit tray in the mix. We butter our bread and take our first bites to file the edge off the stomach growls.

Then comes another growl. Sort of. A furry thing made the noise. A half-grown and obviously male Russian Blue cat. The feline stares out of Olga's bedroom door at us, asking who dares to enter his orbit without permission. The cat places his long legs forward and plants his paws to give his torso a good stretch.

The handsome blue boy has the telltale heritage of striking green eyes. Wide-open eyes survey his environment as the cat strolls over to ask what we're doing.

Selena replies, "You're a beautiful boy. I'd pet you if I weren't eating."

Selena turns her eyes up at me. "Look at him. A charmer. I always wanted a Russian Blue kitty. My mom raised Himalayans, so I guess there was no room for another breed, but I always admired the Blues. Heard they have a mild temperament as well."

"Yes, they are sweet animals," I reply. "This kitten was at the back-door begging when Olga spotted him. Momma Olga didn't have the heart to let him go hungry. Now he's a fixture here. Usually, she keeps him outside or in the barn, or the greenhouse during the night, but she may be afraid to do so tonight with such frigid weather."

"What'd she name him?" asks Selena, mesmerized by the handsome smoky-blue feline.

"Actually, I'm the one who named him. I named him 'Oliver' after Oliver Twist since he is an orphan like me."

Selena smiles at the irony. "You are a beautiful Ollie, yes you are." The cat rubs Selena's leg a little more before sitting down on the floor beside us. Ollie is determined not to miss a thing.

Before long, Momma Olga is serving up two warm bowls of salmon stew in fresh dill cream sauce. Delish. Selena blows a spoonful to cool, and pops it into her mouth to enjoy the outrageous combination of flavors before asking, "Do you like dogs or cats, Sergei?"

"I always wanted a golden retriever. They're gorgeous and seem so affable. I would love to own one, but my lifestyle has prevented it. Perhaps one day," I consider while cooling a spoonful of the stew.

"We had a golden when I was growing up. Named him Buffett. After Jimmy Buffett, the musician. Buffet was my dad's dog. Dad took him everywhere, including his office. Buffett was a fixture there. And yes, he was an absolute sweetheart. Dad didn't leave the waterway in his boat without his first mate on board. Mother was second mate."

"What was he like? Buffett, I mean," I ask, curious.

"Beyond awesome, but Dad had to have him trained. Mom got upset because when he was young, Buffett would knock you over when someone opened the door to go out. Then the dog would take off and we wouldn't see him until the next morning. Buffet was proud to show off all sorts of things he had gathered for us in the yard: A trash can lid. Other people's clothes and shoes and a sundry of garbage. Even a bag of beer. All over the front yard. I mean, a retriever retrieves."

I'm tickled. "I bet he was so damned cute it was hard to be too upset with him."

"For everyone except my mom. Dad had an invisible fence put in, but Buffett would jump it. Not to mention, he would jump into the intercoastal, swim across, and be gone for a day or so. That's when my mother shipped the dog to boarding school for training."

"I know something about that. He should have swum to Russia. He and I could've hung out as two misfits."

Selena winks at my remark. "Buffett did well after training, though. If Dad said 'stay,' the dog wouldn't move for days, if necessary. Not until Dad commanded otherwise."

"I have experience with that as well," I add. "Military."

Selena smiles at me. I love her smiles. "I have a curious question," she says.

"Shoot," I reply while stuffing another bite of buttered bread into my mouth.

Selena is pondering, as if she doesn't quite know how best to form her question. She more or less leads me into the discussion. "Is it true that during Soviet times, circumcision was banned since it was considered a religious ritual?"

"Yes," I say simply while taking a sip of stew.

"And is it not true that day care workers and physicians and other childcare servants were obligated to report this infraction?"

"Yes, that is true," I say, taking in a tasty bite of salmon from the stew, then dropping my spoon into the bowl.

Olga is on her way to deliver two salads but looks at me with concern, as I'm sure I'm flushed white. Selena looks at me with the same concern.

"Are you alright, Sir?" asks Olga in Russian, a little more formal than usual.

"Fine, Olga. I just realized something that I had forgotten. It's okay. Don't be worried," I say, touching the old woman's sleeve. Olga sits down the salads and removes the soup bowls casually and goes back to her business, but the wariness doesn't leave her eyes.

"Selena, I can't believe it. It's literally been in front of me this whole time. Do you think that I'm Jewish?"

"It's possible, but you may also be from a Muslim family. Then there's the possibility that your mother or father were from another country with strong beliefs about circumcision. Like the US."

I blink, then fall with my back against the booth, trying to process all the things my circumcision might mean.

"I'm sure there were pockets of people, although not nearly the numbers seen in America, but I'm sure there was a percentage of Christians, or otherwise with non-Jewish or Muslim backgrounds, who held strong feelings affirming the need for circumcision. In the US, many new parents still consider it a matter of future cleanliness, which is a medical myth. However, this pervasive belief is the main reason for baby boys receiving circumcision in the US."

I look at her as though I'm too far gone in shock to understand what she's saying.

Selena clarifies, "All I'm saying is that you could be from any background. I wouldn't grab on to any one idea without more proof. What I don't understand is how you stayed under the radar all your life."

"Is it possible the reason my mother vanished was because someone cut a little meat off the end of my cock?" I try to ask it like a simple question, but I'm sure my face is red because I'm angry now.

"I have no way of knowing. Neither do you, it seems. All I'm saying is to think back. Never know what you can remember. Was there a professional who saw your penis about that time as a boy?"

"Damn Selena. That is asking me to remember a lot."

"I'm not thinking that you'll remember, but just in case you do, maybe there's something that you can learn from it. It's likely insignificant, but it's there."

I feel my eyes wander to another planet, then return to earth. "I'll think about it, but not now. Right now, all I want to dwell on is you. Us. This is 'us' time."

Selena smiles with sweetness.

I shift gears. "Was considering a troika ride sometime over the next days while we are here. The ice storm is predicted to develop into a snow front that is following behind it. I wouldn't want to risk injuring the horses, although there are mules in the barn as well as the nags. Best to get a good coat of snow rather than riding on top of ice. Perhaps the day after tomorrow."

"Well, I don't know about you, President Radkov, but I'm sleeping in this morning. It's almost my usual wake-up time. A gal needs her beauty rest."

"I already cancelled my workout with my morning trainer. Although, I'll have a conference call to get vital updates around nine, but you can sleep. I'll come back to bed when it's over."

"I don't envy you that. I'll do my best to keep your side of the bed warm," she says.

I can't help but show my dimples while the two of us finish our salad. Selena's presence makes me smile. All I need to feel happiness is her smile. Olga serves us yummy langoustines and shrimp with several types of extraordinary sauces that make the seafood taste like it fell from heaven. Selena thinks the one sauce made with mangos, ginger, and soy is out of this world. We finish an entire bottle of wine but pass on dessert.

"Like that plum sauce a lot too. As they say in the South, that Olga can throw down some food," comments Selena.

A sated and happy couple, we return to the chamber. Back to our sanctum. A sanctum we slide into as easily as old clothes.

"Can I wear your clothes to bed? They're so snuggly," asks Selena as she bunches the sweatshirt and crosses her arms to pull it close to her body.

"Absolutely not," I tease my lady. Yes, she's mine. I know that as well as I know my name. Dr. Selena Frederick is my beautiful lady. Mine.

"Too bad, they're mine now," shoots back Selena.

We cover ourselves with heavy fur blankets and spoon in the massive bed. Selena pulls her ankle-length hair around and stretches the bottom of her tresses around my backside. It's warming. I love the feel of her hair around my torso and wish I was indeed naked, feeling her strands around my skin.

Instead, I hold her close to warm her in the cold of the falling dawn this Siberian morning, enjoying the smell of lavender in her tresses. Damn, what a woman.

PART SEVEN
A DIFFERENT KIND OF PRESIDENT

CHAPTER 51
ONCE UPON A TIME IN SIBERIA

I HEAR a ringing in the middle of my dream. *Not possible to be my wake-up call*, I sleepily process in the middle of my luxurious dream, wherein I saw my mother again. A young mother, as she was when I was a boy. My mother hugging me, while crying and covering me with kisses. Stating how she has missed me, with her tear-stained face. How I have been in her heart every moment since the last time she saw me.

I sit up straight in bed.

The red phone is ringing. Shit. When I pick it up, a familiar voice is on the other end.

"Will I need to dress?"

"Yes."

"Okay. Put some coffee on."

The voice replies, "Already done, Sir."

"Oh, and conference in Smoltsky after a list of expenses is completed. He holds the national purse strings," I add.

Selena awakens with a groggy smile. "Time for your daily update?"

"No, Selena. Duty calls. My country's president is needed. No idea how long this will take. Stay and sleep. Be back as soon as I can."

"I'll keep your spot in bed warm," says the sleepy American beauty as she lays sideways to extend herself over where I had been. Snuggling down into my pillows, she sniffs them with a smile, as though she is enjoying the smell of me left on the soft pillows and sheets.

I have time for only a quick smile. A quick second to acknowledge the warmness in my heart as I watch this lady in my bed fall back to sleep. I'm sure I love her. Sure.

Without delay, I put on my robe and a pair of moccasin-style bedroom slippers. Pausing at the chamber door, I look at Selena already back asleep, lying across where my body had been. Feelings for her form a ball in my throat that doesn't allow me to breathe. I stroll back to the bed and kiss the side of her face. It's the first moment I'll be without her since we met. "I'll be back soon. Sleep well, Sunshine."

Selena lets out a sleepy, "Ummmm..." and snuggles down tighter into the covers holding her dreams.

The next time she awakens, I'm lying beside her on top of the bed coverings. "Sergei, why don't you get back under the covers?"

"Just laying here enjoying watching you sleep, Sunshine."

"Oh my, you have my giggle box starting early this morning. Or is it late? I'm really not sure. Either early or late, pick one."

"Now you have *my* giggle box. Is that what you call it? Anyway, you have jump-started it this morning."

Selena looks at me with wide-open eyes and her smile. I might not perceive what a "giggle box" is, but I understand the phrase "jump start." My knowledge is vast and diversified, but I don't know everything. I know enough to understand my lady's giggle box is something I want to jump-start every day.

Selena rises a small amount in the bed to kiss me with her sweeter-than-average lips and lies her head back on the pillow. "Are you able to get some sleep now?"

"Yes, for a while at least. While I was up, I got my updates, so I can sleep past the nine o'clock hour, but I'm afraid I'll be in demand more than I would care to be today. Something very grave has happened."

"I'm sorry, Sergei," says a sincere Selena, rubbing my sleeve. "Anything at all I can do to help?"

"Yes," replies her man. Yes, I'm hers. All hers. "Hold me for a moment." I mumble, "Feel very sad right now."

Without a word, Selena's arms wrap around me. Holding me close and providing me with her heart's warmth. I linger for a few moments and coo a simple "Thank you" in her ear. "I'm so happy you are here today with me, my Selena. This is the worst day of my administration so far."

"I'm glad, too," replies Selena with compassionate eyes. "I realize you can't share some burdens with me, but I'm here."

"It's not a burden as much as grief. I can share some of it with you because it will soon be on the news. Hell of a thing for Russians to learn in the middle of such a severe ice storm."

"Okay," is Selena's reply.

"The day before yesterday, there was a confirmed kidnapping of an American student in Moscow. I sent Spetsnaz to track and find the culprits. Spetsnaz found them. In the early hours of this morning, the team attempted to rescue the American and his roommate, who was a security operative. The American was shot in the head and killed by the kidnappers. Russia lost two of her Spetsnaz agents, as well as my operative who was protecting the American while posing as a fellow student."

Selena's eyes enlarge as I unfold this bad news. She keeps silent and lets me tell the event causing me so much grief.

"This has caused an international incident. The kidnappers aren't even from Russia. These thugs were from part of the former Soviet Union. The idiots in the West can't seem to figure it out. No wonder they think us their enemy. Their ignorance over who we are is overwhelming. Over thirty years has passed since the breakup of the Soviet Union and the end of communism. Yet Washington politicians look at a hundred-year-old map."

"Geez," is all Selena says in disgust. "Hopefully they'll figure out at least that part soon."

"As well they should. Among other things, but the least of my concerns, is that it makes Russia look bad on an international stage. I'll prepare a speech later in hopes it will work out some kinks. Before that, though, I'll need to call four families who lost loved ones. Will sleep awhile first, though. We've not notified the families. I want to wait for them to be notified and give them time to begin dealing with their grief."

Selena nods. "When you say, 'four families,' I assume you are going to call the American family as well?"

"Yes, that is just and right. I want to have more facts about the young man before I make the call. All I'm sure about is that he was an American University student majoring in Russian, participating in an exchange program."

"Are speech writers preparing your speech, or will you do that yourself?"

"I will do it myself. I know what I need to say. That part won't be hard. What will be hard is saying it."

Selena empathizes. "I understand. I have two hands ready and willing to help in any way possible."

"Thank you," I smile as much as a president as I do as a man. "I'm going to try my best to tailor my words so that the world understands this is terrorism. And it's time all civilized peoples get on the same page. You might help with research when we wake up. There're a few facts needing research where you can aid my limited team here at the dacha."

"As we say in America, I'm your huckleberry."

I smile. "I'm familiar with that one."

Selena's face returns my smile, but changes. "Sergei, it's a small matter, and may not even be of concern to anyone, but I wonder how it would be if Russia, out of sheer kindness and good will, shipped the American boy's body home at Russia's expense? An act of goodwill."

I raise an eyebrow but don't speak.

My lady makes her point. "Many of your experts will say that's like Russia admitting wrong, but it's not—it's going deeper to the heart. It's demonstrating that Russia is a civilized nation of decent and caring peoples. The family may not need the financial help, but it's a matter of goodwill. More a matter of saying, *I'm sorry for your grief, and I'm showing it.*"

"You, young lady, think out of the box," I express.

"Well, I never thought boxes were much good for thinking in. Just saying. Sergei Radkov is a different kind of Russian president. This president does things differently."

"My security team might just send you back to America if they heard you say that," I jest.

"I'm sure they would." In her conspiratorial voice, she whispers, "Let's not tell 'em." Sleepily, she pulls a handful of my sweatshirt toward her and lowers me to her for a kiss. "And you, President Sergei Radkov, need to get under these covers with me and get some sleep."

Admiring her curves and placing my hands around her glorious bump where the covers lie, I make an alternative suggestion. "I'd like to know more about this round bump right here. It seems to give me wild and passionate ideas. In and out of the box."

"Well, President Radkov, if you want to know more about that bump, then you'll need to be well rested. Once you're rested, I promise you an exemplary adventure. Maybe me on all fours." Selena's voice lowers back to her conspiratorial tone. "Hands on the bed, ass in the air. In fact, I might hold on to one of those sturdy bedposts to support me," Selena says, rolling her eyes while lying in the most enormous bed I'm sure she's ever known existed.

I often consider how this bed could house a military aircraft carrier. I look at all four corners of the bed. "How about you hold on to *that* one, at the foot of the bed? That way I can see you in the mirror for a little extra delight, and *sooooo* can you." I make Groucho Marx eyebrows.

Selena laughs at my funny face. "Okay. Deal, President Radkov. You sleep, and when you get ready, I'll be ready to hold on to your bedpost for dear life."

With a twinkle in my eyes, I give her a kiss and rasp, "Beautiful American woman, beautiful Selena of my heart, you are on like a pot of neck bones."

Selena chuckles and pulls back the covers to allow me to slide in.

I wrap my arms around Selena's curves, and she twists her long hair like a rope and lets her hair loose around my lower torso and backside. I kept the fire roaring in my chambers despite the presidential interruption. The snow falls in sheets of snowflakes the size of my fist, and these hands make a big fist. Like two lovers, we fall asleep while listening to the awareness of the other's murmured heartbeat as the fire makes its crackles.

Sergei and I arise four hours later. Sergei's team might like not having a haggard president addressing the world on terrorism. Glad he slept.

Each of us meanders to our separate showers while the staff delivers a buffet of Olga's brunch to the room. A door leads to the next bedroom from the toilet space. I wrap my towel around me after indulging in a marvelous-smelling lotion of honey and ginger. The ladies made sure I had everything a woman could possibly need, including a large round hairbrush, to wrap my curls. Wonder where that came from? I smile.

I tiptoe into the next bedroom chamber as though I'm avoiding waking a baby. Not sure why I tiptoe. Just developed into a habit, I think.

Having my clothes picked out for me gives me a grimace, but it's only for a few days. Surely, I can manage. Much to my surprise, the outfits are lovely. There is matching jewelry, including gorgeous matching earrings that dangle just the length where I like them to fall. Everything is neatly arranged across the bed in sets. They arranged underwear and bra choices in a vertical line. To boot, they're the type I wear. Now I wonder where *those* came from. God, I hope it was a cousin. One I don't know.

I scrutinize the clothes carefully. I'm careful that the outfit I choose doesn't make me look like a harlot. I'm bothered. When Sergei and I were walking back up the stairs to his chambers from the kitchen, I heard the security guard mumble, "Shlyukha." Whore. I'm not sure if Sergei heard it. Maybe not since he was talking at the time, and on the other side. If he did, he didn't react.

I'm sure of the translation. It's one that Alexei taught me that night I was so drunk. Maybe Sergei heard it and thought nothing of it, but I sure did. I don't like it. No woman likes it and shouldn't be called that. I don't believe in it. Not degradation. Maybe that's what the staff thinks of me. Shlyukha.

I can see Elizabeth Frederick's "I told you so" eyes rolling in heaven. Sorry to disappoint you, Mom. Yes, I've been loose with Sergei, but I don't regret it. I'm not sure of anything anymore. Certainly not what's going to happen when our time together is up. I'm not thinking about that now. When I leave here, the one thing I'll hold in my heart is that I've loved this man as completely as I can. Shlyukha. I hate it, but shlyukha be damned.

I choose a pair of navy-blue pleated pants and a rosy-pink sweater made of angora with a large cowl neck. I don a pair of mosaic earrings with a multicolored pattern containing pink-and-blue colors. A long-chained golden-heart locket fits around my neck and drops mid-length on the sweater. I adore it.

Next comes perhaps the most perfectly fitting half boots I've ever worn. I choose to keep them on my feet after trying them on for size. Upholstery-style cloth outlines the outer boot with a blue background displaying pink flowers, their long green stems swirling about my feet. Now, these are kickin'. Oh yes! This is very Selena! Take your shlyukha and shove it.

Walking out of the toilet, I smell the buffet offerings in the chamber and see Sergei with his one ear plastered to a phone while taking copious notes, sitting at a two-person table set up near the doorway. Still tiptoeing, cross the carpeted rug and fix myself a cup of coffee with milk. Sitting the cup down quietly on the table, I return to the pot and refill Sergei's cup with the stout black liquid.

"Just make it happen," are the only words I hear Sergei say as he hangs up. At least, I think that's what he said.

"Wow, Selena. You look lovely in your clothes. I like them on you."

"As well, you should. You bought them."

Sergei gives a big grin in reply.

"We don't have to discuss this now," I continue, "but I'm more than capable of reimbursing you for them."

"I think you know better. I'm so pleased you have found them to your liking. The shoppers did an excellent job. I'll have to find a special treat to thank them."

"Whatever you do, be sure you send a thank-you note from President Radkov. Such things go a long way. It did for me. And by the way, you should know that I adore this locket."

Sergei dimples a grin. "Selena, you have the best of ideas. It's obvious you come from a land of charm and hospitality."

"That I do," I reply with a vigorous nod of certainty.

"Speaking of hospitality, let's grab some of that buffet food that Olga has cooked up for us," says Sergei.

"Now, that's hospitality at its best," I say while arising with Sergei from the table.

"Madame," says Sergei with his best hospitality grin as he passes me a plate.

All these offerings. I can't decide where to begin. Not a huge porridge fan, but I like the look of the rice porridge with lemon. Turns out Olga has a better-than-average recipe. Sergei hands me a bowl and I fill it up. Health-conscious, I allow a piece of bacon, a small ham slice, and mushroom with peppers quiche onto my plate.

"Is that all you are going to eat?" asks Sergei. "We might eat dinner late, so stocking up will be a good idea."

"I was going to eat my porridge, then go back for salad, then blinis if I have room."

"Ah, you are a sectional eater?" asks Sergei as he helps himself to copious amounts of fish, sausage, and bacon servings, along with eggs Benedict, salad, blinis, and porridge.

"Oh, don't you worry about my nutrition, President Radkov," I assure him. "I'll get my share, believe me."

"I'll not worry," says Sergei. "I've seen you eat before."

I look indignant. "If my hands weren't full of calories, I'd smack your ass."

"And I'd enjoy it," says the teasing president with a little hip bump on mine.

The two of us sit down to enjoy our meal like longtime companions. "If you want to work on what you must while we eat, it's alright with me," I offer.

"The people of Russia have their president around the clock every day of the year, or so it seems. I have you but a fleeting amount of time. All I'm asking is to only enjoy a quick meal with you," replies

Sergei. With his boyish grin adds, "And then, I'm going to put you to work."

"Oh, is that your plan?" I say, smiling back up at him.

"In some ways, I already have put you to work. I considered the process of the American family dealing with their son's death. Of course, I couldn't go to the burial and make it a political spectacle, but I'm sending several of my top people," assures the Russian president. "Included are my vice president, Secretary of State, Prime Minister, Smoltsky as Chairman, of course. And the US ambassador from Russia, as well as other ambassadors in the region. Russia's condolence will be well represented." He gives a sigh. "Thank you, Selena, for making me realize President Sergei Radkov is a different kind of president. That is what my people need most. Someone to remind them who they are."

I stop my fork's motion while I listen to Sergei's words. A heartfelt warm smile crosses my face. "You give me too much credit. I do, however, admire the way you're handling it. The Americans will see your earnestness. Russians will see it too. The world will see."

"Well, it was you who caused me to understand that words are one thing and action is another. To the utmost that I can understand the situation, I'm going to back up my words with action. It's easy to send condolences; it's another to show that you mean it," confirms President Radkov.

"I think you're doing that," I say in support.

"Oh, I've barely started. I've already dispatched the ambassador to the Michigan location where the family lives. Once I talk to the family, I'll get a feel for how soon it will be before I can have the ambassador return to the family's home. He has already delivered the bad news. The ambassador is to work one on one with the family, for anything they may need, and to arrange the return of their son's body for burial. It's after ten at night there though. Need to call as soon as we eat before the hour gets too late. Although I imagine they'll be awake until late."

"That will be of most importance to the family," I state, feeling compassion.

"Well, there's things to consider. Of course, law enforcement wants an autopsy and such. I'm of the mind, since a Spetsnaz operative saw a kidnapper shoot the boy in the head before he could get a shot off, that there's no need to do an autopsy here. Not unless there is a discrepancy with the forensics on the ground. I'll follow what the family wants. The Russians can autopsy the outer part of the boy's body, but I'm inclined to send the young man home as he is with bullet still in head, as unseemly and morbid as that sounds," rattles off Sergei.

"If nothing else, it will speed up the return of the body," I agree. "As well, you might consider letting the American medical examiners get a copy of everything that has been done to the body," I add. "Perhaps have law enforcement send a copy of whatever records they can share to law enforcement in the US. Like photos of the bagged gun the kidnappers used. Even pictures of the crime scene. Full disclosure."

"You're wise, Selena," says Sergei, giving a smile then lowering the eggs Benedict hanging from the end of his fork, his crystal blue eyes looking at my face as though he's admiring my soul.

"You already thought of that, I'm sure," I add.

"Actually, I didn't. Our governments haven't worked so cooperatively in the past. If this tragedy can have any meaning for this young man's life, and for the others, then opening a door to better relations between our nations is something that I think might add meaning. I'll make it my mission to bring meaning to his life, and to the other three."

I slow my chewing to listen.

"I've asked Chairman Smoltsky to set up a scholarship provided by the Russian people at American University in Washington, DC. The chairman is bucking it now, but I can expect him to take credit for it when he gets to America. In honor of the victim, the annual scholarship is for an American student who is in their third year of college and majoring in Russian studies to come to Russia as a student at any one of our universities."

"So, the young man was a student at American University, you say?" I ask while gulping in a few swigs of coffee. "By the way, this rice porridge is beyond excellent. Reminds me of what Southerners call rice pudding that my mother used to make when I was a little girl. Delish."

"Yes, and yes," says Sergei, raising an eyebrow to the second yes regarding the rice porridge. "The young man's name was Harold Arthur MacDonald. It's my impression he was a young man who wanted to learn of Russia and its peoples so that he could help build bridges between our nations. This is to honor him," says a presidential Sergei.

"His parents must be very proud of him. They likely realize the good things about their son, but having President Radkov remind them during this call will mean a lot. It's like portraying that you see their son for who he was, and what he was about. Sort of like the artist did with the woman in the painting hanging in the gallery. Painting a portrait of a person, but with words."

"Thank you." Smiling while the fork cools his food, Sergei's eyes gleam. "Lady, I don't know how I've made it without you these past months. I'm glad you're here now."

I blush. "Me too. So, what type of scholarships are you providing for the Russian fallen?"

"Pretty much the same. Russia already provides university study, but these scholarships will aid in special international exchange for Russian students at the universities where the commandos attended, and one at Moscow University where the operative was masquerading as a student and roommate to Harold. His name was Olaf. He allowed himself to be taken with the American. Olaf gave up his life to protect Harold. Selena, this is not information that anyone should know. That is a *top-secret* secret," Sergei says to me in a trusting but firm tone. "It's so that the operatives can continue to provide the utmost safety, and for their safety as well."

"I understand."

After Sergei makes his call to America, we leave the coziness of our warm chamber and go upstairs to the large dining room with books and maps and charts, full of laptops and ringing cell phones. Sergei introduces me to the buzzing crowd. After reseating, once the group has given their standing respect to the president—most simply give me a nod—they go back to their business.

One young man wearing dark-rimmed glasses is in a corner on a phone with a finger in his ear. He gives a simple "Hello" after hanging up on his call. I nod.

"I want an update on what you've been working on," speaks the president. "I'll go around the table to receive such updates. Selena is here to help. She understands that she won't be privy to any top-secret information. She doesn't speak Russian, so you will need to use English.

"If you have classified information, then let me know when you give me your update. In that case, I'll meet with you in the secure room, one at a time. You may go wait in the hallway outside the room when you finish your update here."

"Might I speak with you first, Sir?" asks Vogo, who is standing inside the glass-filled room with its gorgeous view of the frozen Lake Baikal. Sergei speaks with Vogo behind closed doors. President Radkov then comes out to the enclosed room with a flushed red face that extends to make cherry tops at the rim of his ears and flushes all the way down his neck.

Vogo takes the stairs running.

Sergei sits back down. He takes careful notes on each update. I do so as well. Before meeting with staff in the secure room, he leans over to me and somewhat whispers in my ear, not really caring if anyone hears, "I'm going to meet with staff members, then I'm going to call those families. Then I'm going back to my chamber to finish my speech to the nation. I've the bones written, but I'll complete it once I've full updates and made those calls."

"Okay," I say. "I'm here to help, even if it's just to refill coffee cups and keep the pot going." I smile up at this man I adore. This leader. I want Sergei's staff to hear my words more than Sergei. The staff gives me projects to research and lets me in on their brainstorming for an added American perspective. I'm an equal. The hours pass.

In the meantime, President Sergei Radkov is busier than a one-armed paper hanger. Completes his updates, then makes his calls to the families while taking notes and documenting each family's needs. Initiates a conference call with all the principals he put in charge of doing all things that might be of comfort to the four families. God, he's strong.

I make my way to my chamber wherein stands a busy Vogo, who silently points out the listening device planted in the chamber. Truly planted. Within a potted plant. I nod, and Vogo quietly leaves.

I'm grave as I emerge from my chamber wearing a dark navy-blue suit with a tie showing the tractor colors of the Russian flag. It's my favorite tie to wear when I'm addressing the Russianness of my national audience. I need all the help I can get. My heart is dragging the hallway floor tiles, as shit is hitting the fan in every direction. Amid this crisis, I'm walking around with a mole and manipulator in my presence.

"I have my speech. I'm ready," I say to the presidential staff.

A podium is set up. I shake my head. Instead, a Russian flag is placed on each side of a chair next to the roaring fire in the dining room fireplace. "I'll be speaking to my nation and the American people and the world at large from my home, and from my heart to theirs."

I review the notes in my speech as the cameramen and press who travel with the president ready their equipment. The broadcasting site is supposed to be from an undetermined location. I'm aware half of Russia knows my location when I broadcast. Russians aren't stupid people. The military stands ready to help defend the location if necessary. I know damned well the consequences of assuming too much when it comes to readiness. Damned well.

I dispose of my notes. There's no need for a dry run. I don't ask anyone's opinion. I'm a president, a citizen, a Russian speaking from his heart and to every eye in my nation, and in America as the interpreters do their work. Across the world at large, I feel the eyes upon President Radkov.

"To the beloved people of my country, and to the American people, and to freedom-loving civilized peoples wherever you may walk on God's good earth: I'm speaking to you this evening with the heaviest of hearts. Two days ago, a student, who was participating in a foreign exchange program between American University in the United States and Moscow University, was kidnapped. He, along with his roommate, were held for ransom. Immediately, I sent the best operatives of Russia to recover the kidnapped young men."

As president, I continue to unfold the story. I speak of the failed attempts to save their lives. Briefly, I discuss the honor Russia will bestow on the American student who "Sought to walk among us, who sought to know and to understand us, and, during his stay here, was one of us. It's infrequent that the world hears of a person whose mission in life was to bring about the best of things for other peoples. Harold Arthur MacDonald had the right to expect safety when within the borders of our nation, as does our citizenry."

Explain how Russia sent their best to rescue the two students, and how two operatives also lost their lives in the massive gunfight, as well as Olaf. I give another brief explanation how Russia intends to honor their death as well.

"To freedom-loving nations, I say to you that the Russian people will not accept terrorism as a status quo. The toughest Russian laws are against terrorism. As a nation of laws, we will enforce those laws." I'm finished.

Of course, there was no discussion of the information gained by the one surviving terrorist. Nor how Russia is already on its way to render pay back. Didn't discuss the tightening of immigration on the nation of origin. Didn't discuss the loss of up to a half million migrant workers from the host nation of the thugs that had been welcomed into Russia for employment in the past. Russia will welcome workers from other nations instead.

Didn't speak of efforts to ease international relations. As president, I spoke of the facts, gave Russia's stance, and that was it. It's the Russian way.

Selena and the support team for the president give me a fervent hand of applause. In a land now known as United Russia, over one hundred forty-four million people stand up from where they were sitting or standing and bellow cheers for their leader who understands their hearts. Tears cloud my eyes as I receive news of their support.

That degree of support is huge. Usually, after such televised announcements, the Russian people are calling bullshit. Trying to decide which conspiracy theory they are betting on. But today, they understand their president isn't covering up a damn thing. He gave them the truth, and he wasn't grandiose about being Russian with propaganda, but spoke to what we value as Russians. The Russian people that I love accept this with appreciation. Selena is right. I'm a new kind of president.

In the land known as the United States of America, over three hundred million people wonder why America couldn't have a president like that. I laugh at that report.

In the nations now neighboring Russia, millions ask if they are now a nation that will feel fallout from being cut off from the economic benefits of seasonal employment—and let us not forget, *the oil*. It can be so cold, and winter is not completely on us. Don't forget the oil!

In a pub in England, one member of Parliament states, "Rather rough riding old chap, isn't he?"

In France, the people shout, "Viva, Radkov, Viva!"

In a region of Latin America, one man tells a reporter his opinion. "Those terrorist dun messed with da wrong dude. He will fuck them up. You watch! Fuck them up!" Man, I love Latin Americans.

In Africa, people wonder if this might hurt their shipments of food and, please, not another war. No more war!

In Asia, people wonder if they can still visit St. Petersburg.

Airing from a bar in Moscow, a slight whistle is let out by a man with an English background who speaks fluent Russian and comments on my television address over his vodka. "That man's going to change the world, I tell ya. Change the world." I love the man who said that.

CHAPTER 52
OUR LADY

AS SOON AS the cheering subsides, Tina announces to the staff that dinner will be served here in the dining room for all staff members to show appreciation for their hard work. "Olga has promised a feast in two hours. This should give everyone time to return to your quarters and dress for dinner."

The room empties as staff members pick up their belongings and leave for what promises to be a delightful meal. Staff usually eat in the dining area of the kitchen only.

"Are you going to your chambers, Sergei?" asks Selena.

"No, I'm going to fix a drink here, then I'll go to the art gallery and spend a little alone time thinking. Already showered and dressed, but you go ahead."

"Is it okay if I join you at the gallery later?"

"Yes. I'll have Vogo escort you to the chamber," I say.

Selena gives me a brief kiss, knowing my heart is heavy. Quietly she arises, as I buzz Vogo to come to the dining hall.

Vogo comes in, and without speaking, nods to Selena to follow him. I arise and fix a glass of vodka and take the stairs to the gallery. The lights come on and I stand in the room and stare as the beautiful art embraces me. Bypassing the paintings, I plop into a chair underneath the dome in the garden. President Sergei Radkov puts his hands to his face and weeps at the senseless loss of life in recent days.

I've seen much death. Seen the death of comrades while carrying out my orders. Death is not new to me. I've seen more of it than any man has a right to. Yet, somehow in my mind, this is different. Another Sergei Radkov failure. Young men died. It's the young that bothers me the most, although I've seen plenty of youthful death. I raise my glass and speak out loud to the air as I toast the life of the dead.

"To you, brave young men. You, who gave your life to others, and to save innocent Harold. I swear to you with my last breath that your deaths won't be in vain for as long as I shall breathe. To you four." My glass is lifted in the air to toast them, and I take a swig of the clear liquid. I still for a while and let the day and events stir in my mind and in my heart.

For no particular reason at all, I get up and go to the room where the painting of the painted lady hangs. Regard the woman on the wall. "How do I know you?" I ask the portrait. As a belated thought, I ask, "Why am I circumcised?" Take in the painted lady and talk to her as though she's alive, and I know her. "Why was I circumcised?" I ask again. Looking closely, I study her features. "You could be Jewish with your blond features. Doubt from a predominant Muslim area, though. Perhaps you descended from Finns. Perhaps Rus. Baltic regions? Hard to say."

I pull out my phone and dial Moscow. As President Radkov, I request all the information known about the painting from Russia's leading expert. I text a pic of the painting to the top art expert. "Even if you have to send a team of experts, I want to know everything that is known about this painting."

My stare continues, absorbing every strand of the woman's long blonde hair. My mother had long blonde hair like that. Mainly she wore it up in a bun on the top of her head with occasional curls failing loose around her neck. The orphan in me wonders if my hair came from my mother or if my father was blond as well.

The lady has green eyes like my mother, too. Certainly, curvy and shapely like my mother, but I've never seen my mother naked, so I really don't have a baseline to compare. Straining, I recall my mother was tall and slim and always looked pretty in her clothes. It's insanity. I know it. This can't be my mother, yet she has a striking resemblance. That draws me to this painting. The boy orphan wants her to speak to him. Wants her to speak in the voice of my mother.

The gallery door opens, and Selena's voice rings out. "Sergei?"

"Back here with the painting of our lady, Selena." My ears follow the sound of Selena's footsteps until she's standing beside me.

"I brought you another glass of vodka. Thought you might be ready for a refill."

"Yes, I've already emptied one glass," I say with a sad smile. I accept the full glass and put my arm around Selena. "She looks as sad as we do tonight," I say. "That's what I see in her eyes. I feel there's a deep sadness that she tries to hide but cannot. Sadness too deeply embedded into her soul." I'm looking and smiling at my Selena. "You look beautiful tonight."

"Spasiba."

My eyes run down Selena's face while running my hands down her back and around her bump. Selena wore her hair pulled up in a bun with a few loose curls at the nape, the way my mother used to wear hers. The beauty dressed in a flouncy black skirt and purple top with a black silk jacket, boasting artful purple and dark-pink flowers. Sleeves end just below her elbow, cuffed with a two-inch lace of black silk. With black boots, amethyst earrings, and her golden locket, Selena is so stunningly beautiful that it hurts to look at her. My mind leaves the painting and focuses on the live beauty beside me a few moments. Then, the two of us study our lady in the painting.

"I called Moscow to see what I can learn about her. Just curious. Just would like to know."

"Hope they come up with something," replies Selena. "It's like she's ours. It feels as though we need to take care of her in some way."

Damn, she makes my heart gush with love as I take in the woman beside me. This woman I once fancied but am now convinced I will love for all time. Never do I want to see her wear such a look in her eyes as the one worn by the painted lady. I want to tell her of my love. Too soon. Too soon. Don't want to overwhelm her. We've barely been together for twenty-four hours. What a full day it has been. Every second of this day has drawn this woman closer and closer to my heart. I believe I've moved closer to hers. In my imagination, a life without her standing beside me doesn't exist. I can challenge others to imagine, but I can't bring myself to imagine that.

"You want to sit a while in the garden while we finish our drinks?" I ask.

"Sure," she says briefly. "Oh, by the way, Vogo says he'd like to speak to you as soon as you have a free moment."

"Vogo, yes, of course, Vogo," I murmur. "Let us finish our drinks, then I'll take you upstairs to enjoy the night view of the lake while I speak to Vogo before dinner."

"Okay," says Selena as we head toward the garden but otherwise walk in quiet. It's restful in the chair.

"I'm sorry not to be in better cheer tonight. I'll try to improve my mood, but my heart is so very sad over today's events."

"Mine is too," replies Selena softly.

I give her a slight smile, more with my eyes than with my mouth. I yearn to blurt out, "I love you," but no, it's not the right time. Besides, I shouldn't with such a heavy heart. Selena deserves better.

"Tomorrow I'm definitely going to work out at the gym. Maybe that will help me work out some of this frustration."

"Can I work out with you?" asks Selena.

"Of course. I would love it."

"Deal," replies Selena.

"I remember another deal we have," I tease.

"I told you it was at your pleasure," comes my lady's retort.

"Want to skip dinner?" I ask, using my Groucho Marx eyebrows again. I love doing that.

"No. Remember I told you President Radkov needs to keep up his strength?"

"That you did, beautiful lady. And so do you." I have an ear-to-ear grin.

"I'm glad to see a smiling face on my lover," returns Selena with the same grin.

"Would you like to go downstairs?" I ask. "I'm ready to get this

party started."
 Selena chuckles. "Okay, let's go."

CHAPTER 53
THE SERVANT IN TENNIS SHOES

WE WALK COMPANIONABLY to the elevator to go down to the dining room rather than taking the stairs. Selena fears tripping on her long skirt on the steps.

"Okay," I reply as her companionable companion. "Elevator it is. I want to be the only one putting bruises on you tonight."

Selena gives me a noogie as the elevator door closes for the short ride down. I laugh at her doing that. She cracks me up.

I step off the elevator with the elegant woman on my arm. Olga's staff has prepared a lovely table, a large floral arrangement in the middle with slender sticks holding hand-painted papier-mâché birds dispersed throughout it adorning the phenomenal oriental porcelain place settings. My Olga never disappoints.

"It's exquisite!" exclaims Selena. "Once again, Olga has outdone herself. Does the woman ever sleep?"

"She seems to, but I've decided she never stops moving from the minute she gets up. Remember, she keeps the staff, including security, well fed all day, every day. After we eat, she'll feed her staff and the other half of the security team and cleanup crew."

"My, she's one hardworking lady." Selena shakes her head.

"That she is," agrees Olga's boss. "Selena, enjoy yourself in front of the fire, and the view outside. I'm going to catch up with Vogo. The others should arrive soon."

"That I shall," replies Selena as I lean in to give her a little kiss. I'm living for our little kisses. Love 'em.

I'm right. Within a few seconds, two of the fellas who had been with her in the dining room earlier in the day arrive. The two say hello and round up the balls for the billiard table while I'm waiting for Vogo to arrive in the situation room off the dining hall.

"Would you like to play?" asks one of them amicably.

"Love to, but waiting for someone," I reply.

"Selena?" he questions.

"No, I'm not much of a player. I'd like to watch you two play, though," replies Selena, as she meanders over to a spot beside the table. I leave my ladylove in good company.

Meanwhile, I spot Vogo, and we meet in the room he has secured. "How are we going to play this thing about the bug?" questions Vogo.

"I want you to have the cleaning staff go in while we're at dinner. While they're cleaning the bathrooms, I want you to water that poor dry plant and douse the bug. Then bury it deep inside the dirt."

"Oh, that should fix it."

"Did you or Alexei figure out where the listening post might be? Is its range outside of the compound?" I question.

"No, that would put it out of range. It has to be inside the compound."

"Amazing," I reply. It's as I feared. However, I act nonchalant.

"Sergei, we have a traitor, or—"

"Don't say it," I cut him off. "It's not Selena."

"How can you be sure?" retorts Vogo.

"We took a swim before I took Selena into the chamber last night. She removed everything, including jewelry and her hair clips. She only wore a robe provided by me into the chamber."

"I see," says an unconvinced Vogo. "You left her alone in the chamber this morning while you were out. Perhaps in her things on the other side."

"I'm the only one who has the code to the lock on the door to the other room. Selena didn't enter there until I gave her the code this morning for her shower. When she came out, she was in view the whole time. I have thought through this morning in the chamber. She didn't have an opportunity."

"I see," replies Vogo. Reluctant to consent to the improbability but concedes.

"There are two possibilities," I state with certainty. "They brought in the buffet while we were both still in the shower. Then there is the cleaning staff."

"Alexei and Ivan oversaw the cleaning staff today," says Vogo, somewhat ruling out the cleaning personnel.

"Question them both to see if there could have been a breach. Their ears only. As well, follow up on the buffet delivery. We have a mole, and that mole will be caught. They may vex us first but make no mistake about their capture."

"Do you know of any other entrance to the chamber besides the front door or the other side?"

I pause for a minute.

"Sergei?" asks Vogo. I can tell he's wondering what his longtime friend might be holding back. I keep quiet.

"I don't think so." I reply firmly. "Be loose. On the phone. Look busy. Do another sweep after the cleaning staff have left. Do another as we come down for the night. I'll buzz you."

"You got it."

I nod toward the door. "Dinner awaits. Are you eating this shift or the next one?"

"Sergei, I have work to do," says the man with the unrelenting scowl, and he turns to run down the stairs. Vogo. How do I explain Vogo?

"Well, enjoy your meal whenever you take it," I call behind him. And this is my current protector. My head gives a slight shake as he leaves. I know I'm in expert hands despite the attitude of the pissant as I leave to join Selena.

Everyone stands at attention as the Commander in Chief enters the room. I'm not big on ceremony but enjoy a speck of respect after Vogo.

"Relax everybody. Tonight, is a celebration of your hard work. It has taken everyone, and I mean *everyone*, running at two hundred percent today to handle this crisis. Unfortunately, it's a crisis that has not ended yet. We still have much to do. I want to thank everyone for their hard work, especially on this day. That includes staff, security, cleaning crew, and let us not forget Queen Olga and her staff. She and her staff and the other half of our team will eat at second dinner serving. I want you all to give Olga and her charge a round of applause. Without them, our creatures would have worked without comfort today."

"Hear! Hear!" comes a cheery voice from a staff member. The others raise their glasses and cheer, "Hear! Hear!"

"Let us be seated," I reply. "I don't know about the rest of you, but I'm starving."

As soon as all take their seats, the food servants remove hot tureens of steaming seafood bisque from the dumbwaiters and begin expertly ladling the ladies a bowl prior to the men. Other servants follow with bread and butter while leaving copious amounts of fresh bread baskets around the table. The water glasses sit pre-filled, but wine, beer, and vodka glasses are dispensed to the eaters of the steaming seafood bisque.

The staff eats up and cheers one another as their leader stays mostly quiet and lets the others revel in their stories and chatter. Selena and I often find each other's hands underneath the table and squeeze. It's hard to say who looks at the other and smiles the most, Selena or myself.

True to Russian meal protocol, next comes salad, followed by shrimp and langoustines with sauces. "Yum!" Selena exclaims as jazz music softly plays through the surround sound.

The food servants keep bread and booze flowing while imperceptibly removing used dishes from each course. The main course arrives with large pieces of prime rib that swallow our plates. Cheesy potatoes and pickled vegetable bowls sit to the side. Selena says she is sure she can feel her thighs growing.

When all eat until they can't inhale another bite, Olga sends up slices of a triple-layered chocolate cake with amaretto ganache and cream cheese icing, adorned with delightful shards of chocolate curls and fresh raspberries and a sprinkling of confectioner's sugar. As if that's not enough, vanilla bean ice cream on the side served in a chilled bowl. To top off our dessert, they serve a chocolate-enhanced hot coffee with sugar and milk. Everyone groans in disbelief, but most eat all the delectable dessert.

The staff clears the plates as everyone stays a few more minutes to savor the remainder of their drinks. Olga and her team arrive in the dining room as the plates are cleared. I arise and clap. The others take their cue and arise to clap as well. Olga and her team bow in gratitude. A presidential thanks to the team is in order. I walk over and kiss the old woman on the cheek and hug each of her staff members. Once accomplished, I take my leave. I won't need to make another appearance until the second dinner service to thank everyone, so in the meantime Selena and I will have a little time to rest our bellies in our chamber.

Neither of us sits down once inside. Selena walks around and around the room. I follow.

"Damn, I feel the need to walk to work off those ten thousand extra calories," Selena complains, holding her stomach.

"Selena, keep moving. I'll try to catch you, but I don't think I can," I giggle.

"Oh, President Radkov, I think you could catch whatever you want with those big hands."

I throw back my head and roar a chortle. "Selena, you have more confidence in me than I do right now."

"You know what would be a really cool thing for us to do?" she asks.

I give her a raised eyebrow while the two of us stop at the back of the settee. Why do I get the feeling that whatever she proposes is something I'm going to need to think about?

"We should go downstairs and help Olga in the kitchen with the second and third service. We should help with the dishes. Be servants."

"So, you're saying President Radkov should be a dishwasher?" I ask with a quizzical grin. "Do you think the President of United Russia doesn't have enough to do without being a kitchen servant? You have no idea the number of things I'm thinking about this very moment without throwing dishwashing into the mix."

"Well, President Radkov *is* a different kind of president," retorts Selena.

I consider this for a minute. No way. No damned way.

"You know, Olga says most of her team will eat after they serve the second service to the remaining staff. She says they need more space to serve the remaining team members and kitchen staff should eat after everyone else has been served. She wants the second service to be as well-treated as the first, so she decided to have the kitchen staff make a third service," explains Selena.

"This isn't my problem. Management of the dacha kitchens is not something I have the slightest impetus to micromanage."

"That's so like the Olga that I'm getting to know," continues Selena. "I would bet dimes to doughnuts that the kitchen staff doesn't even eat in the dining room. Someone would have to man the downstairs *and* serve the dining room. They're all probably tired and would like to sit down to eat."

Did she not hear me? "I'm not micromanaging the kitchen, Selena." My voice is gruffer than I intended, so I use a more rational tone. "Selena, I'm a hard worker, but not a robot. I need to rest and keep my head clear for issues greater than who eats what, when, and how."

"This is about your team. These are the people standing beside you during the toughest times. Some are high-level. Others clean the toilets. But they're *your* people, Sergei. Your team. These people live and work for your approval."

Is she nuts? God, I'm glad I didn't say that out loud.

Selena jogs to her toilet. Good. Maybe when she comes out, she'll have given up this battle. I take a finger and bend it to chalk one up for the male team.

Then I hear her enter the adjoining chamber. Thought she had to pee. What is that about? I suddenly have a pit in my stomach that this war isn't over. Fuck. Maybe I shouldn't have bent my chalking finger so soon. I look at it like a traitor.

Out bounces Selena in warm-ups and tennis shoes. "I'm going to wash dishes," she declares. "President Radkov can rest as much as needed while his team works."

She makes musical sounds to the theme of Rocky and is pumping her fists in the air.

"Well, not my entire team," I say.

It's too late. She is already out the door.

"Fuuuuck," I squelch as I plop on the settee to pout. Yes, I'm pouting. My damn lip is poking out almost to the floor. I play with the fire. It's stoked. I'm not. My poor willie wonders what happened.

I'm here and she's not. I miss her. Already. Took five seconds. I want to be with her. What happened to her holding on to the bedpost? I do what any whipped man would do.

I change, leaving my suit on the floor, and fly down the stairs.

"Olga!" I shout in a playful tone. "I'm here to clean your dishes. Someone fetch me an apron!" I walk over to the sinks and take my place next to Selena. There are stacks of uncleaned dishes. Only Nik, the man who takes care of the animals and grounds with his son, is working the multi-station sinks with Selena.

The dishes are of fine china, so Olga insists they are to be hand-washed. The glasses are adorned with a fine etching and the utensils are silver. Very little tableware is dishwasher safe. There is a sliding metal unit that holds buckets of dirty dishes as they come down the dumbwaiter. The food is scraped off the plates upstairs, and each bucket is about three-quarters full of one type of dishware and sent down the assigned dumbwaiter. Just as Olga insists. Maybe this is one time she disappoints?

The stainless-steel sinks are compartmentalized into sections. Selena takes the first section. Her job is to rinse off the dirty dishes with a foot-operated spout. She needs to place them into a sink which holds a solution to degerm the plates as well as break down the food and oils that cling to them. I take the next section, which involves washing the dishes in soapy water and putting them into the next sink's rinse water.

My hands are working. My ass is moving. I'm all knees and elbows. My face is sweating, but I'm still pouting and don't speak to Selena.

Alexei comes into the kitchen and takes the job of rinsing each piece well with a spout. Not done. Dishes go into another section to remove spots and make the dishes shine. Rinse again. Alexei sings opera as he works. No one complains. Hell, I join him. In spite of my mood, I begin to have a good time.

From there, either Nik or Alexei moves the dishes from the hot water and mounts them along a long draining board. Olga insists on scalding hot water, so all manage their tasks with thick rubber gloves. Damn, it's hot in Siberia in the middle of an icy blizzard.

In fact, all four of us sweat around the sink, and pieces of Selena's hair fall as her tightly woven bun gives way. Little snippets here and there fall across her face.

Olga notices how hard Selena works. How organized, and how the lovely girl completes her tasks. She not only rinses the dishes piece by piece from the buckets, but soon realizes the value of putting the whole bucket in the sink and letting it fill with water as she rinses each piece. Then, the beauty uses disinfectant soap and a rag to clean and rinse the bucket. Selena finds unused counter space where she lines the area with towels for the buckets to dry before she moves on to the next.

This thrills Olga. It's a conspiracy. These hens won't be happy until they've pecked my eyes out.

Selena's cleaning of the buckets as she toils along comes in handy because soon a call comes from the dining room begging for more buckets. Selena drops off the line to dry buckets on the counter. She dries a little less than half of them and walks the buckets to the dumbwaiter. The beauty with the loosening hair accepts a handful of dirties for her walk back. She repeats the same process on the second half of buckets.

I'm so damned proud of her. She is so on it. So damned... well, intentional. She is prepared with freaking clean buckets. Can you imagine? I would've flipped those dirty suckers right back onto the metal rack. She's so... *it*. I'm can't help but to be so damn proud of her. She's right; these are my people. My team. My support system. Yet here she is, a volunteer working harder than the paid staff.

I am a different kind of president. Hell, she has made me a different man. A different person. My heart fills with the love of her. I lean over and kiss her cheek. And give her a little gloved noogie just like she's given me.

She smiles. All is forgiven.

We use a rag from a bucket of soapy water to clean the dumbwaiter that travels up and the one travelling down with new dumbwaiter loot. As a duo, we toil on, along with volunteer members from the first service, to provide cleanup and help the old woman and her staff. Imagine the president and his lady doing this.

Finally, it's time for me to go upstairs with Olga and company. I do so while wearing warm-ups and an apron. The staff love it.

Here I stand in jersey rather than a suit, as the seated members rise to hail the chief. "Sit down, sit down. This is your time to enjoy." Eyes grow large as they take in the dress and apron on their commander. It's a hoot. I even put on white gloves and help to serve the food. With my big hands, they're tight. I persevere.

Of all the staff joining the service, the ringleader of comedy, Vogo, joins in. This is his wheelhouse. He has the crowd roaring in laughter at my expense. Pissant.

I muse. These are my people. They cook my food. They clean my toilets. They wash my clothes. They provide my security. They serve me—but in the end, I serve them. There is one traitor among them with an agenda, but the rest are my people. My people, except the leak…

It's a story that these people who are present will tell their children, grandchildren, neighbors, and friends. "The White Stallion himself served me vodka. Can you believe it? Served me *vodka*."

Of all my service to my country, this is my best. Selena asked me to do this and I'm grateful. So damn grateful I share this moment with these people.

Selena and I toil. Toil together. Toil apart. Toil upstairs and down. I've never felt happier.

Oh, and then there's the dirty linens. You don't want to know. Let's just say we reached a compromise.

When the meal is over, I stay upstairs to help clean and vacuum and rid the tables of all linens. Olga and her team go downstairs to find most of their work completed. Selena bows to the old woman and allows Olga to regain her charge. Selena moseys over to help Alexei with the dishes but finds most things washed, including the large stock pots.

One by one, lights turn off for the night.

No doubt about it. Sergei Radkov is a different kind of president. Damn, what Selena gives me when I least expect it.

Whew!

CHAPTER 54
AND YOUR LITTLE PIGGIES TOO

WHEN SERGEI and I arrive back at the chamber, we both plop on the settee to remove our shoes. Each of us looks at the other and laughs.

"Woman, next time you decide to make such a suggestion, just go ahead and shoot me," laughs the president-turned-dishwasher-turned-food servant-turned-cleanup crew member.

"You can handle it, big boy," I tease.

"Moved up my briefing by two hours since there will be so much to talk about. That will happen in a few hours."

"Better get your butt into the bed then."

"Selena, I'm too tired to sleep. Would you like to take a swim?"

"As much as I'd like to return to the waters where I first kissed Sergei Radkov, I think I'm going to take a shower. I stink."

Sergei pulls up his sweatshirt to his nose and smells his body odor. I'm sure the smell of dirty dishes and lack of sex are in the mix.

"Whew," he says, lowering his shirt from his nose. "That's bad. What if I wash your back if you wash mine?"

"Oh, I think I can wash more than that," I reply.

Sergei reaches over and draws me into his arms, giving me a kiss that I don't want to end. Body odor and all.

"My place or yours?" I ask.

"Oh, yours. You have more personals than I do. I want to see what you do with all that stuff."

I smile as Sergei stands up to give me a hand. We walk into my toilet, pinching butts and giggling like kindergarteners during recess. We disrobe. Double showerheads rinse our bodies. I put lavender shampoo into Sergei's hair and scrub his scalp.

The odor of lavender invades our nostrils. "Now we're going to smell alike," he teases as I work the bubbles through his strands and steal a quick peck on his lips before I push him under the showerhead to rinse.

"Would you like some conditioner?"

"I can live without it," smiles my man. "On second thought, hit me with all ya got."

After applying the hair conditioner, I soap Sergei's body in circular movements with a loofah. Expertly, this tired lady cleans his body as though I'm a nursemaid. Not intending my gentle strokes to be sexy, but oh Cinderella's man is being driven to sexy distraction.

Even so, he makes no sexual advances. When I finish scrubbing this handsome man's body from top to bottom, Sergei pushes me under the showerhead to return tit for tat. A stolen kiss crosses my lips.

Sergei massages the lavender shampoo into my scalp. Then adds more of the bubble-causing liquid as he works his way down my long tresses.

"My God, you must use a bottle of this stuff each time you shampoo."

"Yes, but I'm worth it," I tease.

Sergei rinses my hair, and I instruct how to apply conditioner on long female hair. Sergei is an attentive student and lets the conditioner soak in while he uses the loofah on my body.

"I'll start with your armpits first. They're the worst."

I guffaw and raise my arms. Acting all sexy woman, I place my raised hands onto the shower tiles while standing at a slant with my butt stuck out like Oliver going for a cat stretch. "Go for it, big boy," I tease.

"Oh, that is *so* cheating," protests Sergei.

"So is dissing my armpits."

Sergei washes my armpits, my elongated body, down my legs and between my toes. He even uses a sandpaper-like scrub gel on my face.

"There are good times to be a man. Plain soap on my face is just fine. Even works as shampoo," he says to the wet air as much as to me.

Next, he rinses my body and my hair under the running water. Assisting me in squeezing water from my mane, he dries it with a towel. Pulling my mane up in another towel, he bundles it on my head. The shower smells of lavender. Sergei says, "Can't wait to sniff your dry hair later when I take you. And I *will* take you." Evil Russian grin. I love it.

Sergei is confident of that. His words make my showered wet woman wetter. God, his confidence turns me on.

Instead of making a sexual advance, he dries every inch of my wet body. I dry his. I sit nude in a mirror-front chair.

Naked, Sergei combs out my wet hair. Next, he flosses my teeth. "Damn, the space between your teeth is tight."

I laugh with an open mouth. "Braces," I slosh out while I try to spit, but Sergei doesn't remove his hands from my mouth. My tired lover grasps my hand signals and lets me spit.

After my teeth are brushed, Sergei looks in the bottom drawer of the bathroom cabinet to find a nail care kit.

"Perfect," he says as he pulls out the nail kit and places it on the ceramic top.

I sit naked as a jaybird laughing my ass off. "Are you doing my nails?"

"Yes, madame. And your little toes too," says Sergei, in a British accent as if he's the American Wicked Witch of the West. "What colors do you foresee wearing today, milady?"

"Red. I see red today," I snort, giggling about "milady."

"Oh, I like red. It matches your lips. Your hot lips and my hot blood."

I try to suppress my laughing enjoyment. It's hard. Damn. He's a bit hard too.

Sergei smiles as his fingers remove the polish from my hands. He tries to work as an expert, but occasionally I have to give him hints.

"Um, the cuticle remover goes on the *side* of the nail, not on top."

"Oh, that makes sense," replies the nude nail technician. With a face of concentration, he carefully lays down one layer of polish on my fingernails.

"That's gel polish. You'll need to turn on that light for me to slide my fingers under it for the polish to set."

"Oh, so that is what that contraption is for?"

I nod an affirmative while relishing his every touch, his every move. Fun and loving.

After Sergei applies two layers of nail polish and a topcoat, he works on my toes.

"Regular polish will be fine for the toes," instructs milady.

"How will I know what is regular and what is gel?"

"It says so on the bottle."

"Imagine that," replies Sergei sarcastically as he removes polish from my toes. Growing confident, Sergei perceives himself quite the expert now. I can tell he's loving painting my toes and does so to perfection. It's slow going. But he does good.

"There're times to be glad you are a man. I love this! Just glad I don't have to worry about it," he confesses.

I omit the part where he should massage my feet and legs to increase blood flow. Give the guy a little break. Right?

"So, what now, milady? Makeup, or should I blow-dry your hair?"

"You're actually thinking you're going to attempt putting mascara on my eyelashes?"

"Did I tell you I'm trained in torture?"

"No, but you don't have to apply makeup. I'm planning on sleeping. Usually, women don't apply makeup before sleeping."

"Ah, I thought you might want to for me."

"For you? Prior to sleeping? Sergei, women *remove* their makeup prior to sleep, but if you have a wild hair about it, then I need to know."

Sergei laughs. "I'm just tugging your leg."

"You mean pulling my leg?"

"Yes, that's it. Damn, I'm tired. I can get an hour or two of shut eye before I go to the meeting if you won't entice me with that sexy body of yours."

"I'll make no promises for later, but for now I want you to sleep and rest, too. Sure, no enticement here," I grin as I wave my hand across my nude body.

"Not until I blow-dry your hair."

I stand. "Hey, it's time I blow-dry yours." I pat the chair for him to have a seat.

"Not yet. Don't you ladies put some of this lotion stuff on your face?"

"We do, but I can do that later."

"Not on your life, lady. Back down in the chair. This is the best part. Tell me what goes where."

Sergei applies lotion to my face and uses the under-eye cream. He gets a kick out of the applicator, which is metal and shaped like an hourglass but has rounded ends. The crazy Russian actually says he thought I did Kegel exercises with it. I chortle.

Then comes what he says is his very favorite: the full body application of this sweet-smelling honey-ginger lotion that lifts his libido. Or so I notice.

"Damn, this is fun, and I'm not even done yet," he says.

My eyes gaze into his through the mirror, loving this crazy man whose sexy body is standing in front of me stark naked, holding a hair dryer in his hand and not taking no for an answer. All while dead on his feet. I might be crazy, but it occurs to me I may never get another chance to love another man. If all I get is today with Sergei, if this moment is it with this man, then damned if I won't take it. Take it to the max.

"Usually I turn my head over like this and pull my hair upside down. I blow-dry the scalp underneath pretty good. After, I'll show you how to roll the brush to make my curls behave."

Sergei gives his best. In a hairstylist demeanor, he styles away with the hair dryer in one hand and the large round brush in the other. When he's finished in the back, he turns off the dryer and asks, "How do you do that big-hair-wavy-thing you do in front?"

I can't answer him for laughing. "What I do here is basically the same, but a little more like this," I demonstrate. "It depends if you want to bring the hair like this in the front toward the face or pull it back more away from your face."

"Oh, I like to see your face," Sergei retorts, giving his statement a playful roar like the hairdryer he turns back on.

"Here," I direct. "Brush back this way from my face, toward the side and back." My hand motions convey my meaning more than my words barely heard over the hair dryer.

Sergei complies, and when he reaches his voilà moment, he looks at me with serious eyes. "You're so beautiful to me, Selena, and not just on the outside. I've had more fun with you the past few hours in the middle of a crisis and dishwashing than I've ever had in my whole life."

I take in his face reflected in the mirror. Absorb it. "Do you find me beautiful even without an eyeball full of mascara?" I grin.

"You don't need mascara, Selena. Not for me. You only need enough makeup to make yourself feel good. Only then is it worth it."

I return the most loving of looks in the mirrored reflection. "You know, mister, it's time to blow-dry your hair and put some lotion on you and brush and floss those teeth."

"Okay, but milady, next time I'm going to shave those gorgeous legs of yours!"

"Next time I'm going to shave your gorgeous face," I reply, along with my own Groucho Marx eyebrows.

"Actually, my hair is almost dry. Let's comb it straight back and let it fall. I'll wet it to style it when I wake up, anyway. I can forgo the lotion. But milady, 'twould be a kindness to you for me to brush and floss my teeth."

With that, I comb back his hair. I have his teeth flossed and brushed in half the time it took Sergei to do mine.

With the final spit, Sergei says, "Bedtime, sweet bedtime... even if it's only for a few hours."

The two of us make our way to bed and pull back the covers. Our naked bodies slide under the warming mass. The ever-burning fire crackles, and the wolf howls. Bodies of Sergei and milady spoon. Sergei smells my hair, indulging in the lingering odor of lavender left by his cleaning, the honey ginger on my neck.

"Intoxicating," he murmurs as his man rises, but he stores his passion inside the bundle of his dreams.

Too soon the red phone rings, and I catch it quickly so as not to awaken Selena. I whisper to the sleeping milady, "Good morning, Sunshine." I don't dress as president. Instead, I throw on my robe and slide on my slippers to trudge to the secure room.

"Is it coffeetime yet?" I ask.

"Yes," assures Vogo while pouring me a cup. Setting the cup on the table, Vogo adds, "Damn Sergei, you look like hell."

"I feel like hell."

"Little woman keep you up all night?"

"Yes. Her name is Olga."

Vogo laughs. "Better stay away from that one. I hear she makes you wash dishes all night."

"Worse. She entices you to volunteer to wash dishes all night. The siren."

"Selena okay with that? Thought she would want you all to herself," Vogo asks.

"It was her idea."

Vogo gives quite the roar of laughter for such a little man. "It was Selena who kept you up all night, after all?"

"Not discussing that today, Vogo. Not while I'm the happiest man alive. Anyone on the remote call yet?"

"Yes, all the principals. I made them wait while you got a few sips of the black juice."

"Damn, I forgot my notepad. I can remember what is on it, but can you scrounge me up pen and paper?" I request.

The meeting begins, and by the end I've little need for pen and paper. Instead of taking so much upon myself, I delegate to staff and have them make all the calls and follow-ups. Team members wear the tasks like a badge of honor. Maybe my dishwashing made them more eager to serve.

Moscow principals were informed of the dacha goings-on the prior night during idle chitchat, but no one speaks of Selena. My dacha staff and assistants understand that might be a deal-breaker for me. Totally unacceptable. Understand the president wants and needs his private time, and they darn sure see to it that I get it. The leak? *Which one of these bastards is a fucking mole?*

The meeting breaks after only half the time I anticipated. I return to my chamber on autopilot to dive into bed, but there lies Selena. Still naked, but half-covered with a mink quilt. She lies upside down on the bed with her head near the prophesized bedpost. Fast asleep. I place a pillow for myself beside her and pull loose the fur quilts. One to cover Selena better, and one for me, and another for us to share.

The region is entering the time of year when almost all day is a dusky dark on the other side of the midnight sun. The fire crackles as I lie beside my love and spoon her in my arms to nostril her lavender and ginger and honey. She is here with me, in my arms. That's all that matters.

Matters now. At least until the moment comes. The moment when…

I don't want to think about it. Not while she is still in my arms. I fall into a peaceful sleep.

CHAPTER 55
HANG ON, IT'S GOING TO BE A BUMPY RIDE

WE AWAKE IN THE AFTERNOON. "What time is it?" I ask.

"Who cares?" retorts Sergei. "My red phone hasn't rung. That is what I care about," he says with a sleepy yawn.

I lean my head on his chest to listen to his heartbeat. *Thump. Thump.* His rhythm soothes me like a baby in the womb, comforted by the heartbeat of its mother.

"We're kind of in a holding pattern right now," explains Sergei about the state of his nation as he fights to break through the sleepiness that could easily reclaim him. "There isn't much I can do to change the weather. VP is taking the lead on that, and doing such an excellent job that there is nothing I need to do from here," says the yawning president. "Others are busy with the families of the fallen, so I must step back and let them do their jobs."

I sneak up on his chest and give him a peck on the lips. Sergei's eyes seem to come into better focus. "Why don't I get dressed? Meantime, why don't you sleep some more, and when you awaken, we can discuss food?" I recommend.

"Food. Oh, my God! That's what started all of this. I never understood there was so much to serving food! Everyone gets a raise. Everyone. I'm serious," says Sergei, making an executive decision.

I give him a knowing chuckle. "Yes, Sergei Radkov is a different kind of president. One who needs his rest."

"I can rest later," says the authoritative president. "Right now, I want to be with you," Sergei says. Kissing my face, he smells my hair for its lavender scent. The honey and ginger are still on my skin from our early morning fun. He's aroused.

I feel his arousal as I run my hand up and down his sides and abdomen and around his navel. I'm wearing a knowing smile as Sergei lies back in a relaxed bliss, soaking in my touch. Without warning, I slide down and awaken him with the wet joy of my lips.

"Ummm," comes Sergei's secret password in our secret garden. "You act like a woman with a debt to pay."

Stopping momentarily, I respond, "No, just a woman trying to please her man."

Something in that statement revs up Sergei's motor. Perhaps he is making too much of the "her man" in my prior sentence. He may be in a half stupor, still in half-sleep awareness, but damned if Sergei Radkov doesn't act determined to find out.

He makes his move. Without warning, Sergei Radkov flips me on my back and puts his head between my thighs and lays his moist tongue on my womanness and presses. All in one movement, I might add.

God, he presses the parts of me that make a woman scream while pulling on my waist and buttocks to evoke the sound. Without hesitation, I give him my noises. Cries that bless God and all his saints.

Slowly, Sergei churns his tongue in concert with his hands, churns my lower abdomen to his rhythm. Hands clutching, he holds down my violently thrashing lower torso. Round and round. His hands caress my bottom while his tongue caresses my hood. I scream as though I'm in a frantic rage. Hell, I *am* in a frantic rage.

Before Dr. Selena Frederick, OB/GYN can say what's happening, I experience an orgasm sent by the power of an unknown God. Sergei Radkov flips me over with expectation as I place my two hands on the bed, then scoot up closer to the bedpost and cling to it. I let out an anticipatory moan before the fun begins.

Anticipation is flushing through me as I view Sergei in the mirror.

His cock in his hand, placing it near my opening. A primal look on his face.

The sounds I make are stirring him. Motivating him. Exciting him. Sergei Radkov lets me have it. Have it hard. Bursts his throb deep inside my chamber. I respond with my own bursts of moaning groans. I've never been taken like this. Never this hard. Feels so good. So erotic.

Suddenly leaning across my back, Sergei asks with concern. "Oh my God, Selena, am I hurting you?"

"No. No, Sergei. It's not pain. I promise. Please don't stop. Don't stop. You're almost making me orgasm again. Pleeeeease more."

He kisses my back, my neck, my face while stilling his throbbing inside me. My sizzling urge cools a little.

Sergei murmurs, "Don't let me hurt you. Promise me you'll never let me hurt you," as the side of his face loves my back.

"I promise," I assure the man holding his wealthy manhood so deep inside my womanhood. The same man who stands so deep inside my heart that he can grab my soul with half a hand.

Sergei's lower torso churns as he makes his way deeper into the chamber of his lover. Deeper. And deeper. So deep he is now, that he's speaking in tongues that even Russians don't understand. Thrusting so hard. So wild.

My groans grow louder. Moans so guttural as the man to the back of me reaches further and further into places of an unknown existence. Together, we explore places untouched by my experience. I'm lost in an erotic forest. So primal. There's a wild animal that exists inside me that I don't know. It's feral. Gurgling. Needing. Begging. Taking. The wild animal screams out inside me. Words. Moans. Sighs. Schizophrenic sounds of awe and dismay.

There is an animal inside of Sergei too. I watch the way his teeth clinch, his lips curl, his eyes roll away before he howls out his primal words. Sounds in animal language, moans of a man-beast, groans of expectation, pants of physical exertion. The fire below flickers up to touch our mirrored reflection. Sergei leans his head on my back as we both watch our mirrored movements.

The man-beast grabs my lower abdomen. Pushes himself as deep as he can. Stills to hold in his beastly cry. His lips curl. His eyes meet mine in the mirror. His lips uncurl to chill me. His tongue licks my full spine as he plunges. Mouth sucks the back of my neck. Words of pleasure moan in my ear.

I blow out air in an extended relaxation phase so he can go even deeper. "Oh yes, deeper baby," I plead.

No man has ever touched me this deep. Sergei has found virgin space inside of me. It's a pleasurable kind of pain as he strives to reach it. I clinch around him, using my inner muscles to pull him in more and more until I'm forced to relax.

Sergei is transported. I watch him leave. He's going where the animal is wilder. Where no human control can channel. Where there's no more giving me more. There's no more waiting. There's Sergei Radkov bending over to kiss my back and neck while holding his throbbing vibration deep inside me. Human Sergei spurts a return to me. "God Selena, I must take you. I must take you now," he pants out one word at a time.

I hold on to the bed posts as if a hurricane wind is trying to dislodge me from the stronghold of a tree. Sergei is holding onto my buttocks and abdomen as if he is the wind, the rain, the hurricane, an ungodly force.

Man and woman yell. They scream. Scream louder. Louder. Louder more. More! Loud. Sigh. Gasp. Pant. Breathe. Breathe shallow. Shallow, as though we both are being revived by CPR. We're flat on the bed. Breathing. Breathing hard now. Breathing fast now. Needing oxygen. Reaching our hands across our flat bodies to touch the other's fingertips. Breathe hard. Breathe deep. Looking into the eyes of the other panting beast. Being transformed. Transformed by touch. Human now.

Sergei mans up his strength to reach and pull me near him. Panting. I listen to his heartbeat and synchronize mine with his. Slowly, methodically, our heart rates come down to normal rhythm as both former beasts close their eyes. Waiting. Waiting for the moment of completed homeostasis after the transformation. Transformation into people linked to one another. Transformation from one beast finding another and both finding their primal selves.

I find myself wanting to shout to the ceiling so loud that God above can hear me, "I love you, damn it! I love you." It's not time. Not while I'm a human that I don't know. Might still be half animal. Instead, I rub my hands up and down her arm and push away her hair so that I can put skin on skin while I massage her back. But soon I will make my shouts. I must. So little time left.

God, I love the way she feels. Nothing has ever felt like Selena. Oh, Selena. How can I let her go? How can I?

"Ummmm," comes the sound of Selena's voice from our secret garden. "So erotic," she mumbles from the delight of my hands on her back.

I oblige her with a hand squeeze to her back and the lowering of my head against hers to squeeze her in closer. I want her so close that she is inside me. I can't get her close enough to me. In me.

"Well, Selena Frederick, what are we going to do with the rest of this lousy day? It's totally gray outside."

"I haven't considered one thing that far ahead."

"Nik said he would be afraid taking the animals on a troika ride just yet. But then, he's quite protective of the animals, and perhaps a little overly so."

"Well, we wouldn't want Mr. Nik to concern himself with the animals," comes the reply of a woman still awakening from an exciting morning. An exciting morning that I've provided for her. "I sort of think animal control is out of our domain," says Selena with a witty quip.

My face cracks open with a smile the size of the Grand Canyon. After a moment of reveling, I ask, "What do you say to a sled ride down the hills here?"

"I-I don't know. I've never ridden on a sled before."

"You've never ridden on a sled before?" I question.

"I can remember a few times when it snowed where I lived, but it was rare. Even then, the snow was light and melted in a day or so. Not much of an accumulation, especially where we were by the sea. I didn't grow up sledding. Then what can I say?" she shrugs. "I grew up. At that point, I didn't realize grown-ups were allowed to sled."

I smile the way only Dr. Selena Frederick can make me smile. "How about I fix us a quick cup of coffee? Then we'll dress, and I'll have a buffet delivered to the gallery. Then we'll take off on a sled ride after we eat. I'll show you some of the landscape." I say as an excited grown-up.

"Is this your way of getting a laugh as I bust my ass?" she teases.

"Most definitely," replies the president of good cheer this morning.

Selena guffaws and gives me her fist noogie of the day. "You're on like a pot of neck bones."

"I'm going to eat some of those neck bones you speak of sometime," I retort.

"Very tender meat," she replies.

"I like tender meat," I shoot back.

I find my clothes that were previously discarded willy-nilly around the bed and don them along with my robe.

Selena sits up in bed and gives me a strange look.

"What?" I ask.

"Oh nothing," she says.

"You're giving me your evil smile."

"Oh, it shows? President Radkov, did I inform you that you are in the presence of an evil woman?"

"Selena. What is it?" I groan.

"Just looking at your crazy, wispy hair and wondering what kind of wild woman I look like. Avoiding the fireplace mirror."

"Didn't earlier," I say in a near snark. My eyebrows raise. Then wiggle.

"There is a time for all things under the sun," Selena retorts.

Damn, she's quick. "Ecclesiastes, right?"

"Yep," she says while sitting on the side of the bed and giving her torso a stretch.

I crawl on the bed to kiss her ruby red lips. "Lady, you have no idea what evil means until I get you up on those hills with a sled."

Pushing the remaining covers away, a coquettish Selena retorts, "I'm going to let you have this one. I'll get you back one day. Soon.

Maybe on a pair of water skis. Can't say when, but I'm aware that I'm out of my element right now."

Smiling a large competitive smile as I help her egress from the bed. I put both my arms around her and hug her tight, my head bent against her cheek as she stands on tiptoes to take advantage of as much body as she can. All I can process is that I like the sound of her getting even with me one day. The idea of her torturing me is a thing to look forward to. A small payoff for the luxury of her presence. God, her presence. Will I have a presence in her life when…?

"You may have done that already with the presidential dishwashing deal," I tease, instead of letting my former thoughts linger.

Selena stands back to look at me, and I wonder what she'll come up with next. We're so competitive with each other. But it's fun, not mean. She may win every competition, but I will give her a run for her money. Can't go too easy on her.

Only two words fall from her mouth. "You pussy."

"Dr. Selena Frederick," I say. "Did you just call me a pussy?'"

"I did."

"So misogynistic. I'm shocked. What would the world think if they heard you say that?"

She grins. "Kinda hopin' we wouldn't tell 'em."

I play-attack her like a bear and chase her around the chamber.

She continues to giggle when I attack her and tickle the hell out of her.

When I stop, she leans the back of her head against my chest. "Sergei, you know I'm only teasing, right? I know what I said was evil."

"I know. That's why you said it."

"It is," she admits. "You know I would only say that between us playing, right? No other time."

"Oh Selena. I will take as many of your pussies as can fill this room."

I tickle her more and she howls with laughter. We're kids.

She cries uncle and I say in a more grown-up and serious tone, "Selena, I don't know if we'll make it outside before nightfall, although there's not much difference between day and night this time of year. God, I haven't even put on the coffee. Moving kinda slow, it seems."

"Tell you what. I'll put on the coffee while you call security and Olga and make them aware of our plans," says the beauty with rumpled hair and a cute butt while walking to the coffee station.

I pick up my phone and push speed dial. We have our first cup of morning coffee in front of the fire while chatting and pinching butts. Our laughter is louder than our sex. Each of us heads to separate quarters to rinse off and change clothes.

Selena wears a red Henley shirt with a plaid overshirt that looks like every plaid flannel shirt worn world-round in chilly winter weather. On top of her lumberjack clothes, she wears a pair of snow pants. With her hair braided and tightly affixed to her head, she looks ready to rumble. And oh, so beautiful. I look like a lumberjack with lingering tea bags under my eyes.

Selena smiles her smile. "I love, absolutely love, your wispy blond hair. And those big blue eyes," she says while walking toward me. "Um, those eyes with your light-blue-and-navy lumberjack clothes. Like 'em," she says while running her fingers through my wispy hair.

I don't let myself think about the next day or so when we'll both return to real life. I just want to love her now. At this moment. In this moment. Ask nothing more. Minute by minute. Each one a minute of grace.

We take the stairs up to the art gallery. "I wonder how our lady is doing today?" I ask.

Making herself comfortable under the dome, Selena replies, "Oh, I think she's probably not even yet dressed for the day."

I laugh at her wit as they deliver the food buffet to the gallery. Both of us eat hardily, knowing we'll be exerting ourselves. Forgotten is the prior night's meal. Our promised workout will just have to wait. Today is "us" day. I've lined things up so, and trust my country is well.

Hell, I trust the world to be well despite all the things happening. Smoltsky and the committee, along with the immigration chief, have drafted an immediate plan that even I believe is hardline. Those old-timers like hard lines. There are times when such things are needed. I consider it's that time now, and not one soul in my country has voiced disagreement. Not even the liberal-media bar-whistler, Joe Cook. However, as a contemplative man, I fear being reactionary instead of smart.

After the video of my statement to the world on United Russia politics, handling the media has been easy. "President Radkov said what he has to say. It's no longer time for talking but action. He's not granting interviews at this time. No, not even to you, Mr. Cook," retells my press secretary. "Perhaps later. He's tied up right now and has restricted everyone's access. Yes, I'll give him the message, but it may be a few days. The president has hardly slept and is quite tired," Tina told Joe. I smile when she tells me about Joe's call.

Outside the dacha, I pick Selena up and twirl her around at the bottom of a hill after steering her first sled ride. I have no guilt for taking this time. Tomorrow and its problems—and worse, its sadness—will be here soon enough. I'm ready. Right now, is right now, I tell myself.

We play like children in the falling snow the rest of the day. Selena says that except for a few snowfalls in Chapel Hill, she barely knew snow until her more mature years. Even then, college kids in the South didn't have sleds. Just snowball fights and attempts by the boys to squirrel a snowball down her shirt. Unfortunately for them, they didn't realize what a fighter she is.

Selena tells me her father was overly protective of his girls early on. She figures her dad had seen enough rape as a physician and wanted nothing like that to touch his girls. She tells me Dr. Joseph Frederick thought such behavior to come from the darkest places in the hearts of men. So does Selena. She was touched by it through her role as a doctor and a healer. The rage from it drives her to continue her healing arts.

She started martial arts at five years old. Attained her first black belt when she was eleven. Accumulated three more and continues to practice her katas and stretches most days, except when she's with a troublemaker by the name of Sergei Radkov. She's an enigma. Genuine shock and awe. Things like having black belts don't faze her, but practicing her art does. She says it's an outlet for her rage.

There's nothing colder than the Siberian winds of ice and snow.

Even with a heavy lined down coat with a fur-lined parka style hat, Selena says her face feels as frozen as Lake Baikal. It's beet-red. Even so, she doesn't turn down a walk beside the lake with me. I would like to walk on top of the lake but assess it may not be frozen enough to walk on. Not taking risks with the safety of my girl.

Instead, I put my arms around her as we walk lakeside to provide her warmth. We then stand for a while on the shore while she digs her head into where I unzipped my coat to let her slide her face inside, warming it. I'm the happiest man alive.

Soon, the two of us make our way inside, with Vogo and Alexei following our every move and standing several meters behind us watching all things moving and still. I whisper into Selena's ear prior to zipping up my coat. "You take the right flank; I'll take the left." I tug my zipper closed. As though making a football play, I whisper, "Are you ready?"

"Yes!"

Hut hut hike.

Selena and I reach down and pick up a handful of snow, and quickly pack it as Selena runs to the right and I run to the left. Selena is kind and gives the older Alexei a body shot while I plant a big one right upside Vogo's head.

"Mr. President," says Vogo. "You're so fucking on!"

The four of us spend twenty minutes throwing snowballs and laughing like children. We hide behind trees and duck to a miss a fastball. Selena slid on her ass once. I was scared the fall hurt her, but the pippin popped up and buried my face with a snowball.

The fight ends with a standoff between me and Selena, wherein stupid me, even after getting pummeled by the pippin, throws his snowball down and plows my body into the American beauty as though I'm making a strategic football tackle. "Six points for the Russians," I scream.

"Yes, but no extra point because I hold the football," she says while proceeding to cream the face of the President of United Russia with the last snowball.

I wipe the snow from my eyes and smile. "Yes, but that's just three points for a field goal, so the Russians win." I pick her up and twirl her as she cackles.

Damn, what fun. Damn, what a woman!

The four of us mosey inside, as Ivan and the perimeter security team remain outside. And, of course, Olga is aflutter, wondering what it is the couple should want to eat. Both say just a warm drink until dinner would be nice, as Vogo and I rack the billiards in the dining area and Selena warms herself in front of the fire. Olga sends hot cocoa up via the dumbwaiter.

"What is this shit?" protests Vogo. "Momma Olga hiding the booze bottle?"

I look at him firmly. I realize the pissant doesn't care if the sun doesn't come up tomorrow, or the next day either. But damn it, I'm the commander, and business is business. I put him in line as much as you can with Vogo. "First of all, you are on duty Vogo, despite our relaxation of the rules over the past hour. Second, there is a bar right over there," I say, nodding my head toward the dining room bar. "I think it would be alright if you walk over to put a thimble of Kahlua or vodka in your drink if you must have it."

Vogo nods but doesn't move a muscle.

I lower my eyes as though intoning, "Enough said."

Pissant? Leak? Mole? I shake it from my head. At least for now.

"Momma Olga sent up her famous cookies. Ooh, yum," says Selena. I think she's hoping to diffuse some of this alpha male tension in the room. "Look at these."

Olga sent up an assortment of Russian tea cakes dripping in confectioner's sugar, buttery Russian sugar cookies, and Russian gingerbread cookies.

Even Vogo drops his alpha male attitude and takes a handful of the delights. I break the balls at the billiard table. Vogo wipes up on the game table after my four ball to the side pocket misses and just lingers at the edge of the pocket mouth.

"Oh, I'm out of practice, my friend. I haven't had time for such luxuries."

Pissant doesn't take mercy upon me and clears the table.

Selena looks up at me with a smile. I melt. Her smile melts me every time.

She's viewing the ultra-beauty of the frozen lake. The Southern American is unaccustomed to such scenery. "I think it's the loveliest scenery I've ever seen," she says. "Mesmerizing. Can envision skating fairies on the icy blue frozen lake."

I'm hugging her from behind in front of the glass window. "Are you warmer now?"

"Oh, you bet. This is a winter wonderland, Sergei. A real wonderland. It's like a land of Christmas card fairytales."

"My country is known as the land of fairytales."

"I've heard that, but I haven't time to visit the areas of Russia typically responsible for such notoriety."

"You're here with me, looking at the oldest and deepest lake in the world now frozen in time. To me, standing here with my arms around you, looking at the landscape... that is my fairytale," I say. With my arms around her and my head resting on the top of hers. I'm so damn in love.

Selena reaches up and pats my arm, smiling at this sweetness as much as I'm smiling inside. She leans her head back up against me. I reach down and give her lips a little peck. Heaven.

"I've never been in a place that I absolutely don't want to leave. I am now," she says, spilling out her thoughts.

She's not the only one. I don't want to leave here either. Absolutely not. Could stand right here forever. But we must. We must leave. I'm trying so hard not to dread that moment. How do you thank a woman for this time? This joy? For the knowledge that I can fill my heart with her love?

I hold on to her tight and bend down to whisper in her ear. "Where and what do you want to eat tonight?"

"I'll be happy with whatever Olga cooks us as long as it's a fraction of the volume she made for us last night. Leftovers are fine with me."

"Agreed. Want to eat up here, the gallery, or in the chamber?"

"I'm of the mind that I would love to eat downstairs again and keep Oliver company, but I'm afraid our presence will displace the staff from their usual eating stations. I wouldn't want to do that."

I move my head and look around to her face. "You're something, you know that? Does Selena Frederick have one selfish or mean bone in her body? You think of others more than you think of yourself. Most women would want the luxury of being served in the opulent dining room. Or if they wanted to eat in the kitchen, they would request everyone else leave. But not you. Not my sweet Selena." I kiss her.

"Oh yes she does," she says after we break the kiss. "You get me riled up and I'm meaner than a junkyard dog," she jests.

"I know what that is," I jest back.

I stand here with my arms tied around my ladylove, watching the snowflakes come harder now. The air smells clean and crisp to our noses even while standing behind the glass protecting us from the outside. Snow is falling NASCAR-fast now, but the lake is still visible with the outside lights on. The fire crackles its warmth for those few minutes while my head lies on top of Selena Frederick's hair. All is right with the world, except the moment when we must leave. When the "gala ball" is over. The icy blizzard is transitioning to snow. My duties are beating at the door. Selena has commitments. Minutes are ticking off the Sergei-and-Selena clock. I won't let myself feel the sadness, I won't.

No matter what, this is a moment I'll remember for all time.

The Older Man: "It didn't go off as planned."

Younger Man: "I told you not to underestimate him."

Older Man: "Yes, he is intelligent. Let us see how he handles the next phase. To answer your question before you ask it: the answer is *soon*."

CHAPTER 56
DON'T MAKE HER MAD

I KNOW how short my peace will be. There are bodies to be buried. There are speeches to be made. There are press conferences in need of preparation. All soon. Very soon. There is the painted lady who haunts me. Something is right in front of me. I sense it. And there is the subject of Selena Frederick. Soon. Too damn soon.

"Heck yes," says Selena. "I'm down with doing a bit of working out. Can we go back to the chamber to change?"

"Sure. Asking the trainers to meet us," I say while pushing the fast-dial button on my phone.

Walking as a couple with my arms around this beautiful lady who melts my world with her smile, we return to the chamber. After a quick change into workout clothes, we trot downstairs. We stop by the kitchen on the way to the gym to apprise Olga of the approximate time of our dinner plans.

"Olga says a lot of the team is eating in their own quarters tonight instead of coming out. Many of them are working on projects."

"I see," says Selena.

"Olga says Oliver would be quite grateful for the company."

"Did she now?" asks Selena with her always-sunny smile.

I thought calling her "Sunshine" this morning was the most perfect thing in the world to say to this woman born in a land of sunshine and who wears sunshine on her face all day, every day. It's saying a lot about a person who can bring sunshine in the middle of a Siberian blizzard.

"I did the most natural and relaxed thing I could think of," I say.

"Just what might that be, President Radkov?"

"I ordered Olga to eat with us so that she doesn't have to eat alone."

"I think that's about as fine as ideas get."

Never met a person who loves people and has as much heart as Dr. Selena Frederick. No wonder the entire world loves her. No wonder I love her. Selena is right—I'm a pussy. Don't have the guts to tell her. I hang my head, realizing what is worse is that I don't know what to do with this love I have. Never loved before. Not this kind of love. And little of any other. Maybe my chest isn't big enough to hold the love she needs.

Never said those three English words to any woman. Never faced wanting to say those words to any woman. Never needing to say them. In my life, I've never been afraid to say anything to anybody at any time. Never. But this? I'm so damned scared, it's pathetic. Most of all, I'm so damned afraid of losing this woman. Damned afraid. But someone, please, anybody, tell me how we can go on? Tell me.

I look up from my deep contemplations as we enter the gym holding hands and meet Johan and Xing. Johan works with me on weights. Xing, a multi-leveled black belt in Kung Fu from China, works with Selena. She told me she never studied Kung Fu and would relish the training. Much of her training has been in Filipino arts, including Balintawak.

Oh, I know about Balintawak. A quick and deadly art developed on an island in the Philippines invaded by the Japanese during World War II. The natives knew they couldn't compete with the steel swords of the Japanese. They only had bamboo sticks. So, these intelligent and enterprising people developed Balintawak in secret and trained using sticks and open-hand tactics. They disabled their Japanese opponents before they could swing their heavier swords.

I look up from my weights after my reps. Toweling my face, I see Selena absolutely killing her flying kicks and has Xing pinned against the wall. If Xing wasn't holding up a cushioned punching bag, Selena would have punched his lights out. I laugh out loud when Selena and Xing reset."

"Damn Selena, don't kill my martial arts instructor."

"Well, he needs to stop taking it easy on me because I'm a girl. I want him to get tough with me. That's how I'll learn. I hold black belts of my own. Xing needs to understand I'm not a five-year-old white belt and seriously train me at my level."

I snicker.

"I mean it, Sergei," she says with a face red not just from the work out but also from feeling pissed.

Can't help but love that face. But I speak to Xing in both Chinese and Russian about it. My Chinese is broken, and so is his Russian. Between the two languages, we can communicate.

Xing assures me, "Girl no, no take easy. She is powerful opponent. Never make her mad."

I laugh seriously out loud now. "Selena, you need to take it easy on Xing. He says he's not cutting you any breaks. Swears he's just outclassed."

"Is that so?" replies Selena. I can tell her hackles are still up.

"Yes. And oh, he said for me not to make you mad, and that you're a dangerous woman."

"Tried to tell ya that earlier," says Selena, breathing hard as she hits the cushion held by the martial artist from China, and knocks it clear out of his hand. "Tell him to get tough and stop treating me with kid gloves or his head will be the cushion next time."

I tell Xing what Selena just said, and watch as she knocks him on his ass. The Chinese man gets up, throws down his gloves and shouts to me in his broken Russian that he's leaving.

"By the way, Xing," I shout back to the man in Russian, "You're fired. Not because you're a martial arts instructor who can't handle my girlfriend. But because you're a professional martial arts instructor who walks out when he can't handle my girlfriend."

Selena stands there with her gloves on, inhaling through her nose and breathing out through her mouth, trying to control her breathing.

Sweat is dripping from her face as she comes over to indulge in a towel while removing her gloves.

"So, he's leaving?" she pants.

"Oh yes he is," I say. "I fired him."

"You did *what*? Sergei, why? Sometimes we all get a little ruffled when doing martial arts."

"Not acting professional," comes my reasoned reply.

Selena gives me a head shake, not understanding. She treats herself to a swig of water.

"Sergei, I think he was frustrated. I'm your guest. Your *female* guest. He couldn't bring himself to be forceful with me, and at the same time, I was unloading on him. Xing was in an unbalanced situation. I think you're being unfair."

"Selena, it's not that Xing can't handle my girlfriend. Honestly, I think that part is hilarious. It's that he got frustrated and left. It's his job to figure it out. He doesn't get to leave. Not the martial arts instructor to the President of United Russia."

"Whatever, you say Sergei. Just promise me you'll reconsider it later."

"My mind is made up, Selena. My security and protection are things I take seriously. It's his job to better train me to protect my life—and also to protect me, if necessary, with his death. Yet he walks out because my girlfriend gets in a few licks. Reconsideration is over, Selena."

She swigs her water again and stands as if mulling it over. I see understanding reach her eyes. Then, just like Selena, out of the blue she asks, "Wait, you said he couldn't handle your what?"

I give an ah shucks shrug. "Didn't quite know how to identify our relationship. What? My guest? Okay, maybe. My lady guest? Sure. My friend? Always. The woman with the world's hottest bump who is sleeping in my bed? Sophomoric, but also true."

"I'll be your girlfriend, Sergei," comes Selena's sweet, teasing smile as she finishes off her water. Damn siren.

"Good, because it looks like I'm going to need someone to protect me until I can find another martial arts instructor."

Selena sprays water from her mouth with my reply. Both of us, along with Yohan, laugh.

"I'll work out on the bags while you finish your session," says the tough lady, changing into boxing gloves.

"You have a spitfire," says Yohan in our native Russian.

"Oh, I'm sure that I do. And damn, what a woman."

Yohan gives me a look of agreement as he helps his president build his physical strength. After the weightlifting, the round muscular man and I run around the inside perimeter of the gym. Then we run up and down the stair steps spaced out across the gym. After a short twenty-minute run, we call it a day with a ten-minute cool down walk. I shake hands with Yohan upon parting.

I mosey over to hold Selena's bag a few minutes for her as her long legs stretch to the top of the bag. My spitfire follows with a series of kicks and punches. "You 'bout ready to go shower for dinner, tough lady?"

"Ready when you are, boyfriend."

I let out a snort. Things are always so easy between Selena and I. Good thing, too. After seeing her fight today, I don't want to make this lady mad. That was one thing Xing was right about.

From the gym, we hold hands like teenagers on the walk back to our chamber. "How about this, Selena? Since ladies take longer, I'm gonna make a few calls while you are in the shower. I've got a string of messages to attend to."

"I bet," comes her eternally easy reply. "I feel just a tad bit guilty for taking Russia's president away from his work. But his country can thank me for giving their president a needed breather."

Selena, with those damned ruby lips, forms a smile on her way to the shower. I watch her disappear behind the closed door. I miss her already. There's a lump scratching my throat. I don't want to be here. I want to be with her behind that closed door and loving her. Loving her while I can. Loving her with all my might. Emptying myself to her. Damn, is that a tear? Oh shit.

I wipe it away and make my first call. Alas, Russia's president has concluded his breather for the moment.

PART EIGHT
PIGS IN PARADISE

CHAPTER 57
PIGS

I LISTEN on the other side of the door as Selena lets the massaging showerhead soothe her muscles and wash away her gym odors. Soon, the mist will fill with her new aroma: the scent of lavender.

I sit comfortably on the settee. First phone punch is to Vogo.

"Clear," he says.

That's all I need. Of all the calls I can make, I call my old friend Joe Cook.

"Cook here," comes the voice.

"Radkov here."

Joe whistles. "Thought you were too busy to talk to me?"

"I am, but I don't forget who my friends are or where I come from."

"You're a good man, Sergei. Can you give me anything on the record?"

"I can't, but a person close to the president can."

"Shoot."

"The body of the American is to be flown back to the states tomorrow in a military transporter. The plane will land at JFK for customs. After takeoff in Russia, the body should be in the USA some fifteen hours later. US Armed Forces are aware and will fly wing once the transporter reaches US airspace. No weapons are aboard the transporter. The US Air Force will also fly wing with the Russian transporter back out of US airspace after refueling. Our militaries are cooperating with each other to return this young man to his home."

"Man, that's a lot of wings for one body. Why not a simple commercial flight?"

"Russia wants to assure the body makes it to America. America wants to assure the body makes it to America," I answer.

"Why JFK? Why aren't they allowing the transporter to land at a US military facility?"

"This you must ask the Americans. Maybe they don't want our pilots to see their installations close-up."

"Will the body go straight to Michigan?"

"Again, you must ask the Americans. Russia is willing to fly the young man all the way home, but this is what the Americans opted to do."

"I see."

"Ah, they made a song and dance about the necessity of customs, but I think that is a smokescreen. Russia is handing over all relevant documents, except a few at the crime scene that deal with Russian techniques. Otherwise, we're one hundred percent full disclosure," I throw in.

"So, you think the Americans are eager to autopsy?"

"I think they can't wait," I reply while taking a swig of cold water. "As well, due to forensics and eyewitness statements, Russia only autopsied the young man's outer body. There was no need to do more. How much the Americans autopsy is up to them. We are sending all records of what has been done here in Russia."

"What else is up?"

"As chairman, Smoltsky is in the US working on the scholarship issue, while Ambassador Yudina is working on the transport of the body and anything else that the family may need from Russia. All they need do is ask."

"What is the tone of the American family? Do they seem to blame you or Russia?"

"Not at all. In fact, they reached out to the family of Olaf, the Russian roommate, with an interpreter. The young American comes from a model family. The parents realize it was a horrible no-win situation and everyone was just trying their best. If Spetsnaz didn't go in, the kidnappers would've killed both boys once they got a payoff. Although high risk, Spetsnaz went in to rescue the boys, and the unfortunate happened. Their sacrifice was the noblest and greatest. Those brave men knew the risks going in. The family also expressed their deepest regrets for the additional loss of Russian life. As well, Harold's family has said positive things about my policy on terrorism and would like to see more cooperation between countries to help prevent such violent acts."

"That's good, Sergei. America will follow the bereaved family. At the end of the day, they'll drive public opinion in the US. Can I say a source close to President Radkov called the American family 'a model family in this time of their profound grief?'"

"You may."

"How about the terrorists?"

"Names of terrorists don't get released. That's now Russian law. Whether in death or imprisonment, terrorists don't get so much as their name. Russia won't release information about which or how many terrorists are dead or who is alive. If dead, they're cremated, and we dump their ashes into a pigsty."

"Damn. How are the accused tried?" asks Joe.

"Those accused of terrorism are tried privately in our military court per current Russian law. If found guilty, they'll be imprisoned under military jurisdiction. I expect most cases will return a guilty verdict. The cases for terrorism meet strong criteria to be tried under such circumstances."

"What happens to terrorists who are found guilty?"

"We won't house those prisoners within the Russian prison population at large. Terrorists won't be allowed a chance to spread their ideological violence. They may be housed in isolation. They may be put in chains to work in a certain pigsty or pick up cattle dung. Their life sentences will be unpleasant, I assure you."

Joe lets out a whistle. "That's rough, Sergei. Especially the pigsty."

"If you live like a pig, then you die like one. It's that simple. Why give you an honorable death when you haven't lived honorably? A life as a herder of swine or shoveler of dung is more than appropriate for the living guilty. You no longer have a name, but an alphanumeric code. Your mother won't even know you're alive. Those mothers must assume their children are dead, because in a way, they are. Every day, as these prisoners herd swine, let us hope they remember they brought this upon themselves. That is Russia's message to terrorists in our land."

"Damn Sergei. That's tough considering all things religious and cultural and all. But now, can I quote you on the 'live like pigs' thing?"

"You may. Look, if these terrorists want to pick a battlefield besides kidnapping the innocent to extort money for weapons or their own pitiful financial gain, then we'll fight them as men. If they feel they must use such victims as untrained and unarmed innocent college boys, then we'll match our weaponry to fit the behavior of the terrorists. Pigs. Pigs who will never receive another visitor. Not so much as a phone call."

"And Joe," I add, "these perpetrators are given basic human rights, beginning with healthcare. In fact, all life-preserving measures are taken if they're injured. Russia prefers them alive, not dead, so that the human swine may serve out their sentence of shame. Russia provides them with adequate and competent legal counsel. This is not a gulag of old. This system is limited only to terrorism of the highest order. Russia doesn't intend to sentence the innocent."

Joe lets out a whistle. "Will there ever be an avenue of release for these prisoners?"

"No. I'm working to help the prison populations at large in Russia. I have experts searching to find means for delinquents in our society to turn their lives around and become productive citizens. But terrorists, no. You may say the source close to President Radkov says he insists those cases be prosecuted without mercy. No exceptions. The letter of Russian law must be followed. Those found guilty of terrorism in my land will no longer own so much as a name. You can say I'm hardline, yea, even extreme on this. I won't live in fear of these people, and neither will anyone in my country. I intend to put a stop to extortion of the innocent. You may quote me directly on that."

Joe lets out another whistle. "Damn, Sergei."

"I mean what I say, Joe. Not in my country. And terrorists won't be placed in a shroud, nor have any funeral rights. I realize the Bin Laden thing years ago with the Americans was different, but in United Russia his name would never have been released to begin with. No one will know which terrorist is alive or which is dead. This is Russian policy. Understand this when you commit an act of terror in United Russia."

"What about the masterminds?" asks the reporter.

"There will be no official release from Moscow."

"I gotcha. How about the country of the perpetrators?"

"That's Russia's secret. That is part of no one knowing who or what is where within terrorist cells. Their host country will figure things out soon enough. Policies will be instituted case by case. I'm sure the country of origin in some cases doesn't want that information known. That's up to them. The host nation is trying hard diplomatically, but President Radkov says no."

"May I quote the source?"

"Yes. Our policy extends to the masterminds, operatives, and financial backers."

"Anything else, my friend?" asks Joe after his whistle.

"Yes, but Joe, you know I must leave something for the Russian media. Perhaps I can add that the pig and boar farmers are not keen to have their swine corrupted by terrorist ashes."

Joe laughs through his whistle.

"You must cross Red Square to have a drink sometime," I add cordially after a pause.

"Give me an invite."

"Soon, my friend, soon."

"You know how to reach me, Commander."

"I do."

CHAPTER 58
CONFIRMED

BEFORE I CAN FINISH my shower, the red phone rings. "Confirmed," is all the voice says. President Sergei Radkov is pleased when he hangs up. It's what I've been waiting for.

I hate the red phone. Damn It! Just want a little more time of my own. Alas, my duty always calls.

Time with Selena without my job horning in. It can't be so, but I crave it. I understand all the reasons. Understand the red phone but hate it all the same. I punch a phone button to gather my staff and principals prior to completing my shower. I enter the chamber wearing my favorite plaid warm-ups.

Looking up from her reading on the settee, Selena asks, "Going casual tonight?"

"Just the opposite. Selena, Russia has killed three people: the mastermind and the two men who financed him, or at the very least the last kidnapping. Possibly others. I must address my country and have a press meeting."

"Can I help?"

"Hold me?"

Selena smiles at my presidential request and makes a brisk stride over to me. The elegant lady is dressed in red. She latches on to her lover and hugs him with tight compassion. "I'm right here," comes her soft words.

I melt as I bend to kiss the top of her head. "I know. I just dislike you being here without me."

"Am I without you? I don't feel as if I'm without you."

I look with adoration at the exceptional woman who has stirred my heart. Both my hands cup her face and I kiss those ruby lips that I want to swallow. Kiss her like a devastating meteorite is going to hit Planet Earth in the next thirty seconds.

"You're right. You're not without me," I say, smiling at this woman of my longing. My reluctant hands release her. Already, as President Radkov, as if in sudden commando mode, I'm spouting off my laundry list.

"The team is assembled in the dining room. They know their assignments. The gallery is the best place to write my words to my people. Open with a brief speech, then take questions. Staff members lined up to field some questions. Selena, might I tell you what I would like for you to do?"

"Ask."

"I can write part of the speech, email it to you, and you can do a first-pass kind of review. Then you can email that to Tina. Tina will do the next pass. Then just the three of us will meet. Can you do that?"

"You know I can."

"Let's go."

"I'll tell you what, Sergei. Why don't I run down and have Olga send us coffee? And how about some soup and salad for while we work?"

"Good idea. I'm starving."

"Great. That will give you time to get started. Only thing is, I don't have my laptop on me."

I pull a laptop from a hanging knapsack pegged in the corner behind my desk. "Here, use my extra," I say. Handing my personal laptop to the American beauty who is right here with me. "My old Mac," I shrug. "Nothing top secret there, only non-work related."

"Oh, so you have pics of your old girlfriends in here?" teases Selena.

"I might," I tease back.

Selena winks and retorts, "Maybe I'll check out my competition later. Right now, President Sergei Radkov has more to worry about than former *or* current girlfriends."

I can't help but to shoot her a smile with a look of love in my eyes. I stand, paused in the moment. I don't want to release it. I want this moment. Forever.

She is locked onto my gaze with the same look in her eyes. Could it be? Could it possibly be?

I blink. The moment is broken. I make a nod toward the door. "Well, we're ready to take on the world, current girlfriend."

"What happened to Sunshine?"

"Oh, she'll be in my bed in the morning."

Selena chuckles. "Stinker."

Once out of the room, I run upstairs, and Selena runs down. Each with our own fervor toward perfection, knowing the next moments will influence the world. One Russian. One American. World changers. Imagine.

I use sign language to bridge the language gap and communicate with Olga. Somehow, I even portray Oliver will be missed. But the President is in red-phone mode again.

The sly old owl has already heard about the red phone. Olga has already started preparing trays. Convey to Olga I will take up a tray of coffee and sundries with me if she can send soup and salad when her team has things ready.

Olga simply hands the tray from the counter. I'm feeling like the girlfriend named Sunshine. The cook extraordinaire has the crew's fare in progress.

At that moment, I understand there is no need for me to worry about a thing. Olga more than has the situation under control. I wonder why I bothered to come down to the kitchen in the first place. Silly girlfriend.

With a sparkle in her eyes, Olga taps me on the shoulder and removes the tray from my hands. Olga hands it off to a kitchen aide. Her crooked forefinger beckons me to come look in the ovens filled with her cooking. Bubbling trays of lasagna.

"Olga, you're the best," I say, and hug Sergei's substitute mother.

Olga doesn't understand a word of what I say, but still understands my meaning. "Spasiba," is her one word. I know that one. Then the old woman kisses me on the cheek. Sergei isn't the only one who loves her.

The kitchen aide helps me take the coffee pot, creamer, and mugs up to the gallery. Let's not forget the meat and cheese with bread tray. Rather, Olga provides us with a cart that we elevator up.

Without speaking, I pour Sergei a mug full of beverage along with one for myself. I don't speak but wait for the president to email me his initial notes. Silently, I write my email address on a napkin and slide it to him.

Sergei's eyes don't even look up, but he knows what to do. He sends his first paragraphs of text to me and writes Tina's email for me on another napkin.

I smile to myself as I consider how wonderful it would've been to have had Sergei as a lab partner during my college days. The man's focus is unmovable. I know many extraordinarily focused people. Sergei wins the blue ribbon. My heart skips a beat when it flips.

The president is churning out paragraph after paragraph without moving his eyes from the text. Never do his eyes stray away from the screen.

I consider him. Sergei is like an artist who becomes one with their painting. Prepare myself to focus on my own focus. Preparing myself to convert his Russian text to English, to read his lines for correction, for spelling, for lack of perception, for providing follow-up, for anything. It isn't my place to discuss policy except as the emails state. That's for Tina to do. I'm ready. I focus my American mind. My keyboard is Russian.

I find the "on" switch. That's about it. What does he expect me to do for a password, anyway? The Cyrillic alphabet flows across the keyboard. To me, it's like the alphabet seen by an infant. Different vowels. Different consonants. Different symbols. Different characters and letters. So much for focus. I sit with my eyes on the computer and don't speak. I mull it over, trying to think of a work-around.

Sergei continues to type like his hands are on fire and his fingers are shooting flames. "Ah, I have the bones. The nuts and bolts," he says.

"Great," I say. My eyes move up to his self-satisfied smile.

"Where is that soup and salad? I'm so hungry. Thinking with a few bites, I can concentrate better and whip this out. Did you see many problems with my text?" he asks while taking in a bite of bread and cheese.

"Oh, lots," I smile sincerely. "Sergei, I'm sorry, but I don't understand a word of Russian. And the keyboard is in Russian, and I don't know your password."

The president moves his tongue across his teeth.

I hope he isn't too disappointed in me. "I think you might need to email your text directly to Tina," I suggest.

Sergei's face turns red, but he doesn't say a word. He leans back in his chair. His head tilts backward. He laughs like a madman. "Selena, I'm so sorry. Please forgive me. My mind was so focused on what I'm going to say that I didn't think about anything else."

"I'm sorry, too. Wish I could be more helpful," I shrug, feeling regret.

"Oh, this coffee helps," says Sergei just as Ivan unlocks the gallery door to let in the soup and salad buffet. "Tell ya what, Selena. Gonna email this to Tina. Then you and I can enjoy soup and salad. When we're finished eating, I'll review Tina's suggestions. Maybe, I can read out the speech in English if there aren't too many problems. You can listen and help me."

"I'm with you, Sergei. For full disclosure, Olga already had the food on the way," I confess. "So far, I've otherwise been useless."

Sergei's fast fingers have the email sent to Tina before he could say, "Bon voyage."

He gives my lips a peck as we begin our partial meal and somehow chat about everything but the whole reason we're sitting in this room. Not intentional, it's just how it's happening. I expected a somber mood, but Sergei is talkative and conversational. Even mention of

Oliver the cat shows up in our chatter between old memories and more recent sled rides.

Before either of us can leave behind the savory Italian soup made with sausage and small pieces of homemade pasta, Tina buzzes Sergei's phone. She tells him her suggested changes are minor. Sergei begs her to give twenty minutes please to finish his salad and tells her to do the same.

"You'll need your energy; the night may be long," says the president to his cell phone.

"Of course, Mr. President. Enjoy your salad." *You and that damned American woman,* is what I perceive Tina is thinking. For some reason, she doesn't seem to cotton to me as we say down south. American shlyukha. That's what she thinks.

Maybe Tina from Crimea doesn't like the idea of her president with an American woman. Bet she thinks this American woman is going to be trouble. Trouble. Yes, I guess I am. I wonder how many others here at the dacha think I'm an American shlyukha.

Tina arrives at the gallery in exactly twenty minutes. "Did you get some salad, Tina?" asks her president.

"Please sit and have some with us," I say, trying to make myself a cordial and likable American woman.

"No, but thank you," replies Tina. "Here are the copies you asked for, Sir," she says to her president. "Here is one for you, Selena. I translated it on a software program. Hope it's not too imperfect."

"I'm sure it'll be fine," I reply.

Trouble. All trouble. Yes, that's me. Although Tina is behaving in an ultra-professional manner. Her body language isn't friendly, though. Maybe it's just her way.

"Tina, can you give us a few moments? I'd like to speak to Selena alone. I'll buzz you."

The Russian woman's back straightens. "Of course, Sir." She leaves the room.

Taking my hands, Sergei begins his narrative. "Selena, there will be text and context in my words that you may question. Some are what you may describe as 'un-American.' They'll make me sound like a brutal man. I want you to remember I'm dealing with brutal people."

"My heart is with the slain, Sergei. I can remember you telling me once upon a time that you have strategically killed. That you didn't enjoy it. Under these circumstances, it'd be hard not to enjoy seeing the demise of these bastards," I reply.

"I try very hard not to think such things and instead remain strategic," comes the president's explanation. "Staying focused on the right thing is how I want to succeed. It's my training, and I believe in it," continues Sergei solemnly. "As you've so simply said, my heart is with the slain."

"Then hard words are justified," I reply, confident in Sergei. Although I've yet to know a single word. "All is well," I add.

We sit beaming at one another. There is something is Sergei's demeanor. His eyes. Admiration? Love? Could it be love? Might he have fallen for me as I have fallen for him? I can't let myself think like this. It's too much, too soon. I've been in love with this man since I first saw his face in that hotel room in New York City. But it's too much for me to expect the same from him.

After a few moments, Sergei relents. "Guess I better call Tina back in."

Our magical moment is over.

"Tina *is* your media expert," I yield and give him a smile. I may not be helpful but damned if I'm going to be Trouble.

Focus, Sergei, I silently drill myself. *Focus*. My fast fingers buzz-in an externally calm Tina to the gallery. Upon her arrival, I explain the protocol I will follow. Making the first run in English and giving Selena a chance to evaluate my body language and words from an American perspective. I want the Americans to understand the death of Harold was an act of terrorism, not a Russian act. It's essential.

Then I will repeat in Russian. Both women nod. I'm sure Tina hasn't considered the American perspective. She doesn't think what any American believes is of concern. I'm sure that extends to Selena.

The dry runs are brief, as is my speech. The three of us leave the gallery and make our way to the dining room, which is also a makeshift press room. I follow up with staff, then change into my suit for the press conference. Live in three… two… one…

My speech is pointed and leaves out much, knowing the press will chew up time with follow-up questions. I discuss Russia taking out the terrorist operatives in separate but simultaneous missions. I don't give any specifics on those missions. Russian policy is not to do so. Neither the terrorists, nor their mastermind, nor their financiers so much as own a home, a nation, a family, a name from this time forward.

Then I drop the big bombshell. "While carrying out their missions, the military recovered a cache of weapons. As well, they recovered an undisclosed quantity of cash, gold, and artifacts. The artifacts are to be researched and returned to their nation of origin. The cash and gold will be deposited into the Russian treasury. Confiscated monies will have three separate purposes."

"First, the money will reimburse Russia and her people for the cost of the missions. I won't discuss an amount, but there's more than adequate enough resources to do so. The second use for this unexpected windfall will be to fund scholarships, in perpetuity, that have been set up to honor the slain men and their families. Third, Russia will use the funds to expand its anti-terrorist training. Weapons were destroyed."

I cite Russian law in the context of any slain terrorist bodies. President Radkov doesn't omit the disposal of the bodies, including the pigsty. "Pigs will be put in a pigsty." I discuss Russian nondisclosure laws regarding terrorist names and concealment of how many are dead and how many are alive.

"Might I remind my compatriots and the world at large of the *fact*" —I signal the end strongly and with a brief pause—"that these terrorists had no beef against Russia specifically. They didn't make demands against our country. Because of our recent political changes, these thugs thought Russia to be a haven for chaos wherein they could extend their murderous empires. I'm making Russia's message clear."

I lean forward on the podium. "Russia isn't a land of murder. Russia isn't a land of chaos. Russia has evolved into a land of free peoples searching to expand those freedoms. Russia behaves the way a civilized nation of free peoples should behave. Putting up with the silly ideas of people who think they can exploit our nation is not in the best interests of United Russia and her free peoples. Russia is a nation of laws. We have made strong anti-terrorism laws to protect the innocent within our borders. Russian law will be enforced."

Looking straight into the camera, I end, "Good night, good people of United Russia. All is well tonight."

CHAPTER 59
YA LYUBLYU TEBYA

TINA'S ARRANGEMENT WORKED. One great thing about a blizzard and being in a remote area, there's no other press present except those travelling with the president. So, Tina used the hills and trees as background, nothing else around that might define our location. Viewers only see in her introduction the same thing being seen all over Russia: snow, snow, and more snow. Icicles, ice, and gale force winds. She decides on a plain wall for my backdrop. I'm pleased with her decision.

My private staff gathers their notes and laptops to make their way downstairs. "By the way," Tina calls out to them. "If you've nothing at your quarters ready to eat, Olga has made lasagna downstairs but says you must wash your own dish and put it in the dishwasher and serve yourself buffet-style from the stove. I would take her up on it if I were you."

Soon Alexei appears at the hallway door with a nod for Selena to follow him. Selena and her favorite tour guide make way to the kitchen. As soon as she and chatting Alexei enter the kitchen, they see me with two plates of lasagna that I've heaped up myself rather than being served. What can I say? It's casual night. God knows I've known how to serve myself for a long time.

We meet at our favorite booth. Selena sits down wearing her sweet smile.

"Sorry, milady, late dinner once again."

Selena answers. "After all that sledding and the workout today, I'm hungry. Again!"

"I know. It seems we're always in some phase of eating at a God-awful hour. But it's not all bad lately, huh pretty lady?" I ask with a wink.

"Not until my thighs reach Jerusalem. At this rate, it won't take long to reach the Holy Land," replies my slim lady.

"Well, if your thighs are going to the Holy Land, then so am I. You know how much I love your thighs," I say with teasing seduction.

Selena shoots me her "noogie look" but keeps her hands on her fork and heaves a bite of the heavenly pasta pie into her mouth. "My God, this is awesome. And so are you," she says.

I give her a wink as I chew.

"Truly, Sergei. Look at your staff. All of them are in awe of their president. You lead. You're presidential. Then you heave up two plates of lasagna while teasing with them. You're Mr. Awesome."

I start to make a teasing response. Instead, I give her a sincere smile and say, "Spasiba."

Alexei takes the next table over. I lean over to speak to him. "By the way Alexei, I saw Ivan earlier. Says he's alright, but I wonder if he has returned too soon."

"Yes, I sent him home yesterday to wait out the blizzard and rest. Said he was sick and throwing up with a fever. Told him to take it easy but not to come back until he was better. Of course, he showed up for his shift. I just sent him back again to where he's staying in one of the outlying units."

"Not like Ivan to be sick. He's just one of those people who is never ill. Guess viruses get us all at some point," I comment.

"No, not like him," agrees Alexei. "Thinks it is just some sort of flu bug. Appears flushed and pale. Best he stays away from the rest of us for now. So, I booted him out."

About then, the Italian-pie cook makes her way over and sits down beside us with her own plate. Oliver is in tow behind his momma.

Little buddy lies down next to our booth as our sworn protector after a Selena leg rub. Can't blame him. That's what I'd do if I lived in his fur.

"Selena was just saying how outstanding this lasagna is, Olga. I must agree," I interpret.

"Spasiba," replies the old woman as she holds her glass for a toast clink. "Toast to love. It is the wine of life's blood."

The fire roars in the kitchen hearth as the staff chats among themselves as they eat. They hardly notice the president is present. That's the way I like it. I shut myself off a lot to work. Perhaps I need to be more like that American president, Abraham Lincoln, and have fireside chats. It's not original, but also not a political steal. I just like the idea, even if it's not my own or anything new. It simply hasn't been used in a long while.

I talk, and people watch as everyone devours the Italian fare. Most plates are cleaned by hungry eaters. For dessert, for wanting partakers, large trays of Olga's cookies are offered. Oh, President Radkov indulges. I wink and nod my way around the serving trays while I heap three plates and take a teasing for doing so.

I defend myself with, "You can have three plates of cookies when you're president."

Fireside chats. Imagine.

Sergei sits a plate piled with cookies in front of Olga and me. "For my favorite ladies" he says before Olga and I appoint him chief interpreter.

"Olga, Selena says these are called Wedding Cookies in America, but she remembers seeing them mostly during the holidays."

"Selena, Olga says she got the pecans from South Carolina, which she thinks is near your home."

"Yes, yes, Olga, Selena says South Carolina is less than an hour's drive to her home. It is very near."

Then in both languages he says, first in Russian, then in English, "Ladies, my mouth is tired. If you guys are going to chat, you must hire an interpreter. Tina's English is quite perfect. For now, my mouth is busy eating cookies!"

We ladies howl with laughter as Sergei Radkov eats a Russian Wedding Cookie and lets a drop of confectioner's sugar linger on his chin. His favorite ladies try to indicate a need for a napkin touchup. Sergei wipes his chin with his fingers and pops them in his mouth and *yuuuums* like a schoolboy.

"He is so bad," I say.

Olga understands every word.

When the President of United Russia, turned fifth grader, finishes his cookies, we say our good nights to Olga and Oliver, who seems to think my legs are the best rub in the kitchen. He doesn't fail to tell Sergei so right to his face. "*Meow!*"

Olga calls the attention monger over with her kitchen treat stash. Then, feline and momma retire to their chamber as Olga tells Sergei she is leaving to study her book on how to speak English. Such a cool lady.

President Radkov does indeed have his fifth-grade boy going on. "Oh, we're going swimming in the pool when we get back."

"Oh, yes?" I question as though I'm the mature one.

"Yes," says the president as we arrive on our floor holding hands. "Because last time I was a gentleman and didn't look at your body coming down those steps, although I truly wanted to peek. This time, I'm looking and watching."

"That's too bad," I retort with a serious face. "Because I stole a peek of you."

"Oh, you so did NOT! I watched you to see if you would, but you were too chicken."

"Chicken? You're the one who didn't peek," I reply factually.

"Oh, I was taking a cue from Ms. Chicken. *Bock, bock, bock!*" says the fifth grader, kicking off his shoes by the poolside.

"Oh, is that how chickens talk in Russia? No wonder you're hard to understand."

"Oh yeah," replies the schoolboy. "I'm the one who speaks English, and you don't know a word of Russian," he says with hands on hips.

"My point exactly," I retort, pulling off my shirt.

"Okay, Miss, okay," says the leader of the largest nation in the world as he throws his clothes off and makes his way into the pool.

Damn, he's fast. I remain up top and tease with a queenlike air as I slowly remove and fold my clothing. I press and crease them with my hands, giving Sergei a snooty smirk. When I take off my bra, I quickly turn my back to Sergei as though to say, "You don't get to see."

That doesn't stop me from shaking my ass at him, though, before I remove my underwear.

Sergei's smile is wide at my girlish play. He says he would like to remain a little fifth grader, but his manhood is growing. As the Russians pronounce, very contra-*dick*-tory.

I drop my underwear and bend over, making sure my ass is high in the air, to pick them up and fold them.

Sergei gives me a lustful groan.

I take the clasp from my hair and use it to snap my twisted mane in place on top of my head. I enter the pool's steps, stepping high like royalty as I make my way down with the aid of my aide's hand.

"Your Majesty," says Sergei, giving a slight bow and taking the queen's hand.

I grossly look the other way with my nose in the air, so as not to look at the man or his growing parts. I break character and laugh at our playfulness and drop my act as Sergei leads me into the geothermal pool's deeper water. Of all things, Elizabeth Frederick enters my mind. I wonder what she would think of me and Sergei now. Shlyukha? I'm discovering that sometimes I'm not my mother's daughter.

As he lets go of my hand, Sergei's palm darts to the top of my head and dunks me underwater.

Not to be outdone by the President of United Russia, I give the inside of my dunker's thigh a bite while underwater. A bite that will cause a raspberry bruise and makes the president howl in pain.

"Ouch! That hurt!"

"You messed up my royal hair," I say in a nonchalant tone.

"Oh, lady, it is so on. Those neck bones are roiling even if you do kick my ass."

I'm laughing so hard I can barely speak. "Never underestimate the value and the power of teeth," I call out to him as I swim then run into the shallows. I dive back into the deep and splash my rival and try every elusive technique I can think of.

Sergei chases me. He catches up with me, and I'm kicking and screaming as he noogies me hard. He grabs me from behind and overpowers me.

I squeal, but I'm not giving up without a fight.

Oh, what does the big bully do? He leans over and makes a big suction mark on the side of my upper neck that will result in a huge hickey.

Shlyukha. That's what they'll all say. American shlyukha. Okay, Elizabeth Frederick. You win. I'm behaving like a shlyukha and I'll have to pay the price for that.

I'm angry. "You bastard!" I yell at him.

"Actually, I think I may be," says a grinning Sergei matter-of-factly. He is so damned pleased with himself. Asshole.

"Ohhhhhh. Sssssss. Oh, I hate that!" I scream at him.

"Do you really?" comes the nonchalant reply from the fifth grader. "Do you give?" comes the question as if from a bored tsar.

"Give? Who the *fuck* do you think you are? Pontius Pilate? Hell no! I don't give! Sex, that is. No sex!" is what falls from my mouth. Feeling like the world's greatest whore, I angrily leave the pool and unceremoniously slam the door on my way into the chamber and run to the toilet.

He doesn't get it. He just doesn't get it.

Sergei stays in the pool, looking like a stunned schoolboy. "What the fuck? I don't get it," he says while I'm leaving. He damn sure doesn't.

Sergei shows up in my toilet wearing his presidential robe, saying he's here to see about his ladylove.

Ladylove? Fuck him.

I'm naked in the shower. I step out and towel myself off without saying a word. I can do the Elizabeth Frederick silent treatment act. Oh, I can. I ignore Sergei partly because I'm afraid to speak while I'm feeling this angry. Maybe I'm overreacting. But then, don't I always over-rationalize? Did or did not this man just disrespect me? I'm not sure. I sit and begin to comb out my wet hair.

"That's my job," says the tsar.

"I'm perfectly capable of combing my own fucking wet hair." Yep. If I wasn't feeling disrespected before, I am now.

"Is that why you're angry, Selena? Because I wet your hair?" He's so sincere. And sweet. Damn him. He can't be sweet *and* sincere while I'm so pissed.

"No," comes my sharp reply.

"What is it?"

I ignore the question.

Sergei steps over and takes the comb from my hand with authority. "What is it then, Selena? I don't know, and I need to know what upset you. We were just playing, or so I thought."

"Yes, I bit you hard to retaliate against you dunking me and thereby wetting my hair. You could've bitten me back anywhere. Just not where you did. Not so that it looks like I have a love bite. Everyone will see and think I'm your American whore. I'm sure some already do. I'm no shlyukha."

Tears of anger, hurt, embarrassment, maybe even betrayal. Yes, that's it. Betrayal stings my eyelashes. I still don't know if Sergei overheard when the man on his security team called me a shlyukha. I should have discussed it with him then. Now, I'm acting like a child.

"Despite my behavior these past days, I'm not your whore, Sergei. And you have no right to demean or disrespect me by making me look like one." Damn, that's too Elizabeth Frederick. I love my mother, but she was straighter than an arrow.

Sergei lets out a long breath. "Selena, I'm sorry. I was playing and not thinking. You must know that I'd never demean or disrespect you."

The president falls on both knees next to me and my tears. "Never." After a few moments' pause, "I'm so sorry, Selena. I would all but kill any man who tried to demean you in any way before I'd have time to give it a thought. Here I am doing it myself, without a thought. God, I'm so sorry," Sergei says with sincerity while looking into my reddened eyes.

"What can I do to make up for it?" he pleads.

Should I tell him? Should I tell him about what the man said? And how others on his team, like Tina, act toward me? Of course not. That's my problem to handle. I need to put on my big-girl panties and grow up. Elizabeth Frederick, I love you, but back off. I'm my own woman now and, for better or worse, can make my own decisions. I try to pop my mother out of my head and send her back to heaven.

I give him a horizontal headshake.

"Then I will tell you now, young lady—and I do mean this, young lady—no one, *no one*, may ever say that you're my whore. Or show that they think it. You're the woman I desire above all women. You're the woman I respect above all women. For me or you or anyone else to think you are my whore isn't a thought that is acceptable to me. Do you understand that?"

I guess he didn't hear when his man muttered that awful Russian word. He gets a vertical head nod this time.

Sergei walks around in the small room for a moment, as though trying to decide whether he's going to say something more. Instead, he leaves me. Just leaves me. Leaves me alone with my thoughts. I guess he wants to be left alone with his thoughts, too. I can tell he didn't like what happened. Nope. Not at all.

So, I blow my hair dry and leave the toilet with my robe on. Reaching into the bar, I take out a water. I ask, "Would you like one?"

"Yes, please."

I sit next to the president and former tsar, who has a book in his hand with the white fur throw wrapped around his torso on the settee.

"What are you reading?" I ask somewhat shyly.

"You're asking the wrong question," states Sergei.

"I am?"

"Yes. The correct question is, what am I reading to you?" informs Sergei, speaking to me as though I'm his ladylove. He has a raised eyebrow.

"I see," I say, smiling as happiness returns.

"So, lay your head here," points Sergei to the pillow in his lap as he makes his ladylove comfortable.

I look up at my lover's lips as he reads from a book of poetry from all over the world. Old and new. Religious passages from the Christian Bible, Koran, Buddhism, Hindus, Mongrels, Old Testament, ancient

Romans, Americans, French, British, Icelandic. You name it. Love songs sung long ago. All about a man who has longing in his heart for one woman. One woman who was made by God—or Gods, according to some poems—for his sake, and only she was made for him. Oh, how those poets believed it to be true.

Somewhere in the middle of the book comes my favorite.

"When a man loves a woman/can't keep his mind on nothin' else/He'd trade the whole world for the good thing he's found…"

I smile, and Sergei returns a huge, satisfied smile and continues. "If she is bad he can't see it/She can do no wrong/Turn his back on his best friend/If he puts her down."

"Damned if I would turn my back," inserts the returning fifth grader. "I would pop him right in the mouth."

"I bet you would," I smile. "Are those not the most beautiful lyrics you've ever heard? God, I love that song. The words. The sound. It's so my song," I expand with a stretch while throwing back my head in reveled pleasure, as though he's describing the best ice cream ever.

"Are the rest of the lyrics in the book?"

"Yes."

"Read them to me, please. Do you mind starting from the beginning? I'd love to think it through with the music in my head from the start."

Without reply Sergei reads the blues-song lyrics made into poetry with his voice until the end. "Cause baby, baby, baby/I am a man/When a man loves a woman."

I've decided it's time. Going to tell her right here and now. Right at the end of this song-poem. At the end of her favorite words, now mine. Read to her from my heart. It's time. It's time to say what is inside my heart. I look down to gaze into those emerald green eyes to be sure she can see my lips as they move. Never said these words to anyone. Not anyone. Now is the time. The perfect time.

My mouth parts with a wide smile. Selena's eyes are closed. The love of my life has fallen asleep like a little girl in daddy's lap.

Very softly, I whisper, "I love you, Selena." President Sergei Radkov makes a major executive decision not to remove this woman asleep on his lap. There is just something about it. A private moment that is all mine but shared with her.

Very convoluted, but I'm happy just to know I've whispered the words to her. As though the words will lie on top of her. Warm her and cover her like the fur throw. Love just being here with her in our room in the moments of her sleep. To look at her face. It's my secret about her. At least for now. God, I love her so.

Soon my head falls to the back of the settee with closed eyelids, and I succumb to sleep. I awaken to the burning fire and the beauty still asleep, unmoved in my lap. Once again, I whisper, "I love you, my Sunshine."

Then I pick up the beauty from my lap and stand up with her weight in my arms.

"I'm carrying you to bed, Selena. We both fell asleep," I say when she stirs.

"Oh Sergei, I..."

"Shhh, sleep now, sweet Selena, my Sunshine. Sleep now," I say to this woman who I regret making feel like a whore. I'll damn sure fix that. I'll damn sure fix that before morning light.

I awaken sometime later from my deep sleep surrounded by large pillows and fur blankets. The heat of a roaring fire warms me with a sleeping Sergei Radkov holding his arms around me. I don't want to awaken him. I don't want to move, but I have to pee. Pee like a racehorse.

I gently roll my covers to the side and slide out from underneath them while rolling from Sergei's sleeping arms. Success! Sergei lies in a deep sleep. I smile as I notice that I awakened sometime in the night to pull my long hair around his naked body.

Sergei had removed both our robes before sliding into bed. He has said he loves to feel my skin on his, to smell me, watch me, listen to my sounds. I love it too. Love having him take all of it from me. Happy are my offerings, but for now, I move on bare feet to the toilet, taking advantage of the Persian rugs to shield my feet from the coldness of the wood floors.

After washing my hands, I alight to the slim table behind the settee holding glasses and fresh water in an ewer. The geothermal pool made me extra thirsty. I throw my head back and gulp down a glass of water. Then pour another.

I don't notice that Sergei has awakened. I respond to his voice by looking into the mirror above the fireplace.

"Don't move, Selena."

"Sergei, I didn't mean to…"

"Shhh. Right there. Just like that. I want to remember you just like that. Your face in the mirror. Your long hair lapping at your ankles. Your green eyes blazing. Yes, just like that," says the throaty voice of Sergei in a half whisper. As though in a trance, he pulls back his covers and sits on the side of the bed. His eyes follow my curves slowly. Slowly, evenly, he moves, as though he's a blender put on its lowest running power.

My eyes follow his movements in the mirror. I'm enchanted as my eyes move with his reflection. Sergei's feet patter like a mindless zombie stepping on broken glass without a notice. A mesmerized man. He stands in front of me now. Looking. Taking me in as though he's never seen my nude body before.

Touches my face with just the tips of his fingers. Down my nose and my lips colored into a cherry rose in the light. Along the angles of my face and down my neck, he moves. He looks like he's going to kiss me, but instead, his fingertips continue down my neck and upper torso.

I swallow hard, but I'm not sure anything passes my Adam's apple. Close my eyes and throw back my head in the throes of ultimate delight. Lips part and a slightly audible "Ummmm" escapes my throat.

Sergei's fingertips round each breast. Lightly. So softly. Oh, the erotica of it all. More firmly, he sends the index finger of his right hand, just the one finger, straight down from my breastbone to my navel. The mirror reflects as Sergei's mouth opens, as though he wants to put his tongue there. Right there. He does not.

Sergei's look takes me in. All of me, without moving his finger. He studies my reflection. My hair is hanging like parentheses around me and clinging to the arcs and lines of my body.

Gently, his left hand pulls back my hair from my bump that he loves. His left hand adores the bump with his right index finger in place. His hand holds there firmly, skin on skin, as his right index finger travels my abdomen, the top of my pubic bones, the roof of my lady hair. Gently, he adds another finger and massages the area beneath my pubic bone.

I breathe shallow. Gasp. Fight an immediate orgasm. Breathe through the impulse as Sergei's travelling fingers move down the inside of my parted thighs. His eyes follow his own movements. His fingertips make their way to the back of my knees and massage the skin methodically, like folding a pair of Sunday trousers.

More briskly, he moves both his full hands down my leg to my ankles and pats for me to put my foot on his knee. I oblige. So does he. Fingertips explore the top of my foot. I want to scream. I do.

"Sweet Jesus!" I cry as though it's Sunday in North Carolina.

Lovingly, Sergei bends his body over and lets his mouth suck my big toe. Sucks as though it were a neck bone.

I swallow air. Gulp it in. I'm aware some people find this sexually arousing, but I've never exactly gotten it. Not until now. Sergei's tongue, mouth, teeth ravage my foot with bites and kisses. Moves up my lower leg to the back of my knee. Kisses. Licks. Sucks. His movements become rapid. Frantic, as though he's impatient. He's gone before I can complete the rasp falling from my mouth.

His mouth makes small bites on my thighs. Takes more time now to move except to the one place he's yet to touch. Both hands grab my bump as his tongue explores. His head lays in my lady hair. The side of his face adores the feel of it. Loves it. Kisses it with tenderness. Sergei stops.

He pulls back his head to adore my woman. Stares at it in awe. Studies it. With his one index finger, he explores. Adores it. Moves his mouth along my adult spot and extends his tongue for one lick. Smacks his mouth and extends his tongue to moisten his lips as though he licked and liked. His hand tenderly moves behind my hair and clutches my bump. My woman is moving into his mouth.

Sergei is like a primal savage exerting caveman noise while putting the moist pressure of his mouth against me. Inside me. Through me. Circles. Lines. Arcs. Segments. Sergei Radkov paints a portrait of erotica.

I struggle to breathe. Pant in pleasure. Throw my head back and scream.

My legs are weak. I can barely stand. Sergei swoops his arms behind my knees and sweeps me up in one motion to bring my body to his chest. He walks steps to his bed. Our crystal blue and round emerald eyes don't leave one another.

Gently, lays down my body across his bed. Slowly. Gently. As if I'm asleep and he doesn't want to awaken me. The bed is so soft that I feel I'm being laid upon the feathered wings of angels. I want to reach up to taste him, but I was too late. Sergei was already on top of me. Between me.

"I must take you now, Selena."

He enters me with the force of his movements. Our eyes never leave the glory of one another.

He's moving.

Moving the way Sergei Radkov moves. The way Sergei Radkov moves when he's inside me. He presses his mouth to me. Drinks me. Quiets me. Quieting me the way he does before I scream.

Sergei makes deep plunges and rapid turns, followed by slow withdrawal. He washes, rinses and repeats. A flurry of Russian words snows in my ear. "Ya lyublyu tebya."

"We are one and the same. It means we are one and the same," he whispers in my ear.

He claims my eyes.

"It means 'I love you' in English. I love you," he speaks over my mouth.

"Ya lyublyu tebya," he says again and kisses me. Plunges his tongue deep inside my mouth, moving to match his lower movements.

Like much of the Russian language, the phrases have different meanings than their English counterparts. So beautiful, "We are one, we are the same." So beautiful.

Sergei wants to share more than his plunges.

I raise my hips and flail against him to steal the energy of his movements. I feel his hands slide down the skin of my back and latch onto my hip bump and pull my naked flesh onto and around him. He grinds. Deep and hard.

I can't speak. I repay him with deep, guttural moans in his ear.

Sergei whimpers. "Your moans are the most erotic sounds I've ever known."

"I love you, Selena, Oh God, I love you," comes his breathless whisper as he speaks over the top of my lips with his blue eyes mixing with my green so close as to make one color. We are one and the same.

"Please don't be angry with me, Selena," he says, kissing one side of my face, moving to my ear. "It's soon, I know it's soon. But I've loved you for so long," gulps Sergei in a wizened voice as he heaves. "I want you, Selena," he pants.

"Your body. Your passion. Your soul. Ya lyublyu tebya," Sergei says, removing his face from the side of mine as he takes my eyes again while churning his body more deeply, more erotically into mine.

Finding the smallest iota of my voice, I eke out, "I want to give you all of those things, my love. I love you, too. I want to be one with you."

Sergei slows his churns, looks at my mouth speak, the words in my eyes.

My lover puts each hand on a cheek of my face as he gazes into my eyes, loving me like the morning sun. "Selena, I've never said these words to anyone. No human being has ever said them to me, and I've not said them to anyone. Please say them again while I make love to you. Please."

"I love you, Sergei. Sergei Radkov, I love you," I say slowly, as I kiss one side of his face and neck, and then the other. I hold his face in my hands.

"I've never said those words to any lover either, nor had them said to me. No. Nothing ever like this," I gasp as somehow, amid all this emotion, Sergei has found a physical part deep inside of me that causes me to heave and blow.

We look into the eyes of the other and we know. Teardrops fall from our eyes as each of us weeps in love and warmth and truth and acceptance and knowledge and erotica.

Sergei puts his lips on those of his ladylove and agitates his manhood. Touches erogenous places. Oh, so erogenous. The tears fall from his eyes and mix with my teardrops. Our eyes open to see the soul of the other as our bodies whirl into a gear. A g-force, an energy, a place where screams escape and moans wail in delight and murmurs of pleasure reach their pinnacle and spread like sunlight on white desert sand. Ummmm. Ummmm.

Two now one; let the end come. We snuggle. "I love you," falls into each lover's ear. Once, twice, and again.

Sergei puts my face in his hands and murmurs, "Ya lyublyu tebya. It means, 'We are one, we are the same' in Russian. I think I said that earlier. I think," he giggles.

"You must go deep to find the beauty of Russian words and phrases. They hide like a gem in the woods. You must enter the forest to find it," he reflects.

Sergei gives my forehead a solid kiss. "You are my heart," he confesses.

I reply to the gesture by saying, "I think I'm the luckiest woman in the world to love a Russian man. There is no other man for me, Sergei Radkov. Only you. It's you and only you I love."

"Say it once more," comes my love's smiled request.

"I love you. We are one and the same. I love you, my Sergei."

Sergei rolls to cuddle me closer to him. "*I love you* is beautiful too. I love you, Selena Frederick, I love you."

I roll on top of him to touch his face. "I once touched your face like this," I say to him. Touching the side of his face, first with the soft side of my hand, then with my fingertips on the angles of his jawline.

"For no reason at all," I continue as Sergei gives me a quick lip nibble. "You were on the TV screen," I confess. "And I was alone in my hotel room. I just felt an overwhelming urge to touch your face."

Sergei watches my mouth speak, and the words in my eyes.

"I thought I had gone nuts, but I felt it. An energy. It calmed me. It claimed me. I knew I had touched something, someone, very deep. Very dear," I say.

I blurt out, "Then I poked you right in that eyeball with my finger!"

I feel the muscles of Sergei's abdomen spasm as he throws back his head to laugh.

Sergei returns my gaze and says, "Selena, I love your humor, your wit, but I didn't know that quality about you until I met you. You surprise me in so many ways, and I love them all. I never dreamed we would make love on that first night and draw so close. Not complaining, mind you."

I wink at him. "So, when did you first notice me?"

"Oh, it was before you noticed me, for sure. I think first on the front of a magazine. My first reaction was all male. I thought you were beautiful, and with a… I guess you could say a rare type of sexiness."

"Ah," I reply.

"Granted, I never could have imagined how sexy you truly are. But then I began to process other things about you. Listened to your words on television. I realized you didn't possess just a rare type or sexiness, but a rare humanity. I had the biggest crush on you. I followed your every word. Then I read your book."

His blue eyes glow and my green ones dance.

He inhales. "Then I read your book. Somewhere along the way I fell head-over-heels in love with you. The first time I kissed your hand, my lips sizzled. Actually *sizzled*. I knew that the feelings I had for you were more than real. They were everything."

———

The fire burns. The wolves howl. More snow falls as the wind plays with snowflakes and drifts them into an art form loved by moving air. Oliver snores downstairs and Olga learns to say "Hello" in English.

Two lovers sleep a deep and kind sleep. Smiles upon lips and REM eyes moving behind lids. Lungs breathe deep and thrust out every bit of stale air.

All is well with the world, my friends. Sergei Radkov and Selena Frederick are in charge. We are World Changers. Imagine.

My eyes fly open. My dream state interrupted. The mole. The microphone. The painted lady. The land-to-air missile. Nefarious, all of it.

Worse is the rapidly approaching tomorrow when Selena and I must part. I tell you my secret plan: I don't have one. I did the only thing possible. After I put Selena to bed, I knelt to pray. I begged God to help me.

Much has been taken from me. Much has been given to me. I begged Him. Begged God, *Please, please, don't let this woman be taken from me.*

CHAPTER 60
WE ARE CLAN

THE SOUNDS of the wolf's cry didn't awaken the two lovebirds in my immense bed, nor the hoot and screech of the mighty Eurasian eagle owl called Bubo bubo by name, nor the crackling fire amassed against the wall. It was a red phone. Man-made. Russian. Not beautiful. Just red.

"Damn, too many people have this number," I complain. "I think I'm going to change my telephone number."

Selena smiles a gentle laugh as I roll over and answer, "Radkov," followed by, "Hold on." I hold the phone to my chest and roll over to Selena, saying, "I love you, Sunshine," and give her a peck on the lips.

"Go ahead," I say in a raspy morning voice as my face covers the phone. "Yes, I got it. Can we fly?" I pause while another voice speaks in my ear. "Yes, yes, return tomorrow. Moscow. Yes. When I get there. No need, Tina is my press secretary. Get with her. Tina can handle the announcement. There's no reason for me to release it personally. Tina can do it now, or when people are actually not asleep. Matters not to me." I hang up.

"Now, I know I'm changing my number," complains the president with a five o'clock in the morning wake-up call. "There's no sleeping late for a president, not even on a frozen vacation."

"Must you get up?"

"Actually, no. The call was just to inform me the autopsies should be complete this afternoon. Ice and snow removal from the Cemetery of the Brave will start tomorrow morning." I let out a yawn before trying to speak further.

"The two Spetsnaz commandos will be buried at the cemetery. Olaf, the operative posing as the roommate, will not. Even his family thinks he had gone back to college and lived a normal life. One day I hope it's possible to tell them and all of Russia his true story, but not now. The family thinks the monies for his burial and to help with family support came from anonymous donors. Some did. Most of the other funds will be from the government. Olaf's family will receive one payout instead of monthly checks."

"I see," comes Selena's listening voice.

"And I really shouldn't be telling you any of this."

"I understand that," Selena replies. "Though it's not like knowing where your nuclear arsenal is hidden. Dear man of my heart, it's not in me to cause harm to any of those families. Any of this information would hurt them."

"This I agree, Selena. This is why we are one. This is why we are the same."

"That's wonderful," says Selena with a smirking grin. "And I don't wish to know where any missiles lie in Russia. President Radkov can be on his own with that one."

"Hmm," is the only reply made by this sleepy president, and the two of us fall back into our love dreamland for another few hours.

The room cools. I awaken and don my favorites to stoke the fire.

Selena gives a yawn and sits halfway up in bed. The happy doctor moves to the bed's edge and puts on her robe and slippers and makes her way to the toilet for what is likely to be the first of nine hundred times she will do so during the day. Why do women pee so much? After emerging, she starts the coffee pot.

"Oh yes, wise choice," I say.

"Um," is all that a bleary-eyed Selena can fumble out of her mouth.

I make a pit stop while she puts out two cups and finds herself a dribble of milk to splash her cup. I return from my bodily function chore and put my arms around this woman that I can now scream "I love you" to.

And I do love her. Yes, I do. And she loves me. Yes, she does.

My arms pull around her front to warm her close and nestle her into my bosom. "Good morning, Sunshine. I love you." My smiling lips touch hers.

"Good morning, man of mine. We are one and the same."

Can't help but smile as I rest my head on hers and just love her. Just love her as the coffee pot spits its last drops. "I call that ready," I claim with presidential authority.

"I'll second that," says Selena democratically. We stroll to the settee and sit down to inhale our first sips of the day.

"We have had busy days here. These days with you just flew by. So fast. So very fast. So much has happened," I admit as I take in another good swig of go-juice.

"Yes," says Selena with melancholy as she takes a sip.

I feel the melancholy too. The tone should go unnoticed on this gray morning in Siberia. Everything seems gray in Siberia. At least, since Selena has been present. The earth tilts so that Siberia should get about five hours of daylight now, but all Selena has seen is gray. Gray clouds threatening ice. Gray clouds with white snowfall.

I know Selena's heart is heavy with sadness. Just like mine. I long for my lover to see this dacha in the spring when the birds are chirping, and Olga's garden is blooming. What is next? Will she see this place again?

Thinking it's too early to be so sad and thinking so deep, I watch Selena's smile cross her face. She takes the hand of the President of United Russia.

"I'm grateful we have had these days to love each other, Sergei Radkov," she says as she opens my hand and kisses my palm.

Love the touch of her hand. The whole feel of her. Not from across oceans and thousands of miles away, but right here. Right beside me. One with me. Oh God, He knows I don't want this to end. It can't end. No! President Sergei Radkov won't let this end. I won't.

Both of us take another swig. Each look away from the gaze of the other, lest we see the elephant in the room. The big pink one. The one that is too ugly to be red.

I know Selena heard what I said on the red phone this morning. Selena tries to make a wince look like a smile as she puts the mug of pale black liquid to her lips to pull in a drag of it.

I watch knowing. I sit my cup on the coffee table. I'm nervous. Scared. Time to kill the ugly elephant.

"Selena, I must go to Moscow tomorrow. I think we'll need to go in different directions then."

Without warning, Selena lets the wall of tears fall.

"Oh my God," she says from embarrassment by her emotional release. She jumps up. "I'm sorry, Sergei, let me go recover. Give me a minute."

I stand and grab to hold her, but she pulls away. "Please, please, let me recover. Please." Selena runs through the toilet into the adjoining bedroom. The woman of dignity doesn't want me to hear her heaves.

I detect hives filling my throat.

I sit back down with the most forlorn look I've ever worn. I want to throw something to break that damn mirror. That mirror that provided me and Selena with so much erotica just last night.

I've known forlorn days. The President of United Russia gazes into the fire for the power of answers but finds it cold. And empty.

I pray under my breath. Look into my heart. Clutch my Solovetsky cross and pray harder. The answer comes. We are one. We are the same. We aren't school children playing at love. We know life. Life knows us. This is what is right. All I need are words.

I'm working hard to repress tears and choke them down. Tears don't want to go lie down and take a nap. Selena's baby girl tears must want to come out and play, too. Even in the Siberian weather. It hurts. Both of our tears want to wail and scream and get their way.

I can hear Selena fighting them. The martial artist is beating them with her "Damn You" stick. My strong lady is forcing the tears to stop. It hurts. Damn, it hurts.

Now more controlled, I hear Selena splash water on her face and brush her teeth. I hear her wrestle eye drops from her bag for the stinging drops to help her red and swollen eyes. She is recovering. I'm trying to do the same.

Brushes her long hair to her ankle bones. I wonder if Selena allows her eyes to meet her own gaze in the mirror. Mine can't. Decorum. She must have it. Professional. She must be. Dr. Selena Frederick was raised as a strong and dignified Southern American woman. I know this. I know my lady.

Selena finds her way back to the settee. "I'm sorry," she mutters, looking me in the eye. Damn, she's strong.

I'm the man she is sure will be the absolute love of her life, and she's as helpless as me.

"I didn't mean to act like such a child. Of course, we must go in different directions." Selena's shoulders shrug. "Suddenly I was filled with a fear that I would never see you again. You," she says softly.

I can only nod. She's the strong one.

"You, the man that for the first time in my life I've allowed myself to fully love. Driven to love. Choose to love," she says with hurt in her voice but understanding in her smile and eyes. "I accepted the whole package when I took our first leap of faith."

I take her hand. "I cry too, Selena. I want to be beside you every moment of every day. I will be, but not like we have been here. Actually better," I say in a tone that Selena doesn't comprehend.

I man up and get down on both knees. I take the hands of the woman I love and speak unrehearsed words. "Selena, I have nothing. I have a job. That's it. That's all I've ever had. When this job is over, I have no idea what I'm going to do with my life. I do have savings. As a former orphan, I was never much of a spendthrift. I really haven't used my presidential salary, except for a gala to meet a beautiful woman." I smile.

"I bank it all pretty much automatically. Professional answers will come in time." I nod with confidence.

I know Selena doesn't care about jobs and savings. Only being with me, the man she loves. I want to give her all the disclosure I can think of.

She remains silent and listens to my words. Damn, she's so beautiful.

Looking at her hands, I hold them tight while she listens. My eyes roll up to hers. "Selena, all I truly have to offer you is what is in my heart. I don't have a family for you to love. You have already met all the family that I have to offer, and they are here now in this dacha. I don't have a babushka momma to love you, except Olga. Nor sisters and brothers, at least I don't think. I never had a father."

Her eyes don't move but watch my moving mouth.

"I've studied families together and studied the behavior of men I thought to be good from all over the world. Never knew my father, who should have taught me how to be a man. How to parent as a man. How to love as a man. My father didn't even have the decency to teach me who I am or where I came from. I think I resent him most for that. I'm unsure how a father is to behave or what makes him a good father to a child, except for what is in his heart. That's all that I have. It's that which is in my chest."

Selena isn't sure where this conversation is going, but tightly squeezes my hands. Her body language signals she understands what is important to this man humbled on his knees. This man, whom she loves. She keeps silent and lets me roll on with my meandering words.

I find myself pinching Selena's hands so tight, they must be ready to explode. My grip relaxes a little, as I'm suddenly aware of my overly tight bind.

"With you, Selena. Only with you, am I sure that I can accomplish anything. Anything at all. With you, only you, can I grow to be a man in ways that I'm currently in default. I do hope to have children. My heart hopes for a family, dreams of it, but has so far denied it to myself." I pause for Selena to consider my words and process them before continuing.

"Then I saw you for the first time. Then I read you and saw you and met you. I can no longer deny myself. I can't deny myself of you. You, with whom I'm one and the same. You, the forever love in my heart." My tone is so gentle and sincere. And sweet. Truthful. I mean for it to be.

Selena's eyes only show love. Her lips only part a slight smile, giving all intensity to her man. To me.

Taking a deep breath, I ask with the strength of my heart, "Selena

Frederick, will you marry me? Will you be my wife? I only have my heart and soul to give you, but I'll only hold one woman within their walls. There will be only one woman for me. Forevermore, it will be you. You are my one. Will you be my wife?"

Selena doesn't speak. She sits stunned. Her eyes never leave mine. I know Selena wasn't sure what she was expecting from this morning, but certainly not me on my knees asking for her hand in marriage. But then, why not? Yes, it has been merely days, but we have both taken leaps of faith that would have never happened with anyone else. Mere days, but we had both admired the other from afar over time and learned of one another through other means.

Only dreaming of knowing each other, but never thinking we really would. That seemed like a pipe dream. A pipe dream that led her to me. To this place. This country. This dacha. This room. This glorious room. This glorious moment. I just want to hear one word, but I must give her time. I know she's surprised. Hell, I'm surprised. She can have all the time she needs.

None of this would have happened without the craziest bravery I've ever performed as a man. Now, that man is on his knees humbled in front of her. That man with the wispy blond hair who wanted to meet her so badly that he created the most ridiculous scheme to get an introduction. Selena connected to me. Has grown to love me. I'm her warrior. I'm her man. Hell, I'm her White Stallion.

Just one word. Please, Selena, give me just one word.

Selena's eyes twinkle, and she slides her butt off the settee onto her knees to face me. Selena takes my hands in hers. Whatever she is going to say is not going to be one word. I know that much.

"Sergei, I had loving parents, and so I know at least one way that a man and a woman love. My parents gave me a good example. Never have I appreciated them nearly so much as I do at this moment. I feel them with me in my heart. My sister Debbie and her husband and my nieces are my only family. I love them dearly, but they live in a place where the land is their heart and life's blood. Their land is not my own. It's not my place. But love them, oh God yes, I do," Selena confirms with a slight nod.

I don't flinch my focused face.

"Then there's Sam. I cared a lot about Sam and perhaps loved him in a sense, but not like you, Sergei. He wasn't mine other than how he was my friend. Sam belonged to someone else, and I was aware of it, and it was never meant for me to take him away or for him to be mine. What happened was only to be one night, to soothe his loneliness, as he'd been separated from the true love in his heart for so long that he was afraid he was losing his vision of her. That's all it was about. Dr. Selena Frederick was simply medicine, and we both understood that. That was the deal. That was the plan. Yet it tore my heart into pieces when he was killed the next day. Somehow, I felt responsible. I knew I needed to heal. Heal from Sam. Heal from the hungry, the wounded, the pregnant women with no fat left on their bodies to nourish another life. I needed time."

I have no expression, only my ears.

Selena continues. I'm not sure she even knows where to take her words. Like me, on my knees.

"And here I am. Here I am with you. With you and feeling a love in my heart that I didn't know a woman could feel for a man. Knowing no other man will be here in my heart. Not here, not in this place," she says, taking one hand and pointing her index finger at her heart.

Damn, I want to kiss that finger. Want to kiss that heart. I remain a focused man and don't move a muscle.

"I don't know where I'm going after I finish my current obligations. I have a medical degree and suppose I can do many things, but I'm not sure what it is I want to do exactly. I'm not even sure if I want to continue practicing medicine. I put all such thoughts in another package to be opened at the end of this journey. But now, I've known Sergei Radkov, and he knows me. I have loved him, and he has loved me. All I know is that I want to love him more. I will never abandon him. I will be beside him. I won't leave him. I'll be one with him," she says firmly.

I suppress the smile that wants to cross my face.

After her strong words, she looks into the eyes of the man she loves like fire loves air and asks, "Sergei Radkov, will you marry me? Will you be my family? Will you father my children? Will you be one and the same with me forevermore?"

I am taken aback for a moment, but then I realize, what in the hell else could I expect from Selena? Beautiful Selena. This is so her. So Russian red is her beauty with her shining ruby lips. Her beautiful long dark hair with emerald eyes that bear fire behind her lashes. Fire. Always fire. Passion. Passion for others. Passion to help others. Passion for me. *For me.* This woman has passion for me.

"Oh God, yes!" I cry. Truly cry as tears fall from my eyes.

Selena cries too. "Oh God, yes! Sergei, I want to marry you. Live my life with you! You and I are family. We are a new clan."

Tears flow from four eyes.

I hold her and rock her and kiss her and love her and cry with her. "Oh Selena, I want to be the father of your children. In my life I've never wanted to father children, but I want to start now with you," I say, moving the coffee table out of the way and throwing down the fur throw covers and blankets in front of the fire.

I loosen her robe and begin to ravage her body.

Selena blows out a breath. Her hand pulls up her lover's face. "Full disclosure, Sergei: I must let the pills flush out of my system first. Look at me, wild man," she says as she again pulls up the face of the ravaging warrior to her eyes. "We have many things to work out. Many. One thing I won't do is have a child without their father's name."

"Selena, these things we will work out, but right now I'm an animal who wants to mate. Mate with the only female who will bear his kind. God, I feel it in my blood. Touch me, Selena. See how I throb for you."

Selena removes my trusty warm-ups and kisses my throbbing. A throbbing that wants to mate. Wants to mate, I tell you.

I pull her to me and rest her on pillows while I whisper, "I'm entering you now, Selena, I must. I'm wild for you. Wild to be a husband to you. Wild to make a baby with you."

Erotica whips Selena to her tail bone as I ravage her. Ravage at moments gently and others, hard. Ravage with authority. President Radkov is in charge. God, I want to make a baby with her so damn bad. A baby to be part of our "one and the same." Soon. It will be soon.

"Can you imagine this, Selena? Close your eyes and *imagine*, beautiful lady. Me inside you like this, and we're creating a child? Do you feel it? God, I feel it," says the man of authority as I slide myself wildly to and fro.

Selena screams with pleasure as her body responds to my movements.

I'm not done.

Holding her tight, I rock her. Lovingly, I rock my throbbing inside of her.

I speak English. I speak Russian. I've lost count of the many languages I speak with fluency. Once it's over twenty, who cares? With tears in my eyes, I may have spoken words in some of them, or all of them, or maybe not—hell, I might have made up a few new languages, I don't know—the words just fly from my mouth as I coo the lady in my arms and in my heart.

She is my warrior companion. Damn, this woman is a warrior in every right. She is warrior enough to imagine. Warrior enough to change the world. We are a clan!

Selena drives my primitive spirit.

"We are one, and soon we'll be making another," says the primal man. "I'm going to plant my seed so deep inside you. It's all of me. It's everything that is within me, given to me by God, to pass on to the children we make. I will give you all of me. Every drop of me," I whisper into her hair.

"Oh Sergei," shouts Selena. Dr. Frederick understands it won't be so, not this time. We can't create life now. But soon. Oh, but I want to create life with her and let myself imagine.

Our bodies rock. We let our screams soar with the eagles and howl with the wolves.

"Selena, I give you my seed. My seed!"

My body spasms and hers rocks with me. It's different this time. Beyond sexual. Beyond erotic. My best description is that we are complete. We are joined. Forevermore. It's better, this beyond. We are one and the same physically, mentally, emotionally, even financially. In every way that matters. One. Thank you, God, for answering my prayers.

The nefarious be damned at this moment. Their time is coming.

We are clan. And with our imagination, we're going to change the world. Me and her, my other.

For the first time in my life, I'm not alone. I hold in my arms my other self. Nothing matters. Not the orphan boy. Not my country. Not those who are plotting to destroy me. Nothing. No one. Just us.

We are clan.

CHAPTER 61
THE "S"

"WANT to eat breakfast in the gallery on our last day?" Sergei asks.

"Always," replies the naked lady on his chest.

Sergei bends down and gives me a tender kiss on my forehead. Both of us so much in love. So very much in love. The thought of it sends shivers down my spine.

I don't know how long Sergei and I can keep our love and our marriage intentions under wraps. I want it to be a minor worry, nothing more. He has enough on his plate without worrying about me and my security. But Sergei, being Sergei, is clear that he wants us to be the ones driving the decisions we make for our lives.

We dress in warm-ups and mosey into the gallery, each of us holding a cup of coffee. We sit like a couple on their honeymoon and Sergei, also being Mr. Presidential, begins a long list of items we need to discuss. "Selena, there's so much to talk about. Our relationship is number one, but the world doesn't need to know about it. Not yet."

"Oh, I agree. Mostly because of security. There's enough on your mind without worrying about my safety. You and I both need to meet our commitments."

"Decided not to run for president when Russia holds elections. Election reform is my top priority," he states.

"Why?"

"Selena, I'm now in my forties. I want to make a life and a family with you. Being president wasn't something I grew up wanting to be. It simply happened. I've had a few lax days here with you, relatively speaking, but ordinarily I'm working day and night, every day and every night. Russia has many issues, and I'm trying hard to resolve as many as I can before I leave office."

"Did you want to run for office before you met me?"

"In all honesty, there were times I considered it with ambivalence. Maybe yes, but not really. It might be best for my country if two or more new opponents enter the ring, following new election guidelines. That will be the genuine test of my effectiveness."

"Yes, but you are forgetting one thing," I state.

Sergei raises his eyebrows.

"Your people love you. You are the White Stallion. President Radkov gives them hope and pride."

"One day that horse will have to be shot. Better sooner than later."

I chuckle. "No one, not even you, Sergei Radkov, will ever kill the White Stallion that is inside of you. Never."

Sergei shoots me a loving grin.

I continue, "There are a few weeks left for which I'm committed. I've not agreed to the next tour. I might consider doing only conferences and that's it. It might help ease security. If so, I can stay with my fiancé in Moscow." I grin.

The food arrives which is more than twenty people can eat. We fill our plates and sit down in the gallery chairs to continue our discussion.

Sergei speaks before taking a bite of food. "The most pressing thing for me, of the most importance, is: what kind of engagement ring does my fiancée want?"

I almost choke on my eggs Benedict. I can't believe he's already thinking about this. "Glad someone is meditating on that. All I can say is I don't want a diamond. Diamonds create the market, from which many evil things arise. Perhaps something mined here in Russia, so long as it's not diamond. Could have it specially made."

"Perhaps an alexandrite, like the one I wore to the ball." I add, with extra consideration on the matter. "Or an aquamarine."

"Um," says Sergei as he chews his quiche. After he swallows, he replies. "Oh, an alexandrite. Fit for a queen. Alas, we both have things on our plates to complete, but you're the one to decide what is next for you."

I shake my head. "I've already decided. *You* are next. Having your child is next. If you don't want me with you in Moscow, then I'll do something else for a while."

"Selena, Selena. I want you beside me every moment of every day. I just don't want you to give up medicine and other things which are important to you." Swallowing again, Mr. President continues.

"Your book is notable work, and you might only get to promote it this once. I don't want to cut the experience short for you. Not your destiny. I never want you to look at me with regret."

"I would never regret having your baby. Then another. Then adopt a few Russian orphans. Who knows?" I say, getting my needling noogie on.

"Woman! Wow!" Sergei says with a mouth full of food that he's trying to hold in while smiling.

Sergei manages his food and speaks. "This is what I think we should do," Sergei says once he swallows it all down. "You should finish your tour and return to Moscow. Or we can meet back at the dacha. We'll talk at that time and decide how to move forward. If the press gets wind of our love affair, perhaps you might need to do a shorter tour or stick to conferences. In the meantime, I'll try to wrap up election reform."

"That is a year down the road. You know it. It's time we commit or not. Why don't we take the next couple of weeks while I'm in country to mull it over," I suggest.

"That's sensible," says the lip-pecking president as he gives me a small touch on my lips to show his agreement. "There are a few things I need to show you, though. The first is personal. I want to share it with you, but it's only between us."

I nod.

"It concerns Our Lady."

"Okay."

"I may recognize the artist's signature. Come, let me show you.

Let's take it off the wall," says Sergei eagerly. "Only able to see the first letter, and only halfway because of the frame. That's why we are taking it apart."

"Sure this is warranted?"

"Yes."

We heave-ho the painting and lay it on a bench with care. Sergei tears open the back of the portrait. The entire portrait doesn't need removal all the way from its frame. Only about an inch or so at the bottom.

"See this curved *S* followed by jumbled letters and the *y* at the end?"

"Yes?"

"The signature is by Andre Smoltsky, Russia's chairman. This was his family's dacha before it was taken from him—or should we more accurately say, was given as a gift to the prior president."

"So, you believe Smoltsky painted this lady?" I ask.

"Yes. And I'm sure it's a painting of my mother."

"How strongly do you feel this is your mother? She is extraordinary but could be anyone," I remark, reading his mind.

"About ninety-nine-point-nine percent sure she is my mother. Remember me telling you about her aquamarine jewelry?"

"Yes."

"*This* is her jewelry."

I study the ring and the necklace adorning the naked lady, who looks so young. So damn young. "Those pieces look specially made," I comment.

"I agree."

"Do you think Smoltsky is, might be…"

"My father? It's possible. Some of our features are alike. Need to think this through, though. Smoltsky knows something about my mother, and I want to know what it is."

"Whenever you have it figured out, invite Smoltsky over for a political drink before you discuss anything with him. Save his glass and drink. There will be DNA. At least then you can test it to see if you two are related. Those results will strengthen your case one way or the other."

"Selena, I've already obtained Smoltsky's DNA. This presidential thing for me was always some sort of play. I didn't know how, but I thought myself a puppet. Events appeared organic, but who showed all those news reels of me the day the former president was shot? The media?" Sergei shakes his head.

"As well, the interpretation should've been, 'This guy is a flunky.' That day at the dacha when the former president was shot was the worst fiasco of my career. Never bought how things played out."

I don't want to argue with him but find myself saying, "That's hard for me to believe, though I suppose it's possible. Not sure the White Stallion part was a plant, though. Truth is, it's the strength of such a beast that the people fell in love with. Some things you just can't plant. Especially good things. Bad things are much more predictable."

I sigh. "Alas, regardless of who may or may not have planted or maneuvered what, Sergei Radkov is in office. An office that's yours until there is a change. It's up to you to use it and execute your duty."

I continue to verbalize my doubts as my wonderful man listens. "Besides, if you're a puppet, why would Smoltsky hand the office over to his son? His unclaimed son?"

"Can't say," replies Sergei. "Maybe he had an idea he could control me, thereby controlling two branches of government," shrugs the President of United Russia. "I don't know, but I will find out."

I object. "Sergei, I don't see Smoltsky as a fool. The first thing anybody will figure out about you is that you're not a man who can be controlled. Besides, this painting doesn't mean he's your father. Andre Smoltsky may have once bedded your mother, either willing or unwillingly, but that's all this means.

"Besides, it's all so far-fetched. Perhaps this lady isn't your mother. Perhaps she resembles her but isn't her. Perhaps Smoltsky has a type. Likes women with long blonde hair, say. Perhaps your mother lent this woman the jewelry or somehow ended up with it later. Could have been sold to the lady. It's no more far-fetched than anything else."

"Your arguments are well made, Selena, but either way, it's possible Smoltsky knows something about my mother. If so, I'm going to find out what it is. Come, there are other things to show you," nods Sergei.

CHAPTER 62
THE TUNNEL

SERGEI RETURNS us to his bedroom chamber with Alexei in tow. "Do a full sweep of the room, please, Alexei," requests the president.

Alexei does so without comment. "Also, check the bathrooms and dressing areas, please," Sergei adds.

Alexei complies and leaves after clearing the room for listening devices.

Sergei takes me by the hand into the presidential bath and dressing area. Sergei shuts the door as though he means to be extraordinarily secretive. "I found something." Reaching behind a shoe rack, he mashes a button. The entire rack of shoes moves along with the wooden flooring. A hole appears with a ladder that seems to extend several floors below to the ground.

"Go down the ladder a few steps," orders the Commander in Chief.

"Russian engineering," I smile and obey.

"Here, Selena, see this button?"

"Yes."

"That is what closes the hatch. The hatch is battery operated. If the power goes out, the hatch will manually open and close. The only problem is that you will still be working the hatch in the dark. I'm going to leave this small flashlight behind right here near the top. Be careful not to knock it off or drop it."

"Got it."

"There's a hidden light switch here at the top," Sergei points between the first two steps. "And another below."

I'm enthralled but dumbfounded.

"Let's go to the bottom," commands Russia's president.

We finagle our way to the bottom of the steps when Sergei explains, "I understand this seems strange to you and you are wondering, 'What the hell?' If I ever tell you to shelter here, don't question me. If you think I'm insinuating you need to come here, don't hesitate. If you feel you need to come here, don't hesitate—"

I interrupt him. "Do you think we're in danger?"

"Maybe. Tell you about that in a minute."

Sergei continues as a tour guide. "There's a cot here that you can unfold and rest on. If you feel you're in danger of discovery, turn off the lights. Grab this flashlight on the cot. Of most importance, grab this knapsack next to the tunnel door and go through the tunnel."

Sergei's pupils are large from the lack of light and grow larger.

"The tunnel will turn several times. Stay right. Always to the right. Never go in another direction. Got it?"

"Yes." I reply, listening intently to the president and not asking questions.

"Don't forget this backpack. There are several bottles of water. And there are several flashlights with extra batteries. Also, a couple of glow sticks. This should get you to tunnel's end without problems."

I nod.

"I placed a bicycle at the mouth of the tunnel. Did you see the waterfall when you flew into the dacha in the helicopter?"

"Yes, I did."

"That's where you will come out. There is a path that you can take with the bike along the river, but it may have become overgrown with weeds in places. Keep following the river, though. It will take you to the next town. Dump the bike if you think you can travel faster on foot."

Sergei takes a breath, knowing he's firing a lot at me at once.

"You should be able to get help there. If possible, pull your hair up, wear a kerchief or something to disguise yourself if you can. Understand, this would be under extreme circumstances."

"I understand," I say, nodding my understanding. "Should I put something in the backpack now? Something for my hair? It's damp and cold in here, so maybe an extra jacket?" I'm being polite. It's cold as a witch's whistle down here.

"That's a good idea. The next part is up to you, Selena. It can stay or go. This is your backpack. I put in a twenty-two-caliber weapon with extra bullets. The weapon is loaded. Can you handle it?"

"Yes, it's been years, but I've done target practice with a twenty-two caliber."

"Good."

"I hope this is something you never use. But if you think you need to, don't hesitate, even if you must leave me behind," Sergei says in an emphatic voice.

"I would nev—"

"Selena, I'm a big boy. I've been left behind many times before and caught up. I'm trained. You go and you take off. Fast. Don't hesitate. I'll catch up to you, or you may get help that could save both our lives. I know where you're going. Do you understand me?"

The commanding strength of Sergei's voice is apparent. I decide it's best not to argue with one of the best soldiers in the world on soldiering. "Yes," I say.

"Okay. Does the gun stay or go?"

"It can stay."

"Okay, training is over. Which way do you turn if you must take the tunnel?"

"All rights, Sir," I noogie him with a salute.

"Okay, from now on, I'm strapping on a twenty-two and a Suvorov knife as well. I'll hide an American Colt forty-five too. Only you and I are aware of any of this."

"Sergei, what has gotten you so jumpy all of a sudden? Smoltsky?"

"Not exactly. Between my nomination hearings and confirmation, security brought me here to the dacha. En route, surface-to-air missiles were shot at our helicopters. It was obvious our route was known. That meant a leak. A few days ago, a listening device was found in my chamber. I'm not sure how or when or especially by whom it was placed. Only my most trusted team has been doing the sweeps. Somewhere I have a mole. A traitor."

"Might it be a foreign power?" I question.

"It could be, but my gut says no. The listening device was clumsily placed in a plant. The receiver range was short, within the dacha complex. I think the device was placed to implicate you."

"*Me*? What do I have to do with anything? I'm not a spy. I don't know any secrets. It must be for money."

"You're an American involved with the President of United Russia. Our first night together may have been overheard by someone on my team. The mole. There are hardliners who are still very anti-American and dislike this new president in the first place."

"God, I hope it's a foreign power," I mumble.

"Perhaps, but I still have a mole."

CHAPTER 63
THE LAST DAY

I RETURN Selena to the bedroom chamber.

"So, what's on for the rest of today?" she asks.

"Well, milady, we can take a walk by the lake. Or go to the gym. Can stay here in front of the fire. Or go for a swim." At which point I twitch my Marx eyebrows. "And we can do all of these things, but whatever we do, we must eat a wealth of Olga's food."

Selena laughs. "Is that the cold, nearly frozen lake you're discussing? Walk or swim there?"

I pshaw but don't answer.

"Since we are kind of in workout clothes, why don't we go to the gym, then dress for outside and take a pleasant walk, then head to the shower?" Selena suggests.

"I like that idea."

We take off for the gym, then have a wonderful day outside even though blizzard remnants continue to drop snowflakes in sheets from the gray Siberian sky.

"These are some of the largest snowflakes I've ever seen," comments Selena. "Never seen flakes this big in my life."

"We make 'em big here. Siberia is a bit like the American Texas. Whatever we do, we do big. Come on, let me show you our Siberian stables."

Selena and I enter the stables, which house a few nags and mules. "See, I don't understand this. State-of-the-art stable with these rickety old nags and mules," I grumble. It's just not sitting right with me.

"When control of the dacha was handed over, is it possible the animals were switched out? I know little about horses, but I understand there can be an enormous difference in their value. It was a while ago since ownership changed, right? The original animals may have perished or been sold," Selena contemplates. She looks around the stable lacking in animal life for its size. "I would like to vote for sold," she adds.

"Any or all of those things are possible. Nik came here soon after the changeover. He says the stables always had only nags and mules since he arrived. What you suggest may be true, Selena. Who knows, this is Russia," I shrug. "Many things, some things, and absolutely nothing can be true all at the same time," I clarify.

"What I don't understand is why the president wanted this dacha, or why he was, as you said, 'given' this dacha? You said he didn't use it much, yet he kept it shining like a new dime," Selena wonders.

"In America, the main reason would be about wealth. For money, even if it was so the owner might borrow against the property. Here in Russia, it's most likely that it was about power. Yes, power," I confirm in my mind as much as to Selena. "He took it because he could," I continue. "Likely enjoyed doing so."

I mull over the dacha's history. "Whatever happened to the stable horses, they were likely of a good breed. You just don't put in electronic doors for mules and nags."

"I absolutely agree," says Selena. "Although, in America, I've heard of folks doing some pretty extreme things for their beloved animals. This is different, though. What are there, twenty or thirty stalls? This was someone's passion, and perhaps a lucrative endeavor as well."

I continue my theories. "For reasons I don't completely understand, I want to know the history of this place. This Lake Baikal dacha, now a presidential resort, this place. Since my first visit to this dacha, I felt an undeniable connection. It stirs something in me. Now that I'm considering Smoltsky to be my father, maybe it was always a family connection.

"I'm sure of one thing: something went down over ownership of this dwelling. It was beloved. You can feel that in the walls, on the grounds. Everywhere.

"A power play. Some bad blood. Something. I can feel it." I clarify my thoughts with Selena. "As Americans say, 'it would be salt in a wound' for the man who stole your horses to flaunt riding them. That would be a bit of vengeance. But to dispose of the animal empire housed in this building, well, I suppose that would be another thing."

"That may tell you something about the revolution. Do you believe Smoltsky was behind it? Is it possible that revenge fueled the revolution?" asks Selena.

"Someone high up was behind the revolution. I'm certain of that. I'm sure my attempt to negotiate the release of the president and his cronies wasn't part of the plan. Even I didn't know I would do that until it happened," I answer.

I spill my thoughts aloud. "It's impossible to know what would have happened in the end if that furnace hadn't blown up. I don't think I would be standing here as president of Russia," I state as I stroke a nag's nose.

"Certainly, most of the rebels at that dacha weren't people high up in the government. Of course, I only got the media's perspective, but it seems most were ordinary people seeking change," ponders Selena.

"I agree with you on that, Selena."

"So, let us process through this a minute. It may be important," she offers. "On that day, what do you think was meant to happen?"

"I think the president was meant to die, but not the way he did. Probably meant to be thrown in a prison to rot. Yes, in the end, those men died at the hand of revolutionaries, but in a different sequence than what was planned. No one could have known I would address the crowd and try to negotiate their release. But I don't see how the furnace was planned. Unless someone skewed the forensics. I did have a second forensics team come in secretly. No foul play on the furnace."

"So, really, the revolutionaries could have, at any point, gone into the command center, blown the enclosure, and killed those men—or drug them out for a dramatic moment. Say, in front of a firing squad?" asks Selena.

"Yes. Those men were left in that room to sweat. Left to understand that they were not in control. Definite Russian power play. Moscow was silent. They had nowhere to go. They were meant to know that. I'm sure of that much," I respond. "Question is, was it just Smoltsky who had reason to assassinate the president, or were there others? My guess is that there were many. Who they were, and whether any of them played a role in what happened, I can't say. No one knows who was giving final orders. There is no proof of anything," I reason.

Selena's ears listen, and the gears in her brilliant mind whirl. I love it when she is like this.

I continue to ponder. "There is an operative. I will call him, or her, X," I begin matter-of-factly. "He or she put the whole thing together. One player. Maybe Smoltsky—or could be Smoltsky is a pawn, too. Could be Smoltsky had no role at all. Whatever the deal is, our Mr. or Ms. X has covered their tracks. For now, I'm working on flushing out operative X."

"I see," says Selena as a nag nudges her with its head. "Alright, missy, I will pet you, but I didn't bring any carrots. Sorry, sweet girl."

Selena continues to process with me. "So, this X didn't factor in Sergei Radkov being at the dacha that day. Do you think because of the crowd's reaction, the mysterious X decided to use you?" Selena pauses. "Wait a minute. Let's back up a few steps. Why assassinate? Why not simply destroy them? Make them suffer through life and deal with tragedy?"

"Yes," I answer. "X wanted them dead. That is my belief, but maybe that's because I experienced so much death on that day. Possibly even wanted my own."

I look out across the mountainside as sheets of snow continue to pile layers across the landscape. "The intent could have been to capture and imprison. But the risk of bloodshed could never have been ruled out. I cannot say if X meant for the others to die, or just certain ones. If this was not revenge, then it was for power, or both."

"Money?" asks Selena.

"Money in Russia can be made in many nefarious ways without a revolution. If revenge, money may be rooted in that revenge," I say. "Like what happened here."

"Kind of like in America. One thing I can say about this love of mine is that he sure keeps things interesting," smiles Selena as she puts her downy coated arms and mitten paws around me.

"Possible I was at the wrong place at the wrong time," I say after a few minutes. "Fairly sure I'm a pawn, though. I don't know my puppeteer, but I'm convinced there is at least one. That is what my gut says."

"X," responds Selena.

"X," I reply.

"Well, they didn't control you then. I see it as unwise of them to think they can control you now," she says.

I give my sweet girl a smile. We walk around the frigid lake, knowing at some point we will receive a mug of cocoa from Olga. Maybe a few of those cookies. About halfway through our walk I get a text from Tina.

"Oh Selena, Selena. No!"

"What is it?" she asks.

I hand her my phone to show the text. Headline reads, *"Russian President's American Whore."*

"What are we going to do?" questions Selena.

"For now, we should go inside, drink hot chocolate, shower, and process this. Think. For the next hour, this doesn't exist. See what I am texting to Tina?"

"'For the next hour, this doesn't exist,'" reads Selena. "I just hate that someone is trying to ruin our last day together. Let's try not to let them ruin it for us. We'll deal with it, but let's try not to let it get to us too much," she suggests.

"Damn it, there is a mole working here for my puppeteer. These pictures of you and I were taken over the past few days. All are within or outside of this compound. There is one more thing."

"It's almost like a home invasion," acknowledges Selena demurely. "As much as I'm ready for cocoa, maybe we should walk this off a little longer."

"Agreed," I ponder as we meander. "Here's the other thing. They're hurting me in the one place they can: you. That means they're coming after me. That's the other thing, and they know this would piss me off.

I was so afraid of this, Selena. I must control my anger. Let's walk more."

"All that's happened is I've been called a name. I say let's fight fire with fire."

Selena gets raised eyebrows from her lover.

"Joe Cook. Call him. We announce our engagement. This X person then loses control. Maybe we invite a Russian news anchor as well. One American. One Russian. Maybe another foreign correspondent, or a full-fledged press release. This won't be about a headline. It'll be about nuptials."

"Selena, you are brilliant."

CHAPTER 64
ALEXEI!

TWO LOVEBIRDS ARISE EARLY the next morning knowing our time is up. Time at this lake haven has ended. Reality with its ugly tentacles will seep into our lives. Today. Damn it to hell.

Sergei and I eat a quick breakfast, finish packing, and head downstairs to say goodbye to Olga and her staff. I pick up Oliver, who is enjoying one last rub against his favorite pair of legs. I pick him up and adore the beast. Give him a nuzzle and a few strokes. Oliver rewards me with loud purrs and kisses my nose. I'm gonna miss the little bugger.

"Yes, next time I'll bring you treats," I promise.

Alexei has it all worked out. The plan is to have the president and me go straight to Moscow. We'll fly using his presidential jet. The presidential plane is stored in a hangar at the bottom of the mountain a few miles away. The closer dacha hangar seems unsafe to the pilot because of ice on the runway. Makes for hazardous takeoffs and landings. The conscientious pilot likes the safety of the alternate airstrip better.

Alexei has gone through all the safety protocols in his head more times than I know how to count. Sure of it. That process won't end until he has the president and his lady safe in Moscow at Red Square. This is my Alexei. I adore the man and appreciate all he has done for me. My dear Russian friend.

The hanger has been swept and re-swept by security. Alexei phones in an additional security check while I sit in the car. Airplane worthiness has been triple checked, with the pilot waiting behind security checkers on the ground. Snipers in place. Helicopter ground survey done. Alexei orders another helicopter survey of the surrounding landscape.

He arranged for the four Humvees sitting outside the dacha's side entrance for the journey to the airstrip. Its portico is perfect for use during inclement weather. A brick drive makes a lovely circle leading out to the main road. Although the front entrance is much more elaborate with sweeping views of the lake, the side portico is more functional. The journey to the hanger a mere few miles. Those will be long miles for the short man.

Sergei needs to make a few presidential calls in private. I need to call my agent and manager, and most of all, the mountains of North Carolina. Security decides for Sergei and me to take separate cars. We agree so that each of us can complete our tasks.

Although, for privacy, I'm of the mindset that waiting until we board the plane might prove a better option. Instead, I scribble notes on what to say to my agent and manager. North Carolina will be easy.

Alexei continues to click off details minute by minute in his head. Anybody can watch his body language and know this. I wait with him in the second car behind the lead. Alexei is driving me, so my safety is under his control. Sergei is tied up on a call but will join the convoy shortly.

Alexei doesn't like it and grows impatient. Sergei has a skeleton security staff covering him while he's inside. I can hear the thoughts in the tam wearer's head. *Damn Sergei! When will he learn? When will he learn he is now President of United Russia, and he needs to be secure every minute of his life? Sergei, Sergei.* I smile.

Alexei prefers to cover both the president and his lady at the same time when we sojourn outside. Especially in a transitional situation like transport. But it's Sergei Radkov who is president, and the president has given the order. The president won't be long. Alexei looks at his watch. He's wordlessly damning Sergei. His body language is twitching. I silently smile, thinking Alexei actually knew Sergei when he was a young recruit.

Security still has secondary staff like Tina to transport. Alexei handles a lot. I understand his agitation and love him for it.

Two Humvees are decoys for the presidential transport. One at the front and one at the back. Alexei states he's glad Ivan has recovered from his illness. He needs all hands on deck. Ivan will drive the lead car. Vogo will drive Sergei, and Sasha—who I don't know as well—will drive the last car. Alexei knows Sasha, but not as well as he does the others. Sasha is a young recruit from the prior administration. His best guys are covering the front.

Alexei is getting nervous. He's planned and had everything according to schedule, except the president hasn't arrived. His fingers fumble and make light clicking noises on the steering wheel. He turns the heater back on in case I'm feeling chilly.

"Oh my," I say. "Alexei, I forgot my stash of books. Left them in the closet." I'm halfway out of the car. I forgot the items delivered from my Irkutsk hotel room.

"Selena, get back in the car. I'll get them for you," yells Alexei.

Since I'm already almost out of the car, I respond, "No need, Alexei. I can handle it," and off I sprint toward the dacha in an unusual frantic mode for me. I don't want to hold up the rest of the party.

KABOOM! An explosion. Behind me. I turn to stare in disbelief. My car blew up. My car. *My car?* Everyone is rolling out of their vehicles. Alexei's tam is flying in the air.

"Alexei!" I want to run. Run to Alexei. Oh God, there would be no use. Horror and fear and grief swallow me like Jonah's whale.

I'm frozen. Then I swap to triage mode like during my DWB days. I will help the others. Yes, help the others. I'm a doctor. I'll help. That's what I do. My disconnected thoughts are interrupted.

KABOOM! Another explosion. There's no time for horror. There's no time for grief. The whale has spit me out, and I'm swimming in a sea of primal fear.

A hand clutches my shoulder, throwing me to the ground. There's a body over me.

Sergei. Thank God, Sergei.

Sergei yanks me up after the last of the threatening debris falls. "Get behind me," he orders, wielding a Colt .45 handgun. "Make your way toward my chambers. Eyes open," says the soldier in a suit as he walks backward away from the blast zone.

I slip off my mules and leave them behind. Somehow, the wet clacking of the shoes I'm wearing seem inappropriate after what my eyes just saw. We duck behind a portico column to shield us as Sergei scopes out our surroundings.

I'm in shock, but something has taken over my mind as I move on autopilot with this professional soldier. I'm back in a war-torn country. I'm in a jungle. I'm at the edge of somewhere that humans shouldn't exist. I'm with Sergei.

On the run like convicts, we reach the side entrance stairway. With our backs plastered against the wall, Sergei listens for sounds. Not hearing any, he opens the stairway door and looks around with his gun at the ready. "Let's go," he whispers.

Slowing at the top of each stairway, Sergei pauses and looks and listens for what may be ahead or behind us. When we reach his chambers, he signals for both of us to flatten against the wall on each side of the door. He crosses in front of the door to the other side. He signals for me to hold there. I obey. The president types in his security code. The commander flings open the door and leaps inside, brandishing the nose of his Colt .45.

I think it's an eternity before Sergei returns. Braced against the wall, Alexei pops into my thoughts. Alexei. His tam shooting up and gaining altitude, then floating down like a feather in the soiled air. All of Alexei in pieces somewhere in the forest of this peaceful home that Sergei loves. I bite my lip. Not the time to mourn.

Sergei pulls me inside, locking all safety locks behind him. He whispers, "Let's go. You know where." I grab a pair of tennis shoes and run to the tunnel mouth. My soldier, lover, and the President of United Russia helps me onto the ladder. "Here's the flashlight. I must go check on Olga and the others. Wait for me inside. If you hear anything odd, take the tunnel. No matter what you hear or think, don't come back up. Do you understand me?"

I can't speak. A mass of dark hair nods. At the bottom, I don't open the cot. Alone in the dark. Bombs going off in my head. Good men dying up top. Who can sit in this dark dungeon? My nerves are as tight as my father's nautical knots. I pace, trying to regain my sensibility. Sergei is right. I need to stay put. Oh God, Sergei! What if something happens to Sergei?

No! I nearly scream out loud. You're not going to fall apart. Not. Follow Sergei's instructions to the letter. If nothing else, that's how I'll honor him. I wipe my tears. I slide to the tunnel entrance, finding the backpack. A new old trusty. I go ahead and pull up my hair and put on the headscarf for disguise and warmth.

If anyone can survive this, it's Sergei. Believe it. Believe it with all my heart. Someone has taken the life of my friend, Alexei. I will fight whoever is responsible until my last breath.

I turn off the flashlight to save the battery.

CHAPTER 65
DARK IN RUSSIA

FEELS like hours have passed in the dark tunnel. Days. Soon, it will grow dark outside in this part of Russia. Dark from lack of sunshine. Dark from lack of clear skies. Darker still inside this freaking tunnel chamber. Dark.

The tunnel chamber is the blackest black I've ever seen. My eyes can't see my fingers held at eye level. Dark. Dank. Cold. Not frigid like outside, but ghostly cold. Moist. Heavy. The tunnel chamber covers me with its eeriness like a cloak. I shiver.

Voices. Sergei? I can't tell.

Gunshots. One shot firing in a spurt, one after the other. Not a Colt .45. Sergei! What if he's hurt?

I'm halfway up the ladder steps when I remember my promise. I scramble down. Find my backpack and wind my way through the tunnel.

I will know where you are. If Sergei can find me, he will. Otherwise, I must get help. Must.

Come to an intersection where I must go left or right. *Stay right*, I hear Sergei's voice speaking to me. Footsteps behind me? Not sure.

I want to douse the light, but I need it to find my way through the winding tunnel. I will my legs to move faster. Faster in the cold. Faster.

Press on. I'm thirsty but don't worry with the swig of water my mouth aches to take. Should I remove my .22 caliber weapon? That would require stopping. My .22 will be worthless against an automatic weapon. Faster.

Feel heavy, as though I'm on the moon. My legs are shaking, working against the dark weight and frigid air of the tunnel. Working against the dankness. Working against the cold. Working against my fear. Days of long workouts and runs benefit me. Still, I have to will my cramping legs to put one foot in front of the other.

How much longer? How long is this tunnel? No idea. Another intersection. Could go straight or take a right. I take the right but wonder if my pursuer knows where I'm going. Obey Sergei.

Is there air left in this confined space? I battle cramps that are screaming, *No air, no air left*. Fatigue. So much fatigue. Harder. Fight harder. Fight the enemies of dark and the cold unknown.

See a stream of light! "Oh God, I think I've made it!"

Sprint through the cave opening and find the bike. The tires are slit. Damn. There's but one thing to do.

I enter the clearing.

Walk toward the brush beside the river. Or was that part of Lake Baikal? I don't know, but this was the best choice with the directions Sergei has given me. Down past the waterfall. There is a town at the end of the path. I can get help there. Must hurry.

"Where are you going?" asks a voice behind me. I whirl around. Ivan stands wearing his automatic weapon on his shoulder, and a blood-splattered grin.

I don't answer. This is truly a dark day in Russia.

CHAPTER 66
LIKE A PLUCKED CHICKEN

I GLARE AT IVAN.

"Asked you a question." His grin is evil.

I don't respond. Hell, my dry throat won't let me.

"Throw your backpack as far from your body as possible," he commands.

I sling it.

"Hands up."

I raise my hands over my head.

"That's a good girl. Now down on the ground on your belly with your hands over your head. Might want to take you doggie style," grins the evil face.

Actually hope he tries to take me. Poor odds all the way around, but I might have a better chance of getting in a jab as Ivan fumbles. I want to fight him. Want to tell him to fuck off. Want to tell him I doubt if he can even get it up. Spidey-senses dictate otherwise. At least for the moment. Give nothing away. Still, I glare at him.

Ivan gives a little smile at his weapon. "Your choice. I can fuck the dead as easily as I can fuck the living. Once more, on the ground," comes his unyielding voice. The devil gives a brief pause and adds, "Don't think your almighty ineffective American karate will work on me. Although, I would enjoy your impotence."

I want to tell him he's the impotent one. "It seems you have a weapon trained on me. Hardly a fair fight. Put it down and we'll test my impotence," I respond coolly.

"On the ground," sneers Ivan.

I comply, not seeing any options.

Ivan strolls over as though he's on a Sunday afternoon walk. Puts his knees on my shoulders and rope-ties my hands over my head. I thought a little jujitsu prior to being tied may have been my best, if not only, option. But the weapon. Even an accidental firing in that position is likely to be fatal. Perhaps preferred? What do I care what he does to my dead body? It's living that's painful. Either way, it's too late.

Sergei. I must stay alive in case Sergei still lives. I must. I must endure this.

Ivan pats me down, stopping at my ass and giving it a raunchy caress. "Mmmm," he mutters.

I don't dignify him with a response. No matter what, I'll stay calm. That's the only chance I have. Stay calm and think. Don't let the bastard rattle you.

Ivan pats down my back. The monster puts a bandana in my mouth and another around my eyes. Methodically, he flips me over, unzips my coat, and pats down my front, lingering on my breasts and my woman.

I don't flinch.

Alert ears pick up his movements as he walks a few yards away. I want to formulate a plan. Are there any options? Don't give up hope. Do not.

He returns. Ivan fumbles with me, but I can't determine to what end. Whatever it is, it doesn't sound good. Yes, I wish I had fought him earlier on. Gone ahead and taken the bullet. Whatever he's up to, I might be better off dead. Ivan is going to kill me, anyway. After all, it was my car he had blown up.

Hope. I must hope. Hope and think.

Ivan stands me up and pushes me in his willed direction. Somewhere closer to the waterfall, I can tell that much. Is he going to throw me over, tied and bound? Ivan isn't talking. Quiet Ivan... is he following his Plan A? Damn these Spetsnaz guys.

Oh Sergei, I'm sorry if I've let you down. So sorry, my love. And you too, Alexei.

Ivan hoists me up in the air by my arms. A rope pulley system hangs my body from a tree branch. Gravity becomes the enemy of my arms. For whatever reason, I imagine myself as one of those plucked chickens hanging up in a Chinese market. Giddiness. Endorphin overload. My arms stretch out to their fullest. They may pull out from my shoulder sockets.

I'm cold. So damn cold. Just hanging here. Ivan removes the blindfold. "Better you see. At least for me, anyway. Just better," says the grinning man.

I'm sure he was born of madness.

Ivan moves behind me. Behind the tree. My God, a trap. I'm bait. At least I know Sergei is alive. Sergei will come. That's why I'm the bait. I hope Sergei doesn't come. For whatever reason he can't, I hope he doesn't.

Snowflakes tickle my nose. Cold swells my lips. For a person raised in the southern USA, the cold is almost unbearable. For the first time, I wish I were born in Buffalo.

I wish I was a plucked chicken. I've never thought a damned plucked chicken was better off than me, but as my lips and hands grow blue, I become convinced the chicken is better off.

My arms don't just ache, but sear in pain. I want to cry. Tears don't come.

I try to scream behind my bandana gag. The face of my love appears from the entrance of the cave.

"Selena," he cries.

I try to call to him. Want to warn him. Sergei is too panicked to decipher my facial expressions or the mumbles behind my mouth cloth.

Ivan steps from behind the tree with his AK-47 ready. "Hello, Sergei."

Sergei stops in his tracks. The president glances at me but focuses his eyes on his former friend. His friend that he had known the longest. "My God," slips from his lips.

"Yes, brother. Be a good boy and remove your weapons. You know how."

Sergei gives a knowing nod. "Colt forty-five in the back, twenty-two on the ankle," he informs the assailant. With one hand in the air, he gingerly removes the .45 from his back and tosses it. Bends down and removes his .22 from his ankle and tosses that too.

Sergei doesn't look to see the horror on my face. He knows it's there. Doesn't need to see it.

"Now, if you will be so kind as to lie on the ground facing the cave, hands stretched over your head. You know the drill."

Sergei complies. I hope he doesn't plan on letting Ivan take him. Please, no, Sergei.

Ivan walks up beside him. As Ivan moves to bend down over Sergei's shoulders, Sergei makes his move. Then he goes limp, and I can tell he is in darkness. Ivan has hit my love on the head with the butt of his AK-47.

I watch from my plucked chicken perch. The snowflakes wet my hair. I succumb to the pain, the cold, the horror. It's more than I can bear. I share Sergei's darkness as I go limp, and my head falls to the side.

CHAPTER 67
BROTHER

I AWAKEN to water poured on my head. I look up into the face of Ivan as I shake water from my body like a wet dog. Tied to a tree, I see Selena dangling from another across from me. My heart drops. *Focus. You must focus. It's game time.* I know it. So does Ivan. I try to conceive of words that might appeal to my friend. A friend I no longer know. I find none.

Ivan moseys over to Selena. The pail-toting bastard pours water over her head too.

"Wake up, pretty one. You won't want to miss this. Sleepy time is over."

Selena's body shivers to life. So cold. She's so cold. She's blue. My heart shivers. With a swollen face, her eyes can barely open. *Hang on, baby. Hang on for me.* I just hope her heart is still warm and keeps beating.

I want to yell at Ivan to leave her alone. My training states it would be of no use. The words catch unspoken in my throat. Instead, I try to catch Selena's weak eyes. They flicker up at me. "Love you," I mouth.

Selena seems to perk up a little.

Ivan returns to me. The traitorous devil sits down in front of me, stretching out his muscular legs as though he's sunbathing on a beach. We glare at each other. Out of the corner of my eye, I espy Selena. She is doing something with her hands. I'm unsure what, but my instincts instruct me not to look.

Instead, I allow my gaze to focus on Ivan. Ivan, who wears a facial expression that's indescribable to me. Silly, perhaps. Nearly silly?

"Why?" It's not something I mean to ask, but the word falls from my lips despite my lack of intention.

"Why? Because I was paid well to do it. Paid very well, indeed," brags Ivan.

"Might you have asked for a raise?" I quip.

Ivan throws his head back in a maniacal laugh and rolls his eyes. "Sergei, Sergei, Sergei. This is so much better. Want to know who ordered this? Eh, *part* of this? The target is Selena, but I've been paid," shrugs the face of this devil. "What does one extra matter?"

"Who put out the order?" I ask, trying to leave defiance out of my voice as Selena wiggles. She's in pain. That's obvious. In danger of freezing to death too, but I have to keep Ivan talking. Give her more time.

"Well, it was your dear old dad!" replies Ivan, delivering the punch line.

"You mean Smoltsky?" I reply, taking away Ivan's humor.

"You knew?"

"I guessed, but wasn't sure."

"Well, now you know," says Ivan with exaggerated enthusiasm.

"Guess what else, bro? You and I are brothers. Or half brothers, I should say."

"That I didn't know." In earnest I say, "Ivan, you are my *whole* brother. Don't do this."

"Sergei, Sergei, Sergei," Ivan continues with sarcasm, enjoying his condescending tone. "It's my duty. You should understand duty. I wonder if that is what dear old Dad saw in you. Sending you to that fancy English school. Looking out for you at every turn. Protecting you. Me? Noooo. Had me thrown in that orphanage as an infant to rot. Well, his baby boy became a killer. Here I am!" exclaims a jubilant Ivan.

"So what is dear old Dad's motive now?" I ask.

"I'm not sure," shrugs Satan. "Perhaps he's hoping you'll have some kind of breakdown over Selena. Step down from office. That sort of thing. Then dear ole Dad will have removed all barriers to his throne. And of course, with most public reluctance, move into power. This time, perhaps, just perhaps, the people would be grateful for his service."

Ivan continues his bedeviled speech. "Remove all the skeptics. Suppose he expected you to flunk President 101. But, as always, you are Sergei," says the madman using a cool but sarcastic voice. "Got to admit you fooled him on that one. Then along comes your whore."

Selena is still wriggling about.

"What about your mother?" I ask with sincerity. *Keep him talking.*

"Oh, she was one of the Smoltsky whores, I suppose. I found her, you know," says Ivan with a wry smile. "Then, I tortured her."

Speaking conspiratorially, he whispers. "Then, I killed her. Had the funniest expression on her face when she died. Hoping my brother shares the same expression when I kill him. Oops! Half brother."

"How long have you known? Known about our mother? Known we were brothers?"

"As long as I've had horses."

"So, about ten years? You've known for ten years and never said a thing?"

"Well, they do call me Ivan the Silent," he smirks.

"Of all the things you got to do that I didn't, I envied you getting to ride horses the most. When I was a kid, you know," Ivan explains with nonchalance. "You got to do everything, and all I could do was rot in that orphanage and become a killer. So, brother, here I am. A killer. You helped to make me."

I shake my head.

"So anyway, I bought me some horses and taught myself to ride. No point in letting just you and the pissant have all the fun. Dear ole Dad loved horses, too. Offered to take him riding. Guess he's not much on spending time with his prodigal son. And, Sergei, *I'm fucking prodigal.*"

I don't respond. Ivan stands up and moseys over to Selena as though he were out on a stroll. "Have you taken her ass yet? Of course, you haven't," sarcastic Ivan says while touching my woman's bump.

I grit my teeth.

Ivan pulls out a pair of red women's underwear from his pocket. "Remember these?" he asks Selena.

Ivan sniffs the panties with a sense of luxury. Sniffs the crotch with an ogle of insane sexuality. He licks it. "Maybe I should put them on you just so I can take them off again," Ivan says to Selena, then throws the underwear to the ground as though they're on fire.

"Ah, better just to go for the real thing, you juicy woman. You smell so good. Mmmm. Then maybe I'll give you the pleasure of my big cock up your ass," he says slowly. "Hate for you to die without knowing the pleasure."

Ivan didn't find my Suvorov knife sheathed around the inside of my upper thigh. I wriggle. Desperate to finagle the weapon around so I can grab it with my hands. Damn awkward and isn't going well. Fortunately, Ivan thinks I'm wriggling because of my upset over Selena.

He smiles with delight. "You know what's coming next, don't you, bro? My cock, the weapon," says the madman with a mock look at his own horror. "Usually, I would cram it up her ass first thing, but I'm thinking I want some of this woman first," he says, allowing his hand the freedom to touch Selena in her private garden.

I will kill this man. Make no mistake. I will kill my brother.

Ivan's gaze returns to me. "Almost forgot. Know what I did, brother? Crammed my cock up my mother's ass before I killed her. Gave her a taste of the one gift in life that she gave me." Ivan's hands reach his genitals as the smile of the devil I don't know crosses his face while his fondling of Selena desists for a moment as he luxuriates in his storytelling.

"Nothing like keeping it in the family, da, bro?"

I say nothing.

With that, Selena swings herself backward and forms herself into a ball. As she swings forward, she lifts upward and stretches out her leg just before contact. Her movement gives herself enough momentum to kick Ivan straight in the jaw before he can react.

I had hoped she would strike his carotid. Her kick knocks him down, but not out. Shit. Why does his head have to be big as a block of ice and ten times harder? Damn him.

Hoped the strained bending of the birch would break the tree and set Selena free. Instead, the rope that Ivan tied around a burl remains in place as the tree springs back up straight. I'm bound to a cedar with a fat trunk fed by the plentiful water source. Selena's tree is an anomaly. Several thinner trees have grown together to form one fat trunk with fatter branches than is normally seen in this northern region.

Think! I demand of my near frozen mind. Help Selena. I must help Selena.

Tree roots cover the ground, but hell, roots are everywhere. Fuck. Why couldn't Selena's tree break with the force of her motion? Uproot the bastard. Perhaps the limb might give way with the force or slide the rope over the burl. Like everything else in hardy Siberia, the tree stands its ground.

Selena relaxes in a way that is phenomenal to me. Spinning her body like a top with her legs tucked, she unfurls and extends her legs out as she swings forward and up. One hand loosens out of her rope. The other as she falls to the ground.

Ivan crawls like a spider toward his AK-47. I close my eyes. Selena will be lost. At least she won't have to suffer a desecration by Ivan's hands. Frantic, I try to move my knife, but with coat and bindings, it's near impossible. Impossible won't keep me from trying.

Before Ivan's fingertips reach his weapon, shots fire. Two AK-47s. One from the mouth of the cave, the other from a hillside. Ivan looks down. There's nowhere else to go. Before the shots can reach him, the highly trained soldier of United Russia scrambles and throws his body over the cliffside and down the waterfall.

CHAPTER 68
FIND HIM

VOGO STEPS from the mouth of the cave and runs over to the side of the bluff where Ivan rolled over. He opens fire and sprays his weapon down into the gushing water.

A body never surfaces.

Bruised and battered, Alexei runs limping down the hill.

Scrambling to her feet, Selena dashes over to me. Her eyes see nothing else but me. This nearly frozen woman, who was tortured and hung from a tree long enough to freeze into a solid mass in the Siberian cold, sees absolutely nothing but me. The warmth of her heart fills me.

"I have a knife," I direct her.

"Where is it?" Selena asks rapidly.

"Right now, it's in my ass crack."

Selena lets go of a laugh and a tear at the same time. Her purple and blue hands hold my face. Blue and purple lips kiss mine, which must be the same color by now.

"How did you get it in your ass crack?" Of all things to ask, she asks that.

"When I pulled it from my outer thigh, I slipped it around my thigh to hide it between my legs on my inner thigh. I think that's why Ivan missed it. He knows I usually carry knives around my lower leg."

"Okay," she says, moving behind me to locate my sheath.

Selena didn't even notice the beaten and torn but still functioning Alexei limping down the hill. Selena looks up, aghast. "My God, you're alive!" she exclaims. The beauty jumps up to bear-hug her friend. "How did you—?" She can't finish her sentence.

Vogo moves over to cut my ropes after emptying his weapon into the swirling water. Alexei explains his return from the dead. And me? I retrieve my knife from my ass crack.

"I had turned the Humvee off after the inside became heated while we were waiting," explains Alexei. "It was starting to get cold again, so I was turning the ignition to get the heat going right when Selena decided to get out. I heard a catch, a click. I thought the worst and rolled out. Rolled behind a portico column right as the car blew. I yelled for Selena to get down, but there wasn't enough time before the blast."

Alexei is removing his coat and putting it around Selena as he talks. "Put it on Sergei, around his head. That will give him the most heat," demands the doctor in charge.

"On it," says Vogo as he removes his coat to put around my head. Remind me to never call this man a pissant, never.

Alexei insists on putting his coat around Selena once she has removed her wet one. The frozen woman buries her frigid hands into the sanctum of the coat's pockets.

"Snowmobiles are on their way to take you both to the infirmary," says Alexei.

Adjusting Alexei's coat closer to her body, Selena replies to Alexei, "You're going to the infirmary, too, my friend."

"No, I'm alright. Cuts and bruises," he says.

Vogo hands Selena her recovered knapsack.

"No, you are. And so am I. We're all going," orders the American doctor, taking command while she pulls a scarf from her knapsack and plops it on my head.

My head?

"No Selena," I say. "I'll freeze to death before the President of United Russia wears a fucking floral babushka scarf on his head. Besides, you need it most. You're the coldest. Put it on your head and don't argue," I say like a firm president who absolutely has had enough.

Everyone gives a smile and a headshake.

Unbound now and warming, I instruct, "Keep this under your hat for now. The public needn't know about it. Period. Not yet. There is something we must do first."

"We have dead to explain, Comrade," replies Vogo, who forgets the "Mr. President" thing more than he remembers it. That is fine. I will forever forgive him. A friend who has your back is worth a hell of a lot more than any title. Just don't tell Alexei I think that.

"I know," I reply. "Saw the agent who likely surprised Ivan in my chamber. He's the security man usually posted between my chamber and the kitchen stairwell. The guy you recruited from Moscow, Alexei."

Alexei's head nods sadly as we all stand close together.

"Notification will be delayed for a few days," I say. "I'll release everything at one time. Including the agent's death as a patriot in the line of duty. For now, we give up nothing. Not even that I'm alive."

All heads nod. Heads of my most loyal.

The snowmobiles arrive. Per Selena's insistence, we all head to the infirmary. Including Vogo, whose primary assignment is still to protect his president. The warmed intravenous fluids, blankets, and warm broth returns me to something resembling life. Selena is recovering, too, and says I'm going to be a good patient, or else she is going to kick my ass.

"Touché, Miss Blue Lips," I say. "But your beautiful bump is going to stay in this bed next to me. My doctor is here. You, madame, are now a patient. Surrender your charge, woman. Time to be a doctor-patient, 'cause I have plans for you later."

Selena guffaws. "Yes, Sir." She just had to noogie me.

Alexei is bandaged and sewn up in a few places, but it'll take a hell of a lot more than a bomb to put that old goat out of commission. I love this man.

I assemble my security team around my hospital bed. I brief the team on the one and only one objective. "I'll secretly be flying back to

Moscow overnight with Alexei and Vogo, and, of course, Selena. Sasha, you're the lead here. You have one and only one directive: find Ivan."

"Sir, do you think Ivan's body might wash up downstream?" questions Sasha.

"No," I say firmly. "Find him. He's alive. I would bet the Russian treasury on that. Take him alive if you can. Doubt he will allow that, but your directive is to try. It won't be easy. Whatever you do, don't underestimate this man. He is sly and skilled. This is one hell of an assignment, but I need Alexei and Vogo in Moscow. Bring in every resource you need. I'm sending you help from operatives around the country, including professional trackers. Top secret to all investigators. For now, your job is to find him. FIND HIM! FIND IVAN!" orders President Sergei Radkov.

CHAPTER 69
ONE LAST THING

THE NEXT MORNING, Andre Smoltsky walks the hallways to his office, passing the security checkpoints. There's a nervousness in his walk. Fidgety. Agitated. The chairman likely hasn't heard from Ivan. Heard nothing about the dacha. I'm sure he's cursing his prodigal bastard son in his head as he makes his way to the one place he believes he can close the door and think. His bastard prodigal son. I'm his bastard prodigal son too.

Smoltsky will act oblivious to anything that happened at the Lake Baikal dacha. I'm sure of that. He'll come to his office as usual this morning. It's his only real choice. His preference. His seat of power. Well, his seat and his power will be turned upside down this morning.

The chairman's pace slows when he notices Vogo and a rather swollen, bandaged, and beaten Alexei standing at the checkpoint before his office. Smoltsky nods as though he plans to walk past them and enter his office as though there's nothing amiss. First, the president's security pats him down. He's not amused.

Oh, but there is something amiss this morning, Andre Smoltsky. Yes, there is.

Smoltsky finds me inside. My presidential ass is sitting in the chairman's chair. My relaxed feet are propped on top of the chairman's desk, with an open newspaper in my hand.

"What are you doing, Sergei?" asks Smoltsky.

"Well, it seems, Chairman Smoltsky, I'm reading the newspaper. Like the sports section? I read the Moscow hockey team is performing well this year," I reply without moving my eyes from the page.

"Why are you here, Sergei?" asks the Chairman coolly.

I lower the newspaper.

"Well, *Dad*, I want to ask you something, and it's not to borrow your car for the dance."

With that, Smoltsky falls into the chair opposite me. "You know then?"

"Yes. But I have one question for you," I say nonchalantly, folding the newspaper and placing it to the side. Smoltsky's bastard son leans forward, closer to his old man.

"Where is my mother?"

"I wish I knew, Sergei," says the chairman.

Smoltsky receives a raised eyebrow from me.

"It isn't like you think, Sergei. Your mother and I were in love. Times were different then."

"Why don't you enlighten me?" I ask, wearing my White Stallion persona, though allowing my voice a hint of sarcasm.

"Your mother was from America, Sergei," says my father in a soft tone. "Her family immigrated from Poland to America. Her father died when she turned seventeen years old. A year or so later, her mother died. Your mother had this idea that she wanted to go to Poland for a year to study after her second year of college."

The old man continues with a faraway look. "She went to Warsaw. All seemed well the first semester, but then something happened. The money didn't arrive from America for her second semester. With her fluent English and Polish, she accepted work at a publishing house translating books." The old man took a deep breath but continues.

"Tried to earn enough money to return home. A short time later, the powers that be determined the publishing house where she worked produced unacceptable propaganda. I was the commander in charge of shutting it down."

"So, you saw a beautiful young woman and took what you wanted?" I ask, not cutting dear ole Dad any slack.

"Nothing like that. Yes, she was young and innocent. So very innocent," says Smoltsky dreamily.

I'm quiet as Smoltsky continues his narrative.

"Some of my men wanted to force themselves upon her. Your mother was a young and beautiful American. As commander, I stopped that nonsense. Took her under my wing to protect her from the others."

"How very gallant of you," I comment.

"Sergei, we fell deeply in love and became lovers. I had made a political marriage. My wife and I had two daughters, no boys. A loveless marriage, but necessary for both of us. I moved your mother to the outskirts of Moscow to be closer to her. When you were born, I felt so happy. Finally, I had a son. At the same time, I began to rise in the Party. Back then, the Party was everything," says the old man as though he was recalling a horror story. "Everything."

"You want to know what I remember?" I ask without waiting for a reply. "Rather, what I don't remember? I don't remember anyone calling themselves my father. I do remember your weekends away with my mother when she left me with a babysitter. I also remember being put to bed and hearing Momma and a male voice going at it in her room when I awakened from my sleep. Nooky time, Dad?"

"Sergei, what you remember is true. I visited your mother as often as possible. Both of us agreed you shouldn't be aware of my identity. Both of us had to be careful. The less said about the three of us, the better. Sometimes, before I left, I would sneak into your room and watch you sleeping. Watch you growing. My boy."

I want to puke. "How very poignant. But what happened to my mother?" I ask forcefully.

"I don't know, Sergei. I swear that to you. The love of my life disappeared. Vanished without our boy. I looked for her everywhere. Every gulag. Searched every record. If I learned of a safehouse, I would go to see if I could find her. Nothing. I was the new rising star within the Party. Someone in the Party found out about us and decided that if my liaison with you and your mother became known, things could get messy. My wife hailed from a politically high-up family. I don't know who gave the order. And I don't know who enforced the order, but I believe someone did. This is the only explanation I have."

He looks earnest as he continues his sickening story. *My* sickening story. "I tried to provide food for you while I searched for her. Saw you growing thinner. Left food for you when I could. As you know, that was limited. That's when I made the call for you to be picked up."

A light bulb flicks on in my head. *We have orders.* I ask, "So, this son that you loved so much... you were his private benefactor. Then, later arranged for him to become president, only so that you could have him killed?"

"NO! Sergei, you were never to be killed. At the dacha, when the former president was killed, the crowds went wild for you. Shouting 'White Stallion! White Stallion!' I couldn't help but be so proud of you, Sergei. My son. Yes, I did put you up for nomination, but you were the one the people wanted."

He holds up a firm hand. "But Sergei, I wasn't your benefactor. I tried to find out their identity because I thought they might lead me to your mother. But I was never able to uncover who they were. I know you searched, too. Believe me when I tell you, everything in my search led to a dead end.

"So, just kill Selena, then, and of course before that, the Russian president?" I ask, changing the subject.

"I'm proud of having that fucking bastard killed. That man. A monster," sputters the chairman, aka dear ole Dad, while shaking his head. His ire is so intense that he has trouble finding his words.

"The people—*our* hungry people—wanted him dead. I simply helped to make that happen. Selena is an American. She will ruin you. Just as your mother would've ruined me. You've come so far, Sergei. I couldn't let that happen."

"Oh, so you decided to ruin me instead with her death?"

"You would've survived that. Just as I survived losing your mother. Life goes on. It must. But you wouldn't have survived what your love for her would've done to you politically."

"Just like your love for my disposable mother? And Ivan's too, come to think of it."

This man either has blinders on or is lying. I don't argue his point about Selena. Instead, I ask about Ivan. "Why was there no benefactor for Ivan, or at least no help from you?"

"I didn't find out about Ivan until recently. Ivan's mother was nothing to me. Only with her once, you see. A bar pickup. Not of any consequence," waves off my father, as though having his illegitimate children in an orphanage wasn't something worth his concern. "Ivan's mother put her infant boy into that orphanage. I didn't know about it until Ivan told me. Was never in touch with his mother again. Wouldn't have known how to reach her if I wanted," shrugs the man I'm trying hard not to hate.

"Besides, it was hard enough siphoning money for you. I did it for your mother. The beautiful woman that I loved and never forgot." He trails off.

"You siphoned *what* for me? Wait, the clothes at Vogo's..."

"Yes," says my father as though he has been redeemed. "Vogo's father and I were close political allies. I arranged your stay with Vogo's family as often as possible. It was me who did that," says my father proudly, until his fiery face of ire returns. "At least until that bastard of a president had Vogo's father murdered. I know it was his doing. And probably your mother too. Couldn't prove any of it," says Smoltsky, shaking his head. "And had my son protecting him just to irk me. Do you know how that ate at me?"

I say conclusively, "Let me get this straight: You are behind the coup that killed the president. I take his place. Then I become involved with Selena, who wasn't up to your standards. So, you sent your other son, Ivan, to kill Selena. Does that in any way *not* bother your parenting conscience?"

He's exasperated. "Ivan came to me, threatening. The man was already a killer. Everything was his idea. He volunteered to do it—for an extorted price, that is. The boy is a killer worse than the devil himself. Killed his own mother. Tortured her too. I could only imagine what he might do to me."

I ignore his cowardice. "Tell me about the Lake Baikal dacha. How did it end up in the former president's hands?"

"That bastard always hated me. We were rivals. Yes, I rivaled him," says the chairman, feeling proud and justified. "He found out about your mother and me. Threatened to expose me if I didn't sign over the dacha. I loved that place. It had been in my family for generations. I was making a fortune breeding racehorses there, too. But mainly I raised horses because I loved it. Loved the horses. Loved the races. Oh, they were such proud animals on race day. Loved the lake. It was my happy place, don't you see? The only place where I felt happiness."

His face is crimson now. "The horses disappeared like your mother after I signed the dacha over to him. I suspected him of taking your mother, but alas, there's no proof. Never any proof. He took everything from me."

The man in front of me was existing somewhere in outer space. Existing with his memories, along with clouds of self-justification.

"Why was I circumcised?" I ask.

"Oh, your mother was adamant about it. I warned her against it. She thought if your 'state' was discovered, she could refer to her American heritage and claim it was not religious. A cleanliness thing."

I had nothing else. Wanted nothing else. I was done. Done and disgusted.

I look into the face of my father and say, "Andre Smoltsky, you are under arrest for the murder of a Russian president. The murder of everyone who died at the dacha during the coup. The attempted murder of Selena Frederick, the attempted murder of Alexei Polkhy, the murder of a special agent, the destruction of state property, and any other charges the Russian legal system deems appropriate."

I don't allow this poor excuse for a man to interrupt my speech. "You will be imprisoned in solitary confinement in the same dungeon where you and your ilk once sentenced perceived dissidents to reside."

Alexei and Vogo stand at the door entrance and take the cue to enter. "You may have the distinct honor of handcuffing Chairman Smoltsky and transporting him to his new home," I say to them.

Gleefully, Alexei handcuffs the chairman. Then bangs my biological father's head on the desk.

"That is for the agent who died because of your plotting," says Alexei.

Vogo, being Vogo, and damn well not one to be left out of the ongoing action, bangs the chairman's head on the desk again. "That's for attempting to kill Dr. Selena Frederick. Any man should die for that, and I hope you do."

Vogo surprises me. He never really liked Selena, and especially disliked me being with her. What can I say? He's Vogo. Figure him out if you can.

"You have nothing on me. Only the word of Ivan. A madman!" screams the bloodied Smoltsky.

I, President Sergei Radkov, known as the White Stallion, pull my cell phone from my shirt pocket. "I beg to differ, Andre. I think *you're* the madman."

I grin at Vogo. I just have to ask. "'For attempting to kill Dr. Selena Frederick?'"

Vogo's brown eyes turn up to me. He shrugs. "I decided I like her after all. She's a good lady, and your lady. This ass wipe is going away for what he tried to do. Nobody messes with my president or his lady."

Vogo. Only Vogo.

The End.

EPILOGUE

INTRODUCTION OF SELENA to my people is to be televised from the presidential salon in a short while. Yesterday, I spoke with my Russian people after Smoltsky's arrest. My people will love her as much as I do. I just know it.

I held nothing back yesterday. First, I gave them the joyful news of my engagement to Selena. I told my people who she is, including the scope of her past work, and the fact that she is an American.

I told the sordid facts about my orphan history and the recent unfolding of events that led me to discovering the identity of my father. And then all the rest. Discovery of Ivan as my half brother, and of our extended history since the orphanage. Alas, the events that unfolded at the Lake Baikal dacha and the imprisonment of Smoltsky, my father.

My people know it all, including Smoltsky's role in the coup against the prior president. Even the Lake Baikal history between the former president and Smoltsky. Losing a security agent at Lake Baikal, and the responsibility Smoltsky must take for so much loss of life. The coup and the killing of the prior president is being referred to as the Victory Day Massacre. My father is the mastermind and killer.

Yesterday's ordeal lasted three hours. The media asked me many questions, and I answered them all. The truth is out there. If any

Russian ever thinks I might lie to my people, they only need look at yesterday. I imprisoned my own father. If that doesn't speak to my truth, I can't say what might.

My father. Even he doesn't get to kill presidents, much less attempt to kill Dr. Selena Frederick. My father is a role model in reverse. He stated his motive to do away with Selena was to help me. Afraid she would ruin me, just like my mother. I can't explain it to you. Not exactly. Other than to say I knew my mother. My mother was not a person someone could ever consider might be their life's ruination. Neither is Selena Frederick.

Out of the same mouth spoke this man, saying he loved my mother. Sorry, Dad. I've known what it is to love a woman now. If the love of her will ruin me, then let it be so. There'll never be a time from the moment of that press conference that I will hide my love of Selena. You can't love someone and make "ruination" your primary concern. Especially if they are innocent of any wrongdoing. It doesn't work that way. Sorry, dear ole Dad. You never loved, nor understood it.

Now, it's time to introduce my fiancée to my people. If they hate her, then they do. I'll resign if my people are so shortsighted as to hate her because she happened to have been born in America.

"You look so handsome in your suit," says my smiling fiancée while straightening my tractor-design tie.

"And you are beautiful," I say to her as I place my lips on hers.

"I want you to talk the most," I say. "I will, of course, talk some too and support you. But I want you to lead with me beside you."

My beauty looks up at me with her ruby red lips surviving the purple from a few days ago. Always smiling, my lady.

"Mr. President, you are not just a different kind of president, but a different kind of man."

"Nervous?" I ask.

"No," she says. "You are beside me."

What a woman. "That I am," I say.

Joe Cook and Ihar Popov, a Russian journalist, will be our two interviewers. They arrive at the same time. I give them a handshake, and so does Selena. They review protocol with us.

"Mr. President," says Joe Cook, "we would appreciate, because of recent events, a few questions with you first. Say, maybe two each. Then we'll introduce Selena. We'll speak in Russian during the Selena portion, and we think it would be awesome for you to translate. Let people see your speaking interaction. Since he's playing on home turf, Ihar will start first and introduce you. I'll go second and introduce Selena. Of course, Ihar will explain the language protocol to our viewers to kick things off. Sound, okay?"

"Perfect," I say. "But understand that I want the Russian people to get to know Selena. Please, once you introduce her, direct most of your questions toward her. Of course, I'll pitch in, but let Selena lead. She is accustomed to being interviewed and I'm sure she will do well. Agreed?"

"Yes, Mr. President," agree both men.

Selena smiles. "How's your prostate, Joe?"

All but Ihar laugh at the joke. My sweet Selena is the first to notice Ihar doesn't get it and reaches out to touch his arm. "It's a private joke. Don't let Joe get away without him telling you about it later." Ihar nods.

The crew is ready for our live interview. The two journalists take their seats in the presidential salon.

"Two... one... and we're live."

Ihar explains the purpose of the interview and the language protocols. He introduces me, and I walk into the salon and shake the hands of both men for the camera. I take a seat on the settee, where Selena will sit beside me in a few minutes.

After a little chitchat, Ihar begins. "Mr. President, it has been an eventful week for you, ending with you imprisoning your father. How devastating is that for you?"

"Actually, it was more devastating for me to imprison the chairman of the Russian houses. I learned of my biology this week, and that man is not truly my father. My father never claimed me nor knew me. I don't know him. What I've learned of him is not to my liking. The man is a murderer and has committed crimes in my country. In fact, I consider him a domestic terrorist. Imprisonment is appropriate pending legal evaluation for a military versus a criminal trial. That will be left up to our legal authorities to decide. That is not something I will have a hand in. And the name of a domestic terrorist is not normally given. But due to the high-profile nature of the case, Andre Smoltsky's name had to be released. The people have a right to know what happened to the chairman and former president."

"Are you angry at your father?" asks Joe in Russian.

"I'm not angry with Smoltsky. There is nothing for me to feel anger over other than his actions. We share biology, that is all. Am I disappointed in who my biological father is? Yes and no. Yes, because of his crimes. I would have preferred a law-abiding Russian. Had it not been for his crimes, I may even have been overjoyed to learn I had a father such as Chairman Smoltsky. No, I'm not upset with him, because we only share biology. We're not two men who think alike. We're not of the same mind. I suffer no loss personally. He's not someone I will miss having in my life because he was never in it."

"Do you think Chairman Smoltsky nominated you for president because he knew you were his son?" asks Ihar.

"That is a question that I asked him when we last spoke. He said no. He told me it was because of how the Russian people reacted to me at the Victory Day Massacre. Might a bit of nepotism have played a role in the mind of the chairman? I can't say. It's a question for him to answer. I can only tell you what he said to me."

"Mr. President, there are a million questions to be asked, and I'm sure they will all be answered in time. So, I'm going to ask you the most important question," states Joe. "Are you ready?"

I nod.

"Mr. President, are you in love?"

Joe. Only Joe. Of all the hard-hitting questions he could ask, he asks me that.

"Yes," I say with my mouth split open and my teeth hanging outside my lips. "I'm so in love with this lady that I can't stand it."

With that, Joe introduces Selena. The beautiful lady, who still has swelling in her face after Lake Baikal. She walks into the ornate salon wearing a smoky lavender dress with a purple weskit. She's wearing alexandrite jewelry and emerald green eyes that sparkle.

Her swollen face, if possible, makes her appear more beautiful because she doesn't fret over it. It's a sign of her recent suffering and she wears it like a badge of honor.

Selena hugs each standing journalist and me, too. Smiles. She bows in front of the camera as if to a live audience. Well, the truth is, there is a worldwide live audience. The lady from North Carolina settles beside me. Smiles.

Ihar asks the first question. "Dr. Frederick, you look wonderful, especially considering the way you just survived the ordeal of your attempted murder."

"Thank you."

"What went through your mind during the ordeal?"

"The first thing I realized with the car bomb was that it was *my* car. I was the target. When Ivan captured me, I knew I would likely die. He had failed to kill me with the bomb and had pursued me to complete that task. Ivan enjoys torture. As awful as it was, in the end it was his torturous delay that saved my life. Otherwise, he would have simply shot me and escaped. I felt anger, pain, cold—such cold!—fear... all the things you would expect. Most of all, I felt the need to survive. Simply survive."

I felt her shiver when she spoke of the cold.

"What was the worst part of it for you?" asks Joe.

"Thinking Sergei might have been killed. I heard gunshots before I took a secret tunnel to escape. I heard shots up top, but I didn't know who got shot. I was halfway up the ladder to see if Sergei may have been injured when I remembered the president's explicit instructions to me. He told me that no matter what I heard, I had to take the tunnel and get help. Not to go up top. I did as I was ordered by the president, who is more than just a different kind of president. President Radkov is the world's best soldier. I followed his orders. Still, I was concerned about his fate. Choosing to take the tunnel was the only way I could honor him if the worst had happened."

"When were you the most afraid?" asks Ihar.

"The whole time. I think even when I was unconscious, I was afraid. Only a miracle could save us. But President Radkov and I received a miracle. Two of the president's security team arrived and opened fire on Ivan. If not for those brave men, we wouldn't be alive today. The president and I owe them our lives. They were our miracle. They're Russian heroes."

At some point, I put my arm around Selena. I was sitting beside her but wanted to be closer. Wanted to hold her. To touch her. I looked into the camera and interpreted.

"On a happier note, you're an engaged woman," says Joe.

Selena brightens the world with a smile.

"Yes."

"Got a ring yet?"

"Yes, I'm wearing it," she says, showing the camera her ring.

"It's a Russian Alexandrite. I was wearing it when I met the president. It was a little loose because I was wearing it over a pair of formal gloves, but I had it adjusted. I leased my jewelry for that event, but the president was able to purchase it outright. I was also wearing this dress the night I met him."

"It's a gorgeous rock," comments Joe. "Dress too."

"It is," Selena remarks after my interpretation.

"Dr. Frederick, what will you do once you're married? Will you practice medicine?" asks Ihar.

"All our plans are preliminary. As you know, I'm still promoting my book around the world. I'm attending and sometimes speaking at human rights conferences. However, the price tag for security will be so high now that I'm engaged to Russia's president. A president who is trying to increase the fortunes in his country's treasury. I don't want to add additional cost to his country. What we are considering..."

She looks over at me. "Is it okay for me to divulge this now?" she asks me before speaking.

I nod.

"Tentatively, we're discussing the coordination of my book promotions with overseas trips by the president. Similarly, trying to meld those with human rights conferences when they occur where the president is conducting business. That way, security will already be accounted for. The conferences that I attend will be those that are relevant to my new role in Russia, which I guess now is a good time to discuss."

"Please do," says Ihar.

Selena inhales deeply. "I'm a trained physician, but again, security is an issue. No patient wants to be examined by their doctor with security present. So that's not feasible. As you might expect, the plight of orphans in Russia is an issue that is dear to the heart of the president. What he's asked me to do is work on a project to improve the plight of Russian orphans. I'll begin with improvements in healthcare, nutrition, and education. As well, if I may, I would like to tell Russia what their president is doing at his own expense to save on costs."

"Of course, Dr. Frederick," says Ihar.

"I know I'm a giddy schoolgirl right now because of our impending nuptials, but I think Russians already understand they have a different kind of president. This man is a World Changer. He is devoting most of his talent to his country and his people, but I'm of the belief his good works will ripple and change the world. This president, this man, is farming parts of the presidential dacha. Some of it with greenhouses. As well, the land surrounding some of the prior president's former homes and those of his oligarch's, is now being used to farm. Farmers will use unconventional tools such as composting on those estates. The food will be shipped to orphanages in Russia. As well, extra food will supplement nutrition in schools in the poorer communities within Russia.

"As well, he is installing greenhouses on the grounds of northern orphanages. In more southern Russian regions, he is creating garden spaces for the children to learn to garden. Agricultural college students can volunteer and help the kids learn gardening while receiving college credit as an internship.

"At harvest and planting time, federal employees can donate a day from their office to garden at one of the farming sites. Even their president plans on donating a day or more. You can expect I will be donating my time as well."

Selena looks at me, then at the camera. "Russian people, behold your president!" I'm almost embarrassed to interpret.

Joe, Ihar and Selena stand in ovation. So, do I.

When we sit back down, I chime in with a laugh, "I wasn't clapping for myself. I was clapping for the success of these programs, and for this brilliant woman with her brilliant ideas, along with the people in my administration she has drawn in. Drawn in, and excited them to be part of this project. Yet she credits me and not herself. And you can see her enthusiasm. Talk about a World Changer! This woman has changed the world with every step she has ever taken. Russian people: behold the woman who will be Russia's next First Lady."

We're up on our feet again. Selena, too. But she turns to me and claps as though the ovation is for me. What a woman. Just love her.

Settling again, Joe gives Selena a hardball question. "Do you think being an American will be a disadvantage to you here in Russia? Inhibit your other works on your platform? Yea even, your accomplishments as a World Changer?"

Selena answers slowly. I almost jump in, but she starts.

"There are many beautiful women in Russia, and women of beauty. Yet God created me thousands of miles across the ocean for Sergei. And He created Sergei for me. I'm sure of that. Who am I to question the works of God? To deny His joy for me? For whatever reason, it's me who Sergei loves, and I love him. I'm no more responsible for the conditions of my birth, including where I was born, than are the orphans of Russia."

Selena swallows and continues after my interpretation. "As far as my endeavors in the past, let me be clear: my husband-to-be is a World Changer. I intend to change the world right beside him. President Radkov has given me an assignment that affects some 700,000 Russian citizens, who are children. That's a real opportunity to change the world. As far as my platform, I think my new role extends my platform, instead of retracting it."

I jump in. "Any Russian who doubts why I love this woman after hearing this is not listening. You love who you love. And I love this woman who happens to have been born in America. Selena told me she has been treated better here by every Russian she has encountered than anywhere else in the world. This is why I love my good people and feel so much pride in them. I think most Russians will appreciate Selena for who she is and for her spirit of service to the Russian people. She is a woman who dares to imagine a better world and seeks solutions to change it for the better. I'm inspired by this woman. If ever you doubt if your imagination can change anything, then just look to Dr. Selena Frederick. I do."

We take more questions concerning the wedding, Selena learning Russian, our desire to marry soon and start a family, and where we might live after my presidency. Finally, we bring the interview to a close, but Joe asks one more question.

"Are you afraid of being revisited by Ivan?"

"Yes, I say. Make no mistake. This man has the best military training Father Russia can provide, including the ability to disguise. Ivan is a madman and very dangerous. A man who kills without mercy. I ask for the help of my Russian people. Law enforcement's major thrust right now is to find this madman. We've set up a hotline if you think you have information. Let's find him.

"My people, help me find Ivan."

ACKNOWLEDGMENTS

Thanks to all my readers for your readership. I hope you have enjoyed reading this book as much as I've enjoyed writing it.

Whether you purchased this book through Amazon or not, I hope you will go to **amazon.com** and leave a review. Your input is valuable for two reasons.

First, because as an author, it feels good to know folks actually enjoyed reading your work. Or if not, what sorts of things I could have done to improve your entertainment. Also, if I made errors that you would like to share with me.

You can always reach me at deedeblakeauthor@gmail.com and deedeblake.com.

Second, authors live and die by your reviews. It's not just sales, but reader reviews that drive Amazon promotions and advertisements for authors. So, you are more valuable than you know!

The Russian Orphan is currently in screenwriting for a television series. Such things take time, but I can't wait to see it on screen!

Also, I'm working on two sequels, for this the first of the World Changer series. *We Were Lost* will deal with what happened to Selena's parents and Sergei's mother. Teaser: there will be a wedding. Wonder if my evil antagonist will show back up and try to spoil things? And I promise all sorts of unlocked doors at the presidential palace on nuptial night…

Find Him will deal with the search to find my madman antagonist. He's a slippery one. Think he'll die in the end, or is he too evil to die?

Stay tuned.

Deede Blake

ABOUT THE AUTHOR

 **Deede Blake** graduated from the University of North Carolina at Chapel Hill School of Pharmacy. She was an Algernon Sydney Sullivan Award Winner for her early humanitarian efforts, as well as a Bristol Achievement Award winner.

A scientist by training, an author by passion. A poet, song writer, short story writer, essayist, former novelist, world traveler. You can probably find her adventuring somewhere that no American has ever been…

Prior to book release, *The Russian Orphan* manuscript was chosen to be offered as a television mini- series. It is currently undergoing screenwriting, stay tuned. Sequels coming soon: *We were Lost* and *Find Him* to complete the World Changer Trilogy. For her next two sequels, Deede is committed to research among the Mongolian nomadic peoples, Africa, and the Philippines to delight her sequel readers.

She has two grown children and two cats. Her daughter hopes to welcome foster children into her home in September 2023. Deede is ecstatic to have new additions into their family. She lives in Myrtle Beach, South Carolina. She stays part-time at her partner's home in Ocean Isle Beach, North Carolina.

Made in United States
Troutdale, OR
07/19/2024

21317338R00329